GRACE RIVERS;

OR,

THE MERCHANT'S DAUGHTER.

A TALE.

BY THE AUTHOR OF "ADA, THE BETRAYED; OR, THE MURDER AT THE OLD SMITHY;" &c.

LORD HAWKSWORTH AND HIS ASSOCIATE AT FLODANG'S.

CHAPTER I.

THE SNOW-STORM.—THE MOTHER AND SON.

"How the wind howls, mother! There again—and the snow is so deep in the garden! What's that? Did you not hear a voice?"

Widow Woodfall put down her knitting-needles, and listened attentively as her son Harry thus addressed her. She listened for several minutes, but all was still; and, shaking her head, while a tear glistened in her eye, she said—

"My dear, it was only the wind sighing and moaning among the trees and chimneys, and yet I did think I heard something. Heaven help any poor creatures that are out on such a night as this. Oh! how little those think who are sitting in their warm, happy homes, with everything around them that makes comfort, even in the height of the winter's tempest, of the breaking hearts that are wandering about exposed to every gust that blows, and the many, the very many, my dear, who know not, on such nights as these, where to lay their weary heads. Your poor, dear father, Harry, may—may—"

The tears gushed to the widow's eyes, and she could say no more.

"My father, you have often told me, mother," said the boy, "was killed on board the vessel his own courage had taken."

"So—so they told me, Harry. So they told me; and there was one who came to me in my wretchedness and widowhood, to tell me that his last words were a blessing upon you, my dear. 'Heaven help and bless my boy,' he said, and then expired. In the deep ocean—and not where I can longer near him—dashed by the surges—he lies—yes, I am denied the consolation of weeping at his grave."

The widow wept bitterly, for this was always a subject that called up all her feelings, and from which, when it crossed her mind, she was sometimes hours in recovering.

"Mother—dear mother," said Harry, "don't cry now—my father is in Heaven. His battles, cares, and troubles are all done. We have still to go through with the fight, for young as I am, mother, I have seen enough of the world to know some of the great difficulties a poor lad has to contend with who is without fortune, friends, or——"

"Hush! hush! my dear, you have that which is better, far better than gold or a thousand hands to clasp yours in seeming friendship. You have industry and integrity—rare qualities, my dear Harry, most rare qualities."

The wind which had been calm for some moments, now, as if it had been gathering strength from all quarters of the earth, air, and ocean, swept round the humble home of the widow with a fearful violence that seemed bent upon destroying everything that marred its fury. It howled, screamed, and then blew such a parting blast, that the mother and son looked at each other in momentary alarm.

"This is a terrible night, my dear," said the widow.

"It is, mother. I never in my life heard such wind."

He approached the little casement as he spoke, and shading his eyes with his hands, he looked out upon the dreary night.

"It's snowing hard, mother," he said, "but the wind will scarcely let it fall. It tosses the great flakes here and there, and even catches up masses from the ground, and dashes them about as if they had but newly falln. Hark! There comes the wind again."

With a low moan as if approaching from hundreds of miles off, came the howling wind—nearer and nearer then it came, sweeping our cities, towns, villages, fields, rivers, and scattering dismay in its progress until it swept over the cottage and garden of Widow Woodfall, like a hungry lion roaring for the animals to come forth to be destroyed. And what misery and woe had not that same gust of wind accomplished ere it reached so far! Many a gallant bark it had met upon the pathless ocean, and as it howled with fury by, there had arisen that last despairing cry from earth to Heaven for its mercy. The gay vessel was wrecked! Then the same wind had roughly assaulted many a lordly hall and lofty building, stripping off roofs and tearing down ancient gable-ends. It had wandered too into forests, and torn up trees by their clinging roots from out that soil in which they had lived hundreds of years—like a pestilence it had left the awful signs of its presence in its track.

The rich man had, as he heard the howling blast, drawn himself closer to his warm fire-side, and smiled; the poor had sighed, and the houseless wanderer had sat him down, in may cases benumbed with cold, weary with travel, and faint with hunger, to die.

"Mother, that was a fearful hurricane," said Harry. "Did you ever hear the like?"

"Once—once, my dear."

"When was that, mother?"

"It was when old Mathew Freeman

turned out of doors his own child. Poor thing—poor thing. Some say she perished in the storm, but others say she was seen since in great want and misery. She should have come to me. 'Twas very cruel of her not to come to me. We are poor, Harry, but were we poorer, we would give to destitution."

"We would, mother. Oh, if the rich and great did but know the way to real happiness, how very joyful would their lives become, and what pain and suffering would be spared to many who now die of broken hearts from poverty and woe! If I were rich, mother—if I had wealth, such as I have read of as possessed by many in this land, how happy I should be in the happiness of others. Mother, I would have some ancient noble hall; a cheerful fire of forest logs should blaze upon the ample hearth, and lend a ruddy glow to the palest, wanest face, that showed itself within the magic of its blaze. There should be good old English cheer for all who came, and songs and tales, and many a merry jest. The sick at heart should smile, the cold and weary should have warmth and rest—the hungry food. Oh, mother, what a hall I would have; an old English hall, dear mother, such as we read of, but may never—never see again."

"No, my boy, we shall never in England see them again. The nation has changed its habits. Does the snow still fall, my dear?"

"It does, mother; but the wind is scarcely so high. We shall get no sleep to-night, unless it moderates, and that's unlucky, as I go to Mr. Quickset's to-morrow for the first time. I don't think I shall like the law, mother."

"My dear, you may be more happy than you imagine; but was I not telling you, just before that first gust of wind, about poor Grace Trueman?"

"You were, mother, and I would like much to hear about her."

"You shall, my dear; but you must not mind me crying a little, because I always do when I think of her—poor, dear girl. How very beautiful she was! It was just such a night as this on the tenth of January, only two years ago."

"The tenth, mother!—why, this is the tenth!"

The old woman trembled, as she lifted her hands, exclaiming:—

"Is it, indeed, Harry? I did not know it. This the tenth, and just such a storm of wind and snow as happened two years ago! Something is surely going to happen, Harry; and may Heaven in its mercy make that something a happiness to poor Grace Trueman, wherever she is."

"Tell me how it came to pass, mother, that a father could ever turn his own child to the door unheeding of the fury of the elements, and turning asunder every natural tie that bound him to her."

"It was very wicked, my dear; but old Mathew Trueman was a proud man."

"A proud man, mother? Oh, if people would be proud of doing right—proud of relieving instead of inflicting misery—proud of being greeted by blessings instead of curses—how great and noble a thing this pride, which is now the parent of so many vices, would be, mother."

"It would, Harry. They say, from an obscure origin, Mr. Trueman made his fortune, and was and is worth more than a hundred thousand pounds. So he could not bear the idea of his daughter, who he wanted to wed some nobleman, whose property might make him be glad of the match, should become the wife of poor young Rivers, one of his clerks."

"Rivers, then, loved the merchant's daughter?"

"He did, and a nobler, better heart never beat in a human bosom."

"And she, mother, she loved him?"

"She did, my dear Harry—she loved him with her whole heart. Where Grace Trueman loved it was with no stinting measure. Bless her—bless her! —I think I see her now with her quiet smile and her sweet face gliding about the house like an angel, so happy and so beautiful, loving her stern, harsh father, waiting upon him until even his heart would soften, and he would call her his beautiful child, and pass his rough hard hand across her brow, muttering always something about a coronet."

"She must have been very beautiful."

"She was, Henry—she was. You know I nursed her after her poor mother died, and a fairer, better, more loving gentle girl never lived."

"I should have liked much to see her, mother."

"You would have loved her very much, Harry; but you never saw her, for you have not been home with me quite two years, as you know."

"I often wished to be home with you, mother."

"And I would have given worlds to have had you with me; but I was, as you know, forced to go to service, as a nurse, to enable me to support you after your poor father's death."

"And now, mother, we will never part. Was Grace Trueman fair or dark, mother?"

"She was —"

"Hark! what was that?" cried Henry, suddenly starting from his seat, as a low moaning sound came upon the air, during a lull in the wind—a sound that was evidently not produced by the raging element. "Did you hear it, mother?"

"Hear what, my dear?"

"I am sure I heard some voice in a tone of deep sadness. There, again."

A low plaintive noise at this moment met their ears, singing. Sometimes the notes would be completely lost, and the wind whirling round the houses carried the sound away in another direction, and then some few of the words spoken would come clearly and distinctly to their ears, and with a painful pathos bespoke the heavy heart of the singer. The voice was a female one, and it was a very sweet voice, although sad and solemn; still, what it might have been, had she who owned it been the child of luxury, instead of a wanderer on such a night, without a home, there was ample evidence to show in the liquid trembling tones that appeared as if forced from the depth of a bruised heart.

Neither mother nor son spoke, as if fearing to break the spell which that voice had cast over the gloomy night. The wind lulled, dying off in the far distance, with many a sigh, as if its power for that time was gone, and it was moaning at its defeat by some higher intelligence. It would seem that the mournful singer was approaching the house, for the sounds became more and more distinct, until, after a pause, she who uttered those melancholy tones commenced a sad ditty, to which the widow and her son listened, as if entranced.

The words—the tones—the exquisite pathos of the singer, all combined to give the simple ballad an air of reality, that was at once painful and admirable.

"The bleak wind is blowing,
  And cold is the air,
Oh, pity—pray, pity
  The children of care.
The snow it is falling
  Upon my babe's breast,
And hunger is breaking
  Its slumber and rest.

"We are homeless and houseless,
  A mother and child—
A long night is coming,
  The tempest is wild;
My little one's moaning
  Is breaking my heart;
Oh, pity its hunger,
  And we will depart.

We are cold, we are weary;
  My babe's sweet blue eyes
Are now dimmed with tears,
  You may hear its low cries;—
Its soft little hands
  Are cold as a stone;
We shall die—we shall die,
  All friendless and lone."

Deep sobs followed this pathetic appeal, and Harry Woodfall sprang towards the door, exclaiming—

"Mother, dear mother! they shall come in here. They shall have my—my supper—my breakfast—my—my dinner to-morrow, and the next day. God help them, poor things!"

The widow rose from her chair; she grasped her son's arm, and her lips moved for a moment without producing any sound. Then she gasped—

"Henry—it is Grace."

"Grace Trueman?"

"Yes—yes—I know the voice. Heaven have mercy upon her father!"

The widow's feelings overpowered her, and she sunk upon the floor, while Harry flew to the door to admit the wanderer and her child.

Before, however, he could withdraw the bolt that kept it close, a loud scream burst upon his ears—a scream of such terrible intensity that for a moment he recoiled a step.

"Help—help!" shrieked a voice.

There was then a brutal laugh; and just as Harry had opened the door a man's voice cried in loud and savage tones—

"Found at last!"

Harry was nearly blinded for a moment by the storm of snow, hail, and sleet, that flew in his face; but he plunged forward up to his knees in the snow drift.

"Hilloa!" he cried. "Who's there?"

No voice replied, and in vain he strove to pierce the obscurity of the night with his eyes. Large flakes of snow kept darting into his face with a vehemence that was extremely difficult to stand against.

"Who called for help?" he shouted.

"What's the matter, Harry Woodfall?" said a neighbour from a window.

"I hardly know," said Harry. "Did you hear anything?"

"Yes; I heard a screaming."

"Have you a lantern?"

"Yes; wait a minute, and I will hand it out to you. Good gracious, what a night!"

"Who called for help?" again shouted Harry; but there was no reply, and he was fain to wait until the lantern was handed out to him by the neighbour from the window. Harry, however, did not find it of much assistance, for the snow, now that the wind had much increased in violence, came down so thickly, that he could see nothing two feet from where he stood.

"'Tis very strange," he said; "the poor creature is gone, whoever she was. Heaven help her! To attempt any search without the least knowledge of the direction she went in, would be absurd. I have done my best. Poor thing—poor thing! Could it really have been Grace Trueman, or has my mother been deceived by some fancied resemblance in the voice? I hope she was."

With the lantern in his hand, he walked slowly back through the snow to his home. As the light cast a dim halo around it he thought he saw something not quite so white as the surrounding snow. He stooped—an exclamation of surprise escaped his lips.

A dead child, or insensible from the cold, lay half buried in the snow, within a few paces of his door!

CHAPTER II.

THE FOUNDLING.—THE WIDOW'S KIND HEART.—A VISITER, AS UNEXPECTED AS UNWELCOME.

HARRY was for a moment so astonished at the sight before him, that he stood regarding it without acting then immediately upon the impulses of his generous heart. It was, however, but for a moment that surprise held him motionless; for then, throwing down the lantern, he stooped, and taking the little innocent from among the snow, he rushed into his mother's humble home with it so precipitately that the good woman, who sat in her chair trembling, and much affected, screamed aloud.

"Hush, mother, hush!" cried Henry. "For the love of Heaven look at this."

He laid the child on her lap, all covered with snow as it was, and all other feelings in the widow's breast were immediately absorbed in intense astonishment.

"See to it, mother!" cried Harry. "The poor little thing is dead, I fear."

"Dead, Harry! Good heavens, no. Where did you find it?"

"By the door-step, mother. This is, no doubt, the child which its poor mother sung of in so plaintive a strain."

"Then, as there is mercy in Heaven," exclaimed the widow, "this is Grace's child."

"If she who sung was Grace, mother, there can be no doubt."

A low moan now came from the cold lips of the child. The warm air of the room had begun to exercise a beneficial influence upon it, and the vital energies were beginning to be restored.

"It is not dead, mother!" cried Harry. "See—see, it opens its eyes. Are they not beautiful? Warm the poor thing by the fire, mother. May Heaven preserve it."

"Run out and get some milk, Harry," said the widow, as she busied herself in taking off the snowy garments of the child.

Harry was gone in a moment, and Mrs. Woodfall, with tears of sympathy in her eyes, soon divested the child of its cold, damp, clothing, and wrapping the little thing in a warm blanket, she chafed its limbs, and in a few moments Harry returning with the milk, a small quantity warm was administered, and then the child looked in the face of the widow with that earnest gaze that children will so often regard a stranger with, giving us an impression that deeper powers of thought and perception are in action within their young hearts than we would otherwise suppose.

The widow smiled—the smile was reflected on the face of the child. It nestled in her bosom, and was soon in a quiet, dreamless slumber.

Harry was affected almost to tears as he sat opposite to his mother gazing upon the child that lay thus sleeping in her arms.

"Mother," he said, "I—I——"

"What, Harry ?"

"I will work for that little one. God has sent it to our care. I will work for it, mother."

Tears started to the widow's eyes as she replied,—

"Harry, this little one makes me feel as if the last eighteen years had been but a dream. It is the image of what its poor mother was at that age which it is now. This little girl has the same soft, winning smile, that even in her cradle made Grace Trueman so very beautiful. There are here the same long glossy ringlets. Oh, my dear Harry, it seems to me but some dream."

"Then you feel sure, mother, that this child is Grace Trueman's ?"

"I do, Harry. As Heaven is my judge, I do. All circumstances conspire to make me sure of it."

"Then, mother, what can have happened to induce her to leave it in the cold snow, and rush so precipitately from our door ?"

"Alas ! I know not, Harry. 'Tis to me most mysterious. She may return. Poor, poor Grace !"

"But, mother, if she should not ?"

"Well, my dear, we may leave that to Providence."

"And, mother, you will ——"

Mrs. Woodfall understood what Harry meant, and she clasped the child closer to her bosom as she said,—

"I will do my duty, Harry."

"God bless you, mother ! I knew you would take care of the poor foundling. Far from being a burthen to us, mother, it will be a comfort; it will be something for us to talk about—something for us

to love and watch over. On the long winter evenings, when I am away, mother, this little one will keep you company, and wile away the tedious time."

"It will, Harry—it will. We will call it by its poor mother's name."

"Grace Trueman ?"

"No, Harry—Grace Rivers."

"Rivers was Grace's father's clerk, then, mother ?"

"Yes; they married secretly."

"And what became of him ?"

"Alas ! I know not, Harry. He was generous, noble, brave, and handsome."

"Indeed, mother ? And did not such qualities do much for him ?"

"Under other circumstances they might ; but he was poor, and lived with Mathew Trueman, who had no appreciation of such virtues."

"Ah, mother, how many a gallant and noble heart has been crushed by the blight of poverty; how many a bright spirit, born with powers to bless and delight all, has gone to the silent grave unwept for and unknown, because the mere struggle for bread has exhausted the energies which, under happier auspices, would have been felt in their happy influence through the world."

"It is true, Harry. Poor Frank Rivers was all that could be wished, and Grace loved him as surely never one fond, faithful heart yet loved another. He, too, seemed to have given up all thought and hope that was not wound up with Grace. But Mr. Trueman scorned him and his suit, and left them to want, misery, and wretchedness.

"'Tis *he* is to be pitied, mother. He, the harsh father, who could turn his back upon his innocent child, and only because she acted in accordance with the dear suggestions of that one feeling of all others, which has followed us from Heaven—love."

"Ah, Harry, you have read, I fear, too many romances," said his mother. "Here you are but fourteen, my dear, and you converse on subjects far beyond your age."

While the mother thus spoke in apparent chiding, there was no mistaking the look of pride and pleasure she cast upon her boy, as she in her inmost heart rejoiced over his early genius and precocious intellect.

"I do love the romances," he said,

"and I believe, mother, that if they contain pure principles, and be read with a proper spirit and appreciation of the beautiful, they tend to raise and exalt the mind above many of the petty evils of existence."

A heavy knock at the door at this moment arrested the attention of both mother and son, and so unusual a circumstance was it that any visiters should come to them at such an hour, that they felt irresolute for a few brief moments whether to open the door or not.

Another knock, louder than the former, forced upon their minds the necessity of immediate action, and Harry, rising, said,

"Never fear, mother—never fear. I'll see who it can be."

He opened the door. The snow was still falling in large flakes, and, covered all over his breast and shoulders with it, a man above the middle height appeared on the threshold.

"The Widow Woodfall lives here?" he said.

A cry burst from the widow's lips, as she heard his voice, and she said,

"Close the door, Harry—close the door. Keep that bad man from our home."

"Indeed?" cried the man, with a brutal laugh; "it will take both of you, I think, to do that, and then perhaps you may find me too strong for you."

He placed his foot within the doorway, and not suspecting Harry of being so prompt or so resolute, both his head and foot got a severe jam between the door and the door-post, as the boy tried to close it.

"Curse you, you beggar's brat!" said the fellow, "I'd wring your neck for sixpence."

The boy was not to be so easily defeated; for, stepping back, while his cheeks burned with indignation, he caught up a stout broom handle, and before the man was aware, brought it down upon his head with a whack that made him look utterly confounded, and converted the widow's solitary candle into hundreds, that danced before his eyes in the wildest disorder.

"Help! help!" screamed the widow, rushing to the door; "neighbour's, help!"

The man seemed to have just sense enough left to be aware of his great danger now; for with a bitter oath he made a random blow or two at the boy, and then a rush towards the door of the cottage to escape.

The widow's cries had, however, roused some of her humble neighbours to her rescue, and before he could cross the door step, he was seized by a man taller and more powerful than himself.

"Not so fast!" cried his captor,—"not so fast, my fine fellow. What have you been doing?"

"Hold him!—hold him!" cried Harry; "I believe he would have murdered my mother."

The fellow writhed in the grasp of the strong man who held him, but it was of no use. Several others were now hastily coming up, when the villain suddenly drew a knife from his pocket, and opening it before any one could be aware of his diabolical intention, he stabbed the man who held him, muttering as he did so—

"Fool! you may take that for your pains."

The shock of the wound caused the man's hands to relax their hold, and before any one could lay hold of the assassin, he darted off, and disappeared in the snow drift.

"I'm a dead man," said he who was wounded; "neighbours—these are my last—words."

His strength forsook him, and he fell upon the door-step, the blood from his wound dyeing the snow with its crimson tide.

"Is all this some awful dream?" exclaimed the widow. "Can it be real? Am I awake? Harry, my boy, Harry, speak to me."

Before her son could make any reply, a cry from the child attracted her attention, and she sprung into the cottage. The little innocent lay where the widow had placed it in her fright and confusion —namely, on an antique covered chair, and now the noise appeared to have awakened it, for its mild blue eyes were fixed upon the door-way.

Mrs. Woodfall clasped the child to her breast and burst into tears. The wounded man was now lifted inside the cottage, which was soon filled with anxious neighbours eagerly inquiring who had done the deed.

"I know him too well," said the widow

A surgeon who had been sent for, now hastily entered the room, and proceeded to examine the wound, which he declared to be of a dangerous character.

"I know I am dying," said the man, "I feel it—I am certain—I charge you all to find out my murderer. Help me home. Thank Heaven there are none to mourn for me. I have neither wife nor children. Help me—help——"

He fainted away from loss of blood, and several of the compassionate neighbours took him in their arms and carried him to his own house.

The widow's cottage was presently restored to its former quiet, and Harry placed a bar carefully across the door before he spoke a word; then turning to his mother, he said—

"Mother, who is that man?"

"Oh, Harry, do not ask me now. For more than a year now I have thought him dead."

"You know him, dear mother?"

"Yes, yes, Harry—I do know him, and I have my doubts if he be human or some fiend in mortal shape."

"I should know him again if I were to live a hundred years without seeing him," said Harry. "There was a scar across his forehead."

"Yes, yes," said the widow, "there was. Oh, my Harry, shun that bad man as you would shun all evil."

"Who is he, mother?"

"Mark Hilliard is his name."

"Well, mother," said Harry, who saw that his mother was much agitated, "compose yourself. You need be under no apprehension now, dear mother. The villain will never, I think, again tempt his fate by coming here."

"Would to God I had never seen him," said the widow, mournfully. "His hatred against poor Grace and Rivers is so great—so terrible, that now he has once fancied—or perhaps seen that her poor infant is in my care he will haunt us, Harry, day and night."

"Haunt us, mother—why should he?"

"His enmity to this poor babe's father is so great that he will revenge himself upon it, or upon those who succour it; but Heaven's will be done. I look, Henry, upon this little innocent as a sacred trust from Heaven, and I will do my duty by it, through peril or through safety; besides, it is Grace's child—bless her—I loved her ever, Harry—I think I see her now with her mild blue eyes fixed upon her father's face as he would be speaking harshly to some one, and then she would lay her little head upon his breast and whisper to him, 'father, you did not mean it? Tell him you spoke only in anger.' Even he, the stern, cold Mathew Trueman, was sometimes subdued by her gentleness; but now—now—my poor Grace—my poor Grace."

"Oh, mother," said Harry, "if she had but staid here we would have tried to make her happy."

"We would—we would. Is that the snow again, Harry?"

The boy went to the window and shading his eyes with his hand he looked forth.

"Yes, mother. The large flakes are coming down so quick and fast that I can see nothing beyond the window."

"Go to your rest then, Harry. Go at once. Let us bar our door as securely as we may, and this little innocent will be refreshed by the morning."

Harry placed, in addition to the ordinary fastening of the door, a piece of wood slanting from the floor of one of the panels, so that it would have been impossible for any one to break in without smashing the door to atoms.

The widow warmed some milk in case her little charge should awaken, and then with the usual affectionate good night and blessing to her son, she retired to rest for the night, leaving Harry to make his own bed upon the sofa, which was his only resting place, as the humble abode could boast but of two rooms.

"This is all very strange," said the boy, after he had lain down, "very strange. What a rascal that man looked to be sure. Well, I'll work for the little child—who knows but it may grow up to be a comfort to my mother in her old age, and a little wife for me. I love poor little Grace—I—I—won't go to sleep for an hour or so—no—that is I —good night, mother—dear—dear—mother—mo—mo——"

Harry, in spite of his resolution, was sound asleep, and peace, innocence, and repose reigned in the humble home of Widow Woodfall.

CHAPTER III.

A RETROSPECT.—THE AGENT AND THE MERCHANT.—AMBITION, AND A CORONET.

NINE years before the events we have recorded in our last chapter, Mathew Trueman, one of the richest merchants and largest importers which England could boast of, sat in his own little dingy private office in Thames Street, indulging in one of those delicious day dreams which the rich and fortunate have so rare an opportunity of falling into, but which, by the bounty of Heaven, are not altogether confined to that class, for while radiant hope still

"Springs eternal in the human breast."

the poor, the needy, and even the destitute may construct those airy fabrics of the imagination that cheat reality for a time of its miseries, and shed the delightful feelings of prosperity around the veriest wretch that ever fortune buffetted.

But Mathew Trueman, the rich merchant, the possessor of numberless vessels skimming the wide ocean from shore to shore, some loaded with the balms, gums, and spices of Arabia, while others toiled through the surging waves with their rich cargoes of silk from eastern looms—he, the arbiter of the fates of hundreds who were in his employ—a man whose very word "on Change" was worth a thousand pounds, in the shape of unlimited credit to him he so much honoured—had not he, Mathew Trueman, with his iron countenance, and his cold, hard heart, ample materials for day dreaming?

He sat for some time in silence trimming the end of a pen, then a smile, not of mirth—for Mathew Trueman scarcely knew what that was—but a smile of exultation passed across his face as he muttered—

"Yes, that will do. It must succeed. There can be no reasonable doubt. Lord Hawksworth must be accommodated—of course. I began business with three-and-a-penny; but I can accommodate a lord when I like—I have several of these scions of nobility under my thumb. Yes, that's it exactly, under my thumb—the thumb of the rich merchant. They accuse me of usury, do they?—humph!—that sneer shall cost him dear who lets me hear it. Let me look again."

He took up a peerage that lay before him, and commenced reading at a page which had been doubled down.

"Humph—Lord Hawksworth—eldest son of the Earl of Montjoy. Yes, yes, born 18—, of course, and now at the precious and delightful age of eighteen. My Grace, my beautiful Grace is seventeen this day—seventeen—ah—humph—and I began the world with three-and-a-penny. I could roll her up in cloth of gold—I could cover her with diamonds, each one worth a German principality. I could—I will make her vie with the richest, the highest, and in my old age she shall shed a—a—lustre over her father from the blaze of her coronet. She is dutiful, good, beautiful—humph!"

He remained now silent for many minutes, lost in a pleasing reverie, when the door was gently opened, and a clerk put in his head, saying—

"Beg pardon, sir, but——"

"Way for the Earl and Countess of Montjoy," said the merchant, giving utterance to his thoughts. "Ha! that's the countess's father, ha!"

"Sir?" said the clerk.

"Her coronet becomes her. Grace—Grace!"

"Sir?"

The merchant started to his feet, and faced the intruder.

"How dare you, sir, intrude upon me?"

"I—I only came, sir, to say that Girkins is here, sir."

"Girkins?—d—n Girkins!"

"He says, sir, that Nubbles and Sweetbread's house have closed."

"Failed?"

"Yes, sir."

A livid hue overspread Trueman's face, as he muttered—

"Curse them, they are deep in my books. Are you sure, idiot?"

"Girkins says so, sir."

"Show him in here."

The clerk disappeared; and in a moment, as if it were by magic, the whole current of his previous thoughts had changed, and with a knit brow he began writing the names of the men who had failed.

"Curse them," he muttered, "and I

have so much of their goods on commis-sion, which I suppose I dare not touch. Impudent scoundrels! But I'll see what is to be done. Of all the things on this earth, I do hate a man that fails. I never failed—never thought of failing —began the world with three-and-a-penny."

"Mr. Girkins, sir."

A mean-looking man, dreadfully marked with the small-pox, entered the mer-chant's room, and from the obsequious manner in which he came in, and the impossibility there seemed of his ever recovering from the profound series of bows with which he advanced, any one might have supposed that he held Mathew Trueman in great and special reverence.

"So, Girkins," commenced Trueman, "these cursed fellows, Nubbles and Sweetbread, have gone?"

"If you please, Mr. Trueman——"

"If I please? I don't please at all."

"Oh, no, certainly. Dear, bless me —a *lapsis* merely—I really —"

"Where did you hear it—when did you hear it, Girkins?"

"Not an hour ago, Mr. Trueman, if you please, from Blaggs and White. I'm afraid ——"

"Afraid of what?"

"That Blaggs and White are shaken."

"The devil!"

"Oh, yes, sir; if you please, Mr. Trueman, you are looking uncommonly well to-day, sir, really ——"

"Never mind my looks," cried the merchant with petulance, as he rung a small hand-bell, which was answered by a clerk.

"Oh, it's you, Hilliard, is it?" said Mathew Trueman. "Go and make up in round numbers, Nubbles and Sweet-bread's, and Blaggs and White's ac-counts, and let me know what are the amounts."

"Ah," said Girkins; "of all the men —gentlemen, I mean, for business—well, no matter."

"What are you muttering about, man?"

"Eh!" cried Girkins, as if he had been suddenly taken by surprise.

"What do you mean by 'of all the men for business,' and then 'no mat-ter?'"

"Pray excuse me, sir, if you please. I was only presuming to think that if England has reason to be proud of her mercantile position, she should be proud of her merchants, and among them who should she be so proud of as Mr. Mathew Trueman?"

This was a powerful dose of flattery, and would have sickened any one with a weak stomach, but Mathew Trueman had been fed at the delicious fount of flattery so long by all around him, that like an opium eater, he could take a much larger dose than he began with, and he answered Girkins with a much smoother brow.

"Pho, pho, Girkins. I know what's what as well as most men. I began with three-and-a-penny, and I'm not ashamed of it. I swept out Marks, Fogglestone, and M'Cree's warehouse for two years when I was a boy; I put them in the Gazette when I grew up, ha! ha!"

"Wonderful, astonishing man!" said Girkins, lifting up his hands; "and may I venture to humbly inquire after the beautiful and accomplished—oh, Hea-vens!—lovely Grace?"

"She's very well."

"Thank Heaven."

Girkins devoutly crossed his hands upon his breast, and seemed to be giv-ing himself up for some moments to silent prayer. Then as he shook his head, he said—

"Mr. Trueman, I often think that——"

The door opened, and a clerk appeared with a slip of paper on which the ac-counts were noted down, and which he handed to Mr. Trueman with a mock kind of a flourish, and then bowed him-self out.

Trueman looked after him and mut-tered—

"I don't like that fellow. His aspect is not of the right sort."

"Rough spun, rough spun," said Girkins. "I happen to know him, if you please, Mr. Trueman, and I can humbly take upon myself to say that Mark Hilliard is——"

"Two thousand four hundred and sixty-five pounds, three shillings and a penny," read the merchant from the slip of paper, not heeding what Girkins was saying.

His face turned of a bilious yellow with passion, and dashing the paper on the table, he cried with vehemence—

"There's scoundrels! Two thousand four hundred and sixty-five pounds, three-and a-penny! Of all the infernal scoundrels—they shall never have their certificate as long as they live. Three-and-a-penny! The villains! It's a robbery—a dead robbery. Now, you call yourself a lawyer, Girkins?"

A very faint blush of colour came into the cheek of Girkins, as he said—

"I was before my little difference with—the Chancellor."

"Oh, I recollect. You were struck off the rolls as an attorney," said Trueman, coarsely.

"Most unjustly," muttered Girkins; "and now, if you please, I will call myself an agent."

"Very well, call yourself what you like; but go now and make all the inquiries you can about Nubbles and Sweetbread, you understand. See what can be done. Bolster 'em up a little, if possible, and I can in a month convert all the goods I have on commission into actual sales—keep the money on account, ha!"

"What a man—a wonderful brain, constantly in deep thought," ejaculated Girkins, than whom a greater scamp there did not exist unhung. "May I now humbly inquire if you have seen Lord Hawksworth?"

"No. I expect him here."

"Nor the colonel?"

"No."

"Ah—I was thinking as I came down her from the West end. It's foolish of me—very foolish, indeed."

"What's foolish?"

"I—if you please, I came through Hyde Park; I saw the *elite* of the nobility—the ancient aristocracy; I saw them blazing with diamonds, and some of them were a—a—, if you please, beautiful. The sun was shining in unusual splendour. There were lords and ladies, dukes, earls, and two of the blood royal. Oh, what a throng; but—but among them all—among the highest, the noblest, the proudest, I saw none, as I am a living man—no, not one who could have graced a coronet, or shed a new lustre on her station like your own daughter, Grace."

"Ah, indeed," said Trueman, his eyes kindling with pleasure; "that is your opinion, eh, Girkins?"

"It is, if you please, and always under favour, sir, from my heart it is, sir. I fell, sir, into a train of reflections, and I said to myself, where among all these is to be found the clear, active intellect, the accurate judgment, the endless resources of mind of one who wears no coronet, but the imperishable one of his own genius, which has risen him from—from——"

"Three-and-a-penny," put in the merchant, at once adopting the fulsome flattery to himself.

"Ay, from three-and-a-penny to a princely fortune," continued Girkins.

"You are about right there, Girkins," said Trueman. "I have raised myself, and as for what you say about my Grace—bless her and make her always rich—it's very strange; but—but—some such thoughts have once or twice come across my own mind."

The merchant with all his subtilty was far inferior to Girkins, who for the last month had been dexterously insinuating such thoughts into Trueman's head, but so dexterously and so finely that the merchant verily believed the idea to be the coinage of his own brain, and when Girkins now spoke out upon the subject, he only wondered at the curious coincidence of their thoughts.

"Have I indeed," muttered Girkins, "had the honour of thinking for once in the same way as Mr. Trueman? It's enough to make me imagine my fortune made."

"I was thinking that Grace merits some high station," said the merchant. "I have no one in the world but her to look to, and—and—I would like—but no matter now—no matter."

"Lord Hawksworth—"

"Eh?"

"Sir?"

"You said Lord Hawksworth, Girkins?"

"No, sir—you said Lord Hawksworth, if you please. Mr. Trueman—you were in thought—a kind of reverie such as great minds sometimes falls into, and then after remarking that Grace would become well some high station, you mentioned Lord Hawksworth—the heir of one of the oldest earldoms in the kingdom. The representative, when his father dies, of a long line of illustrious ancestors, and the possessor of many hereditary honours and distinctions. Oh, sir, Mr. Trueman, if —if——"

"If what?"

"If poor Girkins were to live to see the beautiful Grace Trueman—a—a—"

"A what, Girkins?"

"A countess!"

"Ay; a countess—a countess," repeated the merchant, as if delighted with the sound. "And what if I say she shall be a countess—I who began with three-and-a-penny?"

"Then she is a countess," said Girkins.

"Ha! I believe I can do something."

"Everything."

"You are partial, Girkins; but—I think,—incline your ear, Girkins. I think that it is possible that by young Lord Hawksworth coming here often he may—you understand?"

"See and admire the beautiful Grace," put in Girkins.

"Ay; and then by my accommodating him——"

"Truly, with money on his bills——"

"Yes, yes, Girkins."

"You may——"

"Hush! hush!"

The door opened and a clerk announced—"Lord Hawksworth!"

CHAPTER IV.

A SPRIG OF NOBILITY.—THE MERCHANT'S DAUGHTER.

EARLY dissipation had begun already to leave its traces on the countenance of the young man, who now walked, or rather lounged into the merchant's room. He was of a slim make, and dressed in the very extreme of the mode, which, happening not to agree very well with his shrunken-looking figure, made him look much worse probably than he otherwise would.

His hair was of that most disagreeable of all light browns, which is destitute of all warmth, and more nearly resembles dust than anything else. Upon his face sat the most dissatisfied smile it was possible to conceive, only that to-day it was a little languid, owing to a head-ache

his lordship had as a small result of the previous evening's amusement, combined with, to use his lordship's own words, "the ex—ces—sive—ly horrid hour" he had got up at, in order to keep his appointment with the rich merchant.

"Your lordship's most obedient servant," said Trueman.

"Ah! how do—how do?—morning."

His lordship thought it fine to clip his words, and even to drop as many of them from a sentence as possible.

"Yes, ah! uncommon tired. Horrid thing! Got up at twelve, ah!"

"Your lordship is not an early riser?"

"Early! ah, frightfully early! up at twelve. Ah!"

Now, Mathew Trueman knew very well in his own heart that the man before him was an execrable puppy, and destitute of either sense, discretion, or the common feelings of kindly consideration which should adorn his class; and Mathew Trueman, likewise, as well as he could love anything, loved his daughter Grace; yet at that moment he was pondering in his own mind upon the chance he had of bringing about an union between his beautiful child and the titled puppy before him, because he was a lord and heir to an earldom. Yes, Mathew Trueman, rich, independent Mathew Trueman, would sacrifice his child, cringe, speak in a low reverential voice, call vices by polite appellations, because this man was a lord!

Alas! what a poor consolation to Grace, for a broken heart, would have been a coronet!

"Ah—ah!" said Lord Hawksworth, after a pause; "recommended to you by Girkins. Ah! do something in the way of money. Ah!"

"I shall be happy to accommodate your lordship," said Trueman.

"Thank you!—ah! regularly out of cash. Run a race with constable, and wan't it!—ah!"

Lord Hawksworth intended this for wit, and gave a languid smile, which produced a laugh from Trueman, who said,—

"And yet I dare say your lordship started with more than three-and-a-penny?"

"Ah!—what?"

"Three-and-a-penny, ah! That was my capital, sir; and now, a—hem! I believe, without hurting myself, I can oblige a lord."

"Impertinent, low vagabond!" thought Hawksworth.

"Had him there!" thought Trueman. "Make him consider himself obliged."

"Well, ah!" said his lordship, after a slight pause, "I want to raise the circulator, ah!"

"Money, my lord?"

"Ex—act—ly, ah!"

"Your lordship is under age."

"Yes; but my friend, Colonel Noland, will, ah! lend his name to my bills, you see, ah! and I pledge my honour to take them up."

"The colonel," remarked Trueman, "does not stand over well in the money-market; but with your lordship's honour as a further security, something may be done."

"Ah, by G—d! something must be done, old fellow! Jenny wants money."

"Who, my lord?"

"Jenny Dunois. I—I—ah, took a lodging for her; reasonable, twelve guineas a week only, ah!"

Trueman looked a little startled at this disclosure, and said,—

"What sum would your lordship consider your necessities require?"

"Ah, the colonel says that forty thousand worth of bills will do for a start."

Mathew Trueman gave a great start himself at this, and said,—

"Forty thousand, my lord!"

"Ah, yes, about that. The revenues of the estates of the earldom are thirty-two thousand a-year."

Mathew Trueman drew a long breath.

"And," continued the young man, "the earl is old, ah! I shall soon be of age, very —"

"It's a large sum, your lordship; but I will speak to my commercial friends, and give you an answer when and where your lordship may please."

"Ah, I'm staying at Flodang's just now; you can send there."

"The colonel to be bound?"

"Yes."

"And your lordship's word of honour as a nobleman and a gentleman to take up the bills when your lordship comes of age?"

"Yes, exactly—that's it, ah! Must go now. Morning, Mr. Freeman."

"Trueman, my lord."

"Oh, ah, Newman. By—by, ah—morning."

"Your lordship may depend upon my utmost exertions to accommodate you."

"Ah, yes. By—by—ah."

Lord Hawksworth was languidly moving towards the door, when it was opened, and a vision of so much grace and beauty presented itself to him, that even he drew back with that involuntary respect which innocence, beauty, and virtue ever succeed in exacting even from the most vitiated of the human race.

A young girl stood in the door-way in an attitude which some rare sculptor might have sought in vain to imitate. Half springing forward, yet half retreating, for she had, not knowing that any one was with the merchant, bounded to his room, and, with her usual buoyancy of spirits, had forgotten to ask if he were alone or not. She was attired in simple white, relieved only by a small edging of lace. Her beautiful and luxuriant hair hung half on her bosom, half on her shoulders, in exquisite disorder. Her beaming lustrous eyes, the heightened colour on her fair cheek, and the striking attitude she assumed as she would have retired on seeing a stranger, all combined to render her in the eyes of him who gazed upon her most fascinating. Palled as Lord Hawksworth had been with much pleasure, and used to the artificial charms of many, the fresh, natural, and exceeding loveliness of the merchant's daughter came upon his bewildered senses like a burst of sunlight from an universality of gloom. Even he, with all the cool assurance which he had been educated in, and which is the principle inculcated into the minds of noble personages in early life, even he stood confused and abashed; such power has youth, purity, and innocence over the worst of men, or at least the silliest, and those who least really appreciate these qualities that lift humanity so near to Heaven.

Now had Mathew Trueman, with all his wild ambition to see his daughter admired by a heir to an earldom, worked his keen sagacious brains for a striking mode of first presenting Grace to Lord Hawksworth, he would not have done so more effectually—by way of making an impression—than had by accident been brought about.

For the space of about half a minute, neither the father, his child, nor their visitor spoke. Then, however, the merchant, as he saw Grace, with a deep blush, was gliding away, broke the silence, by saying to her—

"Grace, my dear, you can come in This is only a friend."

"Yes, yes," said Lord Hawksworth, "'pon soul most love—ly; come in—yes—charming. Was there ever such a blaze of concentrated beauty? Ah—ah —pray come in."

Had Lord Hawksworth said nothing, and tried for once in his life to look a little modest, Grace would, in obedience to her father, have entered the room; but as he recovered his surprise, he recovered his assurance and impertinence; his bold offensive stare, Grace could not and would not endure. His muttered expressions of admiration she did not hear, or she would have been more annoyed still; but as it was, she turned her face to her father and said, quietly—

"I will come again, father, when you have no one with you," and then vanished from the room.

Lord Hawksworth made two steps to the door, as if he would actually have pursued her, but Mathew Trueman did not wish matters to be on so very easy a footing as that would imply, and he said—

"My lord!"

"Eh?—ah. Uncommon lovely," said Hawksworth, slinking back to his chair, annoyed at his own precipitancy.

The merchant saw that his visitor's eyes would not wander from the door, through which had passed the dazzling vision of beauty that had made so great an impression upon him, and in his own heart he exulted that the first step—always the most difficult—was so successfully taken in his wild ambitious scheme of encircling his daughter's brow with the cold weight of a coronet, which was to stand in lieu of happiness—a very mockery of the trusting and affectionate heart.

Hawksworth seemed quite to have sunk into a reverie, and the merchant smiled to himself as he thought—

"'Tis of my child—my beautiful Grace, he thinks. He is now imagining her blazing with diamonds, and a countess's coronet upon her brows."

Lord Hawksworth was really reflecting upon the possibility of accomplishing the ruin of the merchant's beautiful child, and he no more dreamt then of a coronet than as if there had been no such thing in existence.

"My lord?" said Trueman.

"Exquisite, upon my soul," muttered Hawksworth, musingly.

"My lord?"

The young man started and turned to the merchant, saying—

"Oh—really—Mr. a—a—Glueman."

"Trueman, my lord."

"Beg pawdon—Trueman. That was a—your daughter?"

"Yes, my lord."

"Ah—a—handsome girl—very."

"She is considered very beautiful, my lord," said the merchant.

"Considered?" exclaimed Hawksworth, actually for the moment betrayed into a fit of energetic feeling. "She is an angel!"

"You flatter my poor girl," said Trueman.

"No, dem—dem—no, ah. True, she's a Hebe—a divinity."

"She is accomplished," said the merchant, "she has wit, manners, tact and wealth—wealth beyond what many patrician daughters of this land can aspire to. When my child marries, with my full consent and approbation, she shall be presented on her wedding day with two hundred thousand pounds.'"

"Ah! two hundred thousand?"

"Yes, my lord."

"Ah, ah; you must have made a deal of money, Mr. Shewman."

"Trueman, my lord."

"Beg pardon—never in my life could recollect people's names. Quite a peculiarity of my family—we never could."

"That is a mattter of no consequence, my lord, and, as stated by myself, I will inquire among my personal friends, and see if your lordship can be accommodated."

"Ah, yes—I'll call again to-morrow."

"I will wait upon your lordship at your hotel, if you please."

"No," said Hawksworth with eagerness, "I will call here to-morrow."

"As you lordship pleases," said the merchant, secretly smiling at the young man's eagerness to visit him, and guessing the attraction.

In a few moments Lord Hawksworth had got into his splendid cab (which was not paid for), and trotted from Thames-street, not, however, without casting a curious glance up at all the windows of the house, with a forlorn hope of seeing the beautiful Grac Trueman at one of them.

CHAPTER V.

THE REFLECTIONS OF AN AMBITIOUS MAN.—THE MEETING ON THE STAIRCASE.

WHEN the merchant was alone, he rubbed his hands together, and smiled several times. Then he spoke half aloud, as he shut his ledger with a bang.

"Fortunate, most fortunate," he said. "All as I would have wished it. Yes, Lord Hawksworth, I will purchase a coronet for Grace at the price I mentioned to you, only if you are the vendor, I will lend you beforehand half the sum at fifty per cent., so shall we be quits more easily than you imagine. He was evidently much struck with Grace. He could not keep his eyes from the door. I cannot ennoble myself, but the father of the Countess of Montjoy will be somebody; and then Grace—she did not seem much to like Hawksworth —pho—pho—use is everything—she don't know him. He's good-looking, decidedly—and—and a lord, and an earl in perspective."

The merchant rubbed his hands again, and smiled to himself in the most pleasant and contented manner imaginable.

Ah, how different would have been the expression upon his face had he known that Grace from the one look she had given to her father's visitor, had taken a great dislike to him—one of those dislikes common to every young girl, but which are very rarely got over.

Moreover, another circumstance had occurred just as the merchant was enjoying himself so much by noting how struck Lord Hawksworth was with his daughter—a circumstance which would have driven him almost frantic, had he known it, trifling as it was.

It arose thus:

Mathew Trueman made always a great boast of sacrificing everything to his business, the comforts of his small household included, so that Grace in her route to her father's private counting-house, had to pass along a passage, from which opened a glass door to the clerk's room.

Now, it so happened upon this occasion, that as Grace herself was passing this glass door, it was suddenly opened from within, and some one coming out hurriedly, nearly ran against her.

Grace looked up, and to her surprise, she saw that the person was a stranger to her, although being without his hat, he seemed to belong to the establishment. He was a young man with a pale, pensive look, but redeemed by an appearance of high intellect, which glowed in every feature of his face, and lent to his eyes a sparkling lustre, that except when in very gentle moods, was almost painful to observe.

He seemed for the moment as much, if not a great deal more surprised at the sight of Grace, than she was at the sudden meeting with him, but quickly recovering himself, he bowed to her, and said—

"I hope my foolish precipitancy in opening the door has not alarmed you?"

"No," said Grace, and her sweet musical voice seemed to linger in his ears like a tone from Heaven. "No. 'Tis I should have been foolish to take alarm."

She longed to say, "Who are you?" but she could not, and with a low curtsey she passed on, leaving the young man rivetted to the spot with admiration.

And Grace, too, when she got to the foot of the stairs, must needs turn her head to see if the very handsome young man was gone. Their eyes met; it was but for a moment. Grace blushed, and made a bound up the staircase, much vexed with herself for looking round, and in her eagerness to escape, she made a false step.

In a moment, and it seemed to Grace as if he must almost have made one jump from the glass door to the staircase, so quick was he, the strange young man was by her side, and ready to assist her to rise.

She had, however, recovered herself without assistance.

"Good Heavens! are you hurt?" he cried.

"No, I thank you," said Grace, blushing a still deeper scarlet.

"I am very thankful—for——"

There was a pause of half a moment, and then their eyes met again.

"You are quite sure you are not hurt?" stammered the stranger.

"Oh, quite," said Grace. "Good morning."

"Good morning."

Grace ascended the stairs, but she heard him say—

"Now indeed the sun has gone out. Oh, how beautiful!"

The young girl hurried to her room, and bolting the door, she sat down by her dressing-table, and burst into tears.

When she had relieved her overwrought feelings, she said—

"How foolish I am. Why do I cry? It was very—very silly of me to look round as I did, and yet he cannot think ill of me for doing so. No—his manner showed—Oh, Grace—Grace, what are you saying?"

She now remained for some moments in deep thought, and then she said in a low, gentle voice—

"Who can he be? So young, so—handsome. I—how very foolish I am to think in this manner of an utter stranger, and who may have a bad heart for all I know. Oh, no; a bad heart never beamed forth such feelings as are evident in his face. No—no. But who is he?—who can he be? I never saw him before to-day, I am quite sure of that, because—because—nothing."

How long Grace remained communing with herself and smiling the while, she knew not, until she was aroused by some one knocking at her door.

Grace sprung to her feet, and her first glance was at the glass. Her eyes still showed the traces of her recent tears. She hastily poured some water into a glass to wash them with, but again the knocking came, and the voice of her nurse, Mrs. Woodfall, addressed her—

"My dear—my dear—it's only me."

"Coming, nurse, coming," said Grace, upsetting the water in her agitation.

There was no resource now but to open the door at once, which, with trembling hands, she did, and her kind-hearted nurse came in.

"My dear," she said, "what is the matter?"

"The—the matter, nurse?"

"Yes, my love."

"Oh, the—the matter?"

"Why, goodness gracious, my darling, you have been crying."

"Crying, nurse?"

"Yes, my love, your eyes are quite swollen. Ah, my poor dear Grace, who has been saying a harsh word to you?"

"No one, nurse—no one, I assure you. But—I—I broke a glass, you see."

"But you did not cry for that, my darling, I am sure."

"No—no, I——"

"Ah, now I am sure your father has been busy, and in the hurry of a moment has said something to you which you have taken as unkind; but I'm sure, Grace, he loves you tenderly."

"He has said nothing, nurse. Sometimes, indeed, when he is tormented, as he says, by business, there is harshness in his manner; but I know it is not real."

"You are right, my dear. But what a sad thing it is that people should make themselves so unhappy after money. Folks begin life by wishing to make money, because they hope to enjoy it, and they end by its becoming their master, and they its most abject slave."

"Yes, nurse, yes."

"But, my dear," said the old woman, kissing Grace, fondly, "you have not now told me what vexed you."

"I—I wasn't exactly vexed."

"Were they tears of joy, Grace?"

"No—no, nurse, I will tell you. I was so foolish as to stumble on the staircase, and—and you see, nurse,—stumble on the staircase."

"Well, my darling, and you hurt yourself. Was it your ancle, my dear?"

"Oh, no, nurse; I did not hurt myself at all; but—but—a—gentleman came, and—and would have helped me up, but I had got up before he came, so—so I came to my room, and being a little flurried, I may have cried."

"A gentleman?"

"Yes, nurse."

"Ugly?"

"Ugly—ugly? Quite the reverse; he was as handsome as—as—as—"

Poor Grace had been caught in a very simple trap, and the moment after she had spoken, she saw how she had committed herself, and looking reproachfully at her nurse, while her face was suffused with blushes, she said—

"Now I'm vexed with you, nurse."

"With me, my dear?"

"No, dear nurse, no."

The kind-hearted young creature threw herself into her nurse's arms, and burst again into tears.

"Well, my dear, I won't provoke you any more; but I will give a guess as to who the handsome young man with the black eyes and the voice can be. A long time ago, Grace, I am told your father was in business as a partner with a Mr. Rivers, but in a few years they quarrelled and separated, your father carrying on the business, and Mr. Rivers betaking himself to the army. Well, poor man, he was killed in some battle or another, and left an only son an orphan, and it seems he died very poor indeed, and the poor child was knocked about from one to another, till an aunt of his adopted him, and brought him up till her death very respectably; but as she had only a small life annuity, it perished with her,

HENRY WOODFALL DISCOVERING THE CHILD IN THE SNOW.

and then poor Rivers—that is the son, Mr. Francis Rivers—was left alone in the world, and I understand from little Tom Hackey, the errand-boy, that he has come into your father's counting-house to-day as a junior clerk for the first time."

"Then it was he," faltered Grace.

The door was opened by a female servant, who said—

"Oh, if you please, miss, master's disengaged now, and wants to see you, miss."

"I'm coming," said Grace.

CHAPTER VI.

A NEW PIECE OF COMEDY.—THE USEFUL CREATURE.—THE FELLOW CLERK.

YOUNG RIVERS, the merchant's new clerk, for it was he that Grace had had the little adventure with on the staircase, remained for a few moments after she had disappeared from before his enraptured vision, in a reverie of delight.

"Who can that be?" was his thought. "Did ever mortal man imagine aught more beautiful! Am I dreaming, or is this reality? Am I in my senses? Did I for one moment touch her hand, or is it only fancy? Here, in a house devoted to business; here to exist in so uncongenial a soil, one of the fairest, best, dearest! Oh, it must be a day-dream. It can't be real. It's very provoking, though. Well, I have something to dream about now, however—something to speculate in my imagination about. After this I shall believe in ghosts, goblins, sprites of all kinds, and particularly visions of lovely girls with long flowing hair and blue eyes of heavenly tenderness and——"

"Master's a-coming," cried a voice from the passage.

Rivers was down the few stairs in a moment, and he saw in the passage a lad of about fifteen or more, and presenting in his dress and appointments a most nondescript appearance.

Rivers looked at him in amazement, and an idea came across him that this might be another creation of his brain.

"Are you the new cretur?" said the youth.

"The new what?"

"The new cretur."

"Who do you mean?"

"Oh, you know. Is your name Rivers?"

"It is."

"Oh, then you are the new cretur. How de do? How de do?"

"I am very well, I thank you. May I presume to inquire who you are?"

"Tom Hackey."

"Very likely, but what are you?"

"They calls me the fag. When there's anything uncommonly dirty or disagreeable to do, I'm the cretur! If anybody's in a passion, they kicks or pinches me. If anything's broke, I always comes in for a blowing up. If master writes a letter never so much too late for the post, it's always my fault."

"Why, you are the scape-goat of the establishment then, it appears?"

"I don't know what you mean about being a goat in the establishment, but I know I has lots to do and five bob a week."

"I dare say your abilities, like most geniuses, are underrated," said Rivers.

"I believe yer. You're a sensible chap, I think, and I'll give you a bit o' friendly advice, when you tosses with Hilliard."

"Toss with who?"

"Mark Hilliard."

"Who is he?"

"Him in the office. You must have seed him."

"I did see a person in the office, but we have not yet exchanged a word."

"Very good, when you toss with him, mind as you make him bring down his tin with a hard dab, and have something put over it afore you cries heads or tails, or else he'll do you as brown as possible."

"I have no doubt," said Rivers, "your caution is very friendly, but as I never tossed in my life, and never intend, why you see I am in no danger of being done brown, as you say."

"Very good. 'Hang out the banners on the outward walls, the cry is still they come.' Ah! ah! ah! ah!"

"Good God, what's the matter?" cried Rivers, at this sudden outbreak.

"Are you struck all of a heap?" said Tom Hackey, recovering himself, with difficulty, from the violent attitude he had thrown himself into.

"I must confess," said Rivers, laughing, "I'm rather struck."

"Thought you would be. People generally is. I flatter myself as I can come Macready rather—just a few——"

"Oh, can you?"

"I believe ye. I ain't such small drink as you thinks for, when I really comes out. 'High reaching Buckingham grows circumspect.' Ah! ah! ah!"

Rivers could hardly restrain his laughter, and Tom Hackey resumed—

"I believe you like it. You can't help it. It's human natur."

"It's remarkably good, I dare say."

"What do you think of this?"

Tom Hackey threw himself into an attitude, and rushing down the passage, exclaimed, "'A horse, a horse—my kindom for a horse. Bind up my wounds. Bring me another horse. A horse—a——'"

Mathew Trueman at this moment appearing, the stage-struck hero fell into his arms, and was immediately saluted by half a score of hearty cuffs.

"You scoundrel!" cried Trueman.

"Murder!" shrieked Tom.

"You infernal villain! how dare you make this noise here?"

"The Thane of Fife's got a wife," mumbled Tom. "Murder. Call out the guard. Oh, my head! Hang out his body on the beetling rocks."

"Take that," said the merchant, giving Tom Hackey a parting box on the ear, "and mind me, if ever I find you idling your time again in this most disgraceful way, you leave my service at once, with a pretty character."

"I only," began Tom, "was a-going to——"

"Silence, sir."

"I was only a-going——"

"Will you be off, you scoundred?"

"I only was a——"

The merchant made a rush at Tom, who now precipitately retreated, having, as he well knew, by former experience, put his master in a towering passion by answering him.

But then how delightfully prudent a man was the rich merchant, even in the smallest matters of business. He would not discharge Tom Hackey, because he well knew that there was but a small chance of his ever again meeting so patient—so really hard-working, and at the same time, last, though not least, so honest a drudge.

"Oh, Mr. Rivers, you are here, are you?" said Trueman, when Tom had left.

"I am, sir. I—was coming to you."

"You will generally find me in my private room, Mr. Rivers."

"I was only wishing to ask you, sir, what hour I should be here in the morning?"

"You must attend by eight, alternately with Mr. Hilliard."

"Very well, sir, I will be punctual."

Rivers bowed to the merchant and walked into the office, whither his employer followed him to give directions respecting some work which he wished done immediately.

Such, however, was the confusion that poor Rivers was in, regarding the appearance of the beautiful girl in the passage, that he could scarcely at all comprehend what the merchant was talking about, and when the latter said—

"You will make exact copies of the letters for me, Mr. Rivers," the young man replied, to the great surprise of the merchant,

"Yes, my darling."

"Sir?" said Trueman.

"Sir?" repeated Rivers, reddening to the very roots of his hair.

"Are you awake, Mr. Rivers?"

"I believe so, sir."

"Then, I doubt it, sir," said the merchant, throwing the letters down before him, and walking out of the counting-house.

"Oh, what a madman I am," thought Rivers. "Either I have been dreaming, or I am in the same house with the most beautiful young creature that ever mortal eyes beheld, and here I am foolish enough to risk my immediate discharge by non-attention to the commonest business. Oh, Francis Rivers, think more calmly, and do not dash your own cup of happiness from your lips."

As he made these reflections he set about busily copying the letters, but what was his horror to find, upon comparing his transcript with the original after he had done one to find that he had actually commenced it with the words—

"Beautiful vision," instead of "Dear sir."

He tore up his copy of the merchant's letter in despair, and threw the fragments into the fire, when as he did so, he found that his fellow clerk's eyes were intently fixed on him.

There was something in this man's looks that Rivers by no means liked; a lurking expression of low cunning was ever present upon his dark, sallow countenance, and the smile that drew down the corners of his mouth, was anything but a pleasing or a mirthful one.

"It certainly is a fact," thought Rivers, "that there are people with whom we have never exchanged a word, and of whom we know nothing good or bad, but who, nevertheless, one shrinks from instinctively, and this fellow-clerk of mine, I see, will be a favourite aversion."

By the cunning smile that flitted over the features of the other, it would seem that he almost guessed the nature of the thoughts that were passing through the mind of Rivers, and after a few moments' silence, he said, in a coarse tone of low familiarity—

"Well, young fellow, I suppose we shall be better acquainted by and bye?"

"My name is Rivers, sir," said the young man, who was far from being used to such a mode of address.

"Very well, and my name is Mark Hilliard, so they say. I repeat, we shall be better acquainted, and no offence I think is in that."

"None, whatever, Mr. Hilliard," said Rivers, who began to think it would be foolish of him to show any temper for a little want of the good manners of society in his fellow clerk.

"I should think not," said Hilliard. "Oh, mum's the word. Here comes old dot-and-go-forward—d—n him!"

The merchant entered the office, and advancing to Hilliard, he said—

"Mr. Hilliard, have you finished those invoices, for Malta?"

"Yes, sir. Here they are," said Hilliard.

"Very well. Now, if you please, you will get on as quickly as possible with the entries of those papers I gave you yesterday."

"Certainly, sir."

Mathew Trueman was about leaving the room, when Hilliard said—

"Beg pardon, sir, but a poor relative of mine has rent to pay to-day, and if you could oblige me with a couple of sovereigns—"

"Mr. Hilliard," said the merchant, "you know I don't like this irregular mode of doing business—you must take your salary at its stated periods, if you please."

"Case of extreme emergency, sir," added Hilliard.

The merchant with a vexed air laid down two sovereigns, and said—

"This is the last time I shall make any such advance, sir."

He then walked from the room, without looking to see what progress Rivers was making in his letter-copying, to the young man's very great relief.

CHAPTER VII.

THE TWO CLERKS.—THE QUARREL.—THE FIGHT.—A VILLAIN'S REVENGE.

THE moment the merchant was clear of the counting-house, Hilliard placed the thumb of his left hand upon the extreme tip of his nose, and spreading out the remainder of his digits, he said—

"Go to the devil, old cut-and-come-again. You forget your I O U, old stick-in-the mud. D—n you, I'll swear you out of these two sovs when my quarter comes round."

Rivers looked amazed at this unblushing piece of rascality, and Hilliard observing his glance of mute astonishment, muttered something about "a spoon," and then said aloud—

"Honour bright, Mr. Rivers—no peaching."

"No what, sir?"

"Peaching."

"I really don't know what you mean."

"Do you mean to say you are so verdant as not to understand a little slang?"

"I don't understand slang at all, sir. I have been educated among gentlemen."

"Oh, indeed. Well, peaching means sneaking in to the governor, and telling him what I say. Now you understand?"

"I do understand you, sir, and, in reply, would strongly recommend you to protect yourself."

"Protect myself! What do you mean?"

"I mean, sir, by never saying anything that you are ashamed to hear repeated."

"Oh, dear! bless us all—amen. Hokey-pokey—gammon."

Rivers took no notice of these various expressions of incredulity on the part of Hilliard, but went on with his writing calmly, resolving that he would not allow his temper to be ruffled by anything his companion should say.

"Well, now," said Hilliard, after a pause, "you are right to be cautious. It might have been a plant on you, you know, to find out what sort of stuff you were made of. But all's above board with me. When I say a thing I mean it; I'm rough and ready."

Rivers merely nodded his head in reply to this, as intimating that he heard him, but did not consider that he had anything to do with his roughness or his readiness.

"Mark Hilliard says what he thinks,"

continued the other, "and thinks what he says. He's always alike, d—m me!"

Still Rivers made no reply.

"Come, come," continued Hilliard, "I dare say you are a good fellow, though you look so demure. Tip us your daddle."

Rivers conjectured that he might mean shake hands, by seeing the outstretched hand of the other, and he replied:—

"I think, sir, that if any value is to be attached to the process of shaking hands, we ought to know each other a little longer before we exchange that pledge of friendship."

"Oh, indeed!"

"If," continued Rivers, "you consider it merely an unmeaning form, pledging me to no opinion—no companionship, I am perfectly willing to take your hand."

"Damme! you may take it or leave it."

"Then I prefer leaving it."

"You do?"

"I do."

Hilliard bent his brows upon Rivers, and his face assumed a demoniac expression, as he muttered:—

"Do you mean to insult me?"

"No," said Rivers.

"Then what the devil, sir —"

"Silence, sir!" said Rivers, in a tone that at once cowed his companion, who was evidently only making the experiment to see if the other would be bullied easily.

"Silence, sir!"

"Oh, silence, eh?"

"Yes," said Rivers. "I will not be spoken to by any one in the manner you were assuming."

"Assuming, eh?" said the much discomfited ruffian, with a pale cheek.

Rivers made no answer, and after a pause Hilliard added,—

"You have insulted me, sir, and d—n me if I don't have satisfaction!"

Rivers turned full upon him, and said, calmly:—

"You are a fool as well as a rogue!"

The dark face of Hilliard turned perfectly yellow, as he cried,—

"What, sir? Curse me, how dare you?"

"How dare I!" said Rivers, whose blood was up, in spite of his prudent resolution. "How dare I! Why, if you were as courageous as you are cowardly, I dare."

Hilliard quailed beneath the glance of Rivers, but he bethought him that he might yet make a last desperate effort to get the better of his fellow-clerk; for the idea of sitting down in the same office with a man who had out-bullied and brow-beaten him the very first day, was too much for him to bear.

He trembled for a moment, partly with passion, and partly with fear; then he said:—

"Young fellow, you don't carry it off that way. Mark Hilliard isn't to be put down by such a boy as you are."

"Well, sir?" said Rivers.

"It isn't well, sir, and for half a pin, I'd punch your d—d head for you!"

Rivers smiled, and at the moment he received, being off his guard, a blow from Hilliard that nearly staggered him.

It was but an instant that Rivers paused, and then before Hilliard could follow up his brutal attack, he sprang upon him, and with one blow, which knocked aside all guards and fell in the middle of his face, he sent him sprawling to the farther end of the counting-house, where he fell with such a crash that the house shook again from top to bottom.

Before Hilliard could rise, Mr. Trueman stood at the door of the office, with looks of astonishment and rage.

"What is all this?" he cried.

Rivers turned to him, and said—

"Sir, I have knocked down that scoundrel in self-defence."

"Defence?"

"Yes, sir; I was attacked by him for I know not what."

Hilliard sat on the floor, stanching the blood from his face with his handkerchief, and the merchant looked at him for a few moments in silence, then he said, in a tone of forced calmness, although his voice trembled with passion,—

"You leave my service this moment, Mr. Hilliard."

The bewildered scoundrel shuffled to his feet, and in an abject, whining tone, said,—

"If you discharge me, sir, I don't know what will become of me."

"You have discharged yourself, sir. Do not say that I discharge you. Think you that I can have my counting-house made an arena for your blackguard disputes?"

"I do not think, sir," said Rivers, "this will ever happen again."

"You know, sir, there's nobody knows your discount customers so well as I do," whined Hilliard.

This remark seemed to have some effect upon the merchant, who was largely engaged in a peculiar kind of usurious business which would not bear any very strict scrutiny. Hilliard saw him wince, and he followed up his advantage by adding—

"You know, sir, White and Moses offered me anything to go to them."

"I don't know any such thing," said Trueman; "but if I was sure this would not occur again, I might ——"

As the merchant rather appealed to Rivers as he spoke than to Hilliard, Rivers replied—

"I don't think it will occur again, sir, if that is your only difficulty as regards this man. He will not attack me again, and I am quite sure I shall never be the aggressor."

"Upon condition, then," said the merchant, "that I hear no more of this, Hilliard, I feel inclined to overlook your very bad conduct."

"Thank you, sir. I am sure I never intended it should come to this. After I had refused White and Moses ——"

"Well, well," said Mr. Trueman, "I don't want to hear any more about it."

"Very well, sir."

"Come, now, let me see you shake hands and forget it all."

"There, sir, you must excuse me," said Rivers. "I never give my hand to a man who I do not esteem, or in common courtesy to one I have reason to think badly of."

"Oh; pho, pho," said Trueman; "shake hands."

Hilliard held out his hand, but Rivers, with respectful firmness, said—

"I cannot, Mr. Trueman, take that man by the hand; he made a most wanton and unprovoked attack upon me; and had I not happened to be the stronger, which he is now aware I am, I might have been severely injured by him."

"Well," said Mr. Trueman, "look ye here, both of you. I will have no quarrelling in my counting-house, and upon a repetition of what has now oc-curred, you shall both leave this establishment within an hour."

"I am willing to leave it now, sir," said Rivers, "if you are dissatisfied with my conduct."

"The next time, Mr. Rivers," said the merchant.

"I can only say that I will not be the aggressor," said Rivers.

"I'm not going to interfere with him," muttered Hilliard. "If he don't want to be companionable, I'm sure he needn't."

"Silence—silence," said the merchant. "Let the matter drop now. I will hear no more from either side about it."

Rivers turned to his desk, and went on with his letter copying, while Hilliard obsequiously opened the door for the merchant, and held it while he passed out of the counting-house.

Then, as Rivers had his back towards him, he shook his clenched fist, and swore to himself a horrible oath of vengeance against him.

"I shall never be content till you're hanged at the Old Bailey, my spark," he muttered; "and it will go hard with Mark Hilliard unless he contrives to let you in to some pretty scrape yet. Curse you, I'll beat you one way if I can't another. I'll have my revenge. But the first thing I must do now, is to make as good friends with you as I can. That goes d——y against the grain, but I must do it."

CHAPTER VIII.

THE GENTLEMAN AND THE AGENT.—A PAIR OF ROGUES.—THE CONSULTATION AT BERNARD'S INN.

EVERYBODY knows Bernard's Inn, Holborn, but everybody does not know that in it, at the period of our tale, which was not very long ago, there lived in a dingy set of chambers, up three flights of ricketty stairs, one Jonas Quickset, an attorney-at-law, and constantly at law with somebody was he.

Mr. Quickset was a small man, with a hook nose, a sallow physiognomy, and an eye that looked for all the world as if it were ashamed to be an eye, for it winked and blinked, and shuffled about in its orbit from the floor to the ceiling, and from the ceiling to the floor, when any other pair of eyes encountered it. Nevertheless, there was one thing which Mr. Quickset's eye always looked at steadily, and had never so much as winked at for forty years, and that was Mr. Quickset's interest.

We have spoken of Mr. Quickset's eye in the singular number, and now we proceed to explain that we are fully entitled so to do, seeing that that very clever and far-seeing professional gentleman had but one eye.

Mr. Quickset's business consisted of a number of dirty jobs which his more respectable brethren were ashamed to have anything to do with, for notwithstanding what ill-tempered people will say, and one-sided writers will write, there are men in the law of as high honour, liberality, and gentlemen, as are to be found in any profession whatever; but it is the fashion with many persons to condemn a whole class for the errors and knaveries of a few individuals of it.

Mr. Quickset, however, truth compels us to state, was a very great rogue—a monstrous rogue—he lived and luxuriated in roguery. It was a part and parcel of his very nature, and he could no more help being a rogue than he could help looking the little despicable wretch he did look.

He and Mr. Girkins had been engaged together in many transactions, and, in fact, Mr. Quickset would have attracted the same notice from the Lord Chancellor that his friend Girkins had, only that the particular piece of roguery which had struck the name of Girkins from the roll of attorneys could only be perpetuated in one name, so the more wily Quickset had shuffled out of it, leaving the whole onus upon the shoulders of Girkins, while he was, if it succeeded, to have equally the profits.

The fates, however, were adverse. Girkins was struck off the rolls, and Quickset remained on them, so Girkins became that most suspicious of all characters, an agent for anything, everything, and nobody, who wanted any business transacted through the instrumentality of another—he, Girkins, being not at all particular with regard to the honesty of the transaction.

The hand of union, therefore, between Girkins and Quickset was by no means broken, and the agent worked very well indeed with the attorney, who still by the act of parliament remained a gentleman, and by act of parliament only.

Mr. Quickset was sitting alone in his chamber, when a gentle knock announced a visitor, whereupon, graciously opening the door with his own hand, he admitted Mr. Girkins.

"Ah, Girkins, how do ?"

"Tolerable, thank ye—middling."

"Take a seat."

Girkins sat down, and after solacing himself with a pinch of snuff, he said—

"I think, Quickset, we may work a little affair that I have in hand, rather comfortably than otherwise, I should say."

"No doubt of it," said Quickset.

"Why, I have very little doubt of it."

"I should say you have none."

"It amounts to none."

"I know it, Girkins. You are a safe card. Study is the word."

"It's a money affair."

"Accommodation ?"

"Yes."

"Oh, discounts, I suppose ?"

"It will be done that way, I believe."

"Who's the man ?"

"Why, in rather a roundabout way, I heard that a certain young heir to a certain earldom was in want of a certain amount of cash to carry on the campaign till he became of age."

"Exactly."

"When he does come of age he has a large sum quite independent of his father."

"Very good."

"So that, you see, if the present earl's life should drop, and he is seventy, we have our man tolerably safe."

"But his bills are worth nothing."

"They are not negotiable."

"Certainly not, and should he be inclined to repudiate them, you know, when of age, we are all in the wrong box."

"My dear Quickset—a—hem. You don't quite yet know all the little circumstances connected with this case."

"Of course not."

"Exactly. Well, I will explain."

"I am all attention."

"The party is found who will make the advances."

"Oh !"

" Yes, and all we have to do is to get as large a finger in the pie as we can."

" Of course."

" Certainly. Then another party who is likewise to have a finger in the pie, will put his name to the bills as well. My dear Girkins, mind you don't let too many fingers be put into this pie."

" No more than I can help, you may depend."

" I am aware of your discretion and abilities."

" Thank you."

" Oh, I mean it."

" I know you do. Now you are an attorney, and I can let you in for all the legal part of the business, you see."

" For a con—si—der—ation ?"

" Ex—act—ly."

" Half ?"

" Agreed."

" Now then for the particulars."

" You shall know all, my dear Quickset, for you are perfectly aware I have no secret from you."

" Curse him, he is going to tell me some thundering lie," thought Quickset.

" The best way is to tell him the truth, and then he never acts upon it, because he never believes it," thought Girkins.

" Well, the particulars."

" Are simply these. This young nobleman wants forty thousand pounds."

" All at once ?"

" Yes."

" Very good."

" Along with his bills, he offers his word of honour as a nobleman and a gentleman, that when he comes of age he will not repudiate them on the plea of minority."

" Gammon."

" So say I."

" Of course. Why, he'll swap a few horses with a parcel of black-legs like himself, and then turn bankrupt."

" Very likely ; but I beg to remark that that is nothing to us, Quickset."

" Not a bit, if we keep your names off his paper."

" Decidedly ; but the most precious feature in this cause is, that the man who is willing to advance this forty thousand pounds, or twice forty thousand if it should be wanted, don't want back a single penny of it."

" Indeed ?"

" True."

" How do you account for that ?"

" He'll do it for the honour of the transaction."

" What an infernal liar this Girkins is," thought Quickset, in the recesses of his heart.

" He's swearing to himself now, and don't believe a word of it," was Girkins's thought.

" You don't mean that ?" said Quickset, aloud.

" I do."

" How do you make it out ?"

" Easily."

" Then, pray explain."

" I mean with you to be strictly confidential. The young nobleman is Lord Hawksworth."

" The only son of Earl Mountjoy ?"

" The same."

" He is indeed a pigeon worth the plucking."

" He is."

" And this gentleman who will lend so much money for the honour of the thing—who is he ?"

" Mathew Trueman, the rich merchant."

" He ?"

" Yes, he."

" Now, Girkins, you are joking."

" I never was more serious in my life, Quickest, as you will yourself presently admit."

" Go on—go on."

" Mathew Trueman has a daughter— beautiful as an angel, and he has set his heart, with a little friendly nudging onwards by your humble servant, upon getting her a titled husband."

" I begin to see."

" I thought you would. Well, this extravagant, weak, muddled-headed young lord is just, as he thinks, the very person to be struck with the beauty of his daughter—so he will lend him money, until his only means of extrication will be by making the daughter a countess, on condition of the father crying quits with him."

" Oh, that's the plan, is it ?"

" It is."

" It will fail."

" Of course it will for two reasons. Ay, for three."

" And they are ?"

"These. Firstly, Lord Hawksworth will repudiate the debts, when he becomes of age. Secondly, like all vain fools, who have nothing but a title to be proud of, he is proud of his, and will not marry the merchant's daughter, however much he may admire her; and, thirdly, she, the daughter, will most probably run exactly conter to her father's wish, and quash the whole affair, if even Lord Hawksworth were willing to make her his wife."

"Upon my word, Girkins, you know what you are about. I never heard anything more luminously and clearly stated."

"I have taken some pains with the parties, I rather think, and come what may, there must assuredly be some nice pickings out of the transaction for so able a professional gentleman as Jonas Quicksel, Esq., Attorney at law."

"Assisted by Mr. Girkins, agent, &c."

"Exactly."

"Well, Girkins, if you can bring all this about, I shall consider you a very clever fellow. Good-bye."

TERMINATION OF THE QUARREL BETWEEN THE CLERKS.

CHAPTER IX.

THE FATHER AND DAUGHTER.—GRACE'S NOTIONS OF A HUSBAND.

BEFORE Grace went to her father she satisfied herself that all traces of her recent tears were gone, for although she could stand the questioning of her nurse, she would have been sadly troubled by the same sort of inquisitiveness on the part of the merchant.

It was after Mathew Trueman had settled, or fancied he had settled, the quarrel between his clerks, that Grace made her appearance, in obedience to his message in the small private counting-house, which had been so recently occupied by Lord Hawksworth.

The merchant's face was stern and clouded when Grace entered, but the sight of his beautiful daughter soon brought a smile upon his harsh, rugged features, and he said, as he extended his hand—

"My dear, you need not have run away when you came here before."

"You were busy, papa," said Grace,

"Not very; that gentleman was more a friend than a customer."

"Indeed!"

"Yes—Grace—my dear—did you—see—him?"

"Yes, papa."

"Oh! I thought you had not."

Grace made no reply to this, for she did not think it required one; and after a pause her father said, while he looked with fondness in her beaming eye—

"My beautiful Grace, how happy your old father will be when you have contracted some noble alliance, every way worthy of you, and, perhaps, a coronet is resting gently on those brows."

"Oh, father, I am not ambitious."

"But you should be."

"Should be?"

"Yes, to be sure."

"In all that I have heard or read, the wise, the great—I mean the great in mind, not the mere adventitious circumstance of rank—and the good, have ever decried ambition."

"Wherefore?"

"As a deadly foe to content."

"Oh, nonsense—nonsense! What would have become of me if I had not been ambitious, Grace? Perhaps you don't know that I started in life with three-and-a-penny? Ah!"

Grace ought to have known, for she had heard it above a thousand times, and always accompanied by the concluding "Ah!" which the merchant seemed to consider clenched the matter for ever.

"Yes, father; but the honest, praiseworthy exertions of industry I do not call ambition."

"Don't you, Grace?"

"No, father."

"Then what do you?"

"That wild envy of others possessing fancied advantages above us, that constant restlessness for station, and to be ever what we are not, until, as I have read, the mind loses even its appreciation of virtue and its reverance of right, in its mad desire to attain its objects, which seem at a distance so bright and alluring, but which ever lose their lustre on a closer approach."

"Romantic rubbish!" cried Trueman, as he had no other answer ready.

"I am content," said Grace, "without pining to be other than what I am."

"That's all very well till you have the chance, you know, Grace. Never pretend to be quite contented, but always, as I did, when I had but three-and-a-penny in my pocket, fix your eyes upon the next round in fortune's ladder, Grace. Ah!"

Grace never liked these conversations with her father, for her extensive reading, and natural good judgment, told her that he was wrong; and she now endeavoured to get rid of the subject by saying—

"You sent for me, father, for something?"

"No, my dear, I only sent to say that I was alone now, as you had gone away on seeing a visiter with me."

"I merely came to see you a moment, father, and, of course, went away when I saw that vulgar-looking man with you."

"What—what?" cried Mathew Trueman, his whole countenance exhibiting the most unequivocal signs of astonishment.

"Is he not so, papa?"

"Not so?"

"Yes; I thought he stared at me most unlike a gentleman."

"Why—why, bless my heart, he is a gentleman; he must be a gentleman."

"Must be, papa?"

"Yes, he's a lord—a nobleman; eldest son of an earl; estates, dignities; House of Lords; coronets, walks in processions; visits kings and queens. A gentleman, indeed, I should say he was. He never began life with three-and-a-penny in his pocket; he's extravagant, too, as all noblemen ought to be."

"Then, papa," said Grace, with an arch smile, "he may end life with three-and-a-penny, if he began with more."

"No fear of that; oh, when a nobleman squanders away all he can get, he must be kept by the public, of course; always is; either a sinecure altogether, or he is made some stick or another in waiting; so, you see, Grace, there is no chance of an earl or an earl's wife, eh? ever coming to three-and-a-penny. Ah!"

"An earl's wife, papa?"

"Yes, I said an earl's wife. Oh, what a wife for an earl you would make, my Grace."

"I, papa?"

"Yes, you."

"I never thought of being anybody's wife."

"But whenever you do, mind you think of a title, and a coronet, Grace, for you shall wed with some noble of the land, or my name ain't Mathew Trueman, and I didn't begin business with three-and-a-penny in my pocket; ah!"

"Father?" said Grace.

"Well—well, what makes you look so pale?"

"Am I pale?"

"You are, indeed. Bless me, girl, what's the matter with you?"

"Nothing—nothing."

A fearful surmise had come over Grace's mind of the truth, namely, that it was one of her father's schemes to match her, without the sanction of her heart, to some glittering title, so that he might catch some of its refulgent beams and gratify his own ambition to be allied with aristocracy of birth.

A shudder passed over her frame as this supposition occurred to her, but the next moment she rejected it as absurd, and with a smile she turned to her father, saying—

"I hope mine may be a happier fate than what is called a noble alliance. I am too young, for many years, to think of marriage; but if I do love ever, it shall be some one mild and gentle in his manners; some one conveying the Heavenly stamp of intelligence in his face; one who, from the power of a glorious intellect, will command the respect of mankind; such a one only would I wed, and as such a one would not have poor, foolish, romantic Grace Trueman, why, you see, father, I shall remain with you always as I am now."

Trueman was silent for a moment, and then he said in a low tone—

"But suppose you should find some nobleman with all these virtues and excellencies besides."

"Then I should say it was a thousand pities he had his title, because nature had conferred upon him so much higher a nobility."

"Yes; but nature's noblemen don't wear coronets, you understand, Grace, ha!"

"They wear hearts, father."

"Pho—pho! all romantic nonsense. No such thing; they generally wear coats out at the elbows, and seedy hats."

"Well, father, you see your Grace will be condemned to live single, then.

I will cheer your declining days; and when the hours you devote to business are over, you will always know that you have one warm, loving heart to welcome you to your 'ain fireside.'"

There was something in this picture of domestic happiness that staggered the merchant for a moment; but then he thought of "the countess's father" being spoken of, as himself, and Mathew Trueman was in a moment the ambitious man again.

"No, Grace," he said; "you must never be sacrificed to the peevish whims of an old man. Some one will fall in love with you—the feeling will be mutual; and, while St. James's bells ring their merriest peals, you will be converted from Grace Trueman into Lady something, or perhaps the Countess of something."

Grace shook her head.

"What think you of that picture?" said her father.

"It has no charms for me."

"No charms?"

"None; and, besides, hangs upon so many improbabilities, father."

"I don't know that."

"But are they not evident?"

"No; certainly not. How?"

"As thus: first of all, some one must fall in love with me—then, that one must be a nobleman—two improbabilities."

"I don't see that they are such great improbabilities."

"Well, father, there is a greater to come. I might not fall in love with the nobleman, you know, father."

"You—you don't mean to say, Grace, you would be so mad as—as——"

"As what, father?"

"To refuse an alliance which would bring honour, distinction, and—and—a-hem! upon us?"

"You forgot happiness, father."

"Well; happiness, of course."

"Is happiness always of course?"

"Nonsense, girl, nonsense. You read so many novels, I know you do, that you forget common sense, and that I began business with three-and-a-penny only in my pocket—ha!"

"Father, let us quit this profitless and ungracious subject," said Grace.

"Oh! certainly; only common sense is common sense. Come, come, don't look so gloomy about it; we shan't fight, as young Rivers, my new clerk, and young Hilliard have done already this morning."

"Fight, father? Rivers?"

"Yes; well, I never saw such a girl: a little while ago you were quite pale, and now you are altogether as red."

"How dared Hilliard——"

"Eh?"

"I mean—that is—I—nothing——"

"Oh, that is a very satisfactory explanation. Well, well, go away to your nurse, Grace; but don't be so foolish as to take all these absurd notions in your heard you have been talking to me about."

"Was Hilliard hurt, father?"

"Not much; but Rivers got the better of him."

Grace breathed more freely.

"Yes," continued the merchant, "he knocked him sprawling into a corner. I believe it was all because Rivers has some nonsensical notions, something like yours, of not shaking hands with anybody he don't esteem, and all that rubbish."

"Good-by, father," said Grace, rising, and looking more beautiful than ever, since the mention of Rivers's name.

CHAPTER X.

TOM HACKNEY AND THE DRAMA.—THE LOVER'S SECRET.

WHAT was related to Grace Trueman by her nurse concerning Rivers was true, so far as it went, and there were many other circumstances of which she knew nothing, but which, nevertheless, lay at the bottom of the merchant's heart, like the worst dregs of his moral existence.

Mathew Trueman had, to use a mild term, out-generaled his former partner, the father of young Rivers, and had contrived, when the business became flourishing, to oust him from the concern, by quibbling concerning the articles of partnership for some time, and leading him such a life of humility and vexation, that, not being at all a business-man, he was glad, eventually, to get out of the concern, a comparatively ruined man, leaving Mathew Trueman to enjoy the fruits of their united capitals and industry for the previous five years.

This affair, at the time, Mathew Trueman thought a fine stroke of policy; but when, as years rolled on, he began to find that the mere account at his bankers did not bring to him that lively sense of satisfaction and "lightsome happiness" he had foolishly imagined, his conduct to poor Rivers would rise up before his scared imagination, and terrify him.

When, therefore, the son of the man he had thus injured applied to him for employment in his counting-house, he eagerly seized the opportunity of at once accepting him as some sort of expiation of his conduct to the father.

These were the true circumstances that brought Francis Rivers into the merchant's counting-house; and the young man, being ignorant of his father's wrongs at the hands of Trueman, felt grateful for a timely reception, which he placed all to the credit of his employer's good heart.

The merchant, however, looked upon the employing of Rivers as an investment of so much good against so much bad, as if Heaven kept a debtor and creditor account of men's actions, and cast up a balance occasionally, to see how the account stood.

This is by no means so uncommon a delusion as some may imagine, for there are many thousands of "very respectable people" who do the same thing, as, for example, some tradesman who swindles everybody all the week, but piously attends his parish church three times on a Sunday, a process which we heard an old lady of decidedly evangelical principles, once describe as "rubbing off as you go on."

This, then, was the account Mathew Trueman kept with his conscience. "I robbed the father, but I employ the son. I turned the father out of my counting-house, but I take the son in," a species of logic which, if it answers at the great bar of Heaven, will be urged by sinners, high and low.

But to return to Rivers. What a new existence seemed now to have dawned upon him, since the beautiful vision of the merchant's daughter had burst upon his senses. As yet he knew not who she was, and his great anxiety now was, as to how and when he could procure information concerning the lovely girl, with whom he felt, henceforward was to be found his only happiness in this world.

Love is a plant of rapid growth. It germinates, buds, and blooms in a moment; and such was the love which, lightning-like, had flashed across the heart of Rivers for the unknown girl he had met in the merchant's house.

He felt that his destiny in life was fixed. He had an object for all his thoughts, something to dream of, and amid the silence of the night he had now an interminable subject of delightful reflection.

Oh, what airy fabrics of the imagination could he not now raise story by story, until they touched Heaven in their giddy altitude. Sometimes he would fancy himself walking with the beautiful maid of his heart, along the margin of some limpid stream, while, in a low murmuring voice, he spoke to her of love, and she hung upon his arm, while he could just perceive the gentle quivering of her long silken eye-lash, as it rested on her damask cheek, and felt, by the light pressure of her hand within his own, that his words were not unwelcome to her ears. Oh, such dreams as these were bliss indeed! Rivers forgot all his quarrel with Hilliard, he forgot his very existence. A new and delightful subject engrossed all his thoughts, all his fancies.

Not a word was exchanged between him and Hilliard for the remainder of that day, and although Rivers plied his pen laboriously in copying a mass of correspondence for the merchant, he did not find the time hang heavily on his hands, but after an hour or so, came to do his work mechanically, while his thoughts were far otherwise occupied, and in imagination he was conversing with the girl who had gained entire possession of his noble, honest heart.

At one o'clock Hilliard took his hat from a peg in the office, and casting a look of mingled hatred, scorn, and defiance, at Rivers, he went out to get his dinner.

Rivers heard him close the office-door, and it was a great relief to him to find, upon glancing round, that he was alone.

He put down his pen, and leaning his head upon his hands, he gave himself up to a delicious reverie, wherein Grace figured, of course, as the presiding genius

of all the thoughts that sprung up in rapid succession in his brain.

How long he had remained in this state of dreamy contemplation, he knew not, but he was aroused by some one saying—

"Well, I hears you. You needn't keep on repeating of it like a old poll parrot."

Rivers started from his position of thought, and looking hastily round, he saw Tom Hackey, the singular errand-boy, regarding him with looks of intense astonishment.

"What's the matter?" said Rivers.

"How should I know?"

"Oh, I thought you said something."

"So I did, but you said something first."

"I—I! Oh, no. You mistake, I did not speak; in fact, I did not know you were here."

"No doubt o' that ere. You was in one o' them studies as people calls brown."

"Oh, was I?"

"Yes, you was. How you was a smiling away. My eye, for all the world like an old pair o' bellows, you was."

"But I never knew that a pair of bellows, old or new, smiled."

"Well, what's the odds. It's a *simetar*, ain't it?"

"A what?"

"A simetar. When you says one thing's like another, you know."

"I suppose you mean a simile."

"Ah! that may be the out and out way o' saying it, but I always calls it a simetar."

"Well, but, Tom, there's a right way and a wrong."

"Very likely; but I'm a poor fellow, and only has five bob a week, so the wrong way does for me all the same."

"As you please; but what did I say?"

" 'Oh, lovely,' says you."

"Nonsense."

"You did, you know you did—or else you would not get all on a sudden so red; why, the red lion a top of the street's nothink to you."

"Pho, pho; you imagined it."

"No, I didn't. 'She's lovely,' says you—'a divine *creter* she is,' says you. ' Her eyes,' says you, 'is like stars as is twins;' then you shakes your head, and says, with a sort of a smile, says you, 'No, no, no, no, no,' says you, 'it's the stars as claims to be like her eyes,' says you. Then you heaves a sigh as was enough to blow the great ledger off the desk, and you says, 'Fate, fate, fate,' says you."

"Impossible!"

"Well, then, if it wasn't fate, it was fat!"

"You rave, boy, you rave. Here's half-a-crown for you, and—and mind you don't repeat this ridiculous story to anybody."

Tom Hackey pushed back the half-crown, and with a shake of his head, he said—

"I do'sn't want the money—mums the word. I sympathises with you."

"What?"

"You are in love. I knows you are. There you goes, blushing away like a house o' fire. I knows as you're in love, and so is I."

"You?"

"Yes, to be sure. Let's be confidential. 'Tis not alone my inky cloak, good mother, nor customary suits of solemn black, but I have that within which passeth show. These but the trappings and the suits of woe!'"

"What has Hamlet to do with it?" said Rivers, laughing heartily.

"Everythink. Hamlet's romantic, so am I, Tom Hackey. Hamlet's always making *sallallyquashies*, so is I, Tom Hackey."

"Making what? Bless me, what an extraordinary word!"

"Oh, you knows what I means. 'To be or not to be—that was the kevestion.'"

"Perhaps you mean soliloquies?"

"Well, I said so. My love is like a torrent. Ah, down, demon, down! Ha! ha! ha! My blood biles, my heart grieves, liquid fire toddles through my brain, and my stomach aches like madness. Ha! ha! ha! Revenge! revenge! I must have revenge!"

Tom Hackey, as he uttered these sentiments, possessed himself of the office-ruler, and assumed an attitude of intense defiance to all the world at large.

"Who are you to be revenged upon?" said Rivers.

"Oh, nobody; that's only a speech."

"Whence from, for goodness sake?"

"I seed that at the Surrey; it's called 'The Pool of Gore! or, the Fifteen Murderers of Finchley Common.' It's a out-and-out piece, it is."

"So I should think from the specimen you have favoured me with; but your state of mind must be rather dreadful, if such sanguinary speeches are expressive of it."

"Oh, I can come the tender. 'I wish as I was a pair o' gloves on your hand. Oh, Juliet—Juliet—Juliet! I'll forswear my name, and be no more Tom Hackey."

"You are quite a genius," said Rivers.

"I always was. I begins to think old Mat would feel the loss of me."

"Old who?"

"The governor."

"Upon my word, everybody here seems to have some singular name for Mr. Trueman."

"In course. Who art thou, villain? Thy name—thy lineage—quick, draw and defend thyself. Ha! ha! ha!"

"I'll make you defend yourself," said Mr. Trueman, putting his head in at the door.

"Th—dev—governor!" said Tom.

"Get out, sir. Have you been to your dinner, Mr. Rivers?"

"No, sir."

"Tut, tut; why, I told this fool, who is quite mad with a theatrical mania, to stay in the office while you went to dine."

"I—I forgot," said Tom; "but I'll run out and get him a saveloy and a buster."

"Silence, sir! You can go when Mr. Hillard comes back," said the merchant.

"He's in love, sir, and don't want no *witals*," remarked Tom Hackey.

"In love, are you, Mr. Rivers?" said the merchant. "Ah! you redden. Well, if your affections are engaged, it's perhaps all the better for you. I always think when a young man has once formed a firm and honourable attachment, he has a much better chance of success in life."

"Oh, Heavens!" exclaimed Tom Hackey. "Upon the beetling rock I——"

"Silence, sir! Come and take a snack with me, Mr. Rivers. This is my luncheon time; but you can manage to make a dinner of what's on the table, I daresay."

"You are very kind, sir," said Rivers.

"Not at all. Mind the office, Hackey."

"First in my dear love the office comes, and, oh, next—oh, oh!"

"Now, listen to me, sir," said the merchant. "You shall leave my employment if I hear any more of this rubbish."

Tom only muttered to himself—

"Can such things be, and overcome us like a summer's cloud?"

"Come with me, Mr. Rivers," said the merchant.

Rivers followed his employer, who thought to himself, as they went upstairs—

"I'm glad this young fellow's affections are already engaged, for he might get up a hopeless passion for Grace. She is very beautiful, and in every way calculated to inspire such feelings."

CHAPTER XI.

WORLDLY ADVICE—THE PRIDE OF MONEY.—RIVERS'S ANXIETY.

WHILE Mathew Trueman, the rich merchant, would have turned quite frantic with rage at the presumption of his clerk daring to fall in love with his daughter, he could not control the silly vanity of showing to Rivers his beautiful child, and hence his invitation to him. He wished to dazzle and confound him with the beauty of Grace, and then never again to allow him the honour, as he conceived it to be, of seeing her.

How little the wily and deep-thinking merchant thought that a mere trifling accident had that morning marred all his designs for the future, and that the very entangled heart, which he congratulated himself Rivers had, was filled solely with the image of his own beautiful child.

But so it is with all the schemings and contrivings of man. His deepest-laid plots, his most artfully and cunningly-devised schemes are ever at the mercy of the merest accident, when down topples the whole fabric he has raised in his imagination, upon what he thinks so secure and inimitable a basis.

And thus it is that fools have fortune, and talent is clothed in rags; the accident has favoured the fool, and confounded all the reasoning of the man of deep research. Who shall, then, say that such and such a thing shall be? No one who knows aught of human nature, or who has studied the progress and various computation of human events.

Could Mathew Trueman have believed it possible that in five minutes, while he was conversing with Lord Hawksworth, something had occurred which— But we will not anticipate. We will let the crafty man work out to his utmost his craft; we will let the pure, the innocent, and the highminded obey Heaven's behests. Our duty is to chronicle events more than to reason upon them.

Rivers followed the merchant listlessly, for, as he understood him, he was to lunch with him alone; but when he ascended the same staircase up which the beautiful girl, who had made so great an impression on his heart, had disappeared, a hope sprung up in his bosom that he might see her, and he trembled with excitement and an anxious expectation as step by step he followed the merchant into the dining-room.

A handsome and elaborate luncheon was laid upon the table, together with wines of several description; in fact, the luncheon was as like a dinner, with the exception of being composed of cold viands instead of hot, as any one thing could be like another.

The merchant was extremely gratified at the look of admiration which Rivers cast upon some really beautiful paintings which hung in the room and he said—

"Ah! Mr. Rivers, I see you are a judge of art. I got that Claude a bargain—three thousand guineas only."

"'Tis a fine specimen, sir."

"So they say; but, come, we will waste no precious time—you can come up another day and look at my paintings."

"Thank you, sir."

"And in the meantime we will attack the luncheon. Ah! Mr. Rivers, it is something to begin with three-and-a-penny, and go on till you buy a Claude for your dining-room at three thousand guineas—ah!"

"It is, indeed, sir, and reflects the greatest credit on the honourable industry that has achieved so much."

"Three-and-a-penny ain't much to start with. Ah!"

"Certainly not, sir."

"Bless me, where can Mrs. Woodfall and Grace be? My daugher, Rivers, and her nurse, a worthy old soul, always lunch with me."

"His daughter!" thought Rivers.

"Some folks think my Grace handsome," continued the merchant; "but you shall judge for yourself, and it may be well for you, Rivers, that your heart is already engaged."

"Ye—ye—yes, sir—I—oh, yes."

"Confound it, you fellows in love, whenever the subject is mentioned, begin such a course of stammering and hammering, that it's quite impossible to make out what you mean."

The merchant rang the bell as he spoke, and a servant appearing, he said—

"Tell Mrs. Woodfall and your young mistress that I am waiting luncheon for them."

"Yes, sir,"

"So you are in love, Rivers? Well, you can't do better. Are you quite engaged?"

"Sir, I do not mind confessing to you that I have registered a vow in Heaven, that if I do not wed the dear object of my heart's fond love, I never will think of another."

"He's booked," thought the merchant. "Well—well, when you have made a little money, you had better marry her."

"I will strive, sir, to merit her."

"Very properly spoken, my boy. I knew your father very well. You have heard as much—how he married for love only; but do you take my advice, the advice of an old merchant, who has seen someting of the world, and mind when you do marry to have a little money into the bargain—you'll find it an amazing set off against any little future disagreeables that may arise, you may depend."

"I cannot barter my affection, sir."

"Ah, that's childish jargon—barter your affections—trash! Marry a beggar and you'll be very glad to barter your affections for bread and cheese. I've seen something of the world, I should think. Began with three-and-a-penny—Ha!"

"We view this subject very differently, Mr. Trueman," said Rivers.

"Of course we do. You are a romantic boy, and I am an old merchant. You are in love, and I am not, you know."

"Exactly, sir."

"Well, I rather think that makes some difference, don't it?"

"A great deal, sir."

"Very great. Now you are in love with some poor girl with a prettey face, I know you are. You have as good as said so."

"I don't know, sir."

"Oh, nonsense! Well, what's the consequence? Eh—a large family—poor people always have large families—of course. Twelve children, or somewhere thereabouts—a second floor taken unfurnished, and doomed to remain so—pail outside the door for the children to be sick in."

"Sir, really——"

"Oh, it's all true—I know all about it. Lodged in an attic above such a family—watched the whole proceedings. Husband took to drink—wife thumped the children—children screamed—and had all the diseases they possibly could."

"You draw a gloomy picture, sir."

"Of course I do. Poverty is always gloomy—nothing in the world so cheerful as money, Rivers."

"I believe it's a great assistance, sir, to a light heart," said Rivers.

"It's everything—heavy purse light heart—light purse a heavy heart, as a matter of course. Now take my advice, Rivers—fall in love with some rich man's daughter."

"I have thought of it, sir."

"The devil you have."

"Yes, sir. I am in hopes that she I love so truly may be a rich man's daughter."

"Oh," said Trueman, reassured. "That's right indeed, certainly. That's quite right."

"Curse the fellow," thought Mathew Trueman. "I began to be afraid he was going to take my advice, and then he might have begun with falling in love, or pretending to do so, with Grace; and now I come to look at him, upon my word he's rather good-looking than otherwise."

While those thoughts were passing through the merchant's mind, Rivers was in an agony of suspense to know if the beautiful girl he had met on the staircase was the merchant's daughter or not, and his impatience converted each moment of delay into an age.

He was not doomed much longer to be kept on the tenter-hooks of despair, for just as the merchant exclaimed—

"Where can those females be?"

The door of the room was thrown open, and the enraptured gaze of the young man fell upon the reality of all his dreams—the living incarnation of all his hopes—in Grace Trueman, the rich merchant's daughter.

CHAPTER XII.

THE MEETING OF THE LOVERS.

RIVERS, by being half-prepared for the apparition of beauty that suddenly

THE BURGLARY AT THE MERCHANT'S HOUSE.

burst upon his senses, had sufficient command over his feelings to prevent himself from uttering any exclamation, or betraying more feeling or confusion on the occasion than might have been perfectly natural in a young and exceedingly modest man, and was rather gratifying than otherwise to the merchant, as testifying to the great effect his daughter's charms had upon a stranger.

Grace, however, all unprepared as she was for a sudden meeting with the person who had occupied her thoughts ever since her first meeting with him,

turned very pale and red by turns, being scarcely able to seat herself at the table with any degree of composure.

Luckily for her, her father was too intent upon catching the effect his daughter's wonderful beauty had upon Rivers, to notice her confusion until she had very nearly succeeded in conquering it.

"Well, Grace," he then said, "you need not put yourself out of the way. This is only Mr. Rivers, my new clerk. Mr. Rivers, this is my daughter Grace."

Mr. Rivers rose and bowed, and Grace, stealing a glance at him from under her eyelashes, bowed likewise, when they both resumed their seats.

"Now for luncheon," said the merchant.

Rivers knew no more what he was eating or drinking than the man in the moon. Sometimes he would take a tiny piece up on his fork, as if he were determined to dine upon homœopathic doses, and at others he eat for a few moments as if for some desperate wager.

"A glass of wine with you, Rivers," said the merchant, condescendingly.

"Thank you, sir," said Rivers, and poured the wine into the salt cellar.

"Why—why, Rivers!"

"I beg your pardon, sir, I—I really—"

"Oh, that's always the way with you fellows in love."

Grace slightly started, and Rivers upset the decanter in a moment.

"There again," cried Trueman. "Upon my word, Rivers, you are sadly confounded."

"I beg ten thousand pardons, sir, I—I was, I confess, thinking."

"Of your beauty, ah!"

Rivers bowed.

"Grace," said the merchant, "Mr. Rivers is deep in love—engaged to some exquisite damsel, and has no eyes for other charms. He is chin deep—ha—ha—ha!"

Rivers felt a strong inclination to jump up and strangle his host, while Grace turned of a deadly pale hue.

"Yes," continued the merchant, 'he's booked and posted—done for!"

"I—I really, sir," stammered Rivers.

"Nonsense, nonsense."

"You mistake, sir."

"Why, didn't you tell me you had been head and ears in love for Heaven knows how long—and was now?"

"I—I said now, sir, now—now."

"Well, of course, now—now."

"Ye — ye— yes, sir, exactly, sir. Miss Trueman, now—now. Exactly—to-day."

"Come—come, I won't torment you any more," said Trueman.

Grace breathed a little freely, as she whispered to her heart—

"Now—now, to-day. Yes—he loves me!"

"Come now, Grace," said her father.

"You shall sing a song, and then we go to business again."

"Excuse me, father, to-day," said Grace.

"No excuses."

"I implore——"

"You nonsense! Come, let's have one of your old ballads."

Grace saw there was no escape, and in a voice which, although it was low and tremulous at first, Rivers thought the music of another sphere, she sang the following ballad:

"When nature from its sleep released,
Blithe morning reddens in the east,
And scatters with a lib'ral hand
Her gem-like dews o'er all the land:
And from his nest with eager spring
The lark doth rise, and rising sing:
While the fair new-born day I see,
I think of thee—I think of thee.

"At noontide, when to shun the heat,
Embow'ring shades are my retreat;
Where falling water, cool and clear,
Wake music to the listening ear;
I seek, perchance, the world of dreams,
And weave a thousand airy schemes;
Thro' all an angel form I see,
And think of thee—and think of the.

"And ever at the evening hour,
In daisied fields, or jasmine bower,
Whether I tread the haunts of men,
Or steal to some romantic glen,
To look on the descending sun,
His daily course of glory run:
Oh! brighter than his beams to me—
I think of thee—I think of thee.

"When night has donn'd her starry robe,
And darkness mantles o'er the globe,
And Cynthia, with her tender ray,
Makes the night lovelier than the day;
When I have joined my hands in prayer,
Resigning all to heavenly care,
The world denounc'd, and fancy free,
I think of thee—I think of thee.

"Dear lady, when Time's hasty snows
Do on my wrinkled brow impose,
The same mild influence still shall last,
To bless me as in all the past.
In hope, in joy, in pain, or strife,
Thro' all the chequer'd scenes of life,
Thy tenderness my theme shall be;
I'll think of thee—I'll think of thee."

"Well done," said Trueman, "but not so well as you usually sing, Grace."

Grace hung down her head and said nothing.

Rivers only thanked her by a look, but that one look said more to the heart of Grace Trueman than would the most laboured panegyric upon her singing.

"Well," cried the merchant, looking at his watch, "we have ten minutes to spare; you sing a song, Mr. Rivers."

"Who, I, sir?"

Grace looked up a moment, and their eyes met. He read in them the words, "do sing," and being really a fine singer of tenor songs, he, with great feeling, sang the following:—

"Oh! love is like the rainbow,
    That passes ere an hour!
Oh! love is like the beauty
    That decks the summer flower.
'Tis like to the cameleon,
    Which never is the same;
'Tis like the timid antelope,
    So sweet, but hard to tame;
Or like the gentle crescent moon,
    Whose light so briefly shines;
Or like her sister-stars, that fade
    When pensive night declines.
'Tis like the crystal of the lake,
    When rippled by the breeze:
'Tis like the perfum'd zephyrs
    That play among the trees;
'Tis like all beauteous sounds and sights
    Which this fair world supplies;
Yet! oh, I found it most complete
    In my dear lady's eyes."

"Well done—well done, bravo!" cried the merchant. "That's enough for to-day, and for ever," he muttered to himself, "for, d—e if I don't think this cursed fellow, with all his pretended constancy, is casting sheeps' eyes at my Grace, confound his impudence."

The merchant now rose, saying—

"Well, we must indulge ourselves no longer, Mr. Rivers.

"I am at your service, sir," said Rivers.

Grace rose, and bowing nervously, walked from the room.

"Beautiful," said Rivers.

"Eh?" said Trueman.

"The—the—Claude, sir."

"Oh, the picture."

"Yes, sir, I said, beautiful!"

"So it is—so it is—cost a pretty sum, though. Three thousand guineas out of a man's pocket who began with three-and-a-penny, ha!"

———

CHAPTER XIII.

HOPES AND FEARS OF RIVERS.—A WALK AND AN INTERRUPTION.—A HUMBLE BUT DEVOTED HEART.

OH, what a new and glorious existence seemed to have opened to the poor merchant's clerk, when he thought of Grace, the beautiful, the gifted Grace Trueman, not more rich in all the varied charms of person than she was in mental loveliness.

"Now," he exclaimed, "I have, indeed, something worth the living for! Now, indeed, have I a pursuit in life, more alluring than the soldier's glory, the statesman's power, or the miser's gold. From this happy, happy day, I date my life. I did but breathe before, but now I live, indeed, in the dear love which swallows up all other considerations in the vortex of its mighty passion. Oh, Grace—Grace, if Heaven should so far bless me as to make you mine, how sweetly would our days glide onwards. In some quiet cottage by a silver stream, whose gentle murmurings should woo us to repose, we'd live. We would have no thoughts that were not of each other. The days should pass in love and thankfulness to Heaven for our pure happiness. Oh, could I realise such a picture of peace, contentment, and affection, kingdoms might change masters, ambitious man might rise or fall, and mankind vex themselves with the thousand cares of life—cares created by themselves, while I was happy, having reached the proudest height I e'er aspire to—To love and be loved by Grace."

Busied in these reflections, Rivers leaned his head upon his hand and saw not the triumphant leer with which he was regarded by Hilliard, who, although he affected to be writing, held his pen suspended from the paper to note the many smiles that flitted over his companion's face, and to endeavour to gather from its changes the subject of his thoughts.

At length, with a deep sigh, Rivers suddenly looked up, and in an instant Hilliard's eyes were glued to the ledger before him. Rivers had not noticed that he was an object of so much attention to Hilliard, and he endeavoured to bend his mind to what was before him; but the image of Grace Trueman would flit across the page he was striving to fill with dull, uninteresting characters. The memory of every word she had spoken, the lingering melody of every tone haunted him perpetually, and he longed for five o'clock, when the office would close, and he would be able to seek some sweet retirement far from the crowded streets, to think freely of the love which he felt would henceforward be the blessing or the bane of his existence.

At length the welcome sound of the clock as it tolled the hour of five came upon his ears, and Hilliard at the very instant dropped his pen and sprang from his stool, while Rivers, with nervous haste, began to sort the letters he had written.

Tom Hackey then entered the office, and with a familiar nod to Rivers, he said—

"Well, so here's five o'clock at last. Haven't I been waiting for it a long time, rather? I always puts away the great ledgers, and just pops things a little square for old Mathew before I leaves."

"Do you?" said Rivers, as he put on his hat, and hurried from the room.

"Well, I never!" cried Tom. "What a hurry he's in."

"Now, idiot," exclaimed Hilliard, as the poor fellow stood unconsciously in his way.

"The same to you, sir," cried Tom, in a similar voice.

"I tell you what, young fellow," said Hilliard, "some of these days I'll make you bite your tongue for your impertinence."

"Bless us, you don't say so?" replied Tom Hackey. "How about St. Andrew's watch-house, eh?"

This seemed to be a sore question to Hilliard, for with a muttered oath he left the office. The fact was, that Tom Hackey, once passing down Holborn Hill, had been attracted by a crowd at the door of the watch-house, and upon pushing his way forward to ascertain the cause, he found Mr. Hilliard had been apprehended on strong suspicion of picking a gentleman's pocket of his watch. The next morning Hilliard was discharged from want of evidence, with a

caution by the magistrate, and the affair never having reached the ears of Mr. Trueman, Hilliard was in a fright continually that Tom Hackey would some day take it into his head to relate it.

Having promised, however, at the earnest solicitations of Hilliard, that he would not mention the circumstance, the poor fellow was far too kind and conscientious to break his word, and although he did occasionally taunt Hilliard with the affair, he never had the least idea of carrying it to the ears of Mathew Trueman.

In love as in rage we equally require exertion to allay the excitement of the mind, and Rivers, when he was fairly clear of the office, set off walking westward at a tremendous pace, his mind the while busy with thoughts of Grace and her beautiful beaming eyes, which seemed to dance before him as he went.

"Oh, if I could but win a fortune for her," he said; "if I could in some manner make myself more worthy of her than I am, I should be happy; but poor and dependant as is my position in life, will Mathew Trueman ever bestow the hand of his darling child upon me? He surely loves her; but he is, I fear me, one of those men who love rank and gold and all those adventitious circumstances which, in the eyes of so many persons, surround a man with such a halo of glory, while honest poverty may rot unnoticed among the busy throng."

While pursuing these reflections, Rivers had no more idea of where he was going than any one else had for him, and when he reached the corner of Fleet Street, being impeded by some persons, he, in a fit of abstraction, turned and proceeded towards the City again, whither he had not proceeded far, when the voice of Tom Hackey met his ear, as he exclaimed—

"Hilloa! are you going back?"

"Back! where?" said Rivers.

"To the City, to be sure. I thought you was in never such a hurry to get away."

"Why, so I was," smiled Rivers. "Thank you. Good evening."

"Oh, but I want to speak to you."

"Won't to-morrow do?" said Rivers, who wished then for no companion but his own thoughts.

Tom was silent for a moment, then he said—

"Mr. Rivers, I'm only a poor boy, and not fit company for you, in course, though if you was to see me do Richard at our private theatricals, you wouldn't think me none so dusty.—'A horse—a horse—my kingdom for a ——' "

"Fool!" shrieked an old gentleman, upon whose most sensitive corn Tom Hackey had stepped in his theatrical fervour.

"Sir, I begs your pardon," said Tom, "I didn't see you. I supposes as the horrid pang is a going away?"

"I'll give you some pangs, you villain!" exclaimed the old gentleman, shaking his walking-cane, and stamping with rage and pain.

"Come along," said Rivers; "you should be more careful in the streets, Tom."

"So I should; but, like many great actors, I'm rather carried away by my feelings.—'Bind up my wounds—ha—ha—ha—'twas but a dream.' "

"Good evening," said Rivers. "I really cannot allow you to walk by my side if you behave like a maniac."

"Well, I won't," said Tom. "You may depend as I won't. But will you let me say to you all as I've got to say to-night, instead of to-morrow?"

"If you particularly wish to do so, certainly," said Rivers; "but the public street is not a very good place for a conference."

"Where was you a-going?"

"I was going to walk right on until I came to some place where at least I could see a few trees and a little grass growing."

"Then you needn't go very far. There's the Temple Gardens. Come, then, and I'll tell you what's worth knowing, because it may keep you out o' mischief.'

"Indeed? Well, I may as well walk there with you as elsewhere," said Rivers; "and I can but thank you for your proffered communication."

The two strangely-associated companions walked down Fleet Street until they reached the precincts of the ancient abode of the Templars, now devoted to far different purposes, and passing through the gate by Whitefriars, they were soon in that pleasant spot of verdure by the river's bank, which has been trodden by many of the greatest and the highest personages connected with our country's history. They sat down upon one of the most retired of the benches, and then Tom Hackey fixed his eyes upon the face of Rivers, and a strange expression came over him—an expression so different from that he ordinarily wore, that Rivers was both surprised and alarmed.

"Mr. Rivers," he then said, in a voice that was evidently struggling with some great emotion, "I wish to speak to you about something that you may think very odd of me to—to mention."

He turned away his head a moment and Rivers thought it was to hide a tear.

"Tom," he said, "I shall be most happy, I am sure, to be of any service to you. Make a confidence with me, if you think proper, and I will hear you patiently, and advise you to the best of my judgment."

"I—I had made up my mind," said the poor fellow, "when I was a-dusting of the passage to tell you what I'm going to tell you now—it's about Grace."

"Grace?" cried Rivers, starting as if a bombshell had fallen at his feet.

"Yes, Grace Trueman. Oh, Mr. Rivers, is she not most beautiful? When first I went to the office and saw her, I thought she was some angel, and I used to move about softly, and think of her as if she was really one; but then one day she spoke to me, and it was so kind and so sweet a voice, that I have often wakened up in the night and thought I heard it again. She—she shouldn't have done it; Mr. Rivers, she shouldn't have spoke to me like that—bless her—but she should have spoke harsh and unkind to me, she should."

Rivers listened in astonishment to this, and as Tom's feelings would not allow him to continue speaking, he said—

"But why should you object to her speaking kindly to you? Surely you would rather be spoken to kindly than harshly?"

"Yes—yes," said Tom, while the convulsive twitching of his face betrayed the emotion he was trying to conquer; "yes, I would rather be spoken kindly to by you, and by Mr. Trueman, and by everybody but Grace."

"And wherefore make her an exception?"

"Oh, she shouldn't," he said, as a tear fell upon the gravel walk, "she shouldn't speak so like an angel, and look so like an angle. because then a poor, hopeless, wretched fellow would not love her as I do—as I do."

CHAPTER XIV.

THE WALK IN THE TEMPLE GARDENS. TOM HACKEY'S CONFESSION.

THE poor fellow leaned his head upon the elbow of the wooden seat, and there was a silence of several moments' duration, for Rivers' mind was full of painful emotions. There was something so genuine and so sincere about the manner of the lad, that Rivers was shocked to find that the beauty of Grace had made such an impression upon him, at the same time that he seemed so feelingly alive to his want of hope.

"Is this, Tom, what you wanted to tell me?" he said, in a kind tone.

"Not all, not all," sobbed Tom Hackey. "I should hardly have thought to tell you this much, and no more, because you love her too."

The colour in an instant mantled in the cheek and brow of Rivers, as he said—

"I love her! I—I, Tom?"

"Yes—oh, Mr. Rivers, don't deny it. Don't say you doesn't when you does. You can't help—I know you can't. You love her. It would be very odd if you didn't. Bless her, everybody loves her."

Rivers felt much affected at the earnestness of the poor fellow's manner, and he said—

"Tom, you must recollect you brought me here to say something to me, not for me to confess to you my feelings."

"Oh, it's all the same. I've been a good while at Trueman's, and everybody knocks me about; but, as I tell you, one day Grace came home from somewhere she had been on a visit, and I saw her when she first came into the house. From then I used to hide in corners to see her go by, as she walked out with her nurse, Mrs. Woodfall, and I was so happy, because sometimes I had a letter to put in the post, or something that took me out of doors, so I could follow her, and she used to walk here."

"Here?" echoed Rivers, and the place was immediately in his eyes invested with a thousand charms it had not worn before.

"Yes—here, and she used to rest herself upon this seat." What a delightful seat it instantly became to Rivers!

"I will come here every day," he thought.

"Yes," continued Tom Hackey, "she went on that way for a long time, till one day Mr. Trueman called me into his counting-house, and giving me a letter out of those that had come for him, he says, 'You will find my daughter in the drawing-room; give her that letter, and tell her it came under cover to me.' Then he said, 'Well, Hackey, what are you staring at?' for I could hardly stand or move, with the idea of going into the room where she was, and speaking to her. Well, Mr. Rivers, I did go—stair after stair I went up, and I thought I should have *falled* down at every one, till I came to the door. It was a good while afore I could knock, and when I did, she says, 'Come in,' says she, and then I couldn't go in, and while I was trembling, she comes to the door and opens it, and I nearly falls down stairs. Then says she, 'Do you want me?' and I says, 'Yes,' says I, 'here's a cover, miss, as comed under a father, to your letter.'"

"What?" said Rivers.

"I'm only a telling of you what a nice hash I made of it. Then she takes the letter, and her hand touched me just here."

Tom Hackey showed one of his knuckles to Rivers, as he spoke, with great pride.

"Ah, yes," said Rivers, "and then?"

"Then she said, 'Thank you,' and it wasn't the words, Mr. Rivers, for they was simple enough; but—but I don't know what it was, my heart came up in my throat, and—and—I—I—cried—a I do now—just as I do now."

He leaned his head upon his hands and burst into tears.

Rivers rose, and paced up and down upon the green sward in deep emotion by himself.

"Oh, Grace—Grace," he said, "all

that know thee, must adore thee. This poor fellow's state is but a type of mine. E'en as his heart is desolate and hopeless, so may mine be. His love is as true as mine; but as for Mathew Trueman, he is quite as likely to look with contempt upon me as upon poor Tom Hackey. And even should I win the gentle heart of poor Grace, can I wed her to povery and want? No—no; perish the selfish thought. Locked in my own breast will I keep the fondly cherished secret of my heart, until I can unblushingly avow it to the world; which shall not be until kind fortune has enabled me to offer Grace a home as well as a loving heart."

Alas! lovers' vows of prudence are like the fleeting beauties of the rainbow—a moment beautiful, and then lost for ever.

He walked back to the seat on which he had left Tom, and approaching him, he said, kindly—

"Come, cheer up. We cannot have all that we desire in this world. You should make yourself happy in knowing that Grace will ever speak kindly to you, and think kindly of you."

"I do love her," said Tom; "nobody ever loved anybody half so well. I would jump into the river there to save her a pain; I do love her; and so do you, and that's what I principally came to talk about. I think she will love you."

Rivers felt his heart beat quickly.

"I've told you now how I love her," continued Tom; "but you know it's quite absurd for a poor ignorant fellow like me to think of Grace Trueman, and it would have been a good deal better if she'd given me a box o' the ears instead o' speaking kind to me, or if she'd shied the poker arter me as I went down stairs, that would have been better; but she would make me love her, you see, so don't blame me; but what I want to say is, that I hope she and you will be as happy as a long day in summer; and if you do ever tell her you love her, and she listens to you, like a young bird learning a new delicious song, mind you are always kind to her; never say a harsh word to her. Treat her gently, and love her always. Make her very—very happy; and poor, forlorn Tom Hackey will find a little consolation to

know that her mild, sweet voice and pretty smile ain't thrown away; and some day when you are sitting by your own fire-side you may tell her how the poor boy loved her, but how he wished only for her happiness, and prayed for her and blessed her always. Tell her not to be angry with poor Tom Hackey for loving her."

There was a few moments' silence now, during which Rivers was much perplexed to know what to say to the simple-minded young lover, whose affections were so pure and rare that he wished the happiness of the beloved object rather than his own. At length, he said—

"This subject, Tom, will be a painful one to you, and we will not renew it after this time. Nevertheless, as you have given me so fairly your confidence, I will show my appreciation of you and your generous feelings by avowing to you that my happiness in life now depends upon Grace Trueman."

"I knew it—I knew it," said Tom. "I seed it in your eyes, I did. As for not talking agin about Grace, it's a pleasure to me to hear her name, and I'd a great deal rather sit here and talk of her than go to a feast."

"Well, if you ever found such a pleasure," said Rivers, "I can, too, and we will, if you please, make this a frequent place of meeting."

"But—but——"

"But what, Tom? Why do you redden and look confused?"

"You know I am but a poor lad employed to do odd jobs about the office, and you are a gentleman."

"My dear Tom," said Rivers, "it is the mind and not the station that makes the gentleman. If all who call themselves gentlemen, and pride themselves upon their rank, had such really kind, honest, noble hearts as yours, the world would be a happier one than it is."

"Then you don't despise me?"

"Despise you? I honour you. Your generous feelings towards Grace are as rare as they are most commendable."

"Well, well. It's very kind of you to say so; but we will then meet here, and I can tell you all I have heard of Grace during the day, and you can now and then, just when you like, tell me how you love her and how happy you mean to make her. Now, good-by, for I'm going to rehearsal."

"Rehearsal, Tom?"

"Yes. I belong to the Buskinians. We gets up private plays, and uncommon well we does 'em, too, I can tell you. I suppose you wouldn't come some day?"

"Yes, I would, Tom, and I have no doubt I shall be much amused."

"Well, then, you shall come and see me act Richard next week."

"I will, with pleasure."

"Some of these days, you know," added the poor fellow, who was evidently struggling with his feelings, "who knows but I may become a popular actor, and then Grace may come and see me? I should be very proud then : poor Tom would scarcely know himself. But these are all dreams. There now ; there's the old Temple clock striking seven, and I shall be fined threepence if I ain't in Catherine Street by a quarter past. Good-by, Mr. Rivers ; I shall see you to-morrow."

So saying, Tom Hackey, with a tear glistening in his eye, hastily left the garden.

It wanted yet an hour or more to the dusk of the evening, and the gardens, illumined by a bright yellow sun, which sparkled on the river, too, as it glided gently by, as if laden with a freight of molten gold, looked so beautiful that Rivers could not leave the spot. Moreover, it had a great charm for him, for had not Tom Hackey told him that Grace had not only frequently walked there, but that that very seat was the one she chose on which to rest herself after the walk?

"How strange," thought Rivers, " is human destiny. Here am I, deeply in love, and clerk to a merchant, and have made a confidant, all within the short space of twelve hours. Oh, what a happiness it would be to me if Grace, some evening, were to come here and permit me to address her. Then if I could summon courage to tell her how I loved her—love—love? No—no. Have I so soon forgot my prudent resolutions of endeavouring to acquire something more worthy to offer her than a poor dependant heart? Be still, my selfish feelings ; I must control my passions until I am in different circumstances. Oh, what a

villain I should be to deprive her of the home she has, with none other to offer her but such an one as she might shrink from. Ah, cruel fortune, to use me so scurvily—I am friendless and poor."

He rose from the seat to pace the gravel walk by the bank of the river, and he thought it must have been his good genius which caused him to turn his eyes towards the gate, for as he did so, without knowing why, he saw Grace and her nurse descending the stone steps leading into the garden.

The rich evening sun was lighting up the face of the merchant's daughter—it was glancing like threads of gold among her hair. Oh, how beautiful she then was, as, with her quiet, seraphic smile, she listened to some kind discourse from her nurse, and little dreamt of the fond heart that was beating as it would burst its bonds in the breast of Rivers.

CHAPTER XV.

THE MEETING OF THE LOVERS.—AN ADVENTURE.

RIVERS withdrew among the trees, for he was fearful that her nurse might advise her to leave the garden if she saw him, and from among the shadows cast there he watched with all a lover's pure intensity of feeling the form of her he adored, as she walked lightly over the verdant sod towards the very seat upon which he had been sitting, and behind which he was even now ensconced among the trees.

His heart beat high with emotion—he trembled, and for an instant a mist seemed to come over his eyes as he gazed in rapture upon Grace, who, now that she was seated, he could hear her say to her nurse—

"Then, dear nurse, I will wait here for you while you go to Fleet Street and purchase me the colours."

"But, my dear, I shall get them wrong," said the nurse, " for you know I am ignorant about them."

"No, nurse, they have each proper names, which I have here written. Do you go while I stay here and dream of the old Knights Templars who used to walk about in these gardens."

"Well—well, take care of yourself,

my darling, I shall not be gone long," said the nurse, as she walked away, leaving Grace so near to Rivers that he could almost have stretched out his hand and touched her.

Now a fear came over him that she might think he had lain in wait for her, and dogged her to the gardens, and rather than she should think so, he would have foregone the pleasure of see-ing her at all, and with a sigh, he thought—

"Must I go even now that I am blessed by breathing the same air with her, and that my whole nature seems refined by her presence? Ah, no, I will remain here in concealment, and—who is this?"

As Rivers spoke in a low tone to himself he saw two men some distance from

THE QUARREL IN THE COUNTING-HOUSE.

Grace Trueman, but evidently from their gestures talking of her. That one of them was Mr. Girkins, and the other Lord Hawksworth, he did not entertain a moment's doubt, for he had seen both these persons at Mr. Trueman's, and they were neither of them very easily forgotten. The close, sharp, thin lips of Girkins, and his shuffling gait, combined with a peculiarity about his keen grey eyes, would have pointed him out among a thousand; and as for Lord Hawksworth, who that had once seen the effeminate-looking fop, could ever again forget him?

"What can this mean?" thought Rivers, as he saw Hawksworth turn and nod to Girkins, who instantly with a quick step left the garden.

Lord Hawksworth then commenced, with great labour, drawing on a pair of straw-coloured kid gloves, and as he did so, slowly approaching the seat on which was Grace Trueman.

Grace had her eyes fixed upon the water, which was gliding by in so much beauty, and she was not aware of the presence of Hawksworth until he stood opposite to her, intercepting part of her view, and with a grin upon his countenance, which he meant to be fascinating, but which was really more like the contortions of an ape.

A very slight cry of alarm came from the lips of Grace as she saw the figure before her, and she half rose from her seat; but it seemed as if she had been ashamed of her fears, for she immediately again seated herself, and remained quietly looking on the river.

Rivers was in the very act of springing forward as Grace moved, but so suddenly had she recovered her presence of mind that it had a similar effect upon him, and he, too, shrunk back into his former position, feeling that at present he was scarcely justified in interfering, but rejoicing within his heart that he was there to protect his beloved Grace against insult.

Lord Hawksworth, with all his effrontery, paused a moment before the awe-inspiring dignity of beauty and virtue, and could scarcely screw his courage up to address the merchant's daughter; but any feeling of delicacy was but very transient in such a mind as Hawksworth's, and after a few moments' irresolution, he said—

"Ah! I have the honour of addressing Miss Grace Trueman?"

Grace turned her mild, lustrous eyes upon him, as she said calmly—

"I do not know you, sir."

"No—no, doubtless; but we shall be better acquainted. Do you know, I consider you the most charming girl in London? Upon my soul I do."

Grace rose to walk away, but Hawksworth interposed in her way, saying—

"Nay, now, my angel, you really shall not go; upon my honour you sha'n't. I'm a peer."

"Behave, then, like a gentleman," said Grace.

"Ah, so I can. Your beauty is enough to set mankind at war. Upon my honour I never did see your equal. You really shall not go. Nay, I insist upon a little conversation."

"Do you mean, sir, that you will detain me by force?" said Grace.

"Such gentle force," replied Hawksworth, "as may just suffice to make a young lady listen to a compliment. You positively shall not go."

He still kept in her way, and Grace glanced round the gardens in search of succour, when Rivers, pale as a marble statue from suppressed emotions, stepped from behind the seat and confronted Lord Hawksworth.

Grace for a moment did not see that there was a third person added to the party, and it was only on Hawksworth starting back several paces, and exclaiming in a voice compounded of surprise and fear—"Who the d—l are you?" that she turned quickly and saw and recognised Rivers.

"Mr. Rivers?" she cried, with a delighted animation.

"The same, lady," he replied, "and your servant ever."

She immediately stepped to his side, and gliding her arm within his, she said, with a confiding earnestness that went to the heart of Rivers—

"You will protect me?"

"With my life—with my life," he cried.

"How dare you——" commenced Hawksworth.

But before he could proceed further, Rivers interrupted him by saying, in a voice of thunder—

"Beware, sir! you are safe at present."

"Oh, indeed!" exclaimed Hawksworth, skipping several paces backwards so that he might be ready for a run, should Rivers show any disposition to attack him. "You are a fine fellow. I must tell old Mathew Trueman to look better after his daughter."

"I will return to you in one moment," said Rivers, as he quietly disengaged Grace's arm from his; but Hawksworth saw the action, and guessing its purport, he flew from the garden with the agility of a dancing master.

"Oh, that such a man as that should be one of England's nobles," said Rivers.

"Is he so, indeed?" said Grace.

"He is, Miss Trueman; but I will forget him in my joy at rescuing you from his impertinence."

"I was getting alarmed," said Grace, with a smile ; "but how came you so opportunely, Mr. Rivers ?"

"Why, I—I was—that is—I am—"

Grace laughed. Oh, what music was that laugh to the heart of Rivers.

"I am a bad one at an explanation," he said, "more especially when I am very much interested. Is not this garden beautiful ?"

"It is, Mr. Rivers ; moreover, I like it for its historical associations."

"It has an interest that way," said Rivers, although in his heart he thought its modern and present associations far transcended any others.

Grace now again sat down on the garden seat, and Rivers stood by her side, enjoying more happiness than the whole of his former life had ever presented to him.

And Grace looked so confidingly up to him, and seemed so satisfied with his presence, that it is more than probable she was as happy as Rivers. How completely, too, was Lord Hawksworth, and the poor nurse, and Tom Hackey, and everything, forgotten by Rivers, as his whole soul was filled with the ecstasy of being near to and remaining with the merchant's beautiful child.

"I shall ever love this garden," he said.

"Love it ?" said Grace.

"Yes ; the human heart has in it well-springs of holy affections that make spots dear to us by associating them in the mind with what is dearer still."

"My nurse is to meet me here," said Grace.

Rivers was ashamed to confess he had played the eaves-dropper, and, therefore, tried to shift the discourse by saying—

"I will myself spare you the recital of this little adventure to your father, by telling him in the morning how happy it made me to be the instrument in rescuing you from that insolent puppy."

"No—no," said Grace, a sudden suspicion coming across her mind that her father might not receive the adventure in the same light that she did. "No, I will tell him at some fitting time. Leave that to me, Mr. Rivers. But here is my nurse; we will tell her, and she shall advise us."

There was something inexpressibly delightful to Rivers in the manner in which Grace spoke of him, as if he were an old friend; and we, as honest chroniclers, must confess that he very uncharitably wished Mrs. Woodfall a long way off as he saw her descending the garden steps.

"One word," said Rivers, in an agitated manner, "one word before we part. Will you again make this place beautiful by your presence ?"

Grace was silent for a moment, and then in a low, soft tone, which fell like the melodious breathing of an Eolian harp upon his ears, she said—

"There is a reason against my coming here, for he who was impertinent to-day, may be so to-morrow."

"But," faltered Rivers, "he who was your protector to-day, may be so to-morrow."

Grace made no reply, but walked forward a few paces to meet Mrs. Woodfall.

"At least," thought Rivers, "she has not said she would not come. There is hope in that."

The young man remained alone for some moments, while Grace, as he supposed, was recounting to Mrs. Woodfall the circumstance which had thrown her into his company, and then the pair advanced towards him, and the widow said—

"Mr. Rivers, you have saved my dear Grace from insult, and I thank you, for I love her as dearly as if she were a child of my own."

"I should, indeed, have been spiritless," said Rivers, "had I acted otherwise than I did. My presence here was purely accidental, and I thank Heaven that I was here, as my presence was in danger of being required."

"It was my fault," said Mrs. Woodfall, "for I might have known that my dear, beautiful Grace would soon attract around her all the beaux in the Temple."

"Now, nurse," said Grace, "you are trying to spoil me as usual, and to make Mr. Rivers think me a vain girl."

"Spoil you, my darling ? That is impossible."

"Nay, 'tis easy to spoil perfection," said Rivers, "as the slightest breath will for a moment cloud the pure surface of a mirror."

"A very pretty compliment, Mr. Rivers," said Mrs. Woodfall; "but we must be going home, or you will do more to spoil my dear child than her poor old nurse."

Grace held out her hand to Rivers, and as he took it in his, and felt the small taper fingers, a thrill shot to his very heart, and he felt as if he could have stood on that spot for ever, provided he might still gaze into the pure depths of Grace Trueman's eyes, and feel her small hand clasped in his.

The nurse roused him from the almost reverie into which he had fallen, by saying—

"Good evening, Mr. Rivers."

He started, and Grace started sympathetically, for it would seem as if she could have left her hand in that of Rivers for some time longer with most exemplary patience.

"Good evening," said Rivers; "shall I be your escort through the city?"

"No," said Mrs. Woodfall, decidedly, "'tis better we should go alone, as we came alone. This meeting, recollect, is purely accidental."

There was decision in her tone and manner, but still nothing of a very discouraging tenor; the fact being, that Mrs. Woodfall was exceedingly prepossessed in favour of Rivers, and had a great many old-fashioned notions about love at first sight, and young people being born for each other, &c., which induced her to look upon the sudden acquaintanceship, and evident growing affection between the handsome young clerk and Grace, with no sort of pain or displeasure.

"If they love each other," she reasoned, "I am quite sure they ought to marry, and a handsomer couple could not be found. I hope to see my poor Grace happy, in spite of all my fears that her father, in his great love for money, would worry her into a marriage, the principal object of which would be to increase his consequence, instead of his daughter's happiness."

"Farewell, Miss Trueman," said Rivers.

Grace said nothing, but the one eloquent glance that she gave Rivers was worth more than all the tongue could have uttered.

In another moment he was alone in the Temple-garden. The sun had dipped below the horizon, and a moaning wind began to sweep over the river. The birds were singing their evening hymn as they retired to their roosts. The long dark shadows of the trees were mingling together into dull heavy masses, and the finely streaked colours which lent a glory to the eastern sky were fading away.

"She is gone," said Rivers, "and with her has gone all that was rare and beautiful—she has gone, and the sun no longer shines upon my heart—she is gone, and all is dreary desolation. Oh, did ever human heart love like mine? Here I swear by yon murmuring river—by yon pale crescent in the eastern sky—by earth, sea, air, and by Heaven, never to love another—never to think or dream of any one but my own, my beautiful Grace. Heaven register my vow."

Even as he spoke the wind increased in strength, and a black mass of clouds came from the south, piling themselves up like gloomy battlements in the sky. Then one vivid flash of lightning lit up the face of nature, and in the short space of five minutes all the beauty was gone, being surrounded by gloom and storm.

"Is this ominous?" said Rivers, as with a shudder he left the garden.

CHAPTER XVI.

THE PROJECTED MURDER.—HILLIARD AND HIS VICTIM.

TURN we from the pure feelings of Grace Trueman and her lover to a darker page in human history, a page spotted with blood, and over which is cast the shadow of guilt and despair.

When Hilliard left his desk in the merchant's counting-house, he hurried along Cheapside and Fleet Street until he came to Temple Bar, when, turning down a dirty and obscure thoroughfare, he entered New Inn, and walking hurriedly along two sides of the square, he dived into a dingy doorway on the third, and then ascending the creaking ancient staircase, he paused not until he was opposite a door, on which were painted the words "Mr. Noble." At this door then he paused, and a change came over his dark and swarthy features; he turned of a ghastly paleness as he whispered to himself—

"Shall I go back now, or—or shall I persevere? D—n it, faint heart never won fair gold! It is but a few minutes' work, after all, and the reward is immense. I have heard that fellows feel something as I do now at their first mur——curse the word, I cannot speak it! I am an hour, too, before my time, and waiting on such an errand is none so pleasant. Well, I can't walk for an hour, so I must knock. I am cold to the very heart. It's very odd, but I never felt so strange before. What can be the meaning of it? I must have some drink, and it's better to have it in these old chambers than anywhere else, as I am now at the door, or else I shall have all this nervousness over again, I suppose. I won't shrink now; no, d—n it, after persuading Wilson for six months to murder his master, am I to hang back? Curse that word hang! What made me use it? It's an uncomfortable one. But here goes."

He now knocked at the door of the chamber, and in a few minutes the lock turned, and a young man appeared in the entrance.

"Well," said Hilliard, "what's the matter now? You look as pale as ashes."

"I pale! Am I pale?" said the other.

"As a ghost."

"Well, you are rather so, Hilliard. You don't look well."

"Nonsense! I am quite well. Stand out of the doorway and let me in, will you?"

"Yes—yes!" faltered the other. "Come in, but you are early. I did not expect you till seven, you know. But I am glad you have come, for never in my life did I find the chambers so lonely as they have been this dreadful day."

"What do you mean by dreadful day?" said Hilliard, as he walked into the first room of the three that composed the set of chambers, and held his hands close to the fire that was burning in the grate, although the season was so far advanced.

"Ah! you are like me," said Wilson; "you are cold and shivering."

"It's a lie!" cried Hilliard; "I am no such thing."

"Well, well, don't speak so loud; I ma,and have been since I set foot in the chambers this morning. I never passed such a day."

"We are alone here?"

"Yes; he will not be here till eight. He has gone to his dinner."

"His last dinner," muttered Hilliard. The other shuddered.

"What are you trembling and gasping in that way for, Wilson?" cried Hilliard. "You are as weak as a cat. Why, you have been six months making up your mind to this job, which is to make you comfortable, and clear you of all your difficulties, and now you don't seem to fancy it. What do you mean, I say?"

"Oh, nothing, nothing," said Wilson, with a sickly smile. "I always was, you know, nervous, and surely this is an occasion when one may be allowed to feel a little more than usually so. You are trembling yourself, Hilliard, you are, indeed."

"I tell you I am not," cried Hilliard, grasping tightly the back of a chair as the only means of assuming a degree of steadiness and nerve which he was very far from feeling.

"Well, I am. I can't help trembling."

"No, I know you can't," said Hilliard; "you are a poor creature, and I don't know what you would do without me; you'd get into a pretty mess. Now, tell me, are you quite positive that Noble, your governor, will have that sum of money you mentioned about him to-night?"

"I am quite sure," said Wilson, who was the clerk to Mr. Noble, a respectable solicitor.

"You are?"

"I am. The three thousand pounds is trust money, and to-morrow he intends investing it. Well, rather than take it to Clapham, where he resides, I overheard him say he would sleep in the chambers to-night with it, and early to-morrow proceed to the city; so, you see, if he comes in and tells me he is going to sleep here, there can be no manner of doubt upon the matter."

"Very good," said Hilliard, "that's all clear enough, certainly, and a very good job it is for you, Master Wilson—the making of you for life, I should say."

"Yes, I—I hope so; but you will have the most, you know, Hilliard."

"The most? What do you mean by that?"

"Why, you know, you make out that I owe you so much at cards."

"Well, and so you do; and if I were to drop a note to old Noble, to tell him what a gambler you had been, you know very well he would discharge you at once, and you would never get another situation as long as you lived. Then, of course, you would soon be begging about the streets."

"Yes; I daresay that is all very true," said Wilson; "you have a great knowledge of the world, which I never pretended to."

"Of course I have," said Hilliard. "Here you have been dreaming away your existence with old Noble since you were a boy for fourteen shillings a week; but times will soon be changed with you."

"Yes, very soon."

"Now, you recollect what you are to do. You are to take a solemn oath—I believe you are religious, Wilson?"

"My mother was."

"Ah! very well, that's much the same; you are to take a solemn oath, and I another, that we will, under no sort of circumstances, betray each other."

"That is but fair," said Wilson.

"Of course, it is but fair; because then, in the event of any accident occurring to one, the other may feel himself perfectly secure and safe."

"Yes—yes; that is right."

"Well, after your oath, you are to take your share of the money, and go at once to Liverpool: you will have a good start before you; and, when you are there, you take the first vessel you see going anywhere. I should advise some eastern port. America has grown so common, that, when any one is missed, the officers look there quite naturally, and the only chance of safety in the United States is, that all being rogues alike, it is very hard to pick out one in particular from among the lot."

"Then you would not advise me to go there?"

"Certainly not."

"Very well; I will take your advice, then, as you know the world well."

"Do so. Now I think we understand each other, with the exception of merely casting up our account. Give me a pencil. Well; here's three thousand pounds to be divided—fifteen hundred for you, and fifteen hundred for me; then you owe me seven hundred and sixty at cards."

"A large sum."

"Large nonsense. You don't dispute it?"

"Oh, dear, no."

"Very good. That reduces yours to six hundred and ninety, you know."

"Ye—yes."

"Then you want me when you are gone to send your old mother, anonymously, two hundred pounds?"

"Yes—and you will swear to do it, Hilliard?"

"Of course I will."

"Thank you. That will give me great consolation."

"Certainly. Well, then, that reduces yours still further, and the gross amount you will have to receive will be four hundred and ninety pounds. Now, I'll toss you to make it six hundred or four hundred, giving you the odds, you see."

"But you always win."

"Nonsense! Persevere at tossing, and you must win eventually. Come on, heads or tails?"

"Heads," said Wilson.

"Tails, it is," cried Hilliard. "Well, you had your chance; you will now receive a net sum of four hundred pounds. No small matter—quite a little fortune for you, Wilson, eh?"

"Yes, but not to be compared with what you will have."

"And which you might have had but for the chances of fortune. You are hard to please, Wilson."

"No, no—not at all; I merely made the remark. I meant nothing."

"Oh, very well, then; only it's hard to hear a fellow grumbling when he is going to get four hundred pounds for nothing."

"For nothing, Hilliard? Do you think we can ever be happy again after what we are going to do?"

"And are we happy now?"

"No, not very."

"Then what difference can it make? You do talk the cursedest trash that ever I heard. You are an odd fellow, Wilson. There's old Noble. He can't have many years to live, and suppose we deprive him of one or two of them, and perhaps save him some long and painful illness;

I think we are doing him a favour than otherwise, do you know, and I am quite sure I have done you one, by putting you up to the whole affair."

"I should never have thought of it without you," said Wilson. "But what shall we do till eight o'clock?"

"Play at cards, to be sure."

"No, no; I shall lose all."

"No you won't," said Hilliard, who had made up his mind to leave his poor miserable dupe the four hundred pounds. "You won't lose anything, for I am out of luck to-night; but the cards will help to pass the time."

The cards were then produced, and the two men who had agreed that evening to deprive a fellow creature of existence sat down to amuse themselves until the time should arrive for the execution of their terrible purpose.

The effort, however, to distract their minds from the awful subject which filled them was in vain, and by half-past seven they, with one accord, ceased playing, neither having been a winner—a state of things which was brought about by the management of Hilliard, who, with his simple and weak-minded companion, could win or lose at pleasure.

Wilson was one of those men who, while they are utterly destitute of moral restraints, frequently go through life without any flagrant deviation from the right course on account of wanting the courage to do wrong. Beyond a petty peculation in making up an account, Wilson, unaided by the more daringly wicked spirit of Hilliard, never would have got; but once associated with him, he unconsciously, to himself, became his slave, and the ready agent of his villanies, although the crime they now contemplated was of so awful a character that the trembling spirit of Wilson shrunk from it aghast, and it was months before he became sufficiently familiarised with the idea to reflect upon it without falling into a perfect agony of fear.

The cards were but removed, and Hilliard was about to make some remark, when a double knock announced Mr. Noble.

CHAPTER XVII.

THE MURDER.—A SCENE OF HORROR.— THE DISAPPOINTMENT.

"HE must not see me here," said Hilliard. "Hide me somewhere."

"Hush! hush! He will hear your voice," said Wilson. "Get into that closet. You must hold the door shut, for it has no kind of fastening."

Hilliard promptly ensconced himself in the closet, and Wilson hastened to the door to let in his employer.

Mr. Noble was a man verging upon sixty years of age. His hair was of a silvery whiteness, and his face was furrowed more by study in his profession than by the ravages of time.

"Wilson," he said, as he stepped into the chamber, "I shall sleep here to-night."

"Yes, sir," said Wilson, and the words almost stuck in his throat.

"You can go whenever you like," added Mr. Noble, "and be sure to be here early in the morning, as I have to go to the city on business of importance as soon as possible."

"Certainly, sir," was the reply, and the agitated, husky voice in which the words were uttered, struck strangely upon Mr. Noble's ear, and turning to his clerk, he said—

"Are you unwell?"

"Un—well, sir?" gasped Wilson.

"Yes—why, bless me, now I look at you, you are dreadfully pale. You had better go home at once, Wilson."

"I—am not very well, sir," replied the trembling clerk, "and I will go home very soon. I have some letters still to enter in the book, and I never sleep unless the business of the day is concluded."

"A good plan," said Mr. Noble, "but sickness, you know, is a sufficient excuse."

"I would rather stay, sir, a little longer."

"Oh, as you please—as you please."

Mr. Noble passed into his own room, which was the next one on the suite, the third being fitted up as a bed-chamber, in case he should ever have occasion as he had now, to sleep in London.

"He—he—has the money," gasped Wilson; "he will sleep here to-night;

he has business in the city early in the morning. Yes, he evidently has the money about him, and—and, he will be murdered."

Wilson sunk into a seat, and such an awful sickness of the heart came over him that he thought he must have died.

"Oh, God! oh, God!" he muttered, "shall I even now rush out into the lane and call for help? Shall I save him at this, the eleventh hour?"

"Hist!" said Hilliard, cautiously opening the closet-door, "hist—hist!"

Wilson beckoned to him to come out, and when he was near enough to him to grasp his arm, he laid hold of it with frantic eagerness, and whispered—

"Hilliard—Hilliard, let us give it up, let us even now give it up, and leave him to live. Oh, think again, Hilliard, if I suffer now, what will be my pangs when the awful deed is done?"

Hilliard's face assumed a dark and demoniac expression, as he said—

"Listen to me. If you dare to falter now, I will be your destruction. Shrink from the accomplishment of what you have already gone too far in to retract, and even now I will denounce you as having made the proposal to me to murder Mr. Noble. Your pale face, your faltering tongue, your evident confusion, all will assist to condemn you, and you will reap the bitterest fruits of crime, but none of its rewards."

"God help me—God help me," said Wilson.

"Hush—hush! He has the money?"

"He has."

"Then the deed must be done. There are double doors to the chambers. No sound can reach the open air."

"Do not ask me—do not ask me," said Wilson. "I cannot stir, I can scarcely speak."

"You must assist. And now for the oath. You swear?"

"I swear," gasped Wilson.

"By your soul's salvation, not to tell that Mark Hilliard was with you in the murder of Mr. Noble?"

"I swear that," said Wilson.

"'Tis well—'tis well. Now you must be ready in case of need to assist me."

"I cannot—I cannot."

"You must and shall."

"Spare me—oh, spare me, Hilliard.

I will kneel to you, pray to you; but, oh, spare me this deed. Let me sit here while you do it. I will give up another hundred, if you please. But let me not see it, or have act or part in it."

"Coward!" said Hilliard, "is it thus you shrink at the last moment from what you have pledged yourself so deeply to do?"

"I cannot help it, Hilliard—I am quite unmanned."

"I take you at your word, then. You shall have but three hundred."

"And you will spare me from all participation in it?"

"I will. Sit you here and leave me to do all. Our after proceedings shall be as before arranged. You will take your three hundred and begone immediately that I tell you all is accomplished?"

"I will—I will."

"You swear it?"

"Yes. As I—I give up now all hopes of mercy hereafter, I swear it. Oh, spare him even yet, Hilliard. It may be better. Fancy your hands eternally stained with blood."

"Pshaw!" cried Hilliard, "when I set my mind upon a thing I will carry it out, even should it bring me to the gallows."

"You are bold and resolute, but I, alas! am not. If I had your spirit, Hilliard, I could do it, but I have not. You know I am weak."

"Peace—peace!" cried Hilliard, "peace, I say."

He took from his pocket as he spoke one of those truly formidable instruments called self-protectors, composed of two lumps of lead, connected by a shaft of twisted whalebone.

The moment Wilson saw the weapon, he covered his face with his hands, and would not look up again; for a few short seconds, then, Hilliard stood by him with a bitter smile upon his face, such as might indeed have been worn by some malignant demon, exulting over the fall of a mortal soul. Then he slowly walked towards the door of the inner chamber. His hand was upon the lock, and he was upon the point of carefully opening it, when he heard a chair moved, and the footsteps of Mr. Noble advancing towards the door.

Hilliard stepped on one side, and in a

moment the door opened and Mr. Noble said—

"Wilson, let me have a light."

He stood half in one room and half in the other, when Hilliard, with a blow that went crashing with a hideous sound through his skull, felled him to the ground.

At the sound of his employer's voice, Wilson had looked up, and he saw the deed done. A scream burst from his lips, and he rushed to the farther end of the room, shrieking—

"Mercy—mercy! Oh, God, have mercy!"

"Peace!" cried Hilliard, in a loud voice. "Such another cry, and it shall be the last you have breath in this world to utter."

There was an awful silence then in the chamber. Mr. Noble lay upon his face on the threshold of his own room,

THE QUARREL BETWEEN LORD HAWKSWORTH AND RIVERS.

and Wilson stood with his arms out-stretched before him against the wall on the opposite side of the apartment, gazing with protruding eyes and distorted visage, as if some hideous spectre had suddenly blasted his eye sight.

"A light—a light," cried Hilliard.

"On—on the table," gasped Wilson, in a sepulchral voice, "on the table."

"By Heaven and hell," cried Hilliard, "if you move not I'll smash you."

"Mercy—mercy!" cried Wilson, sinking on his knees. "Oh, have mercy! I dare not die."

There was a low knock at the chamber door at this moment, and terror seemed to freeze up every faculty of Wilson's mind, while Hilliard said in anxious accents—

"Who is that?—speak, who is that?"

"I had forgotten," said Wilson,

wringing his hands. "We are lost. It is the laundress—she comes at this time to clean the chambers."

"D—n her," cried Hilliard. "Go tell her that Mr. Noble is very busy and cannot be disturbed."

"Yes, I—I will try."

Wilson crawled to the door, and gaining his feet with some difficulty, he opened it a small distance, and said—

"You must come again—Mr. Noble is busy."

"Lor, Mr. Wilson," said a female voice, "how odd you speak."

"You must come again, Mr. Noble is busy," was all that the agitated man could say.

"Well, I hear you," said the laundress, "but I can't come till morning now. Good night, Mr. Wilson."

"Good night," said the clerk, as if he were half-choked, and when he had shut the door he tore off his cravat, and opened his shirt-collar, crying—"Air—air! for the love of Heaven, let me have some fresh air!"

"You can open the window now," cried Hilliard, "it is of no consequence."

Wilson staggered to the window, and opening it, he hung across the sill like a dead body, drinking in the fresh, cool night air as if it had been water.

Hilliard proceeded to the table, and there he found a candle, which he speedily lighted by the dying embers of the fire, and then holding the light above his head, he looked down upon the body of the murdered man. As he did so a faint, hollow groan came from the supposed dead, and Hilliard started several paces backwards, exclaiming—

"By — he ain't dead yet."

"What's that?" said Wilson, hastily turning round.

"Nothing particular," replied Hilliard; "who would have supposed the old man had so much life in him? He groaned just now."

Wilson sank into a chair, and covering his face with his hands, bowed himself to and fro, moaning awfully in the bitterness of his heart.

Hilliard regarded the body for some moments with a fixed and steady gaze, although his hand shook as he held the light, and he drew his breath hard and thick, as he strove to say with composure—

"If he ain't quite dead, we must finish him, that's all about it. Have you a knife?"

"No—no—for God's sake, no," cried Wilson; "use no knife—that would be too horrible. Let me not see blood—no blood—no blood."

"Why, there is plenty of blood where he lies," said Hilliard. "Come and look at it."

"I—I look at it?—not for worlds."

"Then here goes to make sure," said Hilliard, as with the leaden weapon he still held in his hand, he dealt a heavy blow upon the head of Mr. Noble. His victim, however, felt it not. In that last groan his soul had parted from its earthly tenement, and was with its maker.

"He's safe now," said Hilliard. "We have but to take the money. Come and help in the search. In which pocket does he keep his money?"

"I would not touch him for kingdoms," said Wilson, "and I know not where to direct your search."

"You are of great assistance, truly," sneered Hilliard, as, setting the candle down by the side of the murdered man, he commenced searching his pockets, with the hope of finding the large sum which had been the inducement to commit the horrible deed which had just been consummated.

Pocket after pocket, however, was searched in vain. Nothing was found upon the body but a purse containing a small sum, and a pocket-book, in which there appeared nothing but memoranda.

"Where is the money?" cried Hilliard, looking up, and the dark veins on his forehead swelling like whipcord, as he glanced furiously at Wilson.

"It must be about him," replied Wilson. "I am certain he received it to-day."

"He has it not with him," roared Hilliard, starting to his feet, and his eyes glaring hideously, with the, to him, dreadful thought that his crime, after all, might be profitless.

"He may have taken it from his pocket and left it in his own room," said Wilson.

"Oh, yes — yes — yes," muttered Hilliard, sinking into a chair and wiping the perspiration from his brow. "I did not think of that. Of course, it is there."

"Or in his pocket-book, in notes?"

"No. There are no notes in the pocket-book. There it is. Look for yourself, while I search the next room."

Hilliard threw Wilson the pocket-book, and the first memorandum his eye fell upon, before Hilliard had taken away the light, made him give a cry of agony and horror, that at once transfixed his companion to the spot as if he had changed to stone.

"What—what now?" he gasped.

Wilson rose, and tottered towards him with the open pocket-book in his hand.

"Read—read," he said, as his trembling fingers indicated the page.

Hilliad read as follows :

"MONDAY.

"Rec'd. of H. G. Noble, Esq., three thousand pounds, to be inserted by me in his name, in such of the public securities as he shall to-morrow make choice of. "CHARLES FEARNSHAW,

"Stock Broker."

Hilliard gave a deep groan, and dropping both the pocket-book and candle, all was darkness in the dismal chambers.

CHAPTER XVIII.

THE MORNING. — RIVERS AND HIS FRIEND TOM.—THE COMING OUT IN "RICHARD."

THE morning dawned fair and beautiful after the storm of the preceding evening ; Rivers never felt such a delightful exhilaration of spirits in his life as when he hastened to the merchant's house. Thames-street even looked lovely in his eyes, for was it not the abode of her he loved?—the beautiful Grace Trueman! And was it not of itself a dear pleasure to be conscious of being in the same house with her, and to have the chance, remote as it was, of seeing her? No longer did the counting-house and all its paraphernalia of books appear dull and heavy in the sight of Rivers. It appeared to him as if everything had borrowed a charm from the presence of his beloved Grace,

and over and over again he blessed his happy destiny which had brought him into the rich merchant's service, since it had given him an opportunity of earning so dear a reward as a bright smile from the beaming eyes of his lovely daughter.

There was but Tom Hackey in the office when Rivers arrived, and Tom, shaking his head, said—

"Oh, I knew you'd be here early enough. What's brought me here every morning never so early, but because once in about a month Grace gets up and takes a fancy to water a lot of plants as she's got at the back of the house. Then I brings her jugs of water, and she always says, 'thank you Tom,' and gives a smile that's enough to make a bird fall off a tree for envy."

"I perceive I am nearly half an hour before my time," said Rivers, looking up at the office clock.

"In course you is," said Tom, laying the dust in the office, as he spoke, with a tin can of water, by the aid of which he produced various fanciful curves and devices on the floor. "In course you is ; but she's a-bed now, bless her. I says to Susan a little while ago, 'Susan,' says I, 'is your young missis up?' and she says, 'Lor, Muster Thomas, how can it matter to you?' Then I says, 'I want to know if she's got out o' bed, bless her,' says I. Then Susan, she says, 'I tell you what, Muster Thomas, Miss Grace ain't got out o' bed ; but I can't see,' says Susan, 'what business it is o' yours,' says she, ' whether she's in bed or out on it,' says Susan."

"Then she is not up?" said Rivers.

"Sartinly not," replied Tom ; "and you won't see her this morning, except it's a wery great wonder."

"Ah, well," said Rivers, with a sigh, as he pulled off his gloves abstractedly, and put them into the letter box, "I must be content even to have the chance, Tom, of seeing her."

"So you must," said Tom ; "but don't have your gloves sent in to old Mathew along o' your letters."

"Along with the letters? Dear me, I made a mistake."

"Summon the castle-guard, and hurl him from the ramparts," cried Tom, fencing with the shovel. "My mother had a maid called Barbara, and she let the worm in a bud feed on her dainty cheek. 'She never told her love.' Ha—ha—ha—ha!"

"Upon my word, you improve," said Rivers, laughing in spite of himself.

"Yes—yes," said Tom. "When the wind is south west, I know a hawk from a handsaw. I am, as you perceive, a little less than kin, and more than kind."

"I perceive you have a great theatrical genius."

"Do you?"

"Indeed I do."

"Really now? Well, I'm quite delighted to hear you say so, 'cos I'm going to have a night."

"A night? What do you mean?"

"Why, the way we pays our expenses is by each on us having a night, and then we sells the tickets among our friends, and it's as broad as it's long in the end."

"Oh, is it. Well, I will be a customer for one ticket on your night, Tom."

"Will you, though, really—boxes?"

"Yes."

"Two shillings it is. Don't say you will if you'd rather not. I'm to do Richard, the crook-backed tyrant. Listen to this,—'High reaching Buckingham grows circumspect.' Lead on to the tower and be d——d."

"I don't recollect that in the play," said Rivers.

"No—it's a new reading, quite new. But it's tremendously effective. It always brings down the house, that does. We've only introduced it lately."

"It's quite an innovation."

"Oh, that be bothered. Then we smother the children on the stage, after making them dance a double hornpipe in fetters."

"Indeed?"

"Yes! One of the murderers we make run after one of the children behind a screen, and then you know we have a stuffed child, that he brings out holding by one leg, and its throat cut, while the other one is sat upon by the other murderer."

"Upon my word, in addition to murdering the children, you make rather a slaughter of Shakspere," remarked Rivers.

"Yes, we slaughter everything. Tear them asunder. Throw them into the deepest dungeon in the castle of Cumfoocleum! Ho—ho—ho! Give 'em to the vultures!"

Here Tom went through a pantomimic broad-sword combat, and finally ended by giving the office door a tremendous poke with the broom-handle, just as it was being slowly opened by some one.

"There now," said Rivers, "you have knocked somebody's head."

"And that somebody will knock his head," said Mr. Trueman, coming in rubbing his forehead.

"The devil!" said Tom.

"So, sir," cried the enraged merchant, "you are at your tricks and absurdities again, are you? Now, you leave my establishment."

"Most reverend, grave, and potent signors," said Tom; "'tis true that I have ta'en away this old man's daughter——"

The merchant was so enraged that he rushed forward to inflict condign punishment upon Tom, but Rivers stood in his way, and said respectfully—

"Remember, sir, who you are, and who he is. Pray forgive him this once. The hour is early, and your appearance was scarcely expected for some time yet."

The merchant paused, and he felt his vanity rather tickled by what Rivers had said.

"I thank you, Mr. Rivers," he said. "It certainly is far beneath me to chastise him. It is early."

"I believe you have found him honest and most trustworthy, sir?"

"I have, certainly."

"Then put up with a harmless eccentricity, which, perhaps, stands in place of what in another might be some serious fault."

"At your intercession, then, Mr. Rivers, I am inclined to look over it," said Trueman; "but, hark you, Tom—don't let me hear any more of this absurd acting about the house."

"Oh, dear, no, sir," said Tom. "Friends, Romans, and countrymen, lend me your ears; I come to bury Cæsar."

These last words were not uttered till the merchant was out of ear-shot, and then Tom laughed and said—

"He won't discharge me, Mr. Rivers.

He knows when he's well off, as well as most men."

"But, nevertheless, you should not trifle with your means of subsistence, Tom. For my sake be more careful, for, by taking your part, I make myself to a certain extent answerable for you."

"He shan't complain of me any more, Mr. Rivers," said Tom. "For your sake I will do more than for anybody else's, except one, except one."

The half hour before the commencement of business soon passed away, and the merchant, coming into the office, asked if Hilliard had arrived.

"No, sir," said Tom, "he ain't come yet."

"Always late, always late," muttered Mathew Trueman, as he walked into his own room.

"Yes, you may well say always late," muttered Tom. "He's useful in his way, or he'd pretty soon be sent to the right about. I've heard him boast that old Mathew dared not discharge him. My eye, who's this so early?"

Tom pointed through the office window as he spoke, and upon Rivers looking in the direction indicated, a blush of anger crossed his brow as he saw the dissolute Lord Hawksworth dismounting from a horse at the merchant's door.

"That is a fellow called Hawksworth," said Tom; "I suppose he comes here on the old errand that so many of the young bloods creep up Thames Street on, to crave money of old Mathew."

Rivers said nothing, but he bent his eyes over the letters he was copying, and determined that if Hawksworth interfered not with him, he would take no sort of notice of his lordship.

Rivers, however, was not doomed to be let off so easily for his gallantry in the Temple Gardens, for it appeared that immediately after his *fracas* with the merchant's clerk, Lord Hawksworth had proceeded to his friend and confidential adviser, Mr. Girkins, who had greatly alarmed him with regard to the injurious effect such a circumstance was likely to have upon the mind of a young enthusiastic female like Grace Trueman, and concluded by saying to the amazed nobleman—

"Your lordship will find that a woman will forgive everything in a man but cowardice, and it is necessary for the success of your lordship's projected intrigue with the merchant's daughter that you should do something to rescue your character from the reproach which this clerk is sure now to take every opportunity of casting upon it."

A very slight infusion of the blood of one of his lordship's ancestors, who had fought and bled at Agincourt, must have lingered in the veins of Hawksworth, for his cheeks reddened at the idea of Grace Trueman considering him a coward.

"I will do something," he said, "to prove to that girl that it was only that I thought it an ungentlemanly thing in her presence to engage in a personal contest with a low ruffian."

"Precisely," said Girkins, obsequiously. "Every one must be fully aware that such was your lordship's motive in not chastising the scoundrel on the spot."

"Of course it was," said Hawksworth, quite pleased that he had succeeded in putting the affair in such a light.

"Then your lordship can take your own opportunity to chastise the fellow's insolence."

"I will go and cane him."

"That would be just the thing. Grace Trueman would be sure to hear of it, and she would directly give your lordship credit for being a man of spirit and great command of temper."

"I will do it, on my soul I will do it."

"The sooner the better."

"To-morrow I will, you may depend, Girkins. I have set my mind upon making this merchant's daughter my mistress, and it is not a trifle that shall stop me. I will ride down to Thames Street early to-morrow morning, and cane this impertinent clerk in the merchant's office."

"Do so. Certainly it is a good plan," said Girkins. "Oh! what pleasure will await your lordship! You will soon be able to raise a large sum of money from this merchant, and you will have frequent opportunities of pressing your suit with his really beautiful daughter."

"She is an angel."

"I never, indeed, saw her equal. But your lordship's admirable conversational powers, aided by your personal recommendations and your rank, will quite bewilder the young thing, and she will fall readily into your lordship's arms."

"Upon my word I think so too. I believe there are not many women who would say nay to me—a box at the opera —a handsome carriage—servants, and everything in style—eh, Gerkins?"

"Not many, indeed, your lordship."

"Well, good evening. I will do what you advise me, the first thing in the morning. But you are quite sure this fellow is one of old Trueman's clerks?"

"Quite, your lordship. You heard Grace call him by the name of Rivers?"

"Yes; certainly she did."

"And he is a tall, dark young man, moderately stout, with curly hair, and sparkling black eyes."

"The same; d—n him!"

"Then it is he; and I would further advise that you give Mathew Trueman a hint to discharge so presuming a person."

"I will. You advise well, Girkins. Upon my word, if I were a king you should be my prime minister."

"I humbly thank your lordship."

Lord Hawksworth departed, and after fortifying himself with a great quantity of wine over-night, he retired to rest, desiring his servants to arouse him early, as he had to cane an impertinent fellow the first thing in the morning.

Hence then, the early appearance of his lordship in Thames-street, and hence, likewise, his exceedingly pale face and trembling knees; for when he arrived at the merchant's door he found that he had set himself a task that was not very agreeable, and if he could by any means have caned Rivers by deputy, he would have been specially glad to have done so.

For a moment he thought of going back, but then shame made him forego that prudent step, for what could he say to Girkins? Moreover, he was inflamed by the beauty of Grace, and he would venture something for her sake.

"I will do it," he muttered. "My sudden appearance may frighten him, and he may be afraid to lose his situation, so he may put up with one blow, which will satisfy me, and then I shall ride off and take some means to let Grace Trueman know. And, besides, if he should be very violent, somebody will interfere, so there can't be much harm done to me at the worst."

Reasoning thus, his lordship entered the house, and seeing the word "office" painted upon an oval piece of glass let into the upper panel of a door, he pushed it open and stood within a few paces of Rivers.

CHAPTER XIX.

THE FRACAS IN THE COUNTING-HOUSE. —AN IMPORTANT HALF HOUR IN THE DRAWING-ROOM.

RIVERS heard the door open, and fancying it was Hilliard or Mr. Trueman, he just glanced from the letter he was writing, and his eyes met the pale face of Lord Hawksworth, who stood grasping in his hand a small riding cane. For a moment neither of them spoke, and then his lordship said—

"You are the young man who was insolent to me in the Temple Gardens last evening, when the presence of a lady alone prevented me from chasting you as you deserved?"

"I am the young man," said Rivers, "who rescued a lady from your rudeness in the Temple Gardens; but as regards the latter part of your remark, it is untrue, for it was your own want of courage and power that restrained you from resenting the manner in which I treated you."

Lord Hawksworth turned very pale, as he said—

"We shall see that, sir. I have come to cane you."

"I am employed here," said Rivers, "in my capacity of a clerk. Will your lordship give me your word of honour that nothing that passes now between us shall be reported by you to Mr. Trueman?"

"Yes—oh, yes," said Hawksworth, thinking by Rivers's quiet and subdued manner that he was thoroughly cowed and would put up with the caning for the sake of retaining his situation.

"Very well," said Rivers, "I give you a like pledge, on my honour. This is purely a personal affair between us; so now I shall kick you into the street."

Before the words were well out of his mouth, Rivers had descended from his stool, and seizing Lord Hawksworth by the collar, he dragged him to the outer door, and with one kick sent him into the middle of the road.

The whole affair was done so suddenly, and with so little bustle, for Hawksworth was too much astonished to make even an unavailing resistance, that before Tom Hackey could shut his mouth, which was wide open, from amazement, Rivers was sitting quietly on his stool again, and writing as if nothing had happened.

"Gracious me," he then exclaimed, "I never in all my life did see such a go as that ; I could dance on my very head, I'm so pleased. There he goes. He's got on his horse, and going away like mad. Bravo—bravo—bravo !"

Tom was patting Rivers on the back when Mathew Trueman came in.

"What are you doing that for ?" he cried.

"Encouraging of him, sir," said Tom.

"Encouraging him to what ?"

"Nothink, sir."

"I'm sure you've been at your ranting again; I heard some confusion. You have been acting, you rascal."

"No, sir—there's only been a little interlude atween the acts," said Tom, "called ' Kick him Out ; or, the Biter Bit,' sir."

"Let me hear no more of your nonsense. Now, Mr. Rivers, have you finished those letters ?"

"Here they are, sir."

"Ah, that will do ; and, by-the-by, now I am here, I may as well tell you that if a nobleman, by name and title Lord Hawksworth, should come here when I am out, you are to treat him always with the greatest attention, and let Mrs. Woodfall know he is here. You understand me ?"

"Yes, sir."

Mathew Trueman then walked from the office, at the door of which he met Hilliard.

"Late as usual, Mr. Hilliard," said Trueman.

"I have been unwell, sir," said Hilliard, and his ghastly pale face fully bore out his assertion. He looked twenty years older than he looked the day before.

"You do, indeed, look very ill," said the merchant. "I will excuse you to-day."

"Thank you," gasped Hilliard, as he reeled to the outer door like a drunken man.

"Humph," said the merchant, "that is the effect of some debauch last night. Confound the fellow, he is very useful when he is sober, but of late that has become rather rare. He will die some of these days in a kennel, and a good riddance he will be ; he knows too many of the discount transactions I am engaged in to make it safe to discharge him, or he should never again darken my threshold."

"Mr. Rivers," said Tom, "did you see Hilliard ?"

"No," said Rivers, "I did not look up."

"Well, I wish you had. I saw a poor wretch brought out to be hung once on a cold, damp morning, and he looked just as Hilliard looks this morning. I never seed such a face."

"His voice sounded peculiar," remarked Rivers.

"I believe you," said Tom ; "he's been up to some pretty game last night, I'll be bound."

"Ah," said Rivers ; "such men as these are our greatest enemies. I fear he is a most unprincipled fellow."

"In course he is. He's just the chap to do a murder, and be hung for it some of these days."

"That is going a little too far, Tom. A man may be most dissolute and abandoned, and yet shrink with horror from imbruing his hands in the blood of a fellow creature."

"Well, that's your opinion, and t'other's mine; and here's the postman and the newspaper boy."

A bundle of letters was placed before Rivers, and he was about to take them into the room where the merchant usually sat, when Tom cried—

"Stop a bit ! Let's see if there's any for *her*."

"For Grace ?"

"Yes. Because—because, then I shall be told to take it up stairs, and—you can go instead o' me."

"No, Tom," said Rivers ; "it is a pleasure to you to go, and I cannot act the selfish part your generosity would allow me."

"Here is one. 'To Miss Trueman, care of Mathew Trueman, Esq.'—Ah ! this comes from some of her old school acquaintances, I know. Some girl as she used to play at leap-frog, and buttons, and marbles, and all that kind of thing with."

"Why, Tom, these are not exactly the amusements of young ladies at boarding-schools."

"Oh, I forgot. More they ain't. They walks along two-and-two, they does, so uncommon proper; and the Missis, she squalls out—' Miss Trueman, your sticking out your elbow.—Miss Jackson, how dare you wink at that ere blue-bottle?—Miss Smith, what do you mean by giving that skip? You is a disgrace to this here school, you is, Miss Smith, *cus* you!'"

Rivers laughed as he took up the letters, and left the room with them.

Mathew Trueman was in his private office, and when Rivers laid the letters before him with the one addressed to Grace uppermost, he said—

"Oh, here is one for my daughter. Let it be taken up to the drawing-room, Mr. Rivers. Send Hackey with it."

"Yes, sir," said Rivers.

When he got back to the counting-house he handed the letter to Tom, saying—

"There, you are to take it up-stairs."

"Then, I don't mean," said Tom. "I told you I wouldn't, and I won't."

"I shall be back in half an hour," said Mr. Trueman, just putting his head within the counting-house, and then withdrawing it.

"He's going out," remarked Tom; "he always says half-an-hour, 'cos he thinks as that makes everybody look sharp; but he'll be gone an hour or more, I'm sure, for he's gone to the wharf, I know. One of his Indiamen comed into the Pool late last night."

"Take the letter, Tom."

"I sha'n't."

"Nay, you ought to take it."

"Then I won't. Take it yourself, and—and—you may see Grace, you know."

"So may you."

"One word's as good as a hundred, and I sha'n't take it," said Tom. "I've made up my mind, and if you don't take it, she won't have it at all, and I shall be discharged, I supposes."

Rivers said nothing for a moment. Then turning to Tom, he remarked—

"Can you love Grace and act as you do?"

"Love her?" said Tom. "Can I love her? I love the very ground she walks on—the air she breathes; I love her better than I can tell you. I think of her all day, and dream of her all night. I've got a glove that she dropped upon the stairs, and I wouldn't part with it for all Mathew Trueman's money. Do I love her? Oh, Mr. Rivers, you need not have asked that. She is all the world to me; but do you go with the letter, and tell her that Tom gave it to you to bring, and then she will think kindly of me for about a minute, perhaps. Go, Rivers, take it. I shall live to see you and Grace very happy yet, I'm sure. You were born for each other; and when you have a home of your own, and Grace is your wife, I should like to die."

"No, Tom, there could be no happiness for even Grace or myself founded on your misery."

"Go—go," said Tom.

Rivers saw that it would be cruelty to torture his feelings by remaining, and taking the letter, therefore, he hurried from the office.

The staircase was ascended in two or three bounds, and then Rivers tapped gently at the drawing-room door, with his heart in a wild flutter of excitement. He waited some minutes, but no answering voice from within replied to his summons. Then he knocked again, but all remaining still as before, he gently turned the handle of the door, and looked into the room. It was vacant. Rivers entered with a sigh as he thought—

"After all I must leave the letter on the table, I suppose, without seeing Grace. This room will for ever be hallowed in my recollection, for here I passed a delicious hour in company with her I love so fondly, so truly."

"Mr. Rivers," said a voice.

The young man started. Grace stood in the doorway. She was attired in a plain morning dress, and her long silken hair fell upon her shoulders in wild and beautiful luxuriance. Rivers could have knelt and worshipped her. For a moment or two neither spoke, and then, after a pause, with faltering accents, he said—

"Here is a letter, Miss Trueman, which, being addressed to you, I have presumed to bring you."

"Thank you," said Grace, as she reached out her hand to take the letter, and then their eyes met and were instantly withdrawn again in confusion.

"I hope," said Rivers, "that you avoided the storm of yesterday?"

"Not quite," replied Grace. "We had to seek shelter. You escaped it?"

"Yes, I—that is—I don't know."

Grace laughed, and turned the letter over and over in her hand as if its outside were deeply interesting.

"I beg your pardon for intruding upon you so long," said Rivers.

"It is no intrusion," said Grace, in so low a tone, that only the quick perceptions of a lover could have caught the fairy sounds.

"You are kind to say so," said Rivers. "I believe I am foolish this morning, for I have not handed you a chair."

THE ROBBERY OF THE MERCHANT BY HILLIARD.

"Thank you. I—I saw from my window the man whose rudeness you saved me from last evening. Did he come to quarrel with you?"

"Nay, Miss Trueman," said Rivers, "the whole affair is beneath your notice."

Grace cast down her eyes and sighed.

Rivers never afterwards could tell what possessed him at that moment, or what gave him courage suddenly to act

as he did, but he advanced towards Grace, and taking her unresisting hand in his, he said—

"Grace, this may be the happiest as well as most miserable moment of my existence, but were my life dependent upon my silencing the feelings that now flow from my heart, I must say that I love you. I am all unused, dear Grace, to the studied expression of my feelings; but if you will not scorn the devotion of a heart that, whether accepted or rejected, will ever beat for you, and you alone, tell me but that you forgive this wild declaration—that you will permit me now and then to look upon you—that you will think pitifully, if not kindly, of the poor clerk who ventured to love you, perhaps forgetting what he was, and what you are."

His voice faltered, and he ceased speaking. Grace sunk into a chair, and burst into tears.

"Oh, forgive me!" cried Rivers, frantically, "for causing you this pain. I will fly from you for ever—never more shall your kind heart be tortured by the manifestations of a love which it is not likely you can return. I am poor and lowly, Grace, and elsewhere I will carry my aching heart. The proceedings of this morning shall seem to me but as a dream, and I will reserve to myself but one consolation—to pray for your happiness. May Heaven shower its choicest blessings on your head. Farewell for ever!"

He moved towards the door, and Grace still wept bitterly. He could not leave her thus, and returning, he knelt before her.

"One word—one word, dear Grace," he said, "to tell me that you forgive me; but a word, and you shall never see me more."

Her small hands were over her face, and the tears were trickling through her fingers. She tried to speak, but sobs choked her utterance. Rivers remained in the position he had chosen in intense anxiety. Then she slowly dropped her hands from her face, and her eyes met his. The tears hung upon her silken lashes, but there was joy in the eyes themselves. He took her hands in his, and covered them with kisses.

"Grace, dear, dear Grace," he cried, "shall I fly from you for ever?"

She shook her head, and the long clustering ringlets of her hair fell like a veil across her face. He rose, and clasped her for one moment to his heart. Then he parted the hair upon her brow, and with one burning kiss ratified his love. She looked up in his face with a beaming smile—a smile such as a seraph might wear before the throne of Heaven. Grace was happy, and Rivers, ah! what a new and glorious dream of joy was lighting up his soul. He glanced around the room, to convince himself of the reality of all around him. Could it be possible that he had declared his love for Grace, and been accepted?

"Dear Grace," he said, "are we dreaming?"

"If we are," she replied, softly, "may we never awake."

CHAPTER XX.

THE WILY POLICY OF MATHEW TRUEMAN. — THE INTERVIEW, AND THE PROPOSAL.

TOM HACKEY was perfectly right when he said that Mr. Trueman would be a long time gone from his office, for it was nearly twelve o'clock when he returned, and by that time Rivers was at his desk writing, or at all events attempting to write, although, as may be supposed, his mind was tolerably pre-occupied.

The interview, so full of joy and interest, which he had so recently had with Grace, seemed to him, when he was once more in the merchant's counting-house, more like a dream than a reality, and he was more than once tempted to go up-stairs again to endeavour to see Grace, and ask if it were really true that he had seen her, and declared to her his heart's fervent passion. Thrice he asked the wondering Tom Hackey if he had been up stairs at all; and it was only upon Tom's repeated assurances that he saw him go with the letter in his hand, that Rivers could be brought to believe that such was the fact.

"Well, did you see her?" said Tom.

"Yes, I did see her. Oh, Tom! she is surely some angel sent from Heaven by my father to make life beautiful to me."

"What did you say to her?"

"I scarcely know. I am so bewildered with her wondrous beauty, that I know not what she said or what I said."

"Oh," said Tom, "did you say as you wished as you was a glove upon her hand, like Romeo?"

"No, I don't think I said that, Tom."

"Oh, well, it ain't much matter. You love her, and I daresay she loves you; but I tell you what, you'll find that Lord Hawksworth is rather in the way, you will. I haven't no great notion of him in the gentleman line, I can tell you. He'll do you some ill turn."

"I defy him."

"Oh, that's all very well. Recollect Macbeth, when he thought as Birnam Wood couldn't by no manner of means move to Dunsinane, and yet it came, you see, notwithstanding."

"True, Tom, most true; but I don't think my danger quite so great as Macbeth's."

"Wery good; but you are coming to my benefit to-night?"

"To-night? You did not tell me it was to-night."

"Yes, but it is, though."

"I can come, but not—very—early."

"Oh, I suppose you'll be in the Temple-gardens till eight o'clock?"

"Why, to tell the truth, Tom, I shall. But after that hour I shall be able to fulfil my engagement with you."

"You are going to meet Grace?"

"I am, Tom. Your conduct towards me warrants me in candour to you. I am going to meet Grace."

"Then you—you have told her——"

"I have told her I love her. That's if I do not dream, Tom."

"And—she?"

"She did not feel very angry with me."

"I knew it," said Tom; "I knew it would be so; but it's rather sudden—I expected it—I don't know how I shall get through Richard to-night. Never mind me, Mr. Rivers. You know I love her too, and though I know she would never think of a poor fellow like me, yet when I hear that there is no hope at all, even though I knew it before, I must feel it, Mr. Rivers."

"Believe me," said Rivers, with emotion, "that the only drawback upon my happiness is, that your heart is sacrificed. But be of good cheer; you will find some other."

"What!" cried Tom, "find another like Grace Trueman? No, Mr. Rivers, she is quite alone in her beauty and her kind heart. You might possibly find in space another sun as bright as that which shines upon us, but there is no equal to Grace, and I must still love her even now."

"A love like yours, Tom—so pure, so disinterested—honours its object."

"Well, well, be it so. I was making up my mind to say no more about her; but I can't. I recollect a poor fellow I knew who lost his only child—a child so very dear to him that it made up all his happiness; and you see, Mr. Rivers, he agreed with himself that he wouldn't never mention it, and the consequence was, that he was always trying to remember to forget, and it made him so miserable; so, after all, I will talk to you about Grace. It will be a pleasure to me."

"I shall always talk of her to you, Tom, with pleasure, and you must love her, and talk to her, and see her as you would a sister."

"I will, I will. But here comes old Mathew Trueman, so no more at present from your humble servant, Tom Hackey."

"Have you the daily paper, Mr. Rivers?" said Mathew Trueman.

"Yes, sir; here is the *Times*."

"Ah, I want some paper that can be relied upon. The *Times* is useful for its advertisements, but you cannot rely upon the truth of another word in its columns. There has been a dreadful murder in New Inn."

"A murder, sir?"

"Yes, a Mr. Noble, a barrister, has been barbarously murdered. It appears his clerk had left the chambers, but forgetting something, came back late at night, and found his master murdered."

"It seems a shocking affair," said Rivers.

"It is. I heard it from a mercantile friend on 'Change. By-the-by, Tom, did you give my daughter that letter?"

"I did, sir," said Rivers.

"Oh, you did?—Very well. It's of no consequence, only it takes you from your work, Mr. Rivers, and Tom is not so importantly occupied. By-the-by, I wish to speak to you, Mr. Rivers. Will you follow me into my office?"

"Certainly, sir," said Rivers, rising and following the merchant, in no very pleasant frame of mind, 'for he was apprehensive that something of his recent interview with Grace must have come to his ears by some means. His fears, however, upon that head were speedily allayed, for when Mathew Trueman reached his counting-house, he said—

"Mr. Rivers, you may be aware that

Hilliard has been a long time with me, and understands my business well. Now, lately he has contracted such drunken habits that I think he and I will soon part, and in that case I should wish you to be enabled to take his place. For the purpose, then, of enabling you so to do, I shall commit to your charge one of the pieces of business which should have come under the hands of Hilliard."

"I shall be happy, sir, to be useful to you," said Rivers, "in any way that lies within my power."

"Then, Mr. Rivers, I will confide entirely in you. A young nobleman, Lord Hawksworth, a son of the Earl of Montjoy, and heir to very large possessions, wishes to raise a sum of forty thousand pounds upon his contingent estates."

"Yes, sir."

"Well, in addition to that, I rather think, Mr. Rivers, an alliance will take place between my daughter Grace, and his lordship."

"An alliance, sir?"

"Yes—I mean a marriage. Grace would well become the ancient coronet of the Montjoys. It's lustre would not be tarnished by resting on her brow."

"Tarnished, sir!" said Rivers; "she would lend a new lustre to a crown—that is, I—I——"

"You what, Mr. Rivers?"

"I humbly presume to think so, sir."

"I am glad my daughter enjoys so much of your good opinion," said the merchant, drily.

"I am quite sure, sir," stammered Rivers, "from the little I have seen of Miss Trueman, that wherever she shall fix her *choice*, she will bring happiness in her train."

"Her choice, Mr. Rivers, upon which you lay so much stress, will, of course, be in accordance with her father's wishes."

"Such is not always the case, sir," remarked Rivers; "but if I have one fervent prayer above another, it is that her choice and yours may coincide."

"Thank you, Mr. Rivers. You will assist me in my interviews with Lord Hawksworth occasionally, and I shall confide in you to make copies of all the important, and, in some cases, secret documents and letters that must inevitably pass between us."

"I shall abide by your instructions, sir."

"My daughter shall be the wife of a peer," added Mathew Trueman; "of that I am quite resolved, Mr. Rivers."

Rivers said nothing to this, but he thought—"If she does, I must enter the muster-roll of nobility, then; for no one's wife but mine shall she be, while I have life, health, and strength."

"You quite understand me, Mr. Rivers?" said the merchant, after a pause.

"Perfectly, sir."

"Very well. You may retire now."

Rivers rose and hurried himself out of the room in a state of mind easier to be imagined than described.

"Good Heavens!" he thought, "is it possible there can be found a father so blinded by the meretricious glitter of a coronet that he would deliberately sacrifice his child for its reflected beams, merely upon his own name? No, Mathew Trueman, you may fancy that Grace, who has been bestowed upon you by Heaven, was sent to become an instrument for working out your mercantile schemes, but you shall find yourself mistaken. She shall never want a warm heart to love her and an arm to protect her, while I possess the one or the other. I do deeply regret now that I gave my word of promise to that puppy, Hawksworth, not to reveal the scene that has passed between us; and yet, perhaps, 'tis better as it is. If we are true to each other, which we shall be, no power on earth can harm us."

Mathew Trueman's reflections were of a widely different character from those of Rivers, for the moment the young man had left the office he smiled, and fell into a pleasing reverie.

"All succeeds," he said, "according to my wishes. This last is, I flatter myself, a master stroke. My mind has been quite tormented since yesterday with the thoughts of some peculiar glances that passed between my Grace and this young spark. Now, however, I do flatter myself I have extinguished all feelings of the kind, if he were really so presumptuous as to have entertained any. He would hardly put himself in competition with a lord, although there is no accounting for the impertinence of some young men. And, besides, I shall be gradually bringing him to take Hilliard's place, by which means I shall get rid of Hilliard. I was foolish to think for a moment this poor devil, Rivers, would have any scruples about the peculiar money-lending business I make so much profit by. He will make himself useful, of course ; Grace will be a countess, and I a happy man."

CHAPTER XXI.

THE PANGS OF CONSCIENCE.—HIL-LIARD'S CONDITION.—A BILL OF THE PLAY.

LORD HAWKSWORTH was, as the newspapers say, in a state of mind easier to be imagined than described when he left the merchant's counting-house after his adventure with Rivers, and every dark passion of his heart was stirred into life and activity against the young man who had exposed him to so much degradation. Lord Hawksworth only wanted one faculty to make him a man to be much dreaded—that faculty was courage, which had he possessed to a sufficient extent to enable nim to carry out the dark designs of his heart, would have hurried him into tne commission of the worst of crimes.

As it was, however, he has ever compelled to resort to the assistance of accomplices for the perpetration of any act of vengeance ; and now that his breast was boiling with rage against Rivers, he made a solemn determination to himself that, cost what it might, he would destroy him.

"I have now in full play," he muttered to himself, "two of the strongest passions in human nature—love and hatred. As I love that enchanting girl, the merchant's daughter, so do I hate Rivers, his clerk, and as I am determined to possess the angelic Grace, so am I determined upon the ruin of this champion of hers who, if he be not disposed of comfortably, will be a perpetual source of annoyance to me."

Having exerted himself sufficiently to make these reflections, Lord Hawksworth took his way to a street leading from the Strand, where lodged his con-fidential adviser, Girkins, who he intended at once to inform of the circumstance that had occurred, with only such slight variations as might represent him, Hawksworth, in a little more favourable light.

Alighting from his horse, he knocked at the lodging-house in which Mr. Girkins resided, and had resided since his little misunderstanding with the Lord Chancellor. Girkins was an agent for such scions of nobility as Hawksworth in rather a large way. He made quite a service of it, and hence the appearance of his lordship, who was well known, did not create the sensation in the house which it otherwise might, and he was quietly ushered into the front parlour with an assurance that Mr. Girkins would attend upon him directly.

In a few moments the agent entered the room, and one glance at the countenance of Hawksworth assured him that the interview with Rivers had been an unpropitious one for his lordship.

"Girkins," said Hawksworth, speaking rapidly, "it is beneath my rank to be engaging personally with low persons, such as clerks and others. I shall turn over this vagabond clerk of Trueman's to your tender mercies. Involve him in some very serious scrape, and I will stand any charges whatever."

"Humph! May I ask if your lordship has seen him to-day ?"

"I have."

"And—and may I hope ——"

"Never mind what occurred. I am still not satisfied. So mark me, Girkins, next to the accomplishment of my designs concerning Grace, the merchant's beautiful daughter, I hold dear to my heart the punishment of this most insolent plebeian."

"Very good, your lordship," said the complying Mr. Girkins. "All shall be as your lordship wishes. I am to understand, then, that I am honoured with these commissions ; first, the obtaining a loan of forty thousand pounds from Mathew Trueman."

"Yes, certainly."

"Secondly, the—the—" seduction Mr. Girkins was going to say, but he altered it to the more polite phrase of "possession of Grace Trueman, and the ruin of this young man, Rivers."

"That is all I wish you to do at present," said Hawksworth. "And now, hark ye, Mr. Girkins, I would rather that you rid me of that young fellow some other way than by telling old Trueman what has occurred. It might go round to the girl, and—and then, you see, she might think it strange."

Even Hawksworth was ashamed that Grace should think so very meanly of him as he deserved, and Girkins quite understood the feeling that actuated his customer, and shaped his reply accordingly.

"I quite agree with your lordship that it would be extremely impolitic to say one word to Mathew Trueman concerning his clerk, Rivers. Now, he has another clerk, by name, Mark Hilliard, who I think could be most advantageously used for your lordship's service. If I do not much mistake him, he is just the person to be of essential assistance."

"Let it be so then; only do you manage everything, for Heaven's sake. You know I cannot be tormented. I swear, that should it cost me twenty thousand pounds, Grace Rivers shall be my mistress."

"More difficult things than that can be accomplished," said Girkins, with a sickly smile, like a faint gleam of white sunshine on an early day in spring. "You may, at all events, depend upon my most devoted service. There is one little matter, however, which requires immediate attention."

"And what may that be?"

"Simply this, that we cannot get on without funds."

"Oh, as to that, it is easily arranged. Let me see : I have credit with several jewellers—I will order a few hundred pounds' worth of jewels, and you can get them converted into cash."

"Certainly, your lordship. I know of a tradesman who would be happy to serve your lordship. By-the-bye, he has now a dressing case, that if your lordship will give me an order for, he will be most happy to supply you with."

"What's its value?"

"Eight hundred pounds."

"A good price for a dressing-case," remarked Hawksworth; "but we must have money, so there's the memorandum. Convert the article into cash as quickly as you can, and let me have some, for I have not twenty pounds left."

"I will attend your lordship to-morrow, and we can then go together to Trueman's, and then urge him to make haste in your affairs. You may likewise catch a glimpse of his daughter."

"That will do, Girkins. Come to me at twelve. Good-day to you."

In a few moments Hawksworth was trotting towards his splendid chambers in the Albany, quite heedless of the immense mass of liabilities he was heaping up around him, and fancying himself quite a fine fellow, and a man of uncommon spirit, because he made a principle of gratifying, or, at least, endeavouring to gratify every vicious or extravagant whim that found a place in his imagination.

When Hawksworth was gone, Girkins paced his room for some moments in silence. Then flinging himself into a chair, he muttered—

"The coward! He has let this young man Rivers get the better of him. Curse on these love affairs! Were they not such very useful auxiliaries in money matters, because they stultify the judgment, and for a time make the most mean and avaricious liberal with their cash, I would never be an agent in them. Hawksworth never will succeed with that girl. Well, what matter—I shall succeed in all I wish, and that is to get a good share of the forty thousand pounds which this Mathew Trueman will lend, upon the likelihood of his own inordinate vanity being gratified by an alliance with nobility. Ha! ha! what puppets are such men in hands like mine. I play with them as I please. Their passions are the weapons I turn against them. One man is avaricious, another vain, a third ambitious, a fourth extravagant, and he who can seize upon those points in human nature will be successful. Have I been successful? Not yet, not yet; but I shall be—I must succeed, for who can cope with me in intrigue—who can draw out the very pattern of a deep-laid plot equal to me? Pshaw! untoward circumstances may hitherto have thwarted me in my ambitious schemes, and in my pursuit of wealth; but the time must come when superior address must meet its reward. I shall yet live to be rich, and to raise myself above the station in life from which I have been degraded. Struck off the roll of attorneys, I am now nothing, unless I can show the world that I have money. Then it will be my very humble servant, if I were an incarnate fiend. I have learnt that much in my intercourse with human nature."

Hugging himself thus upon the errors and perversions of intellect which had been his ruin hitherto, Girkins left his lodgings, in order to proceed to Barnard's Inn, to enjoy a consultation with his friend, Jonas Quickset, Esq., who was not yet struck off the rolls, but continued a gentleman by act of Parliament, not on account of superior honesty, but because he had not yet been found out in any overt act which could make him amenable to the bar of the Chancellor.

Mr. Girkins crossed the Strand, and made his way up Drury-lane, intending to proceed through Clare-market, and so on by Lincoln's-inn, towards his place of destination; but as he neared the purlieus of the market the sky became overcast, and every appearance indicated an approaching shower. Girkins stood up in a mean door-way, lest by spoiling his then only suit of black he should be placed in the dilemma of not being able to proceed upon his nefarious business without a renewal of garments, a measure just then easier to be contemplated than carried into effect.

The sky grew darker each moment, and then large drops of rain came splashing down with a heavy dull sound upon the pavement, spreading themselves out in starry rays, like bullets discharged against an iron target. Then a gust of wind whirled along the streets, catching up stray straws, dust, and every light article that encumbered the thoroughfare, whirling them along furiously, and then suddenly letting them go again, as if the wind had burnt its fingers.

A calm of some moments now succeeded, and then came the shower in earnest, pouring down till the dashing spray from the house-tops and pavement made them appear as if enveloped in steam.

Girkins drew as far in the door-way as he could get to avoid the splashes that darted in upon him, as if purposely aimed against his breast. Not a soul for some moments was visible in the street. It seemed as if in an instant all the population of London had found shelter somewhere until the shower had wreaked its fury on the deserted streets.

Just as this reflection crossed the mind of Girkins, he heard one solitary footstep approaching the door-way from the westward, and surprised at the slow measured pace at which the person, whoever he was, was proceeding at, the agent peered round the door post to observe him, and with a tone of surprise, he ejaculated—

"Mark Hilliard—'tis he, drenched to the skin, and yet to all appearance unconscious of it. This must either be some strange perversity of temper, or he is in deep abstraction. Well met, however; I will speak to him."

Resolving to address him when he reached the door-way, Girkins stood close to the step, and would have carried his intention into effect, had he not been struck with astonishment at the awfully pale and haggard countenance of Hilliard. His lips were of a blueish white —his eyes blood-shot, and uneasy looking, and his face altogether of a ghastly paleness, which made him more resemble one of those awful creations of the imagination, called vampires, than aught human.

The rain dashed upon him, but he seemed utterly unconscious of it, walking on slowly and listlessly, muttering something apparently to himself, for his lips moved as if he were giving a faint voice to some inward cogitations.

So surprised was Girkins at the appearance of Hilliard under such circumstances, and evidently in so terrible a state of mental and bodily distress, that he suffered him to pass him before he could recover sufficiently to address him.

"Why—what can be the matter with him?" said Girkins, as he strained his eyes in staring after Hilliard. "He looks like a ghost himself, or as if he had just seen one. Why, he no more knows it rains than how to transmute metals. I never in my life saw any one look so perfectly wretched. The shower is abating —I'll follow him. Is he suffering merely from the effects of a drunken carouse last night, or has he really been doing something which sits uneasily upon his memory? Surely the latter must be the case. I never saw anybody look as he does but once, and that was a poor devil who was hanged for murder. I'll follow him; it may be that if he has committed some crime, I may make him a more useful tool than even I dreamt of. Yes, Master Hilliard, your looks and manner betoken some circumstances of character to make you fearful of all men and the slave of him who will take the trouble to terrify you. I will follow and see whither you are going with such an awful expression upon your face."

Keeping Hilliard in view, Girkins stepped from the doorway, and following him through Clare-market, he saw him dive down a narrow court, situated near the back of Wild-street, Drury-lane.

Hilliard never once looked round, but presently entered a dirty, mean house, with an open doorway, and which was evidently let out to the lowest and vilest characters.

"So, Master Hilliard, you are housed, are you? Well, as I want a conference with you, I shall take the liberty of beating up your quarters, although they are certainly not the most salubrious."

With these words, Girkins entered the wretched house, determined to inquire from room to room, until he found the object of his search.

CHAPTER XXII.

GRACE TRUEMAN AND HER FRIEND.— THE CONSULTATION.

FOR the whole of the day, Rivers was in a state of mind which, from its extreme agitation, could scarcely be considered as other than positively painful. The hours appeared to him to pass away with a slowness unparalleled, and before the hour for him to leave the office in order to dine came round, it seemed to his mind as if he had been a month without seeing his beloved—his beautiful Grace.

"There's one o'clock," said Tom Hackey; "why don't you go and get your dinner, Rivers? You won't get none if you don't go now, unless you make what I call roast veal of old Mathew's pens by frizzling 'em in the fire, and then eating of 'em up."

"Oh, yes, I'm going, Tom. Did you say you had roast veal?"

"There you go agin," cried Tom. "Why, ye don't know what you is a-saying of. I never comed near anybody

like you. Go at once; stand not upon the order of your going, as Lady Macbeth remarked to the gentlemen as was invited to supper, but go at once."

"Well, I'm going; and mind, tonight I shall come to your benefit."

"Do; you'll open your eyes above a bit, I promise you. Here's one of our bills—a rum un, you'll find. Lot's for the money, you'll say, but I don't grudge none on it. Here you are. What do you think o' this? 'For the benefit of Octavius Junius Delacourt.' That's my theatrical name for to-night, and if it ain't a dasher, I don't know what is. Richard the Third will be performed, previous to which Hot Codlings will be sung by the celebrated clown, Grinallday. Between the acts a double hornpipe in handcuffs and fetters; after the tent scene, Mr. Flewsun will sing the celebrated comic song of Has your Uncle sold his Boot-jack? To be followed by a romantic drama, in two acts, entitled, The Slimy Demon of the Dreary Waste; or, the Slaughter of the Sanguinary Sausage-man. The talented Miss Caroline Jenkinsiana will, during the piece, dance the Cachuca on her head, amidst a shower of real fire——"

"Upon my word," said Rivers, "you have an assortment of attractions."

"Oh, that ain't half of it. It won't be over, I can tell you, very early. Then there's a combat of the Mysterious Stranger and his Six Babies with the Blood-red Ruffians of Rugby Hollow. That's dreadfully exciting."

"So I should think. You may depend upon my being there."

"We've lots o' singing, too," cried Tom, as Rivers put on his hat. "There's a young lady coming out by particular desire, on'y it's thought as she'll soon go in agin."

"Well, well, Tom, I will be there."

Rivers hurried from the office, but what appetite had he for dinner? His spirits were in too great a state of excitement, and his mind was too full of the image of Grace, to permit him to sit down in a tavern.

"I will take a walk rapidly for an hour," he said, "and that will calm me."

With this determination, he started off at a rapid pace, and crossing Southwark-Bridge, found more relief in the exertion of hard walking than he could have experienced from any other course of proceeding.

"We suffer equally," he thought, "from too much pleasure or too much disappointment. I don't know that I have felt so much true happiness, as well as so much intense anxiety, in my whole life before, as I have this one day. Can I believe my own voice when I tell myself that Grace loves me?—that she,

the very personification of all that is lovely, good, and admirable, loves me— a poor clerk, one buffeted about by evil fortune?"

Suddenly Rivers relaxed his speed, and turned pale, as he thought to himself—

"What have I done? Won the affections of a young, artless girl; one used to every luxury of life, one who has never had a wish ungratified. Am I—can I be justified in dragging her

LORD HAWKSWORTH MEETS WITH AN ADVENTURE IN THE STREETS.

from the dear enjoyments—the comforts of a home to share my poverty? No, no, I am not such a villain. Oh, Grace! I will love you—I will adore you; you shall be henceforth the polar star of my existence, but I will not sacrifice you. I will wed you either with the consent of your father, or I will acquire a home for you myself which shall be such as I can without a blush offer to you; or I will, if the effort kill me, tear myself from you for ever. My love for you shall not be selfish. I cannot bring

poverty and all its train of ills upon the head of her I love."

These considerations cast a gloom over the heart of Rivers, and he relaxed in his speed, walking but listlessly back to his office, as a voice seemed to whisper to him—"What hope have you? How can you ever make a home for Grace Trueman? Despair, Rivers, despair— poverty is your portion, and the portion of all who are so unhappy as to link themselves to your fate."

And how was Grace occupied during

the hours that sweetened her interview with her lover? What were the feelings that agitated her young guileless heart, after she had all but confessed the secret love which had so strangely and so suddenly sprung up in her bosom for the poor dependant clerk?

Like Rivers, she for some time could scarce persuade herself of the reality of what had passed; and then, when she thought over all he had said, and recollected each look of passionate love and deep sincerity of heart which he had cast upon her—of her short acquaintance with him—her, perhaps, too trusting confidence, she burst into tears, and sobbing as if her heart would break, she exclaimed—

"Oh, that I had a mother!—Oh, that I had now a mother!"

Poor Grace from her earliest infancy had never known a mother's care; and although the place of a parent had been supplied, as far as it could be, by Mrs. Woodfall, her kind and considerate nurse, yet there is something so holy—so full of love, differing from all other affections, however great and sincere, in the tie between a mother and her child, that Grace, even when she felt herself most happy, most cared for, and most loved, would revert to her motherless state, and sigh for the parent of which she had been so early deprived.

As Grace covered her beautiful face with her hands and wept in the bitterness of her heart for some moments, she was not aware that some one had entered the room, and was gazing at her with unfeigned astonishment, and a grief nearly equal to her own. The unexpected visitor was a young lady of the name of Amelia Dearbrook, who had been a dear friend and companion of Grace's at school; she had now called to make a confidence with Grace upon a subject similar to that which occupied the mind of the merchant; and being told that Grace was up stairs, had thus unannounced come so suddenly upon her. But Amelia's love was all sunshine—friends had consented—there was ample fortune—not one cloud appeared to dim the clear heaven of her joy, and she had come to her cherished companion, Grace Rivers, to pour out in her ears the fulness of her young heart's joy.

"Grace—dear Grace," she said, as she flew towards her, and clasped her in her arms.

Grace started, and glancing through her tears, she felt as if Heaven had almost answered her prayer, by at such a moment sending to her so dear a friend—one on whom she knew she could confide, and whose advice would be as judicious as it would, she knew, be kind.

"Amelia—dear Amelia, is it really you?"

"It is, Grace; but I should be better pleased to find that this was not really you. There are tears upon your cheek, and your bright eyes are dimmed with weeping. What has happened, Grace?"

"I ought not to weep, Amelia, for—for——"

"For what, Grace?"

"For this has been, perhaps, the happiest day I shall ever know; and yet I could not stop my tears, dear Amelia."

"Tears of joy, Grace?"

"Not all of joy. Yet my heart tells me I should not be sorrowful; but you know, dear Amelia, that when we are too happy, we are ever most disposed to find some misery to act as the shadow to the close of the sunny landscape."

Amelia turned aside to hide a sympathetic tear which started to her eye. Then arousing from her emotion, she said, with a smile—

"Will you forgive me, dear Grace, for hazarding a guess, founded on my own experience, of the state of your heart?"

"Yes, Amelia. Do guess—I would rather that than tell you."

"You are in love, my Grace?"

"In love, Amelia?—I—that is—in love?"

"Yes, your eyes, cheeks — your blushes, dear Grace, all express it; but you will not deny me the truth when I tell you that—that I—own I am going to be married?"

"I give you joy, Amelia, and well may he be married who will possess such a treasure as yourself. Well I know your heart, Amelia—it is full of kind and noble sympathies."

"A truce to compliments, Grace. But tell me at once who it is that has raised a flutter in your little heart?"

"Alas! Amelia, my love is clouded

by many cares. I fear my father's approbation may be wanting to him upon whom my heart is fixed. Thus was it that I wept—even in the midst of my joy, and thus is it that now the dim shadow of coming ill seems to rest upon my soul."

"You fear your father's disapproval, Grace? Is your lover unworthy?"

"Unworthy? No—a nobler heart, I am sure, never beat in human breast; but, Amelia, he has that fault which I know in my father's eye nothing can or ever will exterminate—he is poor."

"But your father is rich, Grace, and he loves you."

"He is rich, Amelia, and he loves me, but he wishes to be richer, and his love for me has lately become rather a pride than an affection. He is ever hinting at high projects, and more than once has emphatically declared that none but a nobleman should ever with his consent become my husband."

"But he surely will not barter you for rank?"

"He cannot, Amelia, were he ten-times my father. Yet I love him, and such duty as a child should give ever shall he have; but the affections, my Amelia, are given to us by Heaven."

"You are right, Grace. But tell me who is he upon whom your young heart has fixed its love?"

"One poor and lowly. He is a clerk to my father. Hush! some one comes."

The door opened, and Mathew Trueman made his appearance. There was an air of satisfaction about his manner and a smiling serenity upon his countenance which it seldom wore. He had reasoned himself into a belief that all his schemes were succeeding well, and he already looked upon his daughter as the future Countess of Montjoy.

"Well, Miss Dearbrook," he said, gaily, "we have not seen you for a long time, but we are always happy to see you; and believe me, whatever important changes may take place, we shall always welcome old friends—a-hem! She may come to some of our magnificent parties when my daughter is a countess," thought Trueman to himself, as he drew out his handkerchief and waved it with a pompous air.

"You are very kind, Mr. Trueman," said Amelia; "I never desert old friends, let them be circumstanced how they may. Friendship is as dear to me in a cottage as it is in a palace."

"Oh, I—I did not anticipate a change for the worst, Miss Dearbrook," said the merchant, who was excessively vexed that his words had been so misconstrued. "I merely meant that—that some people as they advance in the scale of social rank get proud and haughty, but we are not such."

"I never imagined for one moment," said Amelia, "that my dear friend, Grace, would alter in heart, whatever she might do in outward circumstances."

"I don't much like the girl," thought Trueman; "we will cut her when Grace marries.—I trust you will do us the favour of remaining to lunch, Miss Dearbrook?"

"That I cannot, Mr. Trueman, thank you. Mine is a mere passing call to bid adieu to my dear Grace, previous to my leaving England for a continental tour."

"A continental tour? Bless me! Are you going to be married?"

"I believe I may answer yes, for you, Amelia," said Grace.

"To an earl?" said Trueman, abstractedly.

"No, sir, merely to an honest man," said Amelia.

Trueman started, and bowing, with a supercilious smile, he said—

"Permit me to wish you all imaginable joy, Miss Dearbrook."

"Thank you, sir," was the calm reply; and then as Grace rose, Amelia bowed to Mr. Trueman, and followed her dear friend from the room.

"Humph! an honest man," muttered Mathew Trueman—"an honest man. Was ever heard the like of that? By Heavens, that sounds as if she knew my secret intentions with regard to Grace. An honest man—of course, that means a poor man. All poor devils that have not one farthing to rattle with another in their pockets, are amazingly honest men. Oh, dear, of course, an honest man; d—n honest men: I hate them; that girl has quite annoyed me with her cold countenance, and her honest man. I began the world with three and a penny, and I should like to know what I should have been worth if

I had been an honest—Pshaw! What am I saying? Confound the girl."

CHAPTER XXIII.

THE MURDERER.—A SCENE OF WOE.

THE first door at which Mr. Girkins knocked in the miserable house whither he had followed Hilliard, was opened by a squalid-looking woman, with one child in her arms, and another holding by the skirts of her dress.

"What now?" she cried, in an insolent tone, as if prepared for something disagreeable.

"I only want to know," said Girkins, "if you can tell me which room one Mr. Hilliard occupies."

"Oh," said the woman, "I thought you came after some money. It's the two-pair back."

With that she gave the child a rough shake for crying, and slammed the door in Girkins's face.

"A pleasant abode has Master Hilliard," thought the agent. "He spends all his money, doubtless, at public-houses, and never thinks of a home. The two-pair back; well, here I am."

By mistake, however, Girkins opened the wrong door, and as he did so, a low agonised voice met his ears, and he saw a man kneeling by the bed upon which lay, apparently, a dead body. Two other persons were in the room, who, although they were evidently not closely interested in the sufferings of the kneeling man, yet appeared to listen to him with an interest that prevented them from hearing Girkins open the door.

"May the curse of a broken heart," said he who was kneeling, "fall heavily upon the heads of those who have worked this woe. Oh, God—oh, God! save me from madness! Must the young, the beautiful, and the good, be ever thus sacrificed? Gentlemen, you look at me aghast; you will tell each other I am mad—that will be your conversation—the balm you lay to your consciences. You are the parish doctors, and now with officious zeal you come when it is too late; look at the pale face which in its stillness reproaches you more than a hundred tongues. That was my wife. You know my story well. We fell into unmerited poverty. We sought subsistence by hard labour, but there were many stronger than we were, and we were nearly starved before we appealed to the tender mercies of the parish officers. What was the answer? The workhouse for her, and a pass to a distant county where I was born for me. She clung to me—the lover of her youth, the loving husband of her maturer years—she shrieked to me in her despair not to leave her, and then I begged for the smallest trifle, weekly, to keep soul and body together till perchance happier times should come. It was refused me with taunts. I was driven from the judgment seat of those sinful men, who punish poverty as a crime with blows. We found shelter here—my wife sunk famishing on this, her death-bed. Then I asked for medical aid; that was denied me, because I had rejected the terms of the workhouse kings. I have knelt by her for many hours, and she is dead. You have come too late, she is dead—dead!"

"Ned," said one of the parish surgeons, taking a pinch of snuff from an elaborately chased silver box, which had been the day before presented to him from the vestry in testimonial of his services. "Ned, I was at Clapham seeing my man rack off the Madeira I took out of bond in the Docks yesterday, and couldn't possibly attend even when Smuggles, the overseer, gave an order on the representation of the woman down stairs.

"Well, I couldn't come," said the other. "They brought the order to me, but I really had not breakfasted."

"Paupers are dreadfully ungrateful," remarked the first speaker. "Now, the newspapers will call this a case of neglect, and all that sort of thing, when here we are both quite attentive."

"The man's mad."

"Yes, a decided monomaniac."

"Fiends!" suddenly shrieked the bereaved husband, rushing towards the heartless men, "vengeance shall be mine."

Mr. Girkins made a precipitate retreat from the door, which he had hardly done, when the parish surgeons tumbled out one over the other, and rolled headlong down the staircase, crying murder as loud as their lungs would permit them.

Before Girkins could reflect upon the strange scene he had witnessed, another door suddenly opened upon the landing, and Hilliard, with a face of terror, stood before him.

"What—what is that?" he gasped, for his guilty conscience converted every sound he heard into danger to himself from the myrmidons of the law.

"Mr. Hilliard," said Girkins.

Hilliard started back, and partially closed the door upon Girkins, who hastened forward, saying—

"Nay, Mr. Hilliard, I come as a friend to have some private conversation with you."

"A friend?" repeated Hilliard. "How came you to know where I was, Mr. Girkins?"

"I followed you just now through the rain, and wish very much to engage with you to perform a service which you will find at once easy and profitable."

"Indeed?"

"Yes; but I cannot explain more to you here. Let me come in, and I will convince you how you may serve me, and pay yourself well."

"You can come in," said Hilliard; "I have not been very well, and am rather nervous."

He opened the door, as he spoke, wide enough for Girkins to pass in, and then immediately bolted it on the inside.

"You are cautious not to be disturbed," said the agent.

"I am," replied Hilliard; "I have only lived here since yesterday, and I don't know what intruding people may be in the house."

"There is one in the next room will not trouble you, at all events."

"Who is that?"

"A dead body."

Hilliard started, and a flush of colour came across his face—then departing, and making him look paler than he was before.

"What—what do you mean by speaking to me of a dead body?" he cried. "What have I to do with it? I didn't kill him—I am armed, sir—I am armed."

"Well, Mr. Hilliard," said the astonished agent, "I have no wish to quarrel with you. I'm sure I have said nothing offensive. There is a dead woman in the next room—that is all."

"Oh, that's all—that's all," repeated Hilliard; "what is death, after all?—nothing—it's nothing to be scared at, is it, Girkins? A man must die some time, and sooner or later cannot make much difference to him, can it, Mr. Girkins?"

"Why, I should say it makes no difference to anybody else, but a great deal to the person who dies."

"Well, but suppose a man advanced in years dies—dies suddenly from an accident—is it not better, far better than as if he had not been killed, but allowed to live on to all the miseries and pains of old age? I say 'tis better for him—much better."

"You won't find an old man in his senses to say so," remarked Girkins; "but we have got into rather a disagreeable train of conversation. I trust I may make a proposition to you in perfect confidence, Mr. Hilliard?"

"You may; I will do anything now, because anything would fall short of—"

"Of what?" said Girkins, eagerly.

"Nothing, nothing. Look here," producing a bottle, "if I am to listen to you, and make you rational answers, this must not continue empty."

"I understand you," said Girkins. "There is half-a-crown—get what liquor you like."

Hilliard took up the bottle, and muttering that he would not be long, left the agent alone in as wretched an apartment as it had ever been his lot to see. In one corner was a miserable, dirty, truckle bed, with a patchwork quilt over it, hanging all in rents and tatters—then there were certain'y two chairs, but neither of them safe to sit upon—a small table, one of the legs of which was tied on with cord, and a half of an iron hoop, torn from some old barrel, for a fender. In the miserable grate some wood was smouldering away, and on the hob was a pipkin, which was used by Hilliard for the purpose of heating water with which to mix spirit.

There was literally nothing else whatever in the room, which any one would have thought must be the wretched abode of some one reduced to the last stage of destitution, rather than of a man receiving, at all events, a competent salary for his services; but then the tavern and the low gaming-house divided all Mark Hilliard's earnings between them.

Upon glancing again at the bed, Girkins saw the corner of a newspaper peeping out from a rent in the patch-work quilt; and being anxious to know why it was hidden there so carefully, he drew it completely out from its place of concealment, and found it carefully doubled so as just to present one column to the eyes. That column was headed with the words "Frightful murder!"

"What have we here!" exclaimed Girkins. "This is an account of the murder of Mr. Noble in New Inn, about which the whole town is almost in an uproar. By Heavens, a thought strikes me! Hilliard's awful appearance, his evident terror, his strange observations with regard to dead people, this paper—all tend to but one supposition, and that is, that if Hilliard be not himself the actual perpetrator of the crime, he is in some way intimately connected with it."

Mr. Girkins remained for some moments in deep thought, and then he muttered—

"This would secure him for ever to do my bidding in any way; but is it safe to let such a man know that I have his secret? By G— he might murder me to get rid of the fright of my some day disclosing the matter."

Impressed with this idea, Mr. Girkins hastily replaced the newspaper under the quilt, and in a very uncomfortable state of mind got back again to the rickety chair on which he had been sitting, just as Hilliard made his appearance.

"Has any one been?" he asked.

"No," said Girkins; "I have been undisturbed."

"Well, well, I didn't expect any one. I have no reason—none whatever. There is brandy—will you drink?"

"No, thank you; such a trifle upsets me."

"Humph!" grunted Hilliard; "it takes a d—d large dose to upset me. Why, I have been trying to get drunk since an early hour this morning, and I can't."

"Indeed! that's odd."

"It is rather. The liquor lays in my stomach like cold water: it won't mount to the brain. I cannot get drunk—I wish I could."

"Do you? Now, I should have thought quite the reverse. But how comes it you are not at Mr. Trueman's to-day, Mr. Hilliard?"

"He gave me a holiday, as I felt unwell."

"I am sorry for your indisposition. Perhaps I had better call again?"

"No, no, I'd rather you'd stay now you are here a thousand times—I like company."

He went to the fire, and dragging together the embers, placed on them the earthen vessel containing the water, while Girkins could not but notice the extreme agitation under which he was then labouring.

"My suspicions are confirmed," thought Girkins. "He does know all about the murder of Mr. Noble. My policy will be not to say anything about it, but to keep him in perpetual fear that I do suspect him; while, from the want of certainty of it, he will not be induced to make any desperate attempt against me. To cover one murder, this fellow would think nothing of committing half-a-dozen more."

"You had better take some of this," remarked Hilliard, as from the mantelshelf he took a small mug, in which he mixed the brandy-and-water, the spirit bearing much more than a half proportion to the water.

"No, I thank you, I would rather not. But, now, to business, Mr. Hilliard. Mathew Trueman has a lovely daughter."

"He has, and as proud as Lucifer. I did but take a little notice of her one day, and she sailed off as if she had been a queen."

"Well, be that as it may, there is one who can pay well for any assistance he may receive as regards information of her movements, and so on. Lord Hawksworth, whom you have seen, is desperately in love with Grace Trueman."

"Indeed! Well, I don't wonder at it. But what does he want me to do?"

"Nothing just now, except being upon the watch, to let him know through me anything that happens at the merchant's. Then there is a fellow-clerk of yours, named Rivers."

"Confound him!"

"Ah! confound him I say; for it is more than possible he may mar all. You must keep a special watch upon him, Hilliard, for Lord Hawksworth and myself both suspect that he is casting an eye upon the merchant's daughter."

All the passions of Hilliard's nature were stirred up at the mention of Rivers, and with bitter oaths he declared that he would watch him night and day.

"You must be very cautious in this matter," added Girkins, "and I'm sure Lord Hawksworth will not mind a few hundreds. Understand me, this Rivers must not only be prevented from rivalling his lordship with Grace, but there is a score of revenge to settle against him, which his mere dismissal from Trueman's service would by no means gratify."

"There is a score of revenge on my part," cried Hilliard, "and I must see him at the gallows."

The guilty man paused, and trembled as he thus inadvertently pronounced the word which, of all others, brought terror to his mind. His agitation was not unmarked by Girkins, who added it as another link to the chain of circumstantial evidence, tending to fix the murder of Mr. Noble upon him.

"I mean," stammered Hilliard, "I mean that I will have my revenge. He has insulted me, and I must have my revenge."

"How sweet that revenge will be," remarked Girkins, "when you are actually paid for gratifying it, Hilliard."

"It will; you may depend upon me in this matter, for it just jumps with my own humour. I hate Mathew Trueman, too, and I now hate his daughter. I did love her; but, as I tell you, she treated me as if I had been a dog."

"Ah! it is not so as regards your fellow-clerk, Rivers," said Girkins. "He is treated very differently by Grace."

"Then he shall not have long to boast of it; for, as sure as I am now a living man, I will think of something which shall destroy him."

An expression, such as a fiend might wear, came across the white hypocritical face of Girkins, as he said in a low tone—

"Perhaps if something could be contrived to ruin his character—you understand me, Hilliard—it would touch him more nearly than even an attack upon his life. Such men as he pride themselves upon their morals, their honesty. If, now, some neatly-contrived little

plot were to succeed in placing his character under strong suspicion—eh, Hilliard, would not that be revenge?"

"It would—it shall be done—it shall be done. I thank you for the hint."

"I merely throw it out as a little suggestion," said Girkins, rising. "Now my good friend, Hilliard, you will quite understand that you are to consider yourself as specially retained in the service of Lord Hawksworth, and anything that may occur at Mathew Trueman's, as regards this girl, on whom his lordship has set his mind, you will take care to report to me."

"I want some money," said Hilliard; "I have not one farthing."

"There, then, is a sovereign for you on account."

"Humph!—that won't go far."

"Good morning, Mr. Hilliard; you can drop me a note, or call upon me, if you should have anything to say of importance—and—Hilliard—take care of yourself."

With these words, Girkins walked out of the room, leaving Hilliard standing in the middle of the floor in a state of great terror.

"What does he mean by take care of myself?" he muttered; "what can he suspect—how can he suspect anything? And yet there is a something about his manner that fills me with fears. Does he know all by some mysterious means, or—or does my imagination merely torture me thus?"

He sank in a chair by the bed-side, and then his eye fell upon the corner of the newspaper, and he drew it forth as if compelled to do so by some agency he could not resist. He held it before his eyes, and for the fiftieth time or more read the circumstantial account of the finding of the body of the murdered man in his chambers—the conjectures respecting the precise manner of his death, and the suspicions of the guilt of Wilson, which were fully expressed.

He read it all in a low half-audible tone, and concluded in a whisper with the last words—

"It has seldom been our lot as journalists to record so atrocious a murder. Mr. Noble was humane, just, and charitable. His premature death has created a void in a domestic circle which nothing can ever fill again, and but one feeling of horror pervades all classes of the community."

He deliberately folded up the paper and placed it in his pocket, then tossing off the remainder of the brandy raw, he threw himself upon his bed and relapsed into a drunken slumber.

CHAPTER XXIV.

THE MEETING OF THE LOVERS.—KIND FRIENDS, AND THE SUNSHINE OF THE HEART.

AMONG all the evils of his condition, and amid all the embarrassments of his poverty and his love, Francis Rivers never for one moment entertained a thought of the black treachery that was at work against his peace—his love—his reputation—ay, his very life. Never for one moment in his wildest imaginings did he suppose that there was aught to struggle with but his necessitous circumstances and the pride of the merchant. Minds such as Rivers's are not suspicious, and although, had he been asked the question, he would have been ready to admit that in the short space of two days he had made two enemies, namely, Hilliard and Lord Hawksworth, yet would have shrunk from any one as a libeller of human nature who would have hinted even at the fearful lengths those enemies were capable of going in order to gratify their passions and their revenge.

The day passed at length away, and Rivers, after once more reiterating his promise to meet Tom Hackey at the theatre in Catherine Street, hurried to the spot now so dear to him in association, and where he hoped to meet the object of his love—namely, the Temple Gardens. In an exceedingly short space of time Rivers was in the garden; and retiring to the seat which to him was a hallowed spot, as being the one in which Grace had reposed, he threw himself upon it, and resting his eyes upon the gate, waited with as much patience as he could command the appearance of her who was now all the world to him.

Leaving, then, the anxious lover to his meditations, we shall follow the beautiful Grace, who we hope our readers love as well as we do, to her chamber, where she intended to pour forth all the aspirations of her young heart to her friend Amelia.

"Now, my dear Grace," said Amelia, "there is one thing I wish to advise you to do; that is, to trust implicitly to your faithful nurse, Mrs. Woodfall. You, as well as I, know well her great affection for you, and believe me, I shall have a shade of unhappiness upon my heart when I am far away from you, if I am not sure that you have a friend and adviser such as she I am sure will be."

"Nurse, I think, has guessed my secret," said Grace, with a blush, "although she knows not of my interview this morning with Mr. Rivers."

"Then call her at once, Grace, and let us hold a solemn council of three, as to what is to be done to forward your happiness."

Grace, with a smile, complied, and Mrs. Woodfall soon made her appearance. Amelia warmly welcomed her, and then, with an arch glance at Grace, she said—

"Mrs. Woodfall, our friend Grace has been so very, very foolish as to fall in love, I understand."

"Nay—nay, scarcely so bad as that," said Mrs. Woodfall; "the utmost that she is guilty of is, I believe, a great partiality for one Mark Hilliard, a clerk of her father's."

"Mark Hilliard, nurse!" exclaimed Grace; "you mean Mr. Rivers."

"Oh, Mr. Rivers, my dear? Well, now you have really very candidly confessed it."

"Now, nurse," said Grace, blushing, "you really use me very ill by making me say such things. Do you know, Amelia, that nurse continually makes me confess all my secrets in this same way."

"Then don't have any secrets, Grace," replied Amelia, "but allow me to tell Mrs. Woodfall everything, exactly as it is."

She then, while Grace pretended to be busy reading a book that happened to be lying on the dressing-table, related to Mrs. Woodfall, exactly as Grace had related to her, the particulars of her recent interview with Rivers.

When Amelia had concluded, Mrs. Woodfall rose, and taking Grace's hand in hers, she said, while her voice trembled with emotion—

"Heaven forbid, my darling child, that any one should place themselves in the way of your happiness. I know that where you do love, you love with all your heart ; but still, my dear, this affair has been too precipitate."

"It has," said Grace ; "I have been very foolish, nurse."

"I will not go so far as to say that, my dear, because this young man may be every way worthy of your best affections ; but we must be quite satisfied that he is so."

"How, nurse ?"

"We must see what sacrifices he will make for his love—we must see what pleasure he will deny himself, my dear Grace, for your sake. I will not say but to all appearance he is above suspicion ; and there is only one cir-

HILLIARD DELIVERING THE LETTER TO MRS. WOODFALL.

cumstance which should make caution necessary as regards him."

"What is that ?" said Amelia.

"His poverty, my dear. I do not say that to disparage him, but true love should always consider the means of conferring that domestic happiness upon its object which never can be obtained with very restricted means. I know that when young people love, they forget all such considerations ; but if your father, Grace, should disapprove of Mr.

Rivers, he would be acting exceedingly wrong, under present circumstances, to ask you to share his poverty with him."

"You are quite right, Mrs. Woodfall," said Amelia ; "and I should propose, as a test of this young man's affection, a solemn promise on his part to forego all that he might presume upon after his next interview with Grace, until either Mr. Trueman shall have given his consent to the match, or his own circumstances shall be in a condition to warrant him in making an independent choice."

"Now, my dear Grace, what do you say?" asked Mrs. Woodfall.

"I will be guided by you, my best of friends," said Grace; "and I'm sure that Mr. Rivers will at once accede to all you may propose."

"True love," said Amelia, "should always have such confidence. And now I should advise Grace to fulfil her promise of meeting him in the Temple Gardens, and you and I, Mrs. Woodfall, will accompany her, so that we may compare notes, and come to some judgment with regard to the real feelings and disposition of Mr. Rivers."

"Thank you, my dear Amelia," said Grace. "If you will go with me and my dear nurse, I shall be much pleased."

"Then let it be so arranged, my love," said Mrs. Woodfall; "and be assured that we have no other object in view than your happiness."

"Of that I am convinced," said Grace.

It was half-past six when Amelia came again to Thames-street to accompany Grace and her nurse to the Temple Gardens, and seven o'clock had been solemnly pealed forth by the giant clock of St. Paul's before they reached their place of destination.

Rivers had now been waiting what seemed to him an inconceivably long time, yet he had scarcely ever for an instant taken his eyes off the gate, for he dreaded lest he should lose the first glimpse of Grace and her kind-hearted nurse.

At length, with a flutter at his heart which quite caught his breath, he saw her descending the step, accompanied by the to him unknown Amelia; Mrs. Woodfall followed a pace or two behind. Twice Rivers rose, and was on the point of bounding towards his much-loved Grace, and twice he shrunk back again, as he knew not if she would wish him to address her in presence of the young lady who was with her, and whose presence, for all he knew, might be accidental, and as unwelcome to Grace as it was harassing to him. Then he saw by Grace's manner that he had been recognised. With a flushed cheek he stood by the seat; then, as he observed her say something to her companion,

which was followed by a glance towards him, he thought he need have no further scruple in advancing to meet her, and he did so, trembling with agitation.

Grace paused, and her beautiful eyes were cast on the ground, while her cheeks reflected the heightened colour that was upon his. Within a few paces of her, Rivers paused irresolutely; and then Mrs. Woodfall kindly relieved his embarrassment by advancing and saying—

"Mr. Rivers, this is a young lady, a dear friend of Miss Trueman."

What he said, Rivers nor any one else knew, as he bowed and muttered something about pleasure and happiness.

Then there was another awkward pause, and Grace just lifted her eyes to Rivers's face. It was a look of love which could not be mistaken, and it went directly to his heart. Oh, how happy the poor clerk was at that moment! His confusion vanished, and offering his arm to Grace, which she took in silence, he led her towards the seat he had just left.

When they reached it, Grace and Amelia sat down, and Rivers stood by their side. Mrs. Woodfall felt for the evident distress of the young people, and wished to open the conference herself.

"Mr. Rivers," she said, "without calling in question the affection which a father must feel for such a child as Miss Trueman, myself and this young lady call ourselves her dearest friends. Her happiness is very dear to us, indeed. She has confided all to us, and we have come without disguise to speak to you calmly and rationally concerning this dear child's happiness."

Rivers felt his heart sink within him as Mrs. Woodfall spoke, and in a low voice, as he bent forward so that Grace should hear him, he said—

"That Miss Trueman should have such dear and kind friends, as I am sure you are both to her, rejoices me. And now, in presence of you and of her, permit me to say that my dearest hope on earth is to be worthy of her love— my only wish to contribute to her happiness. I am poor, friendless, and an orphan; my only possessions consist of my honour, and my own indomitable resolution and perseverance. But loving, adoring Grace as I do, wearing her next to my heart as a precious jewel, ever in my sight, I would rather plunge in yon rolling tide than tempt her from a happy home to share the poverty even of the heart that would shed its last blood to save her from a moment's pain. My love is not a selfish passion—it is a love which seeks the happiness of its object more than its own gratification—but come evil, come woe, there will ever be but one bright spot upon my heart, and that will be the shrine of Grace Trueman."

There was a deep sincerity and a pathos in the manner in which these words were spoken that went to the hearts of all who heard them. Grace leaned her head down and a tear fell upon her small white hand, while Amelia, looking up in the face of Rivers, said—

"You have spoken well, sir, and spontaneously made the promise we came here to exact of you. Love Grace well, but love her wisely! I am not one who imagines that without wealth there can be no happiness, but I am one who believes there cannot be true love in the heart of him who would drag a young confiding girl from a home surrounded with every comfort and even luxury, to poverty, perhaps even to want."

"May Heaven confound the wretch who would do so," said Rivers. "Such cannot be love. Believe me, that my fervent declaration to this dear object of my love was the result of accident, not of design. The words came from my lips because they were uppermost in my heart; but base, indeed, were I if I could be capable of presuming upon the few minutes of rapture which I felt this morning. Grace, you do not suspect me of motives other than the purest which could actuate a loving heart?"

"No," said Grace, "no."

"Heaven bless you! 'Tis true my love is great—absorbing; but it has not conquered reason. I will not now ask Mr. Trueman to let me woo his daughter—that would be madness, but I will show him that I can be zealous in his service. I will strive to earn his esteem; and, it may be that at some propitious moment he may listen to my suit, and, for my father's sake, whom he knew well, grant me leave to love his child."

"Well, now," said Amelia, with a smile, "listen to me, all of you. I don't like fathers who choose husbands for their daughters. It is always better where the choice of the parent and the child agrees; but you and I, my dear Grace, must not forget that it is we who marry our lovers, and not our fathers; so, Mr. Rivers, do you deserve Grace, and have her. Strive to achieve independence for yourself; and when you can say, Grace, here is an humble, but a competent and happy home for you, then go to Mr. Trueman, and tell him you love his child, and will strive to make her happy. Should he, as he ought to do, consent to your union, 'tis far better; but, as fathers do not always see with daughters' eyes, if you and Grace be agreed, then marry, and be happy."

"Now, my dear Amelia," said Mrs. Woodfall, who was rather alarmed at this speech, "just consider."

"I have considered," said Amelia, "and I hope to dance at Grace's wedding."

This animated discourse of Amelia's gave a happy turn to the conversation, which was growing very sombre, and a bright smile illumined the countenance of Grace, as she glanced at her friend, as much as to say, "You see, I have not been so very foolish."

Just then a gleam of sunshine shot across the gardens, and fell in all its radiant beauty upon the little group of persons in whom we are interested.

"A happy omen! a happy omen!" cried Amelia.

Rivers took Grace's hand, and said—

"Heaven grant it is. Dear Grace, I am much relieved at heart by this interview, because it places my motives and inclinations in their proper light."

"Well, Mr. Rivers," said Mrs. Woodfall, "I will not say but that I am pleased with all you have said, and now you must promise me that you will not be impatient of seeing Grace, or even run any risk by writing to her, or meeting her often, for Mr. Trueman would force me from her, and you too, were he to discover such a clandestine intercourse, and then our dear child would have none to comfort her."

"I would come and dare him to turn you away," said Amelia.

"I will be cautious," said Rivers.

"Let me hope but for the happiness now and then of seeing Grace here, and I will promise to awaken no suspicions."

"That shall be," said Mrs. Woodfall. "And now, Mr. Rivers, we must positively go, for it's past eight o'clock."

Grace rose, and held out her hand to Rivers, who clasped it for a moment in his.

"God bless you, Grace," he said.

She could not speak, but one radiant glance from her beautiful eyes said more than words. Then Rivers shook hands heartily with Amelia, who in her frank, kindly manner, said—

"Now mind you behave yourself, Mr. Rivers, or I shall call you to a terrible account."

"I will not fear the scrutiny," said Rivers. "Good evening, Mrs. Woodfall. Farewell, dear Grace."

He shook hands with Grace again, and then he was left alone.

Heaven preserve without a cloud the sunshine that reigns in the hearts of those pure and noble beings.

———

CHAPTER XXV.

TOM HACKEY'S APPEARANCE BEFORE A BRITISH PUBLIC.

RIVERS remained for more than half an hour in the Temple-gardens after Grace had left, quite forgetful of his appointment with Tom Hackey, nor was he roused from a reverie into which he had fallen until touched on the shoulder by one of the porters of the Temple, who said—

"Sir, we are going to close the garden."

Rivers started, and complied with the mandate to leave, much astonishing the porter, by muttering—

"Yes, yes! She is indeed cast in nature's fairest mould."

"What does he say about mould?" thought the man. "Oh, I suppose he's a grumbling 'cos he's turned out and can't stay here among the garden mould no longer."

When Rivers left Fleet-street it was nearly nine o'clock, and he bethought himself of his appointment with Tom at the theatre in Catherine-street ——— ———————— ————, so crossing just by Temple-bar he walked down the Strand until he came to the street in which stands that famed temple of the drama, in which many a lawyer's clerk, and barber's apprentice had strutted his hour upon the stage, and where dramatic-striken heroes make night hideous with their awful slaughter of Shakespeare and the regular drama.

Rivers duly presented his ticket, and soon found himself in a box very near the stage. The house was very full, and as the audience seemed to be on very easy and intimate terms with the actors, there was a constant running fire of remarks, from the pit especially, to the various individuals who made their appearance on the stage.

Some gentleman, whose ordinary occupation appeared to be in the ham and beef line, was enacting "the crafty Buckingham," for the moment he made his appearance, there were numerous cries of—

"Now, sausages; how are you off for small germans?—a rasher of streaky bacon—who stuck the mouldy coppers into the cheese?—two ounces of beef cut with a hammy knife—has your mother parted with her Italian iron?" Besides many other questions and remarks supposed to touch the feelings of Buckingham nearly.

Tom Hackey was "on" likewise, and amazingly splendid did Tom Hackey look, only that the wig he wore was a great deal too large for him, and had a tendency to keep slipping right down over his eyes, and reposing on the bridge of his nose, a measure which by no means improved his personal appearance, or enabled him to see the clearer.

Then ensued the scene where the wily Richard endeavoured to tempt Buckingham to his behests, and Buckingham becoming alarmed, hesitates—

"High reaching Buckingham grows circumspect," said Tom Hackey.

"Enough to make me," said Buckingham, "when there's been a fellow in the pit with a red face crying sausages ever since I've been on the stage."

A roar of laughter followed this speech, and it was many minutes before order was restored; but at length the audience condescended to allow the piece to proceed, which it did with the only usual interruptions, till the last act but one, when a few moments after the drop scene had been lowered, Rivers was terrified by the sudden appearance of Tom Hackey in the orchestra, from whence glancing up at Rivers, he cried—

"Just step over and come behind."

"Hurrah! bravo—bravo," resounded from all parts of the house, and as the box was not one which afforded any way of getting shelter, and Tom was pertinacious, Rivers thought his shortest way of getting clear of public attention would be to comply with Tom's request.

The box was not three feet from the orchestra, and with a desperate resolution Rivers put one leg over to step down, which proceeding was immediately hailed with an universal shout from all parts of the house, and all kinds of cries saluted his ears.

"Don't hurt yourself," cried one. "Be careful," shouted another. "Hold on—now the t'other leg. Have you made your will? Bravo, Richard."

Then a facetious gentleman in the gallery suddenly burst out with such an inimitable imitation of a dog being run over, that Rivers very nearly fell down, which so amused the house, that several gentlemen nearly fell into convulsions with laughing, and the man with the red face got up and screamed again, after which he took off his cravat and threw it frantically upon the stage.

Tom Hackey felt amazingly indignant at the uproar which had saluted his friend, and turning to the audience he was presumed to be saying something, for he made various wild gesticulations.

"For Heaven's sake, come away," cried Rivers; "here, is this the door you came up at?"

"I won't come away. I've been insulted," cried Tom. "Is this a British public? Is this a——"

At this moment a piece of orange peel came with so true an aim against Tom's mouth, that for an instant he actually held it in his teeth, to the intense joy of the British public, who cheered vociferously, and cried encore till its, the public's throat, was quite hoarse. In an instant Tom Hackey dived through the little door leading under the stage, and was closely followed by Rivers, who had to run after him, such was Tom's speed; but Rivers paused, where Tom did not for the insulted tragedian stopped not for drop scene or flys, but

bounded on to the stage in the twinkling of an eye.

His appearance seemed to be the signal for pandemonium to break loose, for such a discordance of sounds could scarcely be supposed to come from human throats. Before Tom could obtain a hearing, the gentleman in the gallery had made no less than five dogs be run over, and everybody else was thoroughly exhausted. Then came a bell in the tempest of sound, and Tom Hackey advanced to the footlights.

"Hear him—hear him," cried a hundred voices.

"Ladies and gentlemen," cried Tom.

"Bravo—encore. How are you off for orange pee? Go it, Richard. Silence—order."

"Ladies and gentlemen—The base wretch who threw the orange peel——"

Tom could get no further, for the shout that now arose baffled all attempts to make himself heard.

"The base wretch," he repeated—but it was all in vain, a British audience would not give him a hearing, and at length Richmond came on to persuade Richard to come off.

"I won't come," said Tom.

"But we are all waiting," cried Richmond.

"Off—off!" cried the British audience.

Finally, by the joint efforts of Richmond, Catesby, and half-a-dozen supernumeries, Tom Hackey was carried in great triumph off the stage, and the band struck up the popular air of Jack Robinson for the accommodation of the gentleman who was to dance the hornpipe in fetters and handcuffs.

Great was the delight of the audience when the clever gentleman appeared manacled, and greater still was their ecstacy when he fell down and couldn't get up again, while the band, consisting of two violins and a clarionet, played Jack Robinson furiously, as if by so doing he would be set upon his feet again.

Finally the clever gentleman was carried off amid loud cries of encore, by the stage carpenters, consisting of an old man and a boy.

"How could you think," said Rivers, "of addressing the audience, Tom? They are evidently not people who will listen to reason, and your sudden appearance in the orchestra was sufficiently comical."

"I don't care a pin about their laughing at me," said Tom, "but why couldn't they let you get out of the box without making such a riot?"

"You shouldn't have minded me, Tom. You know the public will laugh at anything, however trifling."

"You have put us all out of the way, Mr. Hackey," cried a super, who was enacting one of Richard's guards. "There's half an apple been thrown on the stage just now."

"Then you go and pick it up," said Tom.

"I sha'n't—don't be giving yourself airs here."

At this moment the act drop was raised, and both Tom and Rivers had to scamper to the side.

"I'll serve you out another time," said Tom to the guard.

"Oh, bother you," was the reply. "If I don't cut you out of some point, hang me."

Scene after scene proceeded, amid cheers, laughter, and all the miscellaneous noises of a private theatre of the lowest grade, until Tom's grand point, which he had shuffled into the last act, arrived, and the insulted guard, instead of Catesby, rushed on to say—

"My lord, the Duke of Buckingham is ta'en."

Now Tom's grand point was to shout out—

"Off with his head!—so much for Buckingham!" and so would he have shouted, but the guard with deep malice aforethought, said—

"My lord, the Duke of Buckingham is ta'en, and *we've cut off his head.*"

Tom perfectly staggered beneath the blow of fate, and for one brief moment there was an awful silence, when the great tragedian recovering from his temporary stupor, shouted in a voice of thunder—

"Then stick it on a pole! So much for Buckingham!" The roar that succeeded beggars all description, and even Rivers joined in the lusty hurrah, which greeted Tom's presence of mind.

Nothing worth further notice occurred during the play, and very shortly the curtain dropped upon the crook-backed

tyrant, after a combat between him and Richard of full twenty minutes' duration, in the course of which there were enough fencing antics played to have made the fortunes of either at Bartholomew-fair.

Rivers would now fain have taken his leave, but Tom insisted upon his staying just to see the gorgeous costumes of the melo-drama, and so he waited and saw women's, and men's, and angels', and nymphs', and devils', all arrayed in due costume to perpetrate a drama of fearful interest, when pleading fatigue, Tom let him go, after receiving repeated assurances that he (Rivers) thought him particularly great in Richard.

Amused very much with the scene he had witnessed, Rivers repaired to a lodging he had taken near Thames-street, and was soon asleep, and dreaming that he was again in the Temple-gardens, with the small soft hand of Grace Trueman in his, and she smiling upon him like the sun looking through snowy clouds.

CHAPTER XXVI.

THE DREAM.—A DISTURBED NIGHT.

WHILE such sweet visions filled the soul of Rivers with joy, he could have slept on for days, nor wished to awake from his visions of bliss. But

"A change came o'er the spirit of his dream,'

and he found that as he walked with Grace in the Temple-gardens, a serpent followed them wherever they went, and that as it fixed its glassy eye upon Grace, she grew paler and paler, until he thought she was dying in his arms.

With a cry of terror Rivers awoke, and sprung from his couch. The first dim streaks of early dawn were blushing in the eastern sky, and he blessed himself when he found 'twas but a dream.

"Yet," he said, "I will sleep no more to-night; a book shall be the solace of my mind until the morn has fully come. Dear, dear Grace, what an awful dream was that!"

Rivers trembled as he seized upon the first book in his collection; but his interest in the simple, touching narrative his eye lighted upon, soon soothed his imagination. It was entitled:—

THE WIDOW'S DAUGHTER; OR, THE ROSE OF THE BOWER.

UPWARDS of half a century ago there stood in the outskirts of London, and near where the Regent's-park has been since formed, a pleasant and retired little ale-house, called the Bower, which, having a large garden attached to it, in which various alcoves, or summer-houses, had been erected, it was the favourite resort of the gallants of the time, who, being confined during the day to the dense atmosphere of the metropolis, were glad, in the evening, to repair here to imbibe, with its celebrated ale, the pure air of Maryle-bone fields.

At the time of the opening of our story, the house, or inn, was kept by the widow Hamilton, whose husband had died some time previously, and left her, together with an only daughter, entirely dependant for a subsistence upon those who patronized the inn with their custom. But fortunately the business of the house had long been a thriving one, and the civility of the widow and the attractions of the beautiful Alice—for such was the name of her daughter — rather increased than diminished their chances of prosperity.

At her father's death, Alice was scarcely fifteen; but already were the graces of her person fairly developed, and it was universally admitted that her symmetrical figure was one of the finest which nature had ever formed. Numerous were the admirers who paid their homage to the matchless charms of the Rose of the Bower, which was the designation by which she was generally known, and many were the lovers who whispered in her ear that they were only happy while basking in the sunshine of her soul-inspiring smile. Indeed, it was almost impossible to gaze upon her lovely countenance, and watch the varied and expressive glances of her light blue eyes, without feeling an inclination to love her:

" She was not violently lively, but
  Stole on your spirit like a May-day breaking;
  Her eyes were not too sparkling, yet half-
  shut
  They put beholders in a tender taking."

*   *   *   *   *

" ———— Around her shone
The nameless charms unmasked by her alone;
The light of love, the purity of grace,
The mind, the music breathing from her
  face;
The heart whose softness harmonized the
  whole,
And oh! that eye was in itself a soul."

So beautiful and so innocent did she appear, that without detriment to his ethereal nature, an angel might have mourned that aught sensual should ever stain the thoughts of one so pure and virtuous. But beauty is too frequently the cause of attracting the passions of man to its destruction; and innocence being too often deemed synonimous with ignorance, it easily falls a victim to the duplicity of villany.

As Alice had numerous admirers she might have selected a husband from among the worthiest, and it is probable when she fixed her young affections upon Lionel Austin she believed that she had placed them upon a worthy object; but worthy or worthless, the love professed for her by Lionel was returned by her with a fervour and sincerity which those only can experience who for the first time have been surprised into loving. Her young heart flew to him as to one upon whom its well-being entirely depended, and it was soon apparent from the great influence which he had acquired over her, that her future career, whether for good or evil, mainly depended upon his behaviour towards her. She loved him with a purity of affection which one so vicious scarcely deserved, and even when his vices became better known to her, the knowledge did not weaken her love or cause that attachment to cease which, even in spite of her better judgment, she continued to bear towards him.

But though she loved with fervour, her affection was carefully restrained within the boundary of virtue, and notwithstanding his blandishments and beguiling promises, Alice kept so firm a guard over her honour as to convince her lover, dissipated as he was, that upon no other terms than those of matrimony could he ever hope to induce her to become his.

Various were the arts to which he resorted to seduce her from the path of virtue, and though they all failed of success, their failure did not deter him from his purpose. It is singular how persevering some men are, and what pains they take to be vicious; and such was the case with Lionel Austin. On the failure of one of his schemes another was immediately suggested to his active mind. There was no project, however degraded, which he would not adopt to assist him in his dishonourable plans; and vexed at his numerous disappointments, he was ever planning and scheming the ruin of Alice, till at length he hit upon a plan which he was positive would ensure him success. Before, however, we proceed to mention it, we will devote a few lines as to the account which this Lionel Austin gave of himself.

In his visits to the Bower, Lionel had assumed the character of a merchant's clerk, and neither Alice nor her mother ever believed him to be other than he represented himself. But like many important personages, he had enshrouded himself in mystery, and as all persons were not so innocent as the Rose of the Bower and her parent, it was suspected that he was not what he appeared. Indeed, rumour had asserted that instead of a merchant's clerk he was a member of one of the most ancient families of the country, and even the heir to a peerage; but from his earliest youth he had been partial to dissipation, and was unfortunately better acquainted with scenes of vice and immorality than were exactly suited to his exalted connexions. Perhaps his taste was of a peculiar nature, and being of a merry, jovial disposition, he was more at his ease with associates of a kindred spirit, though selected from a lower grade in society, than when conforming to the formal manners which prevailed among those of his own station.

The fame of the beautiful Rose of the Bower had reached his ear and aroused his curiosity to such a degree, that he determined to see her, and finding at the interview that fame had not exaggerated her charms, and anxious, if possible, to win her affections, he contrived to introduce himself as a city clerk. How he succeeded has before been stated, and foiled in every attempt at seducing her, but still too proud to marry her, he hit upon a scheme which he believed would enable him, without suspicion on her part, to gratify his wishes and complete her dishonour.

Fifty or sixty years ago, marriages were more easily solemnized, and required fewer forms to render them legal than they do at present. Provided the parties were married by a real clergyman, it was a matter of indifference at what place, or in whose presence the ceremony was performed, and as its legality depended upon the genuine character of him who solemnized it, neither the licence nor the publication of banns were necessary; consequently, a wide door was opened for abuse, and it was easy for a vicious person of the higher classes to entrap a girl whom he professed to love into ruin. He had only to request one of his pot companions to assume the garb of a clergyman, in order to solemnize a pretended marriage, which his victim believed to be genuine and binding. In a few days, satiated by possession, the heartless reprobate would abandon his unfortunate and deluded dupe, and then upon inquiry, the startling fact would present itself to her, that the marriage was a mockery, and that she had been cajoled of her honour by trickery.

This was the notable scheme which, when more open methods failed of success, Lionel determined to adopt to gratify his base passions, and ruin the innocent and unsuspecting Alice.

It is notorious that the youthful noble whom sensual indulgence renders prone to dissipation, is generally surrounded by persons degraded enough to glory in acting as the panders to his vices, and whatever his rank, Lionel had not far to look ere he found a companion willing enough to assist him in his villany. A place for the ceremony was provided, where, unknown to her mother, at the time appointed, Alice secretly met her lover, and the person who volunteered to act as priest, being properly robed in clerical habiliments, and prepared in every respect for the occasion, a marriage was solemnized, which Alice believed to be genuine, and in the arms of her beloved husband she was happy.

Week after week came and went, and the same blissful felicity accompanied her existence. Basking in the sunshine of his eyes whom her soul idolized, Alice forgot the frail tenure of her present transports, and dressed up the future in her imagination, as appertaining to a terrestrial paradise.

Looking upon the world through the medium of love, she could distinguish nothing but happiness, and absorbed in the fond affection of her husband, she troubled not herself to inquire if that affection were unending, or if a period might not arrive when sorrow instead of joy would mingle itself with her existence. The earth seemed depicted to her fancy as a blissful Elysium, where all were joyous and happy; and little did she suspect that—

"No scene of mortal life but teems with mortal woe."

But soon, too soon, alas! the structure upreared by her imagination toppled to the dust, and within one little month, she discovered that her happiness was only an illusion.

The husband of her choice, and upon whom she fondly doated, without assigning the slightest reason for his conduct, suddenly abandoned her, and she knew not whither he had departed. She sought him in every place where he was likely to be found, but in vain. She never saw him again. At length it became apparent that she would become a mother,

THE MEETING OF THE LOVERS IN THE STORM.

and unable to discover the father of her unborn child, for the sake of her reputation, she made every inquiry as to the legality of her marriage, and to her shame and vexation she ascertained, as she believed, that it was a mockery.

Shortly afterwards she became the mother of a fine boy, but her happiness had departed with her treacherous lover. She who but lately shone as pre-eminent in virtue as in beauty, found herself discarded and degraded, for to her sorrow she perceived that she was deemed by the world a guilty and an abandoned creature.

Several years after the occurrence of the preceding events, Alice was reposing in bed with her beautiful boy by her side, when she was suddenly aroused at midnight from her slumbers by a loud and continued knocking at the door of the inn. Her mother was the first to be alarmed, and throwing up the window of her bed-room, she exclaimed to those on the outside—

"What do you mean by knocking here at this unseasonable hour?"

"We want your daughter," was the reply, "if you are the mistress of the house. Let us in quickly—we cannot delay."

"For what purpose do you come hither at such an hour?"

"She must accompany us. Come, quick—quick."

"Whither?"

"To the Earl of Castleton's in Grosvenor Square."

"You have mistaken the house. We know no such person."

"I am positive there is no mistake. This is the house. The earl is dying, and is most anxious to see her. He bade us be sure and not return without her. We have a coach for her reception. Was not your daughter called the Rose of the Bower?"

"She was. I cannot consent to place her in the hands of strangers."

"She will suffer no injury from us," was the rejoinder.

As the curiosity of Alice had been thoroughly aroused by the preceding conversation, she hastily dressed herself and joined her mother at the window.

"How are we to know," she inquired, "that you come from the Earl of Castleton, or that I am the party he wishes to see? Have you any token to assure us of the genuineness of your errand?"

"I was directed to utter a name as a pass-word, in case of an emergency. That name is Lionel."

"Ah! Lionel," repeated Alice.

"You know the name?"

"Too well."

"Will you now accompany us?"

"Yes, but not without my child."

"I have no objection to his going with us. But quick, for the earl is dangerously ill, and unless we make haste we shall be too late to see him alive."

"I will not detain you an instant," rejoined Alice.

In the course of a few moments Alice and her child were in the coach, which proceeded rapidly to London, and in a short time they alighted at a large mansion in Grosvenor Square. A person was in waiting to receive and conduct them to a handsome spacious room, where, on a bed fitted up with rich and splendid hangings, lay an individual far advanced in life. By his wan and careworn features it was evident that disease had made sad havoc in his aged frame, and that in a few hours his earthly race would have run its course.

As Alice, from the messenger's password of Lionel, fully expected to meet once more with her truant lover, she was greatly disappointed on finding that the person who had sent for her was an old man. It seemed strange to her how her connection with Lionel should have become known to the earl, (for such she ascertained the sick man to be by the respectful manner in which he was addressed by his attendants,) and she mused within herself why she was so anxiously and hurriedly sent for to be spoken to by him previously to his death.

Lost in amazement as to the events of the night, she was recalled a little to herself by the earl, who directed his servants to quit the room. When they were alone together, the venerable earl requested her to draw near to him.

"You are, no doubt, anxious to know," he observed to her in an exhausted tone of voice, "why I have sent for you at such an unseasonable hour?"

Alice bowed her assent.

"My object," he resumed, "I will now explain to you as briefly as possible, for I have not long to remain in this world. Pride has hitherto deterred me from divulging a secret which I foolishly believed to be injurious to the honour of my family. But death is no distinguisher of persons; he levels human pride with the dust, and those who boast of their ancestry are not more favourably treated by him than the meanest peasant. The secret which my pride forbade me to divulge I meant to have carried to the grave, out my sufferings this night, and the near approach of the fell destroyer, added to the consciousness that when I die my family name and honours will become extinct—have all determined me to surrender up my pride to truth and honour, and make the final action of my life a just one. Had it not been for a mere accident, I should have been the last of my race. Alas! how I am wasting the few precious moments reserved to me in this life by telling you of things of which you are entirely ignorant. But, to the object of your present visit. You knew Lionel Austin?"

"Too well, my lord," replied Alice.

"He was my son," observed his lordship.

"Your son?" exclaimed Alice, in surprise.

"Yes, my only son."

"The name of Austin was then fictitious?"

"It was."

"Which explains the reason why I was unable to trace him after he so cruelly abandoned me?"

"No doubt of it," rejoined his lordship.

"You said just now, my lord," inquired Alice, "that you were the last of your race?"

"And so I am," he replied.

"Oh, do not say that Lionel is dead?"

"Such is, indeed, the fact."

"Dead! the youthful and gallant Lionel dead?" she repeated.

"Yes, he is dead."

"Oh, God!" she mournfully rejoined, "again to hear of him and find him dead. Alas! this is indeed to drain the cup of sorrow to the dregs."

"And can you mourn for one who used you so vilely; brought disgrace upon your name, and branded you with infamy?"

"My lord, I loved him," exclaimed Alice, with enthusiasm; "and woman's love is of that undying nature that even when fixed upon a worthless object, and her bruised and broken heart is, as it were, torn piece-meal from her bosom, still with her last breath can she forgive and bless the name of her destroyer. The heart which truly throbs for one will never love another. Injuries of the bitterest kind may be heaped upon it, but its love will surmount them all; and, by its fervour of affection and its constancy, will often triumph over oppression. I loved your son, and though by heaping foul dishonour upon my name he injured me, I love him still, and can mourn him dead."

"Generous woman, your virtues deserve to be rewarded."

"Your lordship's approbation is reward sufficient. But when did your son cease to live?"

"About a year ago."

"What was the cause of his death?"

"His reckless dissipation,"

"Merciful Heaven! and did he continue his recklessness to the last?"

"Unfortunately, he did. From his boyhood he loved to frequent the paths of vice, which slowly but surely brought him to an untimely death."

"Was he long ill?"

"Not very."

"I hope during his illness his sufferings were not great?"

"Most excruciating, both mentally and bodily."

"Alas! poor Lionel."

"His disorder was painful, but not lingering; and just before he fell into the delirium which preceded his death, he detailed to me his heartless seduction of yourself. He would then have done you justice; but, to my shame be it spoken, my pride opposed his wishes, and I forbade him to think of such a degrading union."

"Heaven bless and reward him for his wish," exclaimed Alice, "though it came only at the eleventh hour."

"I hope it will," rejoined his lordship, "for he certainly wished to close his life with a good action. Directly afterwards his senses left him, and he died."

"Oh! that I had been present to soothe his expiring moments."

"I wish you had; but it is now useless to regret the past. Shortly after his death, I made inquiries respecting you, and having ascertained that, together with your mother and child, you were in easy circumstances, and did not require pecuniary assistance from me, I determined, rather than risk the exposure of my son's vicious courses, still to keep you in ignorance of the name of him who had dishonoured you; but the termination of your sufferings has arrived. I will not ask if the boy who accompanied you is my son's. Every lineament discovers his paternity; he has not a feature which has not Castleton displayed in it; and when I look upon him, I feel gratified in knowing that my title and estates will descend to one of such a lofty bearing."

"Descend to him, my lord?" interposed Alice. "Impossible! Alas! he is illegitimate."

"It is false," replied his lordship; "his blood is pure."

"What mean you, my lord?"

"To do him justice."

"Justice?"

"Yes. And I do it the more readily because I know that though his mother is of lowly origin, the proudest lady born is not more virtuous or more truly noble. Alice, my daughter, for such I rejoice to call you, your marriage with my son was a legal one."

"My lord, it could not be."

"Why not?"

"It was solemnized by one of your son's dissolute companions."

"But that companion was in Holy Orders, and competent to make the marriage valid."

"Did Lionel know of this?"

"He did not; the fact was stated to me since his death by the man himself, who is also dead. I saw him at his own request, and he gave me such convincing proofs of his being a clergyman, as to make me perfectly satisfied of the legality of the marriage."

"Oh, God! I thank Thee fervently," ejaculated Alice, "that the stigma upon my child's name is cleared away."

"And believe me, that I am happy to rejoice with you," replied his lordship. "Bring the boy near me, that I may kiss him and die in peace."

Alice did as he requested, and having kissed the child, he resumed, though more faintly than before—

"Henceforth your career will be a prosperous one, as I have so arranged my affairs that you will have little difficulty in establishing your son's claim to my title and estates; but I begin to feel exhausted, and need some rest. Farewell! my last earthly act is approved, both by justice and conscience, and I die happy, in the consciousness that ths name of Castleton will continue in yonder boy, and that with the honours of our race he will blend with them the virtues and the noble qualities of his mother."

Before the dawning of the morning the Earl of Castleton breathed his last,

and, as he had intimated, the son of Alice entered without opposition into his title and estates—and by him they were transmitted with honour to his present noble descendant.

As the aged earl had prophesied, the career of Alice was prosperous; and as she had borne afflictions with patience, she was not spoilt with prosperity. The virtues which had characterised her humble station were not forgotten or neglected when she became more elevated, and while her affability won the love and admiration of her equals, her generosity and benevolence endeared her to those who were poor and unfortunate, and henceforward praises and blessings were the constant attendants which followed in the train of the widow's daughter.

A bright streak of sunlight fell upon the page that Rivers was reading. It was the first which had through the realms of space darted from the glorious luminary of the day. He looked up, and an answering smile beamed from his face, as he said—

"How could I allow myself to be so much disturbed by a dream? What ills can threaten my dear Grace, that I have not a heart and an arm to protect her from? None, none; with Heaven's help we shall yet be happy."

Rivers then rose, and took a long morning's walk in the sweet open country, where everything beautiful reminded him of Grace; and as he gathered health from the genial exercise, he gathered likewise strength of heart to bear with whatever frowns fortune might bend upon him, with the dear hope that at last he should, despite the storms of fate, clasp to his heart, as all his own, the merchant's daughter.

Rivers was early at his office, and despite the fatigue of the previous night, he found Tom there, busily thumping the books together to free them from dust, and otherwise preparing for the business of the coming day.

"Well, Tom," said Rivers, "you acquitted yourself well, I think, last night, and deserve much credit for your exertions."

"The tower—ay, the tower!" said Tom, who, after performing any particular part, generally for the next few days went through it all again. "What vagabonds they all was," remarked Tom then. "I never heard such a noise. I made 'em three more speeches after you left. You see this red mark on the side of my nose, Mr. Rivers?"

"Yes, certainly. How came you by it?"

"Why, some fellow threw a butter biscuit whack in my face when I was slain in the second piece; and, lying dead, I couldn't resent it, you know."

"Not very well, certainly. Have you seen Mr. Trueman, Tom, this morning?"

"No, but here comes another beauty."

As Tom spoke, Hilliard, with a hurried step, came into the office. He made several nervous and futile attempts to hang up his hat before he could succeed in doing so, so great was his trepidation; then turning slowly to Rivers, and glancing at him from under his brows, he said—

"Good-morning, Mr. Rivers."

"Good-morning," said Rivers, who did not think it at all worth while to show Hilliard that he cared sufficiently for his enmity to resent it.

"Oh," said Tom, audibly.

"What do you say?" cried Hilliard, facing him with a savage scowl.

"I said—'Oh,'" replied Tom.

"And what do you mean by 'Oh,' sir?"

"What's that to you?" said Tom. "A fellow may say 'Oh' to himself, I suppose, if he likes."

"Don't be insolent to me," muttered Hilliard, as he sat down to his desk, shaking so that he could scarcely unlock it.

Rivers could not but notice the extreme agitation of Hilliard, and he referred it to real ill health, and felt proportionably disposed to answer him civilly, should he address him, which indeed he did as soon as Tom left the office, for the artful villain, in order to carry out the instructions of Girkins, felt that he had much better be on apparently friendly terms with Rivers than the reverse.

"Mr. Rivers," he said, "as we are to sit here in the same room together, we may as well be friends."

"I am no man's enemy," said Rivers.

"Yes, but I mean we may be civil to each other, you know, suppose we have had a little misunderstanding together."

"If you are satisfied, Mr. Hilliard, I am," replied Rivers. "I can only say that I was perfectly willing to be civil from the first."

"Very well, then, we will have no more squabbling. I'm a strange fellow, Mr. Rivers, but when you come to know me you'll find my temper the worst of me."

"I think," said Rivers, who was resolved to prevent the intimacy from going too far, "that when we meet here we can manage to exchange the ordinary courtesies of life without at all troubling ourselves about each other's temper."

"Very well. Certainly. I've been very ill for all yesterday, but I'm better now."

"I am glad to hear you are better," said Rivers.

"Curse him," muttered Hilliard, "he is as cold as an icicle." He then lifted the lid of his desk, and letting it lean upon his head so as completely to screen him from observation, he produced again the newspaper containing an account of Mr. Noble's murder, and read it from first to last. There seemed to be some ban of Providence placed upon the murderer, which forced him thus to be continually reading the record of his own crime, for certain it was that Hilliard could scarcely pass an hour without going through the whole report in the newspaper.

To the great relief of Rivers, Hilliard made but few attempts to get him into conversation during the day, and when the dinner-hour arrived, and Hilliard proposed that they should dine together, Rivers replied coolly that he preferred dining alone; and after that Hilliard said nothing more to him whatever, appearing to have made up his mind that it was impossible to goad him from his indifference into anything like a show of cordiality; so merely cursing him in his heart, he resolved that he would just be on as civil terms with him as he could, and do him all the injury in his power.

CHAPTER XVII.

THE CONSULTATION.—THE FATHER AND
DAUGHTER.—GRACE'S COURAGE AND
DETERMINATION.

A FEW minutes after twelve o'clock, Mr. Girkins, with his usual bland smile and soft step, entered the counting-house of Mathew Trueman, and desiring that his name might be taken in, Rivers undertook that office, and was told to request Mr. Girkins to walk in to his, Mr. Trueman's, own room.

"Thank you, Mr. Rivers—oh, thank you, sir," said Girkins, who was one of those men who are always lavish of their civilities to those they hate and are trying to injure.

"You are very welcome, sir," said Rivers, in some surprise at the extreme courtesy of the merchant's visitor.

"Ah, Mr. Rivers," added Girkins, as he moved towards the office-door, "I knew your father well; a most worthy gentleman, sir—a most noble, worthy gentleman."

"May I ask your name, sir?" said Rivers.

"Girkins—Mr. Girkins."

"I never heard my father mention you; but still, you may have known him well, sir."

"Most justly said. Good morning, Mr. Rivers—good morning, my very dear sir."

"Humph!" said Girkins, when he was outside the door; "my fine spark, we will see if among us we cannot cut your plumage a little. In truth, you are a likely enough fellow to prove a dangerous rival to his lordship, but we have a mode of doing business which will deprive you of your chance. We shall see—we shall se."

He had now reached the door of Mathew Trueman's room, at which he tapped very lightly, and in obedience to the "Come in" of the merchant, he entered the room.

"Ah, Mr. Girkins, I am glad to see you. Pray be seated."

"You are very good, Mr. Trueman," said Girkins, as he sat down on the very edge of a chair, "and, dear me, how well you are looking."

"Why, I am tolerably well," said Mathew Trueman, "and considering how I have stuck to business all my life, Girkins, and likewise considering that I began the world with three-and-a-penny—ah!"

"Wonderful man," ejaculated Girkins. "Ah! Mr. Trueman, England may well be proud of her merchants, and her merchants may well be proud of Mathew Trueman."

"You are very kind to say so, Mr. Girkins; and—and I may say, that the very next thing to doing well is to have people duly appreciate it."

"Who can help appreciating your conduct, Mr. Trueman; a gentleman who began the world with——"

"Three-and-a-penny," said the merchant.

"Exactly, sir."

"And who leaves off with half a million."

"A whole one—a whole one," suggested Mr. Girkins.

"No—no," said the merchant, with mock candour and modesty; "no—must be content with more moderate expectations. It is not, Mr. Girkins, in the power of even a British merchant to make himself a noble, but there is no reason on earth why a British merchant should not ally himself to nobility, eh, Mr. Girkins?"

Girkins placed his hand on his forehead, and affected to be amazingly struck with this remark. He then fixed his eyes upon a huge file of receipts, which hung in a corner, and in an abstracted manner exclaimed—

"Oh, heavens, were there Mathew Truemans in the senate, Mathew Truemans in the church, and Mathew Truemans at the bar, what a nation should we be!"

In a few moments the merchant was once more alone in his private office in that agreeable frame of mind in which Mr. Girkins ever left him.

Mr. Girkins, when he came seriously to reflect concerning Rivers, and the great detriment and obstacle he might prove to the success of his schemes, as far as the beautiful Grace was concerned, felt the futility of attempting, merely by parental authority alone, to separate two attached hearts.

"It is true," he thought, "I may at once declare to Mathew Trueman all that I know and all that I suspect concerning Rivers and his daughter, and such a step would, no doubt, have the effect of causing the immediate discharge of Rivers; but would that advance the cause I have at heart? Would it not rather inflame the incipient passion of Grace, and induce her to yield to some hurried solicitation of the moment, to, perhaps, become his wife secretly, and so confound all my hopes?"

This was a view of the subject anything but agreeable to Mr. Girkins; and after the most attentive consideration of all the circumstances of the affair, he still strengthed himself in his opinion that he was upon the right track in suborning Hilliard to do some great moral injury to Rivers, instead of at once declaring what he, Girkins, knew of his secret meetings with Grace to her father, a course which could only end in an ebullition of rage on the part of Trueman, and a feeling of persecution in the mind of his daughter that might increase to a dangerous pitch her incipient attachment to the handsome young clerk.

"No," he muttered, "I will adopt a more subtle course. At the same time that I open the eyes of Mathew Trueman thoroughly to the secret attachment subsisting between this Rivers and his daughter, I will, with Hilliard's assistance, involve him in some new adventure, which shall shake even the romantic girl's faith in him, and blast his character for ever. I will now to the merchant, and lay the first lines of my plot, a few well-hinted suspicions of this Rivers, which may be recollected hereafter as damning circumstantial proofs of his guilt. It shall be done; and, if I am an accurate reader of human character, which by this time I ough to be, I should say that this young Rivers was just the man to be so entirely overcome with rage at a false accusation that he will never be able effectually to defend himself. We shall see —we shall see, Master Rivers, whether you and your romance are a match for as well-organised a head-piece as ever planned or matured a plot. We shall see—we shall see."

Mr. Girkins departed with the intent of not only hurrying on Mathew Trueman in the business of the extensive loan with Lord Hawksworth, but of, as he called it, laying the first lines of suspicion with regard to the integrity of Rivers.

And this man, this agent, Girkins, was coolly and deliberately proceeding on as nefarious and horrible a transaction as ever disgraced humanity for the consideration of what portion of the ill-gained money which Lord Hawksworth was to receive from Mathew Trueman he could put into his own pocket. Was there ever such a combination of bad passions at work in any three men as were now in active operation in the breasts of Trueman, Hawksworth, and Girkins? The merchant was willing deliberately to sacrifice the happiness of his only child—her whom he had affected to love and cherish to an extravagant degree, for the meretricious bauble of rank—that rank which, like the false, weak glitter of a mock jewel, only makes its wearer contemptible instead of noble.

Girkins, too, was content to do his share in the unholy work, for what he might procure by cheating the cheats; and Lord Hawksworth was perfectly willing, in order to get rid of a few hours' *ennui*, to make the innocent and beautiful Grace the wretched, guilty thing his passions would eventually have left her. Truly, human nature, when viewed in some of its phases, is enough to make those whose hearts are guiltless, shudder at their species, and to induce them to wrap themselves up in the mantle of suspicion, and consider all men their enemies until they have proved their friends, instead of the more generous and ennobling principle, believing all men innocent of evil until proved vicious.

Girkins was ever a welcome visitor to Mathew Trueman, for he cringed to his vanity, flattered his foibles into virtues, and ever left the merchant in an agreeable state of mind as regarded himself, his own extreme cleverness, &c.

It is a sad thing, but no less true than sad, that mankind, in relation to individuals, with very few exceptions, separate themselves into two classes, namely, those who give a man more than his deserts, and, by over praise and adulation, bestow upon him a station and character beyond what he is entitled to, and those who deny him what fairly belongs to him, and act as a compromise to his flatterers by detracting as much as they possibly can from whatever small merit he may possess.

Is it to be wondered at, then, that the mass of mankind turn with disgust from their detractor to accept the horrid poison of their flatterers? The strongest minds will bow before the subtle fiend, flattery, and the greatest philosopher will listen with a pleased and tickled ear to the man who ever praises him, when he will turn with passion and disgust from him who, with only equal insincerity, takes from him the commendation he knows to be his due.

Girkins, then, was ever a welcome guest to Mathew Trueman, and although the rich merchant in his heart despised the poor agent, he was glad to see him, even as we take some appetite-provoking sauce to flavour the viands of existence.

"Come in, Mr. Girkins, come in," he said; "I am always glad to hear how you are getting on, you know, although you have not made a fortune, Mr. Girkins."

"You are very good, Mr. Trueman," said Girkins, "very good, indeed. I hope I have the pleasure of seeing you quite well."

"Tolerable, tolerable" said the merchant, giving himself a slight blow upon the chest as an indication of how much it would take to do him any great corporeal injury.

"Ah!" said Girkins, in affected abstraction, "you are, as I often remark, both mentally and physically, a most wonderful man."

"You think so, Mr. Girkins?"

"Upon my life I do. When I am dining out somewhere and the conversation turns on rich and talented men, I say always, 'Gentlemen, did you ever hear of Mathew Trueman, Esquire, the wealthy merchant? He, if you please, is a wonderful man. He has a head that could rule these kingdoms, ay, and better than they have been ruled since the memory of man.'"

"Now, really, Mr. Girkins," said Trueman, with a complacent air, "you do go a little too far. You know that I only began life with three-and-a-penny."

"I do, sir, and an astonishing and creditable fact it is."

"Why, as to that, it may be, but there are cleverer fellows than I in the world, Girkins."

"Indeed there are," thought Girkins; "but," he added aloud, "now there you wrong yourself, Mr. Trueman, you do, indeed, and even if I lose your esteem and countenance, I must differ from you; I am one of those who speak my mind. It's a failing, a great failing, but I can't help it, Mr. Trueman; and if you were to quarrel with me this moment, I should still say that your equal never was, and I sincerely believe never will be."

"You are partial—you are partial, Girkins. But about this business of Hawksworth's.'

"Ay, about that business. There can be no sort of risk. How he does rave about the——but I really beg pardon; I am, perhaps, intruding in matters that I should not, Mr. Trueman."

"No—no—go on. Pray go on. What —what is he raving so much about, eh, Girkins?"

"Under favour, then, be it spoken, sir, it is your lovely and estimable daughter, so like you, too, as she is, bless her!"

"Oh, he cares about her, does he! What, more than you before told me, Girkins?"

"A great deal more. 'Girkins,' says he to me—you know he always calls me Girkins—'that daughter of Mr. Trueman's should be on a throne, and hang me,'—you know his lordship uses energetic language sometimes—'hang me,' says he, 'if any man but Mr. Trueman is worthy of being the father of such an angel.'"

"Did he really say so?"

"On my conscience."

"Well, it's very flattering, certainly."

"There I beg your pardon again, Mr. Trueman. You will think to yourself that I am in a contradictory humour to-day; but I must say it is nothing but the simple truth, and not flattery at all."

"Well, well, Mr. Girkins, we won't dispute about that, you know; but all I can say is, that I am quite ready with the money whenever his lordship pleases to hand over the bills with the indorsement of his friend; and then as he is not of age—and—and, Girkins—do you think it likely that his lordship may soon make an offer of his hand to my daughter?

When he does, it is quite understood that I give her forty thousand pounds."

"A portion most magnificent," said Girkins, shirking the previous question; "and every way worthy of your noble liberality and your daughter's great beauty. By-the-by, I don't know whether I ought to tell you so or not, as it might do the young man an injury, but —but ——"

"But what, Mr. Girkins? Who do you mean?"

"Your new clerk! That nice-looking young man, Mr.—a—a—what's his name?"

"Rivers?"

"Ah, Rivers; I declare I have given him so little thought that I quite forgot his name; but I saw him in the Regent's Quadrant the other evening with some of the most disreputable characters. It's no affair of mine. He may have, for all I know, ample means for all sorts of extravagances."

THE PAINFUL INTERVIEW BETWEEN THE LOVERS AND MRS. WOODFALL.

"Indeed, but he has not," said Trueman; "and my opinion of a young man of limited means in a situation who is extravagant is, that sooner or later he must some day rob his employer."

"Gracious powers, what a mind you have, Mr. Trueman. Well, I never should have thought of that, although now I hear you say it, it seems so simple a proposition."

"Nothing is more probable; and in addition to that, curse the fellow, I thought I saw him cast a sheep's eye at my daughter."

"What unparelleled audacity!"

"I think so, indeed; but if I were sure, he should not stay another hour in my service."

"Nay, my dear sir," said Girkins, "let me not judge anybody harshly; the young man may, while in your service, conduct himself properly. Besides, I don't want him discharged yet," added Girkins, to himself.

No. 12.

"Well, well," said Trueman. "He shall have a fair chance; besides, he may be very useful to me," thought Trueman to himself.

"I fear I am much intruding upon your valuable time," said Girkins, rising, for he had accomplished the object of his visit, namely, to point the finger of suspicion at Rivers.

"Not at all," replied the merchant. "I am rather sorry to say that Grace does not exactly see the advantages of a union with Lord Hawksworth."

This remark was made with the sort of air which a man uses when he is asking advice of another, and yet does not wish to appear to do so openly, and Mr. Girkins thought it necessary to reply.

"Indeed, Mr. Trueman, that is a matter of deep regret; but I would humbly advise you, above all things, not to press the matter to her, for such very frequently induces still greater obstinacy."

"Am I to be braved and contradicted by my own child?" said Trueman.

"No, no. Oh, dear, sir," replied Girkins, "that would be monstrous, and to such a father as you are, most monstrous: but I intrude. Good day, Mr. Trueman, a thousand apologies for occupying your valuable time so long."

The agent bowed himself out, and although Mathew Trueman would have been glad of his advice with regard to the best means of overcoming Grace's obstinacy, he would not call him back for fear he should lessen his own reputation for ability and acuteness in the mind of his flatterer. Thus was the merchant doubly the slave of his own vanity. He was not only pleased with the rank flattery of his adulater, but he dared not, for fear of decreasing the dose another time, ask the advice he wanted.

"I will to my daughter at once," he muttered, after remaining for some time in disagreeable and gloomy thought. "I will once more argue with her closely on this subject; or, rather, I will command her to acquiesce in arrangements which in after life will wear to her mind a very different aspect from what they do now. Yes, I will to my daughter, and paint to her in as glowing colours as I can the splendour which this projected alliance would cast upon her, and around her and hers.

Mathew Trueman trembled as he ascended his own luxuriously carpeted stairs to seek his own child. There was a small still voice deep in his heart which told him he was wrong, but it was soon overwhelmed in the wild roar of his ambition.

———

CHAPTER XXVIII.

THE FATHER AND CHILD.—GRACE'S DETERMINATION.—THE MOTHER'S MINIATURE.

GRACE was alone, in the common acceptation of the word; but how far from lonely were her thoughts! New creations had risen up in her mind at the kindling power of affection, which, without that strongest of mortal spells to rouse from their slumber in the brain, might never have shed the magic sunshine of their heavenly beauty upon her trusting, gentle heart. She was thinking of Rivers, of his candid and ingenuous avowal of his love; of the manner in which he had conducted himself through the trying interview in the Temple Gardens; and as she so thought, tears of joy that she had awakened such an interest in such a heart mingled with some pearly drops of genuine sorrow, as the many difficulties of her union with Rivers rose up giant-like before her mental vision.

"It may be," she murmured, "that our fates may be to live apart, and if so, I will not repine at the decree of Providence; but if so, I can never love another. Never—never."

Grace had just got so far in her mental cogitations, when she started at hearing her name pronounced, and looking up, she observed her father standing close to her side.

"Weeping, Grace?" he said. "How is this? Twice now have I found you in tears. This is but a poor return for all my lavish care and affection."

Grace might have answered, "It is a poor love which exacts returns," but she merely looked up in her father's face, and said:—

"Sometimes, you know, father, people weep and are most melancholy they know not why."

"Well, well, Grace, dry your eyes; I—I have come to talk with you. I am playing, with heavy stakes, a game in which you are much concerned;—a game which greatly concerns your happiness."

"My happiness, father!" said Grace, who, with an inward shudder, guessed too well to what he referred; "and is there no converse to the picture? May it not be added that it concerns likewise my misery?"

"No, no," said Trueman, as he evaded Grace's eyes; "no, I don't see that, Grace. Lord Hawksworth——"

"Ah!" cried Grace. "Then my heart guessed as much. Lord Hawksworth! It is of him, father, you came to speak. How, then, knowing my aversion to the man, can you talk to me of happiness in the same breath?"

"Grace," said Mr. Trueman, and his voice was slightly shaken, "you are my only child. There is no one in the whole world to whom my heart warms but yourself. I have toiled night and day, and it has been all for you. My exertions have been most successful. I have amassed a brilliant fortune, but it was for no other purpose than that you might arrive at a brilliant destiny."

The merchant paused, and for one moment in his own heart he knew that his own ambition had had far more to do with his early and late toiling than his love for Grace. It was not until her wondrous beauty burst upon him as she passed from the state of childhood to that of girlhood, that he began in his scheming brains to speculate upon her rare charms as an instrument in the cause of his deep seated vanity to become other in rank than what he was. Not that he contemplated sacrificing Grace for that object, far from it; but he belonged to that numerous class of persons who cannot conceive it possible for rank and wealth to be other than co-existent with happiness.

"Can I, dear father," said Grace, "doubt for one moment of your love?"

"You should not, Grace," he said, "and—and, therefore——"

"Nay, father," she interposed, "I know the inference you would draw. Therefore, you would say to me, be dutiful. Now tell me, father, would you be happy in seeing me go to the altar with one I could not love, and perjure myself in the sight of Heaven—even in the temple devoted to God, because a small section of his fellows had agreed to call him you would have me wed a lord?"

"You cannot surely despise the advantages of rank?"

"No, father, I am far from doing so, but there are things I hold in higher estimation."

"Indeed!"

"Yes. One of them is truth."

"Truth, Grace?"

"Ay, father, truth. How could I, loving him not, say, in the face of Heaven, I loved him?"

"Oh, but you know, Grace, these things are done every day."

"They are so, and the result is—ruin."

"But you are young, and cannot see as I do the advantages of such an alliance. Now, Grace, I have no sort of doubt in the world but Lord Hawksworth will propose for your hand."

"But does it follow, that he, like an Eastern Monarch, is to command the love which cannot be dictated to?" said Grace. "Should he offer, refuse him, father, and tell him that which I am sure you feel in your own heart, namely, that you prefer your Grace's happiness to the world's diadem, had he to offer it."

Nothing makes a man look so confused, when he is contemplating any mean or despicable act, as being complimented upon his virtues, and Mr. Trueman for some moments looked about as foolish as it was possible to look after these words had been spoken by Grace, and spoken, too, with an energy and a truthfulness that made them reach even his heart.

And what, then, did Mathew Trueman do? Did he admit that his much cherished child was right, and exult in the noble, virtuous sentiments which adorned her judgment, and thank Heaven for giving him such a daughter? No, he did what hundreds of thousands of people do when they are convinced against their will. He put himself in a passion!

"Grace," he said, "once for all—hear me. I have set my heart on this alliance for you. You will live to thank me for it, and——"

"No—no, father, never. You would live to repent the force which had urged me to a hateful union."

"One of the oldest earldoms in the kingdom," urged Mr. Trueman, "and more honours in perspective. Your wealth and his rank would suffice to place you at once as a blazing star in the eye of the court. Even majesty would smile upon you, and borrow new lustre from your presence, your equipages, your diamonds, your servants——"

"While my heart was breaking," said Grace.

"Nonsense, nonsense."

"It would be the bespeaking a gilded coffin, father, and seeking to find pleasure in gaudily attiring oneself for disgrace. You—you cannot mean, father, to urge upon me this hateful suit."

"But think, Grace. Think again."

"Before this hateful idea arose in your mind, dear father, were we not happy? Did not I ever fly to meet you? Did not I try to coax you from the cares of business, to come up here and hear me sing to you, and were you not happy—far happier then than now, when you know my heart must beat with alarm when I hear your footstep, and you cannot meet me with the smile you used to wear?"

"Girl, girl," cried Mr. Trueman, "do you want to drive me mad?"

"Father——"

"Nay, this obstinacy is beyond everything—here I offer to you a brilliant destiny, which——"

"Which I do not prefer to your love. Let me remain as I now am, your loving and beloved child."

"No, Grace. You—you set your face against me in the only matter that touches me very nearly. I cannot forget it."

Grace burst into tears.

Her grief seemed for a few moments to affect Mathew Trueman, and the words—"Well—well, you shall hear no more about it," rose to his lips; but before they were uttered, a knock on the door announced some one, and the merchant, dreading that however it was might walk in, and become a spectator of a scene he would not have observed,

went quickly to the door himself, and opening it a small width, said—

"What is it?"

"It's me," replied Tom Hackey. "Birnam wood has moved to——No, bless me—no, what was I a saying of? Here's Jones called about the tallow consignment to Malabar. He says all the fat's in the fire, and in addition to that, some thieves——"

"If you don't go down the stairs directly, I'll knock you from top to bottom of them," cried Mr. Trueman.

"Oh, very good," said Tom. "Stand not upon the order of——" A well-intended blow at his head from the enraged merchant, which Tom managed to avoid, stopped the quotation, and as the delinquent immediately made good his retreat, Mr. Trueman returned to his daughter with the small spark of right feeling which Grace's tears had kindled, quite extinguished again.

"Grace," he said, "the time will come when I'm in the grave, and you will think very differently then of your conduct than you do now."

"May you be long spared to me, father," said Grace; "but the heaviest of human calamities surely cannot force the heart to feel that which it does not. Oh, think again, dear father! I have heard you often say we are alone in the world—we have no relatives."

"None but poor ones," said Mr. Trueman; "but that's all the same."

Grace shuddered at the selfish speech, but she made no remark upon a sentiment which had, at all events, nothing to do with the discussion in hand, but continued—

"Let us be happy once again, and this much I will promise you, father, if you wish it, never to wed one who is not approved of by you."

"Pho—pho, I don't want any such promises. No daughter of mine, I'm sure, would be so foolish as to marry a poor man, and if you won't marry him I choose for you, it's of very little matter to me who you have; but mark me, girl, I'm a man of my word: not one penny of fortune shall you ever have of me if you do not receive the addresses of Lord Hawksworth."

"If that were all," said Grace, "I were content with poverty, provided you were still as kind to me in tone and manner, as——"

"Pshaw!" interrupted the merchant, violently; "you don't know what poverty is. With girls like you it's merely a fine sentimental name. You know nothing about it. Now, I do. I have been poor—infernally poor. Poor and more destitute than you can conceive, because you must go through it to know anything about it. I began the world with three-and-a-penny. I've wanted a breakfast—a lunch—a dinner —a tea, and a supper. D—n it, I have! And then I've gone to bed, and could have cried for want of food. Could you endure that?"

"If it were the will of Heaven, I must, and I would pray to God to grant me patience."

"Patience! why Heaven has granted you the chance of being a countess, and you won't take it."

"Father, I will endure the consequences of not loving Lord Hawksworth," said Grace, firmly.

"You will?"

"Yes. Did my mother love you?"

The merchant staggered as if he had been shot.

"Look here," said Grace, opening a drawer in which was a miniature resemblance of her mother; "can you, father, look on that face smiling upon us with all the magic of the painter's art, and say you will make me so unhappy?"

"I—I—" gasped Trueman. "Where, girl, did you get that miniature?"

"I found it in your escritoir."

"I have not seen it for years. How business takes up the time! Your mother's name was Grace."

"Is this like her, father?"

"The very image—the very image. At least, when I first knew her—she went through much suffering; but— but in her coffin she again looked like that, and wore just such a smile."

A big tear rolled down Grace's cheek, and fell upon the glass which covered the enamel.

"My poor mother," sobbed Grace, "and I never saw her—never heard her voice—never saw her smile on me."

"You were not two hours old when she breathed her last," said Mr. Trueman. "She—she blessed you with her last breath."

"Father—dear father, we are friends again."

Grace threw her arms round her father's neck, and hiding her face on his bosom, wept aloud. The stern features of the merchant relaxed; a spasm crossed his face, as, reaching out one hand, he closed the miniature case. Then in a low tone, that was evidently struggling with emotion, he said—

"Grace, we—we will arrange this matter for the present some other way. Promise me that you will not offend Hawksworth."

"I promise."

"Because it may be of vast importance to me, Grace. You understand?"

"I do not comprehend, father; but I will obey you in all that I can."

"Well—well, that is like you, my own Grace; you will be civil to Hawksworth, that is all? And—and—But no matter; we will trust to time."

"If Lord Hawksworth offend not me," said Grace, "Heaven forbid that I should so far forget who and what I am as to offend him."

"That will do—that will do. Now give me that portrait. It raises painful emotions, Grace. I—I will put it away."

CHAPTER XXIX.

INTRODUCES TO THE READER A GENTLEMAN FOND OF THE MARVELLOUS.— HILLIARD'S AGITATION OF MIND.

WHEN Tom Hackey descended from the room where Mr. Mathew Trueman and his daughter were holding their interesting conference, he walked up to Rivers, and whispered in his ear—

"Rivers, there's Grace a-crying, and old Mathew a-blowing of her up like sticks."

"What?" said Rivers, suddenly dropping his pen.

"Don't make a row," added Tom. "I seed 'em through the crack of the door. He's been a-saying something disagreeable to her, and she's a-crying. Oh, I could have—have given him to the vultures, and hung his body on the beetling rock, I could."

"I will go up," said Rivers. "I— how dare he? Are you quite sure, Tom? I must protect her."

"You mustn't do no such thing," said Tom, "cos if you does, you'll make yourself uncommon ridiculous, that's what's you will. I only told you to let you know as there was a screw loose somewhere atween old Mathew and Grace. Bless her! I hope as she'll wallop him well in the long run. Oh, I could——"

Here Tom Hackey found language by far too weak to indicate what he could do to Mathew Trueman, and he made several terrific blows at nothing, striking various heroic attitudes, and terminating the whole performance by exlaiming——

"Come on, villain—come on! Your day of doom is come! Down—down to thingummy, and say I sent you there! Hit one of your own size, do."

"Pray be quiet," said Rivers, "and tell me what was really amiss upstairs."

"I can't," said Tom. "I only know as there was something wrong atween Mathew and Grace. Oh, I could——"

"Well—well, Tom, you have already shown me by numerous gymnastic exercises what you could do. Now, oblige me just by going up again, and see if Grace is—is still weeping."

"Go up again? I cannot," said Tom, "unless I sacrifice myself; but I'll do that rather than another tear should come from *her* eyes. I——"

"No—no, Tom, I was wrong," said Rivers. "Neither you nor I have any right to interfere between a father and his child. As yet, we can but lament that one word not in genuine kindness is ever spoken to her."

Tom Hackey walked to the fire, and after poking it in that manner in which people poke fires when they have an indistinct imagining that the poker would be just as well in the internal structure of some enemy, he returned with that weapon over his shoulder, and addressing Rivers in a small whisper, said—

"I tell you what it is, Mr. Rivers, some of these days I shall come out strong."

"What do you mean?" said Rivers.

"I mean, that I shall do something in the horror line."

"The horror line, Tom?"

"Yes; I mean to be bloody."

"Bless me, you are quite alarming."

"That's just what I shall be. Some day, when Mathew is a-saying of something to Grace, I'll fetch him a topper with this poker as shall astonish his weak nerves."

"Why, I think it would astonish his nerves, be they weak or strong," said Rivers; "but for my sake, Tom, be patient and discreet here. I have no friend here but you on whom I could depend for a kind office—no one to whom I could speak with confidence."

Tom let the poker fall point foremost to the ground as he replied—

"I'll sit like patience on a monument smiling at grief, and with a green and yellow melancholy I'll——"

"Stand a drop of half-and-half, I hope," suddenly interpolated a voice, which belonged to a very singular head, that at the precise moment popped itself within the counting-house door.

"The devil!" said Tom.

"No," said the same. "James Bumbleton Swiggles, at your service. Good-morning, gents all. Hope you're well, and that your respective maternal relatives are perfectly aware of your various absences from home."

"Confound your impudence!" said Tom; "didn't I tell you not to call upon me here?"

"Of course you did," said the stranger, drawing himself quite within the doorway, and exhibiting a faded dandy of the first water. "Of course you did, Garrick Redivivus; but you see here I am, nevertheless. What are you going to stand? I've come to tell you that our next night is on Thursday, the twenty-first—we are going to do Macbeth — a fine cast. I double the three witches. You can have your choice of either one you like of the 'grooms' that Macbeth murders in the king's chamber. Do you take?"

"You be hanged," said Tom. "Be off with you."

"Won't you offer your friend a seat?" said Rivers, who was greatly amused at the oddity.

"Thank you, sir," said James Bumbleton Swiggles, Esq. "You are one of the true breed. A fine figure for junior tragedy."

"I tell you what it is, Swiggles," said

Tom, "you must not come here. Business is business, you know, old brick."

"Old brick!" exclaimed James Bumbleton Swiggles, Esq. "You notice he calls me old brick—an affectionate substitute for my real patronymic—old brick. Poor soul, it's affecting. If I had been brick merely, I would have stood it ; but *old* brick !— There's the rub—it's enough to draw tears from a constable's staff, and make a parish pump cry itself into fits."

"You are as great a fool as ever," remarked Tom. "Where has your wits been wool-gathering this morning ?"

"I have come straight from the temple of Momus here, my dear Tom. How devilish well you are looking, to be sure. What a head."

"Mind your own head," said Tom.

"Head, head," repeated James Bumbleton Swiggles, several times. "Bless my heart and life, that reminds me of a little piece of juvenile tragedy that happened some time ago. Gents, will you have it ?"

"With pleasure," said Rivers.

"Then I must tell you it's a dreadful incident, a very dreadful incident indeed."

"Don't believe a word he says," remarked Tom. "He's always got some infernal anecdote or another."

"Ah, but, my good fellow, this is a true story, mind you, so here goes. You'll stand some half-and-half, of course. If you have tears, prepare to shed them now. Pull out your cambrics.

"It was one afternoon in June, that, sitting at my window, I was disturbed from my studies by a deep savage growl —I never heard such a growl before ; it entered the very recesses of my soul, and caused me involuntarily to lay down my pen, and exclaim—'Good God! what can that be ?' I also fancied that at the same time I heard a faint cry, but upon looking from my window, all was still, and nought seemed to disturb the serenity of the calm sunshine, but the buzzing sound that is always heard in the heart of a large city.

"The growl that I had heard, had completely overpowered me ; an undefined sensation that something dreadful had occurred, came over me, and I left my study at the back of the house, to seek my family, and in their converse get rid of the unpleasant sensations which had possessed me.

"Upon entering the parlour, I found my wife pale and trembling.

"'I'm sure there's something very dreadful happened,' said she, 'did you hear that awful growl ?'

"'I did,' I replied, 'I cannot get rid of the sound from my ears.'

"'It was the most awful noise I have ever heard, James.'

"'You surely did not hear it here, Mary ? It seemed to me to come from the back way.'

"'It did,' returned my wife ; 'I was in my chamber at the time—it almost petrified me.'

"'It was certainly like the growling of a tiger devouring his prey.'

"'Do go, James, and ascertain the cause. I shall be quite unhappy till I know.'

"'Well,' said I, 'I will ; who lives round the corner ?'

"'There is only the timber merchant that keeps a dog,' returned my wife.

"'Do you think,' asked I, 'it was that dog we so often notice, with the noble bark ?'

"'I have my fears, but go and see.'

"Without further loss of time I put on my hat, and upon going into the next street, a crowd of people round the gates of the timber merchant arrested my attention.

"'Did you hear it ?' asked one.

"'Awful !' responded another.

"'Truly frightful !' cried a third, while hundreds inquired what the matter was without being able to get a satisfactory reply.

"'And what *is* the matter ?' said I, pushing myself into the centre of a group of women who seemed conversant with the matter, or at least appeared to be so.

"'Have you not heard, sir ?'

"'No, indeed, I have not,' I replied, 'that is the very information I require.'

"'Well, sir, you shall hear. You must know, I'm charwoman to the family.'

"'Indeed !' said several.

"'And, therefore, I knows all about it.'

"'Well, proceed.'

"'So, you must know,' continued the woman, 'that some time ago, Mr. Whitcomb, who is now dead, (God rest him !) bought a young puppy, and no one used to feed him but little Master Alfred.'

"'What age?' demanded several.

"'The child was about six; but, however, the dog became very fond of him, and he became very fond of the dog; in fact, they were perfect friends and seemed delighted in each other's company, and at last the dog grew very large and strong.'

"'Oh, yes!' interrupted several, 'the Newfoundland mastiff; we know him.'

"'The finest dog I ever saw,' rejoined another.

"'And such a bark!' echoed a third.

"'I have often noticed the animal,' said I, 'it was a fine animal.'

"'Well, my friends,' continued the woman, 'you know this dog was also very much attached to Mr. Whitcomb, his master, and, in fact, would scarcely allow any other person but him and the child to come near him—it was a savage animal; but since the death of his master, it had been very melancholy, and would scarcely eat a bit; and it was shut up in the top workshop, and perhaps forgotten.'

"'And what then?' asked the bystanders.

"'You shall hear. 'Thomas,' said Mrs Whitcomb, this morning to the foreman, 'had you not better give Carlo (meaning the dog) some food?''

"'He will not take it from me,' returned Thomas, "Perhaps Master Alfred had better give it him; they understand each other better.'

"'Well, perhaps so,' said the mother, and immediately called the child to take the meat to the dog.

"'Oh, yes! mamma!' cried little Alfred, well pleased with the errand. 'I'll give Carlo his food; poor Carlo, he has had nothing to eat for a long time.'

"'He then left for the upper workshop, and upon entering, he stayed till Thomas came to call him; upon opening the door, it seems, something ailed him, and he fell down in a fit.'

"'Well, was it so?'

"'Yes, for he was found in that state by the mother, who came to seek her child; upon opening the shop-door, the dog was lying in a corner, very sick, and a portion of the child's clothes in rags about the room.'

"'Good God!' exclaimed several, 'you don't mean to say he had devoured the child?'

"But I do though,' resumed the woman, 'he had devoured the whole of him, except his head and a portion of the legs; the foreman had seen it, as he entered, but it was fearful to enter, and upon regaining the landing outside the door, had fainted with the horrid scene he had witnessed!'

"'Heaven preserve us!' cried several.

"'Great God, how awful!' replied others.

"'And where's the mother?' demanded several of the women round.

"'Walking about the house, raving mad!' replied the charwoman; 'and nursing the child's head, and tossing it up like a ball.'

"I had heard enough. I returned home with a sickening sensation that seemed to choke me; this, then, explained the cause of that awful growl which ever since has caused me to shiver when the idea crossed my mind

"'Well, James, what is it?' demanded Mary, upon my return.

"'It appears something shocking has happened, but I cannot vouch for the truth of what I've heard,' I replied. I was compelled to draw her attention from the subject, for in her then present situation it would have been cruel to have mentioned it.

"I have since learned that the statement of the charwoman was correct, and can only faintly picture to myself what must have been the agonising feelings of the wretched mother.

"My wife has never yet learned the fact as it really was; but now and then adverts to it by the question of—'James, do you remember that awful growl?' The very idea causes a thrill of horror to run through me. Now every word of that's true, on my life."

"Gammon," said Tom.

"Gammon—gammon? Why, I was the baby."

"What?" cried Tom. "You precious humbug. You the baby as was eat up, and his head made a ball of?"

"I—I mean," said the unabashed

James Bumbleton Swiggles, "I am that baby's twin brother."

"There—there, that'll do. Let's have no more of your lies—one is a dose."

"But did you never hear of the unnatural cook, or the baby's pettitoes?"

"No, nor don't want. Be off with you. I tell you what it is, this here's a place of business, so when you wants to see me don't come to it."

"Not come to it, my Roscius? Can aBumbleton Swiggles keep away from a Hackey? Forbid it, ye immorta's. Sooner shall the radiant sun be caught napping on the twenty-fourth of June, and swindle the little birds into sleeping till half-past eleven o'clock, than——"

"Pray can you explain to me the meaning of all this tumult, Mr. Rivers?" said Mathew Trueman, entering the office nearly purple with rage.

There was an impressive silence of some moments' duration, and Tom

MR. GIRKINS FOLLOWS HILLIARD TO HIS LODGING.

Hackey glanced at James Bumbleton Swiggles with an expression which, if translated into her Gracious Majesty's English, would have been—"There, now, you've put your foot in it."

Mr. Swiggles, however, was one of those gentlemen who are continually getting into scrapes, and as continually, by some means which would never have suggested themselves to anybody else, getting out of them. A moment's thought now produced a scheme for relieving Tom Hackey of anything disagreeable connected with his presence, and before one word could be said to Mr. Trueman, he struck a strange attitude, and shouted at the top of his lungs—

"Who gives anything to poor Tom, whom the foul fiend hath led through fire and through flame, through ford and whirlpool, over bog and quagmire—that hath laid knives under his pillow and halters in his pew. Ha! ha! ha!

Do poor Tom some charity. He's just got out of St. Luke's, and trotted on a bay horse, with an extra leg, and a fire-shovel on the bridge of his nose, down Whitechapel."

Mr. Trueman, as well he might, looked amazed at this speech, and made a step backwards, as he said—

"Bless me, he's mad."

"Mad!" cried Mr. Swiggles. "Who says that? Fetch me the donkey that's fond of pork chops, and let him wink at a church steeple, and tell me I'm mad."

"Go for a constable, Tom," cried the merchant.

"Ah, do," shrieked Swiggles; "and let him who goes for the constable be the goer for the constable. Call a con-stable, and let a constable be called, and in his calling let him nothing call but constable—constable—constable! Oh, for a constable, ye gods! Did you ever see a pig frying onions for a blackbird? Whoop—whoop! Hilloa—hilloa!"

With one of those wild cries which the *supers* at a theatre think necessary during the incantation scene in Der Freischutz, James Bumbleton Swiggles, Esq., rushed past the alarmed merchant, and was out in the street in a moment.

"A madman!" cried Mr. Trueman. "How came he here?"

"Oh, he just bolted in as you see he has bolted out," said Tom.

"Really it's quite dangerous to have such a man abroad; he ought to be under restraint; what could possess him to come here? Mind, Hackey, if ever he should take it into his mad brain to pay my counting-house a visit, run for a constable direcdy."

"I will, sir," said Tom.

CHAPTER XXX.

THE MEETING BETWEEN HILLIARD AND WILSON. — A GUILTY CONSCIENCE NEEDS NO ACCUSER.

HILLIARD was in a most terrible state of apprehension the greater part of the morning as regarded the state of his miserable and weak associate in guilt, Wilson. He dreaded each moment that some one would walk into the office and challenge him as a murderer upon the confession of his accomplice, and he looked forward to a meeting he was to have with him at his, Hilliard's, lodg-ings, with a nervous anxiety that totally incapacitated him from all other pur-suits.

There was a wretched prospect from the window of Hilliard's miserable abode, looking, as it did, into one of those crowded churchyards, which a hundred years ago might have been out of town, but which, by the gradual growth of bricks and mortar around them, have become serious annoyances to the living, obtruding beneath their chamber windows and on to their very door steps.

The burying-ground to which we now allude, had been purchased in small freeholds by several wealthy persons many years before the events of our story commenced, and hence there was not in it that frequent and indiscrimi-nate huddling together of the dead, which is too frightfully common in our metropolitan grave-yards, for the ground was only broken when any member of those particular families happened to die.

Since Hilliard had resided at the wretched abode to which he had been traced by Girkins, he had often sat looking gloomily into the church-yard, and holding dark communing with his own sinful thoughts. He knew that he was there unobserved, and from the mouldering evidences of what had once been living, breathing forms like himself, he strove to gather a confirmation of the gloomy philosophy he would fain have argued his heart into believing, namely, that the end of mortal life was the extinction of all being—an utter annihilation of the individual. Oh, how many of the wicked, the vicious—the shedders of man's blood, and the wrongers of the orphan, have striven, with a wild and frantic vehemence, to convince themselves of such a creed, while their own hearts have ever risen up in rebellion against them, telling them with a voice that will not be stifled, that there is a Heaven above, and a day of judgment at hand.

The sun was shining brightly upon the dingy and moss-covered tomb-stones, and the rank grass in the bury-ing-ground was waving in the light breath of a gentle wind, that ever and anon would sweep among the tombs, as Hilliard once more drew the newspaper from his breast, to read again the account of his own awful crime.

It seemed a judgment of Heaven upon him that he could not part with the record of his own deep and dreadful sinfulness; with a wild and strange longing, he could not refrain from reading over and over again the frightful details of the murder, although to do so seared his very brain, and filled him with terrors that shook his guilty frame. Who shall say that the wicked are not punished in this world? What human vengeance could be equal to the mental agony endured by Hilliard each time he gloated over the page which contained, what appeared to him in letters of fire, the circumstantial account of his crime?

He would get to the end of the paragraph, not omitting a single word, and then, as if he had never seen it, commence anew reading, reading on with the same terribly absorbing interest. Then he would crush up the paper and place it in his pocket, with a determination that he would look at it no more; but in less than ten minutes it was again spread out before his eyes, again to peruse those words which were already written on his memory in letters of fire, never, never to be effaced.

It was full half an hour after his time before Wilson came, and the mental agony endured by Hilliard during that interval of suspense we cannot attempt to describe.

What a frightful change was over the face of Wilson since last he had appeared before his associate in guilt. He had purposely disguised his face as much as possible; but what art could produce the striking change that remorse had effected? Truly he might almost have walked through New Inn without being recognised.

His cheeks were sunken and hollow. His eyes looked almost hidden in their sockets, and there was such an expression of shrinking terror about the thin pale lips, as they were drawn slightly apart, that even Hilliard started, and could scarcely for a moment believe that it was indeed the same man whom he had tempted to such heinous sin, who stood before him.

"You are late, Wilson," he then said, as he carefully bolted the door.

"I thought," said Wilson, licking his dry, thin lips, "that some one was following me."

"You—you are sure—it was not so?"

"Yes, sure—it was a man who merely by accident was going the same way. I am sure it was so, for I saw him go into a house."

"Well—well. Now tell me what you mean to do. Stay lurking about here you cannot, you know. I can't support you."

"What am I to do, Hilliard? Recollect you tempted me—oh! what will become of me?"

"If I were in your situation," said Hilliard, "I would cut my throat."

"No—no!" shuddered Wilson, "that I dare not do—I—am afraid of death now—horribly afraid."

"Pshaw," said Hilliard, "why should you be? It's the end of all."

"Are you quite sure of that, Hilliard?" said Wilson. "Oh, are you quite sure? If you could convince me of that, I would worship you—I would implore you to kill me."

"I—I am sure," gasped Hilliard, while his ghastly countenance and trembling limbs belied the words he spoke.

"No, no, no," said Wilson. "We cannot comfort ourselves that way. There is an hereafter, Hilliard—there is a power, and there is——"

"Peace," cried Hilliard, "I did not meet you here to be annoyed by such prating. It's all superstition, I tell you —vile superstition. Come to this window. There—look out—how many sleep there the calm sleep of death—they feel nothing—know nothing—do you not wish you were among them? By Heavens! a funeral to-day."

As Hilliard spoke, the gate—which was at the farther extremity of the graveyard—was slowly opened, and there appeared a funeral train, which with slow and solemn steps wound its way among the ancient grave-stones, while a neighbouring church commenced tolling its deep-toned, sonorous bell for the departed spirit.

Nearer and nearer the train came towards the window at which stood the murderers, who, by some spell, were unable to quit the spot or to take their eyes off the mournful spectacle.

"Where—where are they coming?" gasped Hilliard; "where are they coming?"

"Look, look," said Wilson, and he pointed immediately below the window, where Hilliard had not observed was a new-made grave.

"D——!" cried Hilliard; "do they dig graves under people's windows? Come away, Wilson; come away, we—we can't stay here."

Wilson laid his hand on Hilliard's arm, as he said, in a hoarse guttural voice—

"Let us—see—who it is. I should like to see who it is. Stay, Hilliard, stay."

The clergyman who was to read the funeral service might now be seen wending his way among the timeworn stones towards the brink of the grave; there was an unwonted air of emotion about him. The traces of recent tears were on his cheek, and it was evident that he was in some measure personally interested in the interment which was about to take place. He paused at the brink of the grave, and then as he turned and saw the funeral train close at hand, he covered his face with his handkerchief, and sobbed aloud in the bitterness of his grief.

Then with a great effort he recovered himself, and removing the handkerchief from his face, he said—

"Heaven's will be done!"

The moment his face was uncovered, Wilson uttered a cry of terror, and fell back in the room. Hilliard, nearly frantic with rage, seized him by the throat, muttering in a hissing whisper—

"Wretch! do you want to destroy us both?"

Wilson pointed with his finger to the window, and after several ineffectual attempts to speak, he said—

"It—it—is—Mr. Noble's funeral. The clergyman is his brother. God of Heaven! that I should have come here to see *him* placed in his grave! Save me—save me, Hilliard! Oh, save me from going mad!"

Hilliard slowly relaxed his hold of Wilson, and a shudder came over his own frame. He could not speak. The deep tone of the funeral bell seemed to pierce through his brain, a burning fever dried up his blood, and he could not have removed from that spot on which he knelt had his life depended on it.

Then slowly and solemnly the voice of the clergyman rose as he spoke the service for the dead, and those guilty men were doomed to listen to that affecting recital, which, to their hearts, brought dismay and terror. Each word sounded to them like awful damnation from Heaven for their great crime. Deep groans burst from Wilson's breast; and when the words—"I heard a voice from Heaven saying unto me, write from henceforth blessed are the dead which die in the Lord," he rose with a loud shriek from the floor, and rushing to the window, as if from an impulse he could not control, he shouted—

"Mercy—mercy—mercy! Save me from the torment which is eternal! I—I did not kill him!—I did not strike the blow! I am innocent so far!"

"Villain!" shrieked Hilliard, as he rushed upon Wilson, and dragged him from the window. "Are you mad? Know you what you do? Do you wish to die upon a scaffold? Away!—fly—fly—while you have yet time—seek safety in flight."

The momentary excitement had expended itself, and before the mourners at the grave could recover from their astonishment at the strange interruption, or even notice the features of him who had caused it, Hilliard had unbolted the door, and dragged Wilson on to the staircase of the house.

"Follow me," he said. "You have but one chance now of escape. Follow me, I say."

Wilson mechanically followed the rapid steps of Hilliard, and they gained the street some minutes before it was possible, even had they attempted it, for any of those who were at the funeral to get round to the front of the house.

"On—on!" said Hilliard; and, seizing Wilson by the arm, he dragged him through several courts, which brought them out in the immediate neighbourhood of Drury-lane. Several times he looked behind him, but there was no pursuit; and when he considered they were comparatively safe, he turned to Wilson, and with a howling bitterness, which was only partially controlled for fear of exciting the too marked attention of the passengers, he said—

"Wretch! How dared you run so frightful a risk for me as well as for yourself as you did by your insane conduct just now? Mark me, Wilson, I will not live a life of danger through you; and as true as that we are here both living men, I will kill you if you be not more discreet."

"Kill me?"

"Yes, frightfully I will kill you. I will find some means that shall make you suffer in some measure, even as you have made me suffer from your accursed fears."

"I could not help it," gasped Wilson. "Forgive me, Hilliard; indeed, I knew not what I did."

"A poor excuse."

"It is my only one. Spare me— spare me!"

"You have no hat. Have you money?"

"None—none."

"Then take this half-sovereign, and go to yon shop and buy one; I will wait for you here. Be quick, and mind you awaken no suspicion."

Wilson took the money and soon provided himself with a hat, although by doing so he did excite a great deal of surprise, if not suspicion, on the part of the hatter, who walked after him to the door, and followed him with his eyes until he joined Hilliard, and they together turned a corner.

During the short period of time that he had been alone, Hilliard had matured a frightful scheme for getting rid of Wilson. He determined to murder him, for he considered that his own life was not safe one moment from another with such a man.

"He would tell all," thought Hilliard, "were he but once in custody, and I should not have the slightest chance of escape. He would, in all probability, have his religious fears sufficiently worked upon to become evidence against me, while his own life would be spared. No, by all the powers of h—ll, I will not run such a risk: he shall die! Surely it is a matter of self-defence; and if ever a death was justified by a great exigency, it is this. He shall die—he shall die, and then I shall feel myself safe. Yet what a damnable position have I put myself in! Two murders for nothing—not one farthing gained by either. Curses on my bad luck."

When Wilson joined him they walked on in silence for some moments in the direction of the Strand, and then Hilliard said—

"Wilson, you will be safer out of London than in it, I am quite sure."

"Where can I go?" said the trembling man.

"Here is some more money; I am very poor myself, and can't give you much; but do you go down to Greenwich, and I will see you again to-night."

"You will come to me, Hilliard?"

"I will, you may depend. You know Blackheath?"

"Yes—yes."

"Well, there is a pathway leading to Shooter's Hill; be you there at twelve to-night, and I will meet you, be assured."

"How shall I see you?"

"You will know me by my blowing a whistle twice. Then you can come in the direction of the sound, when, to assure me that it is you, call out, 'What's the hour?' and I will answer you."

"Very well," said Wilson; "at twelve. You will not disappoint me, Hilliard? I have now no one in the wide world to speak a word to but you."

"I will be there, and hope to suggest something that will make to-morrow more agreeable than to-day has been. Recollect, at twelve, precisely."

CHAPTER XXXI.

THE INVITATION TO THE BALL.—GRACE AND HER LOVER.—TOM HACKEY'S ROMANTIC RESOLVE.

WHEN Mathew Trueman came calmly to consider of the compromise he had made with Grace, regarding Lord Hawksworth, he much censured what he called his own folly and weakness in giving way to the sentimentality of a girl, when riches, rank, and everything which to him (Mathew Trueman) presented an alluring aspect, were at stake.

He paced his small counting-house with a knit brow, and an air of troubled speculation. He never, for one moment, would have dreamed of accommodating Lord Hawksworth with the large sum demanded by his lordship's elegant foibles and aristocratic extravagancies, had it not been that he considered the sum as a sort of purchase-money for his coronet, which he longed to see encircling the brows of Grace.

But then Grace herself became the grand obstacle in the way of what the merchant considered his felicitous and extremely happy arrangement. The more he thought of it the greater aggravation it gave him, that he, the far-seeing, calculating, clever-scheming Mathew Trueman, should be foiled, and one of his most daring and favourite schemes thwarted by what he considered the romantic obstinacy of a girl.

Grace's happiness was a question which never, for a moment, agitated the mind of the ambitious father. It was her grandeur, her rank, which dazzled his mental optics, and provided he could see her a countess, and he, himself, a countess's father, he never, for an instant, troubled himself about the aching brow which his child might feel under her coronet, or the beating, throbbing heart that her ermine robe might conceal.

While these thoughts and anticipations were passing through the mind of the merchant, Lord Hawksworth and his friends had not been idle. Upon the prospect of what Mathew Trueman might advance to the young lord, a peer had on that very day lent him five hundred pounds, at only one hundred and sixty per cent. interest upon bills of exchange endorsed, by both Girkins and Jonas Quickset, Esq., Attorney-at-law.

With this sum, as his lordship remarked, he should be able to carry on the war until old Mathew thought proper to bleed freely. One of his first movements was, by the aid and advice of Girkins, to have a magnificent villa residence near Kew, which was replete with every luxury that could charm the senses, and the next was to issue cards of invitation for a fancy dress ball and *fete champetre*, which he determined should come off with *eclat*, if it cost him a thousand pounds, that is, the five hun-

dred he had borrowed and five hundred more, to which amount he trusted to get in debt on the strength of the first moiety in hard cash.

Girkins had insinuated the suggestion concerning the *fete*, for the express purpose of having the merchant and his daughter invited, in order that the brilliancy of the entertainment might dazzle both of them and give Hawksworth an opportunity of making an attempt to press his suit personally, which, whatever might be its failure, would, Girkins knew, amuse him and please Mathew Trueman.

Moreover, Girkins had taken a great antipathy to Rivers, a personal antipathy which was quite an independent feeling in his mind, and for which there was no particular reason, and he thought that the fact of Grace going to the ball at Lord Hawksworth's villa must be specially provoking to him, Rivers, and keep him in a state of agitation and impatience for many hours.

Thus, when Hawksworth called, according to appointment, on the merchant, he was prepared to give him an invitation to the villa at Kew.

Mr. Trueman received his visitor with every demonstration of pleasure at his visit, and it gave him no small pleasure to see Hawksworth's eyes frequently directed towards the door of the counting-house, as if hoped, rather than expected, that Grace might make her appearance.

After some preliminary conversation upon different subjects, Lord Hawksworth said—

"May I venture to hope, Mr. Trueman, that your charming daughter is perfectly well?"

"Perfectly, my lord," replied the gratified merchant. "My daughter is much honoured by your lordship's inquiries, although she is beautiful, and will have a fortune."

"She is positively lovely, Mr. Trueman. She would make a sensation in society. I mean, of course, *the society par excellence.*"

"I am resolved," said Trueman, "notwithstanding I began the world myself with three-and-a-penny, that my daughter shall make some alliance worthy of her beauty and her fortune—that I am quite resolved upon."

"Rank, I presume," said Hawksworth, "will be considered?"

There was a slight tone of raillery in Hawksworth's words which jarred disagreeably upon the nerves of the merchant, and he was silent for nearly a minute before he said—

"Rank, of course—my daughter merits a high destiny; and of what avail has been all my toil for so many years, if she arrive not at it?"

"Ah! what, indeed," said Hawksworth; "you are a close reasoner, my dear sir—extremely close. By-the-by, the man Girkins informs me that you are satisfied, as far as preliminary matters go, to advance me the sum I think I shall require until I come of age, when you are aware I have large property through the will of my uncle, which the trustees will not let me touch now."

"I have the honour to be aware of that fact," said Trueman.

"I have applied to them twice to pay my debts," drawled out Hawksworth, "but they had the beastly insolence to refuse, and the last time the senior trustee had the impertinence to tell me to pay them myself, since I had contracted them. Quite absurd—quite. The difficulty and trouble of getting into debt is quite enough; but the idea of getting out of it again is quite perspiring."

These anti-mercantile notions of his projected son-in-law made Trueman wince a little. "But then he is a lord, and that is all I require. Of course, he makes my daughter a countess—he can't unmake her again."

"As soon as the blank acceptances are ready, with your friend's endorsement," said Trueman, "I shall be happy to advance your lordship the first portion of the sum which I have agreed to place at your service. You will, however, clearly understand that I consider my principal security your own word and honour as a nobleman that, should I require you to do so, you will renew those bills upon your coming of age."

"That I promise on my word and honour as a nobleman and a gentleman," said Hawksworth.

"I am quite satisfied," responded the merchant.

"And now, then, that we have settled the dull details of business," remarked Hawksworth, "I have to request the favour of you and your daughter's company to my villa at Kew to-morrow evening, when I give a little *fête* to my particular and intimate friends only."

The merchant's eyes glistened with pleasure, as he said in a bland voice—

"Your lordship does us infinite honour."

"You will be there, then, about seven, I trust?"

"Assuredly."

"By-the-by, it's a fancy costume affair."

"Fancy costume, my lord?"

"Yes."

"Bless me, I never put myself into a fancy costume in all my life: I must decline."

"Pho, pho," said Hawksworth; "couldn't you come as a brigand, or a robber—or some such thing?"

"I beg your lordship's pardon, but I couldn't do anything of the sort. I think I see myself in a fancy costume, I, Mathew Trueman, who commenced the world with three-and-a-penny, and am not exactly the poorest merchant in London. A fancy costume, indeed!"

"Well, my dear sir," said Hawksworth, who was much amused at the merchant's alarm, "you can come as you are. Your costume will do very well. You might be a real brigand, you know, and disguised in your present apparel."

"If I can come as an English merchant," said Mathew Trueman, "I have no objection; but as for anything else, it is entirely out of my line."

"Then," said Hawksworth, rising, "we will expect you as you are, Mr. Trueman, with your lovely daughter."

"We shall be there, my lord, you may depend; and now will your lordship do me the honour of walking up stairs and taking some refreshment?"

"With pleasure," said Hawksworth, following with alacrity the merchant to the door, which, however, they had no sooner reached than Tom Hackey rushed out of the counting-house opposite, and pointing in the direction of the street, cried in a loud voice,—

"There he goes—there he goes!"

"Who—who?" said Trueman, rushing to the street-door, closely followed by Hawksworth, and on the moment Grace glided from the counting-house, and was up the staircase into the dwelling-house in a moment. But what, say our fair readers, had Grace to do in the counting-house? Simply this. She and her kind nurse, Mrs. Woodfall, some short time since, after the stormy interview between the father and daughter, equipped themselves for a walk, in order to make some purchases in the neighbourhood; but when they reached the street, Mrs. Woodfall remembered something she wished to take with her, and Grace, rather than go up-stairs again, finding that her father was engaged, although she knew not with whom, stepped into the office to await the coming of Mrs. Woodfall. Rivers and Tom Hackey only were there, and to the former the sudden appearance of Grace was like a sunbeam breaking into a dungeon, and at once dissipating all the gloom in which it had been shrouded.

Tom Hackey made one step forward, and his features gleamed with pleasure for a moment; then he shrunk back with a deep sigh, while Grace merely said, "Good morning" to Rivers, for in her flurry she was scarcely aware of who was in the office, or who was not.

"Dear Grace," said Rivers, taking her hand, "there is no one here beside myself, except an attached friend."

"Yes," said Tom Hackey, "I—I'm nobody—I'll look up the chimney, poke my fingers in my ears, and know nothing. Don't mind me, Miss Grace. I'm only poor, unfortunate Tom Hackey."

"Not unfortunate, I hope, Tom?" said Grace.

"Don't say anything to me," replied Tom; "I doesn't want to *expiflicate* what I mean, Miss Grace. I'm quite willing to be blighted like a lily. Don't mind me."

"What does he mean?" said Grace to Rivers.

"Never mind, Grace," replied Rivers, "he means well to us. Let that suffice—a better, nobler heart than his I'm sure cannot be. What an unexpected pleasure is this, dear Grace!"

"It must be a brief one," said Grace;

"Mrs. Woodfall will return directly—we are going out."

Rivers just glanced round at Tom, who was pretending to be attentively examining the fire-shovel, and then he raised Grace's hand to his lips.

"Blessings on you, dear Grace," he said. "This meeting will cheer me for the remainder of the day."

Grace smiled in her sweet way, and Tom Hackey uttered a melo-dramatic groan.

"What's the matter?" said Grace, starting.

"Nothing's the matter with me," said Tom; "but do you know who is with your father?"

"No."

"Then it's Lord Thingumy—What's-his-name?"

"Hawksworth?"

"Ah! that's the cretur. Now I tells you what, Rivers, Mathew will be popping out of his den, and popping in here, and then you know all the fish will be in the fire. Doesn't you think it will, Miss Grace?"

"I should not have come here," said Grace, with an alarmed air. "Oh! Rivers, if——"

"They're a-coming, they're a-coming!" cried Tom; "I hear 'em a-moving of their chairs."

He darted out of the office as he spoke, and was just in time to execute the manœuvre which enabled Grace to leave the office unobserved, and reach her own chamber, where she sunk into a seat, and first wept and then smiled, as she said,—

"I was very foolish, very foolish indeed; but—yet can I regret?"

She then covered her fair face with her hands, and, blushing at her own avowal, she gently murmured,—

"I do love him, I do love him."

In the meanwhile, Mathew Trueman had reached the door, and was pacing up and down the street, saying,—

"Bless me, who was it? Where is he? What was the matter, Tom?"

"There," said Tom. "Don't you see?—a little to the left—there he goes, there he goes."

"Where—who?"

"Why, the mad fellow, to be sure."

"What, he again?"

"Yes; look as far as you can, sir."

"I am—I am."

"Then look a little further, and you'll be sure to see him."

"You scoundrel!" cried Mr. Trueman, turning in great anger upon Tom; but the latter, now that his purpose was accomplished, adroitly slipped back into the office, leaving Mathew Trueman to proceed up-stairs with his noble guest, or leave him in the passage, in order to come after him, Tom, a proceeding which was not very likely; and, in fact,

after muttering some threats against him, Mathew Trueman made a great effort to recover his equanimity, and, turning to Hawksworth, he said,—

"I have to apologise to your lordship for the rudeness of one of my menials; but he is honest, or I would at once discharge him from my service."

"Oh, don't mention it," said Hawksworth, "the fellow appears to be a perfect original."

"He is, indeed, but infernally pro-

THE INTERVIEW BETWEEN GRACE AND HAWKSWORTH IN THE SALOON.

voking. Will your lordship be pleased to precede me?"

"I will follow you, if you please."

With an air of great satisfaction then, Mathew Trueman ascended the staircase, followed by Lord Hawksworth, who was intent upon an interview with the beautiful Grace, let him obtain it by her liking or not.

Grace heard the footsteps approaching, and hurrying to Mrs. Woodfall, he said,—

"Dear nurse, let us go at once; here is a visitor coming, who I would fain avoid."

"Who is that, my dear?"

"Lord Hawksworth."

"Well, my dear, we will try to escape him by pleading that we are going out, but if your father insists upon your remaing, there is no resource but to obey him with the best grace possible."

"I will obey my father in remaining, should he require it," said Grace; "but nothing shall compel me to utter one word to this lord beyond the bounds of the coldest civility. I will let him see that his company is disagreeable to me, and if he have one spark of pride or gentlemanly feeling, he will not torture me with his presence."

The voice of Mathew Trueman was at this moment heard from the landing of the drawing-room floor, calling—

"Grace! Grace!"

"Father?" replied Grace.

"Come down here to the drawing-room."

"I must go," said Grace, "but do you, nurse, come too, and back me in my desire to go out."

Quite attired, then, for the streets, Grace descended to the room where were her father and Lord Hawksworth, the latter of whom had his eyes fixed on the door with an intensity which mightily pleased the merchant, as he considered it indicative of the great mind which the young nobleman had to throw himself and his earldom in reversion at the feet of his beautiful child.

The moment Grace appeared, Hawksworth advanced toward her with a low bow, saying—

"I hope I see Miss Trueman quite well?"

"Do you want me, father?" said Grace, turning to Mathew Trueman.

The merchant darted an angry glance at Grace, who then turned to Hawksworth, and said, coldly—

"I am well."

"And beautiful as usual," added the young lord. "Allow me to hand you a chair."

"I was going out a short distance with Mrs. Woodfall, father," said Grace, "and shall soon return."

"You can put off your walk, surely," said the merchant, "as we are honoured with the company of Lord Hawksworth, my dear."

"I am afraid of dispppointing my nurse," said Grace.

"I had hoped to be charmed with some music," said Hawksworth. "You have informed me, Mr. Trueman, of your daughter's great proficiency in singing."

"She does sing, my lord, although perhaps my partiality as a parent goes far in my opinion of its excellence. Grace, sing one of your ballads."

"If you command me, father, I will," said Grace.

"I do," said Mathew Trueman, biting his lips.

With a suddenness that made Lord Hawksworth quite jump, Grace commenced—

"Unwelcome love is like the wind
    Which blows too roughly by;
A lover's vows should gentle be,
    And wafted by a sigh.

"Unwelcome love is like the sea
    When stormy is the main!
A lover's sighs should gentle be,
    Nor fraught with rage or pain.

"Then fly unwelcome love from me,
    I'll smile when it is flown.
No glittering puppet named a lord
    Shall call my heart his own."

"Father, I shall be back soon. Come, nurse, we shall be quite late; good morning, sir."

Before, then, Mathew Trueman—who was quite aghast at his daughter's independence of spirit—could utter a word, Grace had left the room, and gliding like an apparition of beauty down the staircase, left the house, followed by her admiring nurse, who was as much delighted with her darling's spirit and wit, as Mr. Trueman was annoyed.

As for Hawksworth, he stood staring through the open doorway as if he had been bewitched. The words of Grace's song still rang in his ears, but, alas! the beauty of the merchant's daughter had appeared to him more exquisite in proportion as she hated him with scorn and contempt, and far from sickening him of his pursuit, only sufficed to add the zest of difficulty to it.

CHAPTER XXXII.

THE FETE AT THE VILLA NEAR KEW. THE ROMANCIST.—THE PLOT.

MATHEW TRUEMAN was almost too angry himself to afford any consolation to Lord Hawksworth for the very cavalier manner in which he had been treated by Grace, and all he could do was again and again to assure him that he and his daughter would be at his entertainment, to which he had that day invited them.

With this repeated assurance, Lord Hawksworth took his leave, and hurrying to his adviser, Girkins, informed him of the acceptance of the invitation, and desired to know what then was his plan of operation.

"At this fete," replied Girkins, "your lordship must have some opportunity of conversing alone with Grace Trueman, and urging your suit."

"But how is that to be accomplished?"

"The father and daughter, my lord, must be separated; and if your lordship has sufficient faith in my tact, allow me the conduction of that part of the affair."

"Very likely; I know you are a clever fellow, Girkins; but how do you mean to do it?"

"Thus, my lord:—I am acquainted with two persons, a male and a female, who are not over scrupulous in what they engage, provided they are well paid. They are both very clever and good-mannered persons. It shall be the man's duty to interest Mathew Trueman in some long-winded conversation, while the female shall be enjoined to fasten herself upon Grace, leading her into some room where your lordship may easily find her."

"Upon my word, not so bad a plan," laughed Hawksworth.

"You will find it a good one," added Girkins; "for your lordship may be sufficiently disguised to deny to old Trueman that you were the person, if Miss Grace should prove too haughty."

"Exactly so. I don't dislike that feature of the plan, for I am not in circumstances just now to allow the merchant to go off his bargain as regards the money affair."

With this determination, these two schemers against the peace and happiness of a young innocent girl separated. We will pass over the interval between then and the evening of the next day, merely premising, that, by dint of entreaties and commands, Mathew Trueman had wrung from Grace a reluctant consent to go with him, provided he came away at an early hour, which the merchant was nothing loth to promise.

The villa of which Lord Hawksworth was the temporary and unworthy tenant was beautifully situated within its own gardens, which contained the rarest collection of plants and flowers for many miles round.

The hour of eight had not arrived, when the gay saloons—for it was one of those villas that are mansions in size and splendour—were thronged with company, most of them of a very questionable character, but attired in every variety of splendid costume. Every intoxicating charm which could be collected in one spot was there, in order, if possible, to dazzle and confuse the understanding of the beautiful girl, for whose destruction such extensive arrangements were made, and such diabolical plots entered into.

At half-past eight Mathew Trueman and his daughter entered the gates of the villa. The merchant was attired in his ordinary costume, and Grace, who entertained the same dislike as her father to fancy costumes, went, as she would have gone anywhere else, in her own proper character of a young lady.

The merchant was announced with a stentorian voice, by a servant out of livery, who heralded the guests, and in a few moments the father and daughter found themselves in the middle of "a glittering throng," and walking through a spacious suite of apartments, the doors conducting to and from which were so numerous and so multiplied by looking-glasses, that a progress from one to the other became perfectly bewildering.

"This is a gorgeous scene, Grace," said Mathew Trueman.

"It is, father," said Grace; "and yet I sigh for the hour of our return."

"I wonder where Hawksworth is among all this glitter?" said Trueman, purposely not noticing his daughter's last remark.

Scarcely had the words escaped his lips, when an exceedingly gentlemanly-looking man stepped up to him, and holding out his hand, said—

"I believe I have the happiness of addressing Mr. Mathew Trueman, the celebrated merchant?"

"Trueman is my name, sir," said the gratified merchant; "but I have not the honour of recollecting you."

"For a good reason," said the stranger; "we have never met before;

but Lord Hawksworth, my most intimate friend, said to me this morning early, 'My dear duke,' said he, 'in the evening, if I should not be at hand, pray search out my esteemed friend, Mr. Trueman, and pay him every attention.'"

"You are very kind," said Mathew Trueman. "Bless my heart, a duke."

"Allow me, allow me," suddenly cried the duke, as he took the hand of an elegant female who was near him. "Allow me to introduce to you my sister, the Countess Algernon Mountfair de Lorme Strathhalvoren Como de Medici !"

"Good God," thought the merchant, "what a title !" and he bowed low, saying—

"My daughter, your ladyship—my only daughter."

The countess then, with the greatest condescension, drew Grace's arm within hers, and said—

"Come, my dear, I will show you the lions."

The duke seized Mathew Trueman, and in a moment the father and daughter were separated.

"Really," said Mr. Tureman, "if your grace would be so kind, I would rather remain near my daughter."

"Could you recommend me an investment for about a hundred thousand pounds ?" said the duke.

"Yes, I could," replied Mathew Trueman, forgetting in a moment everything but his per centage on such a vast amount.

"Very well," said the duke; "but to make you quite understand how I came by it, you see, and why I am so anxious to have it invested, I must enter just a little into family particulars."

"Family particulars, your grace ?"

"Yes. On my return from Bath—"

"I beg your grace's pardon, but I don't see my daughter."

"Oh, she's quite safe.   Listen to me."

"But, your grace—"

"Pho, pho—come along. This way. Your daughter is with the countess, of course. You must know, Mr. Trueman, on my return from Bath, in the spring of 18—, I determined to make a stay with our honest old gardener,

Herbert Thompson, who resided at that time in Berkshire.

"At the death of a distant relation, a considerable sum of money had been bequeathed to him, and at the request of my father he left us to reside in a cottage on the estate of his deceased relative.

"I had often heard Herbert speak warmly and in glowing language of the beauty of his only daughter, Millicent, who was residing as hand-maid to a young lady of title.

"I know not why, but I felt an irresistible wish to be acquained with this unknown beauty, and in a few hours after I had conceived the wish, I found myself seated before a simple repast in the cottage of old Herbert.

"I was surprised at beholding the strange alteration which had taken place in the old man's countenance; I had expected prosperity would have heightened the jollity and social habits of the worthy old man; but far contrary seemed to be the case; his once merry laughing eye now seemed dim, and though but few years had passed since I had seen him hale and strong, he now seemed aged and infirm.

"'Surely,' thought I, 'thou hast some hidden cause of sorrow;' the sorrows of the aged had ever been sacred to me, and I now forbore to question Herbert as to the cause of his unexpected change.

"I know not whether it was that long habit had made him conversant with my disposition, but as if guessing at my inward thoughts, he exclaimed—

"'Ay—ay, Sir William, I wonder not that ye should seem surprised at the wreck of Herbert Thompson.'

"'Thou hast indeed judged rightly,' I replied; "it was upon thee my thoughts were bent.'

"'I knew it—I knew it, my young and noble master,' he returned, 'but I will not make thy young and generous heart bleed by a recital of my heartfelt woes.'

"Perceiving that the frame of Herbert now shook with emotion, I refrained from endeavouring to elicit the cause of the sorrow to which he alluded, and tried to turn his thoughts from them, by inquiring after his favourite child. Millicent. Judge my surprise on seeing the cheeks of the honest and venerable old Herbert moistened with his tears.

"'Ah, Millicent!" he passionately exclaimed, 'would to God she were as happy now as when I lived beneath the roof of thy honoured and beloved father. But see—see!' continued he, 'yonder comes my poor heart-broken child!'

"I looked in the direction pointed out, and saw approaching, the form of a young and lovely woman. 'Can it be possible,' thought I, 'that this is the daughter of Herbert Thompson! Surely she steps with the majesty of a queen!'

"'Pardon me, my noble master,' said the old man, 'but it may flurry the sinking heart of my poor girl to behold a stranger; may I ask of thee to step aside till I prepare her for your presence?"

"'Willingly!' I returned, and, suiting the action to the word, I entered an inner apartment of the cottage, which hid me entirely from her view, although I could plainly perceive the features of Millicent.

"'Father,' said she, sorrowfully, as she entered, 'I have been to plant fresh flowers on the grave of my beloved Walter!'

"This Herbert appeared not to notice.

"'Milli, my dear child,' said he, 'one who has ever loved and served thy poor father, has now come hither to visit him in his age and sorrow.'

"'Then God will reward him, as his will is pure towards thee, my dear father,' replied the beautiful but sorrowing Millicent.

"Her voice seemed music to my heart, and with joy I heard her ask—

"'And will not the stranger, dear father, converse with poor neglected Milli?''

"'I will—I will!' said I, entering the apartment, unable longer to restrain myself from the happiness of being near her, for such indeed was the strange influence which the beautiful girl had over me, that I felt I should not henceforth be happy without her company.

"On beholding me, I beheld a look of scorn for a moment visible in her beautiful eye, but which hastily passed away as she exclaimed—

"'No—no! I had forgotten—thou art not the cousin to the young 'squire; thou art the friend of my poor dear father!'

"'I am!' said I, 'and should be proud did all acquaintance so well deserve my friendship!'

"During the short interview, I perceived the eyes of Herbert fixed with devoted affection upon his child.

"'My dear Milli,' said he, 'this is the son of my noble master, beneath whose roof I spent so many years of happiness.'

"'Ah! say you so, dear father?' said she, and, as a shade of deeper melancholy spread over her careworn features, she continued—'to him, then, will I tell the story of poor Walter and his true love, Millicent,' and taking me by the hand, she led me to a seat, and placing herself nearly opposite, she pressed her snowy hand upon her brow, and exclaimed—

"'Be'ore my brain past sorrows rise:
Oh, Heaven, 'twas a fearful night!
Ne'er can my soul forget the sight
Which met my wondering eyes.
Loud roared the thunder through the sky;
Hurl'd by the power of God on high;
The vivid lightning seemed to dart,
And rend the firmanent apart.
A female form, alas, how fair!
(Blue sparkling eyes, and raven hair)
Fled madly through the raging storm,
Shrieking—'Alas, he dies at morn!'
Then came another shrieking by,
'Save him—oh, save him, or I die!
Oh, God, my child—my child!'
Then came a man with hoary head,
Whose reason seemed for ever fled;
Wildly he murmured—'Where? oh, where
Art thou, my son, my hope, my care?'
Awhile he stood in mute despair,
Then, frenzied, tore his snow white hair,
And loudly cried—'Child of my heart,
Can it be thus that we must part?
Can he we've ever loved so well
Have le't his father's home to dwell
With those whose only god was gold?
For which my darling's life they've sold.
Yes—yes! I feel these fears are true;
His mother's heart is broken, too;
And her whose love he long has slighted
Will fall a flower early blighted.'

"Having finished the above, she burst into a passionate flood of tears, which the honest Herbert did not seem to wish to interrupt. Language cannot paint the mingled emotions of love and pity which filled my heart, as the manners of the beautiful Millicent left not a doubt upon my mind that her reason had been impaired.

" ' Thy tale is indeed a sad one,' said I ; 'are the individuals of your narrative known to you ?'

" Millicent fixed upon me a penetrating glance, and sadly answered— ' Yes, I knew them once ; but Cedric Moreton is dead, and Millicent—ah, poor Millicent,' she sighed, ' still lives, a wretched mourner for his hapless fate. But the flowers are fading,' suddenly said she. ' I must away to plant fresh evergreens upon the grave of my beloved.'

" Starting up, she darted away with the swiftness of a fawn, and in an instant was out of sight of the cottage.

" ' Worthy Herbert,' said I, ' let me entreat of you not to hide from me the sorrow which seems to have overpowered the reason of your lovely child, and to have impressed the stamp of melancholy on your countenance.'

" ' I will not conceal it,' said Herbert, ' although its recital must tear open wounds which time has seemed partially to heal.'

" ' I would not willingly give pain, Herbert ; but I feel so lively an interest in the suffering angel who has just departed, that every incident of her life now seems to concern me.'

" ' Thou art indeed right, my young master ; the reason of my beloved Millicent has received so severe a shock, that I fear no time or circumstance will restore her to herself.'

" 'Dost thou not fear then, Herbert, some harm may befal one so lovely ?"

" What has she to fear ?'

" 'That, unprotected, she may meet insult from the rude and worthless.'

" ' There are none here, Sir William, so rude or base as to insult my poor witless child.'

" ' 'Tis well, good Herbert ; and your assertion speaks highly for the morality of the country.'

" ' Yes, my noble master, it gives me pleasure to say I can bear witness to the manly bearing of those individuals whose chief inheritance seems to be labour and honesty. But, to my narra-tive :—A few months after my taking possession of this cottage, I determined on enjoying solely the society of my beloved Millicent, from whom I had been parted since the death of her mother, which occurred in her childhood.'

" ' I marvel much, Herbert, that you have lived so long absent from her.'

" ''Twas the wish for my child's happiness which induced me to consent to her being so long absent from me. Short-sighted mortals that we are ; I little dreamt that by so doing I should occasion her future misery.'

" ' I dare not trust myself to think, Herbert, that the virtue of thy enchanting daughter has fallen a sacrifice to the treachery of some wealthy libertine.'

" ' No ; and I do thank the author of my being that I have cause firmly to believe the virtue of my child to be as pure as the virgin snow.'

" ' Thou hast relieved my heart, Herbert.'

" ' On my informing Lady Julia Walmington, her mistress, that it was my desire that Millicent should come to reside with me, she refused to listen to my wish, and on finding it my determination, the haughty beauty said, she hoped I should one day have cause to regret taking Millicent from her to be the inmate of a vulgar cottage.'

" ' Which wish, surely, good Herbert, you did not allow to give you uneasiness."

" ' At the time I did not, Sir William ; but her wish has since too truly been accomplished. My beloved Millicent had formed an attachment for the son of a wealthy farmer in the neighbourhood ; he was their only child ; upon him they had lavished love and kindness, but, as is too often the case, their love met with a poor return.

" ' Walter was possessed of every accomplishment that could lure the undiscerning to become his admirers. At hurling, wrestling, and in feats of strength, Walter was equalled by none; but he possessed not the all-necessary attribute of a pure, true heart, for he was equally skilled in guile and deception. The latter had been often painted in glowing colours to Millicent by our only relative, my sister Deborah, who had known him from his infancy. Vain

"" her admonitions. My gentle girl saw not a fault in him she loved so truly.

"' No—no, dear aunt,' she would say, ' you cannot know the noble heart of Walter, or you would, with me, believe him to be above deception.'

"' On being informed by my sister that she considered it necessary that I should forbid further intimacy between Walter and Millicent, I determined by all means in my power to prove to Milli that Walter was unworthy of her love; but so gentle and ardent were the assertions she made in the behalf of Walter, that I found it impossible to withstand against them.

"' Let me, dear father,' said she, ' prove him guilty of one unworthy action, and thy child will break the tie that has so long bound her.'

"' Soon—too soon—alas! had my poor Milli a sad proof of his depravity.

"' She was one evening returning from a friendly visit to a honest, but poor widow, when, in crossing a dell, she was affrighted by hearing several persons in converse, some using the most bitter imprecations and blasphemies.

"' Trembling, she stepped behind a spreading oak, in the hope that the speakers would pass on.

"' I tell you what,' said one, whose voice was too well known by Milli, ' thou art a set of weak-minded fools. What harm will a drop of blood do ye ?'

"' No—no, Master Walter,' cried a second, ' we care not how deep or dirty is the work set us, but we will not stain our hands with blood.'

"' Then ye are cowards !' cried Walter, with an oath : ' and although ye are paid for the work, I myself must do the deed.'

"' My poor frighted girl lingered not another instant, but hastened homeward, pale and breathless. A hundred times did she repeat the fearful and awful words of Walter; then would she, starting, shriek, ' No—no! it's a vile plot to deceive me.'

"' I knew not how to act. I obtained an interview with the father of Walter, and endeavoured to elicit from him whether or not he had any suspicions concerning the actions of his son; but I failed to obtain any information from which I could gain any satisfaction.

"' In a few days, however, it was discovered that the mansion of Sir Eustace Stapleton had been forcibly entered during the owner's absence, and a quantity of plate and valuable jewellery stolen; that Thomas, the old porter, had been shamefully maltreated, and that there were little hopes of his recovery. Words are, indeed, inadequate to describe the deep grief of my beloved child on hearing this.

"' On the following evening, Walter entered our cottage, pale and in terror. My Milli threw her snow-white arms around him.

"' Walter ! Walter !' shrieked she, ' swear that you are innocent.'

"' Innocent of what ?'

"' Bloodshed !' shrieked Milli.

"' Milli, thou art as evil-minded as the rest of my enemies. I have come to thee to tell thee how wickedly and strangely I am spoken of, and even here I find another accuser.'

"' No—no, my dear Walter,' returned Milli, ' I did not accuse you; but—but——'

"' But what ?' asked Walter, roughly.

"' I overheard your fearful words in crossing the glen, and this deed of blood seems strangely in accordance with them.'

"' Milli—Milli, thou art wrong. By Heavens——'

"' Before he had time to finish the sentence, our cottage was rudely entered by the officers of justice, who, showing their warrant for the apprehension of Walter, seized him on the spot.

"' A piercing cry burst from the lips of my beloved child—' He is innocent—he is innocent !' and she fell senseless as they dragged him from her arms.

"' One of the confederates had turned evidence against him. The old porter had died of the wound he had received, and Walter's life was sentenced in return for his guilty deeds.

"' I will not pain you by describing the anguish of his parents, myself, and beloved child : from the hour in which the dreadful sentence was put into execution the reason fled from the brain of my own dear child.

"' Now at short lucid intervals she believes herself a looker-on of the fearful scene, and considers Millicent and

Walter to have been her early friends, and with devoted friendship does she visit the grave of the one, and shed tears for the hapless sorrows of the other.

" 'Think you not,' cried the old man, sobbing aloud, when he had ended his recital, 'my sorrows have been deep enough to overshadow my once happy heart?'

" 'They have, they have, good Herbert,' said I; 'but calm the anguish of your feelings; the reason of thy child, I trust in God, will soon return.'

" Here the gentle Millicent again entered the cottage; in an instant she perceived the distress of her parent.

" 'Father, father!' said she, 'why do I see thee thus sad? I will not leave thee! Nay, nay, I will not leave thee.'

" 'Thy father, gentle maiden,' said I, 'is moved to pity by the sad tale of Walter and your young friend.'

" 'Ay,' sighed Milli, 'their love was indeed a hopeless one.'

" 'Methinks, fair maid,' said I, 'the lover scarce deserved the heart of your amiable friend.'

" A sudden gleam of reason seemed to dart across her brain, and she exclaimed, 'We are commanded to judge not, lest we be judged.'

" 'Good Herbert,' rejoined I, 'change of scene might do much to restore you both to your former selves. Come, then, consent to be my guests at——; it will give me pleasure to have the privilege of enjoying the society of yourself and your beloved daughter.'

"Herbert for a while refused; but at length yielded to my earnest entreaty, and on the following day we all three arrived at——. In a few months I had the happiness to behold the beautiful, gentle Millicent in the possession of her faculties, although a deep, calm melancholy settled on her features.

*   *   *   *

" Twelve months had passed since I first visited the cottage of Herbert Thompson; from that hour never had the features of the beautiful Millicent been absent from my heart; every letter I received from the honest Herbert informed me of the still increasing cheerfulness of my beloved.

" With what fond hope did my heart beat as I again entered their cottage: I was met with a hearty welcome from my friend, and a cheerful and smile from Millicent.

" I determined on spending a few weeks in the neighbourhood, during which period I endeavoured to gain the good wishes of the lovely Millicent, and proud am I to say that I succeeded to my utmost wish.

" I was reluctantly preparing for my departure, when I was hastily summoned to the cottage of old Herbert; upon my reaching it, I started in terror upon beholding our old and favoured domestic struggling with the mighty conqueror, Death.

" No painter could give an adequate description of the scene I then witnessed; the young and beautiful girl had sunk upon her knees, and was addressing a prayer to Heaven, while in her snow-white hand she held that of the dying parent: the setting sun cast his golden beams upon the features of the dying man, and descended across the figure of the prostrate Millicent, who seemed a being of a brighter sphere.

" For a few moments my utterance failed me; for, the lovely being rising from her knees, exclaimed, 'He comes not, and I must bear it all alone!'

" 'No, no, dear girl,' I replied, 'there is one present who will share thy every grief.'

" 'See, see!' continued she, 'he is dying.'

" Her voice seemed to recall the fast fleeting senses of Herbert.

" 'Thou art come, my worthy master,' said he, 'and I shall die happy.'

" I will pass over the last moments of the dying man: let it suffice you, Mr. Trueman, to know, that the little sylph-like form who just now glided to my side, and addressed me with, 'Do come, papa, we are almost tired of waiting for you. Mamma says she fears you will be ill by staying so long,' is the first-born of the once sorrowing, but now happy Millicent, whose unsophisticated heart has fully repaid me for choosing a wife from the humble walks of life, where I believe still many a worthy and gentle heart, equally deserving, is past by for those of less virtue, and though possessing wealth and beauty, yet want that essential charm so necessary to a married life—a spirit of meekness and devoid of guilt. You understand me, Mr. Trueman?"

"I'm d—d if I do," said the merchant. "I never heard such a cock-and-a-bull story in my life."

"You didn't?"

"No, I certainly didn't. What the deuce has it to do with your investment of a hundred thousand pounds, I should like to know?"

"Ah," said the duke. "I knew your great sagacity would make that remark, Mr. Trueman. I said to myself, Mr.

Trueman will say, 'What has all this to do with your intended investment of a hundred thousand pounds?' and you have said so. I rather think I am a little judge of character, Mr. Trueman."

"That you may be," said the merchant; "but I never knew such a roundabout manner of conducting business. Now, if you will have the kindness to come to the point, and let me know at once what investment you would prefer for the money—whether

in real securities or in shares. You understand?"

"Not exactly," said the duke. "Pray walk this way, Mr. Trueman, and please to enlighten me with regard to the nature of different securities,—a-hem!"

"I have no objection, my lord; but I should like previously to find my daughter."

"Your daughter is with the countess, of course. You cannot doubt her safety with such a *chaperon*. Pray

make your mind perfectly easy about her. This way, if you please, Mr. Trueman. So I hear from Hawksworth that you began the world with two-and-twopence?"

"Three-and-a-penny — three-and-a-penny," corrected Mathew Trueman. "I began the world, sir, with three-and-a-penny, and I have not made altogether a bad thing of that three-and-a-penny, though I say it as probably should not, sir—my lord, I mean."

CHAPTER XXXIII.

THE GARDENS. — THE SALOON. — THE INSULT AND THE RESCUE. —A TIMELY INTERPOSITION. — HAWKSWORTH'S VILLANY.

WHEN the Countess Algernon Mountfair de Lama Shrohalvoren Como de Medicis drew Grace Trueman's arm within hers, and separated her from her father, Grace certainly made rather a violent effort to save herself from being thus taken by storm by a perfect stranger, and had she not seen her father move off rapidly under the guidance of the "duke," she might have made a complete "scene" in the efforts she made to release herself; but what was she to do, unseconded, as she hoped to be, and ought to have been, by Mathew Trueman? In a moment he was out of sight, and Grace, with a sigh, gave up the idea of freeing herself from the countess's clutches until she should see him again, when she resolved, come what would, to insist upon rejoining him.

"My dear," said the countess, "I hope you are amused by this little *fête?*"

"It may be my want of taste," said Grace; "but I have seen nothing yet very amusing."

"Why, I confess, there has not been anything very absurd yet, my dear."

"Absurd?"

"Yes; absurdities are the only things I ever meet with, or expect to meet with, at these and similar occasions."

"I would rather," said Grace, "look higher for amusement than a passing folly."

"Ah, that's because you are not used to these things; but you will be in time, my dear."

"I much doubt it, madam; I rather dislike show and glitter than otherwise, and am too fond of home and domestic joys to frequent such places as this, except on pure compulsion."

"Compulsion, my dear?"

"Yes—I care not who knows it. I came here at the request, I may, indeed, say command, of my father. The owner of this place is no acquaintance of mine whatever."

Her ladyship gave a slight cough as she thought to herself, "you and the present owner of this place will be better acquainted soon." Then she added aloud—

"Let us take a walk round the gardens. We shall, no doubt, there meet your father in our circuit."

To this arrangement Grace could have no objection, and she allowed the countess to lead her from the saloon in which they were through a French window, and down a flight of steps into the garden. Here, notwithstanding Grace was so far from being pleased at her visit, and that her feelings were not in the best tune to admire anything she saw, she could not help being much struck with the rare beauty of the spot in which she stood.

The odours of thousands of delicious flowers filled the air with perfume, and the lights which were skilfully placed among the trees cast a fairy-like magic over the various tints of the leaves, making the scene look like some dream of romance, rather than a reality, got up by a profligate nobleman, and to be eventually paid for by the credulous Mathew Trueman, who, like hundreds of his class, showed the greatest acumen in raising a splendid fortune from nothing, only to spend it with a reckless indiscretion, such as no one would for a moment have believed him capable of.

"These gardens, I admit, are beautiful," said Grace.

"Yes," added the countess; "they are arranged with some taste, and were so arranged long before Lord Hawksworth ever set foot in them."

To this remark Grace was silent, for she did not wish the conversation, either for praise or censure, to turn upon the man she hated and despised, and whose house she only set foot in, in preference to coming to an open rupture with her father upon the subject.

"I perceive my dear," said the countess, "that you are no admirer of Lord Hawksworth?"

"Admirer, madam!"

"Well—well, I will change the term. I meant to say, that I perceive you dislike him."

"I do dislike him; and I beg that you will allow that expression of my dislike to conclude our dialogue concerning him, for to me it is an unwelcome and uninteresting theme."

"Certainly," said the countess. "I have no desire in the world to bore you about Hawksworth, but I am really dreadfully tired. Do indulge me so far as to step into this room and rest. It is quite secluded."

They were upon a lawn on the other side of the villa at this time, and the countess with the many names stepped up to a window which stood invitingly open down to the very ground.

Grace hesitated a moment, and then she thought to herself, "What have I to fear? One part of the house is as dangerous or as safe as the other." She then followed the countess into the room, which was truly a magnificent one.

There were splendid mirrors on every wall, and rich crimson silk hangings hung from the walls. The roon was nearly surrounded by costly couches, and from the centre hung a chandelier, the subdued light from the ground glasses of which shed a soft chastened brilliancy over every object.

"Well," said the countess, "we will rest ourselves here, at all events; but I am not disposed to catch cold from the window."

As she spoke she closed it, and the short, sharp snap with which it shut, showed that it did so with the aid of some spring.

Grace glanced a little anxiously at the window, and said—

"I did not feel any draught; and I think that really now, since accident does not seem disposed to throw my father in my way, I must seek him with all the diligence I may."

"I dare say, my dear, he is very agreeably occupied with the duke, my brother," said the countess. "Pray sit down on this sofa a moment, and then I will lead you back to the saloon."

Inwardly vexed that she had come so far, Grace did sit down, upon the assurance that it was but for a moment, for her natural suavity and good temper prevented her from offering all the opposition to the mock countess some more firm minds might have done.

Scarcely, however, had she been seated a moment, when from behind some of the hangings which reached to the ground a figure appeared, attired in a superb fancy Spanish costume, which absolutely blazed with sparkling gems.

A second glance told Grace that it was Lord Hawksworth she saw before her.

"Betrayed!" she cried, as she attempted to rise; but the countess rather rudely pushed her into her seat again, saying—

"Pho—pho, child. Afraid of a lover?"

"Madam," said Grace, "was it well done of you to bring me here? Have you no shame, woman?"

A flush of colour spread itself over the countess's face, becoming visible even through the paint that lay thickly on her cheeks, and with a forced laugh that had no gaiety, but much real bitterness in it, she left the room by a door, which she immediately slammed after her, leaving Grace a prisoner with Lord Hawksworth.

"My charming creature," said Hawksworth, "what a delightful opportunity is this to plead my passion."

Grace flew to the window, but it resisted all her efforts to open it, and she could not find the spring.

"Nay, my beauty," said Hawksworth, "you would never be so cruel as to leave me so soon? When we have had a little conversation, I will do myself the pleasure of escorting you to the common herd of guests, who are as inferior to you——"

"Peace, sir!" cried Grace, turning from the window, bending on Hawksworth such a look of haughty scorn, that his diminutive figure seemed to contract to less than its original dimensions. "Peace, I say! How dare you insult me by your fulsome speeches? I demand my liberty this instant, or you shall find that, weak girl as I am, I have that courage which will raise me above this persecution. My cries shall alarm the house."

"Capital, capital," exclaimed Hawksworth. "My dear, you are ten times more beautiful when you are in a rage than when calmness and serenity rest upon your brow."

"Help—help!" cried Grace.

Hawksworth laughed as he said—

"No one can possibly hear. A whole suite of apartments lie between you and the guests. My servants know better than to interfere with me. Come, now, I only want you to listen to me. You are a charming girl, a perfect city divinity, and I love you."

"You are a villain," said Grace, "and I scorn you. If you have one spark of gentlemanly feeling—one sentiment of honour in your whole composition, give me free egress from this place."

"By Jove! I've taken too much trouble and spent too much money to get you here, to let you go so easily. No nonsense now, Grace; I love you—adore you; and I would go through ten times what I have for one kiss from those sweet, pouting lips."

With a pang of horror, such as no pen can describe, Grace saw him advancing towards her.

"Hold—hold!" she cried, "yet a moment. Lord Hawksworth, can you be so dead to all shame—to all honour, as beneath your own roof to insult an unprotected girl? Can you be so great a blot upon the aristocracy you claim to belong to?"

"Just whatever you please," he replied, "always provided you will be mine."

"Never, never, never!" cried Grace. "Once more, sir, hear me; open this window now, and let me go, and I will keep locked within my own breast the occurrences of this night. I will promise even you so much."

"You are very kind," said Hawksworth, "but I don't happen to care one straw what you tell, nor who you tell—a kiss I will have. Haughty as you are, Grace Trueman, I will press my lips to yours, and think myself well repaid for all my trouble."

"Advance at your peril," said Grace; "I am weak, but surely Heaven will give me strength to repel a ruffian such as thou art."

"We shall see—we shall see."

He advanced two steps towards her, and Grace cried again as loudly as she could.

"Help—help—help!"

Hawksworth advanced another step.

"'Tis all in vain," he said, "you may spare your breath, Grace Trueman. No one will heed your cries."

Grace was not, however, without a hope that some one who would shrink from such iniquity as Hawksworth, might hear, and once more she raised her voice in a loud cry for assistance.

"Help—help!" she shouted, and seizing a book that happened to be close at hand, she dashed it with all the force she was capable of mustering through one of the panes of the window.

"Not even your breaking my windows will avail you," cried Hawksworth, as he moved a chair that was between him and Grace. "You are in my power, and I will now have my revenge for the scorn with which it has pleased you to treat me."

Scarcely had these words escaped Hawksworth's lips, when the French window was dashed in from without with such tremendous violence, as not to leave a whole pane in it, or an unfractured piece of the frame-work.

"Grace!" cried a voice.

The next moment she sunk into the arms of Rivers, who stood on the sill of the smashed window in an attitude of defence.

Before, then, another word could be spoken, there was the loud report of a pistol, the bullet from which passed close to the head of Rivers, for it had been fired by the coward Hawksworth, who had provided himself with arms, in case of being interrupted by any one in his interview with Grace.

The shot might have taken fatal effect, for Rivers, as he stood in the gap of the window, was a tolerably fair mark, had not Lord Hawksworth's aim been bewildered at that moment by the sudden entrance past Rivers of a figure in a cloak, hat, and a plume of feathers, who cried—

"A horse—a horse! my kingdom for a horse! Come ruin, come rack, at least we'll die with harness on our back. Hang out our banners on the outward walls, and give the enemy to the wild vultures of the Haunted Glen."

Our readers will have no difficulty in recognising Tom Hackey, who thus rushed into the splendid room, being by his precipitancy, in all probability, the means of saving the life of Rivers.

———

CHAPTER XXXIV.

THE CONFESSION.—MATHEW TRUEMAN AND GIRKINS.—THE FALSE STATEMENT.—A QUARREL.—GRACE'S RESOLUTION.

THERE was silence for a moment or two in that splendid room, for all were too full of their own feelings to speak. Then Rivers first cried in a voice that might have been heard far and near—

"Scoundrel—unmanly ruffian—trampler on hospitality! You shall now meet a punishment you desere. Tom, look to Grace, while I chastise this lordly ruffian."

The lordly ruffian, however, was not one of those who willingly would wait to run the risk of any such conflict as that which was promised him by the infuriated Rivers, who before then would have had him in his grasp, but that Grace clung to him with such frantic vehemence, that the gentle violence he could only use was far from sufficient to shake her off, and leave him at liberty.

Grace was fearful that her lover might be driven to excess, in his indignation at the treatment she had received, and she clung to him more eagerly each moment, for rather would she that twenty Hawksworths should escape the just punishment of their crimes, than that a hair of the head of him she loved should be injured.

The young lord, though, as we have remarked, waited not to run even the chance of punishment, for the moment he saw that his pistol-shot had failed in its attempt against the life of Rivers, he sprang through a concealed door, and made his escape.

"He's gone," said Tom; "let's storm the castle now. Act first—scene second—a jolly blow up. Hurrah! hurrah! hurrah!"

"Grace, Grace," said Rivers, "my own dear, precious Grace, speak to me. Tell me, dearest, you are not hurt. Grace, Grace."

"No, no, Rivers—Francis, I am quite well now," said Grace; "I was only terrified when you came so timely to my rescue; but let us be gone from this place; each minute passed has been

one of pain, and now they have become agonizing."

"Dearly shall that scoundrel answer for this night's work," exclaimed Rivers.

"Let him be—let him be," said Grace,—"he is most unworthy of your resentment. Perhaps all is for the best."

"The best, Grace?"

"Yes," she murmured, "for now surely my father must be able clearly to distinguish between the really brave and noble, and him who only pretends to those titles."

These words were not misunderstood by Rivers, and they awakened a hope in his mind that after all, as Grace said, the very circumstance that had filled him with so much anger and so much intense indignation, might be the means of thoroughly awakening the merchant's eyes to the real character of Hawksworth, and inducing him to discard all idea of allying with such a man his beautiful child for ever.

"Heaven send it may be as you suppose, dear Grace," said Rivers. "But tell me, is your father here?"

"He is, but I scarcely know where to find him."

"Leave that to us. Here, Tom, do you find Mr. Trueman, and bring him here directly."

"Oh, yes—of course," said Tom, "I'll do it; God bless you, Miss Grace. I would have eaten a hole bang through that Lord Hawksworth, before he should have frightened you. I'm off—I'll put a girdle round the earth in forty minutes.

'Merrily, merrily, shall I live now,
Under the blossom that hangs on the bough.'"

Tom darted through the window, and Rivers, taking Grace quietly by the hand, led her to the sofa she had so very recently occupied with the countess, saying,—

"You tremble, Grace. Sit down, and I will be your guard until your father comes."

Grace sat down upon the sofa, and then her feelings, which had been overwrought by the scene she had gone through, overcame her, and she burst into tears.

Rivers held one of her small hands

clasped in his—he pressed it to his lips.

"Grace—my own Grace," he said, "do not weep; you are safe now from the world, for a heart that must be laid low ere you should be harmed is ready to bleed in your defence. These tears fall upon my spirit, Grace, and almost madden me. Oh! that I had the villain in my grasp, who has thus caused them to flow. Be comforted, dearest; your father will be here shortly, and you can leave this hateful place, never again to look upon it."

Grace leant her head upon his arm, and her paroxysm of weeping gradually subsided.

"You are my preserver," she said, gently. "Oh! what do I not owe you?"

Rivers could not resist the impulse for one moment to clasp her to his heart; and let not our fair readers blame the beautiful Grace for submitting to the embrace, for a purer, nobler heart than that she was for one brief moment clasped to, never beat in human bosom. It was strange that such an interview as this should take place between these two young and attached beings at Lord Hawksworth's villa, and in the most superb and costly room thereof!

It then suddenly struck Grace as the most extraordinary thing of all, that Rivers should be there at all, and she said,—

"I owe very much to your timely rescue, but how is it that you are here? You and Tom too?"

"Dear Grace, it was Tom Hackey who was the principal means of bringing me here. He discovered where you were going, and succeeded in impressing me with an idea that there would be some danger to you from the importunities of Lord Hawksworth. We talked the matter over so long, that at length we determined to walk down to this place, and when we had done so it was an easy transition from the high road over a paling into these gardens, where, upon a rustic seat, Tom found the cloak and hat you saw him in."

"So, so, you came to protect me?"

"I did, Grace, and Heaven has blessed my purpose."

She looked up in his face for a moment, and if ever there was a look of love, that was one, and Rivers in his own heart translated it as such. He never felt such a gush of happiness in his life. He could have defied all care —all sorrow—all danger—then, with the consciousness that Grace looked upon him with eyes of affection, and properly, as she truly did, appreciated his love for her, which was one of those rare and beautiful passions knowing no guilt, and made up of sacrifices; for what would he not have adventured for the beautiful girl who was by his side?

At this moment a series of loud coughs met the ears of the lovers, and then a voice cried,—

"A—a—hem!" and the coughs continued.

Rivers could not suppress a smile, for he recognised the voice of Tom Hackey, and guessed the coughing to be a friendly device to let him know that Mathew Trueman was coming.

Tom had had less difficulty than he imagined he should have had in finding the merchant, for Mathew Trueman had become terribly tired of the duke, and had left him some time previously for the purpose of searching for Grace, whom he could find nowhere, as well as of seeing his lordship, who, to his great chagrin, had not yet shown himself in the saloon.

His astonishment at being suddenly laid hold of by Tom Hackey may be imagined but not described, and after the first bewildering moment, the merchant's impression was that nothing but a fire among his warehouses in Thames-street could possibly account for the appearance of Tom at Lord Hawksworth's *fete.*

"God bless me," he said. "There's a fire?"

"Worse," said Tom.

"Worse?"

"Yes—there's a vagabond!"

"A what?"

"A vagabond—a wretch! Follow me, and I will a tale unfold, whose slightest word shall harrow up thy soul, and make thy ancient hair to stand on end like quills upon the fretful porcupine. Follow—follow!"

"He's gone mad," muttered the merchant— "stark, staring mad."

"If ever," added Tom, "thou didst thy dear daughter love——"

"My daughter?"

"Ay, your daughter. Revenge, Mathew, revenge! You've come here with a white waistcoat and patent pumps to have Grace insulted,"

"Insulted! Who dared ——"

"My dear Mr. Trueman, so I've found you at last," said Girkins at this moment, seizing the merchant by both hands, and shaking them with fervour. "I hope you and your daughter are quite well?"

"I don't know that we are, Mr. Girkins," replied Trueman; "but I am busy now, sir, and cannot speak to you."

"Come on," said Tom, waving an imaginary truncheon in the air, and assuming the attitude and manner usually given to the ghost in Hamlet.

"But," persisted Girkins, "I have a most important message from my Lord Hawksworth."

"A message to me?"

"Yes, my dear sir. Pray step this way one moment, if you please."

Tom Hackey shook his head, but he comforted himself with the conviction that Grace and Rivers would neither of them mind waiting a little by themselves, even in the house of their worst enemy.

When Girkins had succeeded in getting Mathew Trueman into a corner, he said, with impressive earnestness—

"I have just seen my Lord Hawksworth, who has gone to make some change in his dress; but he charged me to seek you out, Mr. Trueman, and explain to you a little affair, which he trusts you will ascribe to right feeling on his part, and not to any want of that respect which he, in common with everybody else, feels for you as the first and most enlightened of British merchants. He begs me to say that, with your critical acumen and great powers of observation, you must have seen a feeling manifest in the whole of his behaviour of great admiration for your daughter Grace, from whose beauty a coronet would gather fresh lustre, and who would adorn the fairest court in the world."

"His lordship is—is really very kind," said the much-flattered Mathew Trueman.

"Ah, if you knew his heart tho-

roughly, you would indeed know how very true your words were. But to proceed: He told me to explain this little affair to you, and to add that he hoped he had not seriously offended you by a little circumstance which had entirely grown out of the warmth of his affection.

"What circumstance? I am quite sure his lordship would do nothing to offend me, although I did begin the world with three-and-a-penny."

"Certainly he would not; but it appears that, wandering about looking for you, he by chance came into a room where your daughter was alone."

"I am very glad of it," thought Mathew Trueman.

"His love, then," continued Girkins, "emboldening him, he told her how much he admired her, and would but have imprinted a respectful kiss upon her hand, when she became alarmed from some cause, and, springing from Heaven knows where, your clerk—ay, Mr. Trueman, your own clerk, Francis Rivers, accompanied by that lunatic there," pointing to Tom Hackey, "burst into the room, doing the most extensive damage, and affecting great merit for a pretended rescue of your daughter Grace. A rescue from Lord Hawksworth, an English nobleman, in his own house! I trust, Mr. Trueman, you see how very absurd this affair is, and how very ill Lord Hawksworth has been treated in it."

"My clerk—Rivers—Tom Hackey!" ejaculated Trueman. "Why, how, in the name of Heaven, came they here? I am quite bewildered; surely this is all a dream!"

"Indeed, Mr. Trueman, it is not, and there stands the identical Tom Hackey."

The merchant turned towards Tom, who again beckoned him "the way that he should go," exclaiming—

"Eye of snake and tongue of bat. Put in that—put in that. I consider you, Girkins, as one of the witches, I do; Lord Hawksworth's another, and I dare say there's some other rogue behind-hand to make the third."

"You scoundrel!" cried Trueman; "you are drunk, sir."

"Can't afford it," was Tom's pithy reply. "Are you a coming or not?"

"Excuse me to his lordship for a few

moments," said the merchant to Girkins; "I will see if Rivers really has had the unparalleled impudence to come here."

So saying, he hurried after Tom, who gave the warning coughs of his approach which we have mentioned. When he had got some little distance off, Mr. Girkins smiled quietly to himself, as he said—

"I think I have arranged that little matter. Hawksworth, by his precipitancy, very nearly ruined all. A serious quarrel just now with Mathew Trueman, before he has advanced the money, would be anything but an agreeable termination to the business, which as yet has given me more trouble than profit. However, this affair has brought matters to a climax as regards this Rivers, for Trueman, no doubt, will at once discharge him."

"Father!" cried Grace, as she sprung towards the merchant, the moment he entered the room through the broken window, "father, take me away from this house! Oh, do not let us stay here another moment."

"Why—why, what is the meaning of all this?"

"I have been insulted, father, by Lord Hawksworth, who you must now know for the villain he really is; and, but for the interposition of Mr. Rivers, I should have found no one near to rescue me."

"Oh, indeed," said Trueman, coldly. "Perhaps Mr. Rivers will be so good as to explain how he came here at all?"

"Sir," said Rivers, who was much nettled at the tone and manner of the merchant; "I am your clerk during the hours I have agreed to devote to your service, but out of those hours it is a mere matter of courtesy whether I explain to you my conduct or not."

"So, sir—so, sir—very good," cried Trueman. "Here you come, like a thief——"

"Mr. Trueman," cried Rivers, his eyes flashing with indignation, "were it not that I would pain your daughter, I would make you retract that word on your knees."

"Father, father," said Grace, "you know not what you say. 'Tis Mr. Rivers who has rescued me."

"Pho, pho, I know all about that. All nonsense, I tell you, absurd nonsense. I wonder, Grace, you could make yourself so ridiculous."

"Ridiculous?"

"Yes! Why—Lord Hawksworth only intended a little gallantry; upon my soul, the young ladies were not so terribly squeamish when I was a young man."

"In one word, father," said Grace, "were you or were you not cognisant of what has happened?"

"Oh, I've heard it."

"From Girkins," put in Tom Hackey.

"Thank Heaven," said Grace, for she felt instantly that her father must have been deceived by some version of the affair very different from the truth.

"What now?" cried Trueman. "Upon my word, Grace, I cannot make you out at all."

"Come hence at once, father, and I will explain all to you. Mr. Rivers, for my sake and your own, leave this place quickly. I am much beholden to you."

"Sir," said Trueman, "your intrusion here is the most abominable thing I ever heard of in the whole course of my life. You may go as soon as you like, and take that poor fool who you have induced to come with you away likewise. I am surprised at Lord Hawksworth's temper with you."

"Sir," replied Rivers, "you are labouring under some very great delusion at present, which I cannot pretend to explain. I will leave this place, because to me it is detestable; and remember, that your daughter is now under your protection, and do not leave her, as you have done, to the insults of a libertine nobleman, and the mere chance of a rescue by some one who may feel more acutely than yourself for her insulted honour. In the morning, Mr. Trueman, you will think differently of this affair."

"In the morning I will discharge you, sir, without a character."

Rivers made no reply to this, but turning to Grace, he said, "Farewell! Heaven guard you!"

"As for leaving here yet," said Trueman, "I don't intend it."

"Then here, father, obedience ceases," said Grace. "*I will* go home, and if you will not take me, I will beg the protection of Mr. Rivers."

Rage for the moment seemed to

CHAPTER XXXV.

THE MEETING ON BLACKHEATH.—THE ARMED MEN.—THE PROJECTED MURDER.—WILSON'S DESPAIR.

THE night was dark, and a cold wind swept along the ground, as Mark Hilliard departed to keep his appointment with the wretched Wilson on Blackheath. He walked from the counting-house over London-bridge, and then diving into a collection of narrow streets lying to the right of the main road, he sought out the most dismal and solitary-looking house he could find, and determined there to wait until it was time to proceed on his errand.

The house was as gloomy as the heart of Hilliard, wrapt as it was in its own gloom and misery, could possibly desire. Not a soul was in the low-roofed, dark, dingy-looking parlour; the windows did not seem to have been cleaned for a year or more; and taking it altogether, it was just the place for a man to retire

WILSON SHOOTS ONE OF THE GAMEKEEPERS ON BLACKHEATH.

to, and nurse the dark and terrible fancies of a guilty soul.

In the darkest corner of that dark room Hilliard crept, and having ordered some spirits, which were a long time being brought him by a tottering old woman, who was the only living thing apparently in the house beside himself, he gave himself up to the contemplation of his project for disposing of Wilson by murdering him.

"Curse on my folly," he muttered, "for associating myself with such a cowardly hound. He will bring both me and himself to destruction, if I do not at once put an end to the danger with his life. How shall I do it? How shall I do it?"

"Here's your brandy, sir," said the old woman at this moment, as she placed a glass and a measure on the table.

"How is it, there seems no one but you here?" asked Hilliard.

"The landlord's in prison for debt, and his wife's ill up stairs, so as I come charing now and then, I serve anybody that comes in."

"Ah, very well—there's the money. Some folks are miserable as well as myself," thought Hilliard as the old woman slowly left the parlour. "But how is this murder to be done? Murder? What made me call it by that fearful name? Surely it is a necessary act for my own preservation, and then becomes self-defence."

For some hours he thus sat in solitude, with no communion but his own fearful thoughts. The death of Wilson he was resolved upon, but it seemed to him that were he to sit in that old parlour for an age he should never be able to devise the means of accomplishing his fell purpose. Then he rose and walked into the high road, proceeding at a slow lounging pace towards Greenwich, thinking that the exercise of walking would amuse his thoughts, and possibly render them less painful.

He had not walked above a mile when he was overtaken by one of the short stages, and hailing it, he clambered upon its roof, and was rapidly whirled down the wearisome length of the Old Kent-road.

The night was sufficiently dark to shroud all objects in obscurity, and although Hilliard sat on the coach with several persons, he could not distinguish the faces of any of them, nor, what was probably of more importance, could they distinguish his countenance; had they done so, the conversation which ensued, and to which he listened with breathless attention, and an anxiety that must have been evident in his face, would not have proceeded so glibly and easily.

"So, that man has not been caught yet," said one.

"What man?" said another.

"That Wilson, the lawyer's clerk, you know, that murdered his master in New Inn. It's wonderful to me they don't take him; he can't be far off."

"It will be wonderful to me," observed a third person, "if he be not taken before to-morrow morning."

Hilliard nearly fell from the coach with the sudden start he gave.

"Indeed! How's that?" said the others in a breath.

"Why, an hour or two ago I met Stevens, the officer, and he said to me, 'Well, I think we shall have that fellow who murdered Mr. Noble, soon.' 'Indeed!' says I. 'Yes,' he added, 'we have received positive information that he has been seen in the neighbourhood of Greenwich, or, at all events, somebody so like him as to be well worth looking after.' He mentioned it to me because he knew I lived at Greenwich, and would be more interesting to me on that account."

"Of course," said one of the first speakers. "Well, I do hope they will catch him, for a more atrocious murder has not been committed now for many years."

"You are right, sir. That Wilson will he hung, as sure as fate. He cannot escape long."

"That is certain, he cannot. I'm further told that Stevens intends to make an attempt at his capture to--night, and I dare say he is at Greenwich by this time."

It is needless to say with what breathless attention Hilliard listened to this dialogue, or how deeply he felt himself affected by it. The conversation now turned upon other topics, and the few miles the coach had to go before it reached Greenwich seemed interminable to him. His brain felt as if it were on fire, and when at length the vehicle drew up at the coach-office in the High-street, the senses of Hilliard were in so shattered a condition that he could scarcely dismount from the roof.

With some difficulty, however, he did contrive to do so, and paying his fare, he hastily dived down a narrow, dark turning, which presented itself to him within a few paces of where he had alighted.

When he had got some distance from the coach, he paused to breathe again, and collect his faculties to think what he should do in the emergency that had arisen. If Wilson was taken, he, Hilliard considered himself as a doomed man, for he made certain that weakness or despair would induce his weak-minded associate in crime, upon very little persuasion, to confess the whole particulars of the murder, and so involve him, Hilliard, past human extrication.

"What on earth can I do," he said, "in this dilemma? He may even now be taken, and, if so, my return to London will be the signal for my immediate arrest. I must kill him if he be still at large, as my only chance of escape." It still, however, wanted nearly two hours to twelve o'clock, when he had appointed to meet Wilson, and rather than wander about the town he resolved to proceed at once to the heath, with the hope that his victim might possibly be hiding about the spot he had indicated as their place of meeting, in which case, he, Hilliard, might be able to take his life, and then get back to town without exciting suspicion.

"If he be still at large, he will hear my whistle," thought Hilliard, "and then I can make short work of him."

He walked on down the narrow turning, for he saw the blaze of lights at the farther end of it, and conjectured rightly that it led into one of the principal thoroughfares of the town, from whence he could find his way to Blackheath. Hilliard, however, required constant stimulants to keep him from sinking, and he turned into the first public-house he saw for the purpose of procuring more liquor, without which he felt he should never be able to go through with the business he had in hand.

Standing at the bar of the house were four men, having the appearance of gamekeepers, who were drinking merrily and noisily, and in the bar were several guns, which the landlord one by one handed over to them, saying:—

"Well, you will have a pleasant walk to-night, and both you and your masters will have a fine day's sport to-morrow, I have no doubt."

"Ay," said one, "there's no doubt of that. Here's half-a-dozen guns to carry among us; now, we must take the two extra ones by turns."

"Are you going across the heath?" said a stout man, attired in a half-sporting costume, who was just within the bar, and had been drinking something with the landlord.

"Yes, we are," one replied.

"Then I tell you what; my name's Stevens, I'm a Bow street officer, and have come down to try and hunt out Wilson, the murderer."

"He who murdered the old gentleman in New Inn?"

"Yes. We have had information that he has been seen lurking about the heath. Now, my lads, there are not many hiding-places on Blackheath, and as you are going across it there will be five of us, and by straggling a little we can hunt him out of any bush he may be concealed in. What say you to it?"

"I'm willing," said one.

"And I," said another. "Hang the fellow, I'd go out of my way any day to take a murderer."

"Or a fellow as poaches," exclaimed a third.

"Then we'll have a glass round," said the officer, "at my expense, and be off."

Hilliard stepped noiselessly from the house without ordering anything, for he had not been noticed by the landlord, as the bar was completely blocked up by the four men.

With a face as pale as death, and limbs that trembled under him as he walked, Hilliard staggered down the street till he came to another public-house, into which he went, and ordering some hot brandy-and-water, drank it off at a draught. He then, with a steadier step and more assured air, hastened towards Blackheath, in the hope that he should meet Wilson before it was too late.

In a breast-pocket of Hilliard's coat there were two articles which he took extraordinary care of—one was a double-barrelled loaded pistol, and the other, strange to say, was the newspaper which first gave an account of the murder of Mr. Noble. He could not part with that; to him it had a fearful interest, and he carried it about him, as if compelled to do so by some decree of Providence he could not contend against.

Every few minutes he would pause to listen if he could hear the approaching footsteps of the party he had left in the public-house, but all was still on the solitary road he was pursuing, and which wound round the park, under tall trees, and past the protecting walls of the gardens which were attached to the numerous villas that were dotted al along the road. He felt satisfied that he had got considerably ahead of the men whom he had so much to fear.

"I may still baulk them," he said; "still extricate myself from this alarming difficulty. Wilson's dead body may be found, and they may suppose he has committed suicide through dread of the punishment of his supposed crime, so shall I avoid all suspicion, and in a short time the whole affair will blow over, and become forgotten."

In about half an hour or less time Hilliard reached the heath itself—an impenetrable darkness seemed to cover it like a funeral pall. He had the greatest difficulty in finding the path which he had mentioned to Wilson; but when he did, he pursued it carefully for some distance, with his hand plunged into his breast-coat pocket, grasping the pistol with which he intended to murder his criminal companion.

Suddenly now he paused, for he thought that far off in the direction of the road he had come he heard the sound of voices, and then distinct laughter come upon his ears.

"They come—they come," he muttered; "they are making merry over their projected capture, or they are assuming a careless manner to blind Wilson to their real object."

He then took a whistle from his pocket, and blew twice upon it, but there was no answering sound; and, with a muttered curse that Wilson did not happen to be close at hand, he walked hurriedly onwards along the path towards Shooter's Hill.

After going some couple of hundred yards, Hilliard again blew his whistle, but with the like ill success, and now he saw that he should soon be quite across the heath, for not far in advance of him he observed a high earthen bank, which enclosed the garden of a cottage that was upon the skirts of the waste land.

A little to his left was a large tree, or what appeared to be such in the darkness, although three or four trees growing close together formed the mass of vegetation he took for one only.

It struck him immediately that this was a very likely place for Wilson to be hiding in; but before he again blew the whistle, he laid his ear to the ground, and listened attentively to discover the approaching footsteps of his foes, who he felt sure were close upon his track. He heard one cry to another—

"Hilloa! Bob, any luck?"

"No," said a voice at some distance in another direction. "What do you bring it in?"

"Nothing—nothing; I shall push on to the hill."

Hilliard darted forward, for the voice of him who spoke last sounded very near at hand. He placed the whistle to his lips, and blew faintly twice upon it. There was a slight movement among the trees, and a voice, which trembled so that Hilliard scarcely recognised it for Wilson's, said—

"What's the hour?" as had been agreed upon between them as a signal.

"Hist! hist!" said Hilliard. "Come out; it is I."

There was a shuffling of feet, and Wilson was at the side of his arch tempter.

"There are men on the heath," whispered Hilliard, as he still held the hilt of the pistol in his hand, "who are even now seeking you."

"Seeking me? Oh, God!"

"Yes; you have been seen, and are now hunted like a wild beast."

"Oh, that I were dead!—Oh, that I were dead!" groaned Wilson.

"Are you so wretched?"

"I am—I am."

"Then why not end your miseries and life together?"

"If I survive this night I will throw myself into the river. I have determined on that."

"You swear you will?" said Hilliard, who shrunk from the murder he contemplated with a cowardly fear, rather than any dislike to the deed as a deed.

"I will—I will! What is that?"

Both Hilliard and Wilson shrunk back behind the trees as the slow steps of a man close at hand alarmed them with the thought that it was an enemy, and so it was, as we shall see.

CHAPTER XXXVI.

THE MURDER—WILSON'S CAPTURE.— THE LOCK-UP AT GREENWICH.—THE STRONG ROOM.

"HILLIARD, Hilliard!" gasped Wilson, "do not let them take me. Oh, save me from them."

"You will drown yourself?" said Hilliard.

"As Heaven is my judge, I will."

Hilliard was silent for a moment, and dark thoughts rapidly came across his brain.

"These men will surely shoot him," he thought, "if they have any fancy that he is resisting them. Better they shoot him than I—I don't want to have another murder on my mind—for nothing, too. He comes—he comes. The foremost of those who would take Wilson and destroy me."

At the moment that these thoughts passed with the rapidity of lightning through the brain of Hilliard, from a sudden break in the clouds there streamed forth the light of a nearly full moon upon the scene, lighting up the heath, the cottages, and every object with a brilliancy that rendered the chance of escape now perfectly absurd.

Within half-a-dozen paces of the tree stood one of the gamekeepers, with two guns in his hand. He was looking about, and began apparently to admire the beautiful moonlight, for he turned his face up to the sky, and looked at the bright shining disc as he said in a low voice—

"Well, who would have thought of the moon coming out in this way, after such an uncommonly dark evening, too!"

Hilliard drew the pistol from his breast, and placed it in the hands of Wilson.

"Shoot him," he whispered, "and you will be quite safe. Shoot him, Wilson."

"I—I?" said Wilson.

"Yes—shoot him now. You cannot have a better mark. He must shoot you, or you must shoot him. To prevent yourself from dying a much more terrible death than you purpose, or anticipate, you must shoot him as he stands now."

Wilson's mind was evidently wandering, and he muttered—

"The moon—the moon: That has betrayed me."

The man now turned his back upon the clump of trees, and called out in a loud voice to his comrades—

"Hilloa!—Hilloa! There's plenty of light now. Come on—come on."

"Now—now," whispered Hilliard, "shoot him now."

Scarcely, if at all, knowing what he was doing, Wilson presented the pistol and pulled the trigger. A sharp report rang upon the night air, and with a loud cry, the man fell upon his face weltering in his blood.

Hilliard darted out of the shadow of the trees in a moment, and seizing one of the guns, he placed it in Wilson's hands, saying—

"Present it at them, and you are safe."

Wilson stood like a statue, so bewildered was he, with the gun presented down the pathway, in the direction the men were fast approaching from. Before, however, any of them could reach the scene of action, Hilliard clambered over the mud bank which enclosed the garden close at hand, and muttering to himself—

"They will surely shoot him, and I shall be spared all trouble," he crouched down so as to be completely hidden from observation.

The other three men and the officer had been straggling over the heath, beating the bushes wherever they seemed thick enough to conceal any one; but at the report of the pistol they one and all hurried to the spot from whence it proceeded, and stood for a moment paralysed with astonishment as they faced Wilson with the gun presented at them over the dead body of their comrade.

"That's him," cried the officer.

"D—n him, he has shot Williams," said one of the gamekeepers. "He'll have one of us down now."

"Off—off—don't kill me—don't kill me," said Wilson, "leave me alone, and I'll drown myself to-morrow. Spare me—spare me, now! I sware to drown myself to-morrow."

"Lay down the gun, or we'll fire," cried the officer.

"Till to-morrow—till to-morrow," gasped Wilson. "Oh, spare me till to-morrow."

The officer made a rush forward, and to the despair of Hilliard, Wilson did not fire, which had he done would in all probability have insured his destruction. He allowed the officer to lay hold of the gun and wrest it from his hands, without offering the least resistance.

"Lost—lost!" groaned Hilliard, as he slid down the bank into the garden, and lay concealed in a bed of flowers.

"You will not kill me," said Wilson, "let me be till to-morrow—or take me now to the river's edge, and you shall see me drown."

The officer, with all the dexterity he acquired by long practice, placed a pair of handcuffs on Wilson's wrists, while the three gamekeepers knelt down by the body of their murdered comrade, and ascertained that life was quite extinct.

"D—n him!" cried one, seizing his gun, "I will blow his brains out now, for this job."

"None of that, if you please," said the officer, "just leave him alone. He'll swing for this job, if not for the other. You must all come back now to Greenwich to be evidence."

"That we will, and if he could be hung to-morrow morning," said one, "it would be so much the better."

"Come on," said the officer to Wilson, "you've made a nice night's work of it, my friend."

"You will not kill me?" said Wilson.

"Not such a d—d flat," was the reply.

"Then I will drown myself to-morrow, according to my promise; to-morrow—to-morrow."

"I say," remarked the officer, "between you and me, I think as he's a little touched here," pointing to his head as he spoke.

"If I thought he'd get off on any such account, I'd shoot him here, whether you like it or not."

"No—no, he mustn't get off; never fear, he'll be hung as safe as ninepence. Why, last Old Bailey sessions that was, a feller tried to get off for murdering of his wife and kid, cos he said as he was a *monymania*; but it wouldn't do

for the judge. He says as purlitely as possible, 'you be hanged,' and he was hanged, as this here bright piece of goods will be, you may take your solemn Davy."

"I hope so."

"You may make uncommon sure; but let's push on; we shall have to knock up one o' the Grinidge beaks about this affair. If it hadn't been as he's shot one o' you, I'd have taken him right on to London, by vartue o' my warrant; but here's another affair, you see, as belongs to Grinidge."

"That's true enough, and there's an end of poor Williams."

Wilson's mind was evidently affected, for he did not seem at all conscious of his situation, but kept muttering in a low tone of voice—

"They will not kill me to-night, if I promise to drown myself to-morrow, and I will—I will—I will."

When the party reached the town of Greenwich, they halted at the first watch-house they came to, and the officer from London requested the constable of the night to have a magistrate called up in order to get his authority for carrying the prisoner on to London.

"Why can't you stay where you are, and make yourselves all comfortable till morning?" said the night constable. "Their worships won't be over well pleased at being called up when the prisoner can be kept quite safe this lock-up."

"Do you think so?"

"I'm sure of it, and what's more, you may take my word for it, all they'd do, would be to remand him till to-morrow morning; so you'd have all your trouble for nothing."

"Will he be safe here?" asked one of the gamekeepers, "for I wouldn't have him get away again for all I am worth, not that that's much."

"Oh, he's half a fool, or mad," said the officer. "He'll be safe enough, I dare say. Here, it's only five minutes to one o'clock, suppose we take the night constable's advice and sit up with him till daylight?"

"You can't do better, gentlemen."

"What will our masters say to us for not being at the preserves in the morning?" said one of the men.

"Why, one of you had better go on, and tell them what has happened," suggested the officer. "You know your evidnce will be wanted in the morning."

"Who'll go?" was the general question now among them, until one said—

"I will. It's a pity we all should get a bad name to-morrow, for a thing like this that we can't help; so I'll volunteer to go and tell the whole story. Good-night, or rather morning, comrades. I'll be back as soon as I can get away to-morrow, and my evidence won't be wanted, I daresay, for it would only be the same as your own, for one of us didn't see more than another."

"That's true enough," remarked the officer. "The testimony of two of you and myself will be quite enough."

"Then, good-by, comrades."

"Good-by—good-by!"

"I know what he's gone for," said one.

"What?"

"Why, he and poor Williams were very great friends, and he isn't satisfied to have his body laying by the trees where we placed it."

"Now, Mr. Night-constable," said the officer, "I should like to see where my prisoner is to be placed before I take the darbies off him."

"Come on, then, and I will show you."

The night-constable preceded the officer and Wilson, with a lamp in one hand and a bunch of keys in the other, while the wretched prisoner still kept muttering—

"To-morrow—to-morrow—I will keep my oath, and drown myself in the river to-morrow."

"Indeed, but you won't, my fine fellow," said the night-constable, "for we don't mean to give you such an opportunity of cheating the hangman."

"I will—I will," groaned Wilson.

He was then placed in a small room, which had but one little boarded window to it, and that was far out of reach.

"He'll be as safe here as in Newgate," said the constable; "I consider this as a stronger room than our blackhole, which is only fit for drunken people."

"What's above here?" asked the officer.

"Another room such as this, facing the street."

"Is it secure?"

"Yes; but if it wasn't, how the devil is he to get there from here?"

"Why, not easily, I dare say. Well, well, we will leave him here, and I dare say for the few hours he will have to stay, he will be safe enough."

The officer then took off the handcuffs from the wrists of Wilson, who still kept reiterating his promise to drown himself on the morrow, and, in a few moments the unhappy man was left in total darkness, and to his own gloomy meditations, if his state of mind would permit him the exercise of thought at all, which was very doubtful.

The officer from London, and the Greenwich constable, now hastened back to the comfortable room they had left, and sending for some liquor, they prepared, along with the gamekeepers, to pass a pleasant evening, for the murder of a fellow-creature had but little effect on those rough men.

The discourse which they held turned upon crime, and there was not a murder for the previous twenty years that was not brought upon the *tapis*, and freely commented on by the assembled party.

"Well," remarked the night-constable, "this fellow will swing if ever one did. He seemed a little frightened-looking chap, too, to have done two murders in his time."

"He does," said one of the gamekeepers, "and if I hadn't seen him with my own eyes, fire the gun, I shouldn't have believed him the sort of man to do it."

"Ah," remarked the constable, with a sagacious shake of the head. "You never know how those quiet fellows can come out, till they does."

"That's true enough—pass the ale."

In this and such like discourse they passed more than an hour, while the miserable Wilson was a prey to feelings of the most agonised description. His was a mind which could ill stand the shocks to which it had been subjected, and it was clear that it had in a great measure given way beneath the pressure to which it was unequal.

After he had been left by the constables and gamekeepers in the solitary room to which he had been conveyed, he sat for some time with his head resting on his hands, as motionless as a corpse, and had it not been that at intervals he groaned deeply, any one who saw him might well have supposed that life had fled, and he had gone to render up his awful accounts to the Maker and Judge of all things.

The boisterous conversation from the common room in which his captors were assembled, came clearly to his ears, and oh, how it jarred with the feelings of the murderer's heart, to hear those tones of half hilarity in which the discussion on the interesting theme they had hit upon was carried on.

After a long time he spoke in a low hollow voice, such as might issue from the grave—

"To-morrow—to-morrow," were his words, "they will let me go to drown myself to-morrow. They will surely let me. There is blood now upon my hands—blood upon my brain—upon my heart. I am a murderer. The lightnings of Heaven seek out such as I am. The vengeance of God falls upon such heads as mine. A murderer—a murderer!"

A fearful spasm shook his frame, and he trembled convulsively for several seconds, after which he spoke not, but rocking to and fro as he sat, he continued to moan at intervals like one in acute bodily anguish, who was trying to suppress the manifestations of all he suffered.

Death to such a man as Wilson would indeed have been a boon, for what now was life to him, but a long protracted frightful dream of pain?

CHAPTER XXXVII.

HILLIARD AFTER THE MURDER.—THE ESCAPE FROM THE LOCK UP AT GREENWICH.—WILSON'S AGONY AND DESPAIR.

WHEN Hilliard got over the bank and dropped into the garden on the other side, he was in such a state of fever that had Wilson denounced him on the spot he was scarcely in a condition to have made the least effort at resistance or escape from his enemies. He fully believed that in his agitation and the agony of his feelings, Wilson would call upon him by name, and that his capture would immediately follow. He clasped his hands upon his head, as if to calm the tumultuous throbbing of his brain and enable him to think of some spurious tale to tell that might screen him in his hour of need; but such was his absolute fright, that at the moment his wits seemed to have deserted him completely, and the wily, scheming villain could think of nothing which would be at all likely to meet the least credence from the gamekeepers.

Fortunately for him, Hilliard, however, the danger he apprehended was only in his own imagination, for not seeing him, Wilson thought not of calling upon him for help, and the idea of denouncing him crossed not his mind at all under any circumstances. To drown himself, and so end all his miseries, was the one great impulse of the mind of the wretched Wilson, and in that the thought even of Hilliard and the manner in which he had tempted him, Wilson, into crime, was completely submerged.

It was nearly half an hour after the party had left with Wilson in their charge, before Hilliard summoned courage to leave his hiding-place, and emerge once more upon the open heath. The moon was then riding in a cloudless sky, and a more lovely night had never come out of the heavens.

Far and near the silvery light made all objects clearly visible, and with a more defined and sharper outline than the sunlight, which gives light to so many vapours that the cold moon's rays cannot influence.

The gloomy-looking tower on Shooter's Hill looked as if it were plated with burnished silver, and there was not a tree, a flower, or a blade of grass, that had not borrowed some soft rays of the chaste light to make them beautiful, and tip their trembling edges with a sparkling lustre.

Oh, how much rather would Hilliard that that night had been bleak and dark as his own heart! That beautiful moonlight but ill accorded with the wild murderous feelings of such a breast as his.

When he dropped on the heath from the embankment, he would fain have avoided the sight which an irresistible impulse induced him eagerly to seek, namely, the body of the murdered man, which had been removed under cover of a hedge by his companions until the morning.

Starting at his own shadow, and with a feeling at his heart as if a cold hand were placed upon it, Hilliard slowly walked to the spot where the murder had been committed. It was partially devoid of grass, and where that was the case, dark crimson stains upon the earth showed where the blood of the victim had flowed from his wound.

Then Hilliard glanced towards the spot where the body lay, and he saw the dark still object that but so short a time before had been instinct with life, and health, and energy.

"Well, well," he muttered, "I did not kill *him*. This is no deed of mine; 'twas Wilson's hand that laid this man low, not mine: no one can accuse me of it. What have I to do with it?—

THE CURIOSITY OF WOMAN INDUCES A DISCOVERY.

Why do I terrify myself by coming to look at him?—But what shall 1 do to save myself from my great danger now? Oh! fool, fool that I was to shrink from taking Wilson's life when it was in my power! Then I should have been safe; but now—now—What may be the tale he will tell to-morrow, even if to-night it remains locked in his own breast, from a want of being urged, as he will be, to tell all? Some cursed, meddling man will wring from him what will place me on the gallows! Ha! what sound is that? Some one coming? Yes; it must be. A chance passenger, in all likelihood."

A footstep was evidently approaching from the direction of Greenwich, and Hilliard strove to appear as much at his ease as possible, as he walked with a slow, studied, careless step, to meet whoever was coming, which he thought better than going in the same direction.

No. 17.

The footstep was that of the game-keeper who had volunteered to go and excuse his comrades to their masters in the morning, when they were to meet for a day's sport. His steps were slow and solemn as he came near the spot where the murder had been committed; and when his eye fell upon the form of Hilliard, he said—

"Hilloa! Who goes there?"

Hilliard's heart sunk within him, as he replied, faintly—

"A friend. Why am I questioned thus on the highway?"

"Have you seen a dead body close at hand here?"

"No, no," said Hilliard. "Dead body? No; I have come straight on, and am going to Greenwich."

"There has been a murder here to-night."

"A murder?"

"Yes; a friend of mine has been shot. There lie his poor remains."

"Who—shot—him?"

"One Wilson—a fellow we were all of us trying to apprehend for another murder."

"He must be a sad ruffian."

"Sad, indeed! My comrades are in Greenwich; but I can't leave him I have known so long, and passed many a pleasant hour with, alone on the heath here, though he is dead. No; I'll watch him till they come in the morning and take him somewhere else."

The man, as he spoke, let the butt of his gun fall to the ground with a heavy blow, and then leaning on the weapon, he stood gazing on the lifeless form of his companion in silent sorrow.

Hilliard did not speak for some minutes, for, exceedingly anxious as he was to procure information from the man as to what had passed with Wilson since his apprehension, he was still alarmed at the notion that in his questions the gamekeeper might discover some unusual interest in the affair, and suspect him of knowing more about it than he chose to tell. It was, there-fore, with an indifferent air that carried him to the other extreme, that Hilliard said—

"You have the murderer secure, I hope?"

"We have. He is locked up at Greenwich for to-night. To-morrow will, I hope, see him in Newgate."

"Yes, of course. Locked up in the watch-house?"

"Yes."

"He must be a hardened villain; I hope he has made a clean breast of it and confessed his crimes, and who his associates are, if he had any."

"Nay, I know not," said the game-keeper. "When I came away he seemed half stupid and half mad. We could get nothing out of him, but that he intended, if we would let him go, to drown himself to-morrow."

"Indeed."

"Yes, but he can't have the chance, I should say."

"No—no, certainly. A great vil-lain—good-night, friend, good-night."

"Good-night," said the gamekeeper, and Hilliard slowly walked away towards Greenwich.

"In the watch-house at Greenwich," he muttered, "and has confessed no-thing. I know that watch-house well. 'Tis a place of no great security. If—if I could but rescue him from it before the morning, and then kill him, all might be well—quite well. Is such a thing possible? We shall see—we shall see."

He now walked rapidly onwards until he came to the neighbourhood where Wilson was held in confinement, when he saw the watch-house door open, and a man came out. Hilliard watched him to a neighbouring public-house, at which he stopped, and the door being opened to him, he went in, and presently re-turned with a tin can and some glasses, with which he hastened back to the watch-house.

"My friend," said Hilliard, "are you a constable?"

"No, I ain't," said the man, "but what then?"

"Why, there's a dead body lying on Blackheath."

"Oh, we know that. We've got the murderer safe enough; he's in the strong-room at the watch-house."

"In the black hole, you mean?"

"No, the strong room."

"Ah, that at the back of the common room?"

"I should think so. He's booked for Newgate. So, you saw the body?"

"I did, as I came across the heath, and frightened enough I was."

"No doubt, no doubt. Well, we've done all we can. We have taken the murderer, and mean to take care of him."

"Oh, he must have had some accomplice."

"No—no, quite alone. There was nobody else. He did it all by himself."

"Indeed! What wickedness there is in the world. Good-night."

"It's good morning now, friend," said the man, as he hastened onward to the watch-house, within which in another minute he was safely housed.

Hilliard stood for some time in deep thought. Then he muttered to himself—

"The strong room. I recollect well when once confined there along with an acquaintance for a street brawl, here in this very place, remarking that the only way to escape from that room would be by getting through the ceiling into the room above, and then dropping into the street from its window, which is perfectly unsecured; but then it was impossible to get through the ceiling from below, and hence the carelessness of the room above, and the reliance in the strength of the strong room. Humph! From the room above, though, the difficulty would vanish, and could I, while the men are drinking in the common room, make a hole in the ceiling of that in which Wilson is confined, I might rescue him. 'Twere surely worth my risk. He must be rescued from his present situation or I cannot return to London, for to-morrow he may tell all, and ensure my instant apprehension. It shall be tried."

With this resolve, Hilliard proceeded to the door of the watch-house, at which he listened attentively, and could hear the murmur of many voices.

"Talk on, talk on," he muttered, "it is better for my project that you should."

He then went to the corner of the house, where he knew that fire-ladders were kept in case of need. These were not secured, except by a chain that passed round them, in such a manner that they could easily be lifted out, and Hilliard, selecting the very smallest, after ascertaining that no passenger was at hand, carefully drew it from its place, and with an intrepidity which only the extreme urgency of the case could have invested him with, he placed it against the window of the room, which he knew was over that in which Wilson was confined, and rapidly ascended.

The house was curiously constructed. One part was rounded towards the street, and in this was the principal door-way, which was not the one at which offenders were brought in. A commoner entrance, a few paces to the right, was the one that led to the common room as it was called, and beyond that common room was the strong room, while to the left-hand side of it adjoined a parlour, that the principal entrance led to direct, thus making three rooms on the ground floor. Now, the first floor was only two rooms—that is, one over the common room, and of the same size and shape, and one other, which went over the parlour and the strong room, both without any division.

The reader will now understand that it was to the window of this large room to which Hilliard placed his ladder, from the very door-step of the principal entrance.

Above that door was a lamp, and Hilliard found no difficuly, by the assistance of its iron frames and supports, in clambering in at the window, which, from a sense of the security of the room, was unfastened. He then drew the ladder carefully flat against the front of the house, and tied it by a piece of string to one of the iron supports of the lamp, so that if any chance passenger had seen it, it had far from a suspicious appearance.

He then closed the window, and stood alone in the large room that ran over the parlour and strong room below it.

The lamp shed a few of its beams into the apartment, and placing himself, then, in such a position as to have the full advantage of them, Hilliard drew from his pocket the pistol with which he had intended to take the life of the wretched man he was now so intent upon rescuing from his place of confinement, and touching a spring, he released a short thick dagger from the side of the barrel, which projected about four inches from the muzzle of the weapon, and being held by the spring, formed a very powerful weapon.

"Upon the temper of this bit of steel," muttered Hilliard, "all must depend."

He then knelt down on the floor, which was not covered by any carpet, and began to feel carefully about the boarding. For some time he continued his search, and then rising with an air of disappointment, he took an exceedingly small dark lantern from his pocket, and with the smallest possible noise, lit it by the aid of a phosphorus match.

He kept the lens of the lantern carefully covered from the window, and then he ran it along board after board of the flooring, until he came to a part where a join had been effected. He then stooped, and inserting the point of the dagger with which the pistol was furnished in the join, he strove to prise up one of the pieces of floor-boards by the power he thus acquired.

The steel did its duty well. It trembled, but it did not bend, or if it did, it by its own elasticity returned to the straight position again at each relaxation of the power which Hilliard applied to it. For some minutes the board continued firm, but then, with a creaking noise, the nails began to rise from the joist. After this first movement had been attained all was comparatively easy, and in a few moments he had the piece of boarding sufficiently up to get a hold of it with his hands, when he raised it completely, for it did not extend beyond six feet.

He then listened attentively to hear if any sound indicated alarm among the men who were noisily carousing in the common room; but all seemed the same as before. He could hear the murmur of their conversation, and occasionally a few tones higher than usual would come more distinctly to his ears. He felt himself as yet perfectly safe.

"Now," he thought, "Wilson is very thin, and he can easily get between the joists, if I make a hole large enough for him through the mortar of the ceiling and the laths. But if, in the surprise of the occurrence, he should give an alarm, all is lost."

The getting up another board was now a matter of no great difficulty, and, when that was done, Hilliard placed his pistol in his pocket, and, taking a knife, began to cut away some of the laths, which, encrusted by mortar, presented themselves between the joists which he had exposed by the removal of the boards. As he was thus engaged he heard a clock strike four.

CHAPTER XXXVIII.

THE WHISPER TO WILSON.—THE ESCAPE.—THE VISIT OF THE OFFICER TO THE STRONG ROOM.—THE ALARM.

HILLIARD had chosen his place well when he commenced his attempt to remove the floor boards, for he was just only over the strong room, so that, in climbing up to the opening he intended to make, he calculated that Wilson would have the assistance of the wall, and, in all probability, of the door. Before, however, he now proceeded further, he thought it prudent to make an attempt to speak to Wilson, in order to quiet any fears he might have when he saw bits of mortar falling about him.

He accordingly placed his mouth as close down as he could to what was left of the bit of ceiling, and said, in as loud a whisper as he dared—

"Wilson—Wilson!"

The wretched prisoner heard him, and, fancying himself called upon by some being of another world, he uttered a loud scream, and shrieked—

"To-morrow—to-morrow," in a voice that brought the London officer to him on the instant, with the exclamation in his mouth of,—

"What now—what's amiss now?"

"Take me from here—oh, take me from here. There are strange voices from the other world calling to me. Even now, one of them pronounced my name in dreadfully hollow accents."

"You be d——d!" said the officer, as he locked the door again in a great passion at being so disturbed, and rejoined the gamekeepers and night-constables in the common room.

Wilson covered his face with his hands, and with a deep groan gave himself up to, as he supposed, all the horrors of a communication with some apparition who had come to torment him for his great sinfulness and evil life.

Upon the whole, however, this circumstance was favourable to Hilliard, who had heard all that had passed in the lower room through the very thin stratum of mortar which was only between him and it; and so he thought, for in a bolder whisper he said again,—

"Wilson—Wilson!"

"Save me—save me!" groaned Wilson.

"Wilson, I say."

"Oh, have mercy—mercy!"

"'Tis I, Mark Hilliard. I have come to rescue you."

"Mark Hilliard!" muttered Wilson. "Can this be possible? Oh, no. My disordered fancy cheats me, and conjures up sounds that have no reality."

"Hist, hist!" said Hilliard; "I am making a hole through the roof, by which you can escape. Spread your coat on the floor, to deaden the fall of any mortar."

Wilson began then to think it just possible that it might indeed be Mark Hilliard himself, and he said,—

"Swear on your soul that you are Hilliard."

"On my soul!" said the ruffian.

"I—I shall be saved—saved," faltered Wilson, as with frantic eagerness he took off his coat and laid it upon the floor as nearly under where Hilliard's voice came from as he could guess.

In another moment a piece of mortar fell upon it from the roof, and a gleam of Hilliard's lantern shone into the strong room.

"Can you—save me?" said Wilson. "Oh, God! Hilliard, can you save me?"

"Hush! hush!—not a word," whispered Hilliard.

Wilson looked up, and by the light of his lantern Hilliard saw his face. It was horribly ghastly, looking more like the face of a corpse than of a living being. The lips were nervously retracted from the teeth, the eyes were bloodshot, and the lids had lost all their natural colour, presenting to the eyes but a slaty tinge, which made the whole countenance look like that of some unhappy being in the last stage of some terrible disease.

There was a dead silence for some moments, for Wilson, in obedience to the injunctions of Hilliard, said nothing, and hardened and unfeeling as Hilliard was, even he was terrified for the moment past the power of utterance, as he looked down upon the frightful upturned face that met his gaze.

The sounds of voices from the common room were now distinctly audible, and one of the men was heard to say in a loud voice,—

"Well, if poor Bill is dead, I'm sure he'd be about the last to wish us to pine and mope over it. He was always fond of a song while he lived, and I don't see why we shouldn't have one now he's dead."

"Oh, hang it all," cried another, "let's have no singing."

"Stuff!" cried the former speaker. "Here goes,—

"While we live let's be merry,
  Be grave when we die;
Let's catch every pleasure
  That flits 'neath the sky.
Tears are but rain drops,
  Harsh winds but a sigh,
For the pleasures so beaming
  That onward swift fly.
While we live let's be merry,
  Be grave when we die;
Let's catch each fond pleasure
  That flits 'neath the sky."

"Well, before you give us any more of that," said the London officer, "I shall pay a visit to my prisoner."

"Pho, pho!" cried the night-constable; "I tell you he's safe enough. Why, you quite insult the Greenwich lock-up, you do."

"The Greenwich lock-up, then, must make the best it can of it," said the officer, "for I always see my prisoners before I think of sitting down for the night, or going to sleep."

"Well, if you will, you will."

"Wilson! Wilson!" said Hilliard, in a hissing whisper, "pick up the fallen mortar, and hide it, or you are a lost man. Quick—quick, I say."

With nervous haste Wilson gathered up the few pieces of mortar that had fallen from the roof, and stowed some away in his pockets, while the remainder he placed under the seat he had so long and gloomily occupied.

"Sit down now as you were," said Hilliard.

Even as he spoke the heavy footfall of the officer was heard immediately outside the door of the strong room, and Hilliard had just time to lay himself down over the opening he had made in the roof, when the officer entered the room with a light in his hand.

His voice was thick and husky from the liquor he had already drunk, and he said—

"Well, my fine fellow, how do you find yourself by this time?"

Wilson had covered his hands over his face, and resting his elbows on his knees, was really in as great a state of mental agony as it was possible for any one to be in. It was, therefore, no acting when he answered the officer with a deep groan.

"Oh, in the groaning line, are you?" said the officer. "Well, it's all the same to me. You sort of chaps have different sorts of ways—some of you are all on the snivelling tack, while others of you carry it off with a high hand and a jovial song. But it's all one to me."

"Yes—yes," murmured Wilson, not at all knowing what he said.

"It is yes, yes. Ah, you're a poor fool, you are! I might have spared myself the trouble of looking at you."

With a profound contempt for his prisoner, the officer walked to the door without having looked up to the ceiling at all, which, if he had done, would at once have ruined Hilliard's scheme, and scarcely allowed him time himself to escape, for the hole must have been observed on the instant.

How many people, however, might go into a room, and never dream of looking to the ceiling.

"Good-night," said the officer. "Oh, you are a poor, miserable devil! D—n it, man, you may as well put a good face on the matter—they can but hang you."

Wilson groaned again, and in great disgust with his prisoner, the officer left the room, and banged the door behind him, double locking it in a great passion.

While this brief conversation, or rather monologue, for the officer had it nearly all to himself, was going on, Hilliard suffered perfect martyrdom to apprehension. He felt that the merest accident in the world might upset all his schemes, and involve himself in very great personal risk besides. The falling of the minutest fragment of mortar, a casual glance upwards on the part of the officer from any cause, would have been sufficient to have caused a discovery.

He lay with the stillness of one dead, hiding by his body every ray from his small lantern, and completely filling up, as it were, the hole he had made. Painfully acute, however, as his hearing was, he caught every word which was uttered by the officer, and when he heard the door locked after he had left the room, the feeling of relief that came over Hilliard's heart was like a breath of air to a suffocating man.

For some moments he still lay quite motionless, nor did Wilson gather courage to make the slightest movement. Then Hilliard assured himself that he was much safer than before, for now, unless he or Wilson made some noise to attract attention, the room would be unvisited until the morning.

He slowly rose, and shot a gleam of light from his lantern through the opening, at the same time that in a cautious whisper, he called—

"Wilson—Wilson?"

The wretched man started from his seat, and in faltering accents replied—

"I am here. I am here, Hilliard."

"Come here. Closer, closer."

Wilson staggered to the part of the room immediately under the opening, and again he turned up his awful-looking spectral face.

Hilliard started as he saw that there was blood streaming from his mouth.

In his mental agony, while the officer was in the room, he had bit his lips through, and the trickling blood rolled down on his breast, while he was quite unconscious of what he had done—so completely will mental agony conquer all feeling of bodily pain.

"You have bit your lips," said Hilliard.

"My—my lips?" said Wilson. "I did not know. I really did not know."

"Well, well, never heed it now. Attend to me. You must contrive to climb up by the back of the door, and such assistance as I can give you from above here, until you get through the opening."

"Good heavens, I cannot, Hilliard, I cannot. If that is my only chance of escape, I am lost."

"It is your only chance."

"I cannot—I cannot."

"By hell, if you do not attempt it, I'll blow your brains out as you stand below there. You must and shall try to ascend here."

Wilson's mind was so enervated and weakened, that he fancied he dared no longer refuse, and with a groan he signified that if Hilliard would have it so he would try.

Hilliard then twisted a couple of silk handkerchiefs he had with him firmly together, and then tieing their ends he reached down to Wilson, saying—

"Take off your shoes and then clamber up by the lock of the door, and the moment I can get a hold of your hands I will drag you up."

For a man in Wilson's nervous state this was no easy feat to perform, but nevertheless he attempted it. Carefully divesting himself of his shoes, he seized with both his hands the loop of the handkerchief, which pull Hilliard was easily able to stand, as he had the purchase of the flooring above.

"Now, now," whispered Hilliard.

"I am coming—I am coming," said Wilson, and with great difficulty he clambered with his feet on to the lock of the door. There, however, he was in a very awkward position, and Hilliard could not get a hold of him until he bethought himself of tying the handkerchief across one of the joists of the flooring, which left his hands at liberty.

To accomplish this, however, Wilson was obliged to descend again, but it was soon done, and upon his second attempt, Hilliard leant down and got a firm hold of the back of his collar. For a moment, then, the whole weight of Wilson hung upon Hilliard's hands, and it was as much as he could do to draw him sufficiently high to enable him himself to seize one of the rafters. After that all was easy, and at the expense only of a few bumps and scratches, Wilson found himself safely in the room above his prison.

Hilliard did not then pause a moment, but going to the window he looked right and left to see if any one were coming. To his aggravation, then,

he saw two women standing gossiping on the opposite side of the way. Oh, how he cursed them as the chatter of their tongues came upon his ears, and he was sure they must see him if he attempted to descend from the window, when in all probability they would give the alarm.

The voices of the women came clearly to his ears.

"You must know, Mrs. Green," said one, "that my husband is a most *particular* man, he is. If he doesn't have his butter melted along with his mutton he's dreadful fractious."

"Ah, it's the way with all the men, Mrs. Sadlebrains," said Mrs. Green, "now my husband always skrimages if he's left long with the baby, and he complains as——"

At this moment Hilliard threw a piece of loose mortar at them, and Mrs. Green cried,

"Gracious! what's that?"

"Bless us!" echoed Mrs. Sadlebrains, and forthwith they scampered in different directions, leaving the coast clear for Hilliard to use the ladder.

He accordingly unfastened it from where he had secured it by the lamp, and then turning to Wilson, he said,

"Follow me down this ladder, and then do not speak a word until I address you."

"I will—I will," said Wilson. "You have saved me, Hilliard; you have saved me."

"Indeed," muttered Hilliard. "But before I part with you I will take care to be easy as regards any further trouble you can bring me into."

Hilliard then himself descended the ladder, and holding it below, he beckoned to Wilson, who, with an alarmed air, got out of the window, and followed him.

CHAPTER XXXIX.

TOM HACKEY'S REFLECTIONS.—GRACE AND HER FATHER.—MR. BUMBLETON SNIGGLES AND FEMALE CURIOSITY.

THE adventure at Lord Hawksworth's villa seemed quite of a nature to exercise an important influence over the whole *dramatis personæ* of our narrative.

Rivers left the villa with mingled

feelings of joy and embarrassment, and yet the joy—the pure ecstasy of feeling triumphed, for had not he been at hand in the hour of danger to rescue from insult her who was dearer, far dearer to him than life itself, and had not he told her how very dearly he loved her, and had she not clung to him, requiting his love with that confidence, which is the dearest, best award this world can afford it.

What, then, to him was dismissal from the merchant's, except so far as it involved a separation from the immediate neighbourhood of Grace, and that indeed was a heart-pang to Rivers, for even the counting-house, with its musty ledgers and paraphernalia of business, was interesting and beautiful when he felt that it was separated only a few feet from the beautiful girl on whom he had bestowed his heart's best love and affection, which could know no change.

"What will the morning produce?" was the anxious question he asked himself. "Can it be possible that the father can punish me with dismissal from his service for protecting his child from a villain?"

In these and similar reflections passed the remainder of the evening with Rivers, and he awaited the coming day with an impatience which had the effect of completely banishing sleep from his pillow until near the dawn of morning. But then, when gentle slumber did steal over his senses, was he not amply and fully recompensed for his anxieties? for he dreamt of his own beautiful Grace. Again in the dreamy stillness of the night he told her that he loved her; again he felt the soft pressure of her hand—again he pressed with a gentle fervour his lips to her cheek, and the young lover's heart was happy.

How very different to these were the feelings of poor Grace, as her father, after he had made a virtue of necessity by consenting to go home, hurried her to the carriage, and then on the road either sat in moody silence, or else reproached her in no very measured terms for being so very captious about a little ardent attention from Lord Hawksworth.

"Father," said Grace, "you are ignorant of the character of the man you think so highly of, and of the real circumstances of the case you speak of as being of such slight import."

"Pho! pho!" said the merchant: "I know all about it. There was no concealment; I was told the whole story the moment it had occurred; and all I can say is, that if anybody in the world is to be excused for a little impetuosity, that person is a young nobleman in love with one who he knows perfectly well would grace his coronet. You much mistake, Grace, Lord Hawksworth and his character. He loves you very much indeed, and you should really make a little allowance for the ardour of a lover's feelings."

"Once for all, father," said Grace "I assure you most solemnly that I will not receive Lord Hawksworth in the character of a lover."

"But—but—consider. It is no joke to be a countess, Grace; no joke, I assure you."

"It is no joke," said Grace, "to have one's happiness sacrificed for life for an empty sound."

"Happiness! Why—why—really, you know its a most splendid alliance, and considering that I began the world with three-and-a-penny, I must say that it's not so much amiss to have a lord and a perspective earl running after my daughter. That's my opinion. Ah!"

"Father," said Grace, "to end this discussion at once, I here declare my unalterable determination not to marry that man if he had a crown to offer me!"

"A—a—crown?"

"Ay, a crown."

"What!—you—you utterly reject—him?"

"Utterly."

"Well—I—really—Oh, you will come to your senses some day or another."

"If ever I lose my senses, my first act may be to encourage the addresses of such a man as Hawksworth, but I must lose them, father, before I do so."

"You are mad, now—frantic—quite a lunatic," cried Mathew Trueman, as he threw himself back in his carriage, and then added in an under tone,—

"I will discharge that abominable Rivers in the morning, or I'll know the reason why."

Grace, however, heard him, and in a

GRACE APPEALING TO LORD HAWKSWORTH.

one of voice that made Mathew True-man open his eyes uncommonly wide she said,—

"Father, I owe you much—very much—far be it from me to underrate the duty of a child to its parent, but I here assure you, solemnly that if you discharge Mr. Rivers from your service for rendering me the most signal service in rescuing me from the brutality of Lord Hawksworth, that I will meet him when I can—visit him where I can, and take every possible opportunity of thanking him for his chivalrous conduct."

"You—you will meet him?"

"I will."

"Visit him?"

"I will."

"Why—why—are you mad!"

"No, father, but thanks to the care you have taken in your choice of instruction to me, you have had me taught *gratitude!*"

"Pho! pho!" cried Mathew True-man, "I wish they had taught you a little discretion."

"I hope they have, father."

"But I find they have not."

"Indeed?"

"Ah, indeed! Do you call it discreet to refuse a lord, and an earl that is to be? Upon my word I consider it scarcely proper and virtuous."

Grace could not suppress her surprise at her father's definition of propriety and virtue, but she made no reply, and the remainder of the distance between Lord Hawksworth's villa and the merchant's house was got over in silence.

Of all those, however, who take an interest in Grace and her father, poor Tom Hackey probably felt the most intense indignation, as well as the greatest anxiety on account of the proceedings of the night. The poor fellow had not the same feeling that Rivers cherished in his heart to nerve him against misfortune. True, he loved Grace as fondly, as fervently as Rivers could possibly do, but then to him she was like

"Some bright particular star,"

which he might worship afar off, but never in his wildest dreams hope or expect to approach.

The words of the merchant had sounded the death-knell of the little joy he had in this world, namely that of occasionally seeing Grace, and catching a beaming smile from her lips as she thanked him for some trifling service he had perhaps manœuvred a whole day to have the pleasure—and what a dear pleasure to poor Tom Hackey it was—of rendering to her.

"Ah!" he sighed, when he reached the Strand, on his way homewards; "it's all up now. I shall be discharged, and so will Rivers, poor fellow. We shall never see her more, but must sit like two Patiences on a monument, smiling at grief, we must. What will become of me I don't know, and I don't altogether much care if old Mathew discharges me."

Absorbed in these melancholy reflections, Tom came to the end of Catherine-street, the scene of all his theatrical greatness and glory. He paused involuntarily, and, shaking his head, he said, in a tone of despondency,—

"Farewell, a long farewell, to all my greatness! Tom Hackey's occupation's gone."

"What do you mean by that, my bundle of faggots?" cried the well-known voice of Mr. Bumbleton Sniggles; and Tom, suddenly turning, saw that illustrious character standing close to him.

"Ah! it's you?" said Tom.

"Yes, it's I; but you don't look the thing, my hero."

"No, not exactly; I was, you see, a little curious."

"Curious? Bless me, how odd! I am curious, we are all curious. Curiosity was the ruin of mother Eve, and is one of the chief failings of her female descendants to the present day; but of all the curious characters with whom I was ever acquinted, I never met with any equal to my own wife: she would plot and counterplot to arrive at the information she desired, and I'll be bound to say would not have hesitated to grope to the bottom of a soot-heap if she imagined anything there lay concealed from her, although useless.

"'My dear,' said she to me soon after we were married, 'what have you in that small cabinet of which you always keep the key?'

"'Nothing particular, my love,' I replied.

"'Then why is it always so carefully locked?'

"'I was requested to do so by the person who left it with me.'

"'Strange, very strange, one would think there was something very valuable in it.'

"'I believe it is so, my love,' I replied, carelessly.

"'And have you examined the contents?'

"'Never; it does not concern me.'

"'Well, my dear, what a strange man you are, to have a valuable treasure in your keeping, and not to know the nature of it. Have you the key?'

"'I have.'

"'Lend it to me, and I'll examine it at once.'

"'No, my love, I had rather you would not,' I replied, 'it cannot concern us.'

"'But I should like to know, dear!

"'I am afraid, then, you must exercise the virtue of self-denial!'

"'Oh, very well, my dear!' returned my wife, evidently chagrined, but I plainly saw that she was excited by the most painful curiosity, although no further notice was taken at the time.

"For the benefit of my readers, I can inform them that when the affairs of my friend, Lord D—— became involved, and his goods and chattels about to be brought to the hammer, he had confided to my charge the cabinet above-mentioned, stating at the time 'that it contained a treasure,' but of what nature he made no mention; he, moreover, requested 'that it might not be opened,' with which request I had implicitly complied, and, therefore, was as well as my wife in the most profound ignorance of what was its contents; neither did I care to know.

*   *   *   *

"Lord D—— had now been abroad some years; the cabinet still remained in the closet in my chamber, and no application was made for it; but repeatedly was I pressed by my wife to ascertain the contents; but to all her solicitations I strenuously objected, more for the pleasure of keeping alive her curiosity, and feigning to make a mystery where most probably there was none.

"Her curiosity at last mounted to fever height, and upon visiting the closet one morning I discovered the lock of the cabinet had been disarranged; I returned to my wife and found her labouring under excessive lowness of spirits, of which I appeared to take no notice.

"'My love!' said I, 'some one has attempted to open the casket in the closet; the lock is damaged.'

"'Pray forgive me,' said she mournfully, 'but my curiosity was so great to know the contents that I ordered the carpenter to open it.'

"'It is a patent lock; how did he manage it?'

"'By taking it off.'

"'Which he has done very clumsily; what answer must I return to my friend, Lord D——, to account for the damage it has sustained?'

"My wife was puzzled what to answer, so wisely held her peace.

"'And now, what is the treasure it contains?' I demanded. 'You can now inform me.'

"'Three books in manuscript.'

"'Is that all?'

"'Yes.'

"I was now resolved to examine the books in question, and upon doing so found them to be MSS. of his lordship's, the opening chapter of which was a cutting article on Female Curiosity.

"This, I conjectured, was what had acted so powerfully on the nerves of my wife, for she never after mentioned the subject of the cabinet, and I believe the disappointment she endured preyed so much upon her mind as to lay the foundation of a complaint which ultimately carried her to her grave."

"Ah, very likely," said Tom Hackey, "it must have been either that or your confounded tongue; for in all my life, I never did come near such a talker."

"Me a talker! Why, what will you say next? I have such a hatred of gossiping that I never would marry for fear of getting a talkative wife."

"Never marry? Why, you have been telling me a long story just now about your wife."

"My wife? Oh, did I say it was my wife?"

"Yes, you did."

"Pho, pho! I mean a friend's wife, don't you see?"

"I hear," said Tom.

"Well, my dear fellow, now what do you say to four penn'orth at Johnson's, eh? Close at hand."

"I ain't in the humour, just now, Swiggles," said Tom, "some other time I shall be glad."

"Well, my dear fellow, I won't press you against your inclination—eh? Ah, bless my soul! Really—upon my life —how strange."

Mr. Swiggles accompanied these words by divers pats about his clothing where pockets are commonly situated, and at length, when Tom took no notice of the various hints thus given, he said—

"The fact is, my dear friend—really now—the oddest thing—I've left my purse at home."

"Have you?"

"Yes; honour, honour."

"Was there anything in it?"

"Ah, you are surely a dreadful wag; by-the-bye, have you got half-a-crown?"

"No."

"Eighteenpence?"

"No."

"A shilling?"

"No."

"Hang it—well—misfortunes can't be helped. It's quite absurd, really, but have you got a sixpence?"

"No," said Tom, resolutely.

"My dear friend, never mind then," cried Mr. Bubbleton Swiggles, shaking Tom heartily by the hand. "I'm equally obliged to you as if you were rolling in riches—and wouldn't lend me any," in an under tone.

"Oh, you are very welcome," said Tom. "Good-evening."

"Good evening. Bless you."

"The same to you, and many of 'em."

"Won't bleed," ejaculated Bubbleton Swiggles, Esq., when he had parted from Tom.

"A horrid humbug!" was Tom's remark upon the character and peculiarities of Mr. Swiggles.

Honest Tom Hackey's feelings were, however, too much excited by, and too much interested in what had occurred to Rivers that evening, for such a person as Bubbleton Swiggles, Esq., to occupy for any length of time his mind.

His own discharge, as well as that of Rivers, he looked upon as quite certain, and the gloomy prospect that presented itself then to the poor fellow's mind, so much oppressed him, that he could not find it in his heart to go to his own humble home, but in great anxiety and perturbation of spirit traversed the streets for a long time, indulging dreamy fancies as to what would become of Rivers and himself.

"It's rather odd," he muttered to himself, "but I've somehow took to that Rivers. He's an honest fellow, and I like him. Some people would hate him if they felt like me towards Grace—but I can't—I can't. She loves him, of course she does. I know it—I'm quite sure of it, and he loves her. Very well, I said so, didn't I?"

Poor Tom Hackey was very much in the habit of arguing with and answering himself in this way.

He now proceeded on in silence for some time, indulging in a fancy of how happy Grace might be with Rivers, while he, Tom, although there would be a void in his heart that could never be filled, would derive some reflected happiness from the joy of those he loved. Suddenly then he paused, and, while a tear dimmed his eye, he said—

"Perhaps, if they have a little one they will not mind calling it Tom."

The poor fellow was so pleased with this supposition that it restored him considerably to himself again, and he got rid of some of the gloomy fancies that possessed his brain, as he walked in the direction of Catherine Street, in which stood the temple of the drama, where he, Tom, had won such golden opinion of all sorts of men; where he had strutted his hour upon the stage, and where, poor fellow, some of his happiest, if not his only happy days, had been passed.

"It's well," said Tom, in his quiet, easy manner. "It's well, when what is real in one's life isn't over pleasant, to find out something that isn't, by which we enjoy ourselves, as I've done when I've been acting some character and quite forgot old Mathew Trueman, and the office, and all the disagreeables. Ah, well, if the worst comes to the worst—if old Mathew should really discharge us to-morrow, why, I'll propose to Rivers to learn to be an actor. He's just the thing for junior tragedy, while I could take the upper parts. How well, now, he'd play Iago to my Othello."

This was a very pleasant source of reflection to Tom, and by the time he became immersed in it he found himself at the door of the theatre.

Oh, how pleasant and delightful to Tom Hackey was the excitement and bustle about the very doors! Could he resist walking in? No!—and why should he, if he could? So thought Tom; and in a few moments he was in the very paraphernalia of the theatre.

The piece in progress was a melodrama of the modern school; it was entitled, as Tom found by a scrip of paper pinned to the wall near the prompter's box, "The Infuriated Fugitive; or, the Wild Bandit of the Blasted Hut."

When Tom had informed himself thus far, he turned his attention to the business of the stage, where was a young lady supposed to be confined in the blasted hut, and who had let down all her back hair, the more energetically to display her grief. Moreover, she had wiped off with a damp towel the rouge with which her face had before been liberally supplied, and looked very natural and very pale.

"Oh, powers above," cried the young lady, "what shall I do? Horror—horror! This is the blasted hut. Where is Mandelanouiskeblinski? Oh, where is he now? Ah! but let me not despair. When did the virtuous ever fall victims to the unadulterated villany of a bandit? Spirit of my sainted mother assist me!"

This was the cue for an adagio movement on the part of the fiddle and the flute composing the band, during which the young lady, who had let down her back hair, knelt very slowly and gradually, indeed, in the immediate front of the stage, and was then and there supposed to offer up some energetic prayer that appeared to be addressed to a hole in the roof of the theatre, just above the gallery. Altogether, though, the effect was very striking and fine, and would have been much more striking and fine, had not some one in the gallery, totally divested of sentiment, shouted out in the very midst of the prayer to the sainted mother—

"I say, when did the old un croak? Did she make over her mangle to you?"

To this application and extremely improper allusion to her mother, the young lady, who had let down her back hair, made no sort of answer, and in act, as far as human nature could, she affected to be quite unconscious of the interruption, and concluded the prayer amid a general round of applause, mingled with catcalls—screams—imitation of ginger-beer bottles coming suddenly uncorked—the crowing of cocks, and such an awful admixture of sounds as were enough to astonish any one.

Suddenly, then, a trap immediately behind the young lady was opened, and there arose from it a puff of smoke—accompanied by a smell anything but salubrious, but evidently awful and unearthly, since the same odour always accompanies the exeunt of a supernatural being at a minor theatre.

By the time that the audience had had a good sniff of the ghostly aroma, the sainted mother slowly arose, or was poked up by two stage-carpenters below.

A round of plaudits followed the appearance of the old lady; and, when she held her hands over the head of the young lady, who had let down her back hair, and looked upwards so as to disclose the whites of her eyes only, the applause became tremendous.

Then suddenly from the prompter's box there came the faint crowing of a cock, and the ghost gave a visible start, and then said—

"I must be gone. The morning herald warns me—I must be gone."

The two carpenters below then lowered the ghost down again, the one remarking to the other with a prefatory oath, which we cannot repeat, that it was blowed hard work with them gostesses.

On the present occasion it was very foolish of the dramatist of the Infuriated Fugitive; or, the Bandit of the Blasted Hut, to get rid of his ghost by the crowing of a cock; for if the prompter, whose duty it was to make all sorts of indescribable noises when they were wanted, had been able to crow well enough to drown a whole farm-yard, he would have found many in the front of the house who would have disputed the accomplishment with him, and so it happened that that unfortunate crow produced a scene of confusion which lasted out the melodrama of the Infuriated Fugitive; or, the Bandit of the Blasted Hut completely.

In a moment there was a crowing from some dozens of throats, and the ghost vanished amid such a volley of imitations, more or less accurate, of " the summons of light Chanticleer," that they would have been sufficient to rout the whole world of spirits.

The crowers, however, were not satisfied with dismissing the ghost, but they kept up a spirited contest among themselves as to which could crow best; a contest which seemed much more entertaining than the play, which proceeded in dumb show for the next quarter of an hour, until the gentleman who was to perform the bandit of the blasted hut entered, when it suddenly occurred to one of the audience that some time last year, in the versatility of his genius, the said gentleman had sung a comic song, called, " Cricketty, cricketty, cricketty, whack fal de daddledum," which, as nobody understood, was, of course, highly amusing, wherefore a call for that song was raised, and the bandit of the blasted hut found himself under the necessity of coming forward, and in his own phraseology, " attempting the song."

This was too much for Tom Hackey's notions of propriety as regarded the regular drama; and, after expressing his feelings in no very measured terms to a gentleman who was painting a gaping wound upon his forehead, which he would have to exhibit early in the next act, and who only answered him by a dead fish-like stare, as much as to say—"I really don't know what you mean," he left the house, and repaired to his own humble home.

CHAPTER XL.

THE CONSULTATION AT THE VILLA.— THE SELF-CONGRATULATION. — THE TRIUMPH OVER RIVERS.—THE END OF THE FETE.

AFTER Lord Hawksworth had made his dastardly and unmanly attack upon the unarmed Rivers by firing a pistol at his head, he could not believe himself safe until he was repeatedly assured that the merchant's clerk had actually left the house and grounds—a fact which was affirmed to him by several persons before he again ventured to make his appearance in the dancing-rooms, where his brilliant, heartless, frivolous, and selfish company were assembled.

The great object of the fete, however, was over, and with its failure—for failure it certainly was—the temper of his lordship by no means improved. He, therefore, took but one turn through the saloons in order to show himself to his guests, and then accompanied his privy counsellor, Girkins, into a private room, where, over a bottle of wine, they talked over the night's proceedings, and surmised the probable result.

The sudden departure of the merchant gave Girkins some uneasiness, and he could not help gently hinting to his lordship that he thought he had gone a little too far.

"Upon my word," said Hawksworth, looking alarmed, "I hope not; who would have supposed the girl would have made half such a fuss about a little piece of gallantry at a fancy-ball, where there is always considered some little excuse, you know."

"Ah, who, indeed," exclaimed Girkins; "your lordship is perfectly right, only, you see, that what in high life and among the aristocratic circles is made no noise about at all, is frequently among the middling classes looked upon with a prejudiced eye."

"Prejudiced, indeed, Girkins, but it was all owing to your advice, you know."

"My advice, my lord?"

"Yes, certainly. You projected this entertainment in order to give me an opportunity of pleading my suit to the beautiful Grace Trueman."

"Yes, oh dear, yes—but—but——"

"But what?"

"I did not advise you lordship to plead your cause to the breautiful Grace Trueman quite so warmly."

"Oh, there I may have been a little in error, but the merchant must be smoothed over by having that attributed to the warmth of admiration, and the ardour of my affection."

"That to a certain extent I have already done," said Girkins, "and I have every hope of not only placing matters on their former footing, but of turning this accident to account."

"As how?"

"Thus, my lord. I cannot but consider the appearance of that young man Rivers here as a most fortunate circumstance, view it which way you will."

"Indeed?"

"Yes. For example, he just stepped through your lordship's window in time to save you in the excitement of the moment from carrying the warmth of your admiration so far as to force the merchant to be deeply offended."

"Humph! well, what next?"

"Simply this, that it will go hard with me if I do not so much influence Mathew Trueman's mind against Rivers, who, poor as he is, is the greatest stumbling-block in (our path, as to induce his immediate discharge from his service."

"But you were saying some time ago that you hardly yourself considered such a step would be politic, as it might tend to awaken sympathy for him in the breast of Grace, which might do more to advance him in her favour than any other circumstance."

"True, but I would likewise counsel Mathew Trueman to remove his daughter some distance from her present home, where she will be inaccessible to this young man. His poverty, too, will be a clog upon him—a complete bar to his ardour in pursuing her, even granting him all the inclination to do so which he doubtless has."

"There is something in that."

"Much, my lord. This Francis

Rivers must get some other situation, or he must starve."

"Granted."

"Well, give him the luck to obtain employment somewhere, will not his time be occupied so as effectually to prevent him being very troublesome? and if he get no employment he will not have the means of attempting anything."

"Curse him," muttered Hawksworth, "I will have more revenge of him than the discharge from his situation. His father, you have told me, was in the army?"

"Yes, he was."

"This young fellow may have courage and be able to use his fists as people of his class usually do, but ten to one if he ever had a pistol in his hand. His father was an officer?"

"If," said Girkins, in a low tone, "your lordship would really condescend to fight him?"

"What is to hinder me?"

"Oh, nothing—nothing."

"I am a dead shot, Girkins."

"So much the better."

"I might then rid myself of him that way easily enough."

"But his death by your hands might get you into some trouble."

"Trouble? Oh, dear no. I have a seat in the Lords, and if any very great fuss were made about the matter, I could but insist, you know, upon being tried by my peers, as the greatest mountebank among the nobility has recently been."

"Certainly," replied Girkins. "They would bring you in Not Guilty, upon their honour."

"Of course."

"Then does your lordship definitely mean to say that you will fight this young man?"

"If Mathew Trueman will discharge him, well and good, I will leave him alone; but if he should not, I will put him out of the way with a pistol-bullet."

"Then we may, I think," said Girkins, "congratulate ourselves upon getting the better of this very troublesome fellow, at last. Should he even refuse to meet you, your challenging him will show a great deal of sincerity to Mathew Trueman."

The sound of music came upon their ears frequently as they thus conversed, and Hawksworth exclaimed with an air of vexation and impatience—

"I wish these people would go now, for I really don't want them any longer."

"I do not think," remarked Girkins, "there are any among them with whom your lordship need use much ceremony. Let them remain as long as they please, while you drive to town; it will be absolutely necessary for you to see Trueman in the morning, in order to set yourself right in this affair."

"So it will; so it will. I will be off at once."

His lordship then rang the bell, and when a servant appeared, he ordered his cab to be got ready immediately, in which he very graciously offered Girkins a seat, which was accepted with every appearance of humility and thankfulness for such lordly condescension.

Lord Hawksworth drove to a fashionable hotel at the west end of the town, where he put up for the remainder of the night, and Girkins left him, after exacting a promise from him that he would be visible at a very early hour in the morning, if he, Girkins, should call upon him in company with Mathew Trueman.

The scheme of the wily Girkins was to have an interview with the merchant at an hour before he should see even his daughter in the morning, and thoroughly inflame his mind against Rivers, so that when the business of the day should commence, the young man should get his discharge without being heard in his defence one moment.

A splendid breakfast with Lord Hawksworth at the aristocratic hotel, he, Girkins, thought might be of some assistance in bringing the merchant to the proper frame of mind for his purpose, and obliterating any little unpleasantness that might possibly be on his memory, connected with the preceding night's adventure at the villa.

The plan of operations was by no means a bad one considering the strange character he had to deal with in the merchant, who was one of those singular combinations of shrewdness and weakness, not so unfrequently met with as people imagine.

Girkins, therefore, retired to rest himself, leaving the most strict injunctions that he should be called at a very early hour, indeed.

The gray cold light of early morning was shining faintly upon the leviathan city, when the "agent" rose from his slumbers, and hastily dressing himself he partook of some slight refreshment, and then started for Thames Street, to see Mathew Trueman.

Over night he had penned the following epistle, which he had no doubt would procure him the interview he sought with the merchant.

"MY DEAR SIR,—Girkins has from me something of great importance to say to you, and I trust you will pardon me for sending him to you at so barbarous and unseasonable an hour.

"Believe me, my dear sir, yours,
                "HAWKSWORTH."

"Mathew Trueman, Esq.

With this note in his hand, Girkins rang the servants' bell of the merchant's house, and was answered by a housemaid whose turn it was to light the fires that morning, and who consequently was far from being in the most amiable of moods.

"What might you please to want?" was asked in a tone which might easily have been translated into—"Well, I'm sure, what business have you tottering here so early."

"Mr. Trueman is at home, of course," said Girkins.

"No, he isn't He's a-bed."

"Well, well, so I suppose, my dear. I want a note given him, and I'll wait here, while you knock at his door and hand it to him, you understand."

"I doesn't understand nothing, and so far as taking of notes up stairs at sich a hour as this, I—lor sir—*suttenly,* I'll bring you an answer in a minute— won't you please to sit down, sir, till I come back?"

This sudden and wonderful alteration of tone, no doubt, arose from the natural kind-heartedness of the housemaid, who seeing that Girkins looked anxious, had not the heart to persevere in her refusal, although people who don't believe much good of human nature, and one rather censorious, would say that a five shilling piece, which Girkins slipped into her hand, had had some effect in the amelioration of her feelings.

Be this, however, as it may, Girkins was quite satisfied that his note would be delivered.

In a few minutes the propitiated nymph returned to say—

"Please, sir, master says, as if so be as you'll excuse his bed-room, he'll be glad to see you up stairs."

"Oh, certainly.   Where is it?"

"The two pair front, sir."

"Thank you—thank you."

Girkins rapidly ascended the staircase and knocked with his knuckles at the door of the two pair front.

"Come in," cried Mathew Trueman.

Girkins quietly entered the merchant's bed-room, saying—

"Good morning.   It's really too bad, as I told his lordship, to disturb you thus early, but then he said, ' Yes, it is, Girkins, but I have an apology to make to Mr. Truemen, and I will make it before I break my fast this day. If I were the first English nobleman it would be no degradation to me to apologise to the first of English merchants.' Those were his lordship's exact words, Mr. Trueman. They made quite an impression on me."

"A-hem!" said the much flattered Mathew Trueman; "I must say, Mr. Girkins, that Lord Hawksworth, in many things, knows what's due to a man who has made his own way in life— a-hem!"

"He does—he does."

"And it may be, you know, though I wouldn't say so much to my daughter, that his lordship does owe me some apology for last night, Mr. Girkins."

"That's what he admits; but he is a young man, Mr. Trueman; when the heart is engaged, you know, the judgment is not very active, you know. Ah, if such men of rank, wealth, and influence as Lord Hawksworth could have, in addition to those advantages, the talent, the tact, the real genius of others who have raised themselves from —from——"

"Three-and-a-penny," said the gratified Trueman.

"Exactly—exactly."

"Well, well, Girkins, you know we can't put old heads upon young shoulders."

"Oh, no."

"As for last night, I think there is a little blame on both sides; I have no doubt in the world but that Lord Hawksworth looks upon Grace as his future countess."

"He does, indeed."

"Ah, so I imagine, and so—so——"

"He only wished to kiss her hand."

"And she raised a squall, I understand. Girls were not so confounded particular in my young days. It's all owing to that nonsense about scientific education, and so on; it gives them all sorts of new fangled notions. Tell his lordship to think no more of it."

"I will, but concerning my message. His lordship will see you at his hotel. He has ordered a sumptuous breakfast; but he said, 'not a morsel of this will I touch, Girkins, till you bring Mr. Trueman with you.'"

"Bless me."

"It's a fact—there he is waiting."

THE MIDNIGHT RECOGNITION IN THE CHURCHYARD.

"Well I—upon my word—I hardly know what to do."

"Make his mind easy by coming with me at once; you will be back in plenty of time for business. His lordship was really, when I left, quite affected, and if you refuse his invitation, he will take it very unkind, I know."

There was something very soothing and delightful to the vanity of Mathew Trueman in the thought that a lord and the heir to one of the oldest earldoms was waiting breakfast for him, and would not take a bit or a sup till he arrived.

"If his lordship will wait breakfast for me," he said, "I really suppose, Girkins, I must not disappoint him."

"The disappointment would be very grievous."

"Would it though, really?"

"Upon my honor."

"Well—well. I will come; I will be down stairs in ten minutes, Girkins; but remember, I must be back here by ten at the latest, to business."

"Oh, of course—of course."

"Then wait for me till I join you."

Girkins then left the room, thinking to himself—

"This man's vanity will be his ruin. Flattery attacks human nature on it's weakest side; but who would have supposed an acute clever man of business like Trueman could be led by the nose so very easily. Humph! Well, it's all the better for me, and all I have to do is to feather my nest well before the bubble bursts, for sooner or later Hawksworth will let him in for a good round sum, or I don't know him; and as for his honour—Ha! ha! ha! His honour. Hawksworth's honour! Ha! ha! ha!"

Girkins laughed in such a curious, unmirthful, and discordant manner, that he quite alarmed the housemaid, who was busy cleaning the step.

Mathew Trueman was as good as his word, and, in less than the ten minutes he had mentioned, he descended the staircase, and was led off in triumph by Girkins towards the fashionable hotel were Hawksworth was staying.

Assisted by a hack-carriage they soon reached their place of destination, and Girkins left Trueman in a most magnificent breakfast-room, while he went to apprise Lord Hawksworth of his arrival.

His lordship immediately rose and made a hasty toilet, as he said—

"Tell me, now, your precise plan of operations."

"Simply this," replied Girkins. "Inflame the mind of Trueman so much against the two troublesome personages, Rivers and that pertinacious, insolent lad, Hackey, that he will be induced to write down their dismissals here, which I will offer to take down to Thames-street, while you keep him with you."

"A good plan enough."

"There will be no trouble about it: I will dismiss them both without appeal; and should they be troublesome, I will call a constable and have them arrested."

"Agreed. Go and amuse him, then, while I get ready. Order the best breakfast they can get ready quickly."

CHAPTER XLI.

THE DEATH OF WILSON.—A GUILTY HEART'S UNHOLY TRIUMPH.—THE HOUSE BY THE RIVER.

WITH a frantic eagerness the wretched Wilson clung to the arm of Hilliard, as the latter with rapid steps urged him along the quiet streets in the direction of Woolwich.

"Are we safe?—are we safe?" were the only words which came from Wilson as he followed close to Hilliard, while the cold drops of perspiration stood upon his brow, and his limbs trembled with fear.

"Hush! d—n you, hush!" growled Hilliard. "If you hold me in this manner I will leave you to your fate."

"Oh, no, no, Hilliard, you will not: you have saved me—you will not let them hoot at me as I writhe in agony upon a scaffold. Oh! no—oh! God! no."

"Be still then, or, as I'm a living man, I will. Your manner is enough to bring suspicion on us immediately were we to meet any one. Be still, I say. Damnation, don't hold by me. Let me go."

He roughly tore himself from the nervous grasp of Wilson, who, in imploring accents, said,—

"Well, well, you will let me walk by your side, Hilliard, and I shall think myself safe then. They cannot take me now—we shall escape them—eh, Hilliard? Tell me we shall escape them?"

"Peace, peace. Come on, and don't speak?"

"Yes, yes; I have had such terrible dreams—waking visions—and there has always been a jeering, mocking crowd, and you and I, Hilliard ——"

"Me?"

"Yes, you—pale, and struggling with death. The fatal cord ——"

"Now, by G——," cried Hilliard, "if I hear any more of this I will brain you as you stand. Do you think I'm going to be frightened? That is, I am not frightened—but—but tormented and troubled by your ravings."

"I will be still, Hilliard—I will be still; but, what—oh! what am I to do?"

"To do?"

"Yes. What will become of me?"

"Remember your promise."

"My promise, Hilliard—my promise?"

"Yes; the river."

A spasmodic shudder passed over the frame of Wilson, as he repeated to himself the words—"the river! the river!" He then wrung his hands in an agony of despair as he added,—

"Oh! Heaven—oh! Heaven! Is there no resource but that?"

"None," said Hilliard.

"Ah! Hilliard, save me—save me! make me your slave, but let me live— You will? Ah! you relent—you will not let me die in the cold water. Fancy it rushing through one's brain, Hilliard; flashing like a thousand lights before the bursting eyes. Oh! horror— horror—horror!"

Hilliard trembled himself as this appeal was made to him, for there was something terrible and agonizing in the tone of voice in which Wilson spoke that was enough to curdle any one's blood who heard it. It was like a shrieking appeal from the very grave.

"Speak—oh, speak to me," he added. "Hilliard—good Hilliard, you are thinking of how I may be saved—I know you are. You will not kill me?"

They had now arrived at a dull and lonely part of the road, one side of which was skirted by a high wall, and the other was very near to the river. Hilliard paused and glanced around him, as in a low tone he said,—

"Wilson—Wilson, listen to me. You are, as you know, a hunted, proscribed man. A reward is offered for your apprehension; the whole of society is, as it were, seeking your life ——"

"Yes—yes—but you, Hilliard, you will save me?"

"I cannot."

A half scream burst from Wilson's lips, which was only checked by the imperious "silence!" of Hilliard, which he accompanied by a blow that made the wretched companion of his crimes and tool of his deep iniquity stagger again.

"Yes—yes," he gasped, "you may strike me, Hilliard—you may ill-use me if you please. I will be very abject— very—very; but you will let me live? Life, Hilliard, is still sweet. What wretch would cast it from him?"

"In a word," said Hilliard, "how do you mean to get a living?"

"I—I must beg—beg."

"And be handed over to a constable as Wilson, the murderer, by the first or second person you apply to."

Wilson groaned and wrung his hands again in an agony of despair and fear.

"This will not do," said Hilliard, after a pause. "I am as poor as yourself, and should be reduced to the same alternative as yourself, if, like you, I were well known and suspected. I cannot keep you Wilson; if I could I would, but I can scarcely keep myself—you know that."

"Couldn't I get abroad somewhere?"

"How?"

"I—I cannot die. Oh, no."

"You must, and there's an end of it. Is it not preferable to cast yourself into the river than to be for weeks in a felon's cell, to be brought out finally to be hooted at by a mob who have come to be amused with your execution? Is there, I say, any comparison between the two? What on earth can save you —how can you leave England without money? It is impossible; you have no hope, Wilson. It's an infernal unlucky affair, but we can't help it—we can't help it."

Wilson glanced round him a moment, and then made a movement to escape from his companion; but Hilliard frustrated it by suddenly seizing his arm, as he said close to his ear, in a hissing whisper—

"Beware—beware! You cannot escape me. Fool! do you think that I will risk my own safety by allowing you to be taken? No, I must preserve myself, Wilson."

"Preserve yourself?"

"Yes; another attempt on your part to escape from me, and I will shoot you dead. Madman! Do you for one moment imagine that I risked so much in rescuing you from yonder place in Greenwich for your sake? No, I knew full well your weakness. My own danger made me so enterprising. You would, before the rope got round your own neck, bring mine into the noose— you would, Wilson."

"Betray you?"

"Yes."

"Oh, no—no—no. As I live, no,

Hilliard—I swear on my knees, I swear I would not. Trust me, I would not breathe a word. Your name should never pass my lips."

"In some moment of weakness, you would tell all. But come on—come on. We will discuss this matter further as we walk. Come on, I say."

As Hilliard did not turn towards the river, which was Wilson's great dread, he followed him, still muttering oaths and protestations that he would never betray his—Hilliard's—share in the murder.

The morning was rapidly approaching, and a cold, keen air was blowing from the water, across the flat, marshy land which divided it from the road the two guilty men were pusuing. Now and then, too, a few straggling drops of rain would fall, giving an indication of coming showers, if the wind should last in the quarter it then came from.

Some distance onwards, Hilliard knew there was an old condemned building, which was situated close to the river's edge, and had at one time been connected with a wharf that belonged to it, but with it had gone to ruin and decay. Towards this house Hilliard slowly led his victim, assuring him as they went, with some faint gleam of hope, that after all his life might be spared him a little longer, and he might at least be permitted to have the chance of evading the law.

Hilliard smiled to himself as the rain evidently increased. A better excuse for getting Wilson into the ruined house than under the pretence of avoiding the shower he could not have found, and as they now came by a turn of the road very near to it, he said—

"Well, Wilson, we will talk over the matter again, but we are likely to get wet, I think."

Wilson looked up, quite unconscious of the rain, as with hope in his voice, he replied—

"Yes, good Hilliard, let us talk of it. How could you think that I would betray you? They should torture me first, and even then I would not name you."

"If I were sure, Wilson——"

"Ah, be sure. You may, Hilliard—I betray you? Never, never."

"The rain is increasing. We must get shelter somewhere."

"Rain?"

"Yes—do you not feel it?"

"Yes—now—now I do, but I did not. There is no shelter here, Hilliard. Let us walk close to the hedge, we shall then avoid it."

"What house is that, I wonder?" remarked Hilliard, with well acted indifference, as he pointed to the old wharf and condemned dwelling.

"It looks like a ruin," said Wilson.

"Then it is empty, I dare say, and will be just the place in which, while we shelter ourselves from the rain, we can have a quite conversation about our affairs. Come on, Wilson—come on."

Deceived by his careless, indifferent manner, Wilson made no hesitation about following him towards the house, and in a few minutes they stood by the remnant of a wall which had once enclosed a garden belonging to it on the sideway from the river.

"We must climb this," remarked Hilliard; "by heavens, the shower increases fearfully. Over, Wilson, over, or we shall be wet to the skin in a few moments."

Thus urged, the trembling Wilson scrambled over the low wall, which was in such a state of decay, that he displaced several bricks in his progress; Hilliard rapidly followed him, and the pair then crossing what had at one time been a pleasant spot of garden ground, came to the door. Well Hilliard knew that one door was open, but he made the remark of—

"I wonder if we shall be able to effect an entrance here?" as he pushed what he recollected, for he had more than once visited the dilapidated premises, would yield readily to his touch.

"There seems no fastening," said Wilson, tremulously.

"That's lucky," remarked Hilliard. "Come in, come in, I say—why do you linger there for in the rain?"

Wilson was indeed lingering in the rain, for the shower had increased to a regular pelting mist of rain, which ploughed the very clay, and was soaking the unconscious man to the very skin. Something, however, appeared suddenly to have come across his mind which made him hesitate—a dread of he know not what—a shuddering horror of a danger that made itself known only to his heart by the awful terror of its presence, but showed not its face, or gave the slightest indication of what it really was.

Hilliard saw the hesitation of his victim, and a demoniac expression crossed his face, as he said—

"In the name of Heaven and hell! why do you stand there, when you can have shelter by advancing a couple of steps? Come on, I say."

"Oh, Hilliard, Hilliard!" half spoke, half screamed Wilson. "You mean me fair?—Swear to me by even the faint hope which you can have in the world that is to come you will not murder me!"

"Murder you!—I murder you! What should I get by murdering you? Curses on your false information, I have already done one murder for nothing. I have no desire to do another."

"You mean me fairly, Hilliard?—You really do?"

"Stay in the rain if you have any doubts."

"Well, well, I will trust you. You see now, Hilliard, what perfect confidence I have in you. I am coming. There, now, I am by your side. We may be useful to each other yet, you know, Hilliard,—by far too useful to wish for each other's death. If we two could not now trust each other, who could—who could, Hilliard?"

"Ay, who could?" said Hilliard, as he preceded the frightened companion of his crimes into the interior of the house, the boards of which creaked under their tread, through the empty rooms of which the wind from the river swept with a hollow moaning sound, and which had something inexpressibly mournful and discordant occasionally in it. Each sound went to the heart of the terrified Wilson like a death knell. He fancied that if he could see Hilliard's face, he should be able to form some judgment of his sincerity; but that he could not do, for the early light of morning was much dimmed by the heavy clouds, charged with rain, which had swept across the eastern sky, nearly obscuring the faint beams of the morning sun, which else by then would have been awakening the world to life and beauty.

The sullen dash of the river could now be heard quite plainly as it washed round the old blackened and time-worn piles that supported that portion of the wharf and warehouses which, for convenience, were just over the edge of the stream.

Then Hilliard paused, for he had reached a room on the first floor which communicated with another that faced the river, and from which a door opened from floor to ceiling, for the convenience of a crane, which in the high and palmy days of the old house had creaked and groaned with many a precious burden.

"The rain does not abate, Wilson," he said.

"No—no—I hear it still. How it bounds from the old window-sills, and what a noise it makes upon the water."

"Are you—very wet—Wilson?"

There was a something in Hilliard's tone that sent an icy cold pang to the heart of Wilson, who, in a hoarse whisper, for fear almost deprived him of the power of utterance, said,

"Am I not very wet, Hilliard?—I—I—am not. Oh, no. Besides, it is not much matter, you know, if I were."

"It is no matter at all."

"No—matter—Hilliard?"

"No, Wilson. You surely are not so very, very foolish as to make yourself the frightful spectacle on a scaffold which you say has haunted you so much in your dreams?"

"Oh, for the love of Heaven—for the love of mercy—explain to me what you mean, or suspense will kill me. Your words are dark and mysterious. Your tone of voice is strange and altered. You turn away your face as if you feared I should read some horrible truth in the expression of your features. Oh, speak again, Hilliard! speak to me. This silence to me is full of terrors."

"When," said Hilliard, in a low tone, "I jeopardised my own life to save you from imprisonment, it was under the express stipulation that to avoid the throng of horrors with which you were then and are now surrounded, you would drown yourself in the Thames."

"But life—life, Hilliard. Oh! think of life."

"How can your thoughts be of life?

In your case it is the hangman or the river.'"

"But one is remote."

"And—and the other's near, Wilson. I solemnly swear —"

"No—no—no," shrieked Wilson, "I guess too well the nature of the frightful oath that hovers on your lips."

"Do you? then I may spare its utterance. I will inflict a slight pain upon you to save you from such protracted agony as would drive you distracted. Come, Come."

Wilson held his head with his hands a moment in a strange, frantic manner—then he said,—

"Is this a dream?"

"Fancy it one," said Hilliard. " 'Tis all the same. Some people say that human life is a dream, and I have sometimes myself thought the same. Come, come."

"Where—oh, where, Hilliard? Your words are terrible, and you point to—to— "

" The river which will soon roll over your corpse. As yet suspicion has not pointed at me in connection with the murder of Mr. Noble. If you were dead it never could. If you were dead, too, you would escape great torment and a dreadful execution—for these reasons, Wilson, you must die."

Trembling so frightfully that his teeth chattered so he could scarcely speak, and his limbs shaking in such a manner that it was as much as he could do to stand, he then knelt at Hilliard's feet, and lifting up his hands, he moaned,—

"Spare me—spare me."

Hilliard shook for a moment, as if he were suffering from ague, and then without a word he seized Wilson by the collar of his coat behind. A scream burst from the wretched man, but Hilliard was determined. He dragged him into the next room, and a dash of rain immediately came upon them both.

"Mercy! mercy!" said Wilson.

Hilliard's lank black hair hung like snakes around his face—an unholy fury glowed in his eyes, and he bit his lips till the blood flowed down upon his breast. Still with a desperate and wild strength he dragged his unhappy and screaming associate onwards. They stood for a moment on the brink of the chasm, beneath which flowed the dark troubled tide of the river. The rain was still falling in abundance, producing a thick mist from the surface of the river—the wind howled and shrieked around the house.

"Down, down," cried Hilliard; "d——n— down with you!" Wilson could not be shaken off. He clung with all the strength of despair to his companion—he twined his fingers in his clothing—as easily might, at the moment, iron rings have been unbent as those rigid fingers of the screaming man. To and fro they rolled for a moment on the extreme verge of the deep doorway, and it seemed that if one toppled over, the other must necessarily follow, locked in the wild embrace of death.

There stood a part of the old supports of the crane close to the door-way, but a little apart from the wall. It might be secure, or it might give way with a touch, but Hilliard risked it by twining his left arm round it, while foreshortening his right, he gave Wilson a dreadful blow in the face.

"Down! down!" he said.

The wretched man relaxed his hold. He tottered a moment on the verge of the precipice. Another blow fell upon his chest. With one gurgling shriek he then went with a sullen dash into the river.

Hilliard still held by the rough pillar he had saved himself by clinging to. He strove to look through the mist down into the river, but he could see nothing. The tide merely dashed as before against the old blackened piles.

" He is gone—he is gone," muttered Hilliard. "I am safe—safe—I am safe now."

CHAPTER XLII.

THE FASHIONABLE BREAKFAST.—THE NOTES OF DISMISSAL.—MR. GIRKINS ON HIS AGREEABLE MISSION.—THE ALARM.

WHEN Girkins returned to the room in which he had left the merchant at the fashionable hotel, he was very well pleased to see that he evidently regarded with great admiration the costly preparations for breakfast by which he was surrounded, for the table was completely laid, with the exception of what was actually intended for eating and drinking, and, on a showy dinner-table, or breakfast-table, such matters form by no means the largest items there to be seen.

For example. there were rare and beautiful flowers, in costly crystal and silver goblets; a lofty epergne in the centre of the table, which contained divers inviting condiments upon little shelves. Moreover, the table was loaded with silver plate of every shape and design that could be required for aiding in the consumption of any of the good things the establishment afforded for a rich and most luxurious morning meal.

"My dear sir," said Girkins, "Lord Hawksworth desires me to express to you his very great gratification at your presence, and to say that he will be with you directly he has made some necessary changes in his dress, as he would not for the world sit down with you *en dishabille*."

"Oh, really," said the gratified merchant, "his lordship is very polite—very polite, indeed. I began the world with three-and-a-penny, and I'm sure, Girkins, lords and such-like can hardly be expected to take such pains about me, and to treat me with so much consideration."

"Indeed, Mr. Trueman, Lord Hawksworth knows the value of talent and industry."

"But you know, Girkins, eh? I am but a very simple man—a very simple man indeed."

"No—no, indeed."

"Yes—oh, yes! I am, I may say, a mere mortal—a mere mortal, Mr. Girkins, although I have made a large fortune without any help from anybody. Ah! I have nobody to thank, not I—I stepped into no dead man's shoes. Oh, dear, no! Though I say it, I owe all I have—and that's not a very little —to my own exertions. You, Girkins, may be pleased to say, my own talents; but I say, my own exertions. Early and late I stuck to my business, and so, you see, my business stuck to me, Girkins, and I never for a moment forgot that I was working on a capital of three-and-a-penny only."

"You have indeed done wonders, Mr. Trueman. Indeed, as I often remark to my confidential friends——But, bless me, here is his lordship!"

At this moment Lord Hawksworth entered the room, in an elegant morning costume, for, being a frequent visitor at that hotel, he had a toilette apparatus and a tolerable wardrobe for all ordinary purposes constantly there. He immediately went up to Mathew Trueman, and, seizing him by both hands, he said—

"My dear sir, how can I sufficiently appreciate this very kind condescension. It shows me that the little a—a—what shall I call it, of last evening, is viewed by you in that light which—a—a——"

"Which," continued Girkins, coming to his lordship's relief, "every one would have expected from the clear intellect and great discrimination of Mr. Trueman."

"My very sentiment—my very sentiment!" cried Hawksworth. "Pray be seated, Mr. Trueman, and we will endeavour to do justice to what breakfast they may indulge us with here. A —a—Girkins, may I trouble you to agitate the—the bell?"

Girkins did agitate the bell, and a waiter obeyed the summons ere it had done sounding.

"Breakfast, Charles—breakfast," said Hawksworth. "Let us have something of anything you may have in the house. My dear Mr. Trueman, have you, now, any particular choice for any one thing above another for your breakfast?"

"No; nothing very particular. When I began the world with three-and-a-penny, I used to be very glad of a penny roll and a halfpenny worth of milk, but since then I have had a few breakfasts, I rather flatter myself, of a different description. Eh, Girkins?"

"Indeed you have, Mr. Trueman."

"No doubt, a—a—no doubt," drawled Lord Hawksworth, as he threw himself languidly into a chair. "Charles, be quick; Mr. Trueman does not like to be kept waiting."

Charles left the room after perpetrating the profoundest of profound and respectful bows; but when he had the door fairly closed, a broad grin crossed his face, and he said, in an audible tone—

"A money-lender, of course. I

hope he'll bite, in which case I shall have a chance of getting the eighty odd pounds his lordship owes me."

It was a fact that this scion of nobility—this hereditary and noble legislator, was in debt to some score or more of waiters at different hotels!

"Now, my dear sir," said Lord Hawksworh, "as we perfectly and clearly understand each other with regard to the little affair of last night, will you permit me to ask you if it was known to you that a clerk of yours, and, as I am informed, an errand boy of yours, trespassed upon my premises on that occasion?"

"You may well ask me, my lord," said Trueman; "and I can only say that a more atrocious and impudent proceeding I never met with in all my life. It is totally and entirely beyond my comprehension."

"Then no one else need attempt to understand it, I'm sure," said Girkins. "I confess myself to have been perfectly astounded."

A couple of waiters, now, with great celerity, laid a luxurious breakfast, and when they had left the room, which they did upon Lord Hawksworth telling them he would dispense with their attendance, he again resumed the discussion, by saying—

"You will forgive me, I am sure, Mr. Trueman, for speaking to you with the freedom of a friend on this subject, but really it would be a thousand pities for a lovely and most accomplished girl, such as your daughter, to throw herself away upon either your clerk or your errand-boy."

"What?" cried Mathew Trueman, starting back and upsetting an egg in his intense horror of the proposition.

"I repeat it, Mr. Trueman," said Lord Hawksworth, as he calmly sipped the delicious coffee that spread a fragrance over the room; "it would be a thousand pities; a girl that is fit for the highest rank of life; that would a—a——"

"Grace a coronet, if I may be excused the pun," put in Girkins, who always came to his lordship's assistance when his lordship's oratory was at fault.

"The what!" cried Mathew Trueman, who might well excuse the pun, seeing that he was quite unconscious of it.

"My little jest," said Girkins.

"Jest, sir? d—n me, it's no jesting matter; d—n it, I can't see the joke of it."

"Certainly not," said Hawksworth.

"My daughter throw herself away upon a poor wretch of a clerk, with seventy pounds a year—my daughter—my Grace—my only child?"

"Or an errand boy," suggested Hawksworth.

"With five shillings a week," added Girkins.

"Four—four, only!" screamed Mathew Trueman, with wild vehemence. "He only gets four and his tea."

On any other occasion Hawksworth and Girkins must have laughed outright at this; but the stake they were now playing for was of far too great importance to be trifled with, and they both kept their countenances admirably. They had quite succeeded in their first object, which was to stir Mathew Trueman to a great pitch of passion, so that he would be ready to accept any proposition which should flatter him with a hope of immediate vengeance upon the delinquents, Rivers and Tom Hackey.

"However humiliating," said Girkins gravely, "such a supposition may be, Mr. Trueman, I, as well as Lord Hawsworth, most deeply regret that facts have forced it upon our consideration."

"I will prosecute them both," cried Trueman.

"Upon my word, if I were to do so too," remarked Hawksworth, "it would serve them right."

"It would, my lord."

"But, nevertheless, I shall be satisfied with their immediate discharge from your service without a character."

"It shall be done! It shall be done."

"You are acting in this matter, Mr. Trueman, with becoming spirit, and that energy which any one would expect from your general character," said Girkins.

"I will do it," added Trueman. "Really, the impertinence of low—I mean poor people, of course—is beyond everything and anything. It must be put a check to, my lord. There is, and always will be, a great struggle going on in this country, between those who have, my lord, and those who have not; but poor low people must be put down,

THE QUARREL BETWEEN HAWKSWORTH AND GIRKINS.

and kept down, and all that sort of thing."

"I perfectly agree with you, Mr. Trueman," said Lord Hawksworth, "and I think your sentiments do you great honour. If we had many like you in the House of Commons, it would be a very good thing."

"We have a tolerable sprinkle," suggested Girkins, and then he added, in an under tone of irony, "you are a truly liberal man, Mr. Trueman, however some people might say that your sentiments as regarded poor people were carried the smallest possible extent too far."

"Not a whit—not a whit," said Hawksworth. "Allow me, my dear Mr. Trueman, to assist you to a cup of coffee."

"Thank you," said the merchant, in a great fume. "I will discharge them both. Upon my reputation, I will.

May I never be able to—to—negotiate another bill, if I don't. The insolence of the thing!"

"Unparalleled!"

"Beyond imagination."

"My dear sir," said Girkins, as he deliberately cracked an egg, "will you permit me to take the liberty of suggesting a course to you which will give you little trouble, and perhaps quite answer your views?"

"What course, Mr. Girkins?"

"Why, simply this: that you write the dismissals of Rivers and Hackey from your service. I merely throw out the hint, as being more consistent with the real dignity of such a man as yourself, Mr. Trueman, whose acts, of course, are looked at, and made into precedents."

"I—I—really—will," said Mathew Trueman. "There is something in that suggestion, Girkins, although it is seldom that any one can suggest anything to me that I have not thought of before."

"Then if you approve of the course," interposed Hawksworth, " why not write the dismissals here, and give yourself no further trouble about such very insignificant persons, Mr. Trueman?"

A pang came across the merchant's heart as he thought of the conversation with Grace in the coach on the way home from Lord Hawksworth's villa, and he said, with some appearance of confusion—

"What—here—now—now, my lord?"

"Yes; here is every possible accommodation, and what is more—bless me, it has just occurred to me—Girkins, I daresay, will have no objection to take the dismissals to your counting-house, and settle the whole affair without any disagreeables, while you stay with me and talk over our mutual affairs a little."

"I shall be proud and happy," said Girkins, " to be of any such service to Mr. Trueman, I'm sure."

Trueman looked uneasy for a moment or two. Again his daughter's words occurred to him, and he thought—

"Will she—dare she put in practice the determination she avowed if I discharged Rivers?"

Then a flush of anger came across his mind as he again thought—

"Cannot I discharge a clerk or an errand-boy from my service with any excuse or cause if I think proper? I will—I will do it. They shall go, and —and it will be better, perhaps, for Girkins to do it in the way proposed, for I may then save a scene which might be very disagreeable."

Each moment the plan of operations assumed, to the mind of Trueman, a more agreeable shape. It would be quite pleasant to get rid of Rivers and Hackey without any sort of personal altercation.

"I feel quite inclined," he said aloud, "to do as you have so very kindly proposed to me."

Girkins slowly rose, and slinking like a cat to a sideboard, he returned with pens, ink, and paper, which he as quietly laid before the merchant, while Hawksworth said—

"There could not be a better or a more dignified course, Mr. Trueman. It would be a frightful thing for you some morning to be saluted as father-in-law, and asked for a maintenance from one or the other of these persons."

" I'd—I'd murder them," cried Trueman. " I—I—but never mind; leave my service they shall this day, and if they dare to come to my premises ever again, I will give them in charge to the police."

"A very good thought," drawled Hawksworth.

"A happy thought," said Girkins. "Oh, you have not written the discharges, Mr. Trueman."

" But I will—I will," cried Trueman, as he hurriedly snatched up a pen and nervously dipped it in the ink.

Girkins affected to be arranging his hat by the glass, while Hawksworth lolled back in his chair, looking vacantly at the ceiling.

Mathew Trueman hesitated a moment, and then he wrote—

" I HEREBY discharge from my service Francis Rivers, but will send to him the current quarter's salary when due wherever he may appoint.
                    "MATHEW TRUEMAN."

He then wrote a duplicate with Hackey's name in it, and the alteration of week for quarter.

" I have written them," he said.

Girkins was by his side in a moment, and hastily blotting them, he folded them up and placed in his pocket-book the documents,

" What is the time?" said Trueman.

"Scarcely half-past nine," said Girkins; "I will be back, Mr. Trueman, by a little after ten at the latest."

So saying, without waiting for another word, he hastily left the room, congratulating himself upon having in his possession such means of discomfiture to Rivers and Tom Hackey, who he felt sure were no despicable foes to his schemes.

We will prefer following Girkins to the merchant's counting-house to listening to the conversation between Trueman and Lord Hawksworth, consisting as it did on the one side of vanity, coupled with affected humility, and on the other of a drawling acquiescence in whatever was said, with now and then some complimentary remarks about the beauty of Grace.

CHAPTER XLIII.

THE ATTEMPTED DISMISSAL.—MR. GIRKINS IN TROUBLE.—THE COURAGE OF INNOCENCE AND VIRTUE.

GIRKINS lost no time in throwing himself into a coach the moment he could see one, and then ordering the coachman to drive to Thames Street, he sat with smiling satisfaction in the lumbering vehicle, figuring to himself the scene in which he was about to take so conspicuous a part at the counting-house.

"Had Trueman been in the way now," he muttered, "while this little affair is in progress, some appeal from Rivers, or perchance from Grace herself, might shake his resolution, but I can add to this affair such circumstances of insult as shall anger the hot-headed young man past endurance, and, far from supplicating, he will, in all human probability, commit himself still further by some intemperate violence."

Rivers, after a night of great restlessness, during which his over-heated fancy presented to him in his dreams his own, his beautiful Grace, in various circumstances of danger, from which he was ever trying to rescue her in vain, sought the office of the merchant with a sad and gloomy prognostic of what the day would bring forth.

There was one vision of his slumbers that had exercised a most sickening influence over his mind. It was this—

He fancied that he was crossing some bridge at the dead hour of the night, when a cry, so awful and loud—so heart-piercing and terrible, came upon his ears, that it almost stopped the current of his blood, and drove his brain to madness. Then something in a hissing whisper seemed to say in his ears—

"That was the voice of Grace Trueman."

He then thought that he flew distracted to the edge of the bridge, and looking over the parapet he saw floating with dreadful significance down the black stream the two arms of some one elevated above the water, while the whole of the remainder of the body was concealed beneath the rolling tide.

By some intuition he then seemed to know that it was Grace who was drowning, and with one bound he cleared the bridge and fell into the stream. Down—down he went, while rushing noises and fearful flashes of light surrounded him, and it seemed as if he should never rise again from the profound abyss of waters into which he had plunged. In his despair then he found breath to utter a cry, and that cry awoke him, for he uttered it in reality.

Oh, how glad he was for a few short delicious moments to find himself in his own little chamber, and with what a deep feeling of thankfulness to Heaven did he, after a moment's pause, fervently exclaim—

"It was a dream—it was a dream!"

But, alas, soon the particulars of his vision came upon his memory, and he trembled as he thought of the arms just projecting above the water, and telling so mutely, yet so very eloquently, of the agony that was below its surface.

It required all his reasoning powers to argue himself out of the fear which his dream had implanted in his breast, and even when he told himself how weak and childish it was of him to allow his mind to be shaken by a dream, he still shuddered at it.

As for poor Tom Hackey, he had made up his mind to be dismissed; but with an elasticity of spirits, which the more profoundly thinking Rivers did not possess, he pleased himself with the thought that it might be the making of their fortunes; for, as he said to himself while dressing at an early hour,

"What's to hinder Rivers, with his fine voice and good-looking appearance, from becoming a theatrical star as well as myself, a-hem? We shall be able to star it together, and astonish delighted and enthusiastic audiences. Let me see, how delightful it will be to read a newspaper paragraph commencing in this way,—

"'Last evening one of the most densely crowded houses that has ever been seen within the walls of old Drury assembled to witness the first appearance, after a lengthened sojourn in the provinces, of those two eminent trage-dians, Francis Rivers and Thomas Hackey. *Hamlet* was the piece, in which the Dane was personated to the life by Mr. Hackey, while we never saw a more effective Laertes than was presented by Mr. Rivers. Macready played the grave-digger on this occasion only.' "

By the time Tom had arrived at this climax, he had got on all his clothes, and exclaiming,

" I have set my life upon a cast, and I must stand the hazard of the die," he rushed down the attic stairs towards the street, and at a rapid pace took his way to the office in Thames-street.

And what were Grace's feelings after the interview with her father in the coach, and the conversation which had there ensued ?

Oh, what a weight of woe hung upon her pure soul ! what tears of agony did she weep at the thought that her best—her purest—her holiest feelings were at war with each other : her love for her father, and her love for him who had found a place in her heart, co-equally dear.

The struggle in such a mind as hers was terrible and distressing ; but it was not a long one, for her deep sense of what was right soon enabled her, how-ever painfully, to come to a just conclusion.

That Rivers should be discharged and thrown penniless upon the wide world because he had dared to protect her from the insults of an unprincipled libertine, appeared to her so monstrous a proceeding that she found, as she thought of it, a feeling of indignation rising in her breast, almost to the exclusion, temporarily, of every other feeling.

" It is not," she said, " that he has given me his heart, and that I love him, which makes me think as I do ; no, no. Were he the greatest stranger—the most indifferent person in my affections, I would not sanction so—so ungrateful, unjust an act as to punish him for what he should be commended—bring distress upon him for what should redound to his profit and his honour. Can it be possible that my father's judgment is so much led prisoner by these men as to induce him, otherwise just and clear-headed, to

perpetrate so shameful an act ? He cannot mean it ; he surely will this morning think differently."

Agitated by these and similar thoughts, Grace rose at an unusually early hour, and slipping on merely a loose morning wrapper, she walked across the landing from her own bed-room door to that of her nurse, Mrs. Woodfall.

In a moment she stood by the bed-side of her faithful attendant.

" Nurse, nurse," she said, tearfully, " are you awake ?"

Mrs. Woodfall started from her sleep, as she exclaimed with genuine terror,

" My dear, is that you ?   Are you not well ?"

" Yes, nurse, quite well ; but perhaps a little over anxious, and—and over fearful."

" Fearful, my darling, at what ?"

" The coming day. So, if you please nurse, I will remain and talk with you."

" Certainly ; I will get up, Grace, directly. My dear child, you look quite pale and ill. Ah, how can anybody have the heart to vex you ; *if* all the world loved you as I do, Grace, you would never shed a tear."

" It is a mistaken feeling in one who loves me, I know well, that rends my heart," said Grace. " My father loves me, but he will not let me be happy my own way, because there is no convin-cing him that it is the right way."

" But, my dear, you do not really think that your father will act harshly towards Mr. Rivers for his conduct last night—bless him for being there to protect you."

" I can scarcely think so, nurse," said Grace, as she covered her beautiful face with her hands, and wept. " Yet, I know not why, my heart is very sad."

" Then it's a shame that it should be so ; but cheer up, Grace, I cannot think Mr. Trueman would act as you fear."

" It would be unjust, you know, towards any one."

" It would, indeed."

" I—I am thinking that before break-fast I will see my father and satisfy myself that he will not act in a manner that would so ill become him."

" Well, my dear, if you like, perhaps

it would be as well. Just stay here while I go and see if he is up."

The nurse was not long in ascertaining from the girl, to whom Girkins had given the crown piece, that Mathew Trueman had left the house some half an hour or more before, along with a "gentleman."

"A gentleman! Who was it?"

"Oh, I doesn't know; all I knows is as he was a real gentleman, I'm sure o' that. I heard 'em saying something about a *breakfastes* as they went out."

With this meagre information Mrs. Woodfall returned to Grace, and putting the best possible construction on the circumstance, in order to cheer her, she said,

"My dear, your father has gone out with some one, and you know, if he had intended to say anything to Mr. Rivers this morning, he would most likely have stayed at home to do so, you see, so cheer up and hope for the best."

"I will, I will, nurse."

The next half hour passed in anxious discourse between Grace and Mrs. Woodfall, after which, the kind-hearted girl found herself much comforted by the friendly sympathy of her nurse, who truly loved her with the affection of a mother.

Still Mathew Trueman, to the great surprise of the whole household, came not home, for such a circumstance as his being away from business at the hour of the office opening, was quite beyond the recollection of the servants.

Encouraged by her nurse, Grace began to augur favourably of this absence of her father.

"He will not discharge Rivers," she thought, "and in order to avoid the awkwardness of meeting with him, and telling him so, he has chosen to go out, leaving him to conclude so much, and go on with his duties."

This supposition appeared reasonable enough, and by the time that the hour of commencing business had arrived, Grace had composed herself into a tolerably easy state of mind.

Mrs. Woodfall, whose feelings towards Rivers before were in the highest degree favourable, was so much delighted with his conduct at Lord Hawksworth's fete, that she determined to go down to the counting-house, and thank him on her own part, for his care of her darling Grace.

This she determined upon without saying anything to Grace, and accordingly stepping quietly down the staircase, she turned the handle of the office-door, and popped in. There were both Rivers and Tom Hackey there, and only them, so Mrs. Woodfall walked in at once, and said in her homely and affectionate way to Rivers—

"My dear Mr. Rivers, I have come to thank you for taking care of my child last night, and you too, Tom."

Rivers flushed with colour, as he said—

"Mrs. Woodfall, I hope always to act towards Grace, so as to meet with your approbation. How—how is she this morning?"

"Very well, but a little anxious and uneasy."

"What!" exclaimed Tom Hackey, "has not gentle sleep knit up the ravelled sleeve of care?"

"Leave off your playhouse nonsense now, Tom," said Mrs. Woodfall, "I quite wonder at you."

"What a nurse in Romeo and Juliet you'd make," said Tom, "or even the Queen in Hamlet. 'Tis not alone my inky cloak, good mother, nor customary suits of solemn black. By-the-by, Mrs. Woodfall, have you any idea of where Mathew is this morning?"

"No, indeed, I have not; but, Tom, some of these days you'll get yourself into serious trouble, and be discharged, for your play-acting, and calling Mr. Trueman as you do—Mathew, to everybody. You know as well as I do, that he's a proud man, and would be very angry at it, indeed, if he heard you."

"Let him," said Tom, "he could but take a deep and bloody revenge. I'll have a starling taught to say nothing but Mathew—Mathew—Mathew."

Tom was poking the counting-house fire at that moment, and as was not unfrequently the case, he was seized with a theatrical mania, and flourishing the poker over his head, he cried, as he made a thrust at the door—

"Come on, Macduff, and d—d be he who first cries hold—enough! Come on—ha, ha, ha! Come on!"

It did appear to Tom, that at the moment he struck the door with the end of the poker, it would have opened if he had not, for it moved about an inch perceptibly, although he, Tom, at the moment could not stay his arm. A conviction then came across his mind that it was the merchant who had been upon the point of coming in, and with the exclamation of—

"Mathew, by the infernal Gods!" he made an ingenious attempt to hide the poker, by thrusting it up the back of his coat, where its handle projected in a singular manner from his neck some distance above his head.

Rivers looked vexed and alarmed for Tom's sake, and Mrs. Woodfall shook her head reproachfully. Then the door slowly opened, and Girkins, who had received a severe rap on the nose, put his head into the counting-house.

"It ain't him," said Tom.

"Good morning, gentlemen," said Girkins, as, seeing there was no more danger, he entered the office.

"Mr. Trueman is not at home, sir," said Rivers.

"I happen to know so much, Mr. Rivers," replied Girkins, in rather an insolent tone.

Rivers made no further remark, but immediately turned round to his desk, leaving Girkins to go or stay as it might please him the best.

As for Tom, he withdrew the poker from his back, and after, in dumb show, making several antics with it behind Girkins, he replaced it in the grate.

"Mr. Rivers," said Girkins, "I regret very much interrupting you, sir, but I have something for you."

Mrs. Woodfall appeared to have escaped the observation of Girkins, as she stood nearly behind the door when he opened it, and he had not once turned round, but had, with a demoniac and spiteful sneer, kept his eyes fixed upon Rivers throughout the short time he had been there.

"A message for me, sir?" said Rivers, with unfeigned astonishment, facing Girkins.

"Yes, sir, for you. I believe I am quite right in addressing you as Mr. Rivers?"

"You know well you are, Mr. Girkins."

"Very good, sir; I have done myself the pleasure of coming some distance and at some expense for coach hire, solely on your account, and that of this other gentleman."

"Do you mean me?" said Tom.

"I do mean you."

"Then I'm very sorry you've given yourself the trouble. You may go again as soon as you like. 'Stand not upon the order of your going, but go at once.'"

"Indeed—a-hem!" said Girkins. "Perhaps some one else may see the necessity of going before I do."

"Tom—Tom," said Rivers, "pray be quiet. Mr. Girkins, you say you have some message from some one for me. Who is it from?"

"Mr. Mathew Trueman."

"And to me?" said Tom.

"Likewise from Mr. Mathew Trueman."

"Oh, indeed!"

"Peace, Tom—peace," said Rivers. "Now, Mr. Girkins, let us have the message, if you please."

Girkins, with provoking deliberation, took out his pocket-book, and affected to be looking among the papers for the one he wanted, while Rivers was filled with anxiety, and Tom Hackey looked the same, with amazement.

The unprincipled agent then of his unprincipled employers, slowly produced the two slips that Trueman had been so artfully induced to write at the hotel.

"I have a written communication for you, Mr. Rivers," he said.

"And for me?" said Tom.

"Do not be impatient, Mr. Hackey. I have likewise one for you. I presume they will be found quite explicit, and require no explanation whatever upon my part."

So saying, he handed one note to Rivers, and the other to the bewildered Tom Hackey.

"My discharge?" said Rivers.

"And mine?" echoed Hackey.

Mrs. Woodfall immediately slipped out of the office without being perceived by Girkins, who stood gloating over the two victims of his plotting and manoeuvring.

"I presume that is explicit?" he said to Rivers.

"It is, sir," replied the indignant young man, "but this is not the way in which I shall leave the service of Mathew Trueman."

"Pray, how then will you leave it?"

"With a character which I will have from him that shall enable me to procure other employment."

"And so will I!" cried Tom. "And what's more, old Greengage, or Girkins, or whatever your name is, you may go back and tell old Mathew I——"

The door of the office opened wide, and Grace stood like a statue of loveliness on the threshold.

CHAPTER XLIV.

THE COURAGE OF GRACE.—GIRKINS'S DISCOMFITURE.

FOR a few moments after this sudden and most unexpected appearance of Grace in the counting-house, there was a dead silence, and a paleness came over Girkins's face as he found there was now the chance of a difficulty in the execution of his mission, which he had not at all calculated upon.

"Miss Trueman," he ejaculated, making a desperate effort to recover himself, "I—I hope I see you quite well?"

"My father is not at home, sir," said Grace, coldly, moving from the doorway in as significant a manner as if she had said "Leave the place."

"I know, Miss Trueman, that your father is not at home," said Girkins; "I have but recently left him. He is breakfasting with his friend, Lord Hawksworth."

"When my father is from home," said Grace, calmly, "I claim some right of interference in what passes in this house. What is your business here, sir?"

Girkins was perfectly staggered at the calm courage of Grace, and he shrunk before the steady but beautiful gaze she bent upon him, like an evil spirit before an angel of light.

"My business here," he muttered, "is with Mr. Rivers and that young man, Hackey."

"Grace," said Rivers, "leave me to settle this, I——"

"No, Mr. Rivers; in my father's absence with his enemy—not his friend, as this man pretends—I will act as I think fitting. What message has he brought?"

"Our discharges," said Tom. "Bless you, Miss Grace, he's given us the sack withour judge or jury."

"That paper?" said Grace, indicating the one Rivers held in his hand.

"Is my dismissal from your father's service," he replied.

"Give it to me."

Rivers handed it to her.

"My father will think better of this," she said, reading it, "when he is not surrounded by evil counsellors."

She then tore it into fragments and threw it on the floor.

"Here's mine," cried the delighted Tom Hackey; and Grace immediately taking it, destroyed it in the same manner.

Girkins trembled with passion as he said—

"And—and what account, Miss Trueman, am I to give your father of this singular transaction?"

"You can tell my father," said Grace, "that his daughter sets a higher value on his honour, than his false, hollow friends."

"Indeed! Then I can tell you, young lady——"

"Hold, sir!" said Rivers, in a voice that made Girkins start again—"hold, for your own safety's sake. Dare to breathe one disrespectful word to this lady, and you shall bitterly repent it."

"You are good at threatening," said Girkins, as he prudently stepped a pace backward.

"Do not tempt me to perform my threats," said Rivers.

"Villain, avaunt!" cried Tom. "Thou knit, thou mite, thou soulless maggot, away, or I'll bring the bellows and blow you into the street. Don't I wish we had some damp dungeon here, we'd just pop you in, old Greengage."

"Leave this house," said Grace.

Girkins stood upon the threshold of the door, looking more like some wild animal at bay than a human being. He was evidently nearly bursting with passion, and yet had not the courage to risk the consequences of what he would like to say.

"Leave the house!" repeated Grace.

"Do you hear?" bawled Tom; "you're ordered off. Can't you go at once, or do you want to be kicked out?"

"I—I—I," said Girkins, "d——n!"

Without another word, then, he rushed into the street, foaming with rage.

The moment he was gone, Grace presented the greatest possible contrast to what she had been. All the feminine tenderness of her gentle nature came gushing to her heart; and, now that there was none to see her but those whom she knew loved her, and could feel for her distress, she sank into a seat, and, while tears gushed from her eyes, she said—

"When, oh, when will all this end?"

Mrs. Woodfall, who had been just outside the door, took one of her hands gently, while Rivers possessed himself of the other.

"My dear child," said the nurse, "you have acted nobly and properly as becomes you."

"Grace—Grace, my own dear Grace," murmured Rivers in her ear, "what do I not owe to you? Do not weep! Your tears fall upon my heart. Rather, a thousand times rather, would I be cast forth into the wide world a homeless wanderer than one tear of yours should flow to save me!"

"And so would I," said Tom Hackey, giving his eye a very hard wipe with the office duster, that lay at hand. "Don't you cry, Miss Grace, bless you! It's the worst of all, it is, to see you put out. There's something got in both my eyes, and my throat, too—there is."

The poor fellow could really say no more, for the sight of Grace's tears quite unmanned him.

"Never mind—never mind!" said Grace, as she strove to calm her emotion. "All will be well. My father will surely discover the heartlessness of those who now pervert his better judgment; and remember, both of you, come what may, I, and I only, am responsible for this morning's work."

"No," cried Rivers; "let the blame, if there be any, rest on my head. I would not have one harsh word said to you, Grace, for worlds."

"Nay, nay, leave it to me," she cried, "I pray you leave all to me. My father will say nothing harsh to me. And—and, if he should, I can best bear with it."

Mrs. Woodfall then walked up to Tom Hackey, and engaged him in conversation, for her natural kindness of heart prompted her to leave, if it were but for one brief minute, the lovers by themselves, for she knew that such minutes were to those young, gentle, and affectionate hearts most precious.

Rivers, then, still holding the hand of Grace in his, stooped his mouth to her ear, and said, in those low, sweet accents, which, coming from one in whom the heart is much and dearly interested, have about them so indescribable a charm and pathos—

"Grace, dear, dear Grace, let my fate be what it may—let misfortune lower upon me, and leave me to the cold mercy of a world which knows not much of that heavenly feeling, and I shall, in my heart of hearts, cherish your image as the gentle, beautiful light which shall guide me onward in my pilgrimage, lightening all burthens, steeling my mind against all harshness, and lending even to destruction a heavenly charm."

Grace replied to him through her tears.

"But, Rivers, do not believe that my father can turn you from him on such grounds as those he can only venture to allege. It cannot, will not be so."

"And—and if it should, Grace?"

She was silent for a moment, and then a gentle pressure of the hand was the mute but eloquent answer. It spoke volumes to the lover's heart. It told him that he would not be forgotten, although he might become the victim of prejudice and injustice.

"You will still," he said, "think of the poor clerk, who loved you—who adored you—who would have died for you, dear Grace?"

"Ever—ever!" sobbed Grace.

"Then let fortune do its worst, I am prepared for all. I am as one encased in triple coats of steel. Fate cannot find an arrow in her quiver that can now reach me, and I laugh the world to scorn. Your love, Grace, shall be a palladium between me and sorrow, which shall convert it to joy."

Grace looked up in his face through her tears, and for a moment she forgot everything in the delightful consciousness of being loved by him upon whom she had unreservedly bestowed her heart's best affections.

Could anything that this world could offer in after life equal the exquisite joy of that moment? Like a bright gleam from Heaven it came in the midst of doubt, difficulty, and danger, to bless them for their integrity, their pure affection, their honour and their clinging tenderness, which knew no guile, which suffered no change from time or circumstance.

Then Mrs. Woodfall, after keeping Tom Hackey in check for some moments, so that the lovers were uninterrupted, came quietly up to Grace, and said—

"Come, my dear child, we may do

THE FRACAS IN THE STREET BETWEEN HAWKSWORTH AND RIVERS.

more harm to Mr. Rivers by remaining here until your father returns, than we can possibly do good."

"True, true. Yes, true," said Grace, as she rose. "It is risking too much. Mr. Rivers, adieu! adieu!"

Rivers pressed her hand fervently to his lips as a "God bless you!" testified to his emotion and his love.

Tom Hackey then came forward and said—

"Miss Grace, you will shake hands with poor Tom for once; I will never ask you again."

Grace gave him her hand in a moment, and then the poor fellow, turning to Rivers, said, while a tear glistened in his eye—

"Don't be angry with me, it's the first time and the last."

He then gently kissed her hand, after which he retired to a corner of the office, and said not another word.

Grace walked to the door, and then

once more she turned, and held her hand out to Rivers.

"Farewell!" she said.

"Farewell!" he echoed.

The door closed, and it seemed to him, now that she had gone, as if a sudden darkness had fallen over the counting-house, and he sat down with a deep sigh.

How long he remained in a reverie he knew not, but he was aroused by Tom Hackey, who, gently touching him on the arm, said—

"Rivers, this won't do, you know. If old Mathew chooses to turn us away, he can and will."

Rivers started, and in a moment his precarious situation came full across his mind.

"True, Tom, True," he said; "I fear such will be the case, indeed."

"Then what do you mean to do?"

"Why, I shall compel Trueman to give us both written good characters, which he is bound to do, and then we will try to get employment somewhere else."

"Fiddle-de-dee," said Tom, snapping his fingers, "I've got a better plan."

"Have you, indeed?"

"Yes, I have."

"What is it, Tom?"

"Why, just this. You must go on the stage, where a brilliant fortune—loads of bouquets—benefits—and everything that's pleasant and delightful awaits you. You may depend upon my judgment, Rivers, you would make a grand hit, and old Mathew would be ready to eat his nails off, that he has treated you in the manner he has."

"I am afraid, Tom," said Rivers, with a mournful smile, "that you are too sanguine, and rate my abilities more by your partiality than my own deserts."

"Not a bit—not a bit," said Tom. "You would and must succeed. It would be positive insanity of you to waste your time in a merchant's counting-house."

"I hope I shall have an opportunity, Tom, of being so insane. It is my only chance. This is a time of peace, or else some of my father's old friends might get me a commission in the army, but there is no chance of such a thing, now."

"And a very good job, too," said Tom. "People's own quarrels, I always think, are quite enough for people to fight without putting on an old coat to be shot at for something they don't care, and in one half the cases don't know anything about."

"Well, Tom, there is certainly some philosophy in what you say," replied Rivers.

"There's a great deal if you would but look for it. Take my word, that as far as you are concerned, the stage is the thing."

"I should be glad of anything, Tom, which would promise me an honourable subsistence."

"Of course, but you would like much better to dash up to the stage-door in your carriage as a great star, and know that there was a crammed house that would tear up the benches if you were not to come."

Rivers laughed, as he said,—

"Ah, Tom, a theatrical life has many charms for you, I dare say, who know something of it; but you must recollect that I am quite innocent of its commonest technicalities, and in all probability should be a sad bungler."

"Pho! pho!" said Tom. "You don't understand how these things are managed on the stage. It's all nonsense about learning the profession and that kind of thing. All that is to be learnt you would learn at the flys of a theatre in a week. It comes to this, that everybody has some peculiar way in doing something. Now, if the public happened to like your way of acting you would be a great actor at once; and whether they liked it or not you would be a great actor if you happened to be the son of one."

"Indeed?"

"Yes! Why, you know as well as I what's going on at Covent Garden, now; there is a man, who, because he has a name that is famous in theatrical matters, is bringing on the stage, one after the other, the whole of his family, without any preparation at all, beyond downright impudence, in which they are all proficient."

"Well, that is true enough," said Rivers.

As he spoke Hilliard entered the office; he was ghastly pale, his lips, from his biting them when with Wilson in the house by the banks of the

Thames, were frightfully swollen; he trembled dreadfully, and his whole aspect and appearance was fearfully shocking.

Rivers could not take his eyes off him, although he would have wished anything rather than to be supposed by Hilliard to be taking any notice of him.

Tom Hackey stood with his uplifted hands, in one of which was the fire shovel, looking at him with the most undisguised astonishment, until Hilliard, perfectly aware of the sensation he was creating, turned sharply to him, and said in a harsh unnatural voice,—

"What are you staring at, eh? Did you never see me before, booby?"

"I'd rather see you behind," said Tom, "you look lovely to-day, and no mistake."

"Tom—Tom," said Rivers, warningly.

"If he treats me with any of his low insolence," said Hilliard, bending his brows upon Tom, "I will teach him a lesson of silence, he may remember to his cost."

"Don't bully me," said Tom. "It won't do, Hilliard. If people object to being looked at they shouldn't make themselves so remarkable."

"Remarkable?"

"Yes—you don't mean to say that you look like a human being, do you?"

"Enough, Tom, enough," said Rivers.

"Oh, I've done," said Tom, "only people needn't get in a rage at being looked at."

Hilliard sat down at his desk, and opening the lid, he held it so with his head, while he concealed his embarrassment, by affecting to search for something among his papers.

CHAPTER XLV.

THE STRANGE MASK.—MR. BUMBLETON SWIGGLES' AUDACITY.—THE RETURN OF THE MERCHANT.

RIVERS beckoned to Tom Hackey, and whispered in his ear, "For Heaven's sake, Tom, do not get into a quarrel with that man. Avoid him and make no remark concerning him."

"Well, I won't but did you ever see such a horrid look in anybody's face in all your life?"

"Never, I certainly confess. Hark! there is some one coming. I hear a footstep. Now, Tom, leave all this affair of our dismissals to me, should Mathew Trueman come in and say anything about it."

"But mustn't I——"

"Hush—hush—this may be him. Hush, Tom. For Heaven's sake leave all to me."

The door of the office was opened an extremely little way, and Tom, the moment he saw the face that peered in, uttered a loud groan, and exclaimed,

"That infernal Swiggles again."

"How do? Ah! how do?" said Mr. Bumbleton Swiggles, taking no notice of Tom's unfriendly remark.

"We really can't have you here," said Tom. "Be off with you, there's a good fellow, we are so uncommonly busy to-day."

"Glad to hear it," said Bumbleton Swiggles, walking in.

"'How doth the little busy bee,
Improve each shining hour.'

You have heard that before, I dare say, so I needn't repeat it all to you, my bold Achilles."

"Oh, yes, yes," said Tom, "a hundred times. Good morning—good morning, Mr. Swiggles."

"Yes, it's clearing up," said Swiggles, determined not to take a hint and begone. "We have had some heavy showers in the night—they say there has been a great deal of rain at Greenwich."

Bang went down the lid of Hilliard's desk, at the word Greenwich, and Swiggles cried,

"Bless me, I didn't know that gentleman was here before. Dear me, what a whack that desk lid came down with."

"Yes, it made a good mask," said Tom.

"Mask!" cried Bumbleton Swiggles. "Bless my heart and soul, I'll tell you a story of a mask——"

"Another time," groaned Tom.

"No, no. It won't take a minute. It happened at Naples to a young man I knew, named Marconi, who, as he looked from the window of his chamber at Naples, a crowd of individuals met his view dressed in every variety of costume; there were clowns and harlequins; Punch and Judy; big heads and little bodies, and *vice versa*, while a concert, performed upon every variety of domestic utensil, pots, pans, kettles, &c., filled the air with its discordant sounds.

"'Bless me,' said Marconi, half aloud. 'Really, I did not know it was the carnival.'"

"'Yes, signor,' replied the voice of his valet, who had entered unobserved, 'it commenced to-day.'

"I had not the slightest idea of it, Paulo,' replied Marconi, yawning.

"'How should you, signor,' returned Paulo, 'while you have been fast asleep.'

"'Why, what time can it be, Paulo?'

"'Near two, signor.'

"'And how many hours have I been asleep, do you think, Paulo?'"

"'Near twelve, signor; it was just two when you jumped into bed.'

"'Why, yes, Paulo; you see I must have some sleep, we cannot be up both night and day; if I remember rightly, I was a little so so; but never mind, a short life and a merry one: fetch my masque and domino.'

"'Yes, signor,' replied Paulo, and immediately disappeared; in a minute he returned bearing, the required articles, in which his master was soon arrayed, and joined the group below.

"He had, however, not long been amongst the masquers and tumblers before a female mask drew near with whom Marconi seemed much struck; her person was above the middle stature and *embonpoint*; there was a certain dignity in her movements which rooted his attention, and in spite of himself he turned to follow her.

"After regarding her attentively for some time he mustered sufficient courage to speak—

"'If I might be allowed the pleasure of the company of so handsome a mask I should be extremely happy.'

"'And wherefore?' returned the stranger in a sort of assumed tone.

"'For the gratification of beholding your exquisite form and face.'

"'And perhaps the latter may be less beautiful than you imagine.'

"'Impossible,' returned Marconi, the music of your voice alone would tempt an angel to adore you.'

"'Ha! ha!' replied the mask, 'how you men are given to flatter.'

"'Not at all; I assure you, I speak the sentiments of my heart.'

"'I can scarcely believe you.'

"'You may rely upon my sincerity,' returned Marconi, placing his hand upon his heart.

"'You then are the first sincere admirer I ever met with.'

"'I acknowledge the compliment,' replied our hero, and bent his head; 'but,' continued he, 'do you not find the crowd of maskers oppressive?'

"'I do.'

"'Then let us retire where we may converse more at liberty?'

"'I cannot, at present.'

"'Why?'"

"'There are those to whom my dress is known, and walking with a stranger might excite suspicon.'

"'But you know it is the carnival, and freedom is allowed to all.'

"'It is; but I must beg of you to leave me now.'

"'Will you meet me here at sunset?'

"'Willingly.'

"'Till then adieu, sweet mask,' replied Marconi, as he gazed after the stranger, who had elicited his admiration, as she tripped away.

"When left alone, Marconi felt at a loss how to amuse himself; the mummery of the merry groups which passed him had lost its charm, and he, therefore, returned home, anxiously to await the time of sunset, when he should again meet his inamorato; he, therefore, called Paulo to take away his domino and mask for the present, and resumed his former position at the window, where he lolled away the time, puffing a cloud of smoke from a Turkish hookah that reposed upon an adjoining table.

"Anxiously did Marconi await the hour of sunset; it arrived at last, and as the luminary of the day sunk in the western horizon he again assumed his disguise, and started for the place of assignation; the stranger had arrived before him, and to the imagination of Marconi her shape and air seemed more bewitching than before—

"'How rejoiced I am to see you,' said he, taking her hand.

"'The feeling is reciprocal,' returned the mask.

"'I feel honoured; but now let us retire were we can converse unobserved?'

"'Willingly.'

"'And in the meanwhile let me entreat you to take off the mask which conceals features I feel convinced cannot be but beautiful.'

"'Do you much desire it?'

"'Most ardently.'

"'And if they should not prove what you expect—what then?'

"'I shall acknowledge the obligation, and laugh at the mistake incident to a carnival.'

"'Good,' replied the stranger; 'but suppose I should wish to retain my mask?'

"'I must then endeavour, by what eloquence I am master of, to persuade you to remove it.'"

"'Indeed!'"

"'Those feet are exquisitely beautiful!' continued Marconi; 'and, good Heavens! what radiant eyes peer through that envious mask! My soul burns with the most ardent love!'"

"'And can you love?' demanded the stranger, languishingly.

"'Most ardently.'

"'And with sincerity?'"

"'Such a form as yours I could adore and idolize! Those dulcet tones from that mouth of sweetness ravish my very ears!'"

"As Marconi said this he passed his arm around the waist of his companion, and endeavoured to snatch a kiss from her ruby lips; in the scuffle her mask fell from her face, and disclosed to his astonished view the features of his mother!

"'Bah!' cried our hero, turning suddenly on his heel, to the astonishment of his companion, who stood gazing after him. 'Bah! bah! how I hate these carnivals!' He quickly retraced his way home, and during the remainder of the carnival, did nothing but puff large volumes of smoke from the aforesaid hookah.

"What do you think of that, eh?"

"Oh, very tiresome," said Tom Hackey.

"Tiresome! Bless me, what do you say, Mr. Rivers?"

"I am really, sir," said Rivers, "so much engaged just now with other matters, that I have scarcely been able to listen to your no doubt amusing anecdote."

"Oh, very well, I ain't at all offended; quite the contrary. Now, sir, if you had made a stranger of me, I should have felt hurt, most decidedly; but to prove to you that I am not in the least so, but, on the contrary, very much pleased with your candour, will you lend me the ridiculously small sum of eighteenpence?"

There was something so thoroughly impudent in the manner and conduct of Bumbleton Swiggles, Esq., as he termed himself, that, in the midst of all his troubles, Rivers could not help laughing at him, as he took from his pocket the required sum, and said—

"There is eighteenpence, Mr. Swiggles, and I can assure you, that this morning I am indeed most particularly busy."

"Sir," said Swiggles, bowing profoundly, "I will not intrude upon you one moment; but I really thought my friend Tom was joking."

"Oh, you humbug," said Tom.

"Sir," continued Swiggles, "I have the distinguished honour to bid you a very good morning. Tom, my ancient Greek, good day."

"Good day," said Rivers.

"Oh, be off with you," said Tom, and Mr. Bumbleton Swiggles made his exit.

"You are done," said Tom to Rivers. "He will never pay you that eighteenpence."

"His absence," remarked Rivers, "was cheap at that price, Tom, at present."

The hum of Hilliard's voice came now from under the lid of his desk, which he had again raised as before, and Rivers and Tom involuntarily paused to hear what he was reading. It was but a word here and there that they could catch, but it seemed to them as if he were reading from some newspaper, and so indeed he was. The guilty man was again perusing the account of Mr. Noble's murder.

Their attention was now attracted to the glass door of the counting-house; and, glancing in that direction, they saw the face of Mathew Trueman looking in at them.

CHAPTER XLVI.

THE INTERVIEW BETWEEN GRACE AND HER FATHER.—THE TRIUMPH OF INNOCENCE AND VIRTUE.—MATHEW TRUEMAN IN A DILEMMA.

RIVERS momentarily expected the merchant to enter the office, but, to his surprise, such was not the case, for Mathew Trueman, after indulging himself with a tolerably long look upon those whom he now considered as the most atrocious of delinquents, suddenly disappeared again. The fact was that the merchant had been so astonished at the account Girkins had given him of what had taken place when he attempted to execute the commission with which he was charged, that he resolved to see Grace before he trusted himself to an interview with Rivers, and hear from her own lips if she had really had the singular and unprecedented audacity to behave in the manner imputed to her by Girkins.

He felt, in fact, in a perfect bewilderment, so entirely novel to him and out of all rule did the transaction appear. That Grace would remonstrate with him, that she would protest and weep at what he knew in his own heart was the great injustice he was committing, he could well believe; but her assumption suddenly of an authority to supersede his actual written commands, about which there could be neither ambiguity or doubt, did certainly astonish and puzzle the merchant extremely.

Nor was poor Grace without her deep fears and anxieties, for when the excitement of mind which had enabled her to go through the scene in the office had passed, and she looked back upon her own boldness, she trembled at the consequences which might result from it.

She waited for her father's arrival with feelings of the greatest anxiety, and she continually asked herself, "How will he receive the news of what I have done? What will he say to me when he sees me? Will he discard me for ever—will he curse me as an undutiful child—as one ungrateful? Ah, no! I am not ungrateful, for is it not from gratitude to Rivers that I have endeavoured to save him from the planned villany of those who would work his destruction?"

A small still voice in her own heart told Grace that love had as much if not more to do with her bold effort to protect Rivers than gratitude, and she blushed as she murmured,

"Yes, I do love him—but why do I love him? Is it not because he is full of truth and nobleness? Is it not because I know he has a heart susceptible of the best and highest feelings? Ah! whom should I find like him?"

Grace for a few moments forgot even the terror of her father's expected frowns, as she indulged in a dreamy reverie, during which she pictured to herself how happy she might be as the wife of such a one as Rivers, with whose dear companionship she could pass through life despising its small cares, and rising even above its greater and more heart-rending anxieties.

Mrs. Woodfall then came from her own room to that in which Grace was sitting. One glance at her face told Grace that her indulgent nurse shared with her all her most anxious fears.

"Nurse, dear nurse," she said, "tell me what you think will happen? Will my father be so very angry with me as to leave no hope of forgiveness?"

"My dear, I do think he will be very angry, but still I cannot think that his anger will stand the test of calm reflection. Sooner or later he must and will see that you have, although acting contrary to his expressed wishes, saved him from the commission of a great and grievous injustice; and whenever he is convinced of that, which I think he will be when unbiassed by evil counsellors, he will love you more dearly than ever."

"You really think so, nurse?"

"I hope so, my darling."

"And I hope so too. What has Rivers done but what every gentleman deserving of the name would have flown to do? He rescued me from a villain, and for that shall he be discarded?"

"It would be very wrong indeed, my dear; but just now your father's eyes are dazzled by the false glitter of the coronet which he hopes by the instrumentality of Lord Hawksworth to see gracing your young brow."

"Alas! alas!" said Grace, "I have no such ambition. What to me would be rank and wealth without that deep joy of the heart which is above all price?"

"You would live a life of splendid misery, my dear, and there is only one consolation I have in all this matter, which is, that no power on earth can force you to accept that man for your husband."

"None, none," cried Grace. "It shall never be said that I committed that great sin before Heaven—for such it must surely be—of giving my hand where my heart could not accompany it."

"Master, ma'am, is coming," said a servant, opening the door a little way, and then suddenly scuffling down the stairs again.

"I told the girl to let me know when your father came home," said Mrs. Woodfall. "Do not alarm yourself, dear Grace, but remember your argument is this, 'What has Mr. Rivers and Tom Hackey done that they should lose their situations, and why should you not take every interest in them on account of gratitude for the service they rendered you at Lord Hawksworth's fete?'"

"I understand," said Grace, faintly.

The sound of the merchant's footsteps on the stairs now came upon the ears of Grace, and set her heart palpitating alarmingly. In another moment the door was opened, and more pale and more stern than she had ever seen him in her life, Mathew Trueman stood upon the threshold.

Not a word was spoken for the space of about half a minute by either of the three persons whose minds, each in its own way, was full of the same subject. Then Mathew Trueman, to whom the silence was the most distressing, because he had the worst cause to advocate, said in a low, stern voice—

"Mrs. Woodfall, I have something to say to my daughter."

The nurse cast one compassionate look at Grace, and then, without a word, left the room.

When the door was closed upon her, Mathew Trueman, while his face grew still paler, stepped up to Grace, and said, in a voice that was evidently struggling to be calm—

"How long is it since you have assumed the conduction of my business, and an authority superior to mine in my mercantile affairs?"

"Never, father, never," said Grace, with deep emotion.

"Indeed! Then I have been much misinformed. This very morning I thought proper to discharge a clerk from my counting-house—I beg your pardon, I suppose I ought to call it yours, since you have assumed the control of it—and it appears my orders were treated by you with contempt and derision?"

"No, no, with neither."

"Then I am misinformed again."

"You are misled, father, rather than misinformed."

"I? I misled?"

"Yes, by those who would overcome your better judgment, and persuade you to a course of action that will end in hopeless misery to all."

"This seems," said Trueman, "rather wandering from the subject in hand. What I wanted to know was whether you or I had the management of my mercantile affairs, and whether, when I see a necessity for discharging a clerk, you are to place your veto upon the act, and say, 'No, this shall not be, because it is unpleasing to me.'"

"Father," said Grace, speaking with more confidence than she could have believed herself capable of feeling, "forgive me for what I am about to say, but I do not think that in your own heart you believe it is proper to discharge Francis Rivers from your service."

"Indeed! this is better and better."

"Hear me out, father, and search in your own heart for an answering echo to my words. The discharge of Mr. Rivers never was—never could have been the suggestion of your own mind; for no one that I ever heard of could accuse you of deliberate injustice. I feel assured the act was suggested to you by those who have more, far more at heart the success of some schemes of their own than your reputation or your welfare."

"Suggested to me was it? Well—well, and am I to shut my mind against all suggestions?"

"Against all bad and selfish ones,

yes, father. I pray to Heaven your heart may always remain closed against such. I freely confess that I did dispute your orders, and that I did, as far far as lay in my power, speak with contempt of the messenger, who endeavoured with such deep malice to carry them into effect. Oh, father, which should be the best friend of one who does a hasty act, which by its recollection might embitter the remainder of an existence—he who carries it out to the very letter, and leaves no one circumstance for the mind to lean on for relief, or the friendly hand that stays the procedure until calmer, happier reflection exerts its sway? You may be angry now, father, with me. You may be piqued that your commands were not obeyed; but such feelings will wear away, while the lasting pang you would have felt upon finding that you had, for no fault, cast those two helpless beings upon the cold mercy of the world, would for ever have haunted your breast."

"You—you are strangely urgent in the cause you have thought proper to advocate," said Mathew Trueman, while a slight quiver in his voice assured Grace that he was not wholly indifferent to what she said.

"I am urgent, father," she added, "for all our sakes, I am urgent. What have they done who you would have cast off?"

"Done—done! Why what on earth brought them to the fete at Kew?"

"If they were blameable and indiscreet in going there, the service they rendered me when there should blot out the memory of the fault."

"Grace, we differ concerning that service. Lord Hawksworth loves you, and he assures me that what he said was but in the way of respectful attachment to you."

"Where Lord Hawksworth ten times a lord, father, he speaks that which is false."

"False?"

"Yes, he merits your contempt and mine for his conduct as much as Francis Rivers merits our gratitude for his ready interference. You have found both those whom you would cast from you and do such positive injury to—for who would employ a clerk after he had suddenly been discharged by one of the greatest merchants in the city?—honest and most trustworthy."

"To be sure," said Trueman, catching in a moment at the argument that gratified his personal vanity—" to be sure, they would have very little chance, very little chance, in any firm in the city, after being discharged by me."

"None, father, none."

"Well, I may say none."

"How could you deliberately turn them into the streets to starve, father? Oh! I am quite sure you never took such a view of the question, or not for one moment would you have listened to the insidious advice of those who would gain their own ends at the price of the honour of a British merchant."

Mathew Trueman was evidently softened.

"Why, truly," he said, " as to that, I rather think there are very few people who would induce me to do what I did not think quite proper, and in fact, when any one advises me of anything that is really valuable, I find on reflection, that I thought of it before."

"You will let them stay then, father? Oh! think, now, what power you possess over them, and abstain from exercising it. The whole affair is one of revenge on the parts of those who I am sure would have made you the mere tool for the gratification of their own wicked passions, and then smiled to themselves at the easiness with which they had made you their dupe."

"Me? me a tool?" said Mathew Trueman.

"Yes, the tool of bold, bad men."

"A dupe, too? When, I should like to know, did anybody succeed in making a dupe of me? No, no. If I had been easily duped, I rather think that I should not have been what I am after commencing life with three-and-a-penny."

"Most certainly, father. Then you never saw this thing in its proper light, and you will say no more about it, but let those who have served you faithfully still continue to do so."

Trueman rose and paced the room for some few minutes before he spoke again, and when he did so, it was evidently done with an effort.

"Grace," he said " the plain truth

is, that—that Lord Hawksworth declares this young man, Rivers, stands in his way."

"In his way, father?"

"Yes; his lordship loves you, and he thinks you look upon this Rivers with kinder eyes than you ought. Now, Grace, if you will solemnly promise me on your sacred word, that such is not the case—I—I—will let him stay."

"Is Tom Hackey included, father," said Grace, carelessly, "in his lordship's suspicions?"

"Pshaw! No."

"Then it appears that Lord Hawksworth is for the future to have the dismissal of your clerks. Father, father, can you for one moment imagine that I, your daughter, would act in any way unworthily?"

GRACE INTERCEDES WITH HER FATHER FOR RIVERS.

"No—no; but then—but Lord Hawksworth may, you know, be a little jealous."

"Jealous! Jealous! And are two persons to be exposed to the horrors of want, because a man who I never gave, by word or look, reason to believe that he was otherwise that most distasteful to me, is jealous?"

"Well, well, Grace, I won't discharge them this time; but I expect you will be more complaisant to your noble admirer for the future."

"You are right, father," said Grace, "in retaining those in your service who are faithful."

CHAPTER XLVII.

GRACE'S NOTE TO RIVERS. — TOM HACKEY IN THE KITCHEN.— OTHELLO'S OCCUPATION'S GONE.— THE CONFEDERATES.

HAVING so much easier than anticipated got from her father permission for Rivers and Tom Hackey to retain their respective situations, Grace was all anxiety to communicate the tidings to them, and put an end to the state of suspense in which she knew they must be.

She knew nothing of the sanguine project of Tom Hackey, or she would have felt no anxiety on his account; for Tom, looking as he did upon that day as the last of his service with Mathew Trueman, had allowed his mind to have free scope in the realms of fancy, and had pictured to himself and Rivers such a brilliant theatrical career, that had the merchant come to him and said, "Thomas Hackey, I cannot possibly spare you, you must retain your present situation," he would have felt quite a shock of disappointment, and, in all probability, have given in his resignation instanter.

He tried repeatedly to interest Rivers and get him to enter into the subject, and indulge in the same dream of theatrical renown which was so delightful to himself; but Rivers's mind was too much occupied with thoughts of Grace in all her beauty and innocence, and the precarious nature of his then position, freely sharing with Tom as he did his feelings of the certainty of dismissal, the moment Mathew Trueman had arranged in what aggrevating manner he could accomplish it.

After these repeated attempts and as repeated failures, to get Rivers to go through a rehearsal of several celebrated scenes from Shakspere, Tom Hackey, who could not restrain his own histrionic ardour, repaired to the kitchen, where, from his genuine good humour and odd sayings, he was a great favourite—the cook likewise freely believing him in her own secret heart to be a very great genius indeed.

There was an air of consequence about Tom Hackey, as he walked into the kitchen, which was at once manifest to the occupants of it, consisting then of the aforesaid cook, the footman, and a nurserymaid.

"Hilloa!" said the footman, "what now?"

"What a tail our cat's got," suggested the housemaid, which, being rather an invidious remark, awakened Tom's ire to a certain extent, and made him look more majestic still, as he said—

"I have merely come here to remark that this wooden chair," plumping into one as he spoke, "will one day fetch its money."

The chair gave an ominous creak, and, being rather antiquated, broke down, landing the great tragedian on the kitchen floor, to the great laughter of the cook, who was forced to sit and beg the footman not to laugh any more, as if he did she couldn't leave off, and it always gave her a *crick* in her side.

"I say," remarked the footman, "the chair won't fetch its money now till it's mended."

"At some sale," said Tom, scrambling to his feet, "at some sale a hundred years after this, it will fetch a great deal of money, as the identical one broken by the immortal Hackey, the celebrated tragedian, ahem!"

"Bless us!" said the cook.

The footman suggested his doubts by a remark concerning a mangle, supposed to have been possessed by Tom's mother, and parted with by her for a pecuniary consideration, which was afterwards bartered for a piano-forte.

To this Tom did not condescend to reply, but seizing the lid of a fish-kettle, he struck an attitude, exclaiming—

"Six Richmonds have I slain to-day. A horse! a horse! my kingdom for a horse! Ha'! ha! ha!"

"Well," said the cook, "I never did see nothing ekal to that in all my life."

"I should think not," said Tom. "Fight, gentlemen of England. Fight, bold yeomen. Draw, archers, draw your arrows to the head. Die, villain, die!"

Suddenly then possessing himself of a spit, Tom Hackey made rather too practical a lounge at the footman, who, in retreating to avoid it, knocked his heels against the kitchen fender, and to the immeasurable amusement of the housemaid, and indignation of the cook, sat down with a great splash in the dripping-pan.

Even Tom, although he was taking a tragic flight, could not forbear laughing at so comic an incident, as he shouted,—

"Down, down to Grease, and say I sent thee there!" at the same time that he dealt the footman a poke, which upset him, pan and all, with a great crash.

"Hush, here's somebody a-coming," said the cook.

It was Mrs. Woodfall, who, putting her head into the kitchen, stood in amazement gazing on the scene enacting within it.

"We are only rehearsing," said Tom.

Mrs. Woodfall beckoned him to the door, and gave him a little slip of paper, on the outside of which was written, in a faint, delicate hand, "Mr. Rivers."

"All is well," said Mrs. Woodfall; "Grace has spoken to her father."

"Has she?"

"Yes, and you are to retain your situation as well as Mr. Rivers."

"The deuce I am."

"Are you not rejoiced?"

"Not over. I'm a star, and so would Rivers have been a star. Hang out our banners on the outward walls."

"Take this letter to Mr. Rivers directly, Tom. It is from you can guess who."

"Grace?"

"Yes. Lose not a moment, for I am certain he is in a state of great anxiety."

Tom heaved a deep sigh as he laid down the lid of the fish-kettle, and said,—

"Tom Hackey's occupation's gone. To this complexion must we come at last. Imperial Hackey is not turned away, and still must mingle with the common clay. Oh, that the genius which a world would awe, should ever in a kitchen——"

"Nonsense," said Mrs. Woodfall, pushing him up the staircase. "Take the note, there's a good lad."

"A good lad, a good lad," muttered Tom Hackey. "The ignorance of women is astonishing. To call me, a theatrical star of the first magnitude, a good lad. She might as well call a queen a good woman."

Tom Hackey then paused in the passage, and looked at the superscription of the note.

"Ah," he sighed, "these are the letters written by her dear hand. They look like her, delicate and beautiful. Happy, happy Rivers. What can harm you or give you a single pang of uneasiness, while Grace loves you?"

He then walked quietly into the office and laid the note, without a word, before Rivers, who glanced with indifference upon it, till Tom whispered the one magic word,—

"Grace."

The truth then flashed upon the mind of Rivers, and glancing around for an instant, to see that he was not watched by Hilliard, he pressed the paper to his lips, before he opened it with trembling fingers.

There were but very few words on that slip of paper, but how dear they were to Rivers. They were these:—

"Do not suffer any more anxiety. My father sees his error. All is as usual. Say nothing to him of this morning's proceedings, and he will be equally silent. From your   "GRACE."

Rivers drew a long breath of relief. "I shall still remain near her," he thought—"still breathe the same air—still be sheltered by the same roof. Blessings on you, dear Grace!"

"So you see we are done," remarked Tom Hackey.

"Eh? Did you speak, Tom?"

"Yes, I said we were done."

"How do you mean?"

"Swindled—regularly cut up in bits. You don't mean to say you didn't expect to get discharged?"

"I certainly did expect my dismissal to-day. But, thank Heaven, it is not so."

"Thank Heaven! Well, there's no accounting for tastes. Only fancy a crowded house, Then the curtain draws up five minutes after the proper time, and the people are half mad with rage when you appear. Then down comes the house."

"Indeed, that would be a climax I should not like to my theatrical career, as I might be extinguished in the ruins, you know, Tom."

"Pho, pho. You don't understand. What we mean by bringing down the house is having a round of applause."

"Then I fear it will never be my lot, Tom, to bring down a house."

"Hush! the governor."

Mathew Trueman walked into the office. He proceeded directly up to Rivers, and laying before him a bundle of papers, said,—

"Be so good as to copy these letters, Mr. Rivers."

"Yes, sir."

"And bring the originals to me when you have finished."

"I will, sir."

The merchant then lingered a moment as if he wished to say something else, and Rivers expected a remark about the previous evening's proceedings was coming ; but he was disappointed, for Mathew Trueman, if he had had such an intention, thought better of it, and walked slowly from the office, to the door of which he was followed by Tom Hackey, who indulged in a great many strange attitudes behind his back, such indeed as would have greatly astonished the merchant could he have been aware of them.

When Girkins was so unceremoniously turned out of the house in Thames-street by Grace Trueman, he rushed rather than walked to the nearest coach-stand, and flinging himself into the first empty vehicle he saw, he ordered the coachman to drive as fast as he could induce his horses to go, to the hotel where he had left Lord Hawksworth and the merchant so pleasantly occupied with the good things before them.

The distance was considerable, but still it was traversed in a tolerably short space of time, and, much earlier than he was expected back, Girkins entered the breakfast-room with an expression of countenance that at once indicated his mission had not gone off in the most agreeable or satisfactory manner.

Hawksworth threw himself back in an easy chair on which he was sitting, and Trueman rose as he said,—

"What—what's the matter ?"

"Ah, what's the matter, Girkins ?" cried Hawksworth. "You look like the cream-faced loon who came to tell Macbeth that Birnam wood had come to Dunsinane."

"Matter enough," said Girkins. "Mr. Trueman, I thought you were master in your own house ?"

"And who dares to say I am not ?"

"Daring as the act may be, I am compelled myself to say so."

"Indeed, Mr. Girkins !"

"Yes, Mr. Trueman. Your daughter is a young lady of some spirit where she takes a fancy, I admit. She did all but kick me out of the place with her own foot, Mr. Trueman."

"My daughter ?"

"Yes, Mr. Trueman, your daughter. She tore up your note, sir, and ordered me off the premises, at the same time she declared you should not discharge Mr. Rivers."

"I should not ?"

"Those were her words, sir. You will excuse me for feeling a little natural indignation that you, one of the first merchants in this great country, should be so contemptuously treated by your own child."

Mathew Trueman's cheek flushed, and he breathed hard a few minutes before he said—

"We shall see, we shall see. My lord, excuse me for leaving you rather abruptly, but it seems my presence is rather required at home."

"Make no excuses, Mr. Trueman," said Hawksworth, "but permit me, as a friend to you and yours, to remark before you go, that I have very little doubt, unless you nip the affair in the bud, this clerk — this very chivalrous Mr. Rivers, will do what he will consider the honour of marrying your daughter."

"No, my lord, not while my name is Mathew Trueman. I would see my right hand hacked from my arm first. Never, never, my lord."

"Mr. Trueman, I am more pleased, perhaps, than I feel myself just now in a situation to express, by what you say. Grace is fitted to adorn any station, Heaven knows, and it would be better than downright criminality to permit her to throw herself away upon a penniless adventurer, when she may command the most brilliant and noble destiny."

Lord Hawksworth said these words with a significance of tone and manner that made them to the merchant's mind amount to something very little short of an open declaration of his intention to lay at the feet of Grace his title in possession and his earldom in perspective.

"My lord," he replied, "your sentiments do me much honour, and your lordship may depend that this—this—I don't know what to call him—this Rivers, shall no longer be a positive eyesore to us all. Good morning, my lord."

"Good morning, Mr. Trueman."

The merchant buttoned his coat round him with a perseverance and energy that showed now excited his mind was, and muttering between his clenched teeth maledictions against Rivers, he took his route homewards, where, as we have seen, he was subdued by the magic power of innocence and virtue.

When he was gone, Hawksworth turned to Girkins, and said—

"By Heavens, Girkins, you surely don't mean to say that such a piece of gentle loveliness as Grace Trueman had the spirit and determination to act as you have described?"

"Indeed, my lord, she did."

"What? Take the part of this d—d rascally good-looking clerk so openly?"

"Even so. Talk of gentleness! Why I never saw such fire flash from any one's eyes in my life, and I do verily believe that she would have laid hands on me, and turned me out herself, if I had not spared her gentleness the trouble."

Hawksworth leant back in his chair, and laughed aloud, as he said—

"Ry Heavens, I love her, adore her —she is a perfect angel. I like her ten times better than I did. Why, Girkins, I would have given a hundred pounds to see her turning you out of the house."

"Thank you. I would not put your complaisance to so severe a test."

"But it really must have been a rich scene."

Girkins for once in his life got really angry, and forgot for a moment his usual caution, as he replied with bitterness—

"I think, my lord, that Grace Trueman could kick any one out of her father's office with almost as much grace and ease as could her lover, Mr. Rivers, and with the additional advantage that any one possessing courage, could and would resist the man, while the girl would have to be allowed her own way."

Hawksworth understood the taunt perfectly well, and his face grew deathly pale, as it always did when he was in a great passion. He glanced at Girkins for a few moments in silence. Then in a hoarse voice, he said—

"From this moment we are strangers. I will trouble you to leave the room directly."

Girkins, the moment he had made his ill-natured speech, had repented of it, and he now saw before him all the disagreeable consequences to his prospects, of a rupture just at that moment with Hawksworth.

It was in a tone of a very different character from that in which he had last spoken, that he said—

"My lord, I have served you faithfully for a long period of time, as an agent in many transactions, in the conducting of which, I believe I have given you satisfaction. For the first, and I will take upon myself to say, the last time, I have for one moment lost my temper, and said what my heart did not dictate."

Hawksworth did not reply to this for about a minute, during which time he was thinking—"What shall I do without Girkins—where shall I find his equal for roguery and cunning?" so that the apology came rather welcome; and when he did speak, he said—

"Well, let the matter rest—I will forget—we are all human, and subject to—to—little bits of passion."

"I am your lordship's very humble servant," said Girkins, "and should Mathew Trueman not persevere in discharging Rivers, my serious advice is, for your lordship to shoot him. Then the most that can happen is, your being tried by your peers, and brought in not guilty, upon their honour."

"I will," said Hawksworth, " I will. Do you go now to the merchant's, and ascertain the state of affairs."

CHAPTER XLVIII.

THE DISAPPOINTED AGENT. — THE CHALLENGE.—THE SECOND.

MR. GIRKINS did proceed immediately to Thames Street, in order to ascertain how the merchant had acted, upon reaching his home. When, however, he sent in his name to Mathew Trueman, he was not a little surprised and mortified at receiving an answer to the effect that the merchant was very busy, and would feel obliged if Mr. Girkins would call the next day.

The real fact was, that Trueman had not yet quite made up his mind as to what excuse he should make to Lord Hawksworth for retaining Rivers in his service after what had taken place, and, therefore, it was exceedingly inconvenient just then for him to see Girkins.

Tom Hackey, to whom the message was given to deliver to Girkins, who would not venture into the office, but stood in a state of perplexity on the mat outside, was quite delighted with the opportunity of saying something provoking to the unprincipled agent.

"Mr. Trueman's busy," he said, "and can't be troubled with you till to-morrow."

"Busy—can't see me?"

"No. But if you come about me and Mr. Rivers, I can do just as well."

"What do you mean?"

"Why, we have made up our minds not to leave Mathew yet, though I can tell you we have prospects that would make you jump again."

"Not leave?"

"No. We turned the thing over in our minds, and we are going to stay."

"Do you mean to say that Mr. Trueman consents to you and Mr. Rivers remaining as before in his service?"

"That's just what I mean. He knows he couldn't do without us. Nobody is aware better than old Mathew which side his bread's buttered on. I should say you needn't trouble yourself to come here any more at all."

With a muttered curse, Girkins walked up to the office door, and looking through the oval piece of glass which was let into its upper portion, he saw Rivers sitting very composedly writing. That was at once conclusive evidence, and without another word to Tom Hackey, he left the house.

It is strange how the feelings of one individual towards another will commence in almost indifference, or but a trifling dislike, and then, as a consequence of the failure of the means used to gratify that feeling, grow into positive rancorous hatred towards the victim of the first ill-regulated feeling. Thus, although Rivers had done nothing to Girkins particularly, although they individually by no means clashed, yet so provokingly had the merchant's clerk crossed him in his schemes, so much had he been totally in the way of his most pet projects, that hatred and malice towards him become one of the master passions of that mind, which was, as it were, a complete hot-bed of vices.

The disappointment in his last effort to cast Rivers from his situation, and reduce him to destitution, put the finishing stroke to the malevolent feelings of the agent, and on his route back to the hotel, whither he hastened to communicate to Lord Hawksworth what he termed Mathew Trueman's disgraceful pusillanimity, he vowed that by some means or another he would, before many days had passed, compass either the death or the disgrace of the unoffending clerk.

In the first place, he determined upon urging on Lord Hawksworth to challenge Rivers, whose pride, he believed, would induce him to accept the invitation. Then he, Girkins, knew that Hawksworth was a dead shot—that was a lordly accomplishment which his leisure had enabled him fully to acquire—and what chance was there that Rivers had ever had an opportunity of firing a pistol half a dozen times in his life?

"Why, then, it follows," muttered Girkins to himself, "that this troublesome young man will be shot, and then there will be an end of all anxiety upon his account. The thing won't sound amiss, after all. Rivers's father was an officer in the army—that will be the statement, and Hawksworth will only get a little notoriety in consequence of the affair. Yes, I will urge him to it. The duel shall take place first, and if that should fail, why then—ay, then, I and Hilliard will concoct a scheme, which, while it shall leave him life, shall leave him nothing else."

Full of these resolves, Girkins hurried onwards till he came to the hotel, and then, in as aggravating a style as he could, informed Lord Hawksworth of the triumph of his rival, and the utter failure of the scheme for driving him from the merchant's house.

Hawksworth listened to the recital in silence, although his feelings were to the full as malignant and excited as those of his unscrupulous agent.

"This is Grace's doings," said Hawksworth. "By heavens! she has more power over the old merchant than I could have imagined possible."

"She has, my lord; and while Rivers stands in your lordship's way, I much fear no satisfactory result will be arrived at, either as regards the beautiful girl herself, or Mathew Trueman's pocket."

"Indeed!"

"Yes. You must see that Trueman's only motive for supplying you upon such doubtful security with the heavy loan you require is, that he considers it as part of the portion he would give you with his daughter. The small sums he has already accommodated you with are as nothing, and you may depend upon my judgment in this matter when I assure you, that without something like a definitive offer from you to take Grace as your wife, you will never see the bulk of the money you so much require."

"You really think the merchant has the audacity to wait for such an offer from me?"

"I do."

"Then he may wait."

"Nay, my lord, I would strongly advise your lordship to make it."

"What?"

"To make it. You need not do so in any way to give the merchant a legal hold of you, but just sufficiently to overcome his scruples. There, however, is one condition which must be fulfilled, otherwise all will be useless. This Rivers must be removed in some way."

"But how?"

"Challenge him, my lord, and shoot him. You cannot fail in doing so. You are an excellent shot. I have myself seen you snuff out a candle with a pistol bullet at twelve paces."

"Why, I believe I am a tolerable shot."

"An admirable one."

"But, as I said before, the young fellow's position in life is rather a bar."

"Take his father's position as your justification, and not his. Surely you can without degradation fight a duel with the son of Captain Rivers?"

Hawksworth was silent for a moment, and then he said, in a careless tone,—
"I don't see any particular objection."

"Will your lordship then write the challenge?"

Again, after a slight hesitation, for he could scarcely bring his mind to it, Hawksworth said,—
"Yes."

Girkins was determined that he should not be allowed to cool upon his resolve, and he immediately placed writing materials before him. The challenge was duly penned, and Girkins said, eagerly,—

"I will see it delivered, my lord."

"Thank you," replied Hawksworth, with cold pride. "If there are objections to this young man Rivers as a principal in a duel, there are still more insurmountable ones to you as my second."

Girkins's face flushed with anger, and he would not trust himself to speak, while Hawksworth continued,—

"Having consented to fight with Mr. Rivers, the son of Captain Rivers, I must be careful to do so in a proper manner, and I shall not trouble you any more upon the subject, Mr. Girkins."

"As your lordship pleases," muttered Girkins, rising.

Hawksworth merely nodded his head in acknowledgment of the low bow of the agent, who instantly then left the room, with the bitterest feelings gnawing at his heart.

When he was gone, Lord Hawksworth rose and walked to and fro in silence for many minutes. Then, in a low tone, he muttered,—

"Shall I persevere in this matter, or shall I not? Beauty and wealth on one side, difficulty and the world's sneers on the other. Shall I now recede? No! By Heavens, the loveliness of the merchant's daughter would make her a star of the first magnitude in the circles I could introduce her to—but not as my wife. Absurd—absurd. She shall be my mistress, if such can be accomplished. Her credulous father may lend me forty thousand pounds on my acceptances — which I can repudiate when I come of age, while by force or fraud Grace shall become mine; and this—this Rivers, curses on him! whose life stands in the way of my plans—shall I shoot him? Yes; but I need not kill him. No; I will wing him—maim him. Ay, that will be the plan.''

He then rang the bell, and when an attendant answered the summons, he said,—

"Let my cab be at the door as quickly as possible."

A low bow and an obsequious "Yes, my lord," were the responses, and in the course of a quarter of an hour his lordship was dashing through the streets in his cab at such an unusual pace, that his "tiger" set his teeth and held on convulsively behind, expecting each moment that his impetuous master would run against something and upset them.

All this furious driving, at which all the police politely winked, was to reach Pimlico before a certain Lieutenant Macdonald, a needy Indian officer, should have started from his lodgings to give his daily attendance at the War-office to solicit a foreign appointment.

His services Lord Hawksworth knew he could command, and, further, he knew that the said Lieutenant Macdonald would be by no means particular in sifting the grounds of the quarrel, but would content himself by aiding and assisting a lord in shooting any one he had a mind to put out of the world.

His lordship was just in time, for the lieutenant was exchanging his dressing-gown for his coat when the cab dashed up to the door.

"Well, Macdonald," said Hawksworth, "I'm going to fight a fellow."

"Indeed!" said the lieutenant. "Well, my lord, I beg you will make use of me. By-the-bye, it's really too bad. Here have I been for eight months dancing attendance on the commander-in-chief, and I can't get a colonelcy even in any of the African corps."

"Well, after this affair, I will see what can be done to give you a lift."

"I am very much obliged to your lordship; and respecting this little affair —may I ask, is it to be a *bona fide* kill-your-man-if-you-can duel, or a mere matter of gentlemanly courtesy?"

"Why, Macdonald, there is a fellow cursedly in my way."

"Oh—ah."

"And, you see, I want him him out of it."

"Certainly."

"I don't want to kill him, but I want to hit him so as to put him on the shelf for a few months."

"I understand your lordship. May I ask who he is?"

"The son of Captain Rivers."

"Of the artillery?"

"Upon my word I don't know; but, however, the fellow is in some measure a gentleman by virtue of his father's rank, so I have resolved to fight him."

"Certainly. Just let me know where I shall find him, and where I shall then find you."

"You will find me at the hotel where you know I am staying, and him you will find at a commercial house in Thames-street, in which he has some interest, I suppose, but that's nothing to me."

"Oh, no—no."

"Here is the challenge. Get him to name some friend at once, and have the thing arranged for to-morrow morning, if possible."

"I will. By-the-bye, we must offer him an alternative, of course. What shall it be?"

"Tell him that a public apology for any offence he may have given me, will obviate the duel."

"Ah, that will do. I see this affair will come off, for that is an alternative, with a vengeance."

It was one o'clock, and Rivers was just putting on his hat to leave the office for dinner, when a tap outside the door attracted the attention of Tom Hackey, who, opening it, was accosted by a gentleman of military aspect, who said,—

"Is there a Mr. Rivers here?"

"My name is Rivers," said our friend. Lieutenant Macdonald made a stiff bow, as he said,—

"May I request the favour of two or three minutes' private conversation with you, sir? My name is Macdonald, Lieutenant Macdonald."

"Certainly," said Rivers. "Tom, will you leave?"

Hilliard had already gone to his dinner, and Tom Hackey immediately left the room, wondering very much what the military personage could want with Rivers.

When they were alone, the lieutenant

THE MEETING IN THE CHURCHYARD.

said, as he handed to Rivers Lord Hawksworth's note,—

"Will you have the kindness to peruse that, sir, and favour me with an answer?"

The note ran as follows—

"Sir,—Understanding that your father held a commission in the army, I am induced to waive all considerations of the difference in our respective social positions, and require from you the satisfaction of a gentleman for matters to which I need not here particularly allude.

"The bearer of this, my friend, Lieutenant Macdonald, has full instructions to settle all preliminaries.

"I am, sir,

"HAWKSWORTH."

"Francis Rivers, Esq.

Rivers read this note twice over before he made any remark upon it, and then, turning to Lieutenant Macdonald, he said—

"Are you aware, sir, of the cause of quarrel between myself and Lord Hawksworth?"

"I am not."

"Then I will tell you. Once I kicked his lordship out of this house for insulting myself, and once I rescued from his insolence and villany a lady whom he insulted in his own house. I have no hesitation in proclaiming Lord Hawksworth to be, with the exception of his friend and confederate, a man named Girkins, one of the greatest scoundrels I ever met with."

The lieutenant looked perfectly astounded at this speech, and for some moments glared at Rivers without being able to find words in which to shape his reply.

"I must beg, sir," he then said,

"that you will abstain from making such remarks to me about my principal."

"I have made all the remarks I wish, sir," said Rivers, "and at the same time must beg distinctly to disclaim any wish to act otherwise than courteously towards you."

"Humph! you are very polite!"

Rivers bowed.

"May I trouble you for the name of a friend?"

"Sir," said Rivers, "I detest duelling. I think it a remnant of the grossest barbarism, and deeply indeed do I regret that the usages of society are such that it in some cases must be resorted to. I think in this case, that I am personally degraded by meeting such a man as Lord Hawksworth, but for my father's sake—for the sake of the name I bear, which is as well known as it is respected by many members of your own profession, I feel compelled to waive my own personal feelings, and accept this invitation. If you will leave me your address, I will, within an hour, send a friend to you."

"Sir, that is perfectly satisfactory," said Macdonald, "but before I go I ought certainly to offer you the alternative which my principal has empowered me to offer."

"And what may they be, sir?"

"A public apology."

"For what?"

"All causes of offence."

"That will require, I presume, no answer from me?"

"Certainly not. I have the honour, Mr. Rivers, to wish you a very good morning."

So saying, and laying his card of address on the desk by which Rivers was standing, Lieutenant Macdonald left the office.

CHAPTER XLIX.

THE MEETING ON HAMPSTEAD HEATH. —GIRKINS'S DISAPPOINTMENT AND RAGE.—THE POLICE OFFICE.—THE PRICES OF WINE.

WHEN Rivers was alone, he sat down at his desk, and leaning his head upon his hands he became immersed in deep reflection on his present position. A thousand thoughts came rushing through his brain. His past life, when he was surrounded with comforts and luxuries, of which now he had but a dim perception, rose up before him for a few moments in all the vividness of reality. Then there flashed across his mind the image of Grace Trueman, and he asked himself what would be her feelings if he were to fall in the coming encounter with the unprincipled man who dared him to the field? What would she then feel? Who would there be to stand between her and the evils which were brought upon her by the wild ambition of her father? Then again, who should he, in his present low and friendless situation, get to second him in the encounter which he had now pledged himself to have with Lord Hawksworth?

There certainly were several who would have seconded him, but then Rivers shrunk from exposing them and their families to the consequences which might arise from harassing criminal prosecutions, which, although nothing to men in the situation in life of Lord Hawksworth, would be destruction to any one depending for his daily bread upon his daily exertions.

"I will not," he thought, "involve any one so situated in the possible consequences of this duel."

He then seized his hat and walked hastily from the office, for the excitement of his mind was such that he could think much better when, in some measure, wearing that off by physical exertion.

After walking some distance, he at length thought of a plan of operations as bold as it was original, and that was to proceed direct to Lieutenant Macdonald, and state to him his objection to involve any one in trouble on his account, and offer to accept any one whom he, Macdonald, could recommend: or if he could not, or would not do so friendly an office—which among his military acquaintances he would surely find no sort of difficulty in—he, Rivers, resolved upon offering to come to the field unattended and relying solely upon his, Lieutenant, Macdonald's, honour, unusual and strange as such a course would appear.

When once he had formed this resolution, he lost no time in carrying it into effect, and hastening towards Pimlico with rapid strides, he reached the lieutenant's lodging, where, to the great surprise of that gentleman, he sent in his name. The lieutenant fully expected some one else, on the part of Rivers ; and when he appeared, he looked with a puzzled expression at him, which Rivers quite expected, and he accordingly hastened to explain the cause of his sudden appearance.

"Sir," he said, "when I told you I would accept the challenge of Lord Hawksworth, I likewise told you I considered duelling as a great social evil— so great, indeed, that I would not involve any of those whom I can call my friends in the consequences that may arise from my meeting your principal."

"Do you mean that you will not name a second ?"

"I do."

"Then—then—what are we to do ?"

"Whatever you please, sir. I am quite willing to meet Lord Hawksworth where and when you please, and, if you like, among your own acquaintance, to whom, possibly, the personal inconvenience resulting from the affair would be of no consequence, but, at all events, if it were, would excite no painful feelings to me, to find one who will become my second, I have no objection ; otherwise, I will face my own quarrels alone, for I should despise myself if I brought destruction, which I might do, upon any one else on account of my affairs."

The lieutenant was silent for some moments, and then he said—

"Why, really, Mr. Rivers, this is the most extraordinary way of accepting a challenge that I ever heard of in my life."

"It may be so, sir, and yet the only way in which I can accept it."

"I confess myself rather puzzled, Mr. Rivers."

"I can't help it, sir."

"But what—what can I say ?"

"Say when and where I am to meet Lord Hawksworth, and I will come and fight him with any weapons he may make choice of."

"Without a friend ?"

"I have ever found, when insulted or oppressed, my best friend to be my own strength and courage."

"Well, sir, it appears to me that this meeting must take place, or else Lord Hawksworth, you see, will have an opportunity of impugning your courage."

"If Lord Hawksworth or any one else says anything sufficiently insulting to me, or about me," said Rivers, "I will take measures to avenge myself."

"What would you do ?"

"I would horsewhip Lord Hawksworth."

The lieutenant glanced at Rivers, and there was so much cool courage in the manly expression of his face, as well as positive strength and activity in his person to carry out any such intention, if he once entertained it, that he thought to himself—

"He certainly could knock Hawksworth to pieces, if he felt inclined, and hence the necessity for the duel."

Then the declaration of Lord Hawksworth that he only meant to wound Rivers so as "to lay him upon the shelf," came across the mind of the lieutenant, and he thought—

"I must arrange it in some way, or Hawksworth will be furious." He said aloud—

"Mr. Rivers, do I understand fully that you decline all apology in this matter ?"

"Certainly."

"And you will accept any gentleman as second whom I may choose ?"

"I will."

"Then, unusual as the course is, I will undertake, if you will give me your word to be on Hampstead-heath to-morrow morning by seven o'clock, to bring Lord Hawksworth and a gentleman to officiate for you, in whose honour you may depend."

"At seven, I will be there,' said Rivers ; "and I have to thank you for the trouble you are taking, and assure you that I come to this meeting with a much clearer conscience in the feeling that I am running the risk of injuring no one but myself."

Rivers then left the lieutenant, and being past his time of return to the office even then, he got into the first conveyance he could find, in order to get more rapidly to Thames Street.

In the meantime Tom Hackey was tormenting himself with a thousand doubts and fears, as regarded the message of the strange military-looking man to Rivers, for from the first he presaged that it involved some sort of trouble to his friend. When, too, the hour expired to which Rivers was entitled in the middle of the day, and still he came not back to the office, Tom got into a state of fidget which tormented him sadly.

Hilliard, too, had not come back; but his non-return at the proper time was a matter of no wonder, as he was seldom punctual; while Rivers, whose mind was so much better regulated, was seldom a minute over the time at which he ought to be at his duties.

Tom went to the door, and looked right and left, but no Rivers could be seen—then he strolled into the office again, and sat down, but that he was too fidgety to do for long, and he went to Rivers's desk, which was close to a window, commanding a short view of the street, where, sitting down upon the stool, he tried to wait with some show if not reality of patience.

"Oh, my prophetic soul!" he said, "I'm sure something's the matter. What it can be is wrapped in mystery, like the bottom of the witches' caldron in Macbeth. Where can he be gone?"

Tom happened at this moment to cast his eyes down the sides of his nose, and so straight on till his glance fell upon the floor of the office, when, close to the legs of the stool, he saw lying a folded paper, in the shape of a note. He picked it up listlessly enough : it was open, and, without looking at the superscription, he read it.

It was the challenge, which Rivers had quite forgotten to secure in the agitation of his mind.

For some moments poor Tom Hackey was deprived of the power of speech, and nearly of thought; then, with sudden vehemence, he cried—

"Murder most foul! as at the best it is; but this most foul, strange, and unnatural. They want to murder him now; that's the next dodge, is it? Oh, you villain—you atrocious—oh!———"

These words were addressed in imagination to Lord Hawksworth, after which Tom read the note again, and a cold perspiration bedewed his brow, as he thought with alarm,

"Even now he may be lying dead. They may among them, by this time, have murdered him; yet—no—no—people don't fight duels at one o'clock—that's dinner-time; no—no—before breakfast these kind of matters come off. All's right till to-morrow morning."

Tom then tapped his forehead a great many times very seriously, after which he said,—

"What shall I do?" And as no reply came from vacancy, he again said still louder,—

"What shall I do?—eh?"

Then a shadow passed the window. In a moment Tom scrambled up the letter, and had it in his pocket before Rivers, for it was he, entered the office.

Tom's first impulse was then to speak to Rivers upon the subject, and implore him not to sacrifice his own and Grace's happiness for ever by perhaps killing Lord Hawksworth : or, if killed himself, plunging her who loved him, and clung to him so nobly, in despair; but a second thought bid him be still, for suppose Rivers to be obstinate and quite unmoved by all he, Tom, could say, would he not then be in a worse position for taking some effectual step for stopping the duel than before? because he, Rivers, would be upon his guard against such a movement, while now there could be no possible difficulty if he kept a sharp eye upon the movements of the young man in stopping the meeting.

As hastily, then, as he had at first resolved to remonstrate with Rivers, Tom Hackey determined that he would not do so; but, concealing his knowledge of the whole affair, save him, in spite of himself.

It was very difficult for Tom Hackey to keep the secret with which he was charged, for he was naturally candid to a fault, and when Rivers said, "I am past my time, Tom; has Mr. Trueman made any remark?" Tom was in two minds to say,—

"Yes, you villain, and I know where you have been, and what you have been about; but I intend to be even with you, and you sha'n't fight if you have ever such a mind to it."

Tom, however, prudently kept this speech to himself, and merely replied,—

"No, Mathew hasn't been here, and

if he had, it wouldn't have been much harm, because I should have told him you wouldn't have been late unless you were about some good—a-hem!"

"Well, Tom," said Rivers, with a laugh, "I shall certainly send to you for a character when I want one."

"Ah! do," said Tom, drily. "Here comes another villain."

Hilliard walked into the office and hung up his hat. Then casting around him his usual suspicious look, he buried his head in his desk, and commenced mumbling something, which neither Rivers nor Tom could hear a word of.

Tom glanced towards him, and then touched his head significantly, to signify his belief that Hilliard was not exactly right in his mind, and Tom was to a great extent right just then, for Hilliard had met in a country paper with a long article on Mr. Noble's murder, wherein many speculations were hazarded as to how the deed was committed, and by whom, together with an expressed strong belief that Wilson must have had some confederate, who was at large and unsuspected himself, while he had, in all probability, taken the life of his wretched dupe. All this was too near the truth not to give Hilliard the greatest uneasiness and alarm, for an investigation might arise therefrom as to who were Wilson's acquaintances, and who could be traced to have ever called upon him at his late master's chambers.

As the day, then, wore on, it was not to be supposed but that Rivers's mind was much occupied by considerations of what might be the result of the morning's meeting with Lord Hawksworth.

There were no human beings, with the exception of Grace Trueman and poor honest Tom Hackey, who, he could assure himself, would feel a pang at his death, and he wished several times, although each time he immediately retracted the wish, that he had never met with Grace, now that there was a chance by his death of visiting her gentle heart with grief.

Often and often he repeated to himself Shakspere's exquisite lines, commencing, "The course of true love never yet ran smooth," and with a sigh he would assent to the truth of the proposition in his own case.

It was an immense relief to him when the hour for leaving business came; but before that he had conceived a wish, which in his circumstances was very natural, and which, if he could not gratify, he felt would embitter his last moments, if he were indeed doomed on the morrow to end his mortal career.

That wish was to see Grace again. Again to speak to her, to hear the soft music of her voice, which ever fell upon his soul like flashes of light from Heaven; but how, oh, how was this wish to be accomplished? With Mathew Trueman in the house, and after what had occurred in the morning, how was he to venture upon the extremely hazardous step of endeavouring to effect an interview with her he loved?

At length he thought, if anybody could aid him, or suggest any course by which he could with some degree of safety accomplish his heart's desire, that person would be Tom Hackey.

"Tom," he said, "Mr. Trueman is at home?"

"Yes."

"You don't know if he is going out?"

"No," said Tom.

"Well, Tom, do you know, I wish very much to see Grace this evening, if it be but for five minutes, and no longer."

"The deuce doubt you," thought Tom. "You think you're a-going to be shot in the morning."

"Do you think," Rivers added, "I could manage to see Grace to-night?"

"No, I don't, on second thoughts. There's old Mathew poking about everywhere, like a dog in a fair. It ain't possible."

Rivers sighed deeply, as he whispered,—

"I have something particular to say to her. Tom, will you take a note for me?"

Tom Hackey looked in his face, and with great difficulty prevented himself from saying,—

"You think you have kept it all snug, and you fancy you'll have this fight to-morrow, but you won't." Then he said, "Write the note, and I'll try."

"A thousand thanks, Tom," cried Rivers, as he hurriedly wrote upon a piece of paper, which he carefully sealed up,—

"DEAR, DEAR GRACE,—Will you meet me for a few moments this evening, when and where you please?

"FRANCIS RIVERS."

Tom took the note without a word, and walked out of the office with it.

CHAPTER L.

THE MEETING OF GRACE TRUEMAN AND RIVERS BY ST. PAUL'S.—THE NIGHT BEFORE THE DUEL.

IN a perfect fever of impatience, Rivers waited for an answer to his brief note. Sit quietly in the office he could not, but he paced nervously from the door to the fire, the fire to his desk, and then back again, until the door opened and Tom made his appearance. He said nothing, but placing his finger on his lips, in the fashion of the witches in Macbeth, he looked mysteriously at Rivers. Then it suddenly struck him that a representation of the ghost scene in Hamlet would be more appropriate, and, accordingly, assuming a severe aspect, Tom Hackey backed out again into the passage with a shuffling movement, no doubt intended to represent the ghostly mode of walking, at the same time that he beckoned Rivers, in a saddened and mysterious manner, to follow him.

Rivers was far from slow in obeying the invitation, and walking hastily into the passage, he said—

"Well—well, Tom, well?"

"List—list, oh, list," said Tom.

"Now, my dear fellow, do patronise a little common sense for once. Have you succeeded? What did Grace say, and how did she look? Will she see me? Has she——"

"Stop—stop—stop," cried Tom. "One at a time—one at a time. I have seen her."

"Yes—yes—and——"

"And given her the note."

"Well, Tom—well. What said she? She returned some answer?"

"Of course she did, and I'm coming to it as fast as I can. Bless me, where is it?"

Tom rummaged his pockets for some minutes, during which period of time Rivers was on the tenter-hooks of impatience, until he produced a little crumpled piece of paper, saying—

"There's the answer."

Rivers snatched at it in a moment, and he read the words—

"St Paul's, at half-past seven."

Brief as were those words, they were dear to Rivers, for they were in the handwriting of Grace. Hastily placing the small missive in his pocket, he retreated to the counting-house to wait the hour mentioned. The place of appointment was indefinite; but he said to himself—

"I can keep walking quickly round St. Paul's till I meet her. Blessings on her kind heart for awarding me the interview which—which may possibly be the last."

A shudder came across the frame of Rivers as he thought of the morrow; but he quickly dismissed such feelings from his mind, for he was one who shrunk not from those things which he had once made up his mind to as quite inevitable.

In the meanwhile Tom Hackey stood in the passage shaking his head at Rivers, and muttering to himself his determination to stop the duel.

"Now if I could," he said, "but find out were he is going to fight, it would be a great convenience; but as it is, there ain't the ghost of a chance, unless I watch him, and if I was to tell Grace—well, I don't see why I shouldn't though, after all. Yet, I don't know, it will only annoy her, and I can manage to stop the affair myself. Let me think. There's old Burnby, the private watchman. He's just the creature. I'll speak to him."

The private watchman, who rejoiced in the name of Burnby, was an ancient officer, too old for active service, who the inhabitants of some dozen or more houses in Thames Street retained specially as a scarecrow to protect their premises at night. In an obscure corner old Burnby was accommodated with a watch-box, in which, with reverence be it spoken, old Burnby slept. Moreover, he was wont, when he came on duty, to adorn his person with a flannel nightcap with long lappets, which, coming completely over his ears, and tying under his chin, saved him from being disturbed by any noise short of what might be produced by a piece of ordnance. Nevertheless, old Burnby once caught, though he got away again, a boy, who with malice aforethought was shooting peas through the keyhole of Mathew Trueman's door, and on another occasion he found out a fire, and gave the alarm, for it happened to be in the house against which was the back of his watch-box, so that when his frieze coat began to frizzle and curl up behind, old Burnby suspected there was a fire somewhere, and sprung his rattle.

This was a tremendous feather in his cap, for the "own reporter," of the *Times* called him, in the report, "that active officer;" to be sure, with the usual accuracy of that journal, he was named Bradley, but then everybody in Thames Street knew that old Burnby was meant.

To this specimen of civil authority, then, Tom Hackey resolved to apply in his present emergency; and, accordingly, just as Rivers left the office, he, Tom, also left it in search of the "active officer."

The old man was tying on his night-cap when Tom reached his box, but, seeing Tom's lips move, he conjectured something was being said to him, and lifting one of the ear lappels, he said—

"Eh? eh? eh? Anything wrong—anything lost?"

"A duel," said Tom.

"Eh? what—a shovel?"

"No," bawled Tom. "There is going to be a duel, and you must prevent it—do you hear?"

"Where's my rattle?"

"Bother your rattle! You must meet me before daylight, this morning, at the corner of the street; and we can go and watch at the lodgings of one of them where he is going."

"Bless us all. You are quite sure it ain't a fire?"

"Here's an old pump," said Tom. "I'm afraid he'll be of no use, after all. I only want to prevent the fight, and don't at all wish to get Rivers up to a police-office if I can help it. It would cost him something, and, besides, where is he to get sureties to keep the peace?"

These prudent considerations induced Tom to persevere in employing the old man, who, but for his lack of physical strenght, had as much real legal authority as was necessary; and it was very likely in the present case that he would require the former.

"Don't mention it to anybody," said Tom, "and I will come for you at daybreak, mind."

"Well, I really," said the old man. "Active officers are in very great demand."

"I needn't ask you to be ready," added Tom, " because you'll be asleep, of course."

"Who, I—I sleep?"

"Yes, to be sure, and very prudent it is of you."

Tom Hackey then walked away, reasoning with himself that if he and the watchman hid themselves in the vicinity of the lodging occupied by Rivers at so very early an hour, they could not fail of seeing him come out, when Tom would hire a coach—for which he blessed his stars he had the means, although he guessed the expense would make a considerable inroad in his savings—and follow him wherever he might be going, so as to be sure to be in time to put a stop to the intended combat.

Half-an-hour before the appointed time, Rivers might have been seen pacing round St. Paul's Cathedral in anxious expectation of the arrival of Grace. Oh, what a miserable half-hour was that to the anxious lover. Again and again he asked himself what he should say to Grace to account for asking an interview so urgently, and yet he would not have foregone the delight of seeing her for ten times the embarrssment which he was sure to feel when she should arrive.

The quarter-past seven boomed from the massive clock, and it seemed to Rivers as if that quarter had been a whole hour in gliding by. It struck him as most probable that Grace would arrive at the southern side of the cathedral, first coming, as she would have to do, from Thames-street, and accordingly he there lingered for the last five minutes which were wanting to complete the half-hour past seven.

The clock announced that the time had come, but still there was no appearance of Grace, and Rivers then ran quite round the immense building at great speed to see if she were lingering anywhere else than where he most expected her.

He arrived nearly breathless again at the corner of St. Paul's Chain, but still there was no Grace.

"She cannot come," he faltered. "Some unforeseen accident has detained her, and she cannot come."

Even as he uttered the words a light figure glided up to him, and then paused irresolutely. He sprang forward with her name upon his lips, which was uppermost in his heart.

"Rivers!" she replied, and the tone was the soft silvery one of Grace herself.

He drew her arm quickly within his, and as it reposed upon his throbbing heart, he said—

"Dear, dear Grace, how can I thank you for thus meeting me? Oh, if you saw what joy you light up in my heart by your presence, you would indeed see how truly—how devotedly my every thought is yours."

"Your note alarmed me," said Grace, tremulously. "I hope nothing has occurred that—that should give you pain."

"No, no, Grace, we will not dream of pain now. How much I owe to you, dearest. If I have a joy on earth it is of your making."

It was in a tone of slight surprise that Grace said—

"Then nothing very special induced you to write to me so urgently?"

Rivers felt much confused, for dissimulation was a stranger to his heart, and yet how should he bring himself to say to her—"Yes, Grace, there is something special, and I know not if by mid-day to-morrow I may be among the living." No, he could not so wring her heart, and although it was with an embarrassed tone, he said—

"Cannot you forgive me, Grace?"

"Forgive you?"

"Yes, for breaking an implied contract in the Temple Gardens, which should have prevented me from asking this interview."

"And me for granting it," said Grace, mournfully. "Ah, Mr. Rivers, if my father's heart were kindly disposed towards you—if he looked upon you as —as I do—how happy—how very happy might we be."

"Alas! Grace," he said, "it is rare, indeed, that wealth likes to ally itself in any way with poverty. If we meet again——"

"If, Rivers?"

"I—I mean when we meet again, Grace, as I hope and trust we shall often and often, we may perchance think of some plan for softening your father's heart towards me. Time may do something, especially if he sees me attentive to his interest, and striving to merit his esteem."

"Heaven send it may!" sighed Grace.

"But—but in the meantime, dearest, will you give me in exchange for this some slight memento of yourself, which will be dear to me when I cannot see you, nor hear, what is to me the sweetest music, your voice?"

As he spoke, he placed a small hair ring upon the finger of Grace, who said, in a tone of emotion—

"Why exchange such gifts to-night?"

"To-night, Grace? Surely to-night is as eligible a time as any other. See, we have walked nearly to the Mansion-house."

Grace thought that Rivers was evading her question, and a suspicion, for a moment, did cross her mind that there was something on his mind which he dreaded to impart to her, but Grace's heart was too full of high ennobling emotions to cherish long the remotest doubt of him she loved, and she assured herself that she must be mistaken.

Unclasping from her slender wrist a small bracelet, she gave it to Rivers, saying, in a trembling voice—

"Will that suffice to remind you of me?"

"It will, dear one. And now assure me that you forgive me for summoning you out to-night, upon so little pretence."

A silent pressure of the hand convinced Rivers that Grace's own heart pleaded for him.

They had now walked by the side of the Mansion-house to Cannon Street, and Grace was too near home to render the further escort of her lover safe.

"You must leave me now," she said, very gently. "The time may come, when——"

She paused, and Rivers filled up the sentence, saying—

"When I shall have a right to stand by you and shield you from every harm."

Grace said nothing, but she cast an eloquent glance at the eyes of Rivers, which gave him a pang of the most exquisite misery, for it showed him how truly valuable and rare a treasure he was risking the loss of, along with his life, because he could not make up his mind to resist a custom, which, as a remnant of barbarism, has no equal in society.

Grace could not but hear the deep sigh that came from the bottom of his heart, as he said—

"Heaven bless and protect you, Grace, let my fate be what it may."

She thought he alluded to his depen-

RIVERS RENOUNCES THE UNWORTHY CONDITIONS OF MATTHEW TRUEMAN.

dant and precarious position in life, and she replied in a voice of the most considerate and gentle kindness—

"Wealth, Rivers, ever fails to purchase happiness. The heart must make its own sunshine. It never borrows even a passing ray from the brightest gold that ever beamed for man."

"You are right, Grace. You are right," said Rivers, as he pressed her hand in his. "Farewell, now, till—till——"

"To-morrow," said Grace.

"To—to-morrow—to-morrow," added Rivers. "God bless you!"

Still he lingered. Still he held that still small hand in his, it might be for the last time. Oh, how could he tear himself away?

"I must go now," she said softly.

Rivers started.

"Yes—yes—farewell, Grace. Farewell!"

He tore himself away from her. He

walked some paces, and then he looked back. Grace still stood where he had left her—to reach her again was the work of a moment.

"Once more farewell," he said. "I will watch you to your father's door."

"Good-night," whispered Grace. "Do not say farewell."

The good-night, like Macbeth's amen, stuck in the throat of Rivers, and it was with difficulty he pronounced it, and in another moment Grace was gone. He saw her reach her father's door, it opened, and, for all he knew, she was lost to him in this world for ever. An increased darkness seemed to fall upon all objects. The air felt colder. He gazed round him for some minutes in silence. Then in a low voice, he said—

"At half-past seven to-morrow, on Hampstead-heath. I must be punctual."

Directing his steps then rapidly homewards, he resolved, if possible, to snatch a few hours repose before the coming dawn.

Each hour, however, that passed, his thoughts became more and more wretched; and, after writing a long letter, which he addressed to Grace, and which, should he fall in the ensuing encounter, he intended should be found in his pocket, he threw himself, dressed as he was, upon his bed, and fell into an uneasy slumber.

CHAPTER LI.

THE MENTAL RELIEF.—TOM HACKEY'S GENEROUS CARE OF RIVERS.—THE LONG NIGHT.

WHEN the mind is much oppressed the body may appear to slumber and to be tasting of "nature's sweet restorative," sleep; but such is not then the case, for although the eyes may be closed, and the frame may be quiescent, there is no rest either to the spirit or the corporeal functions.

So it was with Rivers, on that night preceding the day on which he was to stand up before a fellow-man, to inflict or receive, perchance, death. For more than two hours he lay in that half-sleep, during which the imagination, uncontrolled by reason, conjures up a host of images all bearing a remote connection to the one great cause of mental disquietude, but hideously distorted from the bounds of reality or probability.

Exhausted, rather than refreshed, Rivers sprang from his bed as a neighbouring clock struck one. The pealing chimes before the striking of the hour had awakened him. He felt fevered and heated. A whirl of unconnected images filled his brain, and it was some few moments before the wild phantasma of the imagination retreated like demons to their lair, before the God-like presence of reflection which gradually asserted its supremacy in his mental structure.

He felt very cold, and he feared to take exercise to restore the healthful circulation of his blood, lest he should prove a serious disturbance to the people of the house. He was, therefore, compelled to confine his exertions to throwing out his limbs in different directions, by which he succeeded in some measure in restoring a healthful vivacity to his frame.

He dreaded again to lie down, for the confused dreams he had had during his two hours' semi-sleep had far from disposed him to tempt again the sickly embraces of the dreamy god.

"No more sleep," he said, "no more sleep; I shall receive no refreshment from it, and will not tempt it again. There are, however, yet some weary hours before I need start on this errand which my reason is so much against, but which some false feeling which I cannot rid myself of, has prompted me to."

He then lit a candle, and sitting down, re-read his letter to Grace. Then he indulged in a long retrospect of his past life, after which he painted to himself the future as it might have been in contradistinction to what it seemed to promise.

These were gloomy and harassing feelings, but how should he rid himself of them during the few hours, which would under such circumstances be sure to drag a slow length along, which intervened between then and six o'clock, at which hour he intended to start for the rural village of Hampstead?

Sancho, in Don Quixote, says, "Blessed be he who invented sleep," and it was with a similar sentiment that

Rivers, as he reached himself a book, said,—

"Blessed be he who invented reading! Here I shall find solace from care for a while."

He read as follows :—

"The evening breeze rose lightly over the green fields and fast ripening corn, but without scarce disturbing a blade of grass, or an ear of the fields of wheat that were growing in the neighbourhood of Farquar Hall. The country around was romantic and beautiful, diversified by hill and dale, and many rocky and romantic dales were to be seen on the north side of that hall, where the lovers of romance and rugged nature could wander till they were satiated, for a series of views and prospects rarely to be met with could here be found, while many places were totally inaccessible even to the wild adventurous herdsman.

"The inhabitants of Farquar Hall were a singular race of beings, they associated but little with the neighbouring gentry, and when they did it was to exact more deference than was perhaps their due, notwithstanding the talent of its owners, their ancient descent and large possessions. They were what was called a dark, morose race of beings, incapable of associating on friendly and equal terms with any other family. Their own internal and private wrongs and family dissentions were, unlike others, settled among themselves and in secret.

"People of this cast are seldom popular among the peasantry, who, nevertheless, from a kind of instinct alone, yield their respect to people who had exacted it from them for ages. Yet there was no love, no heartfelt feelings of pleasure in seeing their superiors among them.

"The present proprietor was the brother of the late holder—he dying young, leaving an only son, about eight years old, whom he confided to the care and guardianship of his brother, until he should become of age, with all the absolute authority that a father could possibly possess over a child.

"This youth received a suitable education to fit him for the station he was soon to hold in society. His vacations he would spend among the romantic spots in his future estate, and at the hall, under the immediate eye of his uncle.

"The two were never cordial, but this was a feeling which never was exhibited in the family; but a smile was utterly unknown to Beesley Farquar, the uncle; he was, indeed, a morose, and even evil-looking man. But the youth was ruled with a heavier hand than ever his father would have ruled, and yet he rebelled not, but bore it with a stern resignation, which showed that though he respected the authority he durst not rebel against, yet he detested and despised the man who exerted it.

"While at the hall young Farquar, or Master Henry, as he was called by the domestics, amused himself by shooting and fishing alternately, and in pursuit of this object would often stay out very late, indeed—breakfast being the only meal at which he and his uncle met. He was passionately fond of the sports of the field, and would follow them with ardour, often losing himself in the wild and unknown places which he entered, and glad to obtain a guide to more frequented places, and thence home again.

"While out upon one of these excursions, Henry had penetrated through a wood in a direction in which he had never traversed before, and in which he thought it almost impossible to carry a gun. He made the attempt, and at length succeeded; he was rewarded for his trouble, for a beautiful romantic country lay beyond, where there was plenty of game. At length, wearied, he sought some place where he could rest and inquire his way home, but for some time in vain.

"At length, after wandering about for some time, he came to a small, but beautifully situated cottage. It was in a most romantic spot, and evidently tended by the hand of taste, for the flowers and the arrangement at once pleased the senses and the mind of the observer.

"He stood gazing at the place in a mixture of pleasure and curiosity; he felt desirous to enter, and beg the hospitality of the inmates, and yet feared to make the intrusion. These were strange feelings in the breast of a Farquar, and yet they never sought to disturb the privacy of any one—but pride was their impulse—it was not so now. He gazed once more at the latticed windows, which were overrun by the thick ivy which ran all over the cottage, and then at the beautifully arranged garden, when his eyes became rivetted to one spot—he there saw a fresh object that interested him.

"There was a small summer-house, or rather bower, over which was trained the clematis and woodbine; their union produced a beautiful effect, and almost hid the interior from the intrusion of inquisitive eyes. This was at first the object of his attention, but presently another, and a more beautiful sight met his gaze. This was the inmate of the summer-house, a beautiful fair-haired girl, around whose noble brow her flaxen ringlets clung in clusters, hanging in graceful drops on her well formed neck and shoulders, which vied with the lily in whiteness. Her laughing blue eyes completed such a picture of loveliness that had never met the gaze of Henry, even in his wildest dreams of bliss. He was unable to take his eyes from the contemplation of so much beauty.

"At length, however, he became aware that he was, in his turn, an object of curiosity, for the cottage door was opened, and an elderly lady stood at the threshold. He instantly stated his wants, when she at once opened the gate, and ushered him into a neat kitchen. There he found every convenience that could be desired by the better class of people; it was well furnished, and very clean.

"Food was placed before him, which, though homely, was good and wholesome, but showed the temperate mode of living adopted by the inmates.

"The old lady quitted him, and her place was supplied by the younger one, whom he had seen in the garden. On a closer inspection she appeared more beautiful than before, for her features were classically correct, while her clear complexion heightened charms that were never surpassed. Her voice was sweet and soft, while her animated look lent charms to her conversation. Never had Farquar beheld so many excellencies united in one person.

"He felt that he had no power or control over his feelings; he loved—

he felt, he knew he loved her more than any earthly being.

"'How far is it hence to Farquar Hall?' he at length inquired, after they had conversed for some time.

"'Scarce three miles,' was the answer.

"'Indeed, why I have come at least ten miles round before I reached this spot, and I never was here before.'

"'It is an unfrequented spot, certainly, but that is its principal charm to us. After the loss of my father, my mother could not longer bear to move in society, but sought to bury her grief in quiet retirement, and here we have found it.'

"'I should think any one might be happy in such a spot,' said Henry, looking at his companion as if he would have said, if he dared, 'with such a partner.'

"'We have found happiness and content here for some years, and may do so yet, I hope,' she replied.

"Henry having sufficiently refreshed himself, he had no occasion or excuse to prolong his stay, and after thanking them for their hospitality, he begged they would just point out the road he should take as he was an utter stranger in the place.

"'I will put you in the right road,' she replied, 'if you will follow me.'

"This he did with pleasure, and conversed upon many topics as they walked along, and did all he could do to obtain some kind of hint that if he called again he would not be considered in the light of an intruder; but no such hint could he obtain, and he was content to bid the young lady an adieu, and depart.

"'This shall not be the last of our meetings,' he thought, as he turned away and pursued the road that led homewards.

"He had passed over about two-thirds of the space between the cottage and the proud mansion of the Farquars, known by the name of the Hall, and had about a mile to traverse, when he entered a small wood, that occupied about half that distance, and when about to emerge from the other side, thought he heard the voices of some men in earnest consultation; wondering what could be debated in such a place, and believing they were poachers, he approached them cautiously, until he could hear all that passed, though he could not see the speakers.

"'I tell you,' said one, 'the old squire wants to be rid of his nephew.'"

"'And why?' inquired the second.

"'Because, if he were dead, don't you see, he would be the next of kin, and come into all the property.'

"'Ay, I see that well enough,' replied the first speaker; 'but what shall we get by the job, Jack, tell us that?'

"'A thousand pounds between us.'

"'If we get it, it will make men of us for ever,' replied the second.

"'And of that there can be no doubt; but the country would be too hot to hold us, we must be off to America.'

"'That deserves to be thought of more. I don't like leaving the country.'

"'It would not be safe to remain; indeed, I would not attempt the deed if I thought I could not, directly it was done, put the seas between me and England; besides which, the 'squire would not agree to give us the money unless we swear to do so, and we must act upon honour, or else we are not safe.'

"'Very true; and I will go shares in all things with joy—the reward as well as the danger, you know.'

"'Yes, certainly; but there will be but little danger, as he will never see the hand that pulls the trigger.'

"After this they both left the spot, and Henry stood rooted to the spot. No name had been mentioned, and yet the description and circumstances so much corresponded with his own case that he could not mistake them. Could his uncle be base enough to seek his life, that he might seize his property? Could he act so basely?

"He knew not what to think, and yet he recollected that his uncle was a singularly morose man, and while he had never shown any good-will towards him, yet he had never shown any evil, and he was at a loss to understand it.

"Determined to be on his guard, he cocked his fowling-piece, and keeping a wary eye over the road as he went along, he determined not to show any unusual apprehension, lest it might be only a surmise, and that some other person was intended when the ruffians spoke. He entered the Hall as usual and retired to bed.

"The next morning he descended to the breakfast-room, and met his uncle, who showed no signs of having any guilty project upon his mind, and appeared so completely unembarrassed that Henry really thought that he had made a mistake in his supposition, and was even tempted to relate all that he had heard in the wood, but upon second thought he kept the secret in his own breast.

"He went out as usual, but invariably took with him a couple of dogs, who, roving about, would give him timely warning of any one lurking near him. He often went within the vicinity of the cottage, and often cast a longing look over the garden, but he could not see the beauteous maiden who had charmed his soul.

"At length he met her, and renewed their short acquaintance; he was invited in, and met with a welcome reception. The name of the inmates were Bridgenorth, and the daughter's name was Emma.

"Henry made no scruple in declaring his love, and at the same time his inability to marry for two years, until which time he was under the control of his uncle, who was his guardian. To this no possible objection could be offered either by Emma or her mother.

"Mrs. Bridgenorth had but little property; for at her husband's death, much that he possessed reverted to other hands. She had enough to live upon in ease and elegance, but not expensively, and, therefore, if Henry took her, he must do so from pure love and from no other motive. He declared that he should be possessed of a most ample fortune, and with her he would have nothing more to desire.

"He now often visited the cottage, indeed he was a constant visitor, and received by both mother and daughter as the future son-in-law of the one, and husband of the other. These were the happiest hours he had ever known.

"One evening as he was returning home, full of the thoughts of future happiness, he had neglected his usual precautions of being followed by his dogs and carrying his fowling-piece. He had just attained the end of a dark and unfrequented lane, when a shot was fired, and Henry fell to the ground without sense or motion. How long he remained thus he knew not, but when he woke he found himself very stiff and weak. He essayed to speak, but was unable to do so.

"He saw that he was in a strange place, and that he knew none of those who were about him. They were entire strangers to him, and all their conversation was equally unintelligible, being conducted in whispers. In this state, between life and death, he lingered many weeks, and then but very slowly recovered. His wounds had been very severe, but rendered much worse by lying on the damp earth till morning.

"The assassins, believing they had acted with caution, so as to escape all suspicion, remained instead of flying, and were thus secured. Being thrown into prison, the both confessed their crime, and named the author of the conspiracy. Mr. Farquar hearing of this, and knowing they had the means of proving it in their hands, as well by the money as by notes, he came to the desperate resolution of committing suicide.

"This he did by shooting himself, after he had arranged all his affairs, only a few hours before a warrant was issued for his apprehension by the magistrates of the district, who were all horrified by the act.

"Henry Farquar now came into his property, for no one thought of seeking for another guardian for the short time that remained before he could be declared of age. He immediately sought out Emma Bridgenorth, who wept for him as one that was dead, and related all that had happened, and begged her to name a day when his earthly happiness would be complete."

Two o'clock struck from the same church clock, as Rivers, with frequent interruptions, arising from the reflections that occasionally would force themselves upon his mind, despite the endeavour to distract his thoughts from his own situation, finished the tale he had selected for his reading.

With a deep sigh he closed the page, as he said—

"Only two yet? I must, perforce,

seek some more repose, even at the risk of dreams."

Again he threw himself on the bed, and the same disturbed sleep came over him.

CHAPTER LII.

TOM HACKEY AND THE EFFICIENT OFFICER.—THE PURSUIT TO HAMP-STEAD HEATH.—OLD BURNBY'S COU-RAGE.

IF Rivers felt a difficulty in procuring sound and healthful slumbers, poor Tom Hackey was to the full as much tormented, for so strongly his dread of the duel came upon his mind in the silence of his own little chamber that he could not for the life of him remain in it, but felt a relief by going into the open streets, occasionally paying a visit to the watch-box of old Burnby, who he had the satisfaction of finding was always in a comfortable dose and quite impervious to any sights or sounds which might be calculated to disturb or render him unable to keep his appointment, so Tom very prudently let him sleep on, preferring to awaken him at the time he required his services.

Tom then repaired to the street in which Rivers resided, and placing himself on the opposite side of the way, saw the light which beamed from the window, which although it spoke largely of the decomposed state of Rivers' mind yet it was in a measure satisfactory to Tom, because it assured him that Rivers was at home, and that he could not very well leave without him, Tom Hackey, discovering it, and dogging his footsteps.

Fearful, then that as Rivers was so wakeful, he might start at a very early hour, Tom resolved to drag old Burnby out of his box, and insist upon his keeping with him watch and ward some time before daybreak.

Having made this resolve, the kind-hearted fellow took a brisk walk to keep himself warm, and when he heard five o'clock strike he sought the watchman, who was creating quite an alarm by a symphony of rather a noisy character performed upon the most prominent part of his face.

"Hilloa!" said Tom, "hilloa!"

A variation in the nasal tune old Burnby was playing, only responded to Tom's call.

"Plague take him, he sleeps like a top, or I should say like a true watchman, for they certainly beat everybody at that kind of thing. Hilloa, Burnby! Burnby!"

The watchman only shuffled about uneasily, but he would not open his eyes on any such compulsion.

Tom then bethought himself of an expedient, which he put in practice in a moment, by shouting in the old man's face—

"Fire! fire!"

"My coat! my coat! it's a frizzing," cried old Burnby, suddenly seizing his rattle, and making an attempt to spring it, which Tom promptly prevented, by seizing hold of it, and crying—

"Don't be a fool—the thane of Fife had a wife."

"Whose wife?" said old Burnby.

"Ah, never mind, I forgot you knew nothing of theatricals, and it's no matter. Come along, it's time to follow, or at least to watch our man."

"What's the matter—is it thieves?" was the rejoinder.

"No, it ain't, it's murderers."

"Murderers!"

"Yes, to be sure, murderers, and if you stir yourself you will be just in at the death, so come on."

"Is there any reward?"

"Immense! immense! so come along at once."

Old Burnby immediately bustled out of his box, and getting his coat about him, he was about to leave along with Tom, when he suddenly thought of his duties, and placing his hand to the side of his mouth, he shouted—

"Past three, and a cloudy morning—all's right—come on."

Having thus, as he considered, satisfactorily performed his duty, he accompanied Tom towards the lodgings of Rivers.

"You've made a blunder," said Tom. "It's past five."

"Where's the odds," said old Burnby, "when folks is waked up in the night, what need they mind whether it's three or five, I should like to know?"

"None at all," said Tom. "They can only say, d—n that watchman, and go to sleep again."

"Werry good," said old Burnby.

A very few minutes sufficed to enable them to reach the place of their destination, and Tom saw that the light was still burning in Rivers's chamber. He then pushed Burnby into a deep doorway opposite, and ensconcing himself in the same, he determined to wait patiently till Rivers should make his appearance.

"There's a hackney-coach stand at the top of the next turning," he thought to himself, "and when he comes out we can see which way he's going and soon be after him."

It was nearly the half-hour past five now, and Tom found the night air very cold, for he was not so well provided against it as the old watchman, who was enveloped in so many coats and wrappers that he looked like a great dirty bundle of worn-out apparel.

"I say, Mr. Hackey," said Burnby, "did you ever hear how I found out the fire?"

"A hundred times. Why, hang it, you told it me yourself only yesterday. The fire, indeed!"

"You see," continued Burnby, "I was as usual very vigilant indeed, when all on a sudden——"

"Silence—look there."

Tom pointed opposite as the door of the house in which Rivers lodged was opened, and gently shut by the young man himself, who not being able to find sleep or occupation within doors, had determined to start thus early, and take an easy walk to the place of hostile assignation.

"Shall I spring the rattle?" said Burnby.

"The rattle? by no means—why, you would spoil all."

"Just one twirl."

"If you dare, I'll knock it about your head. There, don't you see him? He is walking very slow. He is going direct for Cheapside. Come on—come on."

Seizing the watchman by the sleeve of his outer coat, Tom dragged him at a most unwonted pace towards the coach-stand, where one solitary chariot stood.

"Coach," cried Tom.

"Here ye is," said the driver.

Tom pushed old Burnby in, and then ascending the rattling steps, he said—

"You see that young man just turning the corner?"

"Him with the cloak?"

"Yes. Follow him, but don't seem to do so. You understand—keep him in view."

"I know—what's amiss?"

"A murder," said old Burnby.

The coachman gave a long whistle, and then mounting his box, he awakened both the horses by sundry lashes about their ears, and then the crazy vehicle set off after Rivers, who had as little idea of being pursued by a hackney carriage in which were Tom Hackey and old Burnby the watchman, as he had of the Monument pursuing him up Fish-street-hill at a slapping pace.

It was very easy for the coachman to keep Rivers in view, for there were but few passengers in the streets at that hour, and Rivers went at an easy pace. Twice or thrice he did certainly look at the crazy old chariot, which seemed to be going his way always, but not a suspicion that the circumstance was other than accidental, ever for one instant crossed his mind.

"You are sure that's him?" said Burnby to Tom.

"I believe you," said Tom—"it's all right."

"Murder's coming it strong rather," remarked Burnby. "I haven't been mixed up in an out-and-out murder for a matter o' five-and-forty years now."

"Ah! the old fool," thought Tom. "He wouldn't be half so pleased if he thought there would be no murder at all, and I'll take good care there shan't be."

Rivers walked on directly down Snow-hill, and along Holborn at an easy pace, intending to take the direct high road to Hampstead, where he guessed he should arrive in ample time. The exercise warmed his blood, and imparted a healthful glow to his frame, so that when he reached the corner of Tottenham-court road, he felt, as far as freshness and vigour was concerned, as if he could have walked a hundred miles.

"I must not altogether," he thought, "take a gloomy view of this question The meeting may not be fatal to either party, and I may satisfy this barbarous and absurd code of honour without having the disagreeable reflection of even crushing so insignificant an insect as this puppy of a lordling."

The old miserable horses in the chariot had quite to be put upon their mettle to follow Rivers up Tottenham-court-road, for he had hung his cloak upon his arm, and walked at a rapid pace.

The streets were beginning now to show more evident signs of vitality, and numerous carriages and incongruous vehicles were moving in different directions, so that the old chariot was not so much noticed. Still Rivers, when accidentally he glanced behind him as he crossed the New-road to the Hampstead-road, could not help remarking,—

"It's very odd that that old chariot should have come so very far my way."

The morning now was getting light and beautiful; the sister hills of Hampstead and Highgate rose like a panorama before the eyes of Rivers in all their richness of high cultivation and magnificent verdure. A soft, healing air came fresh from the open country, so very different from the second-hand, pent-up atmosphere which hung about the ancient courts of the city and the purlieus of Thames-street.

The houses now lost their regularity and tiresome uniformity. There were cottages and villas of all grades and descriptions, surrounded by gardens and named according to the whimsical or romantic notions of their various owners.

The first hill now presented itself, up which Rivers toiled at a slower pace; but when he gained the summit, he started off on the level again at a rapid pace—a pace which took its speed more from the buoyancy which the fresh air and healthful exercise had imparted to his frame than from the necessity of hastening, as it was not yet half-past six o'clock.

"Well," thought Tom, "where the deuce is he a-going to? We've come far enough, I'm sure, already. What do you say, Burnby?"

A loud snore was the reply.

"Hang him," said Tom, "he's gone to sleep again. He thinks he's in his watch-box."

On, on sped Rivers; and now the pretty valley was gained which lies just at the foot of the hill upon which the long, straggling village itself stands. There he paused a moment or two and looked about him, which gave the horses a little breathing space, for they had, for them, travelled an unwonted distance, and were quite amazed at the green fields and the trees.

To the right-hand side of the road was a public-house, and ascertaining that there was ample time for such a purpose, Rivers entered its precincts, and inquired if he could be accommodated with breakfast. A prompt reply in the affirmative, and a polite invitation within the bar, f llowed, and Rivers sat down therein, to the great discomfiture of Tom Hackey, who had directed the

coachman to stop, and was wondering if Rivers meant to come out of the public-house again soon.

"Where am I to drive to now?" said the coachman.

"I really don't know," replied Tam.

"Blessed if I does, then."

Tom considered for some minutes, and then giving old Burnby a violent shaking, which partially awoke him, he cried,—

"Come, old poppy-head, wake up.

We must get out of this. Here, coachman, open the door."

Tom got out of the vehicle, and then hauled Burnby after him, when, paying the coachman, he made haste to ensconce himself and the guardian of the night behind a hedge nearly opposite to the public-house, where he could command a view of the door.

"Bless us, ain't you thinking of breakfast?" suggested the watchman.

"No," said Tom; "we must think

of nothing now till we have arranged satisfactorily the business we have come upon. He won't be long, I dare say, and when he comes out of yonder public-house, we must follow him as circumspectly as we can."

"The murderer?"

"Ah, that will do."

With this old Burnby was satisfied, and after waiting about a quarter of an hour, the sound of wheels coming rapidly up the road from town attracted Tom's attention, and, to his great satisfaction, he in a few moments saw Lord Hawksworth's cab drive past, in which was his lordship, who pulled up some few paces from where Tom was hidden, to give his tiger an opportunity of saying to a boy who was lounging along,—"Is this the way to the heath?" and receiving an answer in the affirmative, a slight touch with the whip started the horse on again at a good pace.

Tom knew now that he was all right. He seized old Burnby by the arm, and crying,—"Come on—keep that cab in sight," he dragged him at a quick walk up Hampstead-hill.

CHAPTER LIII.

THE PLOT.—GIRKINS AND HILLIARD.— A GUITY CONSCIENCE ITS OWN ACCUSER.

GIRKINS was one of those men who would, rather than a victim should escape him, do anything short of what would bring upon his head legal consequences to entrap him in his ruin. He had likewise sufficient experience in human actions, and the accidents which beset the best concocted schemes, never to rely for the accomplishment of any object wholly upon one plan, but to have resources of action beside, which, at a moment's notice, he could bring into play before even the vexation of the first failure could have time to annoy him.

Thus, then, although he more than anticipated the probability of Lord Hawksworth seriously wounding Rivers in the duel which he had urged on, yet he would not loose sight of Hilliard, or the plans by which disgrace was to be heaped upon the innocent young man who had committed no crime, but had placed himself, by loving and being loved, much in the way of Mr. Girkins and his schemes.

With this view Girkins determined upon again calling upon Hilliard, and, acting on his fears as before, induce him to arrange some step as regarded Rivers, which, if he escaped the duel, would place him in awkward circumstances at the merchant's. The wily agent thought that the best possible time to see Hilliard would be at an early hour in the morning, for he reasoned with himself—"He must sleep sometimes, and he is more likely to seek his home for repose at some hour considerably past midnight than before it."

About the very same time, then, that Rivers left his house, in order to repair to the hostile meeting on Hampstead-heath, Girkins proceeded to the not very inviting neighbourhood of Clare-market, in search of Hilliard.

He easily again found the wretched house to which he had before traced him, and, ascending the staircase, he, after much stumbling about in the dark, found himself on the landing, which was immediately outside Hilliard's door. A moment's thought recalled to his mind the position of the door with regard to the landing, and he, instead of knocking, took hold of the handle, which, readily yielding to his touch, enabled him to open the door a short distance.

A faint, sickly gleam of light from a wretched candle shone through the opening, and showed him Hilliard, who, with his back towards the door, appeared either to be sleeping on his chair, or too overwhelmed in thought to hear the slight noise which Girkins made in obtruding himself into the room thus unceremoniously.

"Humph!" thought the agent, "there he is, sure enough. Just returned, in all probability, from some drunken carouse, and his hat is on the floor, and the room is redolent of the fumes of liquor and tobacco."

Hilliard moved uneasily in his chair, and muttered, in a low tone—

"Will they never have done? D——n, will they never cease amusing themselves with these conjectures that almost drive me mad to read? Curses on them, and their vile ingenuity! When will they let the affair sleep, as it ought to do?

Another—another—let me see again what they say."

He then fumbled in his pockets till he produced a newspaper. Slowly opening it, till he came to a particular side, he doubled it up so as to have that before his eyes, and commenced reading it in a low, anxious tone, but one sufficiently loud for Girkins to hear, amid the wrapt stillness that reigned around.

"The murder of Mr. Noble," he read. "Our readers will be pleased to hear that a legal gentleman, some time retired from the bar, but of great skill in his profession, has determined to devote the whole of his legal service and knowledge to the elucidation of the mystery which still surrounds the affair of the murder of Mr. Noble, in New Inn. The extraordinary manner in which the criminal has hitherto escaped detection, although not suspicion, for we are assured that the highest legal opinions are against the supposition of the clerk Wilson being the perpetrator of the deed, and that another party is strongly suspected, has invested the affair with peculiar interest. We do hope, for the sake of humanity and civilization, that the perpetrator of the deed will be speedily brought to justice. It would be premature to give the name of the suspected party in this instance."

Hilliard read this paragraph twice over, and then remained silent for some time, after which he muttered, with great trepidation—

"Who do they suspect? Who would it be premature to mention at present? Can they have any clue? Surely—surely not; each day, too, makes the thing safer and safer, especially as he is dead—he only who could have told all. Curses on the country papers, they are ever speculating on some confounded matter which concerns them not. Why, in London a murder is but a nine day's wonder, and then it takes its place among the things of the last century. I —I will read it again. Perhaps I omitted something."

His hands shook so as he again held the paper, that it crackled again, and he could scarcely hold it still enough to read. Girkins, as he witnessed this scene, felt all his suspicions that Hilliard was the real perpetrator of the murder in question revive, and gather

fresh confirmation. He was, however, much too wily and considerate of his own safety to risk making himself *particeps criminis*, by letting Hilliard know how far his suspicions went. It was enough for him, that in the event of Hilliard turning round upon him with threats of exposure, or demands for money, or become troublesome in any way, that he had that means of at once scaring him into submission and silence. He, therefore, thought it prudent to appear only just arrived, and, retreating a step from the door, which he pulled close shut, he knocked at it with his knuckles.

A cry of alarm burst from Hilliard, and he sprang to the door, which he locked in a moment.

"Humph! Confirmation strong. He thinks me an officer."

"Who is there?" said Hilliard from within.

"A friend," replied the agent. "Don't you know my voice?"

"Yes—yes," said Hilliard, as he opened the door; "come in. There are some bad characters in this house, and I am not fond of opening my door to all who may choose to knock at it."

"Certainly not, Hilliard," said Girkins, seating himself. "I have come to speak to you a little more at large about this young man, Rivers."

"Curse him," said Hilliard, as he clenched his fist and shook it menacingly. "I hate him—abhor him. When will you have something done which will bring him to destruction?"

"As soon as you like now. I am not quite sure that you will see him at the office to-morrow; but should he come, mind you, he has escaped a great danger, and then your operations must begin."

"How—how?"

"Surely you can think of some scheme? Has Mathew Trueman much plate about his house?"

"He has plate; I have noticed spoons and forks about of massive silver."

"Well, Hilliard, what think you would be said to any one who was to thin their number a little?"

"It would be hazardous."

"Not at all, if suspicion were excited in another channel. Now, if I were you, and hated Rivers as you do, with no doubt ample cause, I would make such use of him as should put some money in my own pocket, and destroy him at the some time."

"How might that be done?"

"Thus—you say there is plate about—lay hands on it as you can, but be careful to place a spoon or a fork in the desk of Rivers. You understand me?"

"I do—I do. By G—, it shall be done! That must ruin him. There will be a rout about the things stolen, and then I will suggest a search of the servants' boxes and our desks. That will be rare sport. Ha! ha! ha!—What will my proud, haughty, high-minded gentleman say when an evidence against him is produced, which he may argue against for a hundred years and never get over. He will be transported, and a good job too."

"Ay, he certainly is a troublesome young man, Hilliard. You view this matter in its proper light, I see, and be assured that when it is completed you will find those to whom it is satisfactory not ungrateful."

"It shall be done,—it shall be done. A capital plan. Have you a few shillings about you to spare?"

Mr. Girkins winced a little at this, for he by no means liked sparing his shillings. Nevertheless, he reluctantly produced three, saying,—

"These are all I have with me, but when this affair is done, I promise you twenty pounds."

"Agreed," said Hilliard. "It shall be done, and mind you, I hate that fellow so much, that were it not that I want money, and can't possibly do without it, I'd work against him for the love of the thing.

"You are very kind," said Girkins, "but the labourer is worthy of his hire. I never do anything for nothing myself, and I don't expect you. Now, good morning to you, and when next we meet let me hear that all is right, and this—this, what shall I call him—proud, upstart clerk, is humiliated and disgraced. By Heavens! how his haughty spirit will quail before a charge of felony."

"It will—it will. If anything will touch him closely, that will. Depend upon me to do it, for I have two motives, hatred to him, and money from you."

"Humph!" muttered Girkins to himself. "Two as tolerable human motives as could actuate any brain. Revenge and avarice. This fellow is a valuable member of society."

The politic Mr. Girkins then put on his hat to go, when Hilliard did the same.

"You need not be so ceremonious as to show me out," said the agent, "as I found my way up the stairs, I shall find my way down again."

Hilliard burst into a coarse laugh, as he said,—

"Between you and me, Mr. Girkins, there need not be much ceremony now. Men who have each other in their power are apt to neglect the little courtesies of life."

Girkins started and knit his brows, as he exclaimed,—

"Do you fancy I am in your power?"

"Yes; I was in a lawyer's office before I went to old Trueman to manage his bill affairs, and there I learnt what an accessary before the fact meant."

"Curse you," said Girkins, "you would not be believed upon your oath."

"Well, well, I'm going to spend these three shillings in drink. That's what takes me down stairs now. But remember, you are in my power, and I could—along with myself, I grant—transport you, Mr. Girkins."

Girkins was silent for a moment, but during that moment he thought to himself, "I must, come of it what may, let this ruffian know that I have him more in my power than he has me in his, or he will prove a most troublesome acquaintance." Then he said in a low, but clear tone,—

"Hark you, Master Hilliard, you are labouring under a great error when you think of intimidating me by asserting your power of denouncing me for counselling you to commit a felony. If you were in a lawyer's office once, I was once a lawyer, as doubtless you know well, and I know that your unsupported testimony would avail you nothing. Likewise, Master Hilliard, likewise —"

Here Girkins made a meaning pause, which sent a flush of alarm to the face of the guilty Hilliard, who said,—

"What? what? Likewise, what?

What do you look at me in that disagreeable way for?"

Girkins beckoned with his finger as solemnly as the ghost in Hamlet. The trembling Hilliard approached close to him, as if fascinated by the gaze of the agent's eyes, and when he was within reach, Girkins laid hold of his arm, and pulling him yet closer, whispered in his ear,—

"I could hang you, Hilliard!"

"Me—me?"

"Yes, you."

"I—didn't do it! Who says I killed him? It was not I—d————n, what do you mean by saying you could hang me?"

"I think quite enough has been said. You have just this moment criminated yourself. I said nothing about any killing, but you have."

Hilliard sunk into a chair with a deep groan.

"Tush—tush, man!" said the agent, "heed it not; you are safe with me so long as you don't tamper with me, but recollect for the future that 'tis you are in my power, not I in yours. Always bear that in mind, and we shall get on together exceedingly well, Hilliard."

"How—came—you to suspect?" faltered Hilliard.

"Never mind that. Let it suffice that I know all."

The agent thought it extremely politic to affect a much more extensive knowledge than he really had, and having, as he could easily perceive, thoroughly alarmed Hilliard, he once more said, "Good morning,'" and without waiting for an answer, left the room.

When he reached the street, he laughed quietly to himself, and muttered—

"So, the scoundrel begins to threaten. Humph! I flatter myself that I am a little deeper than such a poor rogue as Mark Hilliard. I never made but one very great mistake in my life, and that was what struck me off the rolls. I played off a clever trick, such as is very common—very common, indeed, and I should have reaped from it honour and reward; but I left a loophole open, by which the knowledge of what I had done became too public; I was found out, and became, of course, scorned by those who objected not to the morality of my proceedings, but could not bear any one who was found out. Well, well, I am at war with society, but I think I am getting the better of the conflict, rather."

Hugging himself with this conceit, Mr. Girkins hastened to the hotel at which he expected the earliest news of the issue of the duel between Lord Hawksworth and Rivers.

As for Hilliard, he remained for some time quite stupified by what Girkins had said to him; he could neither move nor speak, and his heart beat as if it would burst its bounds. That the agent should know his guilt seemed to him perfectly inexplicable, and the more he strove to fancy some means by which he could rationally account for Girkins's knowledge of his crime, the more he felt himself bewildered and lost in a maze of conjecture. At length, a conviction began to creep over his superstitious mind that Girkins must possess some more than natural power of reading men's hearts, and he trembled as he thought how with a word he might consign him to a felon's cell.

He then rose, and clutching the three shillings in his hand, he staggered to the door, muttering :—

"Drink—drink—drink! That must drown all care, and it will—it will. Brandy—brandy; I think I should cut my throat without it."

——

CHAPTER LIV.

THE PROCEEDINGS ON HAMPSTEAD HEATH.—THE ALARM OF OLD BURNBY.

TOM HACKEY could have kept Lord Hawksworth's cab tolerably well in sight had he been alone, but it was no easy job to drag old Burnby up Hampstead-hill; it was only, indeed, by dint of pulling him along, and occasionally giving a push between the shoulders, which, if he had not obeyed, would have sent him on to his nose, that anything like progress was made.

The cab, however, did not go at a rapid pace, and, moreover, it stopped again where there were two roads, and the question as to the direct route to the heath was again asked.

"Either road," was the reply, so the

cab went right on up Hollybush-hill, till it emerged upon the beautiful and picturesque heath that lay far and wide before the unappreciating eyes of Lord Hawksworth, who had an exceedingly small appreciation of the beauties of nature.

Tom Hackey, when he saw the cab stop, pulled up old Burnby, and ensconced him in the corner of a shrubbery, where he was nearly hidden from sight.

Two persons alighted from Hawksworth's cab; one was his lordship, and the other, the accommodating Macdonald. The few words they exchanged came distinctly to Tom Hackey's ears, and they convinced him that the combat was fully intended.

"We are too soon," said Hawksworth, looking at his watch: "How infernally provoking if the fellow don't come."

"I think you may depend upon him," replied Macdonald. "I feel certain he will come, but I am looking more anxiously for the second I have provided for him."

"That is a strange proceeding, Macdonald; but, you will bear in mind, come what will of this affair, I have nothing to do with that."

"Nothing whatever, my lord."

"I merely attend to find my man and a second."

"Precisely."

Hawksworth glanced round him now as he remarked—

"This conversation would be imprudent if any one was within hearing, but as there is no one, I wish to say to you to manage to give me all the advantages of light and position you can."

Even the sycophantic Macdonald blushed as he replied—

"Yes. Oh, yes."

Just then there appeared the person who had been provided for the occasion to act as second to Rivers. He advanced, and shook hands with Macdonald, who addressed him as Clifton, and then bowed to Lord Hawksworth, who returned the salute very coldly, and then turning his back, said—

"Macdonald, I ought not to see or speak to this person at all."

"Right," said Macdonald, and then

he whispered something to Clifton, who said—

"Oh, yes; of course—quite right. By-the-by, is that my man?"

"Yes," said Macdonald and Hawksworth, both in a breath.

Rivers saw the party and quickened his pace, when he was met by his second, who, courteously bowing, said—

"Mr. Rivers, I presume?"

"My name is Rivers, and I presume you are the gentleman who will do me the favour of seconding me in this little affair?"

"I shall have that honour, sir."

"Thank you. I am ready."

"Then, sir, if you will wait one moment I will speak to Lord Hawksworth's second about where we are to go."

Rivers bowed his assent, and Clifton walked up to Macdonald, and said—

"We will follow you and his lordship to any retired part of the heath you think will be safe for our purpose."

"Very well," said Macdonald. "We will saunter on slowly."

Clifton then communicated the result of this arrangement to Rivers, who, acquiescing in it, walked with his second after Macdonald and Hawksworth, who took a course to the left over the heath, which would take them to the most unfrequented part of it.

The moment Tom Hackey saw the belligerent parties walk off in this way, he seized old Burnby by the arm, and crying—"Come on—come on," he dragged him after them, dodging behind every tree he came near, which afforded a shelter from observation, in case any of the party should happen to look back.

To follow parties over an open heath was, however, not the easiest job in the world where secrecy was an object, and Tom Hackey expected each moment that Rivers would look back and recognise him. His only comfortable reflection was, that if such a thing should occur, he would immediately bring forward old Burnby, and stop the intended duel.

Singular to say, however, not one of the party of four looked back, for each was intent upon his own reflections, not any of them being of a very pleasant character.

Half a mile of heath was traversed, and then Macdonald, looking round him, said—

"We may go miles here and find nothing but open country. I shall advise that we get over that paling. There is, you perceive, a sort of wilderness, with trees on either side, and I think we shall not find a better place."

"Agreed," said Hawksworth.

"Down—down, old Burnby !" cried Tom, as he saw Macdonald in the act of turning round ; but old Burnby heard him not, and Tom's only resource was to do as he did, namely, seize old Burnby by the leg, and precipitate him into a hollow, where he lay perfectly free from observation, and in a state of great astonishment as to the nature of the attack made upon him.

Tom Hackey glanced up, and to his chagrin he saw the party he was in pursuit of scale the paling with great alacrity, and one and all disappear on the other side.

"Up—up !" he cried, suddenly rising, and tugging away at old Burnby's white coat, a handful of which at once gave way, and sent Tom Hackey sprawling upon his back in a bush of furze, from which he could only extricate himself by rolling out.

The consequence of this delay was, that the combatants got very much the start of their pursuers among the trees, where Macdonald had advised the duel should take place, before Tom Hackey and old Burnby reached the paling. And when they did reach it, how was old Burnby to be got over? That was a question which would have puzzled the Royal Society or the British Association for a dozen sessions, at least.

"If I get over myself," thought Tom, "I shall never get him over, and he's a constable while I'm nobody. I must push him over, and then climb after him."

Acting upon this plan, Tom began pushing old Burnby up the paling, with an intention of casting him bodily over when he got him to the top. This was, however, a long process, and before he could accomplish it, the combatants had made some progress in their arrangements for the duel.

Clifton placed Rivers by a tree, while he went to Macdonald, and said—

"We use your pistols, I suppose ?"

"Yes : your man has none, of course."

"No ; give me one of yours."

Lord Hawksworth, who heard this little bit of dialogue, muttered a curse between his teeth, and considered it uncommonly hard to supply a fellow with first-rate arms to fight him with ; but there was no resource, as Rivers had not been so imprudent as Hawksworth hoped he would have been, as to bring to the field with him the, in all probability, indifferent pistols his means would have enabled him to purchase.

Notwithstanding the hint of Hawksworth, Macdonald did give Rivers fair play as to situation, and the combatants were placed in such a manner that neither had an undue advantage over the other. The sun was not shining, so that difficulty did not exist, and they had both a good light, and nothing to dazzle and distress the eyes.

Macdonald then whispered to Hawksworth—

"Does your lordship wish to say anything now in case of a fatal accident on our side ?"

"Fatal !" said Hawksworth.

"Why, casualties will occur, you know."

"I have nothing to communicate," said Hawksworth, coldly.

Clifton had put the same question to Rivers, who in reply said—

"Should I fall, that is, be killed, you will find some letters in my pocket, which, if you will take the trouble to forward to their respective addresses, will much oblige me."

"I promise you they shall be forwarded," said Clifton. "There is your pistol, and good luck attend you."

"Thank you," said Rivers. He could not help then glancing around him at the beautiful sylvan landscape spreading far and whide to the horizon, and a sigh of regret rose to his lips as he thought it might be for the last time that he could so gaze. Then the visage of Grace Trueman came before his mind's eye, and for one moment he trembled. It was a temporary weakness, and expelled almost as soon as felt. "God bless and protect her," he murmured, and then he would not speak again, for should he fall he wished that these should be his last words in this world.

Lord Hawksworth was placed opposite to him, at a distance of fourteen paces, that space having been carried by his lordship, who fancied himself a better shot at that distance than at twelve paces. All was now ready, and To Hackey had just succeeded in pushing old Burnby up the wall, when he said—

"Lor bless me, Mr. Hackey, here's two *gemman* as is going to shoot each other."

"The devil!" cried Tom, as dropping the watchman, he looked over the palings himself, and saw the forward state the preparations for the fight were in.

At that instant Macdonald cried—

"One—two."

"Hold!" shouted Tom Hackey. "The man that stirs makes me his foe."

"Three!" cried Macdonald; but the surprise of the moment at hearing Tom's voice caused Hawksworth's aim to be disturbed, and although he fired he missed Rivers, whom he had made sure of hitting.

Rivers did fire, but it was carelessly over Hawksworth's head, and at the same moment Tom Hackey rolled over the palings, in a perfect agony of apprehension, lest Rivers had been shot, and rushed between the combatants.

Rivers looked amazed, and dropping the pistol from his hand, cried—

"Tom Hackey!" while Hawksworth bit his lips for a moment, and then cried—

"Be off with you, you insolent scoundrel. How dare you stand between us!"

"How dare I?" said Tom. "Why, you insignificant piece of humanity, do you fancy I'm going to let you make a target of a real man, you odious vagabond?"

"Scoundrel!" cried Hawksworth, advancing.

"Come on," said Tom, "I'll fight you, and d—d be he who first cries hold! enough!"

"What is the meaning of all this?" said Macdonald.

"The meaning's this," answered Tom; "there shan't be any more fighting except it's with fists, in a good old English way, and if it comes to that, I know perfectly well who'll get the better of the affair."

"Tom—Tom, how came you here?" said Rivers.

"I've watched you all night, and followed you here to stop the fight," said Tom, "and you wouldn't have had one shot, only I couldn't get old Burnby over the palings."

"Murder! murder!—Fire! fire!" cried old Burnby, at this juncture, he having just succeeded in getting on his feet. Dragging, too, from a capacious pocket of his great coat, his rattle, he commenced springing it a rate which made it heard far and near.

"Good heavens! what's that?" cried Hawksworth.

"That's old Burnby," said Tom.

"What, Tom," said Rivers, "the old private watchman?"

"Yes, it is that same active individual, and you ought to be ashamed of yourself to give him the trouble to come all this way to take you up."

"He will scarcely succeed in doing that, Tom, now he is here."

"Oh, I quite understand all this," said Hawksworth, "you don't like fighting, Mr. Rivers, and have got your friends to send a watchman to rescue you. Be it so, if you please. You leave this ground a coward!"

"Lord Hawksworth," said Rivers, "I dislike coarse language, but to coarse people it must be used. You are a liar!"

"What? You infernal——"

"Hold—hold, my lord," cried Macdonald, seizing Hawksworth by the arm. "The fellow is undeserving of your lordship's resentment. I pray you to command yourself."

"D—n him! I'll be even with him yet. Your father may have been a gentleman, sir, which was the reason I gave you this meeting, but you are not."

"You are no judge," said Rivers, calmly, "and if you don't take care I shall be under the necessity of kicking you before I leave this ground."

"Hurrah! hurrah!" cried Tom. "Bravo our side."

Hawksworth's face turned the colour of scarlet with rage, and in his passion he would doubtless have placed himself in the way of some personal chastisement from Rivers had not both Macdonald and Clifton held him back, which they did, and were determined to do most effectually.

Rivers then advanced a few paces, and said,—

"Lord Hawksworth, you challenged me, and I accepted your invitation to the field, notwithstanding my rooted abhorrence to duelling. You cannot then say that I refused to meet you. You have aimed at my life—I have not aimed at yours. The arbitrary laws of honour have been fully satisfied by me,

and no stain can be cast upon my name, nor my motives questioned when again, as I shall, I refuse to hazard my life at the requisition of a man I despise. Henceforward be careful how you provoke my resentment, for so surely as you do, I will take my own part in a manner far less pleasing probably to you than the present has been."

Without then waiting for a reply, Rivers vaulted over the paling, and alighted close to old Burnby, who

LORD HAWKSWORTH'S FURIOUS CONDUCT AFTER HIS REJECTION BY GRACE.

thought to be sure that some very sanguinary attack was meditated against him, and in his fright sat down upon a nettle bush, and commenced crying "Murder!"

Tom Hackey, before he followed Rivers, turned to the wondering trio, who were being so unceremoniously left on the field, and said,—

"I despise as much as I pity you all, you wretches."

He then immediately followed Rivers

over the paling, to whom he called loudly. At first Rivers, who was really angry at his interference, was inclined to go on and leave him, but a moment's calmer thought checked the impulse, and he paused.

"Tom," he said, "why did you come after me in this manner? Leave me to be the judge of what my own honour requires for the future."

"What your fiddlestick requires," said Tom. "Do you think I was going to let Grace, who I do believe now I love better than you do, cry her pretty eyes out, and beat her breast because you might be shot?"

"Tom—Tom, you really ——"

Rivers paused, and Tom Hackey, taking his hand whether he would or not, added,—

'I am really one who wishes you well from the bottom of my heart. I am a poor fellow, but—but ——"

He could say no more, for his heart was full. Rivers saw the state of his feelings, and shaking him heartily by the hand, he said,—

"Forgive me, Tom, for my foolish petulance. Thank Heaven, this affair is over without bloodshed upon either side. Do not mention it to Grace, Tom, whatever you do."

" You deserve to have it mentioned, and ——"

" I've got him—I've got him. Don't resist," suddenly cried old Burnby, who had come behind Rivers, fancying him the murderer, who Tom Hackey was merely keeping in talk, till he, Burnby, armed with all his civil authority, could seize him.

"Who is this?" said Rivers, twisting himself out of Burnby's grasp with great ease

"Me—me," cried the watchman. "Now mind, young fellow, what you are at. If you don't let me take you up this minute, you are obstructing me in the discharge of my duty."

"Don't be an old fool," said Tom. "It's all over."

"All what?"

" All over, and your services are not required."

"What—what?"

" You ain't wanted."

"Not wanted? Ain't I to take anybody up? Am I to be always resisted? I haven't taken anybody up but the hardened young ruffian of five years old with the iron hoop, about a month ago, for seven years nearly."

"Nor will you till you turn a little more active, I fear," said Tom Hackey.

" And have you really, Tom, brought him all this way to arrest me as one of the duellists?"

"To be sure I have."

"Then here, Burnby, here's half-a-crown for ron. Go and get yourself some breakfast somewhere, and then get to the city by one of the coaches."

Old Burnby took the halfcrown, although he shrewdly suspected it was a compromise of felony so to do. While he was considering, Rivers and Tom Hackey walked off, when the latter said,—

"The same advice as regards the breakfast that you gave to old Burnby I should like to put into practice myself, for it makes me rather hungry running after people who are going to fight duels."

"Very well, Tom, you shall come with me where I breakfasted, and then we can go to London together."

Rivers then conducted his faithful, but eccentric friend, to the same house he himself had stopped at on his arrival at the foot of Hampstead-hill, where Tom took a hearty breakfast, after which the pair of strangely-matched companions walked together towards the city, discoursing of many matters as they jogged pleasantly down the hill.

———

CHAPTER LV.

TOM HACKEY AND RIVERS AT THE OFFICE.—THE ILL-OMENED INTERVIEW.—THE PLOT FOR THE DESTRUCTION OF RIVERS.

LONG before Rivers and Tom Hackey could reach London, Lord Hawksworth, who had taken another route with his cab, because he would not, if he could help it, pass his late antagonist on the road, arrived at the hotel where he was so anxiously waited for by Girkins.

The moment his lordship entered the room where the obsequious agent was with so many doubts and fears awaiting his coming, he threw himself on a sofa, exclaiming,—

"Don't ask any questions—I am out of patience, and the fellow has escaped unhurt."

"Unhurt, my lord, and you not touched either?"

"Me? What the devil! did you speculate upon my being hit, and be hanged to you?"

"Certainly not; but it is a strange termination to such an affair as this, that you should both retire from the contest without achieving any result."

"Strange as it may appear, it is true. We had one shot, which was in both cases ineffectual. A second attempt was prevented by the interposition of an idiot, who I have seen at old Trueman's occasionally, and who, without doubt, was duly apprised of the affair by Rivers, and desired to put a stop to it."

"Indeed?"

"Yes, indeed, such has been the result of this morning's proceedings; and now, look you, Girkins, I have had some misgivings, as the fellow was the son of a gentleman, about handing him over completely to your tender mercies; but now hang him, if you like—poison him—cut his throat. Do anything you please, so that you rid me of him."

"Your lordship is very accommodating," said Girkins, drily; "and I am very glad your lordship's scruples have so pleasantly dissipated."

"Enough of that, Girkins. What is you plan?"

"Why, my lord, the plain state of the case is this : Mathew Trueman will, I am quite sure, never advance another penny-piece without a substantial offer of marriage from you to his daughter."

"So I think. Curse him, and what he has advanced has only placed me deeper in the mire than I was, for it enabled me to get a thousand pounds more in debt."

"Exactly. Then proposition the second is, that unless this Rivers be got rid of completely, he will some day get up a secret marriage with Grace Trueman."

"Well, if he does?"

"Why, then, my lord, if Mathew Trueman has lent you by then much money on the strength of a proposal from you for Grace's hand, he will, upon that bubble of ambition bursting, at once press you disagreeably for the payment."

"But—but—I am under age."

"The honour of a nobleman arrives at maturity as soon as he is capable of pledging his word," said Girkins in a low tone.

Lord Hawksworth bit his lips, before he replied—

"I understand my position perfectly well. Rivers must be disposed of in order that I may have a clear field for answering the merchant with hopes of my marrying his daughter."

"Exactly—and you will have this advantage, that Grace will not have you, so that you will not be called upon to soil your coronet in expectancy by contact with the daughter of a plebeian."

"Well—well," said Hawksworth, rising. "Recollect what you have to do. Remove Rivers from my path, and leave me a clear stage. Grace Trueman has more than sufficient beauty to induce my constant attention to her, were that fellow out of the way."

"Leave Rivers to me, my lord ; and do you, as your part of the business, make a distinct proposal to old Trueman, to wed his daughter."

"I will."

"Then will you authorise me, upon such proposals, to take what steps I please, in order to fix the matter more strongly upon the imagination of Mathew Trueman?"

"Take what steps you like."

"There is, then, but one more preliminary to be settled—I must trouble your lordship for fifty pounds."

Hawksworth took out his pocket-book, and producing a note for the required amount, said—

"Take it—but remember it is the last advance I can make you till Mathew Trueman obliges me with the means of opening a banker's account."

"That will be soon," said Girkins. "I have the honour to wish your lordship a very good morning."

Hawksworth replied to this civility by a muttered curse, for he was out of temper with everybody and everything; but Girkins little heeded his humour so long as he succeeded in his main object, which was, to pocket as much money as possible.

"Not a very bad morning's work," he remarked to himself, when he had left Hawksworth. "Twenty pounds to Hilliard, for getting up the robbery, which will be the destruction of Rivers, and thirty pounds my own commission on the little affair."

He then walked to his friend the man of business in Bernard's Inn, and the two worthies held a long consultation as to the best method to be pursued in fleecing Hawksworth of the large advance he now had so strong a probability of procuring from Mathew Trueman.

The result, or rather the first in the order of events, of their deliberations, was to push on the affair with as much celerity as possible, and taking advantage of the latitude which Hawksworth had given Girkins, to do something which, although it might not be pleasing to his lordship, would be specially so to Mathew Trueman. That something was a paragraph to the following effect, which was drawn up by Girkins, and highly approved by his legal friend. It ran thus, and duly appeared in the *Morning Post*, on the following day—

"We are informed from authority, on which we can rely, that a marriage is on the tapis between a certain heir to a certain earldom, and the beautiful and accomplished daughter of a millionaire, who, report says, commenced the world with three-and-a-penny. We are not at liberty to publish the parties' names at present, but we have heard that the bride's *trousseau* will exceed in value one thousand guineas, and that there is every probability of the bride's father being knighted at the first court held after the marriage shall have taken place, which will be celebrated with a splendour befitting the rank of the bridegroom, and the splendid fortune of the bride."

"If that don't tickle Mathew Trueman's vanity a little," said Girkins, " I know nothing of human nature, and of his nature in particular."

Having thus put everything in train, as he fondly supposed, for the accomplishment of his object, Mr. Girkins calmed down his rage against Rivers, feeling merely towards him as one man does to another, when he has had against him some deep feeling of enmity and revenge, which he has rather over r satisfied.

How little did Rivers dream of the plots and contrivances which were hatched with a view to his ruin! In his own pure and unsophisticated heart he could never have imagined human nature could have debased itself to such desperate wickedness as that intended by Girkins, and he flattered himself, that now the duel was over, he should experience but little further annoyance from Lord Hawksworth, or his obsequious tools.

Alas! Never had he been in such great danger. Never before was he so much in want of some good genius to protect him from the vile and atrocious machinations of his unprincipled enemies.

When he and Tom Hackey reached the office it was rather beyond the proper hour for the commencement of business, but, fortunately, Mathew Trueman was too much occupied with some private business of importance to notice their non-arrival at the usual hour. As for Hilliard, his absence excited no remark from anybody, for such a thing was by far too usual.

"Well, Tom," said Rivers, "here we are all again in our old quarters, and you may possibly guess who I should be glad to see after the risk of never seeing her again."

"Oh, I know," said Tom Hackey, " you ought to be ashamed of yourself. What would have become of you if I hadn't found the letter?"

"Well, well, we will say no more upon that subject at present, Tom. Let us think of happier things, if you please. Can you contrive to slip up stairs and——"

"No, I can't. Slip up yourself, will you. Why should I be always slipping up stairs and down stairs with notes for you? Some of these days old Mathew will catch me at it, and then I shall slip out of my situation, and there will be a go. Not that I need care much, only, you see, if you didn't come into the theatrical profession along with me, I should never have any faith in those who were to play junior tragedy to my tip-top characters."

"Oh, indeed! Well, Tom, for once in a way I will take my own note up stairs, if you will ascertain for me that Mathew Trueman is in his own counting-house."

"That I'll soon do," said Tom, and he accordingly went to the door of the merchant's counting house, and knocked loudly.

"Come in," said Trueman, and Tom opening the door a little way, put in his head, saying—

"Want any steel pens, sir? There's a man at the door with some."

"No, no, no," cried Trueman, angrily.

"Or files," said Tom.

"No, I tell you."

"Or sealing wax—or lead pencils."

Mathew Trueman seized a book, and hurled it at Tom's head, who, when he had closed the door, bellowed out, in order to keep up in Trueman's mind the delusion of the hawker of pens, &c.; being there—

"No—none to-day. You can call again when you are passing."

"Confound that fellow," muttered Trueman, as he resumed the accounts he was making up, "I don't know if he be most knave or fool."

"It's all right," said Tom, when he came back to the office. "Mathew is booked for some time, or else I'm sure he would have run after me, I aggravated him so."

"And where do you suppose Grace is?"

"She's generally in the small drawing-room."

"I know. I know. If I could see her for one moment, I should be satisfied. I won't write, for notes are dangerous. One moment's sight of her, and one word spoken to her, will satisfy me."

"Be off with you, then."

Rivers walked stealthily along the passage to the foot of the stairs, and then with cautious steps commenced ascending them.

Stairs always creak abominably when one don't wish to make any noise, and it seemed to Rivers just then as if every stair he trod upon was seizing that opportunity of settling down at least an inch lower upon its supports.

The landing, however, was at length gained, and Rivers was upon the point of knocking at the door of the smaller drawing-room, when it was opened, and a servant appeared with a tray on which were some breakfast things.

"Don't be alarmed," said Rivers, as the girl uttered an exclamation; "I have merely come from below on a message to Miss Trueman."

"Lor, how you frightened me," said the girl.

"Is Grace—I mean Miss Trueman—there?"

"No, she's up stairs."

"I am here," said Grace, descending the stairs, for she had heard the voice of Rivers, and had flown on the wings of love to meet him.

The servant girl placed the tray she was carrying upon a slab that was outside the door, and then went down stairs.

"Dearest Grace," said Rivers "I—"

"Hush—hush!" said Grace, interrupting him. "This is very imprudent of you, indeed."

"But I wished for one moment to see you," whispered Rivers; "to hear your voice again. We were both dull last night, and ought of spirits, dear, dear Grace."

"For heaven's sake, go away, now. If my father should come, what could I do—what could I say? Go, Rivers, go."

"I will. I have accomplished my object; I shall now be happy for the remainder of this day."

He took her unresisting hand, and pressed it to his lips, and then as cautiously as before commenced descending the stairs.

He paused when he was half-way down, and looked up. Grace was upon the landing, and a mutual smile was exchanged by those loving hearts. Rivers waved his hand, and descended the remainder of the staircase, while Grace repaired to her own room again, as much pleased at the casual meeting as her lover could possibly be, now that the danger was over of its being observed by her father.

There was one other person besides the servant who saw Rivers ascend the merchant's staircase; that person was Mark Hilliard. He was at the moment entering by the outer door, in the stealthy fashion he always made his movements since the murder of Mr. Noble, and, with a grim smile of satisfaction, he saw Rivers evidently making for a part of the house where he could have no business. In a moment after his satisfaction was marvellously heightened by seeing the servant descend.

"Good—good," he thought. "Fortune favours me. The very man on whom I wish suspicion to light is ascending to the very rooms where valuables are kept, and there is a witness, too. Good—good. Your doom, Master Rivers, is sealed. Before to-morrow evening you shall be committed for trial as a felon—a low, sneaking thief. Well, that is fine work after he has carried it so bravely to me. I have but now to creep up those stairs myself at the first convenient opportunity, and steal something, which I can place in his desk, and he is convicted. Ha! ha! ha! He will, perhaps, be goaded on to cut his throat, rather than endure to be transported."

CHAPTER LVI.

A DAY OF TROUBLES.—THE SILVER TANKARD.—RIVERS SAVED.—HILLIARD'S RAGE AND DISMAY.—GIRKINS'S DISAPPOINTMENT.

So fair an opportunity of implicating Rivers in a crime had not occurred to Hilliard, and he thought might not occur again. When he entered the office it was with a smile of self-complacency, which sat most ugly upon his far from prepossessing features. Without noticing Tom Hackey, he walked to his own desk, and, as usual, burrying his head in it, he remained for some time with his features completely hidden from sight.

"I have him—I have him," he muttered, in so low a tone, that, although Tom Hackey stretched his ears as much as he could, not a syllable of what he said could be distinctly heard. "Ho! ho! ho! I have him. How strange and how pleasant, that he, with all his high-flown notions and his pride, should be at the bar of the Old Bailey, as he surely will be, before I am."

While the villain was thus picturing to himself the probable results of his rascality, Rivers came into the office with a smile likewise upon his face, but how very different a one to that which, like a lurid light from the infernal regions, had for a moment lit up the features of Hilliard with a loathsome mirth.

The heart of Rivers was full of that pure light from Heaven which yet lingers so sweetly in human nature, typical of what it once was in its native purity, and what it may be again in a better and a happier world. He hardly noticed Hilliard, but the latter looked askance upon the handsome and intelligent countenance of him he was about to make his victim with a satanic leer.

Well might he have been taken for the arch-enemy of mankind exulting over some deep-laid plot for the ruin of some soul which Heaven had endowed with high and rare qualities, in order to make it all its own, and protect it from the snares which would inevitably beset its earthly pilgrimage.

Tom Hackey came up to Rivers, and in a low voice said,—

"Well, you saw her?"

"Yes, Tom—yes."

"Oh. Then I suppose all's right?"

"Certainly, Tom. Quite an angel, I—I—mean—yes."

"Oh, I know what you mean. I've come Romeo myself now and then. Oh, Juliet—Juliet, I ——"

"Hush, Tom. Look."

Rivers indicated the direction of the door as he spoke, and Tom, glancing that way, saw Mathew Trueman opening it to enter the office. In a moment the merchant was in the place, and addressing neither of his clerks in particular, he said,—

"Should Lord Hawksworth call here in my absence, show him up stairs, and say that I shall return within an hour."

Rivers made no reply, but Hilliard, suddenly dropping the lid of his desk, said—

"Yes, sir, I will."

"Very well," said Trueman, giving a glance of dislike to Rivers, who he began to hate most cordially and mortally. He then, with a shake of the head, which accompanied a determination in his own mind of getting rid of him the very first opportunity, left the room.

As for Tom Hackey, he looked extremely hard at the ceiling all the while, as if the merchant had not been there at all.

Hilliard then lifted the lid of his desk, so that he might think without being disturbed, and commenced eagerly concocting a plan which should enable him to carry into effect the suggestion of Girkins. His, Hilliard's, knowledge of the house, and the habits of its inmates, was immensely greater than Rivers's, and he calculated how it would be possible for him, during the hour which the merchant said he should be from home, to slink up stairs and steal anything. It was then eleven o'clock, and he concluded rightly, from former experience, that Trueman's hour from home would, in all probability, extend to two, not that the thriving merchant was a man of unpunctual habits, far from it; but he had a habit, from a correct enough notion that nothing went so well in his absence from home, of always mentioning that he would return much earlier than he knew his business out of doors would of necessity detain him.

"He will be home about one o'clock," thought Hilliard, "and in all likelihood later. At half-past twelve the servants lunch in the kitchen. Then will be my time to slip up stairs unobserved, lay my hands upon something, which I can keep till Rivers goes to dinner, when, if he should not lock his desk, as he frequently does not, I can place it within, and damnify his character for ever."

"With an impatience, then, that was wormwood to his mind, Hilliard waited the slow progress of time, till twelve o'clock sounded from the office clock. His conjectures as to the duration of Mathew Trueman's absence turned out to be correct, at all events, each minute was hastening its verification, and, moreover, to his great relief, Lord Hawksworth came not, for although his coming would have given him, Hilliard, an excuse for proceeding up stairs, yet, at the same time, it would have had the effect of proving that he had been there, and *might* have effected the robbery, and *might* have placed some of the produce in the desk of the unsuspecting and innocent Rivers.

The next half hour was one of still more intense anxiety, for two things might during it occur to thwart him; namely, the return of the merchant, or a visit from Lord Hawksworth. As it happened, however, neither occurred, and at half-past twelve Hilliard found himself perfectly at liberty to pursue his wicked intentions.

He waited then seven or eight minutes, by which time he was sure the servants would all be occupied in the only employment they are generally pretty punctual in, eating, and then he shut his desk, and avoiding the eyes of Rivers, walked from the office.

Tom Hackey eyed him as he left, and when the door was closed after him, he said,—

"There goes a fellow, who I am sure would stick at nothing. Did you see the look of him as he went out?"

"Not I," said Rivers. "I fully believe him to be a most unprincipled fellow, and I don't at all like his looks usually."

"He's only fit for a hangman," added Tom. "As he went from here just now, he looked for all the world as if he was going to assassinate some one."

"Indeed?"

"Ah! I shouldn't be at all surprised in a few minutes to hear somebody cry out, 'Help—help—Macbeth doth murder sleep!'"

"I should, Tom, as you are here, for I don't suppose there is any one else in this house so stage-struck as yourself."

"Me—me, stage-struck?"

"Yes to be sure, you know you are."

"Well," said Tom, lifting up his hands, "after that comes a fish, and says, 'pray fry me.'"

Rivers laughed, and continued the occupation he was about, while Tom sat down by the fire-side, rather indignant than otherwise.

Could Rivers, or Tom Hackey, have suspected for one moment what Hilliard was about, what an effect it would have had upon their present placid state. Such, however, never entered their minds, and in these matter-of-fact days all good geniuses seem to have gone fast asleep.

Hilliard, in the meantime, slunk up the staircase, trembling at every step, for his fears of detection were excessive. By the time he reached the landing, the perspiration was standing in heavy drops upon his brow, and he was fain to pause for support, ere he could proceed a step further. He leaned heavily on the banisters, and threw all his faculties into an effort to listen if he could hear the slightest indication of any one being in the room he wished to go to. That room was Mathew Trueman's bed-room, and it was situated on the next floor.

All seemed perfectly quiet, and his next wish was to ascertain where Grace was, in order that he might not encounter her on his way. He cautiously stooped, and peeped through the key-hole of the drawing-room door, but she was not there, and, with a muttered curse, he thought she might be up stairs and see him.

At that moment he heard a door opened and shut on the second floor. That some one was about to descend he doubted not, and, on the impulse of the moment, he walked into the drawing-room.

The next few moments were terrible to Hilliard, for he could think of no possible excuse to offer to any of the household, or to Grace, should she or they enter the room. He heard a light footstep descending the staircase—it paused at the door—a cold shiver came over Hilliard, and he was on the point of making a rush ro escape, when he heard the door of the back drawing-room opened and then closed.

"Luck—luck again," he gasped—and rapidly passing out of the front room in which he was on to the landing, he felt assured he was more safe than he had yet been.

"Now, now," he thought, " for the completion of my enterprise. Mathew Trueman has a silver cup in his bed-room, which was presented to him by some stupid society or other. That I will possess myself of. The old man prizes it highly, and if it be found in the desk of Rivers, he will be so much incensed that he will have no mercy upon him."

Acting, then, immediately under the favourable circumstances in which he fancied himself, Hilliard rapidly ascended the stairs leading to the second floor, and boldly entered the merchant's bed-room, which was furnished and appointed very luxuriously, although its owner had commenced life with three-and-a-penny.

CHAPTER LVII.

THE ROBBERY.—THE SILVER CUP.—THE QUARREL.—THE BAKED MEAT PIE.

GLANCING hastily around him, the guilty man fixed his eyes upon an ancient cabinet, in which he heard the merchant was in the habit of keeping those articles of cost which he most valued, and as the silver cup he wished to possess himself of was nowhere openly visible, Hilliard conjectured at once that he should find it within the cabinet.

A bitter curse rose to his lips as he thought that it might be locked, and that he was unprovided with any means of opening it. Hastily approaching it, he tried one of the drawers, which, to his satisfaction, immediately yielded to his touch, and there, lying upon its side, in order to enable the drawer to shut, was the identical silver presenta-tion cup which, because Mathew True-man set peculiar store by it, he thought would be most likely, if found in the desk of Rivers, to ensure his persecution with all the rigour that could possibly be used.

With a grim smile he snatched the elaborately wrought article from the drawer, and as he read the ridiculous, fulsome inscription that was engraven on it, he muttered,—

"This Mathew Trueman can have no difficulty in swearing to. Rivers, your fate is sealed. You will now find how dangerous it is to defy such men as I am."

The thought then struck him that it would be just as well if he were, for his own special benefit, to secure some other article of value, the onus of having stolen which would comfortably rest upon the shoulders of the unfortunate Rivers, strengthening the case against him, and preventing the likelihood of any suspicion attaching to him, Hilliard.

"If," he muttered, "I could possess myself now of any articles of plate, I know a means of turning such into cash during my dinner hour, and all would be well."

The avarice of Hilliard was so strongly excited by the prospect of making great profit to himself, at the same time that he blasted and ruined the character of Rivers, that he lingered in the merchant's chamber for a longer period than prudence could at all dictate, while he dragged open every drawer in the hope of finding money or valuables which might be readily converted into such. His search, however, was use-less, and the sudden sound of an opening door on the floor above that in which he was committing his depreda-tions, aroused him to a sense of his danger, and the necessity that existed of as speedidy as possible reaching the office again.

Concealing the silver cup, then, carefully he crept to the door, and peering down the staircase to make sure that no one was ascending, he, with a smile of gratified triumph, and malignant revenge, glided noiselessly into the passage.

"'Tis done—'tis done," he muttered, "this night will see Rivers in the cell of a felon ; how conclusive will be the evidence, how frantically agonizing his feelings, and how terrible to him the sentence which shall brand his name for ever with infamy. 'Tis a rare and a delightful circumstance indeed, to be paid for accomplishing one's revenge ; so great is the hatred I bear to this Rivers, so continually has he crossed me, and such accusations against me does his every look imply, that I would fain

THE MERCHANT SPURNS GRACE FROM THE DOOR.

destroy him. Ah! I am paid, and paid handsomely too, for accomplishing my own cherished purpose."

Carefully assuring himself, then, that no part of the silver cup was visible, Hilliard re-entered the office, and his look of fiendish exul ation was so great as he did so, that Tom Hackey, who never scrupled to look him full in the face, could not fail being struck by it.

"What's in the wind now," he thought. "I never saw that vagabond look so pleased before. He's been robbing a church, or murdering some babby for certain. I say, Rivers," Tom then whispered in his friend's ear, "just look at Hilliard, will you. He looks as happy as old King Cole, concerning whom, I believe it is an historical fact, that he was a merry old soul."

"Hush, Tom, hush," said Rivers, "for my sake, as well as your own, do not get into a quarrel with that man ; he is a dark and dangerous character, and one who, I have no doubt, would not scruple to embrace any means which would present him a chance of revenge against those who might awaken his malignity."

"Bother take his malignity," said Tom, "he knows I don't care a pin about him, and that I stare at him whenever I like, and say just whatever I please."

Hilliard, during this brief dialogue, had seated himself at his own desk, and with his head slightly turned on one side, he glared with his deep sunken, bloodshot eyes upon the handsome countenance of Rivers with the expression of a demon.

"How soon," he thought, "will that look of serenity be blasted; how soon it will be changed to one of unutterable woe and anguish. Ha! ha! ha! When he is in prison awaiting his trial I will call and see him, and ask him how he came to be such a fool as to steal the merchant's much prized silver cup. It will be glorious sport then to hear what he says—to listen with a mild, pleasant-looking countenance to his assertions of innocence, and affect to believe him in a manner which shall clearly show that it is from complaisance, and not conviction. Then I will offer to take any message he may please to send to Grace, and to endeavour to console her for his loss when he shall be convicted. If that don't drive him nearly mad I don't know what will."

So pleased was Hilliard with the prospect of perpetrating this iniquity, that an audible chuckle came from his lips, which so astonished Tom Hackey, that he made sundry remarks, as, he wondered what would happen next, and when the sky fell, he presumed that larks would be caught.

Even Rivers looked up for a moment at the devilish leering face of the villain, who, he little suspected, was at that moment rejoicing over his hopes of his utter ruin, and of his moral annihilation:

The young man turned away with a shudder from the contemplation of the face of that man of crime, and he thought to himself, " It is surely a hard fate to be compelled even to sit in the same apartment with so consummate a scoundrel." A sudden thought then seemed to strike Hilliard, which brought with it a mixed feeling of pain and pleasure—of pain on his own account, because there rushed to his mind those things which he would fain have forgotten, and of pleasure at the thought that he should in some measure be able to inflict upon Rivers an injury which should force his feeling in that same frightful channel as his own.

Hiding his head, then, as was his custom, beneath the lid of his desk, he took from his pocket the several newspapers which, by a strange fatality, he seemed condemned to carry about with him; each was doubled in the exact place where the paragraphs appeared which bore reference to the murder of Mr. Noble, and Hilliard, as he commenced reading, thought to himself—

"To-morrow, even he, proud, haughty, Francis Rivers, with all that he calls his high feelings about him, will have a newspaper article to read which will tear his very brain, as these have mine, only that his feelings must be worse, because I am not discovered. I, though guilty, am very safe, while he, though innocent, will read of his examination and committal for trial with a far more exquisite pain than were he guilty."

Even as he spoke the office clock struck one, and so accustomed was he to rush from the irksomeness of his duties, that at the very first intimation that the hour was come during which he should be at liberty, involuntarily he let fall the lid of his desk with a heavy blow, and half rose from his stool, before it struck him how much more important an object it was to him to remain last in the office on that day. He accordingly placed himself in the position from which he had so suddenly and impulsively moved, and awaited with extreme agony for the departure of Rivers and Tom Hackey, which they generally did together.

"Oh !" thought Tom, "he ain't running off as usual—perhaps he's going to pull up a little for lost time—well, there's nothing like it ; but as the ghost in Hamlet says, soft, I do begin to snift the dinner-hour, and must render up myself to mutton chops, which, if they are over done, will raise such fury in Thomas Hackey's breast as shall make each particular hair on the cook's head stand on end, like quills upon the fretful porcupine."

"The late murder in New Inn," muttered Hilliard, as he commenced to read one of the newspaper paragrahs, which was so fearfully and deeply interesting to him.

"The what?" said Tom, "the murder —where?"

"Who spoke of murder?" cried Hilliard, again letting down the lid of his desk, and facing Tom Hackey with a furious scowl, who promptly replied—

" Why you, to be sure. Who else do you suppose has anything to do with such things here?"

" Dare you hint that you suspect—" cried Hiilliard, and then suddenly dropping his tone, he added—"Pooh! pooh! I am nearly as great a fool as you are to heed your railings."

" Thank you," said Tom, " I may be a fool, Mark Hilliard, but I'd rather be a fool and sleep comfortable at nights, going to bed without reproach, and awaking without care, than something else which it isn't necessary for me to explain."

"Curses on you," cried Hilliard, "the injury you have provoked be on your own head."

As he spoke, he moved from his stool with a threatening aspect, but Rivers immediately stepped between him and the object of his wrath, saying, in a determined tone—

" Hold, Mark Hilliard; much as I blame Hackey for being so foolish as to address you at all, when you are altogether unsuited to converse with him, I dare you for your own safety-sake to lay a finger upon him."

"You dare me!" cried Hilliard,

"Yes, I," said Rivers. "Take the warning, and save yourself from the consequences of your rashness."

For a moment then such a gleam of wild rage flashed from the eyes of Hilliard, that it was with difficulty he kept himself from rushing upon Rivers, in which event the coolness and courage of the merchant's clerk would have enabled him to defeat the malice of the villain, who would have gladly done him some injury.

A thought then came like a flash of lightning across the mind of Hilliard of how soon his revenge was to be gratified to the full, and how trifling would an injury be that he could at present inflict upon him in comparison of the certain horror which in the course of a few short hours he should in all probability be able to load his mind with.

"Please yourselves—please yourselves," he muttered in a low voice, "enjoy your triumph—rant away at your pleasure; my time will come."

With that he once more turned his face from them, and again buried it within his desk.

"Well, I know your time will come," said Tom Hackey, "and it strikes me very forcibly, that time will be eight o'clock some morning."

"Fool!" muttered Hilliard.

"Ah, you are a clever fellow," continued Tom, " discretion is the better part of valour. He who fights and runs away, will live to fight another day; but he who never fights at all——"

"Come away—come away," said Rivers, "how can you be so foolish, Tom, as to tempt the violence of that scoundrel; he will some day do you an injury when you least expect it."

"Well, but he provokes one," said Tom Hackey, " and you know when I am provoked I am as a man more sinned against than sinning, and come wind or come rack, at least I'll die with harness on my back."

" I wish you'd be a little more prudent," said Rivers; "we live in very matter-of-fact times, Tom Hackey, and we find the romance of existence hardly ever attracts upon the stage."

" Ah," said Tom, flying off at a tangent. " All the world's a stage, we have our entrances and our exits, and one man in his time plays many parts."

At this moment Tom Hackey, who was far too intent upon his quotations to notice whither he was proceeding, ran against a baker who, at that popular hour of one o' clock, was conveying a huge meat pie, to an expectant family, when down went the pie, and baker, and Tom Hackey, in one mass of confusion. The latter, however, immediately sprang to his feet, and raising a sort of a war cry over the baker, he cried as he rushed down a narrow turning—

" The Thane of Fife had a wife. The owl was a baker's daughter.

> "Full fathom five the meat-pie lies,
>   Of its gravy mud is made,
>   Such the fate of baked meat-pies,
>   Such the words Tom Hackey said."

In a moment then he was out of sight, and Rivers was fain to give the baker half-a-crown, telling him Tom was a little touched in the upper story.

CHAPTER LVIII.

THE CONCEALMENT IN THE DESK. GIRKINS AND HILLIARD.

WHEN Rivers and Tom Hackey had fairly left the office, and Hilliard found himself alone, he sprang from the stool upon which he had seated himself, and lifting his clenched fist above his head, he cried,

"So, now for my revenge, my deep and lasting revenge. Tremble, Rivers, for a crisis in your fate has arrived, which will hurl you to destruction. Who says the enmity of such as I am is innoxious? I have heard of people who, in the full pride and flush of what they call their innocence, fancy themselves lifted up above the assaults and accidents of life; so is it with this Rivers; but let him beware, little dreams he of the precipice, on the trembling verge of which he stands; the very date of this day shall be to him fraught with frightful remembrances, and she, that beautiful, but the once proud and haughty being, Grace Trueman, how she will gasp to find her idol such a thing of clay."

He allowed his hands slowly to drop to his side after this burst of passion, and then in an altered tone, he cried,—

"Did he lock his desk? And yet what matters. I have tools about me which will undo a much more complicated fastening."

He then walked to the door of the office, which he opened just a sufficient distance to enable him to project his head into the passage. "There is no one near," he muttered. "I am unobserved—safely now can I execute my project, and earn my golden reward of the politic Mr. Girkins, at the same time I gratify one of the strongest feelings

of revenge that ever found a place in my breast." Closing the door then cautiously, he crept back to the fire, at which he stood for a moment or two affecting to warm his hands, although the fact was, that at that moment, even his guilt-laden soul was shrinking from the frightful task he had set himself to do.

He buried his hand in his breast, where was the silver cup, upon which he laid a nervous grasp.

"Yes—yes," he muttered, "this will destroy him, this silver cup which Mathew Trueman, in his pride and vanity of heart, prizes so highly, will be found in the desk of Francis Rivers, as it shall be—as it shall be—must be such a damning proof of his guilt, as to ensure his utter ruin. He will be lost —lost beyond all power of redemption; and why should I shrink?—shrink! do I shrink? No—no, only I am aware I have plenty of time, and I am just gloating still over the consequence of the deed I am about to do. And yet I had better place it in at once—at once —yes, at once."

With a slow and timid step he approached the desk of Rivers, and had it been a living thing fraught with danger, as he approached it, he could not have shuddered with greater fear nor turned his face away with more intense anxiety from it.

His ears were painfully acute to the smallest sound; a cinder falling from the grate made his heart beat with frightful violence, and a fancied sound in the passage nearly paralyzed him with fear; he waited, then, for several minutes, without stirring hand or foot, and scarcely daring to breathe lest he should lose the least indication of some approaching footsteps. But as all continued profoundly still, he again muttered to himself,—

"There is no one near; I will hesitate no longer; already nearly half the period of the absence is expired— the desk is open—perish, Francis Rivers —perish. The deed is done which will hurl you to destruction."

As he spoke, he then drew forth the silver cup which lay concealed in the breast of his garments, and displacing a heap of letters which lay in some confusion at one corner in the desk of

Rivers, he carefully placed under them the cup, covering it over with hurried and trembling hands, but still amply sufficiently to prevent its being seen by a mere casual glance in the desk.

To shut the lid and then seize his hat from the peg on which it hung was the work of a moment. His great object then was to leave the office as quickly as possible, and that, too, without observation, a feat which he imagined he had accomplished, although such, as will be seen hereafter, was not the case.

With a frantic speed, which was lent to him by the hurry and confusion of his mind, he rushed to a neighbouring eating-house, whither he was accustomed to repair during the dinner hour, when his pockets happened to be sufficiently well lined to procure him a meal, which was not always the case, for if the preceding night had been, as it too frequently was, a scene of riot and confusion, the chances were that Hilliard arose from his short, fevered sleep in the morning a penniless man.

Such, however, happened not to be the case in this instance; he had enough about him with which to pay for his meal; he mechanically ordered a dinner, but when it came he could not have eaten it, had he been paid pounds for so doing, and after a vain effort to force a morcel down his throat, he abstained from the attempt, and with such a desperate oath that the trembling and affrighted waiter stood aghast, he paid for the uneaten meal and rushed from the house.

Feeling, then, violently in each of his pockets, he could muster up but the small sum of two shillings, and with them grasped in his hot, feverish hand, he dashed into the first public-house that presented its tempting portal to his view.

Staggering up to the bar, he laid down the coins, and in a hoarse, husky voice, uttered the one word "brandy."

The amount of the money he had tendered was handed to him in ardent spirits, which, to the astonishment of the landlord, he gulped down in one draught, saying, as he did so,

"Success—success—may he endure such pangs that he shall descend to hell with the brand of suicide upon his brow, and my curse clinging to him."

He then hastily left the house, and when he had got into the open street, the first idea that rushed through his half deranged brain was to visit Girkins and claim his reward, but ere he had taken half a dozen steps in the direction of St. Bernard's Inn, where that worthy person was most likely to be found in company with his friend and familiar, the attorney-at-law, who was not yet struck off the rolls, the clock of St. Paul's solemnly pealed the hour of two.

Mark Hilliard was not yet so far gone in drunkenness, or mental disquietude, but that he felt the necessity of returning to the office, in order not only to see how affairs were progressing, but to aid by artful suggestions the denouement of the affair which he had put into such an awful state of progression.

"Yes, yes," he cried, "I must be there. I must suggest a search when the merchant shall miss his much-prized silver cup. I must be loud in my offers in any ordeal which shall prove my own innocence, and of necessity Rivers must accede to any proposition that is made, as assuredly he will—as assuredly he will—in the pride of his fancied innocence and security. Yes, yes, I must to the office. I must to the office."

He turned his steps hastily in that direction, and before a quarter of an hour elapsed he was within a couple of hundred paces of the merchant's house in Thames-street. A cry of surprise then suddenly burst from his lips, as some one suddenly touched him from behind, and ready to sink into the earth from very terror, he bounded forward several steps, when his further progress was arrested by the well-known voice of Girkins, crying—

"Mark Hilliard, Mark Hilliard, I would speak with you."

Hilliard turned immediately, and the frightful paleness of his face, joined to the wild rolling of his eyes, results of the state of intoxication he was in, so much alarmed Girkins, that he bitterly repented stopping him at such a juncture.

Drawing him aside in the shadow of a doorway, he exclaimed—

"Good God! Hilliard, what means this emotion? Your looks are perfectly terrifying. What has happened—tell me what has happened?"

"It is done—it is done!" gasped Hilliard; "give me the twenty pounds you promised me, Girkins, for I have done my work. The money—the money, I say, give me the money, for I am penniless, and I have earned it well."

"Hush, for heaven's sake, hush!" said the agent; "you will attract the attention of the passers by in the street. Talk more softly and confidentially, Master Hilliard."

"Yes," said Hilliard, "but I want money—more money. I will be a pattern of caution, but I must have the twenty pounds, Mr. Girkins. What on earth do you suppose such a man as I could do without brandy? By its potent influence alone can I for a brief space get rid of the throng of frightful images that oppress my brain. I must drink, or I shall go mad, or cut my throat. D———n, do you hear me? I must have money, for how am I to get drink without?"

"It strikes me, do you know, Hilliard," said Girkins, calmly, "that you have had quite drink enough already."

"Pshaw!" said Hilliard, "I have but had a half pint of brandy, and that I felt go down my throat like cold water. I am parched and full of thirst, but my brain is proof against intoxication. You have, perhaps, yet to learn that when the brain is full of frightful images, and when the senses are wrapped in horror, liquor loses its power. I am as sober as you are."

"You may be sober, Hilliard, but the brandy by no means improves your appearance; and as for twenty pounds, I have not such a sum about me were you ten times entitled to it."

"Curses!" said Hilliard, "what have you, then? I have yet that to do, for the proper accomplishment of which I must prime myself with drink. God only knows the scene I may have to pass through this afternoon."

"Tell me what you have done," said Girkins, evading the direct request of Hilliard for money.

"I will," said Hilliard as he inclined his mouth to the ear of Girkins, and spoke in a low, hissing whisper, that gave the agent some uneasiness with regard to his own personal safety, for he thought that Hilliard's mind was surely becoming deranged by the constant state of terror he was in, and the too free use of intoxicating liquors.

"The merchant," said Hilliard, "has a small silver cup, which, from some grad nonsense that is cut upon it, he prizes highly."

"Yes—yes," said Girkins, who at once saw the drift of what Hilliard was saying.

"That cup," continued Hilliard, "he kept carefully in his own bed-chamber. Can you guess where it is now?"

"In the desk of Rivers," said Girkins in a scarcely perceptible whisper.

"Yes—yes, and I must have more brandy to carry me through the scene that may ensue. It must flow like liquid fire through my veins, mingling with my chilled blood, and imparting warmth to the icy coldness of my heart. I must not tremble—I must not look so pale and ghastly as you say I do; I must be calm, sir, calm, mild, and temperate, and yet so full of devilish subtlety as to ensure his ruin."

"But, Mark Hilliard, can you really suppose that raw brandy will act as a sedative upon your nerves?"

"Yes," said Hilliard; "I know it by experience. Two fires will extinguish each other."

"Well, there is something in that," said the agent, "and if you really do think, Hilliard, that brandy is necessary to enable you to complete this matter, which is so well begun, heaven forbid that I should grudge you its assistance."

"Girkins," said Hilliard, "how often you use the name of heaven—I cannot—I cannot."

"The use of such expletives are mere habits," said Girkins; "here is half-a-sovereign for you. Come to me to-morrow at Bernard's Inn, and tell me that Francis Rivers is in custody on a charge of robbery in a dwelling-house, and I will complete the sum of twenty pounds."

"You shall see me between the hours of one and two," said Hilliard; "never doubt the success of the plan—it cannot fail."

———————

CHAPTER LIX.

THE ROBBERY.—TRUEMAN'S ANGER.— THE CONSTABLE AND THE SEARCH.

WHEN Hilliard reached the office, he found both Rivers and Tom Hackey there before him, and, notwithstanding that after he had left Girkins he had taken as much more brandy as he had before imbibed, he walked with more than his usual steadiness to his desk, and in verification of his own words, that two fires would extinguish each other, it seemed as if the excitement of the ardent spirits had but succeeded in successfully combating with his nervousness, without imparting any of its own destructive effects to his system.

Not a word was spoken to him by Rivers or Tom Hackey, nor did he feel in any way inclined to open a conversation. His sole mental inquiry was, "When will Mathew Trueman miss his silver cup?" and the oftener he asked himself that question, the more troublesome and distant did the answer appear, for when he came to weigh the subject in all its bearings, he began to think it just possible, and then extremely probable, that the whole of that day, and perhaps the next too, might pass without the supposed robbery being found out.

"What, under such circumstances," he asked himself, "was to become of his promise to Girkins, and where would be his chance of receiving on the following morning the twenty pounds?"

Moreover, there was another risk, which was each moment growing stronger, namely—that Rivers, in some researches through his desk, should himself find the silver cup; and on the instant, as he, in all likelihood, would proclaim the fact, at once removing all suspicion of his own guilty knowledge of the circumstances, and either leaving it in mystery altogether, or pointing directly to him who did it, as having placed it there for the destruction of the young man, towards whom he was known to bear no good will.

It then became importantly clear to the mind of Hilliard, that some means should be adopted, by which the affair should be brought to a crisis, and whether those means were or were not pregnant with suspicion, as regarded himself, was a matter of not so much importance, as that the cup should be found in Rivers's desk, which, coupled with the fact that one of the servants of the household could swear to having seen him on the staircase, must of necessity force a jury to convict him of the robbery.

But how was this to be accomplished? How were the merchant's suspicions to be aroused, and if aroused, how were they to be directed precisely in that channel which should induce him to proceed directly to his bed-room, in order to see that his highly-prized silver cup was safe?

These were propositions Hilliard cursed his own folly that he had not before duly considered, and although he taxed his invention to the utmost, he could think of nothing that was at all calculated to assist him out of the dilemma.

To go at once to the merchant's private room and hint to him anything concerning the supposed robbery of his cup would never succeed, as that would be by far too grossly suspicious a proceeding.

What was his intense surprise, then, and sudden gratification, to see the office door suddenly open, and Mathew Trueman himself enter, furiously excited, and exclaiming—

"I have been robbed, I have been robbed—there have been thieves in my house—I have been robbed this morning. Hackey, fetch a constable directly—yet —no—upon second thoughts I will not let a soul leave this house until I have made an inquiry into the matter. I have been robbed, atrociously robbed during my temporary absence from home."

"Robbed, sir?" cried Rivers, moving from his stool, and at the same time closing the lid of his desk, from which he had just taken a small account-book.

"Robbed?" cried Tom Hackey. "Angels and ministers of grace defend us. Who steals my purse steals trash. 'Twas mine, 'tis his, and much good may it do him, for there is nothing in it. What have you lost, Mathew—bless me, I mean old Trueman?"

Rivers darted a reproachful look at Tom Hackey, as much as to say,

"There, now, I told you you would make some such step as that some day.'

The merchant, however, was too much occupied with his own indignation to notice the extreme irreverence with which Tom Hackey addressed him. All he was aware of in Tom's speech was, that it contained some dramatical quotations, of which he had an especial horror, and turning to him he exclaimed—

"You scoundrel, you shall leve may service on Saturday night."

Hilliard had by this time stepped forward, and, in a low tone, said—

"You robbed, sir? It must, indeed, be an atrocious act to rob you. I beg that you will close the outer doors and cause the strictest inquiry to be made, for all our characters are implicated in such a transaction as this."

"Of course I will," said the merchant, stamping furiously. "They might have stolen my plate, my money, anything but my silver cup, upon which I prided myself so much, and which really reflected so much honour upon me, commencing life as I did with three-and-a-penny, and ending it, I believe, as warm as any man upon 'Change.—Ah!"

"Your silver cup, sir?" said Hilliard, in a tone of great commiseration. "Do you mean the cup the society honoured themselves so much by giving to you?"

"I do, of course I do," cried the merchant. "Don't be a fool and ask questions. Run about, anybody, and find my cup—my cup—my cup. Five pounds reward for my cup."

"Five pounds?" cried Hilliard.

"No," said the merchant, whose avarice just stepped in after his first impulse; "I mean two pounds ten. Thieves, thieves, thieves! Mr. Rivers, how can you stand staring at me in that manner, when you hear I have lost my silver cup?"

"I can but regret the loss of your silver cup," said Rivers; "as even were I to see the article I should not recognise it, since I was not aware of your possession of one."

"Don't be ridiculous, Mr. Rivers; everybody knows about my cup that was given me by the society for the enlightenment of mankind and the advancement of everything."

"Man—proud man," exclaimed Tom Hackey, "dressed in a little brief authority——."

Mathew Trueman made a rush at Tom, and if the latter had not adroitly dodged him round the two chairs that were in the office, he would doubtlessly have satisfied some portion of his vengeance against the abstracter of the cup, by an assault upon the irritating Hackey.

"Tom—Tom," cried Rivers, in a deprecating tone, and Hilliard immediately said—

"Mr. Trueman, may I be allowed at this juncture to beg a particular favour of you, which, I think, as regards this cup business, would be satisfactory to you as to myself and Mr. Rivers?"

"I beg you will not make use of my name," said Rivers. "I decline most emphatically the remotest connection in any manner with you or your satisfactions or dissatisfactions."

Hilliard was nearly bursting with rage, but he controlled himself sufficiently to dissemble, and said, in a mild soothing tone—

"But, Mr. Rivers, you know when a robbery is committed in a house, all persons therein are placed in a disagreeable position until the real thief be found."

"Indeed?" said Rivers.

"Yes, indeed," added Hilliard; "for suspicion must more or less attach to every one."

"Of course," said the merchant, "it must be somebody in the house; who else could know anything of my silver cup? It's been stolen by some scoundrel who knew the store I put by it. It's been done to aggravate me, I know it has."

"As far as regards suspicion attaching itself to any one," said Rivers, drawing himself up proudly, "I acknowledge no such thing. I bow to no such degrading supposition. Let those assume so much as regards themselves as they think proper, finding, possibly, from past actions, abundant reasons; for myself, I not only repel such an insinuation with scorn and contempt, but likewise bestow a small share of those feelings upon him who has offered it."

There was something so manly, so

dignified, and so innocent in the manner of Rivers as he spoke, that Hilliard shrunk a few paces back in conscious self-debasement and guilt, while Mathew Trueman felt an involuntary respect for the man who would not even allow so light a breath to be cast upon his honour.

As for Tom Hackey, he was so delighted that he seized the poker, and exclaimed,—

"He is a man, take him all in all, we shall ne'er look upon his like again! Friends, Romans, and countrymen, I come to speak to Mathew, lend me your ears! the evil that men do—the cup they steal!"

"You infernal scoundrel!" cried Trueman, making another attempt against Tom Hackey, who this time escaped him and ran into the passage.

"I am not so violently virtuous," sneered Hilliard, "that I am afraid of an investigation into my honesty. Have

me searched, Mr. Trueman; have my lodgings searched—my great coat—and have—have—" here his voice faltered, "have my desk searched."

"I'll have everybody searched," cried the merchant, raising his arms frantically. "I'll have a general search—a terrible search—and I'll find my cup if it's above ground, or I'll know the reason why."

Rivers said no more; but calmly sitting down to his desk, resumed the occupation in which he had been dis-turbed, determined to waste no further anger upon persons who evidently had no appreciation of that nice sense of honour which had been instilled into him in early life, and which feels a stain like a wound.

The merchant then, by a sudden impulse, left the office, and standing at the head of the kitchen stairs, which was not many paces off, he shouted,—

"Hilloa—hilloa, there, some of you come here directly, and run for a constable—I have been robbed, my silver cup is stolen. A constable—a constable!"

The voice of the merchant was well known, and in a moment his small but efficient establishment rushed up the kitchen staircase, and appeared with looks of consternation in the hall.

"Fetch me a constable—fetch me a constable," continued Mathew Trueman. "I'll have everybody searched—I'll have the whole house searched. I would not have lost my cup for fifty pounds."

One of the servants instantly obeyed the message of the merchant, and running over to a neighbouring public-house, inquired how and where a constable could be procured, when the host himself, particularly when he came to know that it was the rich Mr. Trueman who required such assistance, volunteered his services, he being a constable in his own right, and snatching the staff, which had hung ingloriously in the bar for a long period, he rushed, that is to say, waddled across the road to Mr. Trueman's, putting the staff as he went into such curious fencing attitudes as never were yet beheld; and had the, to him, gratifying effect of collecting a crowd instanter, who ranged themslves in a semicircle round the merchant's door in expectation of something extremely amusing.

The first person that mine host of the Star and Garter seized was Mathew Trueman himself; but that might be pardoned in the excitement of the moment, and he soon let him go again, upon seeing his own mistake, humbly inquiring whom he should have the pleasure to escort to the watch-house on his, Mr. Trueman's, account.

"I have lost my cup—my cup!" said Mathew Trueman, hurriedly.

The landlord then thought that he would be exceedingly clever, and managing, with a great muscular effort, to wink one of his little eyes, that were almost lost in fat, he said,—

"Did the villain leave the saucer? cos, if it's the same pattern, it will help to identify, you see, sir."

"You are an ass," said Mathew Trueman. "I mean my silver cup."

"Oh," said the landlord, rubbing his nose with the end of his staff, "you means one of them ere with a *kiver*."

"No—no—no," screamed Mathew Trueman, "it had no cover. Are you a constable?"

"Look at me," said the landlord; "why, I could hardly get in at your door."

How his size established his constabulary authority, did not very clearly appear; but it might arise from the landlord's appreciation of a piece of practical philosophy, now well understood, namely, that in England, if a fat man and a thin man contend for any place, honour, emolument, or dignity, the fat man is sure to get it.

"Come along, then," said Mathew Trueman; "all I want you to do, is to take into custody any one whom I may charge with having stolen my cup."

"I'll do it—I'll do it," cried the landlord, flourishing his staff; "show me the villain, we'll see if the Star and Garter can't manage him. First of all, do you suspect anybody in the house?"

"You stand here," said Mathew Trueman. "I don't want your advice."

"Ah," said the landlord, "very well; wilful people must have their own way; show me the villain, and I'll take him."

When Mathew Trueman again entered the office, he saw that the situation of the parties therein was not at all changed. Rivers was calmly writing at his desk, while Hilliard stood in the middle of the floor, hardly able to conceal the feelings of unholy exultation which were swelling in his bosom. Tom Hackey had again entered the office, and was standing by the fireside, watching the strange and rapid alterations that took place each moment in the countenance of Hilliard, and wondering what they could portend.

"I shall search the whole house," said the merchant, "and the boxes of the servants, and—and—then you will not object to my examining this office thoroughly?"

"Pray, sir, as you are here," said Hilliard, "commence with this office, and let me, at least, have the satisfaction of knowing that no suspicion lies at my door. There is my desk, sir, I beg you will search it thoroughly."

As he spoke, he opened the lid of his desk and commenced moving the various articles within it. The merchant stepped up to it, and took a glance of the interior, after which he said,

"No, certainly, my cup is not there."

"Nor here, sir, I hope?" said Hilliard, shaking his great coat.

"No, no, nor there," said Mathew Trueman; then, as he turned to Rivers, he said, in a tone of slight confusion,

"Mr. Rivers, as I have looked into Mr. Hilliard's desk, I cannot very well avoid looking into yours, but I assure you, I have no suspicions."

Rivers made no reply, but merely bowing his head, leaned up from his desk. Hilliard was at its side in a moment; his eyes glistened with a supernatural looking fire, he ground his teeth with a harsh grating noise together, he drew his breath short and thick, and altogether his appearance denoted such intense excitement as astonished all present. As Rivers did not offer to open his desk, the merchant did so himself; book after book was taken out, several quires of paper, some pens, and the heap of letters was then all that remained.

Hilliard's expectation was at its greatest height, he clapped his hands and burst out into a loud harsh laugh, as the merchant removed the letters, and then one glance assured him that the silver cup was *not* there.

CHAPTER LX.

THE MERCHANT'S UNEXPECTED MEETING WITH LORD HAWKSWORTH.—THE PROPOSAL.

IN order to possess the reader of the circumstances which led to the most unexpected fact of the silver cup, which Hilliard had so carefully placed in the desk of Rivers, disappearing, we must follow the merchant on his expedition from home during the time that gave the villain Hilliard the much wished-for opportunity of executing his vile project.

After transacting the mercantile business which he had in view, the merchant was not a little surprised, in an obscure turning in the city, to meet with no less a personage than my Lord Hawksworth himself, on foot, and totally unattended; moreover, there was a quiet unassumingness in the attire of his lordship, very much at variance with the usual ostentations magnificence that characterised his apparel and personal appointments. The reason of this remarkable change in Hawksworth's appearance, and of the quiet and cautious manner in which he was visiting what he usually denominated the infernally low city, was, that a certain Israelite resided in one of the obscure alleys thereof, who had, in Hawksworth's own phrase, done a few kites for him occasionally, i. e., discounted some bills, but had lately become rather sceptical with regard to his lordship's repeated assurances that he was about to marry the only child of the wealthy Mr. Mathew Trueman, and acquire by the alliance an enormous fortune.

The consequence of this want of faith in his lordship on the part of the Jew, was that for more than a month the supplies had been stopped, and his lordship's most vivid remonstrance met by a calm and steady refusal.

Now, however, as Hawksworth had made up his mind to make a decisive step in the affair, and by and with the advice of his privy counsellor, to make, or at least imply a direct offer to the merchant to marry Grace, he considered he was quite justified in calling upon Mr. Solomons, of much wealth but small faith, in order to procure a temporary advance.

This, to a limited extent, he succeeded in doing, but so strong were his asseverations that he was really about to make the offer for Grace's hand, that even the Jew believed him.

As this expedition to the city, however, was one not fraught with honour or glory, or in any way calculated to be gratifying to his pride, Lord Hawksworth had been content to dispense with all those little attributes in which his small vanity usually delighted, and which goes so far in the eyes of the vulgar to make up the ideal of a great man.

Emphatically speaking, and with all due deference to his lordship, he had sneaked into the city and was endeavouring to sneak out again, when, to his absolute horror, he encountered Mathew Trueman so face to face, and in such an obstinately intractable little thoroughfare, that his lordship at a glance saw that, although he had four alternatives of action, only one of which was to meet the purse-proud merchant, that that, with all its disagreeables, was the most agreeable.

In the first place, to get past Mathew Trueman, he must have got over a post, to get back again he must have clambered over a porter with a chest of drawers on his head, and his only other alternative, besides meeting the merchant, presented itself in the shape of a scavenger's cart, into which his lordship might certainly have scrambled, had he been so inclined.

"D———n!" he muttered, " I shall be bored to death now with this old fool, and I suppose, in order to keep my promise with Girkins and my dear friend the Jew, I must make the promise of marriage which this purse-proud merchant has been pestering for so long."

"Your lordship's obedient humble servant," said Mathew Trueman, when he had in some measure recovered from his first surprise at the unaristocratic and common man-like appearance of his lordship.

"Ah! Mr. Trueman, my most worthy and respected friend," said Hawksworth. "Really, it's quite an agreeable surprise to meet you in the city."

"Your lordship forgets," said the merchant, "that we poor citizens, who begin life with three-and-a-penny, might be pardoned for surprise at seeing your lordship on foot, and without the extremely delightful and agreeable little associations connected with your lordship's rank."

Mathew Trueman then, who was shrewd in his way, could not help thinking how extremely like a lord might look to a second-rate haberdasher's shopman.

"Why, you see, Mr. Trueman," said Hawksworth, "unless people of high station and dignity now and then mingle with what you'll excuse me for calling the vulgar throng, it is impossible for them to discharge the great functions they are called upon to exercise with that regard to the well-being of the mass of the community, and of the London merchants, which is so very desirable."

"That is very true, my lord," said Mathew Trueman, "and although a man may commence life with———"

"Exactly," said Hawksworth; "three-and-a-penny—I know, Mr. Trueman; but, as I was saying, when the governor elopes—"

"When the what, my lord?" exclaimed Mathew Trueman.

"I mean that when the earl my father dies," explained Hawksworth, " an event which it is dreadful to think must happen in the ordinary course of nature, I shall, of course, take my seat in the Upper House, when the experience I may gather even in a public thoroughfare like this may become of the utmost importance and advantage."

"That is uncommonly true," said Mathew Trueman, and not a little wondering at the singular tone of expression, he thought to himself, "the sooner the governor elopes, the better I shall be pleased."

A little air of confusion seemed to pass over Hawksworth's face, as he then said—

"Mr. Trueman, since we have met so opportunely, there is a matter which, to me, is of the first importance and—and—and I may say all-important to my future happiness, concerning which I would fain speak to you."

The merchant's heart bounded with delight as he heard these words from the titled creature, who was by descent, and the courtesy of custom, a great man and an able legislator.

"Now, now," he thought, "will my utmost ambition be gratified. Now, indeed, will a coronet gleam upon the brow of Grace, and, as father to a countess, I believe even Mathew Trueman, who began life with three-and-a-penny, will be somebody. Ah! what can he mean, but that he is now about to make an offer—the offer so long expected, so often hinted at, but now for the first time placed in something like a tangible form? I shall be father to a countess, and father-in-law to an earl. I rather think the firm of Brown, Swigsby, Grunt, and Waggleton, which has so often crossed me in my tallow speculations, will open its eyes and let its hair stand on end a bit. Ah!"

These ruminations of Mathew Trueman passed through his mind with much greater rapidity than we have taken to record them, and his face, even to the weak penetration of Lord Hawksworth, was fully indicative of the extreme satisfaction of his mind, although no sound escaped his lips but the occasional Ah ! with which he was pleased to terminate his sentences.

"My lord," he then said, "I shall have the extreme pleasure in now at once accompanying your lordship to my extremely humble and much honoured home, where we can talk over any matters your lordship may please, at our own pleasure and leisure."

This, however, was a proposition which Lord Hawksworth was not disposed to accede to, for he had, at the bottom of his heart, a suspicion that without his well appointed cab, his handsome gray mare, and diminutive tiger, even he, Lord Hawksworth, might be taken for somebody who was nobody; and, even in the eyes of Grace Trueman, he was far from wishing to appear otherwise than surrounded by the meretricious glitter of his rank, which in his utter want of power of appreciation of such a character as Grace's, he believed must ultimately awaken some feeling of pride favourable to his ulterior views ; for although his lordship had not the remotest intention of ever uniting himself to her, yet his vanity was not a little mortified at the supposition that, were he ever so much inclined to the match, she would unhesitatingly reject him, preferring in his stead the penniless clerk, who really possessed from nature that true nobility of soul which he, Hawksworth, could only ludicrously claim from his ancestors, as if intellect and high integrity could be bequeathed along with other personal property by one individual to another.

He, therefore, replied to Mathew Trueman's invitation—

"If Mr. Trueman would not object to accompany me to an hotel, we can, in a private room thereof, talk over the subject which I shall do myself the pleasure of entering upon."

"As your lordship pleases," said the gratified merchant ; "close at hand, in Cannon-street, there is a first-rate establishment, to which I shall have great pleasure in introducing so distinguished a guest."

"Thank you," said Hawksworth, wincing a little at the idea of a first-rate establishment in Cannon-street, "I

shall accompany you with the greatest pleasure."

Quite in a state of mental exultation and elation, Mathew Trueman offered his arm to his lordship, who, taking it in the most condescending manner, the strangely assorted pair walked through some streets in the city towards the half hotel, half public-house, which the merchant had mentioned.

Mathew Trueman had a special reason for taking Lord Hawksworth to this establishment, for he was well known there, and what an exceeding pride and gratification to him for the landlord and all the waiters to become aware of the stunning fact that he, Mathew Trueman, had brought Lord Hawksworth, a *bona fide* lord, presumptive heir to an earldom, and as superior to the Lord Mayor as any one thing could be to another, to hold a confidential confabulation with him in a private room.

"If that don't astonish them," said Mathew Trueman, to himself, "then they'll open their eyes at nothing."

With a feeling of disgust, which he scarcely attempted to conceal, Lord Hawksworth permitted himself to be ushered into the establishment, and Mathew Trueman, who was anxious that the waiters should not be mystified for the moment as to who and what the visitor was, turned to Hawksworth, and said, loud enough for the whole establishment to hear—

"I will order a private-room, your lordship, if your lordship pleases— where your lordship and I can talk over our affairs. By-the-by, I forgot to ask your lordship how the earl, your lordship's father, was."

Lord Hawksworth at that moment would have felt great pleasure in cutting Mathew Trueman's throat, with any blunt or jagged instrument that could have been presented to him. He positively writhed with agony ; and when he saw these half-dirty looking waiters flourish their rather greasy napkins, and exclaim all at once, as if accelerated by some piece of artful and concealed machienery—"Yes, my lord—certainly, my lord—a private room for his lordship —coming directly," he could have almost rushed out of the place, and given up all his hopes of the deep dip into Mathew Trueman's coffers he had so long flattered himself he was to have.

The landlord, too, hearing the unwonted sounds of lordship and lord in his establishment, made a wild sort of rush from behind a kind of bar, where he had been sitting, and pulling off his wig in a demoniac manner, he rushed among the waiters exclaiming—

"A lord and an earl—a private room in a moment—this way, your highnesses, this way."

"Pray don't put yourself out of the way, Mr. Snaggs," said Mathew Trueman, with a patronising air; "his lordship and I have merely some business of importance to settle; all we require is a private room, befitting his lordship's high rank; as for me, you know I am plain Mathew Trueman, nothing in the world but plain Mathew Trueman, a merchant who began the world with three-and-a-penny, ah!"

This was the climax of horrors to Lord Hawksworth, who, with something between a groan and a scream, rushed after the landlord, who was proceeding up-stairs to show the way to the private room.

Mathew Trueman had no resource but to follow, which, however, he was well contented to do, for had he not fully accomplished all that he wished or intended, and was not the whole establishment fully cognisant and aware that he, Mathew Trueman, was in company with a distinguished personage, who had something so particular to say to him that a private room became absolutely necessary?

"Of course," thought Mathew Trueman, "they'll think it's something connected with the government or the internal resources of the country, in which, in a privy council, it has been thought necessary to consult me—ah!"

As for the landlord, and the waiters, and the chambermaids, and the cook, down to the small boy who run errands, and was cuffed by the bigger boy who cleaned boots and shoes, they kept running against each other in the most extraordinary manner, upon the strength of a lord, with a real earl for his father, being on the premises, a circumstance unprecedented in the annals of the house.

"For, after all," remarked the landlady, "what is a lord mayor, who is a lord one year and a tallow-chandler, or a stationer, or a hardwareman, or a saddler next, in comparison to one who is a lord from a babby upwards?"

"Very true," said the landlord; "and do you know I'm thinking of calling that room he is in now the earl's room, for ever afterwards."

"That will be very well," said the wife, "but you will have a dispute between the two clubs as to which shall occupy it."

"The two clubs be bothered," said the landlord; "the earl's room it shall be, and nothing else."

At this moment a violent ring from the bell of the private room at once set the whole establishment in motion, as if they had been connected to it by a galvanic battery. The landlord and the three waiters arrived at the head of the staircase at the same moment, and the latter, giving their master precedence, allowed him to enter the room.

"A bottle of Bucellas," said Mathew Trueman, with an important air.

"Yes, my lord—certainly, your lordship," said the landlord, and making a wild rush down the staircase, he in a few moments reappeared with a bottle containing something as remarkably like table-beer afflicted by a thunder storm as possible. "Can I bring anything else to your lordship?" said the obsequious landlord.

"Nothing, nothing," said Hawksworth, looking askew at the bottle, and making a mental resolution that not one drop of its contents should pass down his throat.

When he and Mathew Trueman were again alone, there was an awkward silence for a few moments, during which Lord Hawksworth was considering in what cautious manner, so as least to commit himself, he should make the offer, which he felt to be inevitable.

CHAPTER LXI.

THE MERCHANT'S EXULTATION.—THE CORONET IN PERSPECTIVE.

IF Lord Hawksworth had a decided objection to the curious mixture named by courtesy Bucellas, Mathew Trueman, in the height of his exhilaration, had not, for he drank several glasses in rapid succession, more, however, to fill up the vacuum that occurred in the discourse than for any predilection for the horrible liquor.

The hiatus in the discourse was as painful to Hawksworth as it was to Trueman, for while it kept the latter in a state of feverish expectation, the former could not be utterly dead to every feeling of honour and honesty as not to feel some degree of mental confusion and shrinking from the deliberate swindling he was about to attempt.

In order to possess himself of Mathew Trueman's money, he was about to attack the weak point in his character, and utter the grossest falsehoods, entailing upon himself the same moral consequences as a man who attacks the weakest part of his neighbour's house, and robs him of his property.

Then again, Hawksworth had the ulterior design of making the beautiful and accomplished Grace his mistress; and so little appreciation had he of female virtue and honour, from his experience of the loose society among which he had been thrown, that he would not admit to his mind that such a consummation was not possible.

He, therefore, felt like many persons who commit moral crimes, not sufficiently loth to abstain from them, but sufficiently fearful of their consequences, to commit with a bad grace and a hesitating manner.

Thus, when Lord Hawksworth spoke to Mathew Trueman, it was in a stammering, bungling way, that ought at once to have convicted him of duplicity; but where abundant vanity once takes impression of the human heart, it will frequently, from its own resources, find a pleasurable reason for every word and act; thus, then, Mathew Trueman believed the hesitation in manner, and the heightened colour of Lord Hawksworth, to arise from his great admiration of Grace, and his fear lest he, Mathew Trueman, should place any obstacle in the way of his wishes.

"You must, Mr. Trueman," said Lord Hawksworth, "upon several occasions, have observed that I could not refrain from looking with an eye of admiration upon your most lovely and accomplished daughter."

"Why, my lord," said Trueman, "I must say, that a man accustomed to the world and to study human nature, as I am, could not help observing your lordship's manifest appreciation of what I may, I believe, without partiality, call the beauty of my daughter."

"She is as beautiful as an angel," said Hawksworth, in a voice of real sincerity.

Mathew Trueman bowed as he said,—

"And, if angels be wealthy, my lord, I may add that she shall be a rich angel; for, as I before took occasion to remark, I shall present her with forty thousand pounds on her wedding day."

"A liberal dowry, Mr. Trueman," said Hawksworth, "and one which few of our oldest nobility can give with a daughter."

"I believe it," said the merchant, giving the table a blow with his fist, which made the bottle of sour stuff (we beg its pardon, Bucellas) jump again.

"Then, Mr. Trueman," exclaimed Hawksworth, "as a sequence to all that, do you know it strikes me very forcibly I ought to marry?"

"I am humbly of your lordship's opinion," said Mathew Trueman; "for when you come to the earldom, after what your lordship is pleased facetiously to term the elopement of your father, you can hardly keep up the ancient dignity of your house without a mistress at the head of it."

"Exactly," said Lord Hawksworth; and then he added to himself, "I have no objection to a mistress, but a d—d one to a wife."

"I am rejoiced," said Mathew Trueman, "to find one so young as your lordship impressed with such admirable sentiments."

"And I hope, Mr. Trueman," said Hawksworth, looking woefully at the bottle, "that we thoroughly understand each other."

"Most certainly," cried Trueman, as

his ardent imagination of the moment had filled up all important blanks in his lordship's communication, so as to make it appear as distinct an offer of marriage as could well be made. In fact, so extremely urgent was Mathew Trueman upon the subject, that his judgment was blinded; and, had Lord Hawksworth said much less, it would have amply sufficed for his object.

The cunning and circumspection, extreme caution, and invariable tact, which had really raised Mathew Trueman from the condition of a poor boy, with the three-and-a-penny he so often mentioned, to be one of the most opulent merchants in the city of London, seemed in that one transaction to have entirely deserted him; but then Mathew Trueman had all his life been an extreme Radical in politics, and that would go a long way to account for his most slavish adulation of title and rank.

He looked upon the whole affair as finally settled; and, although a disagreeable twinge came across his memory as he thought of what Grace had said of Hawksworth, and the trouble there might be in getting her even to listen to his most substantial proposals, yet, he told himself, it can only be trouble, for she can never be so absurdly ridiculous as to persevere in the refusal of an offer of such magnitude, and presenting so many advantages.

Alas! the ambitious and scheming merchant's habits of life were far from enabling him to understand the purity and nobleness of such a character as Grace's, as he had ever sacrificed every generous impulse for the accomplishment of what he considered the great objects of existence—money and power; so he could not for one moment believe that all human nature was not like his nature, and one of his favourite maxims was the grossly fallacious one which thought that if you would know mankind you must begin by study of yourself, for such self-studying might inculcate erroneous impressions with regard to the very next person with whom the individual came into contact. Lord Hawksworth saw in a moment that he had accomplished all he wished, and the easiness with which he had completed his task pleased him extremely.

He determined, while Mathew Trueman was in so amiable a state of mind, to attempt at once procuring a promise which should satisfy all his wishes.

"Mr. Trueman," he said, "I have frequently hinted to you the state of rather disagreeable subjection as regards money matters in which I have been kept by my father."

"Your lordship has certainly said so much," replied Mathew Trueman; "and the great bar to the removal of so disagreeable a state of things has been your lordship's minority."

"I know it," said Lord Hawksworth; "and, as I before remarked, I am willing to sign bills, which I will pledge my honour to renew or pay when I come of age, while a friend of mine in the army will endorse them."

"Yes," replied Mathew Trueman, "I understand all that. Money, my lord, is uncommonly scarce; yet, considering the circumstances by which we are now connected, I of course feel the greatest possible disposition to make your lordship such an immediate advance as shall enable you to support, without favour or affection to any one, your exalted station."

"Why that would be rather desirable," looking very hard at the bottle.

"No one can hinder your lordship from coming into the earldom," said Trueman.

"Certainly not."

"And the entailed estates?"

"Precisely."

"Well, then, my lord, I do not see that you need be greatly indebted to your family; you may bid them defiance, and, with the assistance I shall have the honour of rendering you, exhibit a state and splendour which may well astonish them."

"I am exceedingly indebted to you," said Hawksworth, who was rather amused at the idea of defying his family, seeing that they had defied him for the last two years and a half to such an extent as not to allow him one penny piece in furtherance of his extravagances.

"Your lordship once named a sum," said Mathew Trueman, "which would enable you to place yourself in a position in society you wished."

"I did," said Hawksworth; "and what I proposed then, I propose now—

namely, to place bills to the amount of forty thousand pounds in your hands, which, by-the-by, is the exact sum you say you intend to bestow upon your fair and accomplished daughter."

This was rather an adroit speech of Hawksworth's, inasmuch as it implied a great deal more than it uttered, and the merchant at once translated it into—

"As I intend to marry her, it will be all the same, when you give me the fortune."

Now, Mathew Trueman thought himself amazingly cunning and clever in all this transaction. In the first place he was quite willing to give forty thousand pounds to be father to a countess, and father-in-law to an earl; but then he thought, if the necessites of Lord Hawksworth be so great, why may not I, as well as any one else, make a profit of them? and, if he will give me forty thousand pounds' worth of bills, I don't exactly see why I should not discount

them, he being a minor, and the paper consequently rather bad, at a hundred per cent. so that when he does marry Grace, which, of course, will occur, why I can pay him back his own bills as her fortune."

As clear as two and two make four, Mathew Trueman thought he netted twenty thousand pounds by this transaction, "and if he don't marry Grace, why then I can come upon him for the whole amount, that is all, and it looks

equally clear that I am a gainer that way."

When Mathew Trueman got thus far in his calculations, he gave a loud "Ah!" and then, with a sort of chuckle, said—

"As I remarked, my lord, money is exceedingly scarce, and will, in fact, fetch any price; but rather than your lordship should be put to any inconvenience, I will take the bills for forty thousand pounds, and turn them into cash as cheaply as the present state of the market will allow."

"Upon my word, you are very kind," said his lordship.

"Not at all, not at all," said Mathew Trueman; "between us there ought to be every confidence and friendship."

Lord Hawksworth winced a little at the emphasis which the merchant laid upon the word, us; but he merely said—

"I trust there ever will be, Mr. Trueman, and I'm sure you will excuse me now for leaving you so abruptly, as I have business of the very first importance at the other end of the town."

"Oh! certainly," said the merchant rising; "I am quite sure we shall neither of us have to regret this most auspicious interview."

Lord Hawksworth bowed, and the pair descended the stairs, at the bottom of which was the assembled household waiting to do all honour to the departure of his lordship.

Mathew Trueman nodded familiarly to the landlord as he went out, which, to that personage, sufficiently implied, "I will pay you when I come again," so that Lord Hawksworth, as was always more satisfactory to him, took his leave without disbursing any money.

Mathew Trueman then accompanied him, until they came to the nearest coach-stand, when his lordship escaped from the merchant, extremely well satisfied by the prospects that the accidental interview had opened to him.

It was strange, then, after those two men parted, each congratulated himself with the vast success with which he had cheated the other.

"The consummate ass," muttered Hawksworth, "to imagine for one moment that I am going to mingle my patrician blood with the red puddle that flows in his muddy veins. Grace Trueman has beauty enough to make her a nobleman's mistress; but, as for his wife—ha! ha! ha! such a *mes-alliance* would be truly ridiculous. Let him take my bills, and the captain's too, for forty thousand pounds; what care I? If he would advance me but half the sum, or a third of it, upon them, the old fool shall be a loser; for, as Girkins truly enough says, ' there is no reason on earth why a lord should not be a bankrupt as any one else,' and then let Mathew Trueman, and be d—d to him, make the most of his speculation."

As for Mathew Trueman, his reflections were of a more pleasant and elated character than his lordship's, for it seldom happens to a man of such business tact that he accomplishes two darling objects at one and the same time. It seemed like winning two prizes in a lottery — he was about to marry his daughter to an earl presumptive, and at the same time he made twenty thousand pounds by a bill-discounting transaction.

"Oh!" he said, "that is not so badly managed; I never played my cards better in my life. I have Lord Hawksworth to the tune of twenty thousand pounds either way, and, if Grace does not obstinately and blindly stand in her own light, she will acquire the title of one of the oldest peerages in the realm. Pho! she can't object—object to be made a countess!—could there be anything so absurd? object to make me a father-in-law to an earl! Yet, no, that is not exactly the case. Of course, I mean everything for Grace's comfort and satisfaction, without considering myself in the least. Ah! I never was more disinterested in my life—ah!"

Hugging himself, then, with these fanciful conclusions, and applauding himself most mightily for his extreme care of Grace's interest and happiness, when he was in reality thinking of nothing but his own arrogant selfishness, Mathew Trueman returned home to his dingy-looking house and office in Thames Street, in a more delighted and happy state of mind than he had ever before experienced, for he never had made, as he supposed, such a morning's work, and never had he been to his mind so near the completion of his fondest and most high reaching hopes.

CHAPTER LXII.

THE DISTESSING INTERVIEW.—GRACE'S COURAGE.—A FATHER'S CURSE.

THE merchant's first impulse upon his arrival at home was, without looking into the office, to walk directly up stairs in search of his daughter Grace, for such was his impatience to complete the arrangements upon which he had so much set his mind, that he could not resist at once informing her of the specific offer he supposed to have been made for her hand, and of painting to her more glowingly than he ever had done the many pleasures and advantages which would await her in her new career.

Moreover, and notwithstanding all the merchant's firm convictions that Grace had by no means a deficient share of intellect, and that it would be very foolish indeed of her to refuse an alliance with a lord, he had a suspicion she might do so from personal antipathy, and as he had never put the matter so decidedly and firmly to her as he intended now doing, he was anxious to have the scene over as speedily as possible, in order that he might draw his own conclusions therefrom, and be able to say something of a decisive character to Lord Hawksworth when he should see him on the following morning.

Grace was reading when her father came so abruptly into the room, and one glance of his countenance convinced her that he was quite in an extraordinary state of mental elevation, and that something must have happened of an extremely pleasant character to impart to him so joyous an air and manner.

"Father," she said, as her countenance reflected the pleasant reflection of his own, "when you are pleased I am pleased, and that something has delighted you extremely I can well perceive."

"Why, Grace," said Trueman, "I am certainly not displeased with this morning's work, for the most important step has been taken in an affair which is nearest and dearest to my heart. I have but one hope, and that is, in the shape of a great expectation that you and I will not disagree upon a subject which I am sure it will be for the happiness of us both to coincide in."

A pang of alarm shot across the breast of Grace, for she too well guessed now that a renewal of the most odious persecution she could ever imagine was about to take place, and that something had arisen more than ever to fix her father's affections upon the proposed match between her and the peculiar object of her dislike, Lord Hawksworth.

The colour forsook her cheeks, and a slight trembling seized her as she sat down with her eyes rivetted upon her father's face, in mute, but terrible expectation of some announcement which would open a breach between her and her surviving parent while either of them lingered in mortal life.

She could not have spoken for worlds—she could only look the painful inquiry that lingered on her lips.

Mathew Trueman, who while he had spoken had kept his eyes on the beautiful countenance of Grace, became alarmed at her rapidly changing colour, and not attributing it to its right cause, he hastily took her hand, crying—

"Grace! Grace! my dear Grace, what is the matter? Your looks are quite alarming—what sudden indisposition has seized you? Here, Mrs. Woodfall, where are you? Where the devil are you, I say? Curse these servants, they are never in the way when they are wanted!"

He was then about to rush to the bell, in order to ring a furious peal, when Grace gathered sufficient strength to say—

"No, father—no—call no one. I am better now. It was but a slight passing indisposition. You see I am much better now."

The merchant looked in her face, and seeing some signs of returning colour, he removed his hand from the bell, as he said—

"You are sure you are better, Grace? because; if you are not, I had much better summon Mrs. Woodfall to your assistance."

"No, no, no," said Grace.

"What I have to say," continued Mr. Trueman, "I can say another time. Good news will keep a little, you know, Grace, as well as bad."

The merchant was standing very close to his daughter, so that she could lay her hand upon his arm, as, looking up in his face with an expression of painful expectation, she said in a low, soft voice—

"No, father, delay nothing—say to me now what you have to say, and, let it be what it may, the knowledge of it will be preferable to the state of suspense in which I should remain."

"Well, then, Grace," said Mathew

Trueman, shifting his eyes as much as possible from the face of his beautiful child, " I—I—I met your noble admirer this morning."

" My noble admirer ?" said Grace.

" Yes, you know who I mean. I have as yet given encouragement to but one nobleman to lay his coronet at my daughter's feet."

" Go on, father," said Grace, in a tone of calmness, which he mistook for a partial acquiescence in his views. " I pray you go on."

" Well, then," said Trueman, " I mean, of course, Lord Hawksworth."

" So I thought, so I thought," said Grace.

" Oh !" thought Mathew Trueman, " she don't seem much distressed about it. I dare say she thinks her former folly very much out of place." This he said in an inaudible voice, as, in order to cover the slight confusion he was under, he paced to and fro in the room.

" Well, then, Grace, all I have to say is, that Lord Hawksworth has, in the most handsome and civil manner in the world, proposed to me for your hand."

" My hand !" said Grace.

" Yes ; he is willing to make you his countess, for an earl he will be, as he himself wittily remarks, when the governor elopes."

" Is he indeed willing ?" said Grace.

" Oh, yes—quite, quite !" said the merchant, who thought he was getting on famously ; " he made the offer in that handsome and aff-hand manner peculiar to all the actions of the real aristocracy of this country. It was done in the most gentlemanly manner in the world. I assure you, he is perfectly willing."

" Indeed," said Grace.

There was but little to be gathered from the mere word indeed ; but there was a something in the tone with which it was uttered, that made the merchant suddenly stop in his uneasy perambulations to and fro in the apartment, and fix his eyes upon Grace's face rather curiously, as he said,—

" Well, Grace, have you nothing more to say besides ' indeed,' to such a proposal ?"

" Yes," said Grace, " I have something much more important to say."

" And what might that be ?" said the merchant, feeling a disagreeable qualm suddenly come over him, as he thought that Grace's next words might be some decided refusal of the brillian offer which so much delighted his own imagination.

How great, then, was his relief to hear Grace say calmly,—

" I only wish he had made the offer to me, father, instead of to you."

" Oh ! certainly," said the merchant ; " but, of course, you know, it was natural for him to wish to have my entire concurrence beforehand, and you know, Grace, you are not usually a stickler for forms and ceremonies ?"

" No," said Grace, " I am not ; but in this instance I should have preferred the offer to have been made to myself, because ——"

" Because what ?" said Mathew Trueman, hastily.

" Because," said Grace, calmly, while the colour heightened in her cheeks, " I could have rejected it with all the scorn and contempt which I feel for the wretched creature who has made it."

Mathew Trueman glared at Grace as if she had been a basilisk, and then retreated backwards until a chair stopped his progress, into which he fell with a heavy plump.

There was a dead silence for several minutes' duration, for Grace felt she had got to a respectable climax, and had no wish to detract from the force of what she had said by any useless words, while Mathew Trueman himself was too much stunned and bewildered to speak during that period.

When he did, it was with a gasping effort that he said,—

" You reject him ?"

" I do," said Grace.

" With—with scorn and contempt ?"

" With both those feelings carried to the highest extent," said Grace.

" And you—you—d—n it, do you call a lord a wretched creature ?"

" I consider this lord a very wretched creature, indeed," said Grace.

The merchant jumped from his seat with something between a howl and a scream, and stood glaring at Grace for some moments as if he could eat her up.

As for Grace herself, she turned very, very pale again, for such a scene of alteration with her father was very dreadful to her; but though she was full of gushing tenderness, and fraught with the holiest, gentlest, and kindest of human feelings, yet she had so wrought herself up to the determination of acting as she had done should the present scene ever occur, that she went through it like a species of martyrdom, with abundance of acute suffering, but without a murmur.

Nay, she compelled herself to face her father's stern and almost demoniac gaze, but she spoke not, and Mathew Trueman himself was compelled to break the extremely awkward silence that ensued.

"Girl—girl, how dare you speak thus," he said, "of one whom I have chosen for your husband—who is willing to raise you to a station so far above any you have ever dreamed of being within your utmost reach? What foolish, headstrong obstinacy is this which thus makes you wilfully stand in the way of a destiny as brilliant as—as—as—d—n it, as unexpected."

"I have spoken, father, the feelings of my heart," said Grace; "to you and to Heaven I am never a hypocrite."

"But he will be an earl!" shrieked Mathew Trueman, "he will be an earl!"

"Were he an emperor," said Grace, "thanks to your care of me, and those by whom I have been surrounded, he is the vilest specimen of human nature I ever knew, and should never be my husband."

"Never?" cried Mathew Trueman.

"Never!" said Grace, solemnly.

For some moments the merchant seemed struggling to find some word sufficiently powerful for the depiction of his passion, and then he burst out with,—

"So, I am to have the curse of an undutiful child in my old age. My gray hairs are to be brought in sorrow to the grave, because you stand in the way of the most darling wish of my heart. Gh, Grace—Grace, is this worthy of you?—is this well of you?"

"Father," said Grace in a voice broken with emotion, "the fact that such an appeal from you to me is necessary should prove to you that it is useless, for how strongly must my mind be wrought upon to refuse a wish of yours,

ere it became necessary for you to use such words in urging your desire. Father, father, if the sacrifice of my life were essential to your own existence or legitimate happiness, it should freely be rendered; but although there are ties between the child and its parent that should be great and lasting, yet are we all God's creatures alike, and we must act according with the attributes with which he has invested us. I cannot love that man, and I will not tell such an untruth to heaven as to say I do."

"Trash!" shrieked Mathew Trueman; "garbled nonsense, extracted from the last new novel."

Grace made no reply to this intemperate speech, nor did she when Mathew Trueman, as he paced foaming and fretting too and fro in the room, suddenly seized two books and flung them against the piano-forte, make any remark. Then, turning to Grace, he said, in a tone of subdued passion—

"Now, hear me once for all, Grace. Through a long life of laborious industry, I have set my heart upon making a large fortune for your sake, and uniting you with a nobleman. It is all that I now live for. Cross me in that, and you alienate yourself for ever from my heart. You shall find yourself a beggar with only my curse for your portion."

Grace covered her face with her hands and burst into tears.

"You are moved," cried Mathew Trueman, "and you consent to my wishes?"

"No!" cried Grace, dashing aside her tears; "human nature is weak, but it has not yielded yet. If I were sure to die, father, before mid-day to-morrow, I might promise to wed Lord Hawksworth at sun-set, in order to give you pleasure, and leave this life accompanied by your tears instead of your reproaches. I would then ask pardon of God for the untruth I had spoken, and abide the penalty of my transgression. But I am now young and full of life; you may cast me from you, father—you may leave me to want and its concomitant miseries, and I must find some charitable hand to relieve them. You may curse me, but against that curse I will appeal to a higher power. Once for all, father, I will not be Lord Hawksworth's wife."

"Not for an earldom, and forty thousand pounds for a dowry?"

"No," said Grace.

"D———n! forty thousand devils!'" said the merchant, as he rushed from the room.

CHAPTER LXIII.

THE RAGE OF TRUEMAN.—THE LOSS OF THE CUP.

MATHEW TRUEMAN retired in very great dudgeon to his own private office, where, locking himself in, he gave himself up to such a paroxysm of rage, that, could he have but found any one upon whom to wreak his vengeance, it would have been an absolute luxury.

Gradually then he calmed down, and began seriously to ask himself whether Grace's determination was really of a character not to be moved, or one of those female caprices, to the existence of which such men as Mathew Trueman always give implicit faith, and which might by perseverance be entirely overcome.

The latter supposition was by far the most consonant to his feelings, and the most agreeable to dwell upon: thus, on this emergency, as on many other minor occasions, Mathew Trueman consoled himself with several proverbs, which he imagined to contain the ultimatum of human wisdom, such as, "A continued water-drop, drills a hole through adamant," "A woman's no is yes in disguise," &c., until he began to believe, because he was reluctant to do otherwise, that, after all, Grace might be won upon to accede to the proposition, which pomised as much honour and glory to him, Mathew Trueman, as herself; besides, he had never forgotten the artful insinuation of Mr. Girkins, that Lord Hawksworth would, as soon as possible after his marriage with Grace, procure of the minister of the day a baronetcy for him, Mathew Trueman, as it would be far more agreeable to his lordship to introduce his wife's father as Sir Mathew Trueman, baronet, to his brilliant *soirees* and parties, than as plain Mr. Trueman, the city merchant.

The infatuated man caught at this poor bait, and as he sat uneasily in his office chair, he repeated to himself—

"Sir Mathew Trueman, baronet—ah! Sir Mathew Trueman—there will be an end to a beginning with three-and-a-penny! and I am to be swindled—for it amounts to nothing else—out of such a termination to my career, because a silly girl won't accept of an unexceptionable offer, on the absurdly romantic plea that she is not in love with the man who makes it? Bah! I hate such nonsense. I never was romantic in all my life, and I never shall be, nor did I ever hear of anybody making much money by it. The only romantic thing that ever strikes me is when somebody brings me a bill to cash, when I happen to know that the drawer and accepter are both *bad* men. I won't give it up yet, not I; pretty thing, indeed."

Mathew Trueman was silent for a few moments, after which he clenched his fist, and shaking it in the air, said—

"I wonder if that cursed clerk of mine, Rivers, has got a hold of the girl's fancy. She sticks up for him hard and fast, and but for her the penniless vagabond would have been discharged ere this. Girkins, too, has hinted such a thing, and so has Hilliard, and so, in fact, has his lordship, and that's enough to make a man think it is so. I am sure —and if I was but d——d sure, I'd turn him out of the house this very minute."

While he was speaking, the merchant was mechanically emptying his pockets of divers notes and documents; among which was one which attracted his attention, and he exclaimed—

"Bless me, I forgot to call at Swiggington's and Gobble's, in Fenchurch Street, about that damaged spermaceti. I mustn't loose a minute."

So saying, Mathew Trueman again hurried out of his house, without any of his clerks or domestics being aware of his having returned.

Five minutes after that time, Hilliard cautiously crept from the merchant's bed-room, with the silver cup in his possession, as we have before recorded.

Grace, when her father had left her, remained for some minutes gazing intently at the door through which he had made his furious exit.

Although this was not the first time she and her father had disagreed upon the same subject, yet it was the first time so many decisive words had been said on both sides, and it was the first time that she felt that utter abandonment of heart which now crept so sadly over her.

"Heaven help me—heaven help me!" she cried: "who could have imagined such a source of grief as this dimming the happiness of my early life? This wild ambition of my father has produced, indeed, bitter fruits, and what will be the end? Alas! I dare not ask myself."

She rested her head upon her arms, while convulsive throbs shook her breast; she gave herself up to the most sad contemplation of what would be her fate and that of Rivers, to whom she had pledged her heart's best affections, and whose only crime in her father's eye was that he lacked the accidental circumstance of noble birth and aristocratic lineage.

That she should now be fearfully, hourly persecuted she entertained no doubt; but how to escape such a state of things—how to extricate herself from the endless mortifications and miseries that seemed impending over her, was a theorem she could not solve.

Where, too, was she to seek a friend upon whose advice she could implicitly rely upon such an emergency? Her early school-fellow and dear companion, Amelia, of whose acute intellect Mathew Trueman had ever been in dread, was far—far away.

"Ought I," she said, "to appeal to Rivers himself? or would it be right to compromise my kind nurse, Mrs. Woodfall, in a way that might do her the greatest injury?"

"Certainly, my dear," said Mrs. Woodfall, who had entered the room unperceived, and heard Grace's murmured words; "who are you to compromise, my darling, if not those who love you so tenderly? I have heard all that your father has said to you, for I was in the next room, and could not shut my ears, and I thought if I came out after having heard some of it, Mr. Trueman would be in a worse rage than ever."

"Then you know, nurse," said Grace, "how truly wretched I am."

"I know no such thing," said Mrs. Woodfall; "you have done quite right, Grace, and no wretchedness can last for long for doing that."

"But what can I do?" murmured Grace; "my father seems infatuated with this offer of marriage from that detestable man, and I think we shall never be to each other what we have been."

"Don't think so, my dear," said Mrs. Woodfall; "I cannot, nor never will believe, till I see it, that any father can sacrifice his child to a feeling of resentment, because she will not marry a man she cannot like."

"But what can I do, nurse? These daily persecutions will kill me."

"We must all hold a consultation," said Mrs. Woodfall, "and decide upon what is best to be done."

"All?" said Grace.

"Yes, all, my dear."

"Whom do you mean, nurse?"

"Why, I mean yourself, and myself, and Mr. Rivers, and that honest, good-hearted, troublesome creature, Tom, who, I am sure, would go through fire and water to serve either you or Mr. Rivers."

Grace's dejected countenance cleared up a little at this advice, offered, too, as it was in so kind and friendly a manner.

"How can I sufficiently thank you," she said, "for all your great kindness to me? I have found, indeed, a mother in you, although deprived of my real parent's gentle care."

"Let me see one of your dear sweet smiles again, and I shall be amply repaid," said Mrs. Woodfall.

Grace tried to smile, but the attempt was a sad failure, and she said,—

"Indeed, I cannot, just now, for my heart is too full; but how, dear nurse, am I to communicate with Mr. Rivers?"

Mrs. Woodfall considered for a few moments, and then said,—

"What I shall advise, Grace, is that you write a note, appointing to meet Mr. Rivers to-night, in the usual place in the Temple Gardens, and as this is the dinner hour, and nobody about, I can slip down stairs and place it in his desk without being observed."

"Nay," said Grace, "I will do that; my father is already sufficiently angry with me, and if there be any risk to run let me encounter it."

In vain did Mrs. Woodfall seek to

conquer this resolution, by representing, that even were she seen she should scarcely be questioned by the merchant himself, as she might have a hundred different reasons for going into the office. Grace would not be persuaded, and writing a short note, in which she merely stated, that by seven o'clock that evening she and Mrs. Woodfall would be in the Temple Gardens, where she would expect him, accompanied by Tom Hackey, she prepared with trembling steps and a palpitating heart to descend to the office.

Had Grace been aware of the fact that her father was absent from home, she would have walked courageously enough on her mission; but the dread of meeting him was strong upon her mind, and she trembled so excessively at every step that it took her treble the time it would otherwise to descend the staircase.

Passing then the door of her father's private office was a fearful ordeal to poor Grace, believing firmly as she did that he was within; for what could she say to account for her appearance there, were he suddenly to come forth?

With stealthy steps she crept past the much dreaded apartment, and by the time she reached the office door she was in the greatest state of agitation and alarm.

It was some moments before she could turn the handle, but when she had done so, and fairly entered the apartment, a feeling of pleasurable relief came over her, and she sat down for some moments in the visitors' chair to calm the agitation of her nerves as she proceeded to the execution of her self-imposed task.

Which was the desk of Rivers she knew well, as, upon the memorable occasion when she had so signally discomfited Mr. Girkins, she had taken particular notice of it.

It was some pleasure for Grace, in her present state of mind, to look at the desk at which he sat for so many hours, and as all remained profoundly still and quiet, a calmer and more hopeful feeling began to arise in her breast, and she said to herself, in softly murmured tones,—

"Surely we shall not be deserted by Heaven; my father's heart may yet be inclined towards Rivers, and then how happy—how very happy, should we be. Oh, hope, without thee, how faintly and wearily would human nature sink beneath its heavy afflictions!"

Grace then rose, and slowly approached Rivers's desk—some loose memoranda and blotting paper were lying upon it.

Upon the latter she saw her own name in two or three places, and it was in a voice more of gratification than reproach. that she said, as she tore away the half-sheet on which was her name,—

"Imprudent Rivers! what confusion and anxiety to us all might not even such a trivial act as this cause; and yet can I blame you? Is not your name ever uppermost in my thoughts, and have I not often—often pleased myself that mine is so in yours?"

Grace was now aroused from her state of pleasurable contemplation, by hearing the neighbouring church clock chime the three quarters past one.

She started at the sound, and, hastily drawing her small note from her bosom, she raised the lid of Rivers's desk in order to place it therein.

She first laid it in the centre of the desk; but then she became fearful he might overlook it among the numerous papers that lay there, and seeing some crossed tapes on the inner side of the lid for holding small memoranda, she thought that would be by far the most likely place to meet his eye.

Immediately acting on this resolution, she took her note up again from where she placed it, but in so doing displaced a large letter, when something glittering from beneath attracted her attention.

An involuntary feeling of curiosity prompted her to search farther.

A half scream burst from her lips, and she was compelled to cling to the desk for support, for she at once recognised her father's much-prized silver cup.

CHAPTER LXIV.

THE SAVING OF RIVERS.—GRACE'S SUSPICIONS.—THE CONSTABLE.

FOR some moments, certainly, intense surprise overpowered every other feeling, and Grace stood by the desk gazing at the cup, and unable to form a connected idea with regard to how it could possibly come there. An ordinary mind, under such circumstances, would have been oppressed with suspicious and conjectures of the most excruciatingly painful character as regarded Rivers himself; but never, for one instant, did the slightest dawning of suspicion, as regarded his honour and integrity, cross her mind. Intense wonder was the sole feeling that oppressed her, and her imagination preferred wandering in the maze of endless conjecture, to injuring her lover by one injurious thought.

Pure and honourable as she was herself, she suspected no guilt in others, and far less him on whom she had bestowed her best affections.

Thrice she raised the cup in her hand in order to be sure of its identity, and then when, upon reading its inscription, she could no longer entertain a shadow

of a doubt but that it was her father's, the exclamation that rose to her lips was—

"Gracious heavens! by what strange accident has this cup, which my father cherishes so much, found its way here?"

The more, then, she though upon the subject, the more perplexed she became, and when she heard the clock strike two, it was more an involuntary act than a premeditated one for her to take the cup in her hand, and hurry with it from the office to her chamber.

Her first act, then, was to lock the door, so that the train of her reflections might be quite uninterrupted, and although she could come to no proper conclusion as to how the silver cup came to be in Rivers's desk, yet she could not be long in feeling what a frightful position it would place him in to have it found there.

From this, then, her acute intellect naturally turned to the question of who placed it there, and she shuddered as the thought rushed like lightning through her brain, that some frightful plot must be in progress for the destruction of him who was so dear to her.

"Oh, heavens!" she cried, "it must be so; failing in his removal from the office by other means, his enemies have sought thus fearfully to accomplish his destruction."

Among all suppositions concerning an extraordinary incident, that which comes nearest to the truth is, in the majority of cases, most rational, and hence, when once the idea struck Grace that her father's silver cup had been purloined by some one, and then placed in her lover's desk for the frightful purpose of substantiating a criminal charge against him, she began to see with what extreme ease and likelihood of success such a diabolical plot might be carried into execution; each moment of reflection more and more strengthened her in the supposition, until at length, had she been so informed by one of the conspirators themselves, she could not have felt more thoroughly convinced of the fact.

She clasped her hands and thanked heaven aloud for permitting her to be the happy means of thwarting so fearfully a concocted scheme. Tears of gratified feeling gushed from her eyes, and as she looked upon that silver cup which might have been the source of such exquisite woe, she exclaimed—

"Oh, Rivers! Rivers! what terrible anxieties and dangers seem to beset the course of our attachment! Shall we ever live to know the dear happiness of reciprocal affection without the fearful alloy of such heartrending scenes as I have passed through, and the more dreadful machinations of those evil-minded men who happen to have leagued themselves together for our destruction."

An attempt on the part of some one to open the door, now aroused Grace to a sense of her situation, and the necessity there was for taking some immediate step in regard to the strange business of which she had become cognisant, she resolved to admit no one but her nurse into the room, for she felt confident that her state of excitement would be evident to any one, and dreaded its forming the subject of comment to the ordinary servants.

The voice of Mrs. Woodfall, however, speedily put an end to her fears, and Grace, unlocking the door, immediately admitted her kind friend and confidant.

"Did you take the letter my dear?" said Mrs. Woodfall. "I have been all anxiety about you, and wondered what could have become of you."

"I did," said Grace, "but in the taking it, I have had a fearful adventure,"

She then related the particulars of the finding of the cup, and ended by saying—

"This has been same plot for the destruction of Rivers, and Heaven has permitted me to frustrate it in this most singular and unexpected manner."

For a few moments Mrs. Woodfall looked all astonishment, then lifting up her hands, she said—

"My dear Grace, you are right, for Mr. Rivers is both honest and clever, and none but a knave would have stolen the cup, or a fool left it in an open desk."

"That is precisely my view, nurse," said Grace; "but what shall be done now to discover the wicked perpetrators of this outrage, so that Rivers may be upon his guard against them for the future?"

"My advice is this," said Mrs. Woodfall, "that you keep the cup yourself, Grace, until you hear some inquiry made about it. Of course, it is expected that your father should miss it, and then that it should be found in Mr. Rivers's desk, when the train of consequences which were to ensue, are too frightful to imagine."

"I will retain it," said Grace, "and should there be an alarm in the house that it is stolen, both ourselves and Rivers may have time to note who appears most active in the transaction."

"I have my own suspicions, Grace," said Mrs. Woodfall, "and unless I am very much mistaken, yours are of the same complexion."

"Mark Hilliard," said Grace, immediately. "If there be any one in this house capable of such a deed, it must surely be Mark Hilliard, for, years ago, I heard my father give him the worst of characters, at the same time adding that he was useful to him in a particular branch of his business, or he would not allow him to darken his door-step."

"It is the same name that was trembling upon my own lips," said the nurse; "but, thank heaven, Mr. Rivers will be saved."

"I will take immediate measures," said Grace, rising, "to bring the affair to a conclusion; but yesterday, my father was looking at this cup, and then he placed it in a drawer of his cabinet, which is in his bedroom; from there it must have been abstracted, which could be easily done by any one acquainted with the premises, and the most likely time not to be interrupted. My father shall miss his cup the moment he enters the bed-room."

So saying, Grace at once proceeded to her father's chamber, and opening the drawer of the cabinet as wide as it could come, she left it in that state; so that Mathew Trueman could not fail taking notice of it the moment he should enter the room.

These arrangements were scarcely completed, when the merchant did return, and proceeding at once to his chamber to affect some changes in his apparel, he discovered the, to him, frightful fact of the loss of his silver cup.

It was then that he rushed down stairs in the frightful manner we have recorded, and those proceedings, which in their termination had so stricken Hilliard with dismay, ensued.

We shall now return to the office, taking up our narrative at the moment when the desk of Rivers was opened.

To Mathew Trueman there was no surprise, to Rivers there was none, but to Mark Hilliard there was the most intense and stunning piece of astonishment that he had ever experienced, so confident was he that the cup must be there, that he would not believe the evidence of his own senses, but darting his hands into the desk, he quite astonished Mathew Trueman by the eagerness with which he rummaged its contents, and the look of disappointment and surprise which came over him when he found that the cup was really not there. He cast one glance of fearful fiendish hatred at Rivers, and then with a terrible oath he retreated to his own desk, under the lid of which he placed his head, as was his custom, striving amid the wild excitement and anger of his soul to think in what manner the cup had been removed, for that it had been found by Rivers he did not suppose for an instant, as he had a perception that Rivers would not have acted the hypocritical part which would have been his during the inquiry, had he really been in possession of any information concerning the missing cup.

"By who on earth, then can it have been removed," he thought, "and removed secretly too, for the merchant cannot find it, and no one seems to know anything about it?"

As for Rivers himself, he looked on the examination of his desk with great coolness for some minutes, but when his eye alighted upon the little note addressed to him in that handwriting which, once having seen, he could never forget, his manner as instantaneously changed from the cold disdain with which he had submitted to the mortification of having his desk examined, into an anxiety, a restlessness and agitation, which could not fail of being instantly remarked by the merchant.

Poor Rivers was fearfully apprehensive that Mathew Trueman's eye, as well as his, might light upon the well-known handwriting of Grace, in which case, although he—Rivers—was determined the merchant should not have the letter, yet his observation of it would have brought affairs to a disagreeable climax, and unquestionably cause Grace much disquiet. By good fortune, however, Mathew Trueman did not see the note, and thoroughly satisfied that his cup was not in Rivers's desk, he allowed him to close the lid, as he said to him—

"Mr. Rivers, you seem dreadfully agitated at something. Just now you were all calmness and self-possession; but I must say, Mr. Rivers, that a very remarkable, and what some people might consider a very suspicious change has taken place in your general demeanour."

Rivers drew a long breath of relief, as he took his key from his pocket, and locking his desk, at the same time he said—

"Perhaps, Mr. Trueman, you were right in examining my desk, in common with others ; you must now, however, perceive that such an examination was an useless violation of my feelings ; nevertheless, sir, if you are satisfied I am."

"Upon my word, Mr. Rivers," said the merchant, " you are a most remarkable young man : first of all, you are insulted, and, I must say, looked rather sulky ; then again you seemed like to drop with terror and anxiety at something ; when now you look as pleased as if you had discounted a bill at a hundred and forty per cent—ah !"

As Rivers did not know very well what reply to make to all this, he made none, but contented himself by bowing an acquiescence to the merchant's statement.

Hilliard had heard the merchant's last words, and they at once awakened in his mind a supposition that Rivers might, after all, have found the cup in his desk, before his, Hilliard's arrival, and fearful of the consequences which might ensue of its being found in his possession, had hidden it in the office. He at once let the lid of his desk down, and turning to Mathew Trueman, he said—

"I beg, sir, for the sake of all our characters, you will search here, thoroughly ; I know my own innocence, and, therefore, I have no embarrrssments and rapid changes of countenance."

Rivers quite understood this attack upon him, but he disdained to reply to it, nor did Hilliard, though he looked hard at him, perceive that it affected him.

"I don't see anywhere else to search," cried the merchant, as he looked furtively into the coal-scuttle, "but if it's in the house, it shall be found somehow or another. Here, you Mr. Constable, you keep guard at the door, and don't let any one leave the house, while I continue my examination into this robbery."

Mr. Trueman then ran up stairs, when the first person he encountered was Grace, to whom he said, bitterly,

"Misfortunes never come singly ; I am not only cursed with a disobedient daughter, but there is a thief in the house besides."

"A thief, father ?" said Grace.

"A thief ?" echoed Mrs. Woodfall, coming to the door of the apartment.

"Yes," added the merchant, " my silver cup is stolen—my silver cup that was given me by the Society for the Enlightenment of Everybody and the Propagation of Everything."

"Have you searched everywhere ?" said Grace.

"Yes, I have," continued the merchant, furiously. "I don't suppose I should have done such a thing of myself, but Hilliard so warmly pressed an examination of the counting-house, including his and Mr. Rivers's desks, that I did it, but d——e I could not find my cup."

"That is enough," said Grace, mildly, as she walked up the stairs leading to the bed-chambers.

"Quite," said Mrs. Woodfall, as she too followed Grace.

"Oh, indeed," said the merchant. "That is very consolatory. Upon my soul, you—both of you take it uncommonly easy. That's enough, indeed ! But it sha'n't be enough. I'll not leave a hole or corner in the house unrummaged ; I'll take up somebody, or my name's not Mathew Trueman."

The merchant was as good as his word, and did institute a most rigorous search throughout the whole establishment for his lost cup ; a search which aggravated and annoyed everybody, himself included, without producing any satisfactory result.

The whole of the afternoon was spent in fretting and fuming about his loss ; until, at length, weary, exhausted, and dirty, from poking about in kitchens, coal-cellars, and dust-holes, and quarrelling with almost every one of the servants, he repaired to his own bed-chamber, to restore his outward man to its usual degree of propriety.

Grace and Mrs. Woodfall had been there before him, and what was his astonishment, on a re-examination of the bureau, to find his silver cup quietly reposing at the back of the drawer, from which he had fancied he had missed it.

CHAPTER LXV.

THE CUP RESTORED.—THE NOTE TO RIVERS.

IF Hilliard was before extremely puzzled to account for how the merchant's silver cup got out of the desk of Rivers, he was still more puzzled to understand by what means and by whose agency it had got back to the drawer of the merchant's bureau, for when Mathew Trueman found it there he certainly felt a little conscience-stricken, and after a few moments' thought, he considered the least he could do would be to communicate the pleasing fact that the lost cup was found, to those who had been put to inconvenience by the rigorous search he had made for it.

As regarded the domestics of the household, he merely told the first one that he met that the cup was found, and he cared not whether they were pleased or angry at the course he had taken with regard to it, but he certainly did shrink from walking into his office and confronting Rivers with the information that the cup, about which he had made such a fuss, was, after all, snugly ensconced at the back of the drawer in his bureau.

The only escape which presented itself to the merchant from this disagreeable dilemma was to proceed to his own private office, and then ring the hand-bell, which would summon Tom Hackey to know his wants or his wishes.

"Ah!" thought Mathew Trueman, "that will be the best plan. I don't at all like those cold disagreeable looks that Master Rivers bends on one's face when he's not pleased; I shall certainly discharge him the first opportunity, but, as certainly, I feel that this is not one. How very odd, after all, that my cup should be in the identical drawer in which I had myself placed it, and from which I thought I had missed it; seeing is believing, and as I have seen it there with my own eyes, why, I must believe it is there; although, if such a thing were at all probable, I could almost believe that it had been taken out and put back again; this has been a day of sweets and sours, with a vengeance. I did not think it would have been a red letter day in my calendar commencing as it did with the most auspicious and agreeable meeting with Lord Hawksworth, by which I shall certainly net twenty thousand pounds or more. Then, however, came that disagreeable interview with Grace; and, after that, this most uncomfortable riot about my silver cup; so that, really, I must say that I have been kept in hot water the whole of the day. Well, I suppose I can't expect everything to go smoothly, life will have its troubles to a rich merchant. Ah!"

As Mathew Trueman concluded these remarks, which he considered to be of an extremely philosophical nature, he rung the bell which was upon his table, and in a few moments Tom Hackey put his head in at the door with an inquiring look.

The sight of him recalled to the merchant's mind how deeply he had been aggravated by Tom Hackey's theatrical reminiscences during the recent scene in the office, and as the merchant was not on very good terms with himself, he was very glad of a favourable opportunity of becoming angry with any one else.

"Well, sir," he said, in a tone which was intended to express the utmost displeasure.

"I am very well, thank you," said Tom. "I thought you rung."

"So I did, you scoundrel," said the merchant; "and now, once for all, let me warn you, if I have any more of your theatrical nonsense, I will discharge you without a character."

"Had I three ears I'd hear thee," said Tom.

It was well for Tom Hackey that the merchant's dramatic readings were not very extensive, and in reply to this remark, he merely said,—

"Very well; but mind you are more careful for the future. You may now go and tell Mr. Rivers and Mr. Hilliard that I have found the silver cup."

"What!" said Tom, "after kicking up such a riot? Oh, day and night, but this is wondrous strange! 'Tis pity, tis true."

Mathew Trueman rose in a great rage, but as Tom immediately closed the door, and rushed into the clerks' office, whither the merchant had just then no inclination to follow him, he escaped the personal conflict, and probably the notice to quit, which might have ensued from his rashness.

"Confound that fellow," muttered the merchant; " I believe he is a fool, and I know he is honest, but he is certainly the most provoking wretch that ever lived; and Grace, too, takes his part, and when I abuse him, praises him for singleness of purpose and great probity. I do believe that among her favourites she has the greatest set of objects that can be well imagined."

While the merchant was making these reflections, Tom Hackey hastened into the office, immediately upon his entrance into which he exclaimed,—

"Mathew has found his cup—Mathew has found his cup. All the kick-up has been for nothing; he has just been apologizing to me and said he has found his cup."

D———! where?" said Hilliard.

"Why, d——— is usually down below," said Tom; " where, I have no doubt, you will become duly acquainted with it."

"How dare you speak to me in that style?" said Hilliard, savagely.

"What man dare that dare I!" said Tom, swinging the poker. " Friends, Romans, and countrymen—Mathew has found his cup, I presume, in a hollow tooth or his waistcoat-pocket; but he told me to tell you he had found it, so my mission's ended."

Hilliard immediately put on his hat and rushed from the office.

"There he goes," said Tom, "a good twenty minutes before his time; now, if you or I were to do that, Rivers, we should have old Mathew grumbling at us to-morrow morning, as if something very dreadful had happened. It's my opinion that Master Hilliard knows a secret or two, and could do old Mathew some harm if he chose, nothing to extenuate or set down aught in malice."

"That may or may not be, Tom; at all events, it's no business of ours. I am glad, very glad, that he has found his cup, for it would have been a never ending source of grumbling and vexation to the whole establishment; and now, Tom, be so good as to read that note and tell me what you think of it."

As Rivers spoke, he handed him the small note which Grace had left for him within the lid of his desk.

Tom Hackey took it with a comical expression of countenance, but when he saw, as he instantly did, that it was written in a small, delicate Italian hand, a flush of pleasure and surprise came across his countenance, and the hand in which he held the note trembled in spite of himself.

"It is—it is," he said, " from her?"

"It is," said Rivers. " Read it, Tom; you will see that some part of it concerns you."

Tom Hackey unfolded the note with an air of the most perfect reverence; and when he saw that his own name was really written by Grace, tears of pride and pleasure rushed to his eyes, and he said—

"She has, indeed—she has, indeed, written my name. Ah! Mr. Rivers, will you let me keep this note? It will be very—very precious to me. You can surely spare me this one? You don't know how I have hoarded and doated on a mere scrap of her writing, or some faded flower she had thrown from her bosom. You know I am not jealous of you, Rivers—heaven bless you and Grace, and make you both happy !—But do let me keep this one scrap of her writing that has my own name on it."

"Keep it, Tom," said Rivers, in a tone of emotion; " heaven forbid that I should deny you so small a satisfaction."

"Small!" said Tom; " if I were to become as rich as Mathew Trueman, I should prize this small scrap of paper above all my wealth. How good and kind of her to think of me. She must have known how delighted I would be to go with you and see her. I can sit in some corner, you know, and watch you while you both walk about the Temple Gardens. God bless her! Oh, Mr. Rivers, is there anybody like our Grace?"

"There is not," said Rivers; " but, hark, Tom, six o'clock is striking, and if we wait patiently at the corner of the street, we shall be able to escort Grace through the city to the Temple."

"So we shall—so we shall," cried Tom, eagerly, " and that would be another treat; you shall walk with her, and I'll walk behind, and if anybody dares to look at her, I'll hang his body on the beetling rocks, and give him to the vultures."

"Come along," said Rivers, "come along, and for Heaven's sake, Tom, don't indulge in any of your theatrical rapsodies on the road."

"I won't," said Tom, then casting his eyes round the office, he threw himself into an attitude, exclaiming—"Farewell, ye desks, ye ledgers, and ye day-books. The capacious letter-box, and the old iron coal-scuttle, a long farewell."

Rivers cut short the rhapsody by seizing Tom by the arm, and hurrying him into the street, at the corner of which they took up their stations, and where Tom, to the great annoyance of Rivers, would assume the air and manner of a bandit in a melodrama, and so alarmed several chance passengers by suddenly darting from behind a pump, as if armed with a dagger, and then darting back again, that Rivers was again compelled to expostulate with him, assuring him that Grace would be far from pleased with such vagaries.

This had something of the desired effect, and Tom kept himself tolerably steady for some quarter of an hour longer, when Grace, accompanied by Mrs. Woodfall, made her appearance, to the delighted eyes of her lover.

Rivers was at her side in an instant.

"Dear Grace," he cried, "you know not how you have delighted me by your little missive."

There was a tear trembling on her eyelid as she replied to him—

"Alas! alas! the inducement for its writing was far from joyful; but let us hasten from this neighbourhood, where we are known, and then I will inform you that we have arrived at a crisis in our destiny which may well make us tremble."

Rivers drew her arm within his, as he whispered—

"While we are true to each other, Grace, we may defy destiny."

Tom Hackey then offered his arm very gallantly to Mrs. Woodfall, and thus they walked through the city to the Temple Gardens, which were full of life and animation, presenting a deep con-trast to the anxieties which oppressed those young trusting hearts.

CHAPTER LXVI.

THE WALK THROUGH THE CITY.—THE TEMPLE GARDENS.—AN UNEXPECTED INTERRUPTION.

GRACE's repeated answers to Rivers's supplications on the road to the Temple Gardens to tell him what was the cause of her uneasiness, was the repeated words of—

"Not here, not here; wait until we are at our old seat in the gardens, and then I will tell you all."

It was, therefore, with feelings of the greatest impatience and disquietude that Rivers arrived at the appointed spot of meeting, when, conducting Grace to the seat on which they had before sat on those dear delightful occasions when their young love was budding into the glorious hope of a happy future, he said,—

"Now, dear Grace, take pity on my deep mental disquietude. What is it that blanches your cheek, and brings a tear to your eye?"

"It is the old story, Rivers," said Grace, "but in a new and more dangerous form. Lord Hawksworth——"

An angry rush of colour came to Rivers's face, as he cried,—

"Lord Hawksworth, Grace—has he dared again to renew his impertinent addresses?"

"I may answer yes and no to that," said Grace, "for although I have received no communication from him, or even seen him, yet he has taken a step which has sadly increased my domestic unhappiness. He has, as I understand, made a formal proposal of marriage to me, through my father."

"Which," cried Mrs. Woodfall, "is as hollow and insincere as he is in all his actions."

"The devil!" cried Tom Hackey. "Let him propose; we won't have him on any terms. That's settled; we reject him as a wretch unworthy of notice."

"Hush! hush!" said Rivers. "You have returned an answer to the proposal, Grace?"

"I have," she replied; "its purport you may guess."

"Well and truly, dear Grace," said Rivers; "and how did your father receive the rejection of a suitor so much to his own liking?"

A tear rolled down Grace's cheek as she replied,—

"We are sadly at issue, and I fear an extent of persecution and unhappiness that I tremble to reflect upon. But there is another source of woe more exquisite still."

"Another, Grace!"

"Yes, another. You are surrounded by deadly enemies, who scruple not by the vilest machinations to accomplish your destruction. This very day a silver cup was secreted in your desk."

"Gracious heaven!" cried Rivers. "The cup your father was mentioning as having lost?"

"The same, Rivers, and I cannot be sufficiently thankful to Providence for permitting me to rescue you from that great danger. When I placed the note in your desk which summoned you here, I saw the cup, and myself removed it, else had you been lost beyond mortal power to save you."

Rivers actually trembled as he thought of the frightful danger he had escaped: like a gushing torrent there came over his mind all the fearful consequences that must have ensued had the merchant's cup been found in his desk. How painfully he looked back upon the manner in which he had so haughtily resented the very shadow of suspicion against him. A cold perspiration burst upon his brow as he thought, "God of Heaven, how should I have looked before the eyes of Mathew Trueman and the villain Hilliard, had the cup been really taken from my desk?"

To a man of high moral courage and spotless integrity—to a man of such physical bravery that in a cause he had at heart he could have faced a cannon's mouth, and smiled upon a certain painful death, such a combination of circumstances as would have oppressed him if Hilliard's diabolical plan had been successful, were indeed calculated in their bare supposition to perfectly overwhelm!

Any one would have thought Rivers for a moment stricken by death, for his strength seemed to desert him, and he was compelled to sit down for some moments ere he could recover his composure.

Grace was in the utmost alarm, and the anxiety of Mrs. Woodfall and Tom Hackey manifested itself in their countenances. At length Rivers said with a faint smile,—

"Do not—do not be alarmed. I am better now; but the frightful consequences that might have arisen from that fearful plan did for the moment unman me. What defence could I have made? I should have been told that a clearer case never came before a court of justice, and there is not a magistrate in London who would not have smiled with incredulity at my assertions of innocence. Oh! Grace! Grace! you are indeed my guardian angel!"

"But what is to be done,—what is to be done?" said Grace; "those who contrive one plan will, upon its accidental defeat, contrive another. They will yet destroy you, Rivers—they will yet destroy you, and there will be none but your poor Grace to assert your innocence."

"I beg your pardon," said Tom Hackey, "there's something flown in my eye which makes it water a little; but there will be, Miss Grace, as well as you."

"Heaven only knows," said Mrs. Woodfall, "what will be the end of all this; and as I live, I know not what advice to give you."

"Then I do," said Tom Hackey, raising his voice. "Listen to me, Rivers and Miss Grace, and I'll give you the best advice in the world. I have seen these kind of things arranged all a hundred times. You secretly marry—then virtue is triumphant and villany meets its due reward. Old Mathew Trueman weeps and joins your hands; we all stand in a half circle, and down comes the blessed curtain."

Grace could not suppress a smile for the life of her as Tom spoke, but Rivers shook his head sadly as he said,—

"Alas! Tom, it may be true enough that all the world's a stage, but the great drama of real life seldom ends so pleasantly as the imitations of human nature on the mimic stage."

"Well," said Tom, "that's my

advice: marry, marry, say I, and then tell old Trueman to better himself if he can. What is done, you can tell him, can't be undone. Tell him you intend to play the popular farce of 'Love Laughs at Locksmiths,' to be followed by the favourite play of the 'Honeymoon.' You can tell him, too, that after such a 'Love Chase' you don't intend to be the 'Provoked Husband,' and that if he attempts to send you the 'Road to Ruin,' you must still be 'John Bull,' and achieve for yourself an 'Englishman's Fireside.' "

"Ah, Tom," said Rivers, "Heaven forbid that your bright aspirations should ever be dulled by the saddening mists of reality. But Grace, dear Grace, do you hear Tom's advice? and can you forgive my deep selfishness in making you now, in this extremity of misfortune, an offer of my hand and heart? It might be that your father would relent, and should he not, you would be at

THE DEATH OF WILSON.

least free from the persecutions of Lord Hawksworth, and while I have these hands to work with, you shall not want."

Mrs. Woodfall shook her head, and Tom Hackey exclaimed—

"I'll work for you, too. 'Every One has his Fault,' but mine isn't ingratitude, and I hope after your marriage you won't make me 'The Stranger.' "

Grace was silent for several minutes, then she said—

"Rivers, give me time to think. I will again speak to my father, for I cannot yet believe but that some lingering affection must still remain in his heart for one that may influence his better judgment, and induce him to consult my true happiness rather than the false glitter of a station I covet not. But beware of Hilliard, for he is, I am convinced, your active, but persevering enemy."

"I am sure of it," said Rivers.

"And so am I," said Tom Hackey. "There must be a villain in every piece, and ours is an out-an-outer. I say, Rivers, when you are married, I shall get a little red and blue fire, and set it off in the office, to give a proper effect to the scene."

"I will be upon my guard," said Rivers, "as much as I possibly can against the plans of my enemies; and yet what caution would have availed me against this day's conspiracy?"

"Hear me, Rivers," said Grace; "your danger is more imminent than my own; I may be persecuted, but you may be ruined. This state of things shall not subsist; it is on my account that you have provoked the enmity of these men, and it is fitting that I should rescue you from them. Should my father continue obdurate, you cannot with safety remain in his establishment. You must leave, Rivers, for that is the object of those who seek your destruction, but their disappointment shall be great, for I will leave with you."

"You will be mine—you will be mine, dear Grace?" said Rivers with transport.

"I will write to you to-morrow," said Grace. "We may be poor, Rivers, but we shall not be wholly deserted by that Providence which has already saved you from one frightful evil."

"That's right," cried Tom Hackey; "that's just as things ought to be. If I were getting up this thing properly, you know, I should introduce a song here, and just as it got to the last bar, somebody should come from a practicable door in the flat, and rushing between you, exclaim—'Vengeance shall be mine! Meet me at the cavern of the Red and Green Demon, where vultures shriek, and the wild waves toss themselves into a tumultuous and terrible state of botheration.' Then you ought to say, 'Rash fool, forbear! I defy you to single combat in the Haunted Glen of the Bloody Snake!' Then he ought to say, with two violent stamps on the stage, and a wild unearthly shout ——"

"Pray what ought he to say?" exclaimed the voice of Mathew Trueman, in a tone of suppressed passion, as he pushed himself in the little circle between Tom Hackey and Rivers.

"The devil!" said Tom.

"No, sir," said the merchant, "but you late master, for you are no longer in my service."

CHAPTER LXVII.

THE MERCHANT'S RAGE.—RIVERS'S DEFIANCE.—THE CLIMAX.

A FAINT scream burst from the lips of Grace, as she recognised her father; she half rose from her seat, as if she would have flown from the spot, but then a sudden change of feeling came over her, and it appeared as if on the instant she had made up her mind to abide with calmness and patience whatever might ensue.

As for Rivers, he by an instinctive impulse stepped half way between the merchant and his daughter, and stretching out his arm towards Grace in a protecting attitude, he cried—

"Forbear, Mr. Trueman, forbear. Let not your passion or anger at me overcome your sense of prudence or justice. If there be blame due anywhere it is to me; if censure is to fall on any one, let me alone be subjected to it."

"You tell me to forbear, you scoundrel!" said Mathew Trueman, almost bursting with rage. "Censure, blame, indeed! I'll have you sent to Newgate; and as for you, you shameless hussy, I'll send you somewhere where you will be out of your spark's way. This is no more than what I expected—the secret is now out. You could not marry Lord Hawksworth, forsooth, because you were leagued with this abominable puppy, who seeks to mend his contemptible condition by marrying my daughter."

"Mr. Trueman," said Rivers, "I have a great objection to use harsh language towards you, for fear I should wound the feelings of your daughter, otherwise one single expressive word would suffice to reply to your insinuations."

"Dare you insult me, sir?" said the merchant.

"I never willingly insult any one," said Rivers; "and least of all have I any inclination to insult you; but you must allow me to be as impatient under insult as you are yourself. You have come here, Mr. Trueman, brimful of wrath—let it fall upon me, and me alone."

"No," said Grace; "if there be blame, it is as much mine as Mr. Rivers's. Father, you have wished to unite me to a man whom I not only cannot love, but whom I hold in utter abhorrence and detestation. A desire for my happiness, I am quite sure, has been your only motive; but, believe me, father, you have been mistaken in the means you have taken for attaining that object. Persecuted and unhappy, on account of Lord Hawksworth, can you wonder that I sought for consolation in the society of one whom——"

Grace hesitated for a moment, and then she added—

"Why should I shrink from the truth?—One whom I can love."

Such a flash of exultation showed itself in the countenance of Rivers at this avowal of Grace's, and with such an eager joyful voice did he speak, that Mathew Trueman involuntarily started back a few paces, in fear of what he was about to do.

"You hear, Mr. Trueman, you hear," said Rivers. "Your daughter's happiness must be dear to you. I will believe with her that such is your only object, and the disagreement which has given a chill to both your hearts has been concerning the means. She is dearer to me than a hundred worlds—her happiness shall be my constant care. I would not have the winds of heaven visit her face too roughly. Mr. Trueman, this is a monotonous crisis in all our destinies; by your consent to our union you may make two hearts blessed, indeed, while the sunshine of our joy will be reflected upon your own heart."

"Hurrah! hurrah!" said Tom; "now, Mathew, don't be a fool. If you know what's good for yourself, you'll take out your cambric, give your eyes a bit of a whipe, and say 'Take her.' Then you have nothing to do but look up at the chandelier—no, I mean the sky, as we are on the great stage, and not the little one, and invoke a silent blessing on all our heads."

"Peace, idiot, peace!" cried Mathew Trueman, almost choked with rage. "Hear me, Grace, once and for all; I would sooner see you stretched in the agonies of death before me, than the wife of that man. I solemnly swear that I never will consent to such an union. If you wed him, may want and wretchedness be your portion, and may my bitterest curse ever cling to you!"

"No—no—no," cried Grace; "this is too terrible, too terrible."

"Heed it not, dear Grace," said Rivers, "it is mere raving."

"There you go again, Mathew," said Tom; "you want to make a five-act piece of it, I see. Oh! you unnatural old dog! I fancy I see you repenting some years after this, and searching over your bald head for some hairs to pull out; we shall have to forgive you some day."

The merchant's face became absolutely white with passion, and in a voice of unnatural calmness, he said—

"Francis Rivers, I discharge you, on the spot, from my employment. Mrs. Woodfall, my doors are henceforth closed against you; and as for this scoundrel," turning to Hackey, "I shall give him in charge to the first constable I meet, for abusive language."

"Oh! bother you," said Tom, "you can't do it—you've been getting up the piece of 'The Unnatural Father; or, Vile Mathew, the Terror of Thames Street.' I just care about as much as that for you."

Here Tom, by way of illustrating his argument, pulled a little bit of beaver off his hat, and, balancing the same on the tip of his finger, blew it into the air.

So irresistibly comic was this proceeding, that not one of the party could refrain from watching the little gossamer-like particle, as it floated gently towards the river.

Mathew Trueman, however, was ready to let every little circumstance add as fuel to his indignation, and, seizing Grace by the arm, he said—

"You will accompany me home. As for these discharged menials, they may send for their wages when they think proper."

Grace could not well refuse to accompany her father. The place was too public a one to make any appeal to his feelings, and all she could do was to cast one imploring look at Rivers, and then prepare to leave the spot.

Poor Mrs. Woodfall stood petrified with astonishment and dismay, while Tom Hackey amused himself by addressing an imaginary audience to whom he said—

"Ladies and gentlemen, do not be deceived. Virtue will be triumphant, and villany will fall in the suds. The unnatural father will come to an untimely and terrible end, to the great edification of all young ladies who contemplate getting up a little domestic drama of their own."

Rivers, when he saw that Grace was thus being taken from him, immediately stepped before the merchant, and said, in a calm and dignified tone—

"Mr. Trueman, the day will come when your own heart will tell you you have acted unwisely as well as harshly in this matter—when this day's proceedings will rise up before you in agonized remembrance, and you will feel that you have sacrificed all that would have gilded your declining years with the sunshine of joy by attempting to grasp at a mocking shadow. I am far from one who would attempt to depreciate those holy natural ties which bind a child to its parent; but I am one who believes, and ever will believe, that the parent cannot be too careful not to draw the chain of duty too tightly lest it snap in the process. Reflect on my words, sir. I have no more to say to you. Farewell, dear Grace; we shall meet again, and again, and again, despite every obstacle that can be opposed to us. Difficulties, dear Grace, are love's triumphs."

Mathew Trueman paused a moment, as if searching in his mind for some suitable reply to this; but not finding any language sufficiently strong to express his anger and resentment he merely shrieked—

"Get out of my way, sir—by God, get out of my way."

Rivers stepped on one side, and as he did so, he caught one meaning glance from the eyes of Grace, a glance that repaid him for everything, and filled him with delighted hopes. He watched the retreating forms of the stern merchant and his daughter until they could no longer be seen, then, with a deep sigh, he said—

"Shall this be the end of the beautiful passion which has enthralled my soul? Shall this be the termination of the many brilliant and rainbow-coloured hopes with which my imagination has made beautiful my dependant and almost destitute condition? No, it shall not, it must not be. Despite all obstacles, and all dangers, I will rescue Grace from the persecutions she is enduring, and, if the home I can offer her be but a poor one, it shall, at least, be blessed with content."

At this moment he felt some one touch his arm, and turning, he saw Tom Hackey, who said—

"Well, Rivers, we have fallen on to another spoke of dame Fortune's wheel; what's to be done now? I ain't so bad off, for I've got ninepence, and Mathew owes me a matter of five and sixpence."

"I really don't know what's to be done, Tom," said Rivers; "but where is Mrs. Woodfall?"

"Why, there she is," said Tom, "weeping like a decayed water-spout; but I did not expect that answer from you."

"Then what did you expect?" said Rivers.

"Why, that you had thought of the plan I before proposed to you—on becoming a bright particular star in that hemisphere where it is more delightful to shine in than any other."

Rivers shook his head, as he said—

"I remember, Tom. You fancy me particularly adapted to shine in the theatrical world. But you are mistaken; I am no actor, and I am afraid I feel too acutely the realities of life, ever successfully to depict mimic passions."

"Pooh! pooh!" said Tom; "that's the very thing; the more you feel, the more you'll be able to pretend to feel; but I must immediately speak to Mrs. Woodfall, for I have got two towels and a comb up in one of Mathew's attics."

"And I, too, must speak to Mrs. Woodfall," said Rivers; "for not one among the least of my misfortunes is that I have involved others in their consequences."

"Do not mind me, Mr. Rivers," said Mrs. Woodfall, advancing. "Let us all rather unite, for our dear Grace's sake, and think of some plan which shall contribute to her happiness. Poor thing!

she will now be without a single friend to turn to for sympathy or succour. Her state of loneliness and her persecutions will bring her to the grave unless we can rescue her."

"She shall be rescued," said Rivers.

"She shall—she shall," said Tom. "Let us meet to-night on the Rialto; we must outwit old Mathew some way, and rescue Grace from the chamber in which he will now, no doubt, lock her up."

"We must, indeed, have another consultation," said Mrs. Woodfall, "and the arrangement of a place and time of meeting you may safely leave to me, for, notwithstanding Mr. Trueman's prohibition, I shall proceed instantly to Thames Street, where, I doubt not, I shall have an opportunity of seeing Grace, and ascertaining what her feelings are on this most distressing turn which affairs have taken."

"Do so," said Rivers, "and I can never sufficiently thank you. When shall we meet again?"

"Ay," said Tom. "In thunder, lightning, or in rain? When the hurley burley's done—when the battle's lost and won."

"Now, Mr. Hackey, your nonsense is quite unbearable," said Mrs. Woodfall; "you ought, under the circumstances, to have known better; and what's to become of you, poor simple creature as you are, I can't think."

"Me?" said Tom in great indignation. "Did you mean me, mum?"

"Yes, I did," said Mrs. Woodfall; "and I am sure I pity you from my heart."

"D——you," said Tom, "I am very much obliged to you; but give me leave to tell you, old mother Woodfall, that I look upon you as a female of very limited intellect, and if it was not that I have some respect for you, I should call you an old fool."

"Come, come, Tom," said Rivers, "enough of this—let us agree to meet to-morrow morning at some particular spot, to receive an account of what Mrs. Woodfall has been able to accomplish in the meantime."

"I will meet you both," said Mrs. Woodfall, "in St. Paul's Churchyard; and as for what Tom Hackey says, I know, poor fellow, he means well, notwithstanding his curious oddities. Farewell, for the present, and let us hope for better times to cheer us. I know not scarcely what advice to offer you, for I fear I should be taking a great responsibility on myself by offering any; yet I cannot have my Grace sacrificed even to the absurd fancies of her father, and it seems to me that either he must relent, or among us we must save her from what we might almost call the insanity of his ambition."

"My best thanks and best wishes attend you," said Rivers; "I shall be punctual at the appointment. What hour will be the most suitable and agreeable to you?"

"Ten," said Mrs. Woodfall; and then the three having arrived in Fleet Street, she left them and proceeded to the merchant's house, full of anxiety and grief as to the ultimate fate of Grace, whom she had tended from earliest childhood, and towards whom she felt, if possible, more than the affection of a tender parent.

CHAPTER LXVIII.

THE MEETING OF HILLIARD AND GIRKINS ON KENNINGTON COMMON — THE NEW PLOT.

As the evening of the day on which the above circumstances took place wore on, and became night, a dark mass of clouds hung over the metropolis, and gradually descended, causing the vapour which had accumulated in the air to descend also, thus causing one of those misty, foggy nights, so common to great cities, and London in particular. The rain also descended, but lightly, and continued without interruption for many hours.

The lights of the shops shone dimly through the hazy medium, the raw coldness of the night, added to the rain, soon caused all the thoroughfares to be cleared of passengers, except those, indeed, whose avocations compelled them to be abroad, despite their own inclinations and desires.

Bad as the night was in town, in the outskirts it was worse, for though it had less of the artificial vapour, it had a greater degree of rawness and discomfort.

Kennington Common, at the best of times an exposed spot, either to extreme heat in summer, or in winter swept by the chilly blast of the winds, come from what quarter they may, was on this night a spot which no human being would choose as a promenade; but yet there was one individual who was induced, by some particular and urgent motive, to expose himself to the night blast, and the cold rain, in the most unfrequented part of it.

It was late, and the neighbouring clock had chimed—it was a quarter to eleven, and the man gave many signals of impatience, taking a short and hasty promenade, backwards and forwards, on one spot, anxiously looking around him, and endeavouring to pierce the darkness of the night, and discover if some one whom he sought was yet come.

But disappointment only found vent in a shifting motion in his body, indicative of impatience, while he endeavoured to make the coat collar, which was turned up, protect his face from the driving rain.

Again he resumed his short walk, as if the momentary cessation of motion had become disconsonant to his feelings, and he once more paced to and fro, until the clock again chimed, and he again stopped and counted eleven. He looked in one direction—towards the turnpike, as if expecting those whom he sought to come that way from town; but the night was so dark, that though he could see the lighted lamps at a distance, yet he could discover nothing between him and them.

"Curses on him!" cried Mark Hilliard, for it was he who at that solitary hour had by appointment sought that spot on which he had agreed to meet Girkins. "Curses on him, eleven was the hour, and why is he not here to his appointment? There seems to be some d—d fatality about every scheme that is tried against Rivers. Nothing seems to succeed. Under ordinary circumstances, his destruction must have been certain, but now the best contrived plot that ever entered the brain of mortal man, executed, too, as it was, in an unexceptional manner, has by some extraordinary fatality completely failed.

Master Girkins must again put his ingenuity to the test, for, as yet, this d—d Rivers has certainly got the better of us. What can he—what will he next contrive?"

A stealthy approaching footstep now warned him that some one was at hand, and he leaned moodily against the trunk of a massive tree, as he muttered to himself—

"I presume that is my man. It is like his step."

It was Girkins, and as he approached the appointed spot where he expected to find Hilliard, he cried—

"Hilliard! Hilliard! are you there? 'Tis I. Speak."

"I am here," said Hilliard, in a low, growling voice; "and I have been here some time; and you ought to know I don't like to be kept waiting."

"D—n your impertinence!" said Girkins; "if I kept you all night, you ought to be thankful that I come at last. You are but too well kept, Hilliard, to forget our relative positions. Remember, I know what I know, and that you are completely in my power. Beware, then, of tempting me to use it, or you will rue your temerity."

Hilliard was silent for some moments, for too well he knew to what the unscrupulous agent alluded, and although his natural ferocity of temper and malignancy of spirit induced him frequently to brave the anger of Girkins, yet he never really forgot that he was in his power, and that a few words from him might at any time awaken suspicions that might ripen to his destruction.

"Well, well," he said, "enough of that. Here I am, true to my appointment; tell me at once what you now propose, for you see that fellow has had the devil's luck and his own, and, as yet, we have been able to do nothing with him."

"The failure," said Girkins, "of the last scheme was indeed extraordinary. I cannot myself understand it, but still it is sufficient for us that it has failed, and we must discover some new means of accomplishing our purposes. Now, since your brief note to me, informing me of the failure of the attempt we have made, I have not been unthoughtful of the affair. Rivers must still be committed in a transaction which shall cast a blot upon his character for life. Surely there will be abundant opportunities to accomplish so much, even with great profit to yourself. You and any accomplices you may have must get up a robbery of a more extensive nature than the last, while, by some means, Rivers must be thoroughly implicated in it. There must be such presumptive evidence of his guilt that he cannot escape. I have set my heart upon that man's destruction, and it shall be accomplished."

"Very well, Mr. Girkins," said Hilliard, "it's all very well for you to talk of what must be, but there is another thing which must be likewise, and that is, I must have money. I may be in your power, but still I must have money; and I suppose after the failure of the attempt with the silver cup, you'll be saying I am not entitled to the twenty pounds?"

"Entitled to the twenty pounds?" said Girkins; "how on earth are you to be entitled to the twenty pounds? Do you want your wages without performing your work? Upon my word, Master Hilliard, you have some extraordinary notions about you."

"Then, d———n! Girkins," said Hilliard, "you cannot expect, nor will you get, any good out of me. You may threaten; and I guess, although I cannot see your face, that you are bending your brows upon me in your accustomed manner; but it will not do—I must have money. Without it I can do nothing—I will attempt nothing."

It was far from Girkins's object to come to an open rupture with Hilliard; what he wished was to keep such a threatening circumstance hovering over his head, and yet never approach it; moreover, the agent had had a very liberal share of the advance made to Lord Hawksworth by the Jew, and he was quite prepared to make any advance to Hilliard that he might think politic.

"Well," he said, "you must be perfectly aware that I have reaped nothing but vexation from your attempt to accomplish that for which you would have been so handsomely paid, and upon the strength of which, you will recollect, Master Hilliard, you have already had several small advances from me."

"Small, indeed," muttered Hilliard, with an oath; "so small, that one has actually to chase them through one's memory to remember them."

"But still they were advances, and to such amounts you are certainly my debtor. My consideration for you, however, may induce me to add further to your obligations. I will now take upon myself to advance you five pounds, with the expectation that you will still earn the twenty, by the destruction of Francis Rivers."

"It shall not be from want of inclination," said Hilliard, with an oath. "Give me the five pounds, and what can be done shall be done."

"Understand me, then," said Girkins; "I expect you immediately to attempt something in the style I have suggested to you. Take your measures for a handsome burglary at the merchant's house, and at the same time take care that something is left behind, which shall criminate Rivers—some trifling article which you can purloin from him previously—a glove—a handkerchief—a letter, with his name on it, or anything that can be fully identified and known as his, and that might have been supposed to be left behind in the hurry of such circumstances."

"That I can easily do," said Hilliard, "for in the office he is especially careless of his things, and appears to have no suspicion that any danger can attend him."

"'Tis well, then," said Girkins; "when shall we meet again?"

"When and where you please," said Hilliard; "but I cannot promise you exactly when I shall be able to carry out this new scheme."

"At least, then, let me see you every day until you can assure me that all is prepared. At your own dinner hour you'll always find me in Barnard's Inn."

"Agreed," said Hilliard; "but you seem to have forgotten the five pounds which form so essential a part of our agreement."

"By no means," said Girkins, counting out the required sum. "What I promise, I will perform punctually. Do you the same, and we may remain long friends."

"Well, well, you won't find me backward, for if there's anything I want on earth, it's money, and if there's anything on earth that I hate, it's Francis Rivers."

"Then," said Girkins, in a mocking tone, "my dear Hilliard, it strikes me we need not continue our interesting conversation, so good night to you, and if Providence chooses to assist us in our undertaking, why, it may set about it as quickly as possible."

Hilliard walked away with the polite salutation of a curse, and thus separated these worthies, who, in their extreme cleverness, fancied they could accomplish the destruction of an innocent man, who had nothing but his honour and his integrity to oppose them with.

Hilliard was not at all aware of the remarkable change that had taken place in the position of Rivers during that evening, or he would by no means have calculated so strongly upon the facility with which he could obtain possession of some article of Rivers's for the atrocious purpose he meditated.

Nor perhaps would Girkins, had he been in possession of the facts of which the reader is so fully aware, have taken so much trouble and been so very anxious concerning Rivers; for his principal object—personal revenge—being a subservient feeling in Girkins's mind, and one that he thought would keep, was to oust Rivers from the merchant's house, in order that he and Lord Hawksworth might carry on uninterruptedly the vile machinations which were in progress.

When he parted from Hilliard he directed his steps at once to Barnard's Inn, where he and his legal friend held a long and serious consultation concerning the prospects that were opening to them by the decisive movement Lord Hawksworth had been induced to make in the affairs which had been so very long on the tapis.

"There can be no doubt now," said Girkins, "but that Mathew Trueman would advance to his lordship a sum about equivalent to one half the presumed value of his bills—that is to say, he will receive in net cash a sum strongly resembling twenty thousand pounds, which it will be our faults if we do not aid and assist in distributing."

"My dear Girkins," said the attorney, "you may depend on my most cordial co-operation in so laudable a purpose.

As Mr. Trueman is a man of high character, and generally considered of great mental resources and business tact, it appears to me we cannot do better than follow humbly in his footsteps, and if he considers one hundred per cent. as no more than a proper remuneration for him, I do not see that we should grumble at a similar allowance."

"Very far from it," said Girkins. "I could almost forgive the Lord Chancellor for being so afflicted with virtue one day as to strike me off the Rolls, could I but bring this admirable piece of business some day to so admirable a conclusion as you suggest."

"Exactly," said the other. "Hawksworth would suffer a little, but then when people want bills discounted they must suffer a little, and if he gives Mathew Trueman forty thousand pounds' worth of bills, and gets for them twenty thousand pounds' worth of cash, which we divide with him, leaving him ten, I really think that he ought to consider himself very well off, and that the business has been conducted in an extremely liberal and gentlemanly manner."

"Exactly," said Girkins, with a short dry cough. "Five thousand pounds will be handy to you, and, I may add, particularly handy to me; and I see no reason why our affairs should not progress in the most satisfactory manner, more especially if we can get rid of that fellow who has been such a stumbling-block in our way, and who I more than suspect has wound himself so much round the affections of Grace Trueman as almost to ruin our whole scheme by making the merchant despair of even inducing his daughter to set her cap at a lord."

"Hush—hush! stop—stop!" cried Mr. Girkins's legal friend; "I have no objection, as you are perfectly aware, to a little bit of quiet, systematical, professional swindling, but I decidedly object to be *particeps criminis* in anything which might hereafter bear the ugly name of conspiracy. Now I don't know anything about the person you mention, and what is more, I won't; therefore, my good Mr. Girkins, that is a little episode in this transaction which you must arrange entirely by yourself."

"You are extremely cautious," said Girkins.

"I am; but you must recollect I am still on the rolls, and very many gentlemen in extreme difficulties would be put to great inconvenience if I were not."

"I understand you," said Girkins; "and permit me to add, although averse to compliments, that even among our profession, I scarcely know one to whom I would rather bring a piece of unclean work than to yourself."

"Say dirty—say dirty, at once," said the professional gentleman. "I am not proud; money is always tolerably clean, and let it come through what miry medium it may, it never loses its value or its lustre; but a truce to this—when are the bills to be prepared?"

"I should say to-morrow, or the next day at the furthest," replied Girkins, "for I believe all parties will be equally impatient in the transaction; and as, without the shadow of a doubt, his lordship has this day made his honourable proposal for the hand of the

THE MEETING OF THE LOVERS IN BARNES CHURCHYARD.

merchant's daughter, so there can be no question but that to-morrow he will see the dainty little paragraph I have sent to the newspapers. They are ever willing to insert anything connected with the follies or crimes of mankind."

"Egad, that's true enough, Girkins," said the lawyer; "you are quite philosophical this evening. I shall be careful always to be within at our usual hour of conference—namely, betwixt one and two."

"Then to-morrow, within that hour expect me, and likewise the man Hilliard, of whom I have spoken to you, with whom I have an appointment here. He is a useful spy, and something more."

"An unscrupulous agent," said the attorney.

"Precisely; and now, farewell. I think a clearer prospect never presented itself to us of pocketing a considerable sum of money than the present."

"Good night," said the attorney to Girkins, as he showed him to the door of his dingy chamber. "Be careful of the stairs, they are not so good as I dare say they were some forty years ago." Then he added to himself, "When you are no longer useful to me, I hope you may break your neck down them."

"That's an infernal rogue," muttered Girkins to himself, when he got into Holborn; "when I don't want his assistance any more, I should like to see him hung some morning."

CHAPTER LXIX.

THE ASSIGNATION.—TOM HACKEY'S THEATRICAL FERVOUR.—GRACE'S LAST RESOLUTION.

IT would appear that at this juncture a crisis had arrived in the fortunes of Rivers and the beautiful Grace Trueman —then, likewise, so mixed up were they by the invisible hand of destiny, with the hopes, the fears, the plans, and the machinations of the other personages who occupy an important place in our drama of real life, that a crisis could scarcely arrive in the fortunes of those two in whose actions we are so deeply interested, without, at the same time, producing extensive effects upon those others against whose evil machinations they had nothing to oppose but their innocence and holiness of purpose, and their trust in Heaven.

Grace was fully aware of all the evils of her situation; her father had uttered his bitterest maledictions against Rivers, and there remained to her not the shadow of a hope that he would ever consent to her union with him who had won her best affections; therefore, what endless persecutions might she not endure if, indeed, Lord Hawksworth chose to continue his fulsome addresses.

The tie which had hitherto bound her to her father seemed nearly severed, and the future to poor Grace assumed but a melancholy aspect.

Mathew Trueman nad now arrived at what he considered a crisis in his fortunes; his great object through life had been the acquisition of wealth, but when he grew almost sated with his accumulated hoards, the passion to be something more than he was, to achieve something yet greater than he had achieved, rose strongly in his mind. Commencing life as he had done, with an affected hatred and contempt of those nicknames current in society which make the distinctions of rank, and boldly avowing his opinion that money made the man, it is scarcely to be wondered at that in after life he should cringe to rank with the most slavish admiration, and esteem himself the happiest of men if, through bartering the beauty of his child, along with a large sum of money, for a coronet, he could himself bask in the reflected beams of the glittering bauble.

The very opposition of Grace to the darling scheme of his ambition but strengthened him in it, for he told himself that such opposition was but a difficulty to be overcome; and as he fumed and fretted about the private office, he muttered—

"Ah, I've been overcoming difficulties all my life. I started with three-and-a-penny, and I remember very well it was difficult to get that; then it was more difficult to make six-and-twopence of it. There's nothing but difficulty, of course, and he's the cleverest fellow who overcomes them. Ah, my name's Mathew Trueman."

So did the merchant try to convince himself that by warring against his beautiful child, and endeavouring to sacrifice her, he should be obtaining something which would help to fill his cup of happiness.

Then to Lord Hawksworth, to Girkins, to his legal friend, and to Mark Hilliard, was not the present an important crisis?

How could his lordship support his honourable dignity and represent the peerage properly, unless, by the most atrocious falsehoods, and misrepresentations, he succeeded in getting his bills cashed? Then, if the bills were not cashed, how was Girkins to have any of the proceeds?—how, likewise, was his legal friend to acquire any portion of the plunder—and how was Mark Hilliard to be paid for his atrocious services?

Then to Tom Hackey, was not his discharge from the service of Mathew Trueman the crisis he had always looked forward to, and which was to free him from the trammels of the life he had been leading, and make him a great tragedian, a consummation which he fully believed would arrive? so that, as far as he was concerned, he vexed himself very little about the state of his personal affairs.

But, of all the parties concerned in our story, the one who felt next to Grace, most truly, that a crisis in his happiness, if not in his fortunes, had arrived, was Francis Rivers.

His views and thoughts as regarded a marriage with Grace were widely different from what they had been, for, although from the first moment that his heart had whispered to him that he loved her he looked forward to the more remote possibility of an union with her as the consummation of his brightest dream of happiness, yet, in accordance with the sentiments which he had uttered to Amelia, and which were the genuine ones of his heart, he would indeed have shrunk from taking Grace from a happy home, surrounded with comforts and luxuries, and cheered by the love of a father. "But, now," he asked himself, "was such the case? and by wedding him, and encountering all the risks that might attend his variable fortunes, would she be so unhappy as she inevitably would be in her spendid misery at home, exposed to the addresses of such a man as Lord Hawksworth, and the tormenting persecutions of her father on his account?

"Would not," he asked himself, "poverty with me be preferable to such a fate?—for, at least, she will feel none of that heart-bitterness which arises from harsh words and endless reproaches. What formerly would have been wicked selfishness in me, now becomes a duty, for I owe it to Grace to offer a rescue from her present unhappiness."

It was with feelings such as these, and such reflections, that Rivers, on the morning following his discharge from the merchant's service, repaired to the spot at which he had appointed to meet Mrs. Woodfall.

Tom Hackey was to meet him at the same place, and Rivers had scarcely gained the appointed corner when the poor faithful fellow made his appearance.

"Well, Tom," said Rivers, "how fares it with you this morning? You are true to your appointment."

"Oh, that this too, too solid flesh would melt!" said Tom. "I'm very well, I thank you, but a trifle too fat."

"Too fat?" said Rivers. "How's that?"

"Why," said Tom, "I suppose, with overfeeding. Not that I can particularly accuse old Mathew of doing anything so absurd as to overpay anybody; but such is the fact—I am too fat."

"But how came you to find out that, Tom?" said Rivers. "You don't seem to me to be so very fat."

"Nevertheless, good cousin," said Tom, assuming a theatrical air, and treading on the toes of an elderly gentleman who was passing, "such is the direful circumstance. I should have got an engagement the first thing this morning to run the Apothecary in 'Romeo and Juliet,' but my size forbade it. There's a misfortune for you. Now, I could do Hamlet, for he's represented as little punchy."

"Indeed," said Rivers.

"Yes," continued Tom. "Does not the queen in the fencing scene exclaim, 'Our son is fat, and scant of breath.'"

"Well, I believe she does," said Rivers.

"Well, you see, there's no fighting against facts," continued Tom; "but when I offered to play Hamlet, the agent had the impudence to tell me that he had fifteen Hamlets on his books, and but one apothecary; and that of the fifteen, nine he knew were tolerable low comedians, three more comic singers, and the other three tumblers on the tight rope."

"'Pon my word," said Rivers, "they must be very ambitious gentlemen."

"True, most true," said Hackey. "My name is Norval, on the Grampian hills—but here comes Mother Woodfall. I say, don't you think she'd do the nurse in 'Romeo and Juliet' very well; or, on a pinch, she might double Polonius and the Queen in 'Hamlet.'"

"Hush!" said Rivers. "Mrs. Woodfall has acted the most friendly part towards us, and is highly esteemed for many faithful services by Grace."

"I know it," said Tom, "and do much esteem myself the ancient gentlewoman. Sound clarionets, beat drums, for lo, she approaches."

Mrs. Woodfall at that moment reached the spot, and after a kindly salutation to Rivers, she took his proffered arm.

"Hilloa!" said Tom Hackey, "Mother Woodfall, don't you see me?"

"Indeed, I did not see you," said Mrs. Woodfall; "you poor simple creature, what are you going to do? I am sure it makes me quite unhappy when I think what will become of you."

"Ignorant and presuming old woman," said Tom in great indignation. "What puts it into your old addlepate to wonder at what I am going to do? But since you have taken it upon yourself to wonder, I tell you what I'm going to do. I'm going to electrify the town, and put the povinces into fits."

"Bless me," said Mrs. Woodfall, "I wonder how people can joke at their own misfortunes. You may depend, Tom, if I know of anybody who wants a boy for any purpose, I well let you know, and warmly recommend you, for I believe you are as honest as the day, and if you were not stage-struck, as you are, I do believe you'd get on very well."

"Do you, ancient animal?" said Tom, with great emphasis.

"Old Mother Woodfall's mad. A cursed spite
That I should e'er be born to see her right."

Tom then lagged a few paces behind, ever and anon striking singularly heroic attitudes, which induced some of the passengers to stare with astonishment after him, while others again lurched into the roadway to avoid him, and one nervous old gentleman, in a spencer, ran into a shop, and bolted the door on the inside, to the amazement of the shopkeeper.

"Tell me of Grace," said Rivers; "has she sent me an answer favourable to my hopes?"

"She has sent you a reasonable and proper answer," said Mrs. Woodfall.

"Let me hear it, pray, let me hear it at once."

"It is this.—She thinks that no duty from a child to a parent, taking it in its most extended sense, should be sufficient to induce her to sacrifice herself completely by marrying a man she detests."

"Most true—most true. There could not be a truer, fairer doctrine."

"But," continued Mrs. Woodfall, "she is willing to concede to her father as far as to promise that she herself will marry no one without his consent, if he, in return, will never again mention Lord Hawksworth's name to her, or encourage his addresses. This question she will put to her father to-day, and upon his answer she will act."

"My suspense," said Rivers, in a melancholy tone, "will be terrible."

"You cannot deny," added Mrs. Woodfall, "but that Grace is acting properly."

"I know I cannot," said Rivers. "Everything she does or says is proper; but, knowing my feelings, you must excuse my impatience."

"That I can well do, Mr. Rivers; and I can assure you, that dearly as I love Grace, I would rather see her your wife, with all the prospect of contingent poverty, than sacrificed, for I can give it no other name, to such a man as Lord Hawksworth.

"From my heart, I thank you for your kindly sympathy," said Rivers, "and, should the sun of prosperity ever shine upon me and Grace, believe me, I shall never forget the kind heart that comforted me in affliction."

"This very day," said Mrs. Woodfall, "Grace will speak to her father, and she commissions me to make another appointment with you at the same hour, when you shall know the result, and such further proceedings as may be adopted."

At this moment some confusion of voices behind him induced Rivers to look back, when he saw Tom Hackey menacing several boys who had, being attracted by his extraordinary gestures, jumped to the conclusion that he was a fit object for their merriment, and began persecuting him accordingly with such impish sounds and gestures as boys usually resort to on such occasions.

"Ye young curs," exclaimed Tom Hackey, "why follow ye me thus furious through the streets of Rome? Is this the way you treat Coriolanus? Ye horrid wretches, avaunt!"

Rivers acted much more energetically

than Tom, and, as the boys evidently considered, much more practically; for, upon seizing the foremost, and saluting him with a box of the ears, the remainder took to flight, and so did likewise the one who bore the brunt of the conflict, who, after threatening Rivers with his big brother, and taunting him to come down our court, or hit one of his own size, made off likewise, when (a groan for human nature!) he was unmercifully jeered by his comrades for having, in their cause, "napped it."

"How could you be so foolish, Tom?" said Rivers; "you'll be considered a lunatic if you behave in this manner in the street. You really ought to know better."

"Ah!" said Tom, "it only goes to show the dreadful decline of the legitimate drama; the age is a degenerate age, and the tragedian's occupation is nearly gone."

"I don't know that," said Rivers; "the tragedians may be gone, but their occupations remain, and there only now wants some bright particular star, by its refulgent beams, to revivify the smoul'ering embers of the drama, and make it rise like another phœnix from its ashes."

Rivers, who was a real lover of the histrionic art, spoke these words with a fervour that quite electrified Tom Hackey, who, uttering a loud melo-dramatic laugh, shouted—

"Bind up my wounds—pour manna down my throat—bring me a horse— my kingdom for a stage!—the sock— the buskin—the lights—the orange-peel and the saw-dust—the ginger-pop and the flies—the everything, from the prompter's bell to the thunder box. Gracious powers! is it a dream? ha! ha! ha!"

Tom's minor theatre laugh was uttered so close to the ear of an old lady, rejoicing in about a ton-and-a-half of fat, that she fell down one the pavement with a squash, as if a cartful of blancmange had been upset.

Rivers seized Tom by the collar, and dragged him down Norfolk-street, the end of which they were just passing, and then he said to him—

"Now, Tom, once for all, I will not come out into the streets with you, unless you will condescend to be a little rational."

"Then why do you make such speeches?" said Tom. "I felt, good Heavens, how I felt! By-the-bye, a thought strikes me. Mother Woodfall, are you going home?—or are you going to make a day of it, and have a spree?"

"I am going home, of course, you ridiculous mortal! One really does not know whether to be angry at, or laugh at you."

"Allow me to tell you, Mother Woodfall, that either of those things conveys the greatest insult to a tragedian —you ought to do nothing but weep— now and then varying the scene by a little kicking hysterics, while you wring out your pocket handkerchief into the pit."

"I have no patience with you," said Mrs. Woodfall; "Mr. Rivers, we shall meet again ——"

"At Philippi."

"No such thing; at the corner of Chancery-lane."

So saying, Mrs. Woodfall walked hastily away in the direction of the city; but Tom scampered after her, and, to avoid having the attention of all the passengers in the street drawn upon her, she was compelled to stop.

"You're going home, Mother Woodfall," he said, "and I'm going to old Mathew for five and a trifle that he owes me; so I bestow a dramatic celebrity upon you for ever, by walking with you through the city."

CHAPTER LXX.

THE APPEAL.—FATHER AND DAUGHTER. —THE VOW.—MATHEW TRUEMAN'S AMBITION.

GRACE, after much serious thought and consultation with her kind nurse, had made up her mind to the course of action which had been mentioned by Mrs. Woodfall to Rivers.

Such a promise as that which she now wished to get from her father had been before implied between them. but at all events, not sufficently understood by the merchant to induce a corresponding action.

It was, therefore, that she determined

more particularly to make such a proposal to her father, and implore him to accede to it, for his own sake as well as for hers ; for what but the greatest unhappiness to both could arise from so marked a difference of sentiment on a subject of such vast importance as that which occupied both their attentions?

That she loved Rivers truly and devotedly, and would readily have united her destiny with his, she no longer shrunk from telling herself, but, at the same time, the prospect of an affectionate heart like hers abandoning her father completely, and perhaps entailing upon herself his bitterest malediction, was terrible in the extreme.

"Oh, if he would free me," she said, "from the persecutions of Lord Hawksworth, I could bear a separation from Rivers, with the hope that such a separation would not be for ever, but that the day might come when my father would view him and his feelings with tender regard, and we should all be happy together; but I cannot live the life I am leading, poisoned as it is of every enjoyment, and the dreaded name of Hawksworth steps ever between my father and myself, like a malevolent demon, turning to bitterness our daily intercourse."

What she should do if her father refused to enter into the compact she proposed, she would not then allow herself to think, for it was too painful for her to reflect, as she necessarily must, upon such a refusal.

"There will be time enough—there will be time enough," she said ; " he may yield, and then I shall be spared much painful thought, and even should he remain firm against my prayers, there will be time enough then to think of the days that are to come."

Mathew Trueman had scarcely opened his lips to Grace on their road home from the Temple Gardens, and she was in too great a confusion of mind to enable her to converse with him, so that both parties had had full time to think, without having committed themselves particularly at the first flush of the contested proceedings.

There was one thing, however, which the merchant seemed to have repented of very quickly, and that was the discharge of Mrs. Woodfall, for when he met her in the house afterwards, he rather avoided her presence, than challenged her right to be there, so that for Grace's sake she was determined to remain as long as she was suffered so to do.

Grace knew that by twelve o'clock her father had usually finished the perusal of his letters, and answered such as from their importance required a reply direct from himself.

It was some short time after that hour, then, that she sent a servant with a message to the merchant, to the effect, that when he was disengaged she would be glad to speak with him.

"Tell Miss Trueman," was the reply, "that I will be with her in a quarter of an hour."

During that quarter of an hour the merchant paced to and fro in his little counting-house, and like a person who carefully examines the outside of a letter, and exhausts time in supposition as to whom it might come from, when a glance at the interior would set the point at rest, he wondered very much what Grace could have to say to him, and whether she meditated entire submission to his will, or further defiance of what he considered his proper authority.

"She wants to speak to me," he muttered. " Well, she shall speak to me. It may be, that after all, she has taken a better thought of her position, and believes the title of countess not to be so despicable an addition to her name. So be it, I am ready for any concession; but still I will not reckon upon anything too hastily ; she may meditate further defiance of me and my wishes, and if so, shall find me firm—firm as rock. I will not be bent, not an inch— not an inch. Besides, it is for her own benefit, and what have I striven for all my life, if the very climax of my ambition is to to be thrust aside for the peevish fancy of a girl? It's quite ridiculous—quite—quite. I will go to her at once. What can she have to say to me?"

Thus muttering to himself the merchant ascended the staircase, and entered the drawing-room where Grace was expecting his arrival.

The pale countenance and general anxious expression of his daughter ought to have melted the merchant's heart, but those natures in which the twin passions of avarice and ambition have taken up their abode possess little of the softer feelings of humanity.

Grace, at the first glance she took at her father's face, could have said to herself, "My appeal will be in vain," for she saw nothing there of a yielding character; nevertheless, she resolved to make it, for she considered it in the light of a duty, which, once discharged, absolved her at least of some of the consequences of future disobedience, for then she could tell herself that she had done all that was possible to propitiate her father, and he had rejected all.

For a few moments there was a silence in that apartment, for Grace scarcely knew how to begin the painful conversation, and the merchant was resolved that, as she had sent for him she should herself commence the dialogue.

"Father," she said, at length, when she saw that he would not speak, "I have sent for you——"

"Well," interrupted the merchant, hastily, "I know that, Grace, and I suppose, and hope, it is for the purpose of tendering to me your sincere contrition for yesterday's conduct, and making affairs more pleasant."

"It is with a hope," said Grace, "of greater pleasure, I am sure, to both of us, than we can enjoy in dissention, that I have sent for you, if you will hear what I have got to say. I feel that you have a right of much obedience from me, and that it is very, very sad that there should be anything between us but kind and loving sympathy."

"Well, well," cried the merchant, as he paced to and fro in the apartment, "that is all very right and proper, of course—extremely right and proper. I am glad you are beginning to see your folly—very glad indeed. Refuse a coronet—refuse a coronet, and for what, too—an insignificant clerk, with seventy-five pounds a year, and its expectancies; upon my word, Grace, if anybody else had told me so much of you, I should have denied its truth, and declared that no daughter of mine could act with such absurdity. Only fancy being a countess—just fancy it—the very idea! A countess—bless my heart and life, a countess!"

As Mathew Trueman spoke, he gave his hands so loud a clap together in his exultation, that he made Grace start again, but she said in a firm but low voice—

"Father, you much mistake me; I call upon Heaven to witness my words! I will rather embrace death in its worst form any hour, than that hour should see me the wife of Lord Hawksworth!"

"What!" cried Mathew Trueman, stopping suddenly.

"I solemnly declare," continued Grace, "I never will be the wife of a man towards whom I can entertain no feelings but those of contempt and aversion."

"You will not marry?" roared Mathew Trueman.

"I will not," said Grace.

"Then why—why—what the devil did you say you would for?"

"You mistook me, father."

"Mistook you? Why, d——n it, you sent for me here, and begin talking of peace and duty—pleasure, and obedience, and all that sort of thing, merely to wind up with being as obstinate, undutiful, and as unpleasant as before, d——n it!"

"I have something to propose," said Grace. "You were angry at my meeting Mr. Rivers yesterday, and in that anger you have discharged him from your employment."

"Wonderful feats, truly," cried the merchant, in a sarcastic tone. "I suppose I oughtn't to be put out of my way a bit by an infernal penniless adventurer meeting my daughter, and talking love nonsense to her, in spite of me. Oh! dear me, I ought to have taken it as a thing of course, quite cool and comfortable. Ah! a miserable wretch, with seventy pounds a-year."

"Is a man a wretch, father, because he has but seventy pounds a-year?" said Grace, softly. "There was a time, you remember, when you had but three-and-a-penny."

"Remember!—of course I remember. D——n it, do I ever forget it? But I can't, for the life of me, see what that has to do with the question. Of course I began with three-and-a-penny, everybody knows that, and I've made a large fortune, and can lend money to lords and dukes, and all those kind of things. When that d—d puppy of yours has done as much, I'll say something to him. Ah !"

"The proposal I have to make," said Grace, calmly, "is this—that if you will no longer persecute me with Lord Hawksworth's addresses, nor suffer him to enter this house, at the same time restoring to their situations Mr. Rivers and Tom Hackey, I will solemnly promise never to marry without your consent."

"Vastly polite and civil, upon my soul," said the merchant ; "you surely can't mean to make such frighful sacrifices ?"

"My meaning," said Grace, "is plain, and precisely what I state it to be. I am not much used to deceiving any one, and least of all would I you."

The merchant stopped abruptly in his hurried walk, and said—

"Now, hear me, Grace ; neither that young fellow, Rivers, nor that mad errand-boy of mine, shall ever cross my threshold again, without being given in charge to a constable ; and if you don't marry Lord Hawksworth, I will immure you for ever in some distant part of the country, where at the same time you will be out of the way of your young spark, you will no longer insult me by your presence, and put me perpetually in mind of you disobedience."

"Enough—enough, father," said Grace.

"Oh, that's enough, is it ?" cried the merchant, in a great passion. "Now, once for all, Grace, don't be a fool. Why, good God, girl, do you know what a countess is—a countess is a kind of a sort of a—a—that's what a countess is."

"My resolution," said Grace, "is irrevocable, and I shudder as I feel that there is even a limit of obedience of a child to its parent."

"Look here, Grace," said Mathew Trueman ; "I will give you four-and-twenty hours to consider of it. Consent within that time to receive his addresses, or you leave London for Wales, where you will remain till you come to your senses."

Grace leaned her head upon her hands with a deep sigh, and the mer-chant, after one glance at her, left the room.

CHAPTER LXXI.

THE LETTER TO HAWKSWORTH.—THE MISUNDERSTANDING.—THE CUNNING OF MR. GIRKINS. — THE PLOT THICKENS.

THUS was Grace's first attempt to alleviate the circumstances in which she was placed frustrated by him who should have been first and foremost in prevent-ing the slightest cloud of care from hanging upon the brow of his beautiful child ; but the demon Ambition had taken full possession of the heart of Mathew Trueman, and he retired to his own office with as angry a feeling on his mind as if he were really the ill-used party himself, and poor Grace was treat-ing him very badly.

"Who would have a daughter?" he cried, as he fumed to and fro ; "really, children are quite a curse instead of a blessing ; they never do exactly what you want them. Upon my soul, I could not have believed Grace would have been so desperately obstinate ; but so it is, that's always the way after you have spent a world and all on the education of a son or a daughter, they are the first to turn round and fly in your face."

Mathew Trueman was like many parents. He altogether forgot that his child was a human being like himself, and subject to the same feelings that actuate human nature as he was, but he expected from her resignation, patience, self-sacrificing humility, &c., which he possessed not himself, and which his maturer years had not given, but which he was in a great rage not to find in the youthful breast of his daughter.

In the meanwhile, poor Grace re-mained almost stupified by the sad aspect of affairs. She had fancied that the voice of nature would have pleaded loudly for her, and that her father could not have resisted the appeal she had made to him.

But now she was mistaken—that de-lusion had fled, and she was left to what other resources remained to her afflicted mind.

"Shall I consent to become the wife of Rivers ?" she asked herself ; "shall

I abide a precipitate acceptance of his generous offer, entail upon him an additional burden, which, I am certain, his resources will not enable him to meet? And yet, what would become of me here, exposed to the most frightful of persecutions—no pity, no consideration from him who should be most pitiful and most considerate towards me? What—oh, what will become of me? And what, too, will become of him who has already lost his means of subsistence,

through loving me? Alas! alas! I am very unhappy."

It was a relief to Grace's heart to weep, which she did freely, but as the tears flowed, she felt her spirits revive, and a better hope of the future began to illumine her heart. "Surely," she said, "I have some talent—some accomplishment which, although in happier days was only expected to adorn a leisure hour, may now be turned to more important advantages? There must

surely be employment in this great city for those who are willing to apply themselves assiduously to obtain it. I am acquainted with music and I can draw, those are accomplishments taught to me at a high cost, and why should not I acquire something by again teaching them to others? Then, far from being a hindrance and an oppression to Rivers, I might even be so fortunate as to be an assistance to him."

This delusive thought, and most

delusive it was, presented itself in radiant colours to Grace, and how many a young and gentle heart full of high and noble resolutions has foundered upon the same rock, madly supposing, that in such a place as London, amid the war of conflicting interests, a war more fierce than was ever waged by man against man with the deadliest weapons: a struggle more desperate than was ever entered into by the savagest nations — she dreamt that amidst that war, amidst that unholy struggle, she, armed with but gentleness and patience, would be able to maintain her way.

Alas! poor Grace, little she knew what she proposed to her mind to undertake; little she guessed at the heartlessness she should encounter; little of the villany that would place itself in her way in her struggles for maintenance, and prevent her obtaining that which she sought, but likewise hinder her as much as possible, and deprive her of the enjoyment of that which she had obtained.

But Grace was young and full of hope, and full of ignorance of the world, and its sad ways, so the more she thought over the practicability of assisting Rivers by consenting to a union with him, the more she clung to the idea, and then it brought with it a hope that when her marriage had really taken place, her father, in the necessity of giving up all hope of bending her to his wishes, might relent and accord to her that forgiveness which he would never do while there was a chance that she might be pressed into a compliance with his views; but still she could not wholly resolve upon that course of conduct which should imply immediate acceptance of the offer of Rivers, while she told herself that it was to free herself from an unjust persecution only that she would consent, despite her father's wishes, to become a wife; she likewise felt that every effort should be made to prevent the necessity of leaving her father's home in an unkindly spirit with him.

Then arose one other alternative in Grace's mind, which, hopeless as it seemed, and presenting the most uncomfortable features, she thought herself bound to try; that was an appeal to no other than Lord Hawksworth himself, to ask him if, in the face of her open and avowed disinclination to a union with him, he could so far condescend from his rank and dignity as not to press his offers. Little did poor Grace know what other and more cogent reasons Lord Hawksworth had for amusing the merchant's mind by affecting a desire to make her, Grace, his wife, or she would not have ventured upon the appeal she told herself could surely not be made

in vain, but which would as surely be made in vain as that he, Lord Hawksworth, was a disgrace to the nobility which adorned his name.

Grace, upon this, sought her nurse, and said to her—

"Mrs. Woodfall, my father has rejected my prayer, but still, even yet, before I answer Rivers, I would make one effort not at once to leave my happy home at variance with my only parent."

"What would you do, dear Grace?" said Mrs. Woodfall. "What is there you can do? Your father seems to have got this marriage with Lord Hawksworth firmly in his head, and he will listen to no reason."

"I fear not," said Grace, "unless—"

"Unless what, my dear?"

"Unless Lord Hawksworth himself, from a hopelessness of his cause, abandons the undertaking."

"But how will you get him to do that? Your beauty and your father's wealth, my dear, have together taken too firm a hold of his imagination for him to relinquish the one or the other; more especially as he knows well they must go together."

"Surely, surely," said Grace. "he cannot be dead to all pride, all feeling; some of the ancient nobility that may yet linger in his composition will rise up to forbid him pursuing a heart that despises him? I am determined to leave no room for ambiguity. I will tell him not only that I cannot love him, but that my feelings partake of a negative character as regards him; he has forced me to it, and if I do solicit and obtain an interview with him, it would be to tell him of my dislike."

"My dear," said Mrs. Woodfall, "if you have taken the notion in your head of seeing Lord Hawksworth, and throwing yourself on his pride and his generosity to cease his persecution of you, Heaven forbid that I should endeavour to dissuade you from such a course; if you leave home as the wife of Mr. Rivers without your father's consent, it would please you to reflect, that previously to so doing, you made every sacrifice short of renunciation of all hope of happiness in order to remain."

"You are right, nurse," said Grace. "Let me not have to say, in after years, that anything which could have been done was not done. Repulsive as this man is to me, and loathsome as will be an interview with him, I will still go through it—in four-and-twenty hours my father will come to me again for an answer, which must of course be a repetition of that which he has already, but if, at the same time I gave him such renewed refusal, I cou d tell him myself that Lord Hawksworth had relinquished his pursuit, I could be comparatively happy."

"But how will you see him, my dear?" said Mrs. Woodfall.

"I will write to him," said Grace, "stating my desire to do so, and asking him to come here during the day, when he need not see my father unless he pleases; for a simple inquiry for me, if you previously impress the servants with the fact that a gentleman will call to see me, will prevent any disagreeable encounter that might otherwise take place."

"Then, my dear," said Mrs. Woodfall, "if you write a note I will myself endeavour to get it delivered to Lord Hawksworth, although without the most distant hope of it proving effective in the way you wish."

Grace wrote the note, which ran as follows, being as brief as it could possibly be to express the meaning—

"Grace Trueman wishes to see Lord Hawksworth to-day, any hour after one o'clock, when Grace Trueman will be at home and disengaged."

The letter was sealed and directed to his lordship, and in the course of half an hour Mrs. Woodfall was proceeding with it to the hotel, where Lord Hawksworth she had heard was commonly to be found.

Fortunately his lordship was within, and giving the note to a waiter, who received it with a wink that poor Mrs. Woodfall didn't at all understand, she requested that it might be immediately delivered.

When she was gone, the note was handed round among the waiters, who having duly examined the handwriting, and indulged themselves in various conjectures concerning it, came at last to the unanimous conclusion that it was what they called a billydoo, i. e. a love letter, which the old 'un, meaning Mrs. Woodfall, had brought for some young 'un.

How shocked would have been poor Grace had she known of the construction put on her innocent note; but innocence is its own safeguard, and in its ignorance of evil, it many times escapes the consequences of evil actions.

Lord Hawksworth's surprise at the reception of the missive was intense, and with a jump from his seat, he cried—

"D—n it, she is caught at last. I suppose she wants to ask me whether I really mean to marry her according to the orthodox fashion among tradesmen and other low persons, putting up the beastly banns in a parish church. Well, I must amuse the little creature's mind; she is certainly pretty, nay, positively lovely, but as for marrying—ha! ha! The daughters of these city gentry ought to think themselves sufficiently honoured and distinguished, by being now and then, when nature in a freak has made them handsome, made noblemen's mistresses."

Lord Hawksworth then, with a self-satisfied air and a smirking expression of countenance, walked to and fro in the splendid apartment of the hotel, for the occupation of which it was exceedingly doubtful if he ever paid; then he spoke aloud the result of his deliberations.

"Let me see," he said; "the old fool will lend me his money to a handsome tune, and I shall make his daughter my mistress for at least two seasons —on my soul she deserves two seasons; I shall offer her a barouche and four, a town house and a little villa on the banks of the Thames, with a gilt barge and six rowers in livery. D——e, I think that ought to do. I don't mind being a little extravagant, especially as it ain't my own money. I shall be of age before I am tired of her, and then she may go back to the paternal pigstye in the odious city, and amuse the leisure of the old fool, who began life with three-and-a-penny, by an account of her magnificence as the earl's mistress. I suppose we shall have some vapouring and crying to-day; some girls look well in tears, others swell about the face, and look as if they were recovering from a beastly state of intoxication."

A time-piece on the mantel-shelf now announced the hour of twelve, and Hawksworth, with a start, exclaimed—

"Bless my soul, twelve o'clock; by the time I have made an elaborate toilet, and Charles has brought round my cab, it will be time to visit the dear delightful city beauty. Ah, well, who can help being attractive and all that kind of thing? It's a penalty we handsome fellows pay, that all the pretty women fall into our arms, and even when we least expect it, there comes——"

"Mr. Girkins, my lord," said a waiter.

"D—n him!" said Lord Hawksworth.

"Certainly, my lord."

"Yet stay—curse the fellow, show him up."

"May I hope your lordship's in a state of perfect convalescence?" said Mr. Girkins, entering the room, and taking no notice whatever of his consignment to the infernal regions.

"Ah, very well—very well," said Hawksworth. "By-the-by, Girkins, the merchant's daughter has, after all, surrendered at discretion."

"Grace Trueman?" exclaimed Girkins.

"Yes—why, you seem perfectly astonished."

"I am, rather," said Girkins.

"Are you, indeed? Use accustoms one to these little affairs. I fully expected such a result. She has written to me as a thing of course, and the little opposition she has offered, has added a piquancy to the pursuit. Flowers that are easily plucked, are not worth the plucking, and if the golden fruit of the Hesperides grew on every bush, it would be neglected by a beggar."

"She has written to you?" said Girkins.

"Of course, and here is the note."

Girkins read it, and then said—

"Short, but to the purpose, certainly. I am much surprised, but of course this will expedite matters with Mathew Trueman. You will make the visit, I presume, my lord?"

"It would be positively barbarous not to do so."

"Then," said Girkins, "will you authorize me to make any appointment with Mathew Trueman to-morrow morning at twelve o'clock, in order to complete the money part of the transaction?"

"Authorize!" said Lord Hawksworth; "d—n it, I wish it was to-day at twelve o'clock."

"So do I, and have to wish your lordship a very good morning," said Girkins.

"Ah, be off," was the uncourteous reply. "I've got to dress before I go to the city, and little time to do it in."

When Girkins gained the street, he walked very slowly, and was for a time in a state of complete abstraction from deep thought, then he muttered to himself—

"Written to him, has she? Written to him, and he translates the letter in the manner most agreeable to his vanity. I beg to differ from his most sapient lordship. That letter is for some other purpose, and was written by some far other motive by Grace Trueman, than to throw herself in the arms of such a man as Hawksworth. Contempt and hatred are not passions that easily turn to love and admiration; but still this letter may be of as great importance to the furtherance of my schemes, as if it really meant all that his silly lordship imagines it to be. It shall speak volumes to the mind of Mathew Trueman. It shall open his purse-strings, and I look upon it as the most favourable circumstance for the advancement of this business of discounting the bill, as could well be imagined. Lord Hawksworth has but to keep his counsel, be the result of the interview what it may, and Mathew Trueman shall fall into a snare he little suspects."

So saying, the politic Mr. Girkins hastened to the city, whither he calculated upon arriving long before Lord Hawksworth had finished his toilet, for he knew that upon such occasions his lordship was inclined to the elaborate in point of costume, and liked to present a glittering appearance, like some brigand who has newly plundered a jeweller.

CHAPTER LXXII.

MR. GIRKIN'S POLICY.—THE VANITY OF
THE MERCHANT.—THE ASSOCIATES
IN CRIME.—THE CARD CASE.

WHEN Mr. Girkins reached the city,
he thought himself exceedingly fortunate
in finding the merchant at home,
although a glance sufficed to show him
that Mathew Trueman was not in the
most amicable of humours, in fact, too
short a time had elapsed since the merchant's interview with his daughter for
him at all to recover the equilibrium of
his temper, and it was with rather a
snappish and uncomfortable manner,
that he received the humble salutations
of Mr. Girkins.

"Oh, I am very well," he cried,
"infernally well, and not at all vexed,
and put out of my way, of course, nor
opposed, nor half bullied—oh, dear, no.
A man who has a daughter, must of
course be free from all those annoyances—d—n it, who is it says that he
had rather be bit by a snake than have
an ungrateful child? King John, I
think."

Mr. Girkins humbly suggested it was
a generally received opinion that King
Lear uttered a somewhat similar opinion,
adding, however, he had no doubt that
King John said something of the same
kind.

"Ah!" said the merchant, "if he
had a daughter, he would be sure to say
it. I say it, who am nothing at all but
merely plain Mathew Trueman, a
British merchant, who began life with
three-and-a-penny, and now he is pestered
by lords, dukes, earls, and marquises, to
lend them money."

"Ah!" said Girkins, "there are very
few kings, indeed, that come near you,
Mr. Trueman; you may say that you
manufactured your own sceptre, and
stuffed and wadded your own throne."

"Ah," said the merchant, "there's
something in that. I had it all to put
up myself; but man's born to trouble,
as somebody says, just as the sparks fly
up a chimney. Now, there's Grace,
my only daughter Grace, d—n it, she
won't be a countess."

"He! he! he!" said Mr. Girkins.

"Curse you," said Mathew Trueman

taking hold of the poker, "do you
laugh?"

"My dear sir," said Girkins, "if
you'll permit me to use that familiar
phrase, I beg, with the greatest deference and submission, humbly to presume to differ in opinion with you. I
think your accomplished and lovely
daughter, who is the very image of
yourself, will be a countess, and that
your baronetcy is not far off. I think I
see you, Mr. Trueman, standing by his
Majesty's right hand at the next levee.
I think I see in the dim obscurity of
things to come you in the House of
Commons, pushing the helm of state
this way, and that way, and all sorts of
ways, until the House of Lords get
abominably jealous, and you are made
one of that illustrious assembly; then, I
think, I can see, by looking as far as I
can into the dim obscurity, a change in
the ministry; and by looking a little
further, I see you guiding the state
machine, as premier of this great
country, dispensing favours and magnificence on all around, until—excuse
the pun—the sovereign would never
want change."

"D—n it," said Mathew Trueman,
"you are like the long-sighted youth
who was exhibited a little while ago,
that could see round the corner of the
next street, and look down the people's
chimneys while he was at his own fireside."

"Ah! Mr. Trueman," said Girkins,
"felicitous as your similitude to me of
the long-sighted youth is, and told as it
was in your usual happy manner, I still
must retain my humble opinion, sir. I
may give offence—great offence, sir;
I hope I do not, but I must repeat, that
I fully believe that your daughter Grace
will be a countess, and yourself a
baronet."

"The devil you do," said Trueman.

"I do."

"Why, it was but a few hours ago
that Grace told me flatly she never would
have him, and quite abused me for
making the very offer; as good as telling me, in a round about way, to go
and be d—d."

"Ah! woman—woman—woman!"
said Girkins.

"What woman?" cried Trueman.

"I speak of the sex generally, Mr.

Trueman; wayward, wayward woman. Twisting, twirling here and there and everywhere, like a weather-cock fresh oiled. Saying no, when they mean yes; yes, when they mean no; nothing, when they mean something; and something, when they mean nothing at all."

"D—e," said Mathew Trueman, "if any woman was to serve me so I'd kick her out of doors."

"Woman," continued Mr. Girkins, "is a will-o'-the-whisp—a shadow, a everything, a nothing—but most of all are they incomprehensible as regards their affections."

"D—e, they are incomprehensible altogether."

"One hour," continued Girkins, "a girl will abuse the best father that ever lived, and almost snap his nose off for proposing her a lover, while the next— ah! that such things should be."

"What things?"

"They write to the aforesaid lover, inviting him to tea."

"To tea!"

"Yes," said Girkins, dealing his left hand a great blow with his right, "Miss Grace Trueman, your lovely accomplished daughter, and the very image of yourself, has written with he own hand a note to Lord Hawksworth, asking him to come and see her this afternoon."

"The devil she has!" said Mathew Trueman, sinking into a chair as he spoke, in unaffected surprise.

"On my life she has."

"Do I dream? Can there indeed be such contradictions in human nature?"

"In female nature, yes."

"You don't mean to tell me," said Mathew Trueman, solemnly, "that Grace has written to Lord Hawksworth?"

"She has—I have seen the letter, and his lordship wishes particularly to have a meeting with you to-morrow morning at twelve o'clock, to arrange preliminaries; when, between you and me, Mr. Trueman, speaking as a disinterested friend of both parties, I should say the affair of the bills ought to be settled in order to prevent Lord Hawksworth going anywhere else to borrow money, with which to celebrate his marriage according to his rank. Some very noble personage must give away the bride, and a numerous assemblage of

the peerage will be present at the ceremony whenever it takes place. There will be an account of the ceremony in the *Times*, which, although of course wrong in all essential particulars, will direct attention to more correct reports in other papers."

"Gracious Heavens!" said the merchant.

"It's true, upon my soul," said Girkins. "I could almost stand upon my head with joy. I have done so repeatedly when a boy, and would now, but I fear apoplexy."

"I'll go to Grace at once," said Mathew Trueman, starting up.

"Mr. Trueman—Mr. Trueman," said Girkins, getting between him and the door; "where's your deep knowledge of human nature, and profound knowledge of things in general?"

"D—d if I know," said the merchant.

"Ah!" continued Girkins, "now I see. You say to yourself, with that rapidity of thought for which you are celebrated, I will let the interview take place between these two young persons, without interruption. I will even go out of the house, says you, in order that there be no obstruction to the beautiful interchange of thought, which must take place on such an occasion. I will leave, says you, the earl and his future countess to arrange their marriage between themselves."

"D—n it, so I will," said the merchant.

"I was quite sure," added Girkins, "that your acute intellect would bring you to that conclusion. Ah! there are few people, indeed, that match Mathew Trueman, the British merchant, in deep observation and sagacious intellect."

"Yes," said the merchant, "I'll go out. The best of all possible plans; and to-morrow, Mr. Girkins, if his lordship pleases to come here, and bring with him the bills, I will give him cheques, deducting the amount for discount, at once. I should deeply regret indeed for his lordship to be at all embarrassed at such a time as this. When do you think he is coming to-day?"

"I expect him here very shortly," said Girkins. "He was dressing when I left him at his hotel."

"God bless me," said the merchant, "I must be off as quick as possible. I wouldn't be an interruption to the interview on any account. Where's my hat?"

"Here," said Girkins, handing it to him. "Here is your hat, *Sir* Mathew Trueman."

"No—no—no—really now, Girkins, remember I am not the baronet yet, whatever, a-hem, I may be."

"It was a little slip of the tongue for the moment," said Girkins, "for which I humbly apologize; but I have so accustomed myself, Mr. Trueman, to think of you as a baronet, that almost unconsciously I have prefixed the Sir to your name. I hope you'll excuse me for being just a little premature."

"Oh, no offence—no offence," said the merchant. "None in the least, Girkins. But I must be off. Good morning—good morning."

They parted at the merchant's door, Girkins professing to be going the other way, and Mathew Trueman rapidly walked down Thames-street, until, to his great satisfaction, although agitated, he saw Lord Hawksworth's cab coming up the street.

Fearful then of being seen, and spoiling the intended interview, he ran into a grocer's shop and bought a pennyworth of Spanish liquorice, as an excuse for staying till Lord Hawksworth had passed.

It was far from Mr. Girkins' intention to leave the house so precipitately. He not only had Lord Hawksworth to see, which he resolved to do after his interview with Grace; but he wanted to say something to the ruffian Hilliard, who was alone in the office. Girkins was not satisfied with the success which now appeared to him tolerably certain he should have, in virtually robbing Mathew Trueman of twenty thousand pounds, but still he wished to have his dastardly revenge against poor Rivers, who, if he had committed no other crime against Girkins, had ever stood much in the way of the accomplishment of his schemes.

He found Hilliard just upon the point of departure, for the dinner hour was at hand.

Now Girkins was, even then, not aware of a the discharge of Rivers and Tom Hackey, for Mathew Trueman had felt repugnant to speak of the circumstances of that proceeding. He dreaded that it should get round to Lord Hawksworth's ears that Grace had been detected in a clandestine meeting with one of his clerks; such a circumstance would at once put an end to her prospects of the peerage, and the attainment of his own ambition; therefore was it that he had abstained from mentioning it even to Girkins; and not being, at the moment, able to find any other excuse for the discharge of Rivers, he had not mentioned it at all; in fact, towards the latter part of his interview, he quite forgot it in the multiplicity of new thoughts and feelings that filled his mind.

Moreover, as that discharge, and the causes which had given rise to it, happened to be only known to those parties from whom Hilliard was not at liberty to procure any information, consequently, although his surprise was great all the morning at the non-appearance of Rivers and Hackey, he had no means of accounting for it; and, when Girkins appeared, he was puzzling his brain with conjectures upon that very subject.

It was not to be supposed that Mr. Girkins wore that free-and-easy and composed air which he would have done had he been aware that he was alone, for he had a disagreeable reminiscence of his last interview with Rivers, when he thought it advisable to walk out of the office with unusual celerity, lest his progress should be accelerated by a kick; which, it will be recollected, Rivers had promised to administer to him, in case he preserved not a more respectful tone and demeanour towards Grace than he was then doing.

A glance through the oval piece of glass, let into the upper part of the door, sufficed to let him see that Hilliard *was* alone, and he entered therefore without further ceremony.

"So, Hilliard," he said, "how is it you have the office all to yourself thus early?"

"I don't know," said Hilliard, doggedly; "I have had it to myself all the morning."

"All the morning! Do you mean to say that Rivers has never appeared?"

"Never."

"And Mathew Trueman has not complained of his absence?"

"No."

"Then, Hilliard, you may depend he is discharged," cried Girkins.

"The devil he is—just at the moment, too, when I thought myself so secure in planning a robbery, and palming it off upon him. What's to be done now?"

"I rather think nothing," said Girkins; "if Rivers is discharged, that is sufficient."

"But what am I to do?" said Hilliard.

"Stick to your business, young man," said Girkins. "Industry insures succes, and competence is better than riches. Leave off your idle habits, and adopt frugal and industrious ones.

' Early to bed, and early to rise,
  Makes a man healthy, wealthy, and wise.' "

"Do you fancy—d—n you," said Hilliard, "that I am to be got rid of by a few musty proverbs?"

"I am sure of it, my dear fellow," said Girkins, coolly.

"Then I tell you what, Mr. Girkins—robbery or no robbery, I'll have my twenty pounds."

"How are you to get them?" said Girkins. "I am curious in matters of difficult investigation."

"I'll have you indicted for a conspiracy," said Hilliard, "and blow all your fine schemes about Lord Hawksworth to the winds, if you don't come down to a handsomer tune than that."

"I will have you hung at the debtor's door, at the Old Bailey," said Girkins. "Hung by the neck, in the midst of a hooting crowd, until you are dead—your body afterwards being delivered for dissection, according to law."

"For what?" gasped Hilliard, for he wished, once for all, to make certain how far the knowledge of Girkins extended.

"For the murder of Mr. Noble, in New Inn," said Girkins.

"I—I didn't do it—I didn't do it," said Hilliard.

"I saw you," whispered Girkins in his ear; "I saw you. Be careful and respectful, and I may let you die a natural death, instead of on the gallows. Good morning, Hilliard, good morning.

By-the-bye, it's not very likely Wilson will ever turn up again, is it?—eh, Hilliard? Good morning; keep up your spirits. Look to the ant, thou sluggard, and be wise, as Solomon, or somebody else says."

Hilliard dropped into the visitors' chair with a deep groan.

"Is] that man the devil?" he said. "Where did he get his information? He evidently knows all, and I am indeed in his power. But he will not betray me if I act not against him. Shall I, however, forego the robbery which presents so fair a chance of success, merely because I am not to get the twenty pounds from Girkins? No; my own necessities, as well as my feelings towards Rivers, urge me to its commission—it shall be done. Girkins dare not betray me, although he will not pay me for the deed; and, whether Rivers be discharged or not, I may find some means of implicating him. Ah! his desk, let me search it."

He approached the desk of Rivers, and, finding it open, he eagerly ransacked the contents; to his great joy, he found two or three envelopes of letters, addressed to him, Rivers, as well as a card-case, in which were several cards with his name.

"The card-case will suffice," muttered Hilliard; "it matters not to me if a jury refuse to convict upon it. It will be sufficient to send him to trial, and that will blast his character for ever; besides, Mathew Trueman will always consider him the guilty party, and never for a moment suspect me. If, likewise, he be discharged, the fact of this robbery occurring immediately after would speak much against him. Francis Rivers, you are a doomed man."

CHAPTER LXXIII.

THE INTERVIEW BETWEEN GRACE AND LORD HAWKSWORTH.—THE REPULSE. THE TIGER'S DILEMMA.—A VISION.

THE merchant's skilful manœuvre with the Spanish liquorice fully succeeded, and Lord Hawksworth passed him without ever suspecting the proximity of the man who was so ambitious to become his father-in-law. He drove up in a dashing manner to the merchant's door, and ordering his tiger to ring the house bell, he desired the astonished girl, who appeared in answer to the summons, to take his card to Miss Grace.

This was done, and with a loathsome feeling, Grace saw the name of the man for whom she had sent, in order to make a last appeal to his pride, and ascertain if he had one spark of noble feeling in his whole composition.

"Show Lord Hawksworth up, Mary" said Grace, and then turning to Mrs. Woodfall, she added, "I will make the interview as brief as possible, for the very presence of that man is hateful to me; and after the insult I have received at his hands, no circumstances but the singular ones in which I am placed, would induce me to hold a moment's converse with him."

The message for him to walk up, was duly delivered to Lord Hawksworth who, after ordering his tiger not to

remain with the cab at the door, but keep driving slowly to and fro, with a smirking air, after a gratified glance at his jewelled hands, tripped up the staircase to the merchant's drawing-room, where was, as he thought, the victim of his many blandishments and elegant appearance.

It was a little, but a very little shock to Lord Hawksworth's feelings to find Grace not alone, but he thought to himself, all young girls are timid, and after the bold steps she has already taken

she may be excused for a little affected prudery.

His bow was of the most elegant and recently fashionable kind, and then with a smile, he said—

"Need I say—with what rapture—I received your delightful—little missive, my charmer; your condescension —puts me quite beside myself. I have driven down here quite delirious, and now—don't know how sufficiently to thank you for your—delightful prepossession in my favour."

No. 34.

"You may spare your apologies," said Grace, "for this most disagreeable intrusion. Stern necessity alone, and a wish to preserve those feelings which—"

"Exactly, exactly," said Hawksworth, "my charmer, I understand you completely—you mean to say we can't combat with our feelings, and if we do, love—delightful love—will gain the victory. One season out of this abode of barbarism would etherealize your ideas."

"Sir?" said Grace.

"A barouche with four gray ponies will, I hope, be irresistible, combined with one of those little damp holes they call villas on the banks of the Thames, and the pleasure yacht manned by rowers in fancy costumes. Speak again, my charmer, and let me listen to the music of the spheres."

"Without libelling my judgment," said Grace, "I must say, that I do not understand a word you say."

"Not understand me! I dare say this good old lady quite comprehends my meaning?"

"I have nothing to do with you, or your meaning either," said Mrs. Woodfall.

"If you'll allow me to speak, sir," said Grace, "I will explain to you why I sent for you here; but as I am determined to endure your presence no longer than necessary, if you continue to interrupt me I shall give up my intention, and leave the room."

"I—I am all attention," said Lord Hawksworth, with a disagreeable impression arising in his mind that everything was not so pleasant as he thought.

"I sent for you," said Grace, "to give you a clear and distinct answer—one that would admit of no evasion or circumlocution, concerning the proposal which my father tells me you have thought proper to make for my hand."

"Oh!" said Hawksworth, "the—the proposal, oh!"

"In answer to that," said Grace, "I unhesitatingly reject you. Should not that be sufficient for one assuming the character of a gentleman, and priding himself upon nobility?"

"You are testing my affection, charmer," said Lord Hawksworth. "Ah! ah! there is nobody a better judge of women, wine, or horses, than myself."

"Will it not alarm your pride," said Grace, "to tell you that I despise you, that I hold you in the greatest contempt? Can you continue to amuse a father's ear with your address after receiving such an opinion from a daughter?"

Hawksworth was silent for a moment, during which his colour came and went several times. Then he said—

"You are jesting, Miss Trueman."

"I am serious; I swear by Heaven!" said Grace.

"D——n!" said Lord Hawksworth.

"If you swear here," said Mrs. Woodfall, "I'll send for the footman to turn you out."

"Grace Trueman," said Lord Hawksworth, forgetting for the moment all prudential considerations, "have you the cursed vanity to suppose that I ever intended to marry you?"

Before these words had well ceased sounding in the apartment Grace had left it, and Mrs. Woodfall stayed but to say—

"Sir, you are a disgrace to manhood, and merit the unmitigated contempt of every one."

In a moment then Lord Hawksworth was alone, looking the picture of baffled passion and mortified vanity. What to do he knew not, but his rage was so great that he had not sense to leave the house quietly, as he might have done, and he chose to proclaim his anger and mortification by ringing such a peal upon the bells, that every domestic in the house with one accord rushed up into the drawing-room in the greatest alarm, fancying that some dreadful catastrophe must have occurred.

They burst in in a body, and there, to their surprise, they saw nothing but Lord Hawksworth stand stamping in the middle of the floor upon his own hat.

"What's the matter?" cried half-a-dozen voices.

"Curse you all, get out of my way!" was the reply, and he made a rush from the room, descending the stairs at a hard gallop, cursing and swearing all the way like a maniac. To reach the street was the work of an instant, and then, being without his hat, it became extremely desirable that he should be as speedily as possible ensconced in his cab; but alas! the fates were malignant, and no cab was to be seen, for the tiger had trotted the horse down nearly as far as Cannon-street, and, on attempting to get back, had got fairly blocked in by two coal waggons, a brewer's dray, and a tolerable sprinkling of other vehicles, the drivers of which had got up a sort of ancient concert, and were swearing dreadfully.

In this dilemma his lordship was compelled in the first instance to purchase a hat, which he did at the first hatter's he came to, for the idea of going back to the merchant's for his crushed beaver was too dreadful to entertain for a moment.

That done, he walked in the direction where he saw there was a stoppage of vehicles, for he guessed rightly enough that there he should find his own conveyance.

Now, the effects of precipitancy were fully developed in the conduct of Lord Hawksworth's tiger, for the moment he saw his master he gave the horse an extremely knowing touch on the flank, and endeavoured to make a bolt between two coal waggons, and finding then that that wouldn't do by any means, he drew up so suddenly that the horse stood upon his hind feet for a few moments, and finally backed with such frightful energy, that the pole of a stage coach behind protruded through the cab, dealing the tiger such a whack on the side of the head that he immediately seemed desirous of becoming a postilion, for he lay sprawling on the back of the horse.

His lordship swore, the tiger screamed, and the unmannerly populace laughed, while his lordship was not a little surprised to see from the interior of the cab two other hands besides those of his tiger grasping the reins, while a voice screamed out, "Murder!—police police!"

"Vell," cried the driver of the coach behind, "yer backed against me, spooney. You can't say I drove my pole into yer."

At this moment the stoppage higher up Thames-street ceased, and a general movement of the vehicles in front succeeded; the tiger had contrived to scramble back, and Lord Hawksworth furiously ascended the steps of his cab, where he saw Girkins pale and terrified in the interior.

"D———n! how came you here?" said Hawksworth.

"That's just what I've been asking," said Girkins, pointing to the pole, which at that moment disappeared by the coachman behind backing a little, at the same time expressing a fervent hope that they had had enough of it, and a full belief that they wouldn't back agin him another day, as his pole wouldn't stand no nonsense whatsomdever.

"You—you, I mean," said Hawksworth. "D———e, Girkins, how came you here?"

As he spoke, he threw himself into the vehicle and seized the reins, while the tiger made a wild sort of rush and got up behind.

"Here's a blessed wentilator to our new cab," he muttered. "Well, there's one thing, I can hear all that is said inside through this here hole. What a blessed shame, and we have only had this here blessed cab a week. To be sure, we never meant to pay for it; we only patronize that ere man in Long Acre; but how was the willin with the long pole to know that? Mum's the word; they are beginning to talk."

"Your lordship," said Girkins, "will, I am sure, excuse my presence here, when I tell you I have something of the greatest importance to communicate to you."

"Oh, d——n it," said Hawksworth, "you always have."

"May I humbly inquire which way your lordship is going?"

"To the devil!" said Hawksworth.

"He's getting wicious," muttered the tiger. "He'll be coming it neck or nothing, presently. When he's wicious he puts the wheel in the kennel, and bowls along, trusting to the dispensations of a gratified providence."

"Exactly," said Girkins; "but there are so many different roads—however, to waive the subject, my lord, and to speak of a more transitory state, I have to inform you, as an excuse for getting into your cab, that the rich merchant will, to-morrow at twelve o'clock. advance your lordship twenty thousand pounds upon your lordship's bills."

"The devil he will !" said Hawksworth.

"The devil he will !" said the tiger.

"Curse you, you villain," said his lordship, giving that gentleman's legs rather a savage cut with the whip, "if I hear you speak again I'll drop you."

"There's wice," muttered the tiger; "twenty thousand pounds. Ah! my eye, we'll come it rather on the strength of that ere."

"Yes, I have his own promise," said Girkins. "At twelve o'clock to-morrow the money will be forthcoming."

"You surprise me. What has induced him to come to so sudden a determination ?"

"The prospect of your speedy union with his daughter."

"The prospect, be d—d," said Lord Hawksworth, "The twenty thousand is all moonshine, curse you, if it depends upon that. I have just come away from there, and it's a wonder I escaped with my ears. I left my hat behind me."

"Indeed !" said Girkins.

"Ay, indeed; she is a she-devil."

"Then," said Girkins, with a short, dry cough, "I may be permitted humbly to presume that your lordship's reception was not commensurate with your lordship's expectations."

"Rather the contrary," said Hawksworth, hurriedly. "Billingsgate, I believe, lies in some portion of the world near here, and Grace has been taking a lesson from that proverbially loquacious locality. In a word, she sent for me to abuse me."

"I am all surprise," said Girkins, with another little cough. "It was but a short time since that, meeting Mathew Trueman, I, in my great zeal to do you a service—that zeal which circulates through my whole blood ——"

"Stuff," said Hawksworth.

"In the excess of that zeal," continued Girkins, "I told Mathew Trueman that his daughter had written to you requesting an interview."

"You did ?"

"I did."

"Confound your impertinence, then."

"Ahem," said Girkins; "flushed then with a hope that he would speedily be father-in-law to an earl, he promised, lest your lordship should be embarrassed in making preparations for your lordship's nuptials, to advance the twenty thousand pounds."

Lord Hawksworth immediately put the wheel in the kennel, as the tiger had predicted, and drove at a furious rate for about a mile. Then he turned to Girkins, and said, in a tone of suppressed bitterness—

"It's all up—there'll be no money. An infernal wet blanket has been thrown on the whole affair."

"Gracious powers !" muttered the tiger, his very nose curling up with horror, as he held convulsively by the straps. "Gracious powers ! what a wision of my wages, and arter all to be flummoxed."

———

CHAPTER LXXIV.

THE MORNING.—THE ACCEPTANCE.— THE NOTE TO RIVERS.—TOM HACKEY'S EXULTATION.

"A WET blanket, my lord ?" said Girkins.

"Yes; she sent for me expressly to say, and that in not the most pleasant manner imaginable, that nothing should ever induce her to consent to the match, and then I got angry, and told her I never meant to marry her, so I suppose there's an end to the whole affair."

"I don't know that," said Girkins, slowly.

"Then you are a fool, for I just told you."

"With humble deference to your lordship, I don't know that either. There may or may not be an extremely confidential communication between Grace Trueman and her father before to-morrow at twelve o'clock. I think there will not."

"Well," said Hawksworth; "what then ?"

"Why, then Mathew Trueman, still prepossessed with his notion respecting the marriage, will keep his word."

Hawksworth was silent for a few moments, and then he said,

"What then ?"

"Why, then your lordship walks off, I beg your pardon, drives off with twenty thousand pounds."

"But he will discover his mistake," said Hawksworth, in a whisper.

"There is an old proverb," replied

Girkins, in the same whisper, "which treats of the extreme difficulty of getting butter from a dog's throat. Your lordship understands me?"

"Curse you!" said Hawksworth.

"I am your lordship's humble servant."

"Do you really think, then," said Hawksworth, after a pause, "that there is a chance of getting this money to-morrow?"

"I am sure of it."

"I breathes agin," muttered the tiger, "as the ooman said, when they let her out of the sack."

"But," added Hawksworth, "there is one difficulty. What shall I say if he questions me about the result of the interview?"

"Say that you could not persuade Grace to fix the day for the marriage ceremony."

"D——n it, that's true enough. At twelve to-morrow, you say? Why should I hesitate? This very merchant, himself, has got all his money by trickery. It's diamond cut diamond; eh, Girkins?"

"Precisely; only your lordship is so much the keener jewel."

"By Heaven," said Hawksworth, "it will be a revenge on this girl to turn her own weapons so completely against her, and make her, will she or will she not, subservient to one's purposes. I am confident she would not have me, if I could lay my coronet at her feet; and should the merchant ride rusty about his money, why I can always offer to marry his daughter; and then I am a minor, so that the bills really are of no use."

"And as for honour," said Girkins, "what is that? pooh—leave that to meaner spirits who have their way to push in society; your lordship's rank will always stamp you as current gold among the *elite*. The cream of the cream, among whom alone your lordship wishes to shine. It was well and wittily said by George Villiers, the favourite of Charles the Second, that a diamond shone quite as bright, whether it was begged, borrowed, or stolen; so, my lord, your twenty thousand pounds would shed as great a lustre around you and your actions, as if they had come from the family bankers."

"I will meet you then at twelve to-morrow," said Hawksworth, "at the merchant's house, and if he will discount the bills, let him. I don't see why I should stand in my own light."

"Certainly not, my lord. You may depend on my punctuality; I will now wish your lordship a very good morning, trusting that your lordship is now convinced that this day's work is not so bad a one as your lordship at first supposed."

"The issue has to be seen," said Hawksworth, as he drew up to allow Girkins to get out of the cab. "I shall give you great credit, Girkins, after twelve o'clock to-morrow, probably."

"Contemptible wretch," muttered Girkins, when he was alone. "You may give me credit, if you please, but I will give you none. You shall be the tool by which I carve my way to my own fortune. And of this affair, it shall go hard, indeed, if I pick not a decent competency; but now to Barnard's Inn —the bills must be prepared instantly. Thank Heaven that Grace Trueman and her father are not upon such terms as to make it likely that they will exchange any conversation concerning Lord Hawksworth—we are quite safe—quite. The money will be forthcoming, and what then can Mathew Trueman do? His securities are the bills of a minor, and the word of honour of a lord. Ah! ah! ah! how easily and exquisitely well may thorough men of business be taken in when their passions blind them. Where now is all the tact, all the caution, and all the energy which has accumulated a large fortune as he himself boasts from three-and-a-penny? This twenty thousand pounds will not shake Mathew Trueman's pecuniary resources, but its loss will go nigh to break his heart, for he is wedded to that wealth which he has spent the better part of his life in acquiring. * * *

Grace Trueman had now tried everything; she had appealed to her father in every way, she had appealed to the man who might at once put an end to the persecutions to which she was subjected by withdrawing his suit. All—all had failed, she had met with insult and reproach. Was it to be wondered at then that she should turn with all the freshness of invigorated feeling to the pure noble heart of Francis Rivers, which breathed nothing but generous impulses, and seemed made up of that true nobility, which was wanted by the dissolute and abandoned man with whom she so recently had so disagreeable an interview?

The struggle now between principle and feeling was not of long duration, or rather they combined to direct her in one course; that course was to consent to a union with him whom her heart acknowledged as the only being that would make to her the world a place of pleasant sojourn.

It was the early morning, however, before she communicated her resolution to her affectionate nurse; then she placed a small note in Mrs. Wooodfall's hands, saying—

"Do not blame me. Do not call me rash. Poverty—ay, even want with him I love, is better than the heart's anguish I am enduring. I have consented to become the wife of Rivers."

"Heaven forbid, my dear," said Mrs. Woodfall, "that I should blame you; I will hope that it is all for the best. I will hope that your union may be a blessed one. I will not attempt to dissuade you from it, for I know that both of you will be wretched apart, when you cannot, surely, be so wretched together."

"That is true, nurse," said Grace. "Give him that note, and let him make what arrangements he will, I am his, and his only."

Mrs. Woodfall pressed the hand of Grace in silence, and then hastily arranging herself for her walk to meet Rivers, she slipped down the staircase, and left the merchant's house.

During her absence, Grace, who knew not how soon she should leave that roof, beneath which she had experienced so much joy, and suffered to much unhappiness, collected together the few little articles she could really call her own, and placed them in a small box, which she carefully locked, putting the key in her bosom. This done, she sat herself down, and gave herself up to thought—thought of a chequered character, that little is it to be wondered at that the painful predominated over the pleasurable, for poor Grace stood, as it were, upon the threshold of a new existence The past was full of many conflicting interests and emotions; the future was a blank, which might be filled up with joys or sorrows, which time alone could disclose.

Her father made no effort to see her—they met not at the morning meal, and now that her nurse was out of the house, poor Grace felt lonely and dejected, indeed, for there was not one kindred spirit with whom she could exchange a word.

In the meantime Mrs. Woodfall pursued her way towards the place of meeting with Rivers, which she reached before the hour appointed, but not before his impatience had brought him there, for he had been waiting some time, as also had been Tom Hackey, who, at the urgent remonstrances of Rivers, had consented to behave himself something like a rational being, and not at that early hour collect a crowd around them, which at first he showed a great inclination to do.

Rivers could not gather much from the appearance of Mrs. Woodfall's face, but he thought, if he read anything in it, it was a rejection of his suit.

His impatience would scarcely permit him to speak, and when Mrs. Woodfall, without a word, handed him the note, the superscription of which he at once recognised as being in the handwriting of Grace, his agitation was so great that he could scarcely open it.

When, however, he did so, it was easily read, for it contained but the following words—

"DEAR RIVERS,—I am yours—
               "GRACE TRUEMAN."

"Mine—mine—mine," he cried, as his face glowed with transport. "Tom Hackey, she's mine—she's mine!"

"Hang out the banners," cried Tom. "Let the trumpets bray loud salutation to the morn! Ah! ah! ah!"

"Police—police!" cried an old gentleman, in a spencer, rushing over the road, to the great danger of being run over.

"Tom, Tom, moderate your transports," said Rivers; "my heart seems too big for me, and I scarce know where I am."

"That's moderate," said Tom; "but didn't you say she was ours just now?"

"Mine, Tom, I said she was."

"Oh, well, that's all the same—ours, of course. She's ours—she's ours. 'They are fleet steeds that follow,' said young Lochinvar.' We have tossed with fate, and won it."

"I'll toss you," said a boy, "all your buttons agin mine."

"Come—come—Tom—come," said Rivers, taking his arm. "Mrs. Woodfall, let us go into the Temple—we then can consult at leisure."

The singularly matched trio proceeded into the Temple, where, pacing to and fro in one of its quiet walks, they entered into serious conversation, occasionally broken in upon by Tom Hackey's wild dramatic snatches with regard to the future.

"Listen to me, Mr. Rivers," said Mrs. Woodfall. "I have not opposed Grace's consent to become your wife, for I believe you love her truly, but still we must not altogether lose sight of prudence."

"Certainly not," said Rivers, with a sigh; "of course it shall be my earnest endeavour to procure some employment as quickly as possible, and which I doubt not, although I shall find difficulties, I shall secure; I shall find out some of my father's old friends, and endeavour to make use of their interest."

"Stop a bit," said Tom Hackey; "I live in hopes of a situation—there's Bumbleton Swiggles—you know Bumbleton Swiggles?"

"I do recollect some extraordinary person rejoicing in that extraordinary name," said Rivers

"Well, Bumbleton Swiggles, you recollect you lent eighteenpence to him?"

"Yes, I do, but I have not the slightest recollection of his ever paying me."

"Bumbleton Swiggles pay! he's above it. He told me one day he never paid any little debts, 'Because,' says he, 'it looks like pride, and as if I scorned being under any obligation.' But, however, that's nothing to do with it; Bumbleton Swiggles is quite intimate with a gentleman who frequently nods to the deputy prompter at Covent Garden. There's an opening for me."

"Why, what do you expect to get by that, Tom?"

"Why, I expect at first to do a little of the junior tragedy, and so creep on by degrees."

"Well, Tom, I wish you every success, but if Grace and I are married, I shall not forget my promise, that you shall give away the bride."

"Nor I either," said Tom, "and if I do get a situation at the Garden, you may depend upon me pulling you in neck and heels."

"Thank you; and now Mrs. Woodfall, before suggesting anything from my own mind, let me hear what steps you advise should be taken under my and Grace's circumstances."

"Mr. Rivers," said Mrs. Woodfall, "I have told you that I have not opposed the marriage. I think there is a chance even of mollifying Mr. Trueman's feelings by such a course."

"You don't mean that, elderly female?" said Tom. "Why, you know old Mathew will pull his hair out by the roots."

"That he would be angry, very angry indeed, I can very well believe; but it still remains to be seen whether he can bear actually to part with his only child, and render his home utterly desolate. There are many persons who, while there still remains a chance of accomplishing their objects, will continue violent and obstinate regarding them, but when all chance is lost, and they have nothing to struggle for, they will give up quietly enough. It may be so with Grace's father; when he is actually aware that she is married to you, Mr. Rivers, he may take a different thought of the matter, and though it may take some time before he is cordial with Grace, she may not be so unhappy as she is at present from that circumstance; then I have a fervent hope that her union with you may not be an ill-advised step."

"I rejoice that that is your opinion," said Rivers; "and if the worst of our anticipations should ever be realised, surely with health and strength and a willing heart I shall be able to procure some employment, that with frugality and economy will keep us above the ordinary contingencies of life."

"I trust so," said Mrs. Woodfall. "What I advise, then, is, that you should be secretly married, and that then Grace should take an opportunity of informing her father of it, and soliciting his forgiveness and future countenance; should that be refused, she can then leave home, and trust perhaps to time to ameliorate his feelings towards her and you; an effect, I dare say, would ensue shortly, for in Grace's absence, he would soon find that all his domestic felicity had departed, and that he was striving for nothing; then again the worthlessness of Lord Hawksworth must sooner or later become apparent even to Mr. Trueman, bigoted as he is in favour of rank, so that taking everything into consideration, I do not think the prospect so bad a one as it might at first appear."

"You have given me new hope, new life," said Rivers; "I never can sufficiently thank you, Mrs. Woodfall; but I hope by showing you how happy I can make Grace, to give you, I am sure, the greatest pleasure you can have."

"You are right," said Mrs. Woodfall; "and now, Mr. Rivers, you must excuse what I am going to say. You must be in want of money, for, let you be ever so successful in procuring a situation, it must still be a work of some time. Now, thank Heaven, it is in my power to assist you, for I have been for many years well paid by Mathew Trueman, and now that I am speaking of myself, you may as well know some little of my history. I am a widow, my husband perished at sea, and my one child, Harry, is now at school supported by my wages; those wages, however, have been ample, and until you obtain a situation, and can repay me, here are ten pounds at your service."

"I cannot—cannot take them," said Rivers.

"Nay; but for Grace's sake," said Mrs. Woodfall, "I beg that you will do so. You can repay me when it is in your power. If it were a great struggle, and extreme difficulty on my part to offer you this sum, you might hesitate; but as it is, you need not, for I have it readily at my command."

"I tell you what, Mother Woodfall," said Tom Hackey: "if I do the junior tragedy at the Garden, I'll send you a free admission, though you are a bigotted old female in some things."

"Ah! you poor creature," said Mrs. Woodfall, "I believe your heart's in the right place, though you have not much judgment. It makes me often quite uneasy thinking what will become of you."

"Does it?" said Tom. "I beg you won't trouble yourself, ancient one. It's astonishing the trouble old women are if once they take a crotchet."

"Come, Mr. Rivers," said Mrs. Woodfall, "and recollect I lend it as much to Grace as to you, so quiet your scruples at once, and take it."

"But that I know," said Rivers, "my refusal would much pain you, I would refuse this money; but, for Grace's sake, I will take it, hoping soon that a happier day will dawn upon me, and that I may shortly be well able to repay it."

"That will do," said Mrs. Woodfall; "and now let me tell you, that Grace has left every arrangement to yourself, and will consent to anything you propose."

"Then," said Rivers, "Tom Hickey and I will seek out some little suburban church, where, completely unknown, and without exciting curiosity, Grace and I can be made man and wife with as little eclat as possible."

"Let it be so," said Mrs. Woodfall, "write me a note when and where Grace and myself shall meet you."

"I will," said Rivers, "and inclosed shall be one for Grace, which I will trust to your kindness to deliver to her."

"Of course," said Mrs. Woodfall, "a fortnight must at least elapse, as the banns cannot be published in less time, although this be the end of a week."

"Excuse me," said Tom, "I've done a deed—season your admiration for awhile, and I will relate a circumstance of deep and momentous import. A friend of mine was to play the grave-digger, in Hamlet, about a fortnight ago, and he was grovelled for a skull.

"'Hackey,' said he, 'the skull—the skull's the thing to astonish the groundlings. I want to make a sensation, and I must have a real skull, a *bona fide caput mortum*. What shall I do?' 'Leave it to me,' said I, 'I'll ransack somebody's grave for you, and get you up one.'"

"Good gracious!" said Mrs. Woodfall.

"Yes," continued Tom, "and hearing

that the grim king of terrors had assemb'ed a great host in Barnes' church-yard, I took with me a well known pall to help me on my errand, a smirking rascal, who forsook his comrade, and when I had arrived at the point proposed, the night was drawing on apace, and darkness was upon the tombs of men. I dug, and dug, and dug, but by some strange accident I found myself at the wrong end of the corpse."

"Why, Tom," said Rivers, "you don't mean to assert that you went digging in Barnes' church-yard for a skull?"

"Histrionic ardour," said Tom, "enables a man to do wonders. I did, and got one, too, and just as I was saying to myself, 'Dost thou think that Alexander looked this fashion, and smelt so,' I fell over the sexton.

"'Thieves, said he. 'Hold, my friend,' said I, 'are you the sexton? because if you are, here's half-a-crown

to drink a gentleman's health that was buried here last week. You've kept his grave so neat and trim. Do you kuow who I am?' 'No,' says he. 'Then, says I, 'I am the sub-inspector of rural burying-grounds, and, besides, I have come here to put up the banns of matimony for a friend of mine.' Then he held his lantern in my face and looked very doubtful, upon which I was forced to strengthen my story by giving him some names, and the first that came into my head were yours and Grace's; he took the order and pocketed the fee,

and I shouldn't wonder but there are the banns sure enough."

"Upon my word, Tom," said Rivers, "it was taking a great liberty with Grace's name."

"Well, but as she's consented to be yours, where's the odds? It's all one, you know, in the long run."

"This is the strangest accident," said Rivers, "that ever I heard of; be off with you, Tom, at once, and see if the banns have been put up at Barnes' church."

"I will," said Tom; "and if the

sexton has not bilked me, you may be married next Sunday if you like."

"Well, Mr. Hackey," said Mrs. Woodfall, "you have the most extraordinary jumble of right and wrong that ever I met with—poor creature as you are, I don't know what will become of you."

"Mother Woodfall," said Tom Hackey, "you are an elderly female, with but a limited comprehension. I'm off, lend me sixpence. Old Mathew wasn't at home when I called last night, or else he was denying himself to his creditors, so I couldn't get what he owes me."

"There's a shilling," said Rivers. "I shall be home at my lodgings long before you return, Tom, but be sure you obtain accurate information."

"Never doubt it," said Tom; "I'll be down on the sexton, and if he has played me false, woe be to him."

So saying, Tom hurried away, leaving Rivers and Mrs. Woodfall perfectly astonished at his extraordinary conduct, and the singular manner in which fate seemed to get rid of the only obstacle in the way of the immediate union of Rivers and Grace.

CHAPTER LXXV.

THE PLANNED BURGLARY. — TOM HACKEY'S EXPEDITION TO BARNES. —THE SEXTON AND HIS WIFE.

THE more Hilliard thought over his plan of the robbery at the merchant's house, the more feasible did that plan appear, and in the more agreeable colours did it present itself.

"If it were done at all," he told himself, "it should be done immediately, because it would more resemble an act of revenge and bad feeling on the part of Rivers, consequent on his discharge; but then—" Hilliard wanted particularly to ascertain beyond the shadow of a doubt that Rivers was really discharged, not that it made much difference to him in his view regarding the commission of the robbery, but it would guide him in what he should say in the morning when the burglary was discovered.

With this view he determined to make some remark to the merchant that should produce a reply, from which he could draw an accurate conclusion, and he waited somewhat impatiently for Mathew Trueman to enter the office, in order that he might put his plan into execution.

The opportunity was not long in occurring, for the merchant was commonly fidgetting in and out at least twenty times a day, and the next time he made his appearance, Hilliard said—

"Mr. Rivers has not been here to-day, sir."

"I know it," said the merchant; "Mr. Rivers will not be here any day again. I have discharged him from my service—ah."

"Nor has Tom Hackey been here, sir," said Hilliard.

"No," said the merchant; "I have sent him about his business likewise."

"Indeed, sir? I hope the won't rob the place."

"Rob the place!" cried Mathew Trueman; "bless my heart and life, what puts that in your head?"

"I scarcely know," said Hilliard, pretending to look serious; "but it struck me as rather curious that some days ago I should hear Rivers say to Hackey, 'If old Mathew'—meaning you, sir—'discharges me, it shall cost him more than he thinks.'"

"Indeed!" said the merchant; "a most suspicious speech—a very suspicious speech. You heard him say that, did you, and be hanged to him?"

"I did, sir. Heaven forbid that I should be hard upon any one, or misconstrue an innocent speech to mean anything wrong, but such is the fact."

"Ah! we must keep a look-out, then. I believe that rascal is capable of anything. A man who would—but, d—d it, no matter—if he gives me an opportunity, I'll hang him, as sure as my name's Mathew Trueman—ah!"

Hilliard gave a demoniac chuckle when the merchant had left the room, and he muttered, half aloud—

"A good beginning. We shall see, Master Rivers, if we cannot be one too many for you. You carried it with a high hand while you were here; how will you look at the bar of the Old Bailey? and I think I have as reasonably good a chance of placing you there, as I could well desire. It is seldom that a circumstance occurs so luckily as to cut pleasantly in two ways; but this will do so, for it will take suspicion off my own shoulders and place it upon his, against whom I feel a great hatred. If Girkins will not assist me, he has no possible motive in betraying me, so that a safer robbery was never planned. I will have it all to myself, too. I should be besotted to have an associate in such an affair. Mathew Trueman has quite plate enough to pay me well, and perhaps he may once more miss his silver cup, which, by some d———ble means, got out of Rivers's desk after I had put it there, or dreamt that I had put it there, for the whole affair appears to me so inexplicable, that I sometimes doubt if I could have been awake.

"Let me consider. This is Saturday— a bad night for a robbery, as people are generally up late, and there is a great deal of bustle in the streets—Sunday, on the contrary, is a good day, people scarcely expect such a business transaction on that day. Some of the servants are usually out, and Mathew Trueman himself, as I have been informed makes what he calls a country excursion to Battersea, Camberwell, or Hornsey, and comes home tired. Sunday evening, then, just after dark, will be the time, and I can leave the fastenings of the office window purposely undone, so that I can draw myself in in a moment. It shall be so, it shall be so. I feel some little relief now those infernal newspapers for the last few days have left off their conjectures respecting the murder. I wonder who Mathew Trueman will have in place of Rivers? He can scarcely have anybody who would be so disagreeable to me."

* * * *

Mathew Trueman was so well satisfied in his own mind with the turn affairs had taken, since he supposed Grace had, in her interview with Lord Hawksworth, accepted the proposal to become his wife, that he was more than once upon the point of seeking her, and making friends with her on the occasion, but as often as that did occur to him, he shrunk from so doing, and Girkins's words of "Let well alone," constantly recurred to his mind, about which there seemed to be an undefined fear, that, somehow or another, an interview with Grace would disturb his felicity, therefore he abstained from seeking it; and when the following morning came, his mind was too much engrossed with the expected visit of Lord Hawksworth, and the extremely cunning manner in which he considered he was about to give him twenty thousand pounds for forty thousand pounds' worth of bills, that he had no leisure to think of Grace.

"A glorious hit," he cried, "a plan well worthy of the first of British merchants, who, unless he can shuffle, and twist, and titter, and not be particular of trifles, will never either make money or keep it. What do I care whether Lord Hawksworth is a minor or major, or whether his bills be good bills or bad bills? Forty thousand pounds is the sum I have promised with Grace, and which, of course, combined with her beauty, has induced him to make the offer he has. Now, he brings me his forty thousand pounds' worth of bills, I give him twenty thousand pounds cash for them—a fair discounting price for the bills of a minor and a nobleman, and when he marries Grace, and comes to me for her fortune, I hand him over his own acceptances. Not so bad a move that. Ah, and if anything should happen that he don't marry her, which is quite out of the question now, why, I come upon him for the whole forty thousand, and make money either way. Ah!"

Thus reasoned the merchant, who fancied himself so far-sighted and cunning, when he was in reality being well fought with his own weapons, and foiled in every one of his presumed measures.

But, perhaps, of all the *dramatis personæ* of our tale, Girkins was the most terribly anxious as to the issue of the proceedings which were now apparently so near a conclusion. He considered he had the deepest stake of all in what was going on; he was exceedingly poor, living, to use a common expression, from hand to mouth, and he felt that this was his last chance, in all human probability, of acquiring a considerable sum of money.

If he could get five thousand pounds, which he fully intended to work for, out of the whole amount that was to be wrung from the coffers of Mathew Trueman, and he fully intended to make an effort for even a larger amount, he knew a means of investing it which would return an ample interest, and be sufficient to place him, Girkins, far above those contingencies which continually harassed him, and which made him the slave of many persons whom he really despised, not on account of their want of integrity, but their want of talent, which was continually marring the plans and projects of his politic brain.

As for Lord Hawksworth, he did not allow the affair to give him a great deal of uneasiness; the largeness of his ultimate resources gave him a confidence which such as Girkins could not possibly feel. Moreover, he had no object in the money beyond spending it in riot and dissipation, and Girkins had, for he wished to provide for those contingencies of age which were creeping on him.

Nevertheless, his lordship was well satisfied, angry as he was at Grace, to pocket her father's money, for he reasoned that some one one must lend him money, and it might as well be Mathew Trueman as any one else; there in his mind the question ended, and his only disappointment in the transaction was his evident and complete failure with the proud and high-spirited girl who so scorned his addresses.

This, however, was likewise a subject which did not last very long to the annoyance of the scion of nobility; and although it now and then came across him like a disagreeable twinge, that he had failed in such an enterprise, yet he looked forward to a greater career of pleasurable dissipation with the merchant's money, to allow himself much time to brood over his disappointment with Grace.

Tom Hackey reached the pretty suburban locality of Barnes after two hours' smart walking from the city, and upon making the necessary inquiry he learned, to his great satisfaction, that the banns of matrimony had been duly put up between Rrancis Rivers, bachelor, and Grace Trueman, spinster, for the last two Sundays, and that the same elaborate and wonderful process would be gone through once more. After which,

as the parish clerk somewhat strangely informed Tom Hackey, the parties were *liable* to be married.

"Oh, are they?" said Tom; "do you always catch them after the banns?"

"Not always," said the clerk; "but we consider people *far* gone when they gets that length. Leastways, many of them *is* larks."

"What do you mean?" said Tom.

"Why, we gets a good many eighteenpences by putting up banns between people as hates each other like *warjus*, and then, in course, there's a row, and the banns is put down; but most on 'em as has banns but up is real *wictims*."

"Ah," said Tom, "you pities 'em, do you?"

"Perhaps you ain't a married man?" said the clerk.

"No, I ain't," said Tom.

"Then I wonder you don't laugh all day till you bust. I've been married nine years, and I know it's no joke."

"Well, there's nothing like experience," said Tom.

"More there isn't," said the clerk, "in most things; but in that one case it comes too late. Women are artful, sir, and down upon a few dodges."

"I believe they are," said Tom. "I know one who doubled the ghost of Banquo and Lady Macbeth."

"Do you indeed, sir," said the clerk. "Doubled 'em up, I suppose you mean; but, as I was a-going to say, women is artful, and won't let you have no experience of what they is until they have got you into a line; in consikins, the experience doesn't do you no good, except making you wicious."

"Ah," said Tom, "I am sorry for you. You must take better care another time. I have heard of one scheme of getting rid of 'em."

"A quiet dodge?" said the clerk.

"Very."

"Lor, sir! what is it?"

"Why, you places a pillow on their knees, as they lays a-bed, and you sit down on that to keep 'em from kicking. Then you tickles the soles of their feet like a steam-engine, till they gives up the blessed ghost with laughing."

"Bless me," said the clerk, "I should think that would not be a bad way, and they couldn't bring it in but a perplexity at the inquest."

"Exactly," said Tom; "it would go all the round of the papers, headed 'Awfully Sudden Death.' Something in this ere way:—

"'Yesterday the neighbourhood of Barnes, Mortlake, Kew, Hammersmith, and the vicinity, was thrown into a state of the most indescribable consternation and dismay, by the report, which turned out to be, alas! too true, that Mrs. Quickfidget, the wife of Mr. Rumboozle Quickfidget, parish-clerk, sexton, and undertaker, had departed to the bourne whence no traveller returns, under the most awfully sudden circumstances, leaving her afflicted husband to bewail the loss of his affectionate partner, and three small babbies to loudly lament their love of their mother. By the testimony of their next-door neighbour, the unfortunate woman was heard to laugh repeatedly during the night, thus showing the good terms she was on with Mr. Quickfidget, and in the morning she was found a corpse.'"

"Lor, sir," said the sexton, "you are quite an oracle. If such a thing should ever happen, I hope, sir, that you will not scruple to come over and take your pot and pipe."

"Well," said Tom, "these people whose banns are put up mean to risk it."

"Then you must give me notice."

Tom considered a moment, and then thinking that Rivers would prefer a less public day than Sunday, he said, at a venture—

"Let it be Monday, at eleven o'clock."

"Very good," said the sexton, "very good."

Tom then hastened homewards, while the sexton, slowly shutting the street-door, muttered—

"Tickle the soles of her feet—what an idea; tickle the soles of her feet—God bless me! tickle——"

"What now, you idle, scamping, lazy hound," cried a female voice from the lower regions.

"Nothing — nothing," cried the alarmed husband, opening the door again, and making a rush from the house.

CHAPTER LXXV.

THE MEETING AT TWELVE O'CLOCK.— THE TWENTY THOUSAND POUNDS.— MATHEW TRUEMAN'S REJOICING OVER HIS SUPPOSED GOOD FORTUNE.

IT was ten minutes to twelve o'clock when Mr. Girkins reached the merchant's door, trembling with agitation and excitement now that the hour had nearly arrived which he believed was to make or mar him.

Well he knew from his experience of the world and its vicissitudes that what appeared certain was frequently the very thing that failed, while that which seemed to totter upon the very verge of impossibility would succeed in spite of every prophecy to the contrary.

Moreover, Mr. Girkins was something of a fatalist, and believed that what was pre-ordained would be, in however strange a manner it came to pass; but fatalism, although it ought to do so for its votaries, seldom succeeds, under circumstances of actual doubt and difficulty, in steeling a man's nerves, and Mr. Girkins was quite as agitated and in quite as great a state of anxiety as if he had never heard of the doctrine of fatalism in his life.

The merchant was at home and fully expecting his visitors, but he was somewhat surprised to see Girkins without his lordship, and a faint feeling came across him that, after all, something might be wrong; he was, however, quickly relieved by Girkins saying—

"I have seen his lordship, and he said he would meet me here punctually at twelve. It wants now but a few minutes of that hour, and I dare say he will keep his word."

"Well, Mr. Girkins," said Mathew Trueman, "I must say that I do feel your services in this affair to have been very important, so much so that I think you deserving of pecuniary recompense."

"You are very kind," said Girkins; "I shall leave that subject entirely to you."

"Well, then," said Mathew Trueman, "I think it incumbent upon me, Mr. Girkins, to warmly recommend Lord Hawksworth to pay you handsomely, and I think he will be acting extremely shabby if he don't."

"Some people are so shabby," said Girkins, "that although they acknowledge service being rendered to them, they won't pay at all."

"Ah, hem!" said the merchant.

At this moment the sound of wheels came most agreeably upon the ears of Mr. Girkins, for he thought they could announce the advent of none other than his illustrious patron.

"That is his lordship," he said, "no doubt. You perceive he is punctual, Mr. Trueman."

"People generally are when they have money to receive," said the merchant; "punctuality in all matters of business."

It was Lord Hawksworth, and in a few minutes he was in the merchant's private counting-house.

Mathew Trueman gave him a chair with great affected bustle and humility, and then looking into his pale face—for his lordship had made what he called a night of it on the preceding evening—he said—

"Your lordship does me infinite honour by this great act of condescension; I hope that we meet under the most felicitous circumstances, and that from this moment everything will proceed in the most satisfactory manner as regards a nearer connection between your lordship and your lordship's most obedient servant—plain Mathew Trueman, who began the world with three-and-a-penny, ah!"

"I am quite sure," said Lord Hawksworth, "that everything will be as satisfactory as possible. I was informed by Mr. Girkins that you have no objection this morning to bring to a conclusion the affairs which have been for some time in agitation between us."

"Certainly not," said the merchant; "I may say that after the gratifying conversation I had the pleasure of having some time since with your lordship, I could not think of hesitating at a circumstance which awaited but such a gratifying conversation and its gratifying result, to be as pleasurable to me as I hope it will be to your lordship."

"Yes," suddenly interposed Girkins; "I think a more agreeable party than we constitute at present, candidly speaking, could scarcely be found. The circumstances under which we have met are such as to bring quite throbs of delight to every bosom; here is the first of British merchants, and here is the most noble of noble lords, meeting in the most singular and beautiful manner, under circumstances of the most sweet and endearing nature. You have not forgotten the bills, my lord?"

"D—n you," muttered Hawksworth, "don't quiz."

"My lord," continued Mathew Trueman, becoming quite oratorical, and waving his arm, "women, as Mr. Girkins and I decided at our last interview, are quite females—they resemble, my lord, rusty weathercocks."

"Oiled weathercocks," suggested Girkins, "that turn with the slightest breeze."

"Oil weathercocks," corrected the merchant, "continually making a breeze; my daughter, my lord, is a female as well as the rest of her sex, and however extraordinary her conduct may have been to your lordship at one time, she is now, I feel certain, fully aware of the great honour your lordship intended her."

"D—n it, it's a take in, he's quizzing," whispered Hawksworth to Girkins, for his lordship had not forgotten that he himself had been so imprudent as to let Grace know the real honour he had intended her.

"Hush!" whispered Girkins, "don't be a fool."

"The epistle which, I may say at the eleventh hour," continued Mathew Trueman, "Grace thought proper to send to your lordship, I have no doubt resulted from the serious conversation I had with her, and the manner in which I did myself the honour of painting your lordship's many virtues, and calling her attention to your lordship's exalted position."

"I am very much obliged to you," said Hawksworth, wincing a little, for he had not the most agreeable impression in the world of that same interview.

"And I have, further, no doubt," added Mathew Trueman, "that the manner in which she received your lordship on that occasion was quite consistent with the judicious advice that

I, as a parent, thought proper to give her."

"Oh! quite—quite," said Hawksworth, with a groan.

"May I venture to hope," said Mathew Trueman, "that everything is settled?"

"Decidedly," said Hawksworth. "I never met with such a settler in my life."

"My lord!" said Trueman.

"His lordship means to say," said Girkins, "that his pleasure was so great that it merged into confusion, assimilating to which, in vulgar parlance, may be called a settler."

"Oh!" said Mathew Trueman, "I understand. I can remember my own feelings when I was keeping company with Mrs. Trueman that was."

Lord Hawksworth uttered a deep and solemn groan, which Mathew Trueman merely translated to be an excess of feeling, and continued—

"Bygones are bygones. I was confidential clerk to Slicks, Rickinbottom, White, and Greenfield, and Mrs. Trueman that was, was the only daughter of Mrs. Brown, who kept an extensive milk-shop of the most singular design and pattern, and the old lady came down to a most handsome tune with Matilda, and I made her Mrs. Trueman—poor thing, she didn't last long. She gave in in the course of three years. Death drew a bill upon her at sight, and she honoured it—peace to her *name*. Your lordship's sayings, as I was saying, put me exactly in mind of mine when I was keeping company with Matilda Brown."

Lord Hawksworth groaned repeatedly, and kicked Girkins on the shins during this narrative.

"I always thought," continued the merchant, "that she sacrificed herself to Grace, when she had the measles."

Lord Hawksworth now made a desperate attempt to change the conversation, and he said—

"I understand, Mr. Trueman, that you have no objection to take my acceptances without the endorsement of my friend, the captain?"

"Certainly," said Mathew Trueman. "It would ill become me to require other than your lordship's own signature."

"You are very kind," said Lord Hawksworth. "I have blank acceptances in my pocket-book, which, if you will fill up for forty thousand pounds, I will here, in your presence, accept them."

"There is one thing, my lord," said Mathew Trueman, hesitatingly, "which I will ask of you to give me, and that is the assurance, upon your word of honour as a nobleman, that if these bills are in existence when you become of age, that you will renew them or pay them?"

It was in a slightly altered voice that Lord Hawksworth said—

"I do promise, on my word of honour as a nobleman."

"Then I am satisfied," said Mathew Trueman, and he added to himself, "I have you to the tune of twenty thousand pounds, come what may."

It was indeed amazing that with all the business tact, all the admirable thought and acuteness of character which had raised Mathew Trueman from insignificance to the position he at present occupied, his judgment should be so stultified and his usual sagacity so obscured as to trust to the intangible security of a man's word merely because by hereditary descent, he had become entitled to the prefix of "lord" to his name.

But so it was. Mathew Trueman thought himself safe in any way, and fancied that he had so hedged in his interests that they could not suffer whatever aspect affairs might take.

The bills were produced, and Mathew Trueman himself set about filling them up for the enormous sum specified, while Girkins fixed his eyes upon the ceiling, and endeavoured to pretend he was thinking upon nothing, when, in reality, he was in a state of the most pitiable agitation.

A thousand circumstances flashed across his mind, which might yet interfere with his hopes. Grace might suddenly make her appearance, and say something which would open the merchant's eyes to his real position, or Mathew might himself say something to Hawksworth, which might provoke an angry or an indiscreet reply—or even his lordship might shrink, at the eleventh hour, from the perpetration of the villany he was called upon to practise —but that was a risk which Mr. Girkins told himself was the least of all. Still, however, while Mathew Trueman was drawing ten bills, of four thousand pounds each, Mr. Girkins's condition was far from enviable.

As for Lord Hawksworth, he seemed tolerably composed, and only hummed in a low tone a reminiscence of the last popular opera, during the process of the bills being drawn up, which were to involve him to so serious an extent. That is to say, if he had any regard for that honour which he had solemnly pledged, and that nobility which so ill-accorded with his dishonest disposition and grovelling desires.

Mathew Trueman was too well accustomed to drawing bills of exchange to waste much time in the process, and the important slips of paper were quickly placed before his lordship along with a pen, and the merchant saying—

"Forty thousand pounds on paper, my lord. is a very simple affair; there was a time when I could hardly conceive the existence of so large a sum, that was when I had but three-and-a-penny, ah! but now it's rather a different affair."

"Exactly," said Lord Hawksworth, as in a straggling hand he wrote "Hawksworth" across each of the bills, and pushed them over towards the merchant.

Mr. Girkins breathed hard as he saw Mathew Trueman go to a desk, and return with a cheque-book.

"My lord," said Trueman, as he opened the cheque-book, and held aside the heap of little ends of torn cheques in the first part of it. "My lord, you wish discounted forty thousand pounds' worth of bills, you being a minor. Now, notwithstanding my very great friendship for your lordship, I may be permitted to remark that this is a matter of sheer and downright business."

"Oh, exactly," said Hawksworth.

"Therefore, my lord," continued Mathew Trueman, "I am, in a manner, compelled to treat your lordship in such a manner as I would any other nobleman, being a minor, who might do me the honour to come to me to have his bills discounted."

"Oh, certainly, certainly," said Hawksworth; "I am far from wishing anything else."

"Exactly—ahem," said the merchant. "Then, my lord, the bills of minors, in the city—minors too of great expectations, like your lordship, and great honour like your lordship, are very seldom discounted at all, but when they are it is cent. per cent."

"The devil it is," said Lord Hawksworth.

"Exactly," said Mathew Trueman, folding up the cheque-book again very carefully. "I was afraid your lordship would not like the terms, and, therefore, hesitated to draw a cheque for twenty-thousand pounds, which may be cashed within four minutes and a half's walk from this door."

"Twenty thousand pounds for forty thousand pounds?" said Lord Hawksworth.

"Precisely, my lord; I rejoice to see your lordship has not forgotten your earlier arithmetic."

"Those are the—the—re—regular terms—quite the—the regular terms," gasped Girkins.

"Then, you go halves with me, Mr. Trueman," said Lord Hawksworth; "and every twenty shillings I spend or squander, I must put down another to you."

"That is exactly the case," said Mathew Trueman, picking his teeth with a pen; "we stand equal in the transaction, exactly; so that neither of us can be accused of taking an undue advantage of the other."

"Give me the cheque," said Hawksworth, as if he were swallowing a very large pill.

Mathew Trueman opened the cheque-book again, and deliberately wrote a cheque for twenty thousand pounds, which he pushed across the table to his lordship, saying—

"My lord, I shall leave you and Grace to settle all the other matters between yourselves, and it may turn out that your lordship may never be troubled concerning these bills."

"Upon my soul, I hope it may," said Hawksworth. "If my father, the earl, heard of them, he'd have the gout in his stomach, to a certainty."

"Then I will take good care that he does hear of them," thought Mathew Trueman, "immediately after the marriage takes place." Then he added aloud—

"I trust your lordship will do me the honour, now that we have settled this business, of taking a bottle of wine with me either here or at some hotel in the neighbourhood?"

Lord Hawksworth shrunk immediately from this proposal, for he had a timely recollection of the last hotel in the neighbourhood, as well as the frightful Bucellas, to which he had been introduced by Mathew Trueman, and he said, rapidly—

"Mr. Trueman, I have important business at the West-end, but if you will favour me with a call there, at my hotel, within the hour, I shall be happy to partake of the bottle you mention."

"I shall be proud to do myself the honour," said the merchant.

"Then," said Lord Hawksworth, rising just as the clock struck two, "I will bid you good day for the present, Mr. Trueman, and beg you will not forget your promise."

Girkins likewise rose, but such was his agitation, that he nearly fell over his chair, and he did not know whether he bid Mathew Trueman good day or not, being scarcely conscious of where he was, till he was in the open street.

CHAPTER LXXVI.

THE QUARREL IN THE CAB.—THE RECONCILIATION.—THE DINNER.—MATHEW TRUEMAN'S VISION OF FUTURITY.

GIRKINS drew a long breath, and said—

"Well, that's over—for God's sake, let's go to the banker's directly; a bird in the hand is worth two in the bush, my lord."

Hawksworth without a word jumped into his cab, but Girkins was not slow in following him, for he was determined to stick to his prey. The tiger touched his hat with an inquiring look, for it was his duty to know where his master was going, in case of the party becoming lost in the odious city.

"Glitter, Smash, and Doemhalls, in Lombard-street," said Girkins, "Damme, it's a new firm, but I dare say Mathew Trueman is at the bottom of it himself, or he would never trust them with his money."

It was but a five minutes' drive to the door of the banking-house, and then Girkins and Hawksworth, alighting from the cab, entered the portals of the new and conspicuously showy establishment. The cheque was presented to an old gentleman in a powdered wig, who, after a fish-like stare at the amount, handed it to another, from whence it was passed to a third, from whom it came back again to the old gentleman, who thereupon leaned half across the counter, and said—

"Notes, I suppose?"

"Yes," said Hawksworth, "twenty thousand."

The old gentleman counted the valuable packet over thrice, before he trusted it out of his clutches, and then Hawksworth rolled the whole up into a ball, looking hard into Girkins's face the while, whose very lips were white with emotion, and thrusting the twenty thousand pounds thus crushed up into his trousers pocket, he coolly walked out of the banking-house and sprang again into his cab.

He made no opposition to Girkins following him, and if he had, it is doubtful if Girkins would not have insisted upon it; then his lordship put the horse to his speed, while the tiger, holding fast of the straps with one hand, rubbed the finger of the other sagaciously up and down the side of his nose, as he said—

"We've been to a banker's, and that looks like money; down upon him for my wages to-night, as sure as a gun, and something extra for waiting so long. I wonder if we've got our paper discounted. I didn't think we could fly another kite, blessed if I did."

"My lord," said Girkins, as they together neared the western region o London.

"Well?" said Hawksworth.

"Your lordship has probably forgotten my little commission on this transaction."

"Oh! ah!" said Hawksworth; "you were to have had something, I believe?"

"Your lordship is uncommonly correct," said Girkins, with a sneering tone; "and if your lordship taxes your noble memory a little further, your lordship will recollect that something was said about five per cent. on the amount of bills I could get discounted for you."

"A thousand pounds," said Hawksworth.

"Oh, dear, no," said Girkins; "two thousand."

"Two thousand?" echoed Hawksworth. "Are you mad?"

"I believe not," said Girkins, turning perfectly white with anger. "Five per cent. on forty thousand pounds, amounts, I believe, to two thousand pounds."

"But d—n it, man, I have not forty thousand pounds."

"My per centage," said Girkins, "was to be upon the bills, not upon what you chose to take for them; and as your lordship's faithful agent, I think myself entitled to my commission."

"You may be the agent of the devil, if you like," said Lord Hawksworth, "but I'll see you d—d before you get two thousand pounds out of me."

"If I were the agent of the devil," said Girkins, "I believe I should get more justice than from one of his most despicable imps. You are a d—d infernal sneaking hound."

"Curse you," said Hawksworth, as he struck Girkins across the face with his whip handle, but he was himself immediately seized by the throat with such a terrific grasp, that he dropped the reins, and the horse, feeling himself at perfect liberty, set off at a tremendous pace along Holborn.

"Oh, gracious," cried the tiger, "they are coming it now—here's a shindy. Murder—stop us, stop us!"

Bang went the wheel against the post at the corner of King Street, and away went the party in one grand crash. The tiger went head-foremost into a boot and shoe shop, and Lord Hawksworth and Girkins were picked out of the road scrapings by the passengers, when they instantly fell to pummelling each other like two devils, to the vast amusement of everybody.

The police were called, and they gave each other into custody with many bitter oaths and imprecations, being conveyed in triumph to the nearest station-house.

Upon Girkins's temperament the squabble had acted like the safety-valve to an overcharged steam-boiler, and he became quite cool and comfortable before he had gone a couple of dozen paces.

"My lord," he said, "we both have been to blame—but we are in each other's power; by publishing the particulars of how Mathew Trueman has been swindled—you see I speak plainly—I prevent your enjoyment of the very sum which you now have in your pocket, and blast you eternally in every but the worst society. You know me—I am an unscrupulous agent, and will do anything for money. You may keep me out of that money, which is a mere trifle to you, but which is life and soul to me. So, you see, sir, putting aside all distinctions of rank, and all nonsensical ceremonies, we two scoundrels are necessary to each other. There is an old proverb which says, 'when thieves fall out, honest men get their own'—don't let us be so desperately silly as to allow such to be the case. Now, sir, I provoked you, and I am sorry for it—but you struck me. Now, Lord Hawksworth, let me have one thousand pounds, and still continue your useful agent, or defy and bilk me, and by the God of Heaven, I'll make you rue the day."

There was something both reasonable and alarming in this speech, and Lord Hawksworth began to think he had been hasty, and that he could as ill afford to do without Mr. Girkins, as Mr. Girkins could without him.

"'Tis hard enough," he said, "to receive twenty thousand pounds for forty, without having that reduced immediately afterwards to eighteen. I had no intention to deprive you of your commission, but it was most certainly on cash, and not on bills."

"Well," said Girkins, "I will admit it was my mistake—let us withdraw these ridiculous charges of assault, and hasten to the hotel, where by this time Mathew Trueman may be waiting for us."

"Constable," said Hawksworth, "it's all a mistake, there's a sovereign for you—call a coach—I am satisfied."

"And so am I," said Girkins.

"Oh, then, gentlemen," said the constable, pocketing the sovereign, "I am sure I is—here, cuch—cuch."

In half an hour Lord Hawksworth and Girkins reached the hotel, where, to their great relief, Mathew Trueman had not arrived, so that the besmeared pair had ample time to change their clothing; and each cursing the other in his heart, they ordered a handsome cold collation, to do honour to the merchant on his arrival.

How little did Mathew Trueman think, while he was rubbing his hands in his office, and smiling to himself, what a pretty little scene was being enacted between his projected son-in-law, and the delightful agent, Mr. Girkins. How little he dreamed of the fracas, and the smash, and then the reconciliation, based as it was upon such high and noble principles.

The first thing that aroused him from his reverie, was the arrival of a clerk from the banking-house, with the information that a cheque of his had just been paid, but to which Mathew Trueman only replied, "Very well—it's all right," with a bland smile.

Then he put on his huge blue coat, with the huger gilt buttons, and sallied forth like an exceedingly clever man as he thought himself, to keep his appointment with the noble lord.

The sun was once again sinking towards the western horizon, and every spire and steeple in the city shone with almost regal splendour, and the atmosphere which surrounded such a mass of buildings was somewhat darkened in hue from the surrounding country, by the smoke and vapour incidental to such a collection of human beings, and human habitations, and in some measure dimmed the bright rays that now glanced from the sun.

As the streaming light crossed the various streets at all angles, the burning rays were reflected back by the shop windows, and often dazzled the gaze of the passenger, who chanced to cast his eyes towards the spot. All was bustle and confusion, for at that moment all seemed to be aware that the day was drawing to a close.

Many were quitting their places of business to return to their country villas, a few miles from this scene of bustle and life, while the artisan and shopman saw, in the setting sun, the near approach of that moment when he can abandon himself to ease and amusement, when he can quit labour and court pleasure.

Ere the sun has sunk, the evening clouds come up apace, for a brief space catch his fleeting beams, and gild his departure. Now houses and objects of all kinds grew gradually indistinct—inscriptions could no longer be traced—a gloom seemed to overspread all things, which was soon broken in upon by the lighting of lamps, and the illumination of the shop-windows, as they one after another became too dim to exhibit the wares they contained, to the eyes of the curious.

But that uncertain light, a compound of the sun's departing rays and the light of lamps, renders most things but dimly visible, until total obscuration of the solar rays ensues, when the reflected light of the moon sheds her balmy influence on the earth—then a better light is caused by artificial means, which enables the inhabitants of our cities to transact business at night, with all the facilities of the broad day.

The cool evening breeze is felt to be refreshing by those who travel through the streets, the irradiating heat of which continue till long after sun-set. Now is the moment when the various amusements commence—not all at once, for they vary in their hours—and many are those who parade the principal streets from habit and taste, casting all thoughts of the day's cares behind, and only thinking how the night may be spent to give the most pleasure, though probably in intemperance and riot.

After sun-set, a different race of beings appear to take possession of a city—they have different objects, and different tastes from those who plodded through its mazes during the day.

But what was all this to Mathew Trueman, who saw nothing of the beauties of nature, who drunk not of the artifices of art, except so far as they concerned his own peculiar habits, feelings, and prejudices?

The baronet in embryo—the father-in-law to an earl that was to be, was almost above taking notice of anything or anybody; it is doubtful if he was conscious that human beings were passing him on either side, and brushed rudely past him; he was carried beyond such considerations, and almost beyond that knowledge which momentarily pressed itself upon his senses.

He strode along with the air of a man of more importance than usually belongs to the sons of clay, and barely would he deign to look, as he crossed the streets, to guard against any random vehicle that might not regard him as he regarded himself, but heedlessly endanger his, Mathew Trueman's, valuable life, by knocking him down, and crushing him under its wheels.

"All is as I could wish it," said Mathew to himself, "and that, too, when I least expected it. Who would have supposed such a sudden change would have come over Grace? But it was rank—rank—nobility—that did it—wealth and rank—the ultimate happiness—only reached by the aspiring and talented. Grace will be a countess, and I a baronet—and who knows what else? I shall then leave the city, of course, but I will call there now and then, to receive the congratulations of those who are not so fortunate, so distinguished, as to be baronets, or father to a countess, and father-in-law to an earl—ah!"

As these thoughts passed through his mind, he increased his speed so much, that he soon arrived in the vicinity of the hotel, and in a few moments more he stood on the bottom step of a large flight, that led to the splendid and magnificent hotel where Lord Hawksworth resided.

Mathew Trueman now felt himself somebody, as he ascended those steps, and he asked for his lordship with as confident an air as if he had really acquired the baronetcy which he so much looked forward to, and which he believed himself now without a doubt very nearly acquiring; he did not see the smile of the waiter as he asked,

"Is my friend Lord Hawksworth within?" or Mathew Trueman would have been indignant, if not convinced of how foolish he was making himself.

"Yes sir," was the reply. "His lordship has been some time here. Shall I take up your name, sir?"

"Mr. Trueman—plain Mr. Trueman, at present," said the merchant, "ah!"

"Certainly, sir," said the waiter; "here, Sam, tell Lord Hawksworth that plain Mr. Trueman is here."

"Curse that fellow's impudence," muttered the merchant; "but when I get my baronetcy, I will let them know who I am, and no mistake."

The answer of Lord Hawksworth to the announcement that plain Mr. Trueman was there, was a curse at the waiter's insolence, and an order to show him up stairs, so that in a few moments the well-gratified merchant was shown into a small private drawing-room, which, although of limited dimensions, was furnished and appointed in the most splendid manner.

"My dear sir," said Girkins, "we have quite, in a manner of speaking, waited for you. His lordship was afraid some accident had happened on your road hither, such as an upset in some cursed vehicle."

"Oh! dear, no," said the merchant; "nothing of the kind, I assure you. Business must be attended to, whatever may be a man's position in society, and his ultimate prospects, ah!"

"Certainly," drawled Lord Hawksworth, "certainly—that's uncommonly correct—Mr. Trueman, I have taken the liberty of ordering a little *recherche*, dinner, a kind of discounting repast which I hope, Mr. Trueman, you will find to your liking."

"I am quite sure I shall," said the merchant; "we people of distinction have great similarity of tastes, and I am sure what pleases your lordship is sure to be delightful to me."

"Really, Mr. Trueman," said Girkins, with a scarcely disguised sneer, "you are turning quite courtly already."

Mathew Trueman was quite foolish enough to take this as a compliment, and said—

"A man of the world—a man of the world, Mr. Girkins, can become anything, or everything, and it would be strange, indeed, if a British merchant commencing life, as I may remark I did, with the insignificant sum of three-and-a-penny, could not well and easily assimilate himself to any new prospect that was open to his ambition and spirit of enterprise. By-the-by, Mr. Girkins, you've got a terrible scratch on your nose."

"A slight scratch," said Girkins, "a friendly slight scratch. A little explanation upon an important subject was required between me and a friend, and I believe we did scratch each other's noses by way of awakening attention."

"Bless me," said the merchant, "that was very singular. I have heard of Hottenpots, or some such foreigners, rubbing their noses against each other."

"Exactly," drawled Hawksworth, who seemed, since his acquisition of the twenty thousand pounds, to have stiffened in his manners amazingly. "Exactly; be so good as to ring, Girkins, and ask the wretches here if the dinner's ready. It's frightfully early, I admit, but just ask them."

Girkins did as he was desired, and the answer was that the dinner was just laid in the adjoining apartment.

The three strangely assorted men then rose, and after a polite struggle, to give each other precedence, Mathew Trueman was compelled to walk first, which he did with great dignity, flattering himself that he was making amazing strides towards greatness and nobility, while behind him Hawksworth found time to whisper to Girkins—

"Help me in making him drunk after dinner. I want to know what d—nable crotchet he has in his head about his little spit-fire of a daughter, and what he calls his approaching dignities."

"I will," said Girkins, "for he promised me to recommend you to be liberal, and if he gets very drunk he may do it."

The party now reached the dining-room, where was laid a repast of the most expensive kind, and some wines of the rarest and richest quality, for his lordship had placed a thousand pound note in the hands of the landlord, telling him to get it changed, and deduct his amount, a circumstance which so astonished the aforesaid landlord that he sat down in his own private room, and was full ten minutes in recovering his breath, after which he made up Lord Hawksworth's account, charging every item at its proper cost; then, by an artful insertion of the figure two under the gross amount, succeeded in producing a result equal to double that sum. So that the account stood mathematically thus—

Lord Hawksworth's bill proper, four hundred and fifty-three pounds five shillings and twopence; multiplied by two, equal to nine hundred and six pounds ten shillings and fourpence. One thousand pounds—minus that amount, leaving ninety-three pounds nine and eightpence, which with great reluctance the landlord handed over to his lordship, who, after raving and swearing for about five minutes, was compelled to put up with the extortion; being really quite oblivious of what he had had, and what he had not had during the last twelvemonths.

Truly, Lord Hawksworth's twenty thousand pounds was taking to itself wings, and flying. But to return to the merchant.

Mathew Trueman was too much amazed by the glitter of plate upon the table, and in too great ignorance with regard to the various dishes that were presented to him, to venture upon eating much. Once or twice he took an amazing quantity of what was merely intended to be the sauce, and that being in some instances rather too piquant to be pleasant, he became cautious and fidgety; at the same time that he grew amazingly hungry, for it was long past his own dinner hour, and the savoury steam of the various viands provoked his appetite.

Then, too, another source of great annoyance, was the manner in which his plate was continually whipped from under his nose by the waiters, just as he had turned over once or twice what it contained, and was beginning to think that he would actually venture upon tasting it. He was bewildered by the rapid succession of courses, and once, when he thought he had made a hit in the discovery of a veal cutlet, as he imagined, he lost his chance of verifying the truth of the fact, by being challenged to drink a glass of wine with his lordship; and by the time that digni-

fied and solemn process was over, a custom which is the pest of every dinner table, the tempting dish had evaporated, and was replaced by another, which, had Mathew Trueman been asked his candid opinion of, he would have said, resembled pea-soup half digested.

The dinner occupied a full hour, and finally the poor merchant was compelled to satisfy his hunger with pieces of bread, while he hinted his opinion of the repast by saying—

"Don't you think, my lord, eh, that a good cut off a saddle of mutton, or a sirloin of beef, isn't so bad in its way, eh?"

"Low, decidedly low," said Hawksworth.

"Wretchedly low," chimed in Girkins.

"Oh!" said the merchant, "these thinks all chopped up into little bits, swimming in God knows what, reminds me of the particular family who kept an old black woman without any teeth to chew their food for them, and spit it into their mouths."

The waiters looked aghast at this, and Lord Hawksworth made a wry face, as he drank two glasses of wine with great haste, to settle his own stomach, after so delicious an anecdote.

"I should say," continued the merchant, "that most of the things we've had to-day were decidedly slimy. I tell you what, John or Tom, or whatever your name is," addressing the waiter behind his chair, "you may tell your master that he's an ass, and a d——d fool, or else he'd a sent up a steak and a bottle of porter, rather than all the sloshy stuff we've had in little tureens."

"Yes, sir," said the waiter, with a profound bow.

"And you may go away yourself as soon as you like," said the merchant, "for it's enough to make anybody uncomfortable to have somebody staring at the back of one's head all the while one's having dinner."

"Yes, sir," said the waiter, giving his napkin a great flourish, and looking up to Lord Hawksworth for further orders, who, after a great peal of laughter, said—

"Remove."

The table was cleared with the

greatest celerity, and soon covered with decanters.

"Mr. Trueman," said his lordship, "I am sorry you don't seem to enjoy your dinner."

"Enjoy be d——d !" said the merchant; "I don't know what there was to enjoy. Let's have a good bottle of port and some biscuits. What do they call this d——d house ?"

"It's the Hotel Imperial," said Girkins.

"Is it ?" said the merchant. "I suppose they haven't much custom, and keep a large copper down stairs with a perpetual Irish stew in it. It's a confounded imposition, a regular take-in; they ladle that out into little tureens, and then put some different coloured physic in each to make believe it's something extraordinary, and then they get fools to eat it, begging your lordship's pardon.'

"Wouldn't you prefer," said Lord Hawksworth, "some of the lighter wines to port ?"

"Certainly not ; I don't know what I've been drinking; but it's given me a pain in my inside already."

"The acid wines of the Rhine," remarked Hawksworth, "are considered favourable to digestion."

"So they may be, for all I know," said the merchant; "but I've seen neither rine nor anything else to digest yet."

Lord Hawksworth rose again, and then said—

"Well, Mr. Trueman, I am about leaving the room, and I will order you some port, if you please."

"Thank you," said the merchant, who, like most people, was most prodigiously angry with anything that interfered with his meals. "Thank you, my lord, and if there's a sandwich to be had, I shall be decidedly grateful."

Lord Hawksworth said to the first waiter he met—

"Have you any infernal new, raw, fiery port in the house ?"

"Oh, dear, no, my lord," said the waiter, "we never keep nothing but the very ancientest and finest of wines."

"But I want a bottle or two of another description, and you must get it."

"We'll send, my lord, to some low place," said the waiter, "and get some."

"The low place is your own cellar, and be d——d to you. You know that well enough ; but, hark! you bring in a decanter of such wine as I mention, and put into it half a pint of brandy—do the same to as many more decanters as may be ordered. You understand me, William ?"

"Perfectly, my lord. The singular being as dined with your lordship is to be hocus-pocussed. Missus has got some aquafortis, my lord, if you would like it put in."

"No," said his lordship. "Confound you, do as I order you, and do no more."

The infernal compound was duly set before Mathew Trueman, along with a couple of small sandwiches, which, to show his utter contempt of them, the merchant put into his mouth both at once, making a mental resolution that, when he got home, he would have a steak in the city.

"A full-bodied wine," said the merchant, as he drank a glass of what had been brought him.

"Yes," said Hawksworth.

"A fruity wine," said the merchant, trying as much as possible to look like a connoisseur, for who will confess that he is no judge of wine ?

"Very fruity," said Hawksworth. "It is some of that famous vintage that you hear everybody praise so, you know, but which year it was nobody recollects."

"Exactly," said the merchant. "I've heard of it."

"It would be d——d odd if you hadn't, for everybody's heard of it till they are sick of it."

Mathew Trueman had drunk of the light dinner wines which had been upon the table more freely than was at all prudent, and throwing glass after glass, as he had done, upon nearly an empty stomach, it is not to be wondered at that he should speedily begin to feel some effects from his potations, especially when he came to mingle the doctored port with the acid compounds that were already on his stomach.

At a wink from his lordship, Girkins rose and said—

"My Lord Hawksworth, will you be

so kind as to fill your glass, for I wish to propose a toast, to which I am sure you will most heartily respond; that toast is the health of your lordship's distinguished guest, Mathew Trueman, Esquire. A gentleman as celebrated for everything as for nothing, and one who combines in himself the ultimatum of ultimatums. A gentleman who is as great in one thing as another thing, and who, I believe, I may truly say, reflects quite as much honour on the City of London, as the City of London reflects upon him. A gentleman who, with a manly English taste, has eaten no dinner; but who, it is to be hoped, will eat many dinners yet—dinners which may be neither slimy, nor comparable to those masticated by the coloured female. I am certain, that if any new honours await Mr. Trueman—and who shall be heretic enough to doubt but there are many?—he will sustain those new honours just as he sustained his old ones. My Lord Hawksworth, need I say more in proposing the health of our illustrious friend and guest, Mathew Trueman, who commenced life with three-and a penny? Ah!"

"Hear, hear, hear!" cried Hawksworth.

The merchant was far too stultified with the wine he had taken, and the glasses he continued to take while Girkins was speaking, in order to keep down his modesty, to be at all aware that Mr. Girkins was indulging in a little of that pastime commonly called quizzing.

The health was drunk with great eclat, and then Mathew Trueman, holding fast by the edge of the table, rose to his feet. For a moment the room seemed to spin round with him, and then, as he became more accustomed to his change of position, objects assumed a more stationary character, and he said—

"My Lords and Gentlemen,—For the distinguished honour—proudest moment of my life—feel it in my bussum—never expected to be called to the upper house so soon—quite—quite—incompetent to push about the helm of state—never discounted a bill in my life under sixty-five per cent.—business—is business. A man of business—my lords—is a man who minds his own business—and nobody else's business. I—I—don't know exactly where I am; but this is a most illustrious assembly, and I am glad to see your brother, Lord Hawksworth, and yours—Gir—Gir—Girkins—for d—d—d—me, if there ain't two of each of you (hurrah, hurrah!) Three-and-a-penny. When I look back, I can't help it—tears will come, my lords and gentlemen. It—it's a shock—shocking thing to see a prime minister weeping; but I get twenty thousand pounds either way, and that's no joke. Sir Mathew Trueman for ever! Hip—hip—hip—hurrah! It's a splendid do. I—I—d—me, where am I going?"

At this moment Mr. Trueman's legs doubled up under him, and he made one of those curious dives under the table, which gentlemen frequently perpetrate when they have had what they call the other glass, but which really means the other dozen.

"There's a pretty fellow for you," said Hawksworth; "hang me if I know what he means."

"Simply this," said Girkins; "that, as father-in-law to your lordship, the ministry cannot well refuse him a baronetcy, then he means to go into the lower house, make a sensation, and be called to the upper one."

"Curse the folly of these city people!" said Hawksworth; "I shall leave it to you, Girkins, to put him head foremost into some vehicle, and send him home, and do you be on the look out for a town house for me, order me a proper suite of carriages, make yourself a busy man, and draw out a plan of operations that will embrace a taste for every pleasure that is to be had for money in London."

"And what is not?" said Girkins. "Money, my lord, is the arch-enchanter. Men's souls have a price in London, and, in many cases, it is a very modest one. I shall obey your lordship's instructions, and hope to make myself quite as useful in pointing out how your lordship may most advantageously spend your money, as I trust I have done in assisting you to get it. But do you mean to give up all pursuit of Grace Trueman?"

"Grace Trueman is beautiful," said Hawksworth; "but I don't like trouble and there are more pretty faces than hers. I may yet have some disagreeables with Mathew Trueman, and I don't feel disposed to hurry them in any way."

Lord Hawksworth rose as he spoke, and rang the bell.

"Very well, your lordship," said Girkins. "Your lordship will always find me your lordship's devoted humble servant—as long as you've got any money," he added to himself.

CHAPTER LXXVII.

THE SUNDAY.—HILLIARD AND THE ROBBERY.—TOM HACKEY'S MESSAGE.

THE Sunday came—the Sunday preceding that eventful day which was to make Rivers and Grace Trueman man and wife—the Sunday, on the evening of which Mark Hilliard had determined to make his burglarious entry into the merchant's house, and endeavour to strike so heavy a blow at the heart of

Rivers; for what to him would have been fortune, love, and every other mundane happiness, if his fair fame was branded with such an impeachment as that which the villain Hilliard intended to bring against him?

Little did he suspect, as he wiled away the time with Tom Hackey in the parks and other places of promenade, of the infernal scheme which was hatching for his eternal destruction.

And as little did the beautiful Grace

Trueman imagine the extent of wickedness of even such a man as Mark Hilliard to concoct so diabolical a scheme for the destruction of the innocent, merely for the purpose of temporarily filling his pockets with gold, which would soon be wasted in riot and dissipation, whose only crime was, that he was too virtuous for his,—Hilliard's,—vitiated society.

The merchant had been placed in a hackney-coach by the waiters of the hotel, and as he, Girkins, felt perfectly conscious that the discounting of Lord Hawksworth's bills would assuredly be the very last transaction he should ever have with him, he gave himself but little trouble concerning his safe transportation home, merely giving his address to the coachman, assuring him he would be well paid when he got there.

It was not until late the next morning that Mathew Trueman awoke to a full sense of all the frightful horrors of the doctored port; and, when he did so, he thought that a legion of devils, each of whom actively followed the trade of a blacksmith, had taken up their abode in his head.

His physical faculties seemed quite prostrated; for about half an hour he lay upon his back, doing nothing but groaning; then he rose, and, with nervous trepidation, dressed himself, falling down repeatedly during the process. He was, however, sober enough to feel the full extent of the sufferings, and but a confused recollection came across his mind of the events of the preceding evening; he thought he had made a speech, but he was not quite sure; but, as to what it was about, he was quite oblivious; but, as he drenched his face and temples with cold water, a more vivid recollection slowly returned, and a vision of the indescribable stuff in the tureens came across his bewildered imagination.

"Ah!" he said, "I recollect, or, at least, I begin to recollect; some of those cursed kickshaws that Hawksworth had for dinner have got into my head. It couldn't be the port, for that always agrees with me. Oh, dear, no—oh! cus my head, there it goes again—bump—bump—bump! What shall I do? I can't stay here: let me consider—there's Jenkins has often invited me to his country box, at Wandsworth. I don't see why I shouldn't go now and ruralise a little. Oh, my head! The stages go from Gracechurch Street, and a ride on the outside will do me good. Good gracious, I couldn't shave if anybody would pay me. I must go as I am; and, if I get a little better, Jenkins can lend me a razor. I am quite sure I should cut my throat if I were to take one in my hand."

So saying, Mathew Trueman, in any-thing but visiting costume, walked, in a singular, zig-zag manner, to Gracechurch-street, where, by the assistance of divers porters and coachmen, he got upon a stage that was going through Wandsworth, where we shall leave him to account to Jenkins, in the best manner he could, for his unexpected visit, and the untrim attire in which it was made.

Hilliard was one who detested the daylight: it was uncongenial to his disposition, and the more bright and beautiful it was, the more he detested it, and the more he reviled its vivid effulgence, hating it as he hated everything which was not bad and wicked like himself.

Since the murder of Mr. Noble, he never voluntarily went out during the daylight, and it was only in his absolutely necessary walks to and from the office that he encountered the sunshine, and then he shrunk from it like a guilty thing, as he was, fearful that its golden radiance would, of necessity, bring some of his iniquities to light.

On the Sundays he never, on any account, ventured out: it was his custom on the Saturday evening to lay in a sufficient stock of liquor to keep him in a state of stupefaction during that holy day, which should have been spent in singing the praises of his Maker, and repenting the deep evil that was in him.

On this Sunday, however, on the eve of which he contemplated a crime, a crime far greater in enormity, according to the opinion of all well-disposed and pious persons, because contemplated on a Sunday, he omitted his usual deep potations; and, instead of recommending himself to the throne of grace, as he ought to have done, he employed himself in rubbing up a bunch of skeleton keys; instead of praying to a watchful Providence, he polished up a crow-bar; and, in lieu of the chastening influence of religious observances, he was half the day rejoicing over the accurate workmanship of a jemmy.

Oh, that a man should thus cast away his better reason, and rather, perhaps, than go to hear the preaching of a bishop, dip deep into a puncheon of brandy! But so it is; human nature is weak and frail, and inasmuch as it is composed of dust, it is ever exposing its cloudy and obscure origin. Thus was that holy Sabbath profaned by Mark Hilliard; and, unheedful of that awful judgment which was sure to come, he only praised his own judgment for leaving Mathew Trueman's shutters unfastened; instead of dreading the sound of that silver trumpet which shall call all sinners to the throne of grace, to be precipitated to everlasting torments, or revel in an eternity of gorgeous glory, he was mentally weighing Mathew Trueman's silver spoons, and calculating, with fiendish and irreligious ferocity, the value of his forks.

The day wore on heavily to Hilliard, for he felt the necessity of keeping sober, a necessity of a terrible character to him, inasmuch as it left him to the companionship of his own thoughts, a kind of company that Mark Hilliard was not very partial to.

It was but a dreary amusement to read through those newspapers which he could not forego the perusal of, containing, as they did, the particulars of the crime he had committed in New Inn, as well as the various conjectures which the non-apprehension of the murderer had given rise to.

But the longest day will have an end, the most tardy moments will at length wing their flight into the obscurity of the past, and the long-waited-for evening came at last, dropping like a gentle veil over the fair face of Nature, sweetly quenching the daylight as death approaches the good, who have passed a long career of virtuous and calm existence, and who fear not to pass from a world of uncertainty to one of joy and peace.

The evening was calm and serene—it was one of those lulls of nature which frequently occur when a great change is about to take place in the elemental disposition.

There was a more than natural clearness in the atmosphere, a sure prognostic of rain; and, as the night dropped, not a star was visible in the heavens.

Hilliard looked from his casement with something like a feeling of satisfaction at the darkness and gloom which was rapidly approaching He held out his hand to feel assured that there was the first indication of a drizzling rain

setting in; then the small mist-like shower came thicker and thicker, and gradually the colour of every object changed beneath its influence; the streets became deserted, for a cold and uncomfortable wind at their corners blew the watery mist into the passengers' faces. Curtains were drawn in many a room, and fresh coals heaped on many a fire, while the occupants of those rooms crowded closer to the cheering blaze, and told each other, with a feeling of intense satisfaction, what an uncomfortable night it was without.

Ladies who proposed attending evening service wouldn't go—a likely thing, indeed, they were going to have their best bonnets ruined; and, as for going quite a figure to church, they were not going to do that—not they, to please anybody.

Hilliard resolved to wait another hour, for he thought that by this time the streets would be cleared, and everything as wet and uncomfortable as possible.

The hour passed away, and, secreting his house-breaking tools carefully about him, together with a dark lantern, and plenty of phosporous matches, he locked up the wretched room he inhabited, and creeping silently down the staircase, he stepped out into the miserable, wretched, uncomfortable-looking streets.

The rain was now coming down with that dogged perseverance which has well been described by superlatives, inasmuch as it is always too something.

But this was pleasant to Hilliard, and he chuckled to himself as he crept along under the shelter of the houses, to escape as much as possible from the rain. He liked the idea that every one but himself was being annoyed and vexed by the weather, while to him it was a subject of congratulation, for it afforded him greater facilities in the execution of his project.

There would be less watch on the outside of the merchant's premises, and much less attention to little incidental noises within.

"Yes," he muttered, "yes; all is as I could wish; I would have bespoken such a night; besides, it don't annoy me by its beauty, its twinkling stars, and its moon, with all of which I have proclaimed war. It is the night I like;

a night in which, without regret, I can rail at nature, and steep my senses in forgetfulness and brandy."

In the tolerably long distance between his own wretched home and the merchant's house, he scarcely met fifty people; and when he reached Thames-street, it looked as silent and deserted as if it formed one of the avenues of a city of the dead.

He walked past the house, on the opposite side of the way, several times; there was not a light visible throughout the whole extent, and he muttered to himself—

"Trueman is out—Trueman is out, or there surely would be lights in the drawing-room. Grace, too, may not be within, although what she calls her own room is, now I recollect, at the back of the house."

He then crossed over, and, by pausing, and listening close to the house, he could hear the murmured conversation of the servants, and occasionally a laugh from the kitchen, a good sign they were all well occupied, and far from watchful. The counting-house window was very near to the ground, and might be well secured by its own shutters, which bolted within, and which, in fact, had an inclination to open, if not so bolted. The slightest impulse, however, would keep them shut, and Hilliard, on the Saturday, had, in lieu of the bolt, placed a piece of wood, not thicker than a match, so as to give all the appearance of the shutters being shut; but, at the same time, to allow them to open, with a touch. He looked cautiously to the right and left, to assure himself that no one was observing him, and then he took a long and accurate survey of the opposite houses—every window was closed, every blind drawn.

"Humph!" he said, "the night is decidedly favourable. A person must be curious, indeed, that would put their heads out on such an evening. I am as thoroughly unobserved as if I were in the wilds of Africa. Now, Mathew Trueman, to pay myself somewhat better than what your wages have amounted to."

The slightest touch to the shutters sufficed to open them. The unfastened window was flung open in a moment, and in another Hilliard was in the counting-house.

His next act was to restore things to their former state, and this time he bolted the shutters, but left the window open as wide as it would go, in order to secure himself a good retreat, in case he should require it.

In spite of his villany, and his entire want of compunction, as regarded the commission of the robbery, Hilliard could not prevent himself from feeling a little nervous under his present circumstances, and it required all his thorough conviction of the unlikelihood of his receiving any interruption to enable him in any manner to recover his spirits, and to proceed with his iniquitous adventure.

Cautiously he opened the office door, and putting his head out a short distance in the passage, he listened attentively.

No sound came from the upper part of the house, but he could now plainly hear the servants conversing, and the name of Mathew Trueman coming to his ears accompanied by expressions by no means complimentary, assured him the merchant was from home, and, consequently, that he had nothing to fear from an encounter with him. Then he knew that there was but another male person in the house, and that was a sort of footman, half general servant, who whether such were the terms of his engagement or not, was expected and compelled to make himself generally useful. Him Hilliard scarcely feared, for he felt that, at all events, if he were rendered desperate by being laid hold of, he should at least be a match for the one person who should do so. The most that he feared was a general alarm and a great noise, which, if it should occur, might bring extraneous assistance to his, Hilliard's, danger.

But, of course, something must be risked, and although the worst chances of an undertaking are apt to present themselves rather vividly to the senses immediately after its commencement, and did so in Hilliard's case, he contrived, in the course of a few more minutes, to get rid of some of his apprehension, a process which was unquestionably facilitated by a hearty pull from a small brandy flask which he had brought with him.

"I cannot fail—I cannot fail," he muttered. "I must take care to drop Rivers's card-case and the envelopes of his letters where they will be readily found."

CHAPTER LXXVIII.

THE LOVERS' MEETING.—TOM HACKEY'S PERPLEXITY.—THE PRIVATE COUNTING-HOUSE.

HILLIARD'S next step, now, was to light his dark lantern, and having satisfied himself that it was in a good state, he drew on his feet a pair of large list shoes, which were sufficiently capacious to come over his boots, and feeling in his pockets for the safety of his house-breaking instruments, he congratulated himself upon the prospect of speedily and well accomplishing the robbery.

Just, however, as he was on the point of leaving the office, after casting a contemptuous look around him, for well he knew that in that room there was nothing worth his taking, a very gentle knock came at the outer door.

With a pang of alarm, he immediately rushed to the window, and, on the impulse of the moment, would have attempted to make his escape, had not his acuter judgment told him, that to spring from the window while some one was on the outer steps, would be to insure detection; he therefore waited, with no very pleasurable feelings, the result of the application at the street door.

He heard one of the servants come up from the kitchen, and then, feeling how important it might be to him to hear every word that was uttered, he crept cautiously back again to the door of the office, and listened attentively to the short colloquy that ensued.

To his intense surprise, he heard the voice of Tom Hackey say to the servant girl who opened the door—

"Well, Mary, how is you? Is Mother Woodfall at home?"

"Lor, Mr. Hackey, is that you?" said the girl. "Yes, she is."

"Very well," said Tom Hackey, "I've got something to say to the old gal, if you'll tell her a gentleman's here. I say, Mary, the old governor's out, I suppose?"

"Lor, yes," said Mary.

"So I guessed," muttered Hilliard, between his clenched teeth. "What can this fool want here?"

"Very well," said Tom. "It don't matter to me whether he's out or in, much, and you may tell him I've been here, if you like; but if you do, just add, that he may as well leave out a cheque for that five and odd he owes me."

"Lor, Mr. Thomas," said Mary, "has you gone into the acting line, as you said you would?"

"Yes," said Tom, rushing into the passage. "Bind up my wounds. To be or not to be? that is the question. Whether it is nobler in the mind to suffer the stings and arrows of outrageous fortune, or by opposing, end them? Where's Mother Woodfall?"

"Well, I never, Thomas," said Mary. "You certainly is a great actor."

"I know it," said Tom, "and you are a discerning young female. Come, bustle, bustle; Mother Woodfall to the rescue. Five Richmonds have I slain to-day, and yet not the right one."

"Well, I never," exclaimed Mary, as she ascended the stairs to tell Mrs. Woodfall of her visitor.

Grace's kind-hearted nurse immediately descended to the passage, and when she saw Tom Hackey, she said—

"How could you be so indiscreet as to come here? I beg you will go away again directly. Mr Trueman is certainly not at home, but there's no saying how soon he will be."

"Elderly female," said Tom, "I've got a note for Miss Grace, and it requiring an answer, that answer will I await in this romantic passage."

"From Mr. Rivers, of course?" said Mrs. Woodfall.

"Yes. He's waiting at the corner of the street. All his ideas are in a state of conglomeration, and he's a-wondering if Miss Grace would see him just for a minute."

"Really," said Mrs. Woodfall, "you must both of you be quite mad to think of such a thing. I will take Grace the letter, and you may wait for an answer; but mind, if Mr. Trueman should come home, do run down the kitchen stairs; for I wouldn't have him see you here on any account. You know what a very angry man he is when in a passion, and you must be aware that I am only here upon sufferance myself, and that I am in the greatest anxiety to remain on poor Grace's account."

"I will be deep, uncommonly deep," said Tom, "and frightfully artful. Trust me, Mother Woodfal, lif Mathew should come, he shall know nothing—detect nothing."

"Well, well, be careful," added Mrs. Woodfall, and then she hastened up stairs to Grace with the letter.

"My dear," she said, "here is a letter from Mr. Rivers, which that poor creature, Tom Hackey, has brought, and is waiting for an answer."

"From Rivers?" said Grace, as she broke open the epistle, with a flushed cheek.

It ran as follows:—

"DEAREST GRACE,—You cannot tell how much I prize the privilege of so addressing you. Your brief, but to me so welcome, little note, I have worn next my heart since I was blessed by its receipt. You are mine, dear Grace, and may you never—never regret the confidence you have placed in poor Francis Rivers, who has nothing to offer you in return but an affectionate heart, and a disposition to sacrifice himself, if necessary, for your happiness.

"You say you will be mine, dear Grace; and Mrs. Woodfall says you have left to me the arrangements for our happy, happy union. I write this note, therefore, to say that the singular manner by which the banns were put up by Tom Hackey, at Barnes Church, places it in out power to be wedded to-morrow. Of this circumstance you have, no doubt, been informed by Mrs. Woodfall, and if we do not take advantage of it, dear Grace, we shall break an appointment which Tom has made with the authorities of the church.

"Oh, Grace! let not my happiness be deferred, but rid me of the deep anxiety I must continually feel until you are really my own, and it is out of the power of our enemies to separate us. Say that you will meet me to-morrow morning, at nine o'clock, to ratify that promise which you have so much blessed me by making. Bring with you Mrs. Woodfall, and I will be accompanied by our only honest and really disinterested friend, Tom Hackey. You will get back to your father's by an early hour, without awakening suspicion, and if there is anything then, indeed, dear Grace, to be hoped from the great affection he must surely have for such a child as yourself, it must be speedily realised.

"Tom Hackey will bring this note, and I am waiting its answer at the corner of the next street.

"Adieu, ever dearest Grace, and believe me to be your own—own

"FRANCIS RIVERS.

"P.S.—If your father be not at home, dare I ask you to see me for one brief moment in the passage?—F. R."

Grace seized but upon the two grand points of this letter—the suddenness of her marriage, and the possibility of seeing her lover for a moment on that evening.

"Nurse—nurse," she said, "what shall I do?—what answer can I make him?"

"My dear," said Mrs. Woodfall, "I don't know exactly what he asks."

"He asks me to meet him to-morrow, to be married, and to see him for a moment to-night in the passage. Dare I do either?"

"The first, my dear," said Mrs. Woodfall, "is rather the most important; but ask yourself two questions, Grace, before you answer Mr. Rivers."

"Two questions, nurse?"

"Yes, my dear, two questions."

"And what are they?"

"The one is," said Mrs. Woodfall, "do you love Francis Rivers?"

"Do I love him?" said Grace, blushing; "can you doubt me now?"

"Very well," said Mrs. Woodfall; "the next question is, have you promised to marry him?"

"You know I have, nurse—why do you ask me?"

"Then, my dear, marry him as soon as possible, and if there is any good to result from your union, which I fondly hope there will, delay not its coming. Your situation at present is as unhappy and unsettled as it can well be, and I am sure poor Mr. Rivers himself cannot be happy."

"Then you counsel me, nurse, to marry Mr. Rivers?"

"I counsel you, my dear, to marry the man you love, rejoicing much as I do, at the same time, that he is a worthy object."

"I tremble at such precipitancy!" said Grace.

"Act as you please, and according to your own feelings and judgment," was the reply. "You have been attempted to be coerced into one marriage, Heaven forbid you should be persuaded into another."

"Let me think a moment," said Grace.

Mrs. Woodfall was silent, and Grace covered her face with her hands, while a torrent of thought rushed across her imagination; but there was no absolutely false sentiment about Grace Trueman, and she felt the argument of the nurse, that, having promised her hand, there should be no good reason why she should not ratify the contract at the earliest moment it was sought to be fulfilled.

"You hesitate, my dear," said Mrs. Woodfall; "if so, do not consent."

"No, nurse; I am his, and his only."

"And you will see him to-night?"

"Yes, in preference to writing. My father seldom returns till some hours later than this, and I believe I may see Francis Rivers in perfect safety."

"Heaven forbid, my dear, that I should prevent you. I will go and tell Tom Hackey to bring him, and then you can slip down into the passage, and have a few moments' conversation with him."

Mrs. Woodfall proceeded down stairs at once, and told Tom Hackey to hasten to Rivers and inform him that Grace would see him for a few moments in the passage.

This was a commission which Tom executed quite *con amore*, and he rushed down the street at a great rate to inform Rivers of Grace's acquiescence in his request.

* * * *

As the reader is well aware, Mark Hilliard must have overheard so much of the preceding dialogue as passed between Tom Hackey and Mrs. Woodfall in the passage, and from the latter part of it he became aware that a clandestine meeting was really about to take place between the merchant's daughter and him whom he had all along believed to be her favoured lover.

He felt himself rather in a dilemma, for the thought of having so efficient assistance in the house as Rivers, in case of any alarm, was far from pleasant, although, at the same time, he could not but feel that chance had thrown Rivers singularly in his way, as regarded implicating him in the robbery.

"Perhaps it is as well as it is," he muttered. "I will still pursue my plan, and if I find booty enough in Mathew Trueman's private counting-house—which I may, for I know that he keeps money there from Saturday till Monday—I will forego the spoons and the forks, and leave Rivers's card-case on the floor of that apartment. That, combined with the undeniable fact of his presence here to-night, must certainly convict him."

There was now no one in the passage, for Mrs. Woodfall had gone up stairs again to say a few more words to Grace before Rivers should come; but still the burglar dared not venture from where he was, for he felt that it must take him some moments to pick the lock of the merchant's private counting-house, and, during that brief space, how could he be sure that Rivers would not arrive, and at once crush his hopes by seizing him upon the spot?

"'Tis quite as well that he should go," muttered Hilliard, "before I proceed. Neither Mrs. Woodfall nor Grace can deny the fact of Rivers having been here this evening, and that will be sufficient—amply sufficient for his condemnation. I will wait till this precious love-meeting is over, and will then see how delightful a trap this fine young gentleman has laid for himself."

Mark Hilliard did wait accordingly, and by laying his ear close to the office door, he heard every word that passed in the passage. Mrs. Woodfall came down before Tom Hackey and Rivers arrived, and held the door in her hand, so as to prevent the necessity of Tom's knocking again. She likewise brought no light, for she and Grace agreed that it would be quite as safe, if not much safer, for Rivers to have his meeting with her who was so soon to be his wife up stairs, instead of in the passage, where they might be overheard by some of the servants.

To Tom Hackey all this was delightful, for he considered it highly melo-dramatic in the extreme, and he came down the street after Rivers, making himself look as much like a stage robber as possible, flourishing now and then an imaginary poniard, and darting into dark doorways for a moment, without the slightest necessity, all of which would have put Rivers very much out of the way had he seen it, but he was so intently thinking upon Grace, and what he should say to her, that he paid no attention to Tom Hackey or his peculiarities.

When they arrived at the door, Tom ascended the steps, and knocked three mysterious knocks, saying, at the same time—

"Hist! hist!—be careful—hush! hush! Night has put on her sable mantle. Oh, Romeo—Romeo—wherefore art thou——"

"Now, really, Tom," said Rivers, "this is too bad. I beg that for once in the way, you will be a little rational, and now I think of it, you really needn't come in at all."

"I am very much obliged to you," said Tom; "after the handsome manner in which Grace has consented to marry us, it isn't likely I should behave so queer as not to give her a call when she is willing. Hush! hush! Mother Woodfall; just be so good as to fancy yourself an old duenna."

"For Heaven's sake," whispered Mrs. Woodfall to Rivers, "send that Marplot away—he'll ruin everything if he's permitted to remain here."

"Why, you stupid old pump," said Tom, "you must be beside yourself."

"Tom, you shan't come in," said Rivers, "and there's an end of it," so saying, he took Tom by the shoulders, and pushed him on to the step of the door, adding, "Don't be a fool—there's a good fellow; you know my friendship for you, and I will be with you in ten minutes."

"Oh," said Tom, when he heard the door shut behind him, "that's uncommonly pleasant. Candid advice from a friend—'don't be a fool!' Thank you for nothing. I don't mean to be Re-

markably agreeable this, and mizzling in rain this way, too. Well, I suppose my best plan will be to sit down on this ere top step. It ain't very wet; I have heard that a light heart and a thin pair of inexpressibles go through the world. The light heart may be all very well, but it strikes me that a thick pair —God bless me!—what's that?—would be desirable."

Tom Hackey's exclamation arose from a bright flash of light coming across his eyes from a chink in the shutters in the office—that office which he knew perfectly well was always closed on the Sunday, and never gone into on any consideration, inasmuch as there could be no occasion for so doing, except on some subject connected with the accounts or the business transactions of Mathew Trueman.

"Well," he cried, "I wonder what the deuce that was. I could almost have taken a solemn and natural sort of oath that there was a light in the office. However, it's no business of mine; I ain't on the establishment, and all the interest I have in it is a matter of five-and-odd. Old Burnby is the watchman, and Mathew takes deuced good care he'll always be insured, and as for Grace—oh, d—n it, I don't want her burnt, though, nor frightened to death with thieves either. What shall I do? —make a row? no—kick up a breeze? no—peep through the window-shutters? that's the ticket. What a melo-drama it would make—'The Mysterious Free-booter; or, the Sanguinary Hole in the Parlour Shutter!' Goodness gracious! a three-act piece—beginning with a chorus of villagers, that means nothing at all, and ending in some blue fire, that leaves everything in delightful obscurity, and makes the audience sneeze dreadfully till the next piece comes on."

By this time Hackey had scrambled on to the window-sill, and applying his eye to one of the round holes in the shutters, he took a long and earnest look into the office.

All was darkness, for Mark Hilliard had that very moment left it, and was in the passage.

———————

CHAPTER LXXIX.

THE ALARM.—THE SILVER SALVER.—
DETECTION AND ITS CONSEQUENCES.
THE FLIGHT AND THE PISTOL SHOT.

HILLIARD had heard the whispering between Mrs. Woodfall and Rivers in the passage, relative to his, Rivers's, proceeding up stairs, instead of having an interview with Grace by the door. Impatience then took possession of him, and, moreover, he thought that possibly he might succeed in finding sufficient booty in Mathew Trueman's private office to compensate him for all his trouble, in which case he might be able to leave the house before Rivers should think of doing so.

That Tom Hackey was upon the steps he knew not, or he would, in all likelihood, have come to some different arrangement; as it was, however, he saw no risk in doing as he proposed, and cautiously creeping out of the clerk's

office, just a moment before Tom Hackey clambered up to the window we have described, he crept down the passage, until he arrived at the door of Mathew Trueman's private counting house; producing, then, cautiously, from his pocket, a skeleton key, which, from previous passing observations on the lock, he thought would most readily open it, he cast for one moment the glare of his lantern on the keyhole, and then made as noiseless efforts as possible to unlock that door of which Mathew Trueman, himself, always kept the key

He succeeded with greater facility than he had dared to suspect; and passing into the office, he closed the door behind him, fastening it by the little bolt under the lock, for fear any one should come upon him suddenly when he was unprepared to meet them.

The first object to which Hilliard directed his attention was a large old fashioned secretaire, standing against one of the walls of the room, in some of the drawers of which he had frequently suspected Mathew Trueman kept money for current purposes, those current purposes, to his knowledge, frequently extending to the expenditure of upwards of a thousand pounds in a day.

The locks in the secretaire were numerous and complex; but Mark Hilliard had made picking locks a peculiar study, and few, very few, experienced locksmiths could even equal him in the facility with which he overcame the most difficult pieces of mechanism of that description.

The consequence of this skill was, that in a few moments the locks of Mathew Trueman's secretaire had yielded, and the contents of that cumbrous piece of furniture were at the mercy of the robber.

To his intense disappointment, however, he found nothing to repay him except one solitary five pound note for the trouble he had taken; and, with a bitter curse upon his evil fortune, he began to think what should be his next step.

That next step was one nearly proving fatal to him, for it was to drink up to the dregs the remainder of the flask of brandy he had brought with him, making in all nearly a pint of that liquor which he had taken since his entrance into the merchant's house, upon very nearly an empty stomach.

Mark Hilliard was not to say intoxicated, but he was in that state of daring ferocity which commonly came over him when in a state of half inebriation. He was ripe and ready for anything, however hazardous, and despite his utter want of knowledge of what part of the house Rivers was in, he determined upon proceeding up stairs to the back drawing-room, where was a sideboard, in the drawers of which he knew was kept a good collection of silver plate, with the exception of a few articles that were of daily use and insignificant importance.

The list shoes which he wore over his boots deadened the sound of his footsteps, besides he was so extremely cautious; but had he been much less so, Grace Trueman and Rivers would not have heard him, for their hearts were too much bound up in the delightful interchange of pure and beautiful thoughts they were having with each other to attend to anything in the world besides.

The world was within themselves; and what to them were time, tide, or circumstance, so long as they could breathe to each other in those fervent, low tones, which speak the very essence of pure affection, the feelings which reign without one alloy of selfishness or guile within their breasts.

Mrs. Woodfall, too, after beseeching Grace not to allow the interview to extend beyond ten minutes, for fear her father should return earlier than usual, had repaired to her own room, which was situated in the upper part of the house.

Thus Mark Hilliard, for the servants were all engaged in amusing themselves with gossiping in the kitchen, had but to exercise caution and discretion, common caution, and common diligence, to secure to himself a valuable plunder, and, at all events, descend in safety to the street-door, where, although he might encounter Tom Hackey, he might still be able to overcome his resistance should he offer any, and to escape the consequences of his crime, although he might lose his situation.

To tell the truth, the ruffian did exercise great caution and great discretion, if his avarice stood in the way of his using great diligence, for the plate was provokingly distributed among various drawers, and it was a matter requiring considerable care to place the various articles in his pockets without jingling them together and producing an alarm.

At length, however, he felt certain that he was in possession of the bulk of the property, with the exception of a large silver salver, which he could not think of leaving on any account, since it was nearly sixty ounces, and formed a valuable addition to his already acquired plunder. The salver, however, was a very awkward article to carry; if he emerged with it into the open air exposed, he was extremely liable to be stopped and questioned concerning it; and, moreover, by carrying it loosely, he was depriving himself of the free use of his arms, which he might yet require ere he left the merchant's house.

"I will button it inside my coat,"

he muttered; "it will be quite safe there, and it will escape observation; and in less than a couple of hours after my leaving here, the salver, along with the remainder of the silver, will be in the Jew's crucible, who I know will give me the current price for any booty."

Placing, then, his lantern on the sideboard, he buttoned the salver within his coat, and then, glancing round him, he muttered,

"D—n it, I have done my best; what I have will produce me thirty or forty pounds, at the least; I was in hopes of cash, but that, it seems, was no go, with the exception of this five-pound note, which I shall get but two for, on the risk of Mathew Trueman knowing the number. It would be a foolish risk, now, loaded as I am—a very foolish risk, and I will not attempt it. I may as well be satisfied with what I have got."

He then, walking with difficulty, owing to the really great weight of silver he had with him, nearly reached the door, when, as ill-fortune would have it for him, the rim of the salver, which had only been supported, accidentally, upon one of the buttons of his clothing, slipped off from that frail fixture, and fell with a tremendous clatter to the floor, alarming every one in the house, and filling the mind of Grace with terror and dismay.

A bitter oath burst from his own lips, and for an instant he hesitated whether to make a rush down the staircase and escape with the booty he had, or make another attempt to secure the silver salver. Avarice, at length, prevailed, and stooping to pick up the massive piece of plate, he would, perhaps, have escaped with it, had not, at that instant, the folding doors leading from the front drawing-room been dashed open, and Rivers rushed into the room.

A loud scream burst from Grace, as she, in a moment, saw her lover grasping some one by the throat; as for Hilliard, he was too much paralyzed, for the moment, by fear, to make any active exertion to free himself from Rivers; but then, with the rapidity of lightning, there came across his mind in frightful array all the fearful and bitter consequences of detection. De-

tection, too, with the irrefragible proof of guilt upon him: detection, too, by him of all others whom he most hated, and in whose supposed destruction he was but a little while before felicitating himself.

Such thoughts as these were too much for human nature, and rage and despair lent to Hilliard the courage and energy he really lacked.

With a yell more like that of some ferocious beast than the cry of a human being, he grappled with Rivers; and so sudden and ferocious was his attack, that he succeeded for a moment in wrenching himself from the grasp of his opponent, and nearly reached the door of the room.

Rivers, however, was not so readily to be foiled, and pronouncing aloud the name of Hilliard, as he detected who it was that was making such desperate efforts to escape, he again sprung forward, to seize him. Unfortunately, however, he tripped over the silver salver, which was lying between them, and in his effort to save himself, he fell backwards at the precise moment that Hilliard, drawing a pistol from his pocket, discharged it full in the direction of his face.

The ruffian then rushed down the staircase, and with one blow levelling Mathew Trueman's useful man-of-all-work, who stood bewildered in the passage, he gained the street door, and ran rapidly off towards the purlieus of Tower Hill, where he expected he should be best able to baffle pursuit, if attempted, and where he knew he should find a ready sale for the plate with which he was loaded.

Grace stood transfixed with terror in the front drawing-room during the enacting of this violent scene, which took up less time during its performance than it as taken us to relate.

But when she saw Rivers fall, and heard the stunning report of the pistol, a spell seemed to be taken off her faculties, and with such a cry of anguish, which could only burst from such a heart as her's, in the belief that its best treasure was sacrificed by the hand of an assassin, she flew towards Rivers, who lay motionless, for his head came in rather violent contact with the hard corner of a rosewood chair, which half stunned him, and throwing herself upon her knees by his side, she shrieked his name once, and then dropped in a state of insensibility across his prostrate form.

The greatest confusion reigned throughout the house; the servants ran this way and that, in the most disorderly state imaginable, and the useful man-of-all-work left the house, without any clear idea of whither he was going, nor stopped till he ran against a post in Cannon-street.

As for the female servants, they thought that to reach the passage, and commence what now would have been paid no attention to, because it would only have been considered a private meeting of some class practising singing for the million—namely, a series of discordant sounds and yells, such as may be frequently heard in Exeter Hall now, which is, we believe, licensed by act of parliament for all sorts of humbug.

Then their alarm was still further increased by the suddenly rushing in among them of a disorderly-looking figure, who, if he had not spoken, would scarcely have been taken for Tom Hackey.

"Summon the guards!" he cried. "To horse—to horse! Off with his head—so much for the Lord knows who! Look at my hat."

Tom Hackey's hat certainly bore some marks of recent ill-usage, inasmuch, as instead of presenting the usual cylindrical form of such machines, it was perfectly flat, and on one side of it well plastered with mud.

"Look here," cried Tom. "I was sitting on the step, as innocent as a whole drove of lambs, when somebody comes tumbling over me, without so much as asking me if I wanted a game of leap-frog, knocks my hat off, and, by some singular contrivance, makes me sit down upon it in the middle of the road. Only look! there's a smash! I'll be hanged if I'd stand it, only I can't help it. Who it was, or who it wasn't, I can't take upon myself to say. D—n it, don't laugh, whatever you do! It's no laughing matter, I can tell you. Fancy some of your bonnets that you women are always making such a scrimmage about, being let in for for such a

proceeding! there'd be a regular squall, I'll be bound; something like elderly Nicholas to pay, and no pitch hot."

"Lor, Mr. Hackey, is that you?" said the two housemaids and cook in chorus; "how uncommonly thankful we are."

"I am very much obliged to you," said Tom, "but as far as I am personally concerned, I had rather it had been somebody else. I don't know exactly what extent of frightful damage I have suffered, but I expect it is rather considerable, and decidedly vexatious."

"But we heard a scream," said the two housemaids and the cook again.

"Ah," said Tom Hackey, "it wasn't me; I'd scorn the action."

A loud cry at this moment from up stairs of "Help! help!" came to Tom's ears, and he cried—

"That's Grace's voice!" and then, without a moment's hesitation, he rushed into the house, nor stopped until he reached the first floor.

The door of the back room was wide open, and the first object that presented itself to Tom Hackey's horrified gaze was what appeared to be the dead bodies of Grace and Rivers, lying upon the floor of the back drawing-room

The poor fellow for a moment was perfectly horror-stricken; he could neither move nor speak; and when he did recover his voice it was to call for help in a much louder tone than Grace had used.

At the sound of his voice Grace looked up, for she had recovered from her insensibility, and in accents of the most piercing grief, she said—

"He's murdered—he's murdered! Mark Hilliard has killed him!"

"The devil he has!" said Tom. "Here, help, all of you! bring more light's—run for a doctor—fetch old Burnby—no, hang it, he's no use!"

The servants had by this time ventured up into the room, and Tom Hackey lifted up the head of Rivers, saying—

"For God's sake, miss, compose yourself; he mayn't be dead, after all."

Then, as the numerous lights flashed across his face, Rivers opened his eyes, saying—

"What—what is all this? Good Heavens! where am I?"

"He lives! he lives!" shrieked Grace.

"So I should say," remarked Tom.

"Are you hurt, Rivers? Oh, tell me you are not hurt!" added Grace.

"No, dear Grace," said Rivers; "I think not, although I am so confused just now, I cannot tell. How came I here? Yet, now I recollect. Some one surely fired at me the moment that I stumbled and fell."

"There, you see," said Tom, "there's no harm done, after all. Let me see, I don't suppose there's any bones broken."

So saying, Tom seized hold of one of Rivers's legs, and began twisting it about in a very surgical sort of manner.

"Thank you," said Rivers, rubbing his head; "I am quite sure there are no bones broken, Tom, although there is a bump on my head, certainly; in all probability, my fall saved me from the shot which I now recollect the villain Hilliard aimed at me.

"And look here," said Tom, "here's Mathew's silver salver lying on the floor, with such a bump on it as will aggravate him for a month to think of. It strikes me very forcibly there's been a robbery."

"Yes; this has been an attempt of Hilliard's to rob the house, an attempt which has only failed, Rivers, through you accidental presence here. My father must surely be grateful for the service you have rendered him."

"Query," said Tom Hackey. "It would be rather uncomfortable to explain to him how you came here; and now, you females, one and all, can you take upon yourselves to say—which I sincerely hope you can, although I don't want to bias you for a moment, oh dear, no—that it was Mark Hilliard who ran down the stairs and made me sit on my hat in the road?"

The servants shook their heads, for, to tell the truth, they had seen no one run down, having not themselves emerged from the kitchen till after Hilliard's escape, and Mathew Trueman's useful man had not yet returned from his expedition Heaven knows where, after his fright.

"I can," said Rivers, "take upon myself to swear that it was Hilliard who fired the shot at me, and consequently, he must have been the robber. 'Tis true, I did not see his face, as it was concealed by a mask; but, nevertheless, I am certain it was he. I could not mistake his voice, and he spoke twice during our brief encounter."

"Go down stairs, all of you," said Mrs. Woodfall to the servants; "and let me advise you to say nothing of this affair until you are questioned, which most likely you will be when Mr. Trueman himself comes home."

Upon this, the servants, keeping close together, upon the principle that union is strength, descended to the kitchen, leaving Rivers, Tom Hackey, Mrs, Woodfall, and Grace, in a state of very great perplexity in the back drawing-room.

CHAPTER LXXX.

AFTER THE ROBBERY.—THE PROMISE FOR THE MORROW.—THE MERCHANT'S UNEXPECTED ARRIVAL.

"What is to be done now?" said Mrs. Woodfall. "Here is a most unexpected adventure. Oh! Mr. Rivers, I don't know whether to be sorry or glad that you were here to-night."

"I rejoice exceedingly," said Rivers; "for I may have been the cause of saving you, Grace, from the insults of a ruffian."

"And I," said Grace, as she clung to his arm, "I am so full of joy that you have escaped from the attempt against your life, that all other considerations sink into insignificance. One great grief, Rivers, will swallow up a host of petty evils, and one great joy will have the same effect."

"And I," said Tom Hackey, striking into a theatrical attitude, "how intensely gratified I ought to be. First of all I was turned out on the step in a mizzle, there I remain until I get comfortably wet through—then all of a sudden a fellow comes and bundles over me, neck-or-nothing, and the next thing I discover is, that I am sitting in the middle of the road on my hat. I'm delighted, of course."

"Mr. Rivers," said Mrs. Woodfall, "let me beseech you to go at once. This affair will tell much better in your absence than in your presence, and show a hope from it that Mr. Trueman, by finding out the villany of others, and your own integrity, will view you with a more favourable aspect."

"I have some thoughts of staying," said Tom, "as I am here; that five and odd sticks in my throat, rather, and I don't see why I shouldn't have it."

"For Heaven's sake, go," cried Mrs. Woodfall; "be advised, and go at once."

"Grace," whispered Rivers, "dear Grace, you will remember, to-morrow, at nine?"

"Where?" said Grace, faintly.

"In St. Paul's Churchyard," said Rivers, in reply. "There is a Richmond coach starting at that hour. It passes through Barnes, and will convey us well."

Grace hesitated a moment, and then, when she looked at Rivers's appealing face, said—

"I have given you my heart, Rivers, and I cannot take it back again. I will be there."

"How can I thank you, dearest?"

"Hush! Good-night—good-night; when we meet again, it may be that I shall be able to tell you of some relenting feeling in my father's heart as regards you."

"Heaven send, dear Grace, for your sake, it may be so. Good-night—good-night, my blessings attend you."

Grace cast upon him one look, rich in affection, and then Rivers, turning to Tom Hackey, said—

"Come, Tom, let us go."

"Oh, you are ready, are you?" said Tom. "It's remarkably pleasant to be told to go and asked to come just to suit other people, but I suppose it's all right. Grace, good night, bless you—recollect to-morrow—it would break our hearts to be disappointed. It shall be our efforts through life to gild your existence, and to be continually regilding it whenever it is requisite. Meet us to-morrow, and don't disappoint the sexton. Farewell—dream of us all night. Fancy you are wandering with us in delightful groves, and that nymphs and other people, who have nothing particular to occupy their minds, are kicking up the devil's delight on nature's verdant livery; fancy that, as you lie lapped in elysium slumbers."

"Come along," said Rivers, as he seized Hackey by the arm, and stopped not until he got him to the street door. "How can you be so absurd, Tom, as to keep continually saying 'we,' when speaking of Grace and myself?"

"Don't give your mind to selfishness," said Tom. "Of course, I say, 'cause it is 'we.' Hasn't she consented to marry us, and all that sort of thing?"

Rivers laid his hand on the street door to open it, when a sounding double knock on the other side announced an arrival.

"Mathew, by all that's infernal!" said Tom.

"The deuce it is," said Rivers.

"Let's run into the kitchen, like blazes," said Tom. "You can get into the dust-hole, while I can ensconce myself in the dutch-oven."

"No," said Rivers, "as I am here, I won't hide. You can do as you like, Tom, I'm going to open the door."

"Hurrah, for a row, then," said Tom. "Here'll be a kettle of fish, and the strainer lost—go it."

Tom Hackey very diligently turned up the cuffs of his coat, as if he expected to have a pugilistic encounter with Mathew Trueman, while Rivers opened the street-door, and stood face to face with the astonished merchant.

"Francis Rivers!" said Mathew Trueman, almost staggering off his own steps.

"Yes, sir," said Rivers. "My name is Francis Rivers."

"And how the devil came you here, sir?"

"Come, come, Mathew," said Tom, "don't be insolent; recollect that five and add you owe us. We came for our blunt, and we mean to have it. The tin, Mathew, the tin."

"You—you—cursed insolent—" exclaimed Mathew Trueman, almost foaming with rage. "Watch! watch!"

"There now, said Tom, "you'll make yourself ill. I dare say, now, you've been to dine, and come home on a full stomach. You'll have the nightmare, Mathew, safe as a gun."

"Silence, silence, Tom," said Rivers. "Mr. Trueman, you have too much good sense, surely, to heed what this honest, but eccentric fellow says. I came here uninvited by any one; for an explanation of what has occurred during my presence in your house, I believe I may refer you to Mrs. Woodfall; for myself, sir, I am afraid our further conversation would but provoke anger on both sides; I will, therefore, bid you good evening, sir."

"Upon my life," said the merchant, as Rivers walked past him, "that's cool, however. A fellow comes into one's house, and then declines explaining why, for fear one should be angry. Curse such impudence."

"Mathew Newman, or Trueman, or Blueman, or whatever your name may be, I shall not remain here any longer, for fear I should get into a passion, in which case I might make you feel, above abit. Good-night, Mathew what's-your-name. Take things easy, and don't be violent. Nothing is so injurious to an old gentleman as cultivating his own passions. Good-night, never mind the door. I'll summons you some other day for the five and odd."

So saying, Tom Hackey walked past the bewildered merchant, who turned twice or thrice round before he spoke, and then he said—

"Am I awake—am I Mathew Trueman the merchant—and is this my own house? Hang me if I ain't doubtful of my own identity. Confound them! Ah! I'll let them know I have come home if it is me."

With this, Mathew Trueman laid hold of the knocker, and executed such a tremendous knock, that the servants, one and all, thought that the housebreaker had returned with a strong force to back him, and fully intended taking the premises by storm. It was not until Mathew Trueman had again assaulted the knocker with prodigious violence, that they began to ask each other who should go to the door, not at all suspecting that it was open, or that it was the merchant himself making such an alarm.

A third time Mathew Trueman seized the knocker, and that time he nearly fell down, for it came off in his hand.

Now, to an angry man, who wants to knock very loudly at the door, the knocker giving up the job, and coming suddenly off, is a most aggravating circumstance, and so Mathew Trueman thought, for, after stamping in the pas-

sage in the most alarming manner, he flung the knocker down the kitchen staircase at the very moment the servants, who in a body, had made up their minds to answer the door, were just moving up the stairs for that purpose.

The uproar, however, which the knocker made in its descent, at once altered their determination, and with a simultaneous scream they bolted the kitchen door, and succeeded in entirely disappearing in two huge cupboards that were in that apartment.

Slamming the street-door shut with a frightful bang, the merchant walked up stairs, where the first person he met was Mrs. Woodfall, to whom he cried—

"So, madam, it appears you can explain what appears inexplicable, and can let me know why it is that I cannot be absent from my house a day without finding on my return people here whom I have expressly forbidden to enter its doors."

"I have voluntarily. Mr. Trueman," said Mrs. Woodfall, "undertaken, upon your return, to make that explanation, and I will tell you the truth—Mr. Rivers came here to see your daughter."

"Indeed!" said Mathew Trueman. "Upon my soul, ma'am, you are a remarkably nice old lady to leave in charge of a house; but, curse you—you shall be discharged to-morrow. I looked over your atrocious and d—nable conduct once, but I won't again; the explanation is quite sufficient—oh, dear me, ample, and doesn't admit of a shadow of a doubt. Ah! a nice article you are!"

"Mr. Trueman, you may indulge in what abuse of me you please; when I come to be on my death-bed, thank Heaven, I shall not be able to charge myself with endeavouring to sacrifice my only child to my own schemes of selfish ambition."

"Mrs. Woodfall," said Trueman, "you are the most abominable of old females, and I'll hold no further conversation with you, and to-morrow you leave my service with as bad a character as I can give you."

"But I have something further to say to you, Mr. Trueman. During your absence your house has been robbed."

"Robbed!" shrieked the merchant.

"Yes, the bulk of your plate has been

carried off by a villain, who, but for Mr Rivers, would most likely have robbed you to a still greater extent; and, perhaps, added the crime of violence to that of dishonesty."

"My plate—my plate!" said the merchant, "who has dared to touch my plate? I see it all now—it's a planned thing—a desperate, d——able, planned thing! That scoundrel, Rivers, and Hackey, have robbed me, and were just escaping with the booty when I reached the street door. I see it all. Oh, it's as clear as possible; but I'll have them hanged, transported, and you, too, you old ——, as—what do they call it—*particeps criminis.* Confound you all, I'll go to the police! I'll have revenge, and justice, and law, and, d——me, I'll have everything!"

"Mr. Trueman, you can take what steps you may think proper," said Mrs. Woodfall; "but I tell you, as true as there's a God in Heaven, Mr. Rivers is innocent of that which you would impute to him; the evidence, on oath, of your own daughter will screen him from the charge."

"Pooh! pooh! don't tell me," cried the merchant; "girls will swear anything for their lovers. They will take their oaths that white is black, and black white, but am I a fool—do I look like a fool? I, Mathew Trueman, who have raised myself from three-and-a-penny to what I am now, ah! and am now raising myself still higher; but I'll have justice and law—I will go to the police. They shall be apprehended — committed — tried—hung—transported—and then I'll have vengeance. My plate—my plate!"

So saying, Mathew Trueman rushed down the stairs, and out of the house again like a madman.

CHAPTER LXXXI.

THE POLICE.—THE CHARGE OF FELONY REBUTTED.—THE ACCUSATION AND ITS RESULTS.

A LONG and serious conversation ensued between Mrs. Woodfall and Grace, and although Mrs. Woodfall's fears were much increased with regard to the lasting enmity of Mathew Trueman to Rivers, yet she could not now desire Grace to retract her promise of meeting on the morrow for the celebration of the nuptials, and it was agreed, that happen what might, or what other steps Mathew Trueman should think proper to take concerning the robbery, and by way of carrying out his suspicions of Rivers and Tom Hackey, if those suspicions were indeed real, that she, Grace, accompanied by her nurse, would keep their appointment on the following morning with Rivers.

"Besides, dear nurse," said Grace, "I have it in my power, by my own direct testimony, to free Mr. Rivers from the charge that my father in his anger seems disposed to bring against him, but which in his cooler judgment I dare say he will repent of."

"That is true, my dear," said Mrs. Woodfall, "and, therefore, a subject of great congratulation. Your father walked in two great a passion from me to enable me to tell him who was the real criminal."

Mathew Trueman came back in the course of half an hour, accompanied by two police officers, who, upon searching the premises, at once pitched upon the office window as the place by which the robber had made his ingress, and from thence they followed the proceedings of the burglar to Mathew Trueman's private office, and to the back drawing-room.

"Well, sir," the men then said, "if there is any one you can suspect, we can apprehend him upon the suspicion."

"I do suspect," said the merchant, "one Francis Rivers, a lately discharged clerk of mine, as well as an errand boy, whom I discharged at the same time, and with whom this Rivers is extremely intimate."

"Can you tell us where they reside?" was the question.

"No," said the merchant, "I'll be hanged if I can."

"The inquiry is needless," said Grace, as with a pale face and determined air, she passed through the folding doors of the front drawing-room to the back. "The inquiry is needless—Mr. Rivers is innocent, and so is his humble but true friend, Hackey. I am ready to make oath that Mr. Rivers was conversing with me in the front drawing-room here when the robber, who was in this room, made an alarm by letting fall some of his plunder."

" Indeed !" said one of the officers.

" Oh, pooh ! pooh ! nonsense," cried Mathew Trueman.

" It is as I say," added Grace ; " I can make oath to those facts, and what is more, I saw a pistol fired at Mr. Rivers, in his attempt to secure the villain ; yon wall bears testimony to where the shot took effect, but narrowly missing him it was intended to destroy."

" This young lady's evidence, sir," said one of the officers, " alters the case very materially, indeed, and this Mr. Rivers that you mention will be a valuable witness in the case, instead of a suspected party."

" It's false—false," cried the merchant, stamping with anger. " It's false, every word of it—a mere made up story. Grace, I am ashamed of you ; how can you consent to marry one man, and tell such atrocious lies for another ?"

" Father," said Grace " I know not

what you mean, and at all events, whatever you mean to imply, surely the present time is not the moment to urge it."

" Oh ! dear me," said Mathew Trueman, " you turn wonderfully considerate at all once ; perhaps, as you know so perfectly well who did not commit this robbery, you may know who did ?"

" Yes," said Grace, immediately, " I do know who did."

" You do ! who was it, then ?"

" Mark Hiilliard."

" Pshaw !" cried the merchant ; "likely I am going to suspect a person whom I did not see here, and whom I had not discharged, in lieu of one whom I saw with my own eyes attempting to leave the house, and who was discharged some time before. Does that look probable ?" turning to the officers.

" We can't go upon probabilities, sir," said one of them. " It would be madness to apprehend the person, Rivers, in the face of the testimony which this young lady says she can give in his favour. No magistrate would commit him for trial, and no jury would convict him."

"Not convict him—not convict him?" said Mathew Truemen, "but I will have him convicted; I desire that he may be immediately apprehended; if it costs me a thousand pounds, I'll have him convicted."

"You can't, sir, convict a man of felony just because you wish it. You may go before a magistrate, and make your deposition of the case, and if he will grant a warrant against the person you suspect, I will take him; but unless such is the case, I shall decline, myself, interfering in the matter."

"You're right," said Grace; "exercise your better judgment, father, in this matter. You must feel that a supposition of guilt on the part of Mr. Rivers is contrary to all that we know concerning him, his habits, and disposition; recollect that his father was your friend —I have heard you say your most useful friend. Do not, oh! do not, then, in a moment of anger, commit yourself past the power of retraction."

"Oh, it's all very well your talking," said Trueman; "girls always think their lovers patterns of perfection—that is quite understood; but as I happen to be a man of business myself, I can't enter into all those pleasant little hypocrisies. I will apply to the Lord Mayor, in the morning, and if I don't get a warrant against those two vagabonds, Hackey and Rivers, my name is not Mathew Trueman."

"Then it appears we need not," said one of the officers, "trouble ourselves any further. Good-evening, sir."

"Oh, good-evening to you," said Mathew Trueman. "I'll get a warrant —two warrants. I'm not going to be ridden over—no, not I. And now, Miss Grace, perhaps you will condescend to explain, as we are alone, and I presume I may venture upon the inquiry, how you came to have the confounded assurance to have clandestine interviews with my discharged clerk, after, too, the manner in which you have treated Lord Hawksworth, a manner which I certainly hoped was more like yourself,

and more consistent with my wishes and objects?"

"What manner do you speak of?" said Grace.

"What manner!—what manner! I suppose you will now swear me out that you have given him no encouragement at all, and meant nothing by it?"

"Meant nothing by what?" said Grace.

"Gracious powers!" exclaimed the merchant, stamping about on the floor like a maniac. "I suppose you want to drive me mad?"

"'Tis I who have been driven nearly distracted, father," said Grace.

"Distracted—d—n it! This is a persecution that I have never endured before."

"Do you talk of persecution, father? Can you recollect what I have endured?"

"Have you not encouraged the man —the lord, I mean?"

"I encourage him," said Grace, "with my feelings of utter detestation and abhorrence of his name!"

Mathew Trueman gave a curious sort of howl, and as he threw himself into a chair, he said—

"Girkins was right—Girkins was right—d—n it! Girkins was right. He knows women better than I do, and I begin to be of his opinion; they are all female devils and rusty weathercocks. They don't know their own minds a minute. They are all will-o'-the-wisps, and everything that is changeable and horrid. D—n them up in heaps!" and then came another howl, similar to the former, and Grace really began to think her father's wits were a little distracted.

"Did you, or did you not, send a letter to Lord Hawksworth?"

"I certainly did," said Grace, "but what of that?"

"What of that?—what of that?" cried the merchant. "Am I on my head or my heels? Grace—Grace— you feminine imp—you devil! You'll be satisfied when you've driven me distracted, and made me a ward of chancery."

"And you'll be satisfied, father, I suppose, when I am dead?" said Grace, bursting into tears.

"There she goes—there she goes,"

said the merchant. "That's the way—it's no use talking to a woman—not the slightest—I've done—I've done. Perhaps you'll tell me you don't mean to have Lord Hawksworth after all?"

"Have him!—have him!" cried Grace, with great vehemence. "Before I would associate myself with so vile a specimen of human nature, I would encounter death in its worst form."

"You won't have him?" shouted Mathew Trueman. "You won't be a countess?"

"As I have hopes of Heaven!" said Grace, "I will not have him."

Mathew Trueman got up, and, lifting the chair in which he had been sitting, he flung it against the end of the room, fracturing one of its legs, and making a great noise; after which, he threw his hat into the middle of the chandelier, and then, in a state bordering upon frenzy, he rushed a second time that night from his house.

All this was quite inexplicable to poor Grace. She knew not what to think, and little guessing how artfully Girkins had made use of the circumstance of her sending so innocent a letter to Lord Hawksworth, to get up a false impression in her father's mind, she could not for a moment believe that that had produced his singular conduct upon the present occasion.

"Oh, what a day has this been!" cried Grace, clasping her hands. "What a day of anxiety and terror, of alarm and apprehension. My father cannot, in his calmer moments, dream of accusing Rivers of the robbery which he nearly entirely prevented; but if he does so accuse him, he shall accuse his daughter's husband, for I will keep my promise, and to-morrow morning shall see me the wife of him who has suffered so much persecution for my sake."

CHAPTER LXXXIII.

THE MORNING OF THE MARRIAGE.—THE MEETING IN ST. PAUL'S CHURCHYARD.—MATHEW TRUEMAN'S TROUBLESOME VISITOR.

WHAT a night of deep anxiety was that to the persons in whose interests and in whose fate we hope we have excited in the mind of the reader a kindly interest, as of careful thought, of uneasy rumination, tinctured, too, with happier prognostications. Rivers found it impossible to sleep, for the singular events that had occurred at the merchant's house occupied his thoughts fully, and quite prevented slumber stealing over him. Over and over again he thought over the probabilities and improbabilities of his obtaining employment in London, where was perpetually going on so vast a struggle for precedence in the race of life; where were so many hundreds—ay, probably thousands, better qualfied, from previous habits, for the class of appointments among which he could only hope to procure employment.

He could do no one peculiar thing which but a few others could do likewise, and consequently he trembled when he considered such was the frightful order of things, that he could scarcely present to society an inducement to allow him the means of subsistence.

Time was when parents congratulated themselves and each other, when they had given their children a decent education, because such, they considered, protected them, at all events, against the common contingencies of life; but how far different, of late years, has it been in England, when such decent education even when it runs to extremes, which our forefathers little dreamed of, confers, in many instances, but a patent of starvation upon its possessors! Still Rivers was young and sanguine.

"Surely—surely," he said to himself, "we shall not starve; how few come to such a fate as that in this country!"

He was right; but few—very few are starved to death in this great and Christian country; but how many arrive at the portals of the tombs by a slower process, a process of want, which, although certainly one degree above starvation, resembles, in its effects, as closely as death, by lingering disease, does any of those rapid transitions of mortality to immortality which are so frequent. But to return to our story.

The chill gloom of night still hung over the town, and as yet the gray light in the east had not become visible to harbinger the coming morn. No soul moved along the deserted streets: true, there were here and there a few men, whose duty was to watch over the city, and the peace of the inhabitants, and these were few, and at intervals. Occasionally a knot of them would get together in some dark corner, and discuss the relative merits of their superiors, and now and then turn their keen glances in different ways, to ascertain if any one was approaching; or, probably, from habit, they peered into all imaginable places possible, as well as impossible.

All is wrapped in stillness, and in many streets not even these guardians of the peace are to be found; but see, in the east is a streak of light—it comes like magic—cloud after cloud becomes visible—until the eastern hemisphere becomes dimly illuminated with the gray dawn, which just reveals the outline forms of the giant masses in the city—the tall spires, tapering to the sky, stand out in bold relief, and the morning mist causes these objects to appear preternaturally large—the domes of large buildings—then the chimneys and housetops come to view.

Still all is quiet, as if wrapped in the stillness of death—not a sound to be heard; but, by the time the first tinge of warm sunlight throws its ruddy hue across the sky, the neighbourhood of the markets exhibit a slight stir. Some half-clad human being is seen to shuffle along the streets to his early labour—a solitary cart enters from the country, to deposit its burthen in the mart, and dispose of it to the inhabitants. This is followed by others of the same cast, and a few human beings are here collected, while the other part lay still in perfect quietude and repose.

The early houses for the accommodation of these people are now opening, and the smoke from these fires are the first that ascend to the sky, and greet the morning sun, which has now risen above the horizon, gilding, with his magic beams, all that is in nature, and all that is formed by the power of man. The lingering clouds of night yet stay to kiss the flashing sun-beam, and receive his warmth, while they reflect his splendour, and add an unmatched beauty to the scene.

Life in the city is yet young, though here and there you see the artisan has-tening to his early labour, half-dressed, and but half-awaked, while the smoke from many fires now ascend from their various vents, and tell us that day has begun.

Time wears on, and many shops are opened—many, but not all, for some are aristocratic, and keep later hours, while many of those that are opened are so more for the purpose of admitting that light which is necessary to enable the work people to pursue their calling, and to render the places fit for the reception of the employers' goods.

The busy throng is now increased, and a hum of voices and sounds rise upon the ear and strike the senses, which conveys to the mind more plainly than words can do—the city's up—the town's awake. Like some great giant it falls to rest, and can be but slowly and gradually awakened to new life and energy.

Eight o'clock was sounding from the sonorous bell of St. Paul's, and the hum of awakened energy was becoming each moment deeper and louder, when Tom Hackey and Rivers emerged from one of the narrow courts in Paternoster-row, leading into St. Paul's church-yard.

"We are rather early, Tom," said Rivers, "I think."

"I should say rather, confound you," said Tom; "you know very well you've been boring me since six o'clock to come here, and now we are an hour too soon; we run a good chance of being taken up for suspicious characters, loitering about with felonious intentions; there, now, they are watching us at that corner shop ahead, and there's the baker coming to look at us. How de do, Smith—how de do? Mrs. Smith better, eh? and the little Smiths got rid of the weasels—measles, I mean?"

The baker looked very angry, and went in again, shutting his door with a bang.

"If you go on that way, Tom," said Rivers, "we shall certainly be made suspicious characters of. Suppose we go into Saint Paul's to while away the time?"

"Don't you wish you may get it," said Tom; "there isn't an individual as belongs to Saint Paul's as is up, I'll be bound. A church in this country is always left under the care of Providence, and a strong lock, till there's something to be got by opening it. The dean's asleep, and the canons are all as sound as so many guns; besides, they charges something to go in on a work-a-day, and that's a kind of robbing Peter to pay Paul. You ain't expected to be religious on a Monday morning in this country, and if you will be eccentric, they will make you pay for it extra."

"Ah, well," said Rivers, "we'll walk round and round till Grace comes."

"Ah! I suppose we must. It's dull work enough, that; by-the-bye, have you seen my white waistcoat?"

"Yes," said Rivers, "I couldn't but remark it; but I wish to Heaven you would not wear those singularly large worsted gloves."

"Oh, bother," said Tom, "they are appropriate; I couldn't come kids, so I was forced to give these a dab out in an old flower-pot. Didn't you hear me before you got up?"

"I heard a splashing," said Rivers, "and thought it was rain."

"Bless your innocence," said Tom, "I was washing out this waistcoat, the gloves, and white pocket-handkerchief, and something else that will astonish you when the proper time comes."

"What is that?" said Rivers. "I hope to Heaven, Tom, you are not going to commit any extravagance."

"Commit your grandmother," said Tom, "and make your mind easy. It's a quarter past eight, thank the fates."

Meanwhile, poor Grace Trueman's anxiety and agitation were, if possible, far greater than Rivers's, and she arose at an early hour from a nearly sleepless couch.

Although she did not feel herself a prisoner in the house, she yet thought she might find a difficulty in leaving it unobserved. After a consultation with Mrs. Woodfall, it was decided that the best plan would be to slip out immediately after her father should have gone to his private office and shut himself in, where, at least, he was sure to remain for some time, looking over his early letters.

Owing to his misadventures on the preceding evening, Mathew Trueman was rather late in descending to his office, the consequence of which was, that it was past the half hour after eight before Grace and Mrs. Woodfall had a chance of leaving the house; but it was well they did then leave it, for Mathew Trueman was at that very time reckoning up what money was due to Mrs. Woodfall, in order at once to discharge her, and likewise considering if it would not be advisable to have another explanation with Grace before he should proceed to the Mansion House, in order to apply for a warrant against Francis Rivers for the supposed burglary; and, notwithstanding Mathew Trueman had had a whole night to consider of it, and had made his first faults and hasty impressions, he still, with a dogged pertinacity, affected to adhere to his first opinion, that Francis Rivers, and none but he, had attempted the robbery.

It so happened, then, that about a quarter of an hour after the departure of Grace and Mrs. Woodfall, a departure that was effected with secrecy and safety, Mathew Trueman walked up stairs in order to pay Mrs. Woodfall, and see her out of the house, as well as once more to reason with Grace upon what he chose to call her inconsistency of conduct.

No Grace, no Mrs. Woodfall were to be found, and, to the merchant's still further perplexity, none, even of the household, could give the least idea of whither they were gone.

This was annoying in the extreme to Mathew Trueman; but how far, very far, was he from suspecting the real truth! Had he done so, who knows what excesses he might have fallen into, instead of only sitting down in his office with an air of considerable vexation.

In the meantime, Grace proceeded arm-in-arm with Mrs. Woodfall rapidly in the direction of St. Paul's churchyard, and where was Rivers, expecting her with the deepest anxiety.

The clock of St. Paul's indicated that it wanted but a quarter to nine before Grace made her appearance to the delighted eyes of Rivers. It seemed to him, then, that a purer and more beautiful atmosphere reigned around; the sunlight shone more sweetly; and with an expression of delight upon his features, that not a little puzzled some of the chance passengers who appeared to observe him, Rivers hastened to the side of her he loved.

"Grace, dear Grace," he cried, "you have kept your word with me, and I'm happy. Oh! if you had not come."

"I said I would come, Rivers," was Grace's reply.

"You did, and I ought not to have doubted—nor did I doubt. It was only my foolish anxiety that made the time seem long: but, hark! Grace, nine is striking—the coach will be here instantly —does not nature seem to smile upon us? Have we not a delightful morning?"

"We have, indeed," said Grace.

"Yes, we have," said Tom; "so fair and foul a day I have not seen. Come along, Grace, mind we ain't too late. I was in hopes, whenever you did marry, to have got up a proper affair of it, especially as it is going to be at a little out-of-the-way country place; we could have got, for a few shillings, the paupers of some of the union houses to have executed a village dance and chorus. I don't see why that shouldn't have been managed; but everything has been done in such a hurry, that I have had no notice to look up my proper resources; besides, I ought certainly to have had an elderly gentleman's peruke and lob-wig, as I was to be the papa upon this interesting occasion; and then I could have done it properly, and as it ought to be done."

"The coach is waiting, dearest. Let us hasten. Oh, let us hasten."

"I'll be banged if they take any more notice of me," said Hackey, "than as if I had been Saint Paul himself, instead of being merely in his churchyard. Mother Woodfall, how do you find yourself this morning, mum—tidy, mum, eh?"

"Ah! you poor creature," said Mrs. Woodfall, in the usual commiserating tones with which she was in the habit of aggravating Tom Hackey. "How are you yourself—what do you intend to do?"

"Female—female," said Tom, "I've no patience with you! Come along; don't you see the coach is waiting."

In a few minutes more the party were safely ensconced in a Richmond coach, and it rattled off just as Mathew True-

man started up in his chair in his private office, and said—

"Gracious powers! I never thought of that. She may have gone to have one of her confounded clandestine meetings with that fellow in the Temple-gardens. Gracious me! I'll be off this moment."

The first thing Mathew Trueman did when he left the office was to run violently against somebody, and the next thing he did was to discover that that somebody was in the decidedly jolly stage of intoxication.

"How do?—how do?" said the stranger. "How do, old cock? blooming this morning, eh? up with the lark —man of business—down upon my own luck, rather. Pray, sir, is your name Stewman?"

"Who the devil are you?" said Mathew, quite enraged.

"Don't—don't," hiccoughed the stranger; "drink, and be merry; merry and wise. My name's Bumbleton Swiggles, Esquire; that's what the world calls me, when it wants me. My intimate friends contract it to Bubble, and sometimes Swiggy; humorous, ain't it?"

Bumbleton Swiggles, Esquire, then elevating his voice to an extraordinary pitch, shouted—

"Our Polly is a sad slut,
    Nor heeds she what we've taught her;
I really wonder any man
    Would wish to have a daughter.
            Too ral loo ral loo."

Mathew Trueman got in such a passion at what he considered this crowing over his misfortunes, that he forthwith collared Bumbleton Swiggles, and shaking him heartily, exclaimed—

"You scoundrel—you scoundrel! what do you want here, I say?"

"A pla—pla—place." stammered Bumbleton Swiggles.

"A what?"

"A place, to be sure! I had it from old Burnby, the watchman. You've been discharging somebody here; d—d if I know who it is, or care; but I've come to fill the sit—sit—sit—situation. I hope it's something comfortable. I am amazingly good at broiled kidneys for breakfast, and an easy chair, with a tumbler of grog after dinner. Say the word, down with a quarter's money in advance, and secure me. My father was a shoe-maker, and he married my mother for pure utility. He lived in a cellar, and sold fish, too, on the top of it, when anybody wanted to buy any. So, says he to my mother—

"To mend folks' shoes, and serve the fish,
Some want of help I feels,
And while I drive nails in their toes,
Why, you can skin their heels.

Good of the governor, wasn't it? A rum old blade he was; drunk nine glasses of brandy-and-water at once, and what was better, never paid for them."

"Hilliard—Hilliard," cried the merchant, "turn out this ruffian. Hilliard, where are you? D—n it, there's never anybody here when I want them!"

"Oh, oh," said Swiggles, "I shall repeat the offer; if you don't want me, I'm off. Just lend us five shillings till I see you again."

"Pooh! pooh!" cried the merchant; "no such thing—nonsense."

"Half-a-crown, then."

"No, not a farthing."

"There's a wretch!" said Bumbleton Swiggles. "There's human nature for you. I must go and drink something to recover my spirits."

"Was ever a man so horribly pestered as I have been lately, with one thing or another; I haven't had a quiet moment. If I were not a decidedly strong-minded man, I should commit suicide; but I'll be off to the Temple. Yet, no; I had better go to the Mansion-house first, and get the warrant. Yes, I will, and then I can be down upon my gentleman at once. I'll make you recollect, Master Rivers, coming to my house."

CHAPTER LXXXIV.

THE ARRIVAL AT BARNES.—THE MARRIAGE.—THE RETURN.—THE WARRANT.—AN EVENTFUL DAY.

BUT little conversation could be indulged in between Grace and her lover as they proceeded in the stage-coach, and it was only now and then in whispers that they addressed each other, although the thoughts of both were busy respecting the great change they were about to make in their condition. It is said that people marry in haste to repent at leisure; and however strictly true that doctrine may be in many cases, people seldom indulge in any dreams but of the slightest texture, when they are preparing their necks for the noose matrimonial—thus, dark and full of portending storms, as was the future to Grace Trueman and her lover, they saw no cloud in the sunny sky of their felicity—dreamed of no shadow on the sunny landscape of their joy.

As for Tom Hackey, he amused himself and the rest of the passengers on the outside, while he annoyed Rivers dreadfully by every now and then leaning over the side of the coach, and calling out—

"It's all right—'daresay you'd rather meet the anger of the waves, than meet the angry father.' He ain't coming. 'Rest, perturbed spirit, rest!'"

Then there was an old lady inside who always gave a great jump when any of those interruptions came, and who, at last, became firmly impressed that there was a madman on the outside, who was being conveyed to some private asylum.

Then the usual number of people stopped the coach to ask if it was not going to any other place but its real destination, and one female fairly got in, and just as the man was slamming the door, she asked if he set down at Mr. Smith's.

"Mr. Smith's, where?" said the coachman.

"Why, at Deptford, to be sure," said the woman; "everbody knows Mr. Smith;" and then appealing to Rivers, she remarked, "how stupid some people were."

"D—n it, mum," said the coachman, "we ain't going to Deptford."

"Not to Deptford?" said the woman; "and why not, I should like to know?"

This question was certainly a pozer, and the woman looked quite triumphant, and the coachman was obliged to say—

"'Cause we isn't, that's why, mum. We goes to Richmond, and there's the end of it. Get out!"

"Well, I am sure!" said the woman, "here's impertinence. This, I believe, is a stage-coach, and I am quite certain it was a stage-coach I went to Mr. Smith's last in. I believe, sir," appealing to Rivers, "that a stage-coach is a stage-coach?"

"Certainly," said Rivers; "but I believe, likewise, that there may be two, and one may go to Richmond, while the other goes to Deptford."

"Gracious!" cried the woman, "then this is a wrong coach?"

Then a bright idea struck her, and, turning to the coachman, she said, in persuasive tones—

"My good man, couldn't you go to Deptford, first? Mr. Smith's a corner house, and is new painted throughout. He's gone to great expense."

"No!" cried the coachman, in a tone of aggravation. "I wishes to blazes, mum, as you'd get out."

"Ah," said the insulted female, "I find I am among low people. When a lady wants to go to Deptford, I think it a very hard thing that a common stage-coach won't take her there. An extremely hard case, indeed. I've a good mind to speak to the government or the parish about it, and have it altered."

By this time she alighted, and just as the Richmond coach had set off again, Rivers saw her hailing a Birmingham stage that had just come in.

But such little interruptions as these to a journey are common and incidental; one can only be thankful when too many of them do not occur; and Rivers was truly glad when the coach drew up at Barnes, in order to allow him and Grace to alight.

It wanted, then, a full half hour to eleven, so there was plenty of time for a quiet stroll in the pretty vicinity, before they were required to be present at the church.

Tom Hackey, however, hurried off to his friend, the sexton, and that functionary, with a grave face, said—

"Oh, they are serious, is they? Well, it can't be helped; you know wilful people will have their own way, and there's an end of it."

"Certainly," said Tom. "How's the missus?"

"Hush!" said the sexton, pointing with his thumb over his shoulder; "I'll get my hat, and come out with you in a minute."

The sexton was taking his hat off the peg, when a voice screamed from the parlour—

"Where are you going now, you low-minded wretch? Sot—sot—sotting, I suppose, with some of your beastly low companions. Oh, you are a nice article, you are."

"My dear," said the sexton, in a mild tone, "I am only going, my love—to speak to a gentleman, my dear—to speak about a marriage, my love."

"If you're gone more than a quarter of an hour, you wretch," said the lady's voice, "I shall know where to find you. You'll be in the Green Pig and Frying-pan, you will, or the Cock and Toasting-fork, you low-lived vagabond!"

"Oh dear, no, my dear, not if you disapprove of it," said the sexton. "I shall be back in a quarter of an hour."

When he got some distance from his own door, he said to Tom, mysteriously—

"I've tried it."

"Tried what?" said Tom.

"Tickling, but it wouldn't do. She fetched me such a whack of the head, that it rung again."

"My friend," said Tom, "it strikes me you're a fool! My name is Hackey, and if there was a Mrs. Hackey who spoke to me as your missus speaks to you, I'd skin her. Good-morning—I've got my friends here, and must meet them."

So saying, Tom walked away, and soon found Rivers and Grace near the door of the little suburban church. It wanted but ten minutes now for the hour fixed for the performance of the ceremony, and just as Grace remarked how fine the weather kept, a change took place in the aspect of the day—a cold wind swept across the earth with a moaning sound, and, sensibly feeling the rapid change of temperature, the little party were glad to enter the church, and there to await the coming of the clergyman.

Rivers saw Grace shudder, and he said—

"You must recollect, dearest, we are on the verge of the winter, and these changes are common. Cheer up, Grace; you look pale."

"No, Rivers, it is the changing light. Can I be otherwise than happy?"

Rivers pressed her hand in his, and then the sexton whispered to him—

"Here is the clergyman."

Rivers turned and saw, slowly advancing, a venerable man, who, taking his place in silence by the altar, waited the approach of that pair, who were so soon to mate with each other for better or for worse.

The brief ceremony began; Grace trembled, but her answers were clearly audible; then Tom Hackey, in his capacity of father to the bride, took her hand and placed it in Rivers's. Seven minutes had elapsed by the church clock, and the ceremony was over.

A tear stood in Tom Hackey's eye, which he strove to account for by saying that the sexton had given him a pinch of snuff, and he had, by mistake, put it into that organ instead of his nose.

*   *   *   *

In a few minutes more, Rivers, with his bride, reached the church doors; they walked out together, Grace hanging heavily on his arm, and Tom Hackey bringing up the rear. Neither spoke, for their hearts were too full. The

THE ATTEMPTED ABDUCTION OF GRACE BY HAWKSWORTH'S EMISSARIES.

first who broke the silence was Tom Hackey, who said—

"Grace—no, I beg pardon—Mrs. Rivers, it's getting finer again."

Grace started at the unusual sound.

"Call me Grace Rivers, Tom," she said; "although I am a wife, I need not forget the kind friends of my former life."

"God bless you both," said Tom Hackey. "I'll sweep a crossing for you, any day."

"We know you, Tom, for our kindest and best friend," said Rivers, "and if fortune smiles upon us—believe me, it shall never frown upon you."

"I know it—I know it," said Tom.

"Where is Mrs. Woodfall?" said Grace.

"God bless me!" said Tom, "I have lost the old lady—but here she comes. I declare she's been among the tombstones, trying to get up a cry. Why, you needn't cry, Mother Woodfall, there's nobody marrying you."

Grace looked in her nurse's face, and

she guessed well she had slipped aside to give vent to her feelings.

"Let us get to town as speedily as possible. I have now the one last appeal to make with my father—if he remain obdurate, Rivers, shall I claim a home of my husband?"

"You shall, dearest, and pray Heaven it may prove a happy one. What time will you speak to your father?"

"As early as circumstances will permit—but he shall know that I am a wife before sunset."

"Then I will call," said Rivers, "an hour after that time."

"Do so," said Grace, "this day shall indeed be the most important of my life."

"And here comes a coach," said Tom Hackey, "that will take us back again."

*   *   *   *

Within an hour, the little party were again set down in St. Paul's Churchyard. The quarter past twelve was announced by the cathedral clock as Rivers and his wife stood beneath the shadow of its ancient edifice; Grace then gave the ring to Rivers, saying,

"Keep it, Rivers, till we meet again. Come, nurse, let us now go home, that home which was once so happy, but is now so different."

There was a silent pressure of the hand and mutual glances of affection between Rivers and Grace, which spoke more of the real feelings of the heart than the tongue could utter; then they parted, Grace shuddering at the prospect of the interview she was to have with her father, and Rivers with a heart full of tenderness and devotion towards his young and beautiful bride.

In the meantime, the merchant had fulfilled his threat—he had gone to the Mansion-house, and applied to the Lord Mayor for a warrant against Rivers, and as that important city functionary, although he had been amazingly successful in many mercantile speculations, had not much more sense or knowledge of law than could have been placed in any person's eye without in the slightest degree obstructing the vision, he would have granted a warrant at once to so respectable a man as Mr. Trueman.

But then, there was a fidgety alderman present, who was a lawyer, and he put his spoke in the wheel, and damnified the application, for, by cross-questioning, he got Mathew Trueman to confess that his daughter, and his daughter's nurse, and the footman, were all ready to swear that it could not have been Mr. Rivers who had committed the robbery.

"My good sir," said the legal alderman, "if you were to apprehend this person you speak of, he would bring his action against you, and recover heavy damages."

As for the Lord Mayor, during this colloquy, he sat with about the animated expression of a water melon, and he only gave a slight jump, and said—

"Bless me, what a violent man!" five minutes after Mathew Trueman had whacked his fist on the justice-table, and walked out of the hall with a bounce.

Then the merchant ran with great speed down to the Temple-gardens, where he was doomed to a second disappointment; for, of course, no Rivers, nor Grace, was there; so that he fumed back to Thames-street in the most frightful of tempers, arriving not very long before Grace herself made her appearance.

Then, too, Mathew Trueman was doomed to find that his office had been deserted all the morning, for Hilliard had never come, judging accurately enough that there was ample evidence to convict him of the robbery.

What a delightful state of mind was the merchant in, to receive such a communication as that which Grace had to give him! He had shut himself in his own office, and after upsetting the ink, and throwing a valuable file of receipts into the fire, he solemnly cursed everybody, himself included—he wished that every bank in the country might break, and that every firm in the city might be gazetted.

He d——d Lord Hawksworth, and he d——d Girkins, and finally, he broke three squares of glass in the window, by throwing his private ledger at it, because, with provoking coolness and pertinacity, one of the servants looked in.

Grace entered the house as unobserved as she had left it, and proceeding up stairs, she cried a little in her own room, after which she felt more composed, and ready to meet her father.

The weather was thickening every moment, while an intense coldness superseded the genial warmth of the earlier part of the day. Huge masses of clouds piled themselves up in the sky, and there was one of those heavy foglike atmospheres which frequently hang over London, and sink in every street and court in the city.

Although the day was scarcely half gone, it seemed as if the night had come, and, finally, candles were forced to be burned in the merchant's house before the neighbouring churches had announced the hour of three.

Every moment Grace delayed the communication to her father, which might sever her from him for ever, or, by his forgiveness, open to her a career of happiness beyond what she even, in earlier life, had dreamed of, increased her anxiety, and finally she rose from her chair, saying —

"Mrs. Woodfall, my father does not seek me, and I must seek him, or send for him here, for I can no longer keep this secret from him. I must tell him— I must tell him."

CHAPTER LXXXV.

MRS. WOODFALL'S DISCHARGE.—THE LETTER. — THE SNOW-STORM.

MRS. WOODFALL could not but perceive the extreme agitation under which poor Grace was labouring; and her heart bled for that distress which she knew ought not to have occurred under the circumstances under which that innocent young girl was placed. To feel the existence of such distress was to consider how it could be alleviated, and Mrs. Woodfall said, after a few moments' pause—

"My dear Grace, you shrink, and I do not wonder at it, from informing your father of your marriage."

"I do," said Grace, "but it is a duty which must be accomplished. I know not why I shrink, and yet my heart sadly fails me, and I feel as if I could sink into the earth rather than utter the words, 'father, I am married.'"

"My dear," said Mrs. Woodfall, "an indifferent person can always manage these things better than those who are principally concerned; I will go myself, and tell your father that you wish to see him, and at the same time I will tell him why you wish to see him, so that, you know, he will be prepared to speak to you upon the subject, and you will be yourself spared the necessity of making a communication, at which I do not wonder you shrink."

"But ought I," said Grace, "to shift from my own shoulders that which is disagreeable on to yours? No, my dear nurse, you have done much for me already, much more than I ought even to have expected—much more than I can ever repay you doing. I will go myself; it is fit that I should do so. What I have done let me stand the consequences of."

"But I insist," said Mrs. Woodfall. "Our situations are by no means similar. Your father's anger can be nothing to me to what it is to you. Nay, Grace, say not another word, it shall be so. I may not do your cause any good, but believe me I shall not injure it by any indiscreet advocacy."

"I will not oppose you," said Grace. "You shall tell him if you will, nurse, and Heaven send he may receive the communication with gentleness."

"Hope for the best—hope for the best," was Mrs. Woodfall's reply, and then she hurried from the room in order to carry into effect her kind intention.

That day was doomed to be one of interest, apart from the feeling she entertained for Grace, to Mrs. Woodfall herself, and no sooner had she entered the merchant's counting house, in obedience to his loud and angry cry of 'Come in' when she gently tapped at the door, than he cried—

"Oh, it's you, madam, is it? I suppose you have come for your money and character, confound you! I am not a-going to let you off so easy this time, you old witch! You are a nice article to leave in charge of a house. The duennas in the old Spanish books were fools to you. What the deuce did I employ you for but to look after my daughter?—ah! and nicely you've done it. Here, I can't be away three parts of a day to see my old friend, Jenkins, but what you must let in all sorts of scamps into the house."

"Mr. Rivers was certainly here," said Mrs. Woodfall.

"Oh! dear, yes, Mr. Rivers was here; I know it, and next I suspect Noaks would have been here, and Stokes and Styles, and Heaven knows who else besides."

"Mr. Trueman," said Mrs. Woodfall, "I did not come to talk to you upon that subject."

"The devil doubt you!" said Mathew Trueman, "who the deuce thought you did? But I mean to talk about it—there's your discharge, ma'm, and there's a month's money. Now you may bundle out of the house as quick as possible; and, by-the-by, there's a letter that's come for you by this morning's post, along with my own packet. I have deducted the tenpence for the postage, and now you and I part, ma'm—part, do you understand that? and when you want a place, and the deluded creatures you endeavour to swindle apply to me, I shall tell them to look after their daughters, for that you have an extensive connection with young rakes and blackguards whom you are in the habit of introducing into the house. Do you hear that, Mrs. Woodfall? Now you may go and starve—anything you like so long as you take yourself away from me."

"I quite understood before," said Mrs. Woodfall, "that I was discharged, but I came now to make a communication to you which more concerns you than it does me."

"Oh, indeed! another chap in the house, eh?"

"No, Mr. Trueman, but what I have to tell you concerns you very nearly."

"I don't want to hear anything from you," said the vexed merchant; "go about your business. It's just some artful move to try and stay, of course—women are devils, of course, and as artful as a bundle of friends tied up in a heap. You can't impose upon me, ma'm; read you own letter and be off with you, and mind your own affairs. I won't hear a word you've got to say, and there's an end of it."

"But, sir——"

"Be off with you," cried Mathew Trueman. "Confound you—shall I have to turn you out of my own office?"

As he spoke, he rose with an expression that made poor Mrs. Woodfall think that he was really going to carry his threat into execution, and in her terror, she left the office immediately, without having fulfilled her errand.

With a heavy heart she proceeded up stairs to Grace, to tell her of the non-success of the effort she had made to spare her uneasiness.

"Heed it not—heed it not," said Grace. "It is intended by Providence that I should go through this ordeal, and I ought not to shrink from it so much as I have done; but read your own letter, Mrs. Woodfall, it may concern you nearly."

"It is from the school," said Mrs. Woodfall, "where my boy, Harry, has been so long, since I heard no tidings from his poor father, who, I believe, must be dead."

"Hope for the best," said Grace; "even that anticipation may prove groundless, and some day you may have the pleasure of being convinced that such is the case."

"I have given over hope," said Mrs. Woodfall, as she opened the letter after reading a few lines out of which, she said—

"This happens most strangely; at the moment I am discharged by your father, and ordered to quit his house, I am told by this note that I must myself assume the care of my son."

"Indeed!" said Grace.

"Yes, you shall hear."

Mrs. Woodfall then read as follows—

"MADAM,—I regret to inform you that Mr. James Henderson, who conducted the academy at which your son has been for some years, has suddenly expired, and that the establishment in passing into new hands, who, not knowing you, or feeling for you that friendship which induced the late Mr. Henderson to educate your son at about one-third the usual cost, has declined so doing, and consequently he will be in town somewhere about the time you receive this letter, which I regret very much being under the necessity of sending to you.

"I have told Harry Woodfall to wait at the Cross-keys coach-office until you shall come to him, and trusting you will find his progress and education such as will give you satisfaction, I am, Madam, your obedient servant,

"GEORGE GREEN.

"Late Usher at the Kingston "Grammar School."

"Do not delay a moment, dear nurse," said Grace; "do not delay a moment. Leave me to fight my own battles with my father, and perhaps I may come off better than either of us expect."

"I must go," said Mrs. Woodfall; "but I will call here, Grace, to-morrow, for by that time nothing can have happened of importance, as regards your own prospects, and, thank Heaven, I shall have been able to provide a home, in which I can make you welcome, should this one prove insufferable to you."

"I shall be rejoiced to see you, dear nurse," said Grace, "as a dear and kind friend, I shall be rejoiced to see you; and I trust the remainder of your life will be full of happiness."

"Your happiness," said Mrs. Woodfall, "and that of my dear son Harry, are now my only objects of ambition."

"I shall see you to-morrow—I shall see you to-morrow," said Grace.

Grace strove to assume a composed air, but it was with a thrill of anguish she saw the only friendly heart, at all events, the only one on whom she could call for active succour and assistance, leaving her. She felt herself indeed lonely, and in need of all the courage which innocence and virtue could give her, to support herself under the circumstances in which she was placed. But Grace's was one of those minds which rise with the circumstances in which it is placed, and when least dependant upon the advice and assistance of others, are more capable of acting with energy and discretion.

Thus, perhaps, was Grace more capable of going through the trying interview with her father, now that she found herself quite alone and unaided.

"I will send for him here," she said; "he shall know all. I will endeavour to move him to a better feeling than he has hitherto exhibited. I will paint to him how happy he might be in the companionship of such a one as Rivers, who, while he lightened the toils of his business, would prove a kind companion in his hours of relaxation. I will speak, too, of my own happiness, and I would contrast all that with the desolation that must fall upon him when I am gone —with the want of those domestic comforts he has been accustomed to, and I will ask him if he can be happy, with the knowledge that I am not.

"When his wild dream of ambition is over by my marriage, when the chance of the acquisition of a title through my gilded misery can no longer be present to his imagination, he may relent, and, relenting, seek for a truer and more lasting happiness in those dear felicities of home which can need no change, and depend not on the feverish atmosphere of a court.

"Yes, I will tell him all that, and surely he will be moved. Surely he will feel the truth of that which I assert, and, in feeling it, act as he ought to do, making all happy around him."

By reasonings such as these, she brought herself to a more equable frame of mind than before the departure of her nurse, and felt more firm to go through the interview she determined not to delay in seeking.

Grace would have gone down to her father's private office, but she knew that there she was liable to interruption, and, therefore, she preferred sending for him to the drawing-room, where, should he even feel inclined to speak in those loud, angry terms, which the subject-matter of the discourse might provoke, she would at least be spared the pain of its reaching the ears of the household, a pain which she would have felt more for her father's sake than her own, for she felt that she was blameless.

She then rang, and when a servant appeared, she desired that her father might be told she wished much to speak with him, when he could spare her a few moments of his company in the drawing-room.

Mathew Trueman replied to the message with a decided negative; not that he meant really not to go, but that he was in a decidedly contradictorhumour, and would not go just then because he was asked.

"What does she want now?" he muttered to himself. "Some nonsense, I'll be bound. That girl's never satisfied unless she's having a row with me. Girkins must know a great many women, for he's an admirable judge of the sex. He says they are full of contradictions, and so they are; that what they say one minute, they don't say the next, and what they pretend to mean, they don't mean at all. It wouldn't surprise me a bit, now—oh dear, no, not in the least—if Grace was to tell me that I quite misunderstood her, and that she meant to marry Lord Hawksworth at the first convenient opportunity. It wouldn't surprise me. Some of these days when she is quite in the mind, I must get her to marry him off-hand, and when once she is a countess, she can't very well unmake herself again. Well, I think I'll go and see what she has got to say. Thank the fates, I have got rid of that scheming Mother Woodfall, who, I believe, has been at the bottom of all the mischief, with her cursed demure-looking face, and her Mr. Trueman this, and her Mr. Trueman t'other. D—n it, how I've got to hate that old woman."

Darkness had fallen upon the city by the time Mr. Trueman had made up his mind to attend to Grace's summons. Real darkness—the darkness of the night, and not that caused by the adventitious circumstance of a fog enveloping the streets in its gloomy vapour. The wind had increased to a hurricane, and although much cut up and deprived of its power by the dense masses of houses against which it in vain expended its fury, it still moaned from street to street, and howled round the chimney-pots of the city with frightful violence, while the cold increased every moment, and every appearance indicated that the coming night would be one of fearful violence.

There was every indication, too, by the louring clouds and occasionally falling particles, that a storm was at hand, and that, from the intense cold, it would probably be a snow-storm—and ere the night grew late, the white flakes fell drifting through the air to the ground.

It was a bitter night, for the wind swept the streets, rushing with violence down some cross street, and meeting obstructions in another, eddying round with fearful strength, and sweeping the collected mass of snow in a wreath, that would for the moment deprive the passenger of the use of his visual organs.

A snow-storm in London is perhaps more disagreeable than elsewhere—the numerous currents of air are met in all directions, charged with the keen, cutting shower, which causes the most robust to shrink from the encounter—those thoroughfares, too, where there is much traffic usually become soppy and wet, presenting a scene so truly uncomfortable, that the bare contemplation is bad enough, and the reality direful.

The snow now fell fast and thick, and the housetops presented a curious contrast in colour, and even form, to what they presented a short time before; every projecting mass, every window-sill, every inch that projected forward, became surcharged with the frozen vapour, showing in great contrast to the remaining portions of the buildings, while the pavements and roads of densely thronged thoroughfares became clogged with a mass of mud and snow.

It was while this cheerless state of the weather was obtaining precedence without, that Mathew Trueman ascended the staircase to the drawing-room, in compliance with the summons of his daughter Grace.

CHAPTER LXXXVI.

GRACE'S APPEAL TO HER FATHER.—A STORMY CONVERSATION AND ITS RESULT.—THE RENUNCIATION.

GRACE felt a momentary revival of her trembling agitation when her father entered the room, and it was with a sad prognostication of what would be the result of the interview, that she marked the stern aspect of his countenance, and heard the tones of his voice as he said—

"Well, Grace, so you have sent for me, have you? What now, I should like to know? I suppose you've altered your mind again. Who are you going to marry now, and who are you going to refuse, I should like to know?"

"Father," said Grace, "I have sent for you——"

"I know that, and here I am. Come, what have you got to say—say it at once. Heaven knows, I have had aggravation enough already through your whims and fancies."

"Father," said Grace, "hear me, and, oh, hear me this once with patience. Do not—do not let me plead to you in vain. We've been very happy in the dear love we've borne each other, and that affection of my early life, which might, in the ordinary course of events, have been divided between two dear parents, has wholly fallen to you; until this dreadful subject of my marriage started itself in your mind, we were very happy, and you cannot surely say I was undutiful."

"Undutiful be hanged!" said the merchant, in an angry tone, "you are like the rest of the world, dutiful and agreeable enough when it suits your fancy; but, ah! dear me, quite the reverse when anything of real importance occurs, and you are asked to do something, which I make so dead a point of, as your marriage with Lord Hawksworth."

"Father," said Grace, "my marriage with Lord Hawksworth is impossible."

"D—n it!" said the merchant, "you told me that last night. Did you send for me to aggravate me?"

"But," said Grace, hesitatingly, "it is more impossible now than it was last night."

"More impossible now! What do you mean by that? Have you sent for me to tell me that you have got more infernally obstinate by sleeping on it? Hang it, Grace, but you are enough to drive anybody mad. Will you, or will you not, marry Lord Hawksworth?—that's the long and the short of the matter. If you will, say so; if you won't, you and I are at war upon the only subject I ever made a point of with you, and the only subject I ever should."

"It is now impossible," said Grace; "it admits not of argument. What before lay not within the compass of belief, has now become utterly impossible."

"Why, what the devil has he done now; and what on earth induced you to write him a note to come here and have a private interview with you, if you did not mean to marry him?"

"Father," said Grace, "you seem to be under some strange mistake with regard to that note. Could even Lord Hawksworth have been so base as to misrepresent the tenor of that epistle to you?"

"He neither represented, nor misrepresented," said the merchant; "I had it from Girkins's own mouth that you had written a most affectionate letter to Lord Hawksworth, and that he was coming here to settle the preliminaries."

"A more atrocious falsehood," said Grace, "was never uttered by the lips of man. In sorrow and affliction as I was, in consequence of differing with you upon a subject of great importance, I did wish that there should be an end put to the persecutions of Lord Hawksworth by himself. I thought that, even in his mind, there might be some lingering spark of honour and honesty left, some small portion of pride which would have induced him to discontinue his addresses to one who entertained towards him the feelings of contempt that I do. My letter was a cold invitation to come here, in order that I might tell him how utterly I despised him, how completely I repudiated his addresses. It could mean nothing else—it did mean nothing else."

"The devil!" said the merchant, "and I've discounted forty thousand pounds' worth of bills upon the strength of it."

"Oh! father—father!" said Grace, "how could you for one moment be deceived by that man? Even here, in this very room, he confessed that his purpose in seeking me was of the most dishonourable nature, and that he never for one moment contemplated matrimony, sneering at the very idea of his marrying with one so much beneath him in rank."

"You—you—don't mean that?" said Mathew Trueman, turning pale and trembling in spite of himself.

"Such," said Grace, "was the import of his words; whether uttered in sincerity or not I cannot tell; but, as regards my own belief, I think they were."

"You are mistaken—you are mistaken," said Trueman. "You are mistaken, Grace, quite mistaken. He could not—he dared not—it is impossible. I have his word of honour."

"How is it, father," said Grace, "that you will place such reliance on the word of honour of this man, because he has a title affixed to his name, and yet would laugh to scorn the idea of taking the word of one of your most intimate mercantile friends for a cask of tallow or a bale of cotton?"

"Ah! business is one thing," cried Mathew Trueman, uttering a home truth on the spur of the moment, "and honour is another. You don't know what you are talking about," said he to Grace. "Come, now, I give you a last chance—make everything comfortable and agreeable, and be a countess."

"I have told you, father," said Grace, trembling, "that it is impossible. I have exposed to you the villany which has converted an act of mine—I allude to the letter to Hawksworth—into an encouragement of one whom I held in utter detestation."

"Then, do you mean to say," cried the merchant, rising, "that you sent for me just to din this old story into my ears?"

"No—no," said Grace, clinging to her father's arm in spite of him. "Mr. Rivers—Mr. Rivers, father."

"Curse Mr. Rivers," said the merchant. "Curses on his very name. I shall never be happy till I see that fellow hung. I detest, abhor him. Since the first moment he set his foot in this house I have had nothing but trouble and annoyance. He is an eyesore to me —a cursed eyesore to me, and I hate him."

"Father," said Grace, looking with an appealing glance into the merchant's face. "Father, do not speak so of him; he is noble, generous, and full of high qualities."

"Trash!" cried the merchant, giving Grace a push that, had not a chair received her, would have thrown her to the ground. "Trash! I say; d—n him, d—n him!"

"Father, I love him," said Grace.

"What!" shrieked Trueman. "You have the unblushing effrontery to make such a confession to me? Can you look me in the face, you impudent hussy, and tell me you love a poverty-stricken wretch, who knows as much about book-keeping as a bull does of carving and gilding? D—n it, you are enough to drive any man distracted. You love him, do you?"

"I do," said Grace, "with my heart and soul."

The merchant sat down again, and looked perfectly astounded; but when Grace added—"Father, did you not love my mother?" he stood upon the seat of his chair, in the anger of the moment, as he added in stentorian accents—

No! Do you take me for a love-sick fool?"

"But you must have done so, for I have heard you speak of her."

"A delusion—a delusion," cried the merchant. "One of those things which, like the measles, attacks one only in early life. I might have been labouring under that species of delusion at one time, but I came at last to my senses, and looked upon your mother as I was in the habit of doing upon a dishonoured bill. It's all very fine to draw at a long date upon time for dreams of happiness, and you fancy you've got the old boy to accept it, but it's no go, and if you realize anything, it's at a ruinous discount. Don't talk to me of love and all hat kind of nonsense. If there was a company got up for it to-morrow, the shares would not sell for waste paper."

"But—but—you said you loved her. You swore to love her."

"Well," said the merchant, "I kept my oath. I gave her breakfast, dinner, tea, and supper as long as she lived, and when she died, spoiled my best hat with a hatband. Don't talk to me about love and such stuff! A bill payable at sight is all very well; but love at first sight is quite another thing. I never believe in such nonsense, and never will. Be reasonable, Grace, and smother your ridiculous feelings. There are only two considerations to be thought of in matrimony—rank and money. Now, I've got plenty of money, so you've nothing to do but look for the rank, and Lord Hawksworth is the very thing—a lord at present, and an earl in perspective.

Good gracious! what can you expect more?"

"I called upon Heaven," said Grace, "at our last interview, to witness my oath, as I swore I never would wed Lord Hawksworth. Do you—can you wish me, father, to break it?"

"Then hear me, Grace. I can make oaths as well as you. To-morrow morning you leave London, and your young spark, Rivers, may seek for you in vain. There you shall remain, shut up till you come to your senses, and if you don't marry Lord Hawksworth before the first of acceptances becomes due, I'll never set eyes on you again."

"But, father," said Grace, "if he were to find out my retreat, and I were to marry him secretly?"

"By G—, if you were," said the merchant, "I'd turn you out of doors, and leave you to starve, even if it were such a night as this, when Heaven and earth seem coming together."

"Turn me from your house?" said Grace.

"Yes, as sure as I stand here, you should never cross a threshold of mine. So now you know your fate."

"I do know my fate," said Grace, "for I am the wife of Francis Rivers."

The merchant went backwards till he came to the wall, against which he came with a heavy thump, and then continued gazing at Grace with speechless amazement. Twice he tried to speak, but in vain; his tongue seemed glued to the roof of his mouth, and all his faculties appeared paralysed. When he did speak it was in gasping accents that he said—

"You — you — you—his wife — his wife?"

"Yes, father, his wedded wife."

"No—no—I dream—I dream. Grace, you cannot mean what you say?"

"It is true," said Grace, faintly—"it is true. I am the wife of Francis

Rivers. Father, if you will forgive me this one act of disobedience—if you will look upon me more than ever as your own child—your only one—whose happiness is secured upon a deeper, firmer basis than ever it stood upon before—if you'll consider my husband as he really is, brave, noble, generous, and full of kindly feelings, one who, for my sake, would bestow much affection upon you, we must still be very, very happy."

"This, father, is a crisis in my fate—believe it it likewise one in yours, for anger brings in its train heart-soreness and much bitterness, while the fruits of love and forgiveness are sweet and gentle as the dews of Heaven. Oh! think again, father, of your harsh sentence; let us be a united, happy family: living together in sweet peace and concord. Permit me, and him with whom I have linked my fate, to gild the evening of your days with dear love. Father—father—forgive me. Take me to your heart again. Let the name of that bad man, that noble without true nobility, never cross our lips; let us forget him, and be happy in the dear domestic enjoyments of our own home. Father—father—you will relent—you will relent."

"Never!" shrieked the merchant—"never. To be thwarted thus in the very great object of my life—to be crossed in the very ultimatum of my wishes—in the hour of success, when I had reached the summit of my hopes—and by you, one on whom I had lavished the greatest care and tenderness—I discard you—I discard you."

"No—no," cried Grace.

"Yes," shouted the merchant, in frenzied accents, stamping violently. "From this moment, you are no daughter of mine."

"Father—father!" she cried "think again. Oh! let nature plead for me!"

"No," he shouted. "I have made an oath, and I will keep it. Leave the house, girl—leave the house. If you have married, go to your husband. You are no daughter of mine. D——n, what do you do here? Leave the house, I say—away—away!"

"You cannot mean to execute that threat?" exclaimed Grace. "Think again—think again."

"Once for all, hear me," said the merchant. "Upon this I have determined. It is an act I have long contemplated if, with the desire of driving me nearly mad with which you must be actuated, you should ever act in this manner, throwing yourself away upon a penniless adventurer, and at once making a mockery of my dream of pleasure that I once indulged in."

There was an evident determination in the merchant's tone, joined to a calmness that carried with it more weight than his most violent bursts of passion. Grace might well shudder, as she did, at the aspect of his face. It was perfectly livid with rage. His very lips were bloodless, and he looked more like a revivified corpse than a human being, as, clutching by the side of the table by which he stood, he cried—

"Begone—begone—leave the house—leave the house, I say. I will not have you here another hour."

"Mercy—mercy," cried Grace, as she sunk to his feet. "Send me away, but not in anger. Give me hope that there may come a time, even if it be years hence, when you will speak some kind words to me, and let me know the blessings of a father's love."

"Never—never. Once again, never!" cried the merchant. "I have said it, and though Heaven and hell were to oppose me, I would keep my word. Away—away. Why do you linger? Do you think I am to be moved by your tears? I have seen tears shed in this house from harder hearts to move than yours,—tears from bold, strong men, who knew that I had the power of making them and others beggars if I wished it. Think you that I am to be moved by your tears? You may kneel—you may weep. I have said it, and by the Heaven above us, you go."

Grace rose with a shudder to her feet—she looked around her with a glance of chilly desolation. The lights no longer seemed to illumine the apartment—a cold feeling was at her heart, and she lacked the power to make any further appeal to that justice and that humanity she had hitherto invoked, but in vain; she felt as if her father's words contained the irrevocable fiat of destiny, and there was no farther hope; the storm might lour, the blanching snow-drift might dash against her; she must abide its fury until he came to whom she had plighted her young troth, and the thought of whom alone preserved her mind from distraction.

She mechanically procured her bonnet and a shawl, which, putting on, she stood on the threshold of the door; it was scarcely with a hope that her father might relent for one brief moment, but, if it were, it was soon dissipated, and his stern look left her no hope of mercy.

She walked tremblingly down the stairs,—those stairs she was never again to ascend,—and an unnatural gloom seemed to reign in the passage.

Then she turned once, and, clasping her hands, she pronounced the one word—

"Father!"

"Away!" cried the merchant; "away! I will have a clear house. Away—say no more!"

He opened the door; and, as Grace yet lingered a moment, while the dashing snow-storm blew wildly in the passage, he pushed her on to the step, and closed the door violently after her.

The snow lay heavy at the merchant's door; and, with a shriek of agony, Grace fell into its cold embraces.

Oh! there was no one near to hear or pity her cries; those who had homes to go to were crowding round the cheerful hearth; those who had none, had crept into obscure corners, to shield themselves from the pelting of the pitiless storm; and there lay Grace, the much adored, the delicately nurtured, noble-minded, much-prized Grace Rivers, a prey to the fury of the indiscriminating elements.

CHAPTER LXXXVII.

THE DECLARATION OF MARRIAGE.—A FATHER'S CURSE.—THE DISCARDED CHILD.—GRACE'S NEW HOME.

THE keen, cold winds, blew with violence, howling and whistling past the many impediments it encountered, while the snow fell thick and fast, carried ever and anon in whirling eddies round and round; then would come a sudden lull, while the white flakes fell uninterrup-tedly, till again disturbed by the wild rushing wind, which carried it in dashing showers against whatever obstacle opposed its onward progress.

The snow was deep, and an air of chilly cheerlessness was cast on all around;—the former intense darkness was relieved by the cold purity of the snow; but yet the vision was not assisted, for it fell in such heavy flakes that they could not penetrate far in search of objects.

The streets were nearly deserted, and but the occasional deadened sound of a footstep could be heard.

How long she lay there in a state of half insensibility Grace could hardly tell; but when she partially recovered, she found herself nearly embedded in snow, and so benumbed with cold that she could scarcely move; the flakes were still falling thick and fast, and, as her bewildered senses began to assume a more consistent order and shape, she recollected the promise of Rivers to call for her one hour after sunset, and, as she did so, she heard the neighbouring churches faintly giving out the hour of six.

"He will be here—he will be here!" she gasped; "my husband—my husband—what heart but yours have I to fly to for refuge?"

At this moment some one approached the steps; Grace knew not who the visitor might be, and she shrunk on one side to allow him to ascend.

"Why don't you go home?" said the person; "there—there's a penny, go home. I am quite sure Mr. True-man has a great objection to beggars on his steps."

Grace rose to her feet without a word, and tottered from her father's door; as she walked she sunk ankle deep in the snow, and she thought she would go as far as the first lamp-post, and there wait the coming of Rivers, who, by its friendly light, might see and recognise her.

There were but few passengers in the street, so she could not be well confused by a multiplicity of forms; not that she would have failed in knowing among a million the chosen idol of her heart; but the few passengers who passed were covered by the snow-drift, and, shrouded as they were by cloaks and handkerchiefs, it was difficult to identify any particular person.

Something, however, about Grace's heart seemed to tell her that Rivers was coming, and she strained her eyes along the street in the eager expectation of seeing his much-loved form. A rapid step approached—nearer and nearer came a figure, battling its way against the storm that impeded its progress. Could it be other than he?

"Rivers—Rivers!" cried Grace.

In an instant he was at her side,

"Grace!" he cried; "God of Heaven, is it you? Why are you here?"

"My father," she said, "has discarded me—he has turned me from his door. Oh, Rivers—Rivers—I have no one now to cling to but you."

"And that one, Grace, shall be a host," cried he, in a bold voice; "unnatural parent, that could so behave to such a child; may the time come when—"

"Hush, Rivers, hush!" cried Grace, clinging close to him, "he is my father, still—he is my father, still! Speak not of him, Rivers—I am yours—I am yours—yours only."

"And mine you shall ever be, dear Grace," cried Rivers; "my dearest—best—my wife. Grace, if I cannot give you a rich and pleasant home, I can give you one inhabited by a happy heart, that beats only for you, and will strive its utmost for you. Heaven bless you, dearest, for the trust you have put in me: it is not misplaced. Let us hope that fortune may smile upon us; and then what care we, bound, as we are, in an union of the tenderest affection? Come, dearest, come—lean on me. The snow-storm is now abating. Poor Francis Rivers has a home, such as it is, to take you to."

He drew her arm gently within his; and, supporting her trembling steps, he led her gently down the street; then, calling the first empty conveyance he saw, he handed her into it, and ordered the coachman to drive where he had taken an humble lodging, in a small street leading from Bloomsbury-square, and which, if it wanted the glitter and magnificence of her former abode (for the merchant was profuse in his indoor expenditure), was, at the same time, untinctured with those distressing circumstances that had latterly made that abode one of pain and uneasiness, and worse, to poor Grace, than would have been the veriest dungeon.

Tom Hackey likewise lived in the same house, and much of the sad impression upon Grace's heart was dissipated by the kind sympathy of his honest breast.

*   *   *   *

And was Mathew Trueman happier for the rough act he had committed in turning his own darling child from his door—she who had formed the light and joy of his establishment so long—she who with her gentle voice and sweet willing accents had ever formed so great a relief to the weary, plodding, business habits of his every-day existence?

Unconsciously to himself even Grace had formed the beauty and romance of his existence, and given to his life that charm of variety which had rescued it from the monotony that else would have been insufferable for so many years. She was the kindly household genius that had imparted a purer pleasure to every joy—that invested with a charm, peculiarly her own, every one of her actions, and gathered round the merchant's hearth so many rare domestic felicities, so unobtrusively put forward, that Trueman thought they were his own, and gave not his beautiful child credit for half the happiness she brought him.

In his own words, he had made a clear house, but in so clearing it, he had left dreariness and desolation; and now that he sat down in his solitary-and comfortless-looking drawing-room, a more unhappy man could scarcely have been found within the precincts of the great city in which he had lived so long a life of activity and exertion.

The storm of snow without, and the chilly dreariness within, combined to produce such utter discomfort in the merchant's heart, that he fretted and fumed about his costly apartments with feelings of the bitterest aggravation.

Then, instead of blaming himself for all this—instead of even then seeing his error, and repenting him of his great rashness—instead of then going forth on an errand of peace and reconciliation, he, with a foolish course of reasoning, attributed all the desolation and discomfort he had brought upon himself to

Grace, blaming her loudly for those evils which, had he permitted her, she would have been the first to shield him from ; and then, in the bitterness of his heart, he cursed his gentle and affectionate child, heeding not the blessing that God had bestowed upon him in so rare a gift, and casting away from him as worthless the greatest bounty of Providence.

There was no one at hand to advise Mathew Trueman, and if there had been, it is extremely doubtful if he would have taken such advice. He had no friend who could step in between him and his own passions, and as he sat revolving over the circumstances of the last few years, his hatred to Rivers, and his indignation of Grace, grew stronger every moment.

He thought, with an exquisite pang of alarm, of the fate of twenty thousand pounds which—for the bills were really worthless—he had lent to a dissipated young nobleman on his mere word of honour, one who had long given up all acquaintance with honourable feeling, and who regarded his word merely as a convenience to suit the contingencies of the moment. It never occurred so forcibly to Mathew Trueman before how very poor a chance he had of ever getting back his own money, much less any of the exorbitant interest he had charged Hawksworth for the loan. He had looked with satisfaction upon the marriage of Grace, and had so congratulated himself upon his own cleverness in conceiving the idea of returning him his own bills as Grace's fortune, that the peculiar position of the twenty thousand pounds scarcely ever occurred to his mind ; but now that all hope of those, to him, satisfactory circumstances were over—now that Grace by her marriage had given a death-blow to all his ambitious plans and projects, his great and inconceivable folly in advancing so large a sum to a spendthrift nobleman, and who was a minor, came across his mind in painful contrast to his otherwise accurate habits of dealing, and with a deep groan he confessed to himself that he had spent twenty thousand pounds in the attempt to accomplish something which was certainly further off than ever from probability.

"Oh, how I have been tricked and fooled," he cried ; " and now I've not a clerk in my office, for Hilliard, I suppose, must have committed that robbery, now that he is afraid to venture near the house. If these things get wind, I shall be the laughing-stock of the whole city. What shall I do—what shall I do? What need I of a house, now? What is the use to me of drawing-rooms and chandeliers ?"

As he made this remark, he rang the bell violently, and when the useful man-of-all-work appeared, he said, in a voice of thunder—

"Why are not these chandeliers lighted, I should like to know? Hang you all, am I to have no attention paid me ?"

"We—we very seldom light them, sir," said the useful man-of-all-work, "unless there's company ; but if you'll please to have them lighted, sir, we'll do it, only Miss Grace, sir, says always that she'd rather have the shaded lamp.'

"If I please!" cried the merchant, furiously—"then I do please ; and hark ye, sir, Miss Grace, as you call her, has left my house for ever—for ever—do you hear ?"

"'Ye—ye—yes," said the useful man

"And," continued the merchant, "any servant of mine who mentions her name shell be discharged immediately. You may go and tell that in the kitchen."

The useful man looked quite bewildered for a moment, and then, as Mathew Trueman made a movement of a decidedly hostile character, he rushed down into the kitchen in a frantic state of haste, to assure the servants that young missus had run away, and master was as mad as fury, only he was agoing to have a party on the strength of it.

"A party !" cried the cook.

"Yes, a party," was the reply, "in course he is ; he's ordered the chandeliers to be lighted, and there's a go."

As, however, the old man was proceeding up stairs with a piece of wax taper at the end of a long stick, by the aid of which he was going to light up the chandeliers, he met his master coming down, who then, passing him at full speed, left the house, slamming the street door behind him with terrible vehemence.

That night Mathew Trueman sacrificed so largely to the rosy god, that he got nearly as tipsy as on the occasion of his memorable dinner with Lord Hawksworth — that dinner which had excited in him so much indignation as being unfit for a christian to eat, and consisting of such terrible collections of nonsense.

The following morning was a Tuesday, and there appeared in the *Gazette* an announcement to the following effect—

"Mathew Trueman, of Thames-street, merchant, declining business, hereby gives notice that Messrs. Snapum, Crook, and Flint, of Bedford-row, will pay all claims upon the said Mathew Trueman; and it is hereby requested that all persons indebted to him shall forthwith pay their accounts to the said attorneys.

(Signed)   "MATHEW TRUEMAN."

This announcement was a matter of great astonishment and speculation to the mercantile world. Various were the rumours afloat as to the cause of the sudden retirement from business without the slightest note of warning by the merchant; but none came near the truth, for who could suppose that he would wilfully make such a desolation of his home as he had done?

Mrs. Woodfall called the next day, agreeable to the promise she had made Grace, and then, to her grief and consternation, she had heard what the merchant had said regarding his beautiful child. In vain were all her inquiries. The servants could not give the slightest clue as to where Grace was to be found. They knew no more than what had been stated by the merchant to the useful man-of-all-work; and although poor Mrs. Woodfall too well understood the cause of Grace's sudden withdrawal from home, that in no way assisted her to the discovery where she could be found.

Saddened and disappointed, therefore, she left the house, repairing to the little cottage she had taken on the outskirts of the town for herself and her son, with a vague hope that Grace and Rivers would find her out, for that they were together she entertained no doubt.

All, however, was in vain; no Grace came; and although Mrs. Woodfall perambulated the town, she could find no tidings of the fugitives.

It was duly announced by the newspapers that Mathew Trueman, the rich merchant, had gone to Brighton for the recovery of his health, after the arduous fatigues of business.

Lord Hawksworth and Girkins saw the announcement with a smile of derision, although Girkins wondered what on earth could induce Mathew Trueman to give up business in such an extraordinary manner, and then repair to Brighton, and make no mention of his daughter Grace. His curiosity was greatly aroused, and he made it is business to ferret out the particulars, which he very soon ascertained—for to a man like Girkins there were a thousand ways of obtaining information, not known to the ordinary run of people, more especially as in the present instance that secret was not kept sedulously.

He learned, beyond a doubt, that Rivers and Grace were married; and then, with a triumphant chuckle, he guessed the rest.

"Well," he said, to Lord Hawksworth, "your lordship's flame, Grace Trueman, has married the merchant's clerk."

"Ah! ah! Has she?" said Hawksworth, languidly. "I had really half forgotten her existence; that new dancer at the opera is positively a divine—a sort of sublimified idea of creation. I shall decidedly offer her the barouche, and the barge, and the little damp place on the Thames."

"You could not do better, my lord," said Girkins; "Mathew Trueman has gone to Brighton. Your lordship may laugh at your bills when they come due, and tell him to keep them as valuable autographs."

"Exactly," drawled Hawksworth, who was lounging on a sofa, in a white satin dressing-gown and embroidered slippers.

CHAPTER LXXXVIII.

RIVERS' DISAPPOINTMENTS.—THE STRUGGLE TO EXIST.—TOM HACKEY'S THEATRICAL ENGAGEMENT.—GRACE'S ATTEMPT TO PROCURE EMPLOYMENT.

POOR Rivers found at the end of a

few days his ten pounds sadly diminished; what with the expenses attendant upon his marriage, the payment of two or three little debts at his late lodgings, and the unavoidable current expenses of the few days, that amount was reduced more than one half, and as yet he had failed in every application he had made for employment.

Hour by hour his anxiety was increasing, and it was after the fifth day of disappointment that he sat with his beautiful wife by their humble fireside, striving for her sake to look the cheerfulness which he was far from feeling.

"Grace, dear," he said, "they will not have me yet. I have been to many mercantile houses, and in some of them I do believe there were vacancies; but somehow or other, they listen coldly to my appeal for employment, and when I stated that I would rather not apply to your father for a character, because of his great enmity against me for marrying you, they one and all gave a decided negative to my application; but do not be downcast, dear Grace, I will try again. Surely there is no bar upon me because I loved where not to love would have argued an insensibility very foreign to my feelings."

"Alas! alas! Rivers, what will become of us?" said Grace; "can I do nothing—can I do nothing to lighten the burthen I am upon you?"

"Nay, Grace, you are no burthen," said Rivers; "it is the thought of you that has lent me patience to bear with anything. I could not expect to be successful in obtaining employment so very soon."

"By what strange chain of circumstances," said Grace, "have we been thrown out of the society of Mrs. Woodfall. She knows not where to find us, nor we her."

"So it is," said Rivers; "and in this great city, with its myriads of inhabitants, and its miles of streets, persons may seek each other for years without ever meeting."

There was a low knock now at the door, and when Rivers said " Come in," Tom Hackey just projected his head a little way into the apartment, saying,

"Good evening—I'm going. Don't I wish I may get it!"

"Get what?" said Rivers.

"Why, that extraordinary situation I was telling Grace about. By-the-bye, you were not at home, so you didn't hear anything of it."

"What is it, Tom? I shall rejoice to hear of any good fortune on your part, although I cannot boast of my own luck."

"Why," said Tom, "one of the call-boys at Covent-garden has broke his leg down a trap; its quite providential, and I have some hopes of getting the situation till he is well enough to take it himself. It's five shillings a-week, and I believe there's a few perquisites: but, at all events, it is on the boards, and it is a theatrical engagement. I think I see 'em some day, when somebody don't come, whose got to play something,—the people get furious, the overture's played two times and a half— the prompter's bell rings, but the audience find out that's only a fond delusion, and after being quiet for a moment, they get ten times more furious at such a dead take in. Then the manager stands in the middle of the stage, and tears the hair out of his head by great handfuls—the people in the pit are just wrenching up the benches, and the gods are throwing ginger-beer bottles at the great chandelier. What do you think then?"

"I am sure I don't know," said Rivers, "but I suppose they call in the police."

"No, they don't," said Tom. "Guess again."

"They offer to return the money?" said Rivers.

"No, they don't," said Tom; "don't you wish you may get it?"

"What does happen, then?" said Rivers.

"Why, I, in the beginning of the tumult, have gone into the great tragedian's dressing-room, and, with frantic haste, have attired myself in his dress, which I find hanging on a clothes'-horse to air, and at the moment when the tumult is at its height, when the manager is at his wit's-end, and contemplating having the curtain drawn up, that the enraged audience may see him commit suicide on the stage—at that moment I rush on and offer myself for the part; ring goes the prompter's bell, up goes the curtain, and down comes the house."

"Down comes the house, Tom?" said Grace."

"Yes," said Tom, "that's the way we have of expressing a full round of applause.—I make a decided hit—a palpable hit. I become the great Hackey, and all our fortunes are made."

"For your sake, Tom," said Rivers, "I wish I saw it."

"Good-night," said Tom. "Good-night, I shall be too late; I fancy I see me

A little less than kin, and more than kind.' "

Tom Hackey thereupon shut the door, and hastened to fulfil his theatrical engagement, which he did obtain, through his innocent simplicity and harmless eccentricities, of the really amiable gentleman who had the disposal of the temporary appointment.

The next day brought with it another toilsome walk to poor Rivers, and an equally unavailing one. There was no employment to be had. The most encouraging answer from any was, that he might call again in a few months.

Alas! how was he to live even a few weeks, setting aside months? how was he to provide the common contingencies of life for many days to come? These questions were of fearful import, and as he asked himself, he shuddered at the doubtful answer he was compelled to give. These self-communions caused him to feel faint and heart-sick, and his despair was visible in his features. Grace saw it with sorrow, and said to him in a cheering tone—

"Dear Rivers, cannot I do anything towards our mutual support? I can draw—you have in happier moments proved my skill in that and music. Surely—surely others may require the instruction I have myself had."

"Grace—Grace, do not mention such a thing; you know not the difficulty of obtaining the employment, nor the objection I have of your being the slave of any one."

"I should not be so, dear Rivers—I will try."

"Nay, do not do so; we are not yet driven by necessity, and there is yet near three pounds remaining between us and want. There is yet room for hope. I

will try once again—and surely I shall succeed."

Thus they mutually endeavoured to cheer each other, driving away the gloomy thoughts that were fast creeping over their minds, caused by the ill-success that Rivers had hitherto met with, and the daily decrease of their means of subsistence.

But did the beautiful and tenderly nurtured Grace repine for her former splendid home; did she, by word or gesture, cast a shadow of reproach on him who had taken her from it? Oh, no! His appearance was the signal to call up a more cheerful countenance and impart a sweeter melody to her voice, and yet he never came but to tell her of renewed disappointments—of rude repulses, where, at least, if he met no employment, he need not have met with such scorn and contempt, or rough replies, where a gentle one would have answered much better, and taken away the sting of rejection.

All this poor Rivers had to speak of after his daily wanderings, and hour by hour crept over his soul the dreadful conviction that want could not be far off.

Then what was he to do—how was he to provide against the coming of that dreadful day, when their last shilling should be exhausted, and want—not figurative, poetical want, which luxuriates in its romantic wretchedness over the loss of some cherished luxuries— but actual want—that want which should be felt on rising in the morning by the absence of the morning's meal, stared him in the face.

What, oh! what was he do? He could not tell himself that he was any nearer to the accomplishment of his purpose of obtaining any employment than upon the first day he attempted it; he could not flatter himself, under those desperate circumstances, that any one to whom he had applied had indulged him with a shadow of hope, and day by day he had to commence his weary pilgrimage anew, with even, as he told himself with a shudder, less chances, because there were fewer places to apply to.

At length Grace herself began to tremble at the frightful prospect that was opening before them, and one day

that Rivers had departed with a determination of making some calls at the counting-houses down by the river side—a journey which would necessarily occupy a considerable period of time—Grace, without having communicated to him her intention, wrapped the shawl around her with which she had left her father's house, and went herself forth with the determination to effect something, if possible, towards the alleviation of their condition, although with scarcely a defined idea how to set about it.

The two accomplishments she possessed in the greatest degree, namely, music and drawing, she hoped she knew enough of to render marketable, and it was upon a vague recollection that she had frequently seen announcements in the shop windows of the music shops, that music was taught—such announcements implying that the shopkeeper had permitted the cards of some indigent professor of the art to occupy a place upon his counter, that she walked to some of the fashionable streets to look for a shop of such a description, where there was such an announcement, and where she might have a chance of introducing herself.

In the course of an hour the object of her search presented itself, and by the most diligent search through the window of a respectable music shop, the only announcement she could see bearing upon the subject was—

"The guitar taught by a lady."

This was rather encouraging than otherwise, inasmuch as she, Grace, did not profess that instrument, and it showed that the shopkeeper was not averse to such announcements.

Entering, then, the music shop with a timid and embarrassed air, she said to a respectable looking man behind the counter—

"I have called, sir, to know if you

could recommend me any pupils in music."

"What!" said the man; "a teacher of music are you? How long have you been that?"

"I have not yet commenced, sir," said Grace; "but circumstances compel me to attempt it as a means of livelihood."

"Oh," said the man; "was there no crossing you could sweep, that you hit upon the desperate resolve of getting a living by teaching? Why, you may walk through London on the heads of teachers of all kinds and descriptions, and particularly those of music. Why, they will go for sixpence a lesson anywhere within the metropolis, and in yesterday's paper there's one advertising to go for nothing, because she's partial to genteel society."

"Indeed," said Grace, with an air of deep chagrin.

"Yes, indeed," said the shopkeeper; "if this is the first application, you may as well dismiss the wild idea from your mind. You will never make a single sixpence by teaching, unless you have an immense private connection, or a professional name of high standing."

"I thank you," said Grace, "for your courtesy; but do you think, sir, I should have a better chance in teaching drawing?"

The shopkeeper actually gave a jump, as he said—

"Drawing!—how could you hit upon two such desperate expedients as music and drawing? Why, teaching drawing, it is well known, is the last resource of every artist who has signally failed in his profession. My dear young lady, you haven't the shadow of a chance."

"Alas! alas!" said Grace, "I had hoped——"

"Ah," said the shopkeeper, "that's what a great many persons live upon, though it's not over and above nourishing; but, I tell you what I can do; now and then, if you like, you may earn two or three shillings by copying music, that is, copying the scores for orchestras, a job which I have sometimes put into my hands."

"I am truly thankful to you," said Grace.

"Very well," said the music-seller, " call upon me this day week; and now,

my good girl, you had better go home, for you are certain of meeting no success in your applications, and may possibly meet with a great deal of insolence. Take my advice and go home."

"I will," said Grace, "for I ought to be abundantly satisfied with what you have said to me. I was encouraged to enter your shop, by seeing the placard announcing that the guitar was taught by a lady."

"Oh, that's my sister," said the shopkeeper. "It's a popular delusion; the guitar is not taught by that lady, for she never had a pupil."

Grace reached home considerably before Rivers, and it was with some feeling of satisfaction that she had to tell him the slight effort she had already made had not been altogether unsuccessful, for the promise of the music-seller, a week distant though it was, was at least better than a total failure.

"Alas, Grace," said Rivers. "It does indeed pain me to the soul, that you should be compelled, from your union with me, to attempt making a profit of those accomplishments which should but have adorned a happy leisure."

"And why should I not, Rivers?" said Grace; "the time may come, and quickly, too, when you may procure something that would prevent the necessity of my attempting such resources; but till then, dear Francis, we can but do our best, and by limiting our wants as much as possible, endeavour to make our resources meet them."

"You are, indeed, my good genius, Grace," said Rivers; "and should fortune really smile upon us, we shall be able better to feel the miseries of others and attempt their alleviation."

"We shall," said Grace; "and thus, you see, Rivers, sweet uses may be made of adversity."

CHAPTER LXXXIX.

THE APPLICATION TO TRUEMAN'S LAWYER. — THE REFUSAL. — THE WRETCHED EMPLOYMENT. — THEIR DEPARTURE FROM THEIR FIRST HOME.

BY the end of another week Rivers had expended his last shilling; but then he was promised some employment. It was to keep a tradesman's books, for which purpose he was to attend one hour each morning, the same tradesman having grown too corpulent and idle to do so himself; but then people don't like to give too much for their luxuries, and he paid poor Rivers the magnificent sum of three shillings a-week for the service rendered by him.

Then Grace did get a little music copying from the music-seller, and some weeks she earned the magnificent sum of four shillings, so that together they had about a shilling a day to keep them from absolute starvation. A fortnight's arrear of rent, however, soon produced a serious evil, which it was impossible to fight against, and when affairs were in this frightful crisis, half the rent was suddenly paid by Tom Hackey, who, by nearly starving himself, and by adding an odd shilling or two he had received from the actors to his small salary, managed to realise the amount.

"Tom," said Rivers, when he heard of the transaction, "this won't do; if we come to starvation, we must not pull you down likewise; you have a situation, such as it is, and I dare say one more congenial to your feelings than ever you had."

"I believe you," said Tom; "there's quite an odour about a theatre that's really delicious; it's made up of oil, saw-dust, gas, and paint—I wouldn't miss it for any money. But as to your making any fuss about my paying the rent, that's all stuff; I have had sixpence from one, and a shilling from another, so as to make it quite easy."

"Nay, nay, Tom," said Rivers; "you have been depriving yourself of the commonest necessaries of life; you must have done so to raise this necessary sum."

"You hold your noise," said Tom Hackey. "We've married Grace and we must keep her; I believe [that's the law of the land. I haven't been able to come out yet at the theatre, as I told you I would; they all come with frightful punctuality; but some of these days or other one of them is sure to get drunk, and then comes my chance; 'twas but the other day I was rehearsing Othello behind the flat, and I heard that the stage-manager was rather struck,

for there was a little jealousy mixed up with it; but that we must expect."

"What did he say, Tom?"

"'Good God!' he said, putting his hands over his ears. 'What's that? Just go and tell that gentleman behind the flat that this is a theatre, and not a private mad-house.' Of course, I bolted; it gave me an idea of what sort of sensation I should have made in the front. I'll make them open their eyes, some day."

It was some few hours after that, that Tom Hackey rushed into Rivers's parlour with evidently some new idea.

"Gracious powers!" he cried, "we all forgot—Mathew Trueman owes you some money."

"He does, indeed, Tom," said Rivers.

"A quarter's money, and a quarter's notice," said Tom. "Good gracious! there's a sum—thirty-seven pounds at one fell swoop."

"No, Tom," said Rivers; "I cannot make such a demand. I dipped eight weeks into the quarter, certainly, and I do think I ought to be paid to the day of my discharge."

"Then go to those confounded lawyers in Bedford-row," said Tom, "and have it. It's a good idea—I'll go for my five and odd too. Don't let us be done, Rivers."

Rivers looked at Grace as if he would inquire what she thought of the application.

"It is a just claim," said Grace, "and I do not see why you should not be paid."

"Then I will go," said Rivers. "I wish for no more than to that day on which I was so unceremoniously deprived of my situation."

"Come along," said Tom; "I have just time to go with you; besides, it is nor far out of my way."

"This twelve pounds," thought Rivers, "will be a most seasonable relief, and I am certainly justly entitled to the sum, and can feel no delicacy in seeking for it."

A very short time sufficed to bring Tom and Rivers to Bedford-row, and the office of the lawyers was by no means difficult to find.

"Now, Tom," said Rivers, before they entered, "pray do not indulge in any of your singularities, for our claim will inevetably be doubted. You had better let me speak entirely."

" Well," said Tom, " you may have it all your own way—there's a frightful deal of vanity in the world."

Rivers smiled and entered the lawyer's office, Tom Hackey following him closely.

" I believe," said Rivers to a clerk whom he saw, " you have been advertised to satisfy all claims upon Mr. Mathew Trueman ?"

" Certainly, sir," said the clerk, " we have. Do you come to settle an account, or to receive one ?"

" To receive one," said Rivers.

" I should think so," said Tom ; " to receive one, of course."

" Oh, then," said the clerk, " you had better see Mr. Flukes."

" Very well," said Rivers, " but I don't happen to know Mr. Flukes."

" Oh, he's our managing clerk ; if you tap at the second door you see there, he'll say 'come in ;' then go in."

Rivers did so, and soon found himself in the presence of a little wiry-looking man, with a bald head, who, when the matter was explained to him, said, placing writing materials before Rivers :

" Just write a memorandum that you agree not to insist upon a notice to leave your situation."

" I can have no objection to that," said Rivers, as he wrote the required memorandum. " Here it is."

" Very good," said Mr. Flukes, carefully blotting the writing, " when I see my client, Mr. Trueman, I will take an opportunity of mentioning the affair to him."

" And when may that be ?" said Rivers.

" I dare say somewhere between this and Christmas," was the reply.

" Christmas ?" said Rivers ; " why we have not got through the first quarter of the year."

" Uncommonly true," said Mr. Flukes, " uncommonly true ; but as we have received no instructions about your account, we cannot think of paying it without a special reference to Mr. Trueman, so there's an end of it. If you like to pay me six-and-eightpence now, I'll write him a letter about it."

" You are an extortionate scoundrel !" said Rivers, " and you have cajoled me into giving an acknowledgment that I do not require a warning, merely as a prefatory step to tricking me out of the whole amount. Come along, Tom, we might have foretold that we should waste our time in this application."

" Why, you infernal humbug !" said Tom to Mr. Flukes ; " what do you mean by it ?"

At the same time Tom took up a heavy ledger that lay on the desk, and lifting it in so sudden and threatening an attitude, that down fell Mr. Flukes without being touched, upon which Tom laid the ledger very carefully on the desk again, saying—

" Don't say I assaulted you, you old humbug."

In a few minutes more the friends were in the open air, and Mr. Flukes got up with deep aggravation at his soul, from the fact that Tom certainly had not assaulted him, and that there was a witness to prove he had not, although he, Mr. Flukes, had bumped his head against the fender in a far from pleasant manner.

" Well, Tom," said Rivers, " that hope is gone."

" Yes, it is," said Tom, " quite gone ; but it's always the way if you have anything to do with these lawyers. Never mind, *nil desperandum,* and take things easy. We'll be even with them all yet, some of these days ; until then, let us recollect that

" All the world's a stage,
  And men and women merely players.
  They have their exits and their entrances,
  And one man in his time plays many parts.
  First, the infant lull'd by wild legends in its nurse's arms ;
  Then the schoolboy, dreaming of theatres and Christmas pantomimes,
  Anon the lover of the drama rises full of ambition,
  Making a speech to suit each new occasion.
  Then the actor, treading the stage in tragic hose,
  And after that, when time his locks have silver'd,

The manage r appears, full of wise saws and ancient instances.
Then comes last scene of—the fifth act's termination :
Life's fitful tragedy is over. The curtain drops
On that which once had been the noblest work of God."

So saying, Tom Hackey walked off at a rapid pace to his theatrical duties, and Rivers, with a slower movement, hied him home to Grace, to tell her of the non-success of his application to her father's lawyers.

"Well, Rivers," she said, "we can at least suffer patiently, if it is not in our power to resist successfully oppression. We are young, and the time may yet come when we may look back to all these things, which have made the spring of our existence so dreary and desolate, as but the phantasma of a dream, which with the morning's light has fled for ever."

"Yes, Grace," said Rivers, "we will not yet bid hope good bye. Heaven surely cannot desert one whom it has made so beautiful as you are ; but there is one subject that we must gravely consider, and that is, the absolute necessity of taking some measures to prevent our faithful friend Hackey from sacrificing entirely his own fortunes to our necessities—a thing which I am sure he will do, if we permit him."

"How can we act?" said Grace. "What can we do?"

"It is one of the evils of our destiny, Grace," said Rivers, mournfully, "that to preserve our friend we must leave him. We must go from him, and seek elsewhere a poorer home, where he will not find us ; if we suffer, let us suffer alone, without entailing misery upon others. What we owe here already we cannot pay, and it is honester far to go at once, leaving the small debt behind us, than to increase it without a prospect of meeting the just demand."

"I am ready," said Grace, "I am ready. Whenever it shall please you, Rivers, I am ready to go."

"Then, to-night, dearest," said Rivers, "to-night let us leave this place, in which we can no longer stay with honour."

"Yes, let it be to-night ; let us seek some quiet spot, where at least we shall be unknown in our misery, and while we suffer ourselves, we shall at least not be entailing misery upon others."

This, then, was determined upon, but it seemed like severing the last link that held them to society, to leave poor Tom Hackey, and that, too, without a word of kind farewell. It was, indeed, with a saddened aspect that Rivers could make up his mind to such a measure.

To argue with Tom, and endeavour to persuade him to keep for himself entirely his own scanty earnings, he knew would be a vain and useless task. The only way no enforce such a measure was the one he had adopted, and which Grace had acquiesced in.

Perhaps Poor Grace had not been without a distant hope that a day might come when her father would repent him of his harshness, and, perhaps, she had expected that day would arrive very soon after her expulsion from her home, and its non-arrival had preyed heavily upon her spirits, but, certain it is, that her heart began to sink within her, and on that day she found it hard indeed to fight against the deep depression of her spirits.

Hope was growing less and less distinct within her breast, and although she would not confess it to Rivers, she was beginning to look upon the most melancholy side of their condition.

Little did poor Tom Hackey think that those for whom he would have laid down his life—those for whom he would have sacrificed every earthly prospect, with the romantic generosity that knew no limits, were about in such a manner to leave him, and expose themselves, without one friend to whom they could turn for the most temporary succour, to the cold mercies of a world too full of selfishness and a struggle for precedence to allow humble merit and patient endurance the remotest chance amid the wild turmoil of existence.

That day was, indeed, to Grace and Rivers a gloomy one. They had parted with all they possessed except some of the commonest necessaries of clothing, and their preparations for departure were very quickly made.

They then took a last look around them upon that home which had been their first in the marriage state, and full of disagreeables and miseries as it had been, they had lent a charm to it by their mutual love.

Rivers left a letter for Tom Hackey, in which he explained the reasons for their absence, and then with a small bundle, containing all the worldly goods they possessed, they crept silently from the house.

The day was fast closing in, and night was rapidly making its appearance, and the rain, which had long threatened by the humid state of the atmosphere, now fell in a sharp mist, which rendered the streets greasy and slippery to walk on, and all those whose business did not imperatively demand their continuance in such weather, now turned their steps towards their own houses, where their cheeful firesides would compensate for the disagreeables they had endured without.

As it grew darker, the lamps were lit, and the shop windows here and there displayed lights, until one after another they were all illuminated, and throwing a broad light upon the foot-pavement, enabled pedestrians to pursue their plodding way in a perfect consciousness of the mud and dirt they were walking in.

The sky was hidden from the sight, and he who directed his gaze towards the house-tops, saw but a dark undefinable-looking canopy overhead, that enveloped all the higher structures from his view, until at length, what between darkness and the rain, nothing could be seen above a second story, save where some artizans were at work, and there the numerous lights shone out like a dimly illuminated spot round which was almost palpable darkness.

The rain each moment increased in density, falling heavily, and causing the streets to be deserted by all but a few stragglers, whom necessity alone compelled to be abroad—the poor, the needy, and, perhaps, the evil, and these last not unless they had an object in view that would, in their estimation, compensate them for the inconvenience they must suffer.

A more melancholy and completely miserable state of things cannot happen than a wet night in town; and, bad as it is in the principal thoroughfares, it is still worse in the smaller streets and more deserted parts of the town, which have not the numerous lights that come from the shop windows, and which deprive darkness of some of its gloom.

The wet, splashy mud on the pavement—the dropping rain from the eaves of houses—the overflow of some waterspout, which empties its bursting contents on some ledge, while the element is averted in its course and sent in numerous and copious streams across the footway on the unfortunate pedestrian's head whom chance may bring to that spot, form altogether such a scene of discomfort, that few but the inhabitants of large towns can have any notion or experience of.

On such an evening many of the shops close early, the streets become deserted, and those who are safely housed by a warm fire complacently listen to the sullen pattering of the rain and the heavy footfall of some stray passenger, which sounds more plainly at such a moment than any other, conveying to the mind an epitome of all the disagreeables of a town life, namely, a wet night in the city.

Grace and Rivers wandered through the wet until they came to a suburban district of London, lying a little to the right of Camden Town and approaching the Highgate-road. There they contrived to hire, at a rent of two shillings weekly, a wretched apartment, scarcely defended from the wind and the weather, and there we must leave them for a time with a sigh for their sufferings—a tear for their deep afflictions.

CHAPTER XC.

THE LETTER TO TOM HACKEY.—MATHEW TRUEMAN'S RETURN.—TOM'S INTERVIEW WITH HIM.—THE MERCHANT'S ILLNESS.

WHO could paint poor Tom Hackey's despair when the following letter was handed to him upon his return from the theatre?—

"MY DEAR HACKEY.—Do not think Grace or myself unkind, or unheedful of your true friendship and many admirable qualities, because we have left you in the manner we are now doing. Do not fancy that by so leaving you we do not fully appreciate your kindness towards us, already shown, and all the further kindness which we know you are ready to show.

"Hackey, to reason with you, and tell you you should look to yourself and not to us, I know would be in vain. It is, therefore, with the greatest reluctance that Grace and I have determined, until fortune shall once more smile upon us, to leave you without a knowledge of where we are to be found, for we cannot permit that you should sacrifice yourself so completely as we know you would, to preserve us from the slightest evil.

"Adieu, dear Hackey, and believe us both to be your sincerest and best friends, and with Grace's kindest feelings towards you—I am, my dear Hackey, yours most truly,

"FRANCIS RIVERS."

"P.S. When I can consistently see you, I will inquire for you at Covent Garden Theatre."

"There's a do," said Tom Hackey— "a dead swindle. What'll become of me now? What's the use of marrying us if she deserts us in this way? I'll find 'em out. They can't go far; they haven't got the money, that's one comfort. Let me consider. I've got a good deal of time to myself, for there ain't rehearsal every day, and I'll find 'em out. I won't put myself out of the way about it. I'll find 'em out, and when I do, I'll tell Miss Grace a bit of my mind, that I will, and I'll set about it to-day."

Tom Hackey, however, found that the task of discovering the obscure retreat of Rivers and Grace in London was a task easier set about than accomplished, and one which required more time and more means that was at his disposal.

Still, however, he would not despair, but day after day he trudged about through various parts of the city with the hope of finding some clue to those whom he so affectionately sought.

All was in vain; days accumulated into weeks, and weeks into months. The unhappy Riverses were not to be found, and poor Tom Hackey sunk into a state of complete dejection.

It was strange, indeed, how those three parties, so intimately connected in kindly feelings and mutual sympa-

thies—namely, Mrs. Woodfall, Tom Hackey, and the Riverses, should be ignorant of each other's locality; but so it was. Fate had decreed their separation.

Mrs. Woodfall had tried every means to discover Grace's abode, but in vain; and half broken-hearted, she had at length given up the hopeless task.

A newspaper paragraph then informed Tom Hackey of Mr. Trueman's departure from Brighton to London, and he resolved to put in practice a scheme that had often suggested itself to him of attempting to move the merchant's heart in favour of his discarded child.

"He's got no house in London," said Tom; "what's the use of a house to him, poor wretch? He'll be at some hotel or another, of course, and I might make a grand tour among them, and find him out. If he won't do anything for poor Grace and Rivers, I shall have the satisfaction of telling him what an old rogue I think him, and that'll be a comfort. I'll poke an additional thorn or two into the old wretch's side. I wonder how he gets on with Lord Hawksworth's bills—that was a go. They are renewed, I suppose, as pleasant as possible. Leave me alone, I'll find him out. I think he'll rather give a jump when he sees me."

Full of this resolution, Tom Hackey perambulated the principal streets, inquiring at every hotel for Mr. Trueman. For a long time his search was in vain; but at length, at a magnificent establishment in one of the fashionable squares, he met with the welcome intelligence that Mr. Trueman was there.

"Ah, very well," said Tom; "I want to see him."

"You may send up your name," said the waiter, "but I don't think he'll see you; he never sees anybody."

"Oh, he's up stairs in the first-floor back, is he?"

"No, he isn't," said the waiter; "he's in the first-floor front."

"Thank you," said Tom. "I am such a very old friend, that I can take the liberty of going up stairs. Bless your heart, we were in business together in Thames-street."

So saying, Tom deliberately walked up, and the waiter, after remarking to himself that it was no business of his'n, as he didn't answer Mr. Trueman's bell, gave up all interference in the affair.

In the meantime, Tom reached the door which had been indicated as that of Mr. Trueman's apartment. He knocked twice loudly before a querulous voice from within the apartment cried—

"Come in."

Tom turned the handle of the door, and in another moment stood face to face with Mathew Trueman.

But a short time had elapsed, and yet how sadly was the merchant altered! It seemed as if years had passed over his head; and so amazed was the honest fellow at the changed appearance which the merchant presented, that he stood for some moments staring at him without the power of speech.

Mathew Trueman was scarcely less surprised at the sudden apparition of Tom Hackey, than was Tom at the alteration which so short a time had effected in the merchant's appearance. He was enraged to an excess, and partially rising from his chair, and holding the arms for support, he cried—

"Rascal—scoundrel! how dare you come here? What—what business have you with me? Thief—vagabond!"

"Mathew," said Tom, "mind what you are at. I ain't going to abuse you —that is to say, if you do what you ought, though you deserve it—so don't you abuse me. I have taken a deal of trouble to find you out, and you ought to be grateful. You don't look so well as you did; but I suppose that's your evil conscience, and can't be helped."

"How dare you!" cried the merchant, almost inarticulate with rage; "begone this instant, or I'll have you turned neck and heels into the street."

"If you try any of your violence against me, Mathew," said Tom, "I'll just tell all the waiters, chambermaids, and the cook, and all that sort of thing, in this hotel, what an old wretch you are. I don't want to hurt your feelings, bad as you are; but don't you recollect turning out your own daughter, you old brute, in the snow, you monster on two legs! I only came to make a gentle remonstrance to you, and to tell you you ought to be ashamed of yourself, you hoary-headed old ruffian! There's Miss Grace, bless her heart, after marrying us, has come to all sorts of miseries, and

now she's gone off, nobody knows where, and all through you. Now, I've prepared a little document, just to show you what you ought to do. There it is; it'll only cost you five shillings a-piece to put it into all the morning newspapers. I'll read it for you, as you seem rather bewildered. If you don't think it strong enough, you can put in an extra word or two. Listen to me, and repent, you elderly reprobate. I wouldn't abuse you on any account, but leave you to your own conscience, you shameful old vagabond!"

Tom Hackey then read from a slip of paper, which he produced, the following words—

"'If Grace T., recently married to R., would return to her wretched old father, and forgive him, he may be able to lay his miserable old head in peace in the grave. He will make over to her all his property, and behave dutifully ever afterwards; but if she won't, old M. T. remains a prey to remorse, and means to end his days in a lunatic asylum. N.B. if Tom H. will forgive old M. T., old M. T. will feel particularly grateful to Tom H.'

"There, now, you old sinner," said Tom Hackey; "there's a chance left for you, a kind of last kick—mind what you are about, and we'll all of us take your case into consideration, but remain obstinate, and you are done for—there's no hope for you in this world, Mathew, and very little in the next. Now, don't be obstinate—at your time of life, you ought to know better—give me the money, and I'll put in the advertisement. So, you see, it'll be no trouble to you, old Mathew, and you've nothing to do but down with the blunt."

Mathew Trueman was so paralysed at the quantity of assurance to make this speech, that in silent wonder he allowed Tom to finish it outright, before he attempted a reply—that reply, then, was in the shape of such a pull of the bell, that the silken cord came away in Mathew Trueman's hand, and he had great difficulty in saving himself from falling.

Two or three waiters and the landlord rushed into the room, and then Mathew Trueman, in a hoarse voice, cried—

"Turn him out—turn him out—turn

out that scoundrel—throw him into the street!"

"What's he done, sir? what's he done, sir?" cried the landlord.

"Remove him, remove him!" shrieked the merchant; "remove him, or I will leave the hotel this moment."

This threat had the desired effect, and the landlord became filled with the greatest indignation at Tom Hackey. The idea, as he remarked to one of the waiters afterwards, of that fellow to come and aggravate the rich Mr. Trueman, so as to make him say he would leave the hotel! It was enough to make anybody dreadfully sick of the lower classes.

The waiters, with the assistance of the landlord, laid hold of Tom Hackey, and conducted him down the staircase, which was easily enough done, for having convinced himself that Mathew Trueman did not intend to give any as-

sistance to Grace, he made no opposition to leaving the place. All the remark he made was—

"I wish you joy of that old gentleman you have up stairs—if he gets ill ever, tell him you can't minister to a mind diseased, and to think of his daughter. Whenever you want to aggravate him, tell him it snows, and you wouldn't turn a dog out. If that don't touch him on the raw, I don't know what will—I know the old bloke."

"If you don't be off," said the landlord, "I'll give you in charge to a constable."

"Oh, indeed, spooney," said Tom; "I didn't think you were half so clever. How would you look when you did it? Why don't you stuff a lemon in your mouth? You'd look like a calf's head ready for dressing then. Is that your chimney on fire, or next door's?"

"My chimney? Good God Almighty,"

said the landlord, running out into the middle of the road, "that'll be a second time this month."

Tom Hackey walked away with a feeling at his heart, very much at variance with the heedless character of his discourse. He had made his attempt to induce Mathew Trueman to send for his daughter and had signally failed in so making it, and with despair, he asked himself what he could now do for Grace, or what other means presented themselves of discovering her place of abode.

To these questions he could give himself no satisfactory answer, and poor Tom Hackey, with but the shadow of his former spirits, attended to his duties at the theatre, where his good humour and activity had secured him many friends, so that even when the boy recovered whose place Tom had been employed to fill, they were both retained, rather than part with Tom Hackey, and the other one had a sort of claim upon the establishment, in consequence of the accident.

After Tom's visit, Mathew Trueman had a serious illness, for although he had gone to Brighton for his health, he found that most delighful of all acquisitions gradually decaying—the fever of the mind was preying upon the body, and although there were times when Mathew Trueman felt in his inmost soul that he had made a wretched and frightful miscalculation with regard to his means of happiness, yet pride and anger ever stepped in, and prevented him from acknowledging his error.

Thus was this ambitious man prevented by the same evil passions that had brought misery upon him, from pleasantly enjoying the few remaining years he had to linger in the world. It was months before he rose from a bed of sickness, and then the opulent merchant was the very shadow of his former self, and nothing remained strong and powerful within him, but the rage that ever filled his breast at the mention of the name of Rivers.

CHAPTER XCI.

A LAPSE OF TIME.—RIVERS, HIS WIFE AND CHILD.—DESTITUTION.—THE WILD RESOLVE.—THE SUICIDE.

Two years have elapsed—two long weary years with all their accompaniments of the varying seasons, the summer's heat and the winter's snow, the millions of bright flowers spangling the earth with bright beauty, and the still aspect of the after season, when all is cold and barren, when the sweet flowers seem to have crept in to the bowels of the earth, there to remain until the summer sun shall call them into life and beauty;—two years, to many passing with the rapidity of thought;—two years, like the sunny dream of a sunny night, to those who in the gilded shallop of existence had glided gently down the stream of time, without a passing breeze to ruffle their silken pinions;—two long weary years to the hapless beings on whom fortune had turned a sinister aspect, and whose days had been numbered by items of wretchedness known only to themselves and those, who, with a rare philanthropy, have looked beneath the tinsel surface of society, and marked the deep depths of wretchedness that lay beneath, and heard the sighs of despair which mingle so airily with the music in the floating atmosphere above.

The month was January, and the early evening was beginning to wrap all objects in obscurity,—the white mists from the earth's surface, and from the river, for we are in London, was meeting the denser vapours that descended through the air; chill and comfortless felt the night; occasionally a gust of sleet and rain would dash for a moment in the faces of the bewildered passengers, and then as suddenly cease, leaving them to wonder whence it came.

It was one of those evenings when people set their teeth and breathe hard in the streets, passing each other with great rapidity, and seeking their homes, let them be of what character they might, as quickly as possible.

More particularly in crossing the bridges, did people button their clothing more tightly around them, wrapping handkerchiefs around their necks, taking care that the said handkerchiefs encased their chins, and holding on their hats with great vehemence.

Nine o'clock had arrived, and the streets were nearly deserted, for many business establishments had given over the labours of the day by that hour, and there was no temptation to induce casual passengers to saunter in the public thoroughfares.

Every one who was out on that evening appeared to have somewhere to go to, whither he was bent upon going as quickly as possible. The only laggers in the public streets were the wretched few who had no home to go to—that small per centage of the population who were houseless, and who depended solely and entirely upon chance for the day's contingencies—upon some of the markets, a skeleton of a house, or the dry arch of a bridge for a lodging. The wind grew more cutting and bitter, the rain was mingled more freely with frozen particles, and before half-past nine, a more uncomfortable evening could not well be conceived.

It was not a storm, but a regular set in wretched night, and sufficiently violent to the full to be extremely uncomfortable, and yet not sufficiently so to predicate its subsidence.

There was one man on Blackfriars-bridge, one solitary man, and he sat upon one of the public seats, with his head resting upon his hands, indifferent to the howling of the wind, and the pelting of the shower; his thoughts were too deeply concentrated within his own heart, and his senses to much wrapped up in a contemplation of his own miseries, to heed the external appearance of nature.

That man was Francis Rivers; for more than an hour he so sat, and then, with a deep groan, he rose, and, staggering a little way, for want and misery had done its work upon his manly form, he leaned heavily upon the balustrades of the bridge, and looked long and wistfully into the deep waters, as, with a moaning sound, they rushed beneath him.

"God of Heaven!" he said, in a low tone; "God of Heaven, what miseries have not I waded through for two years—two ages of want, wretchedness, and destitution; and she, too, the bright, the beautiful, and the good, my heart's first, last, only love—the idol of my existence! what is she? Alas—alas! even as one risen from the tomb is she—pale—pale—and wan—privation has done its work upon her lovely form, and our child, too—do I dream, or does the echo of its screams for food still ring in my distracted ears? I—I can scarcely gasp; Heaven help me, for already have I wearied it with supplications."

Again he dropped his head upon his hands, and his whole form shook with emotion; then, like a man who had but been acting a part, he rose, and folding his arms across his breast—

"This night," he said, "we are thrust forth from the miserable house that has long afforded us but a slight shelter from the season's difference. The slight and temporary employments which have kept soul and body together have all failed, all broken down, and we are now beggars, outcasts, thrown upon the wide streets to starve; ay, to starve, unless—unless—yes, there is an alternative, and one that I have hugged to my heart a hundred times. If I cannot live for Grace, by the great God above me, I can die for her; yes, I can die for her—yon dark surging waters can herald me to the grave, and then there are two hopes for Grace when I am dead; her father may relent, when he knows that I, the chief object of his resentment, am lifeless, he may turn again to his child, and bury his anger with me in the silent tomb; or, if he prove obdurate, if his heart be quite marble, some kind souls, who require, ere their philanthropy becomes active, the strong stirring up of some frightful incident, may assist her. Yes—yes; I cannot live for her—I can die for her—I can die for her!"

He paced the bridge to and fro for many minutes; then, in a new strain of deep emotion, he added—

"'Tis hard, very hard to part thus; but it must be done. Do I shrink? No, no; they shall not say that I took the young, happy girl from her brilliant home; reduced her to such poverty, that is seldom found but in the pages of some romance, and then hesitated to rescue her. Although I had to rush through the portals of the tomb so to do, when my sad story is told, it shall have that termination, that my last effort to save her was to die for her.

"And now," he continued, "now for the particulars—the manner—the means —how shall it be done? The river— ay, the river: it shall be so. I will find a grave in its waters, so shall Grace be spared the shock, for she shall not see me lifeless; but how can this be done? —how can this be done? When the tide is running hard and strong to the open sea, I can cast myself into the surging stream, and, like a weed upon the waters, be carried far away—never —never again to look upon what, to me, is more beautiful, more full of Heaven— my wife, and my child; but God so wills it, and it must be done."

It was frightful thus, in the spring of life, to contemplate death for one so innocent, one whose existence was untainted by crime, unmarked by any one deed that could be pitched upon as likely to plant an arrow in his heart, and make life a burden to his soul. It was, indeed, a fearful alternative, to leave thus abruptly those who, under happier circumstances, might have made life so dear to him, earth so beautiful; or, by remaining with them, to insure a gradual destruction, to escape from which there seemed no hope, but which appeared careering on like a frightful demon, who will not be stayed in his fearful progress.

"Yes; I am resolved," he said, " I am resolved; it shall be to-morrow night. I will pray that, until then, we may be permitted to remain in our wretched home; and, before then, I will write to Mathew Trueman, telling him that, ere he receives that brief epistle, I shall be a corpse, and urging him, by all his hopes here and hereafter, to fly to the rescue of Grace, his own child, and save her from the frightful miseries that await her."

Heedless, then, of the pelting of the pitiless storm, Rivers walked to the miserable hovel in which he and Grace, for the smallest possible pittance, had found a temporary shelter, and where it was his prayer that she might be permitted to stay until he had completed his design.

And who would have known the once beautiful Grace Rivers, in the pale emaciated form that rose to meet that husband, who was still dearer to her in poverty and affliction than all the world beside? She strove even to conjure up a smile to welcome him; but it was a sad one, such an one as 'twas painful to see upon her face, because it had no mirth, because it was a very mockery of woe.

"Rivers," she said, "we've been waiting for you—there is something to eat."

"Nay, Grace," he said, "I have dined and supped: I need it not. Your father is in town, I hear. I wonder where poor Tom Hackey is, and Mrs. Woodfall; and, although no friends of ours, I wonder I have never stumbled over Hilliard and Girkins, and Lord Hawksworth."

"What makes you," said Grace, "think of all these people to-night? Any one would think, Rivers, you were going a long journey, and were calling to mind all those you knew before you started on it."

Rivers started as he repeated the words, "a long journey;" and then he added—"a long journey, indeed, a very long journey."

"Rivers," said his wife, "of what are you speaking?"

"Nothing, nothing," he said, in a confused manner—"'tis nothing—but you know life is a long and tiresome journey."

"It is," said Grace, sadly; "and yet how much longer to us would it have seemed, how much more full of woe, had we not had each other, Rivers to lighten the way."

"'Tis very strange," said Rivers, " that your father's heart should never have yearned towards you in all this time. It is his great animosity to me, Grace, that has kept him from you—there can be surely no other reason."

"Do not talk of it," said Grace; "that is a subject that ever vexes you. Two years have passed away, it is true; but, had we been in prosperity, that period would have seemed short, and we should have thought but little of such a lapse of time."

"True—true," said Rivers; "we will drop the subject, Grace, and hope that even a few days will better our condition. I think now I shall be hopeful myself."

Rivers busied himself that night in writing two notes, which he did not show to Grace, and then he requested most earnestly of the people of the house leave to remain there that night and the next, telling them that he had great hopes they would be paid all that was owing them.

This agreement sufficed, and leave was accordingly given, when Rivers again sought the society of Grace for the last time, as he told himself, in this world.

*   *   *   *

A few pence which yet remained to Rivers was forced to suffice for the wants of the succeeding day. He lingered long at home, communing with himself upon his frightful resolution, and each moment the world and its prospects seemed to grow darker and darker. He looked curiously upon every object around him, and he kept telling himself, in a low whisper, that alarmed Grace exceedingly—

"I shall never see that again—I shall never see that again."

The two letters that he had written were singularly characteristic of his state of mind, full of desponding thoughts and sad imagery. One was to Mathew Trueman, and it read as follows—

"SIR,—For two years I have been the husband of your daughter; and during that time, God knows, I have stiven hard to protect her from the evils of penury and want. Such self-sacrifices as I could make, I have made—leaving but one last final one, which should be the last, inasmuch as it precludes a possibility of all others.

"You thrust her from your house—you shut your heart against her because she was my wife. What she then endured, was endured for my sake, and with a holy resignation that was more maddening to me than would have been the wildest impatience, she bore with a meek and gentle fortitude the evils that surrounded us.

"She had a hope, a hope perhaps that bore her up when all other hopes seemed dead, it was that you would still seek her out on some propitious day, and bury in oblivion the sad memory of the past.

"That hope has not been realized, that day has never come, and yet she is your only child. It must be because she is my wife, and it might be, that if I were gone, and the memory of me lost to you by the consciousness that I was in the cold embraces of death, you would open your heart to her in her loneliness.

"I will hope that it should be so, and that she and her innocent child may receive, when I am gone, that succour which has hitherto been denied them.

"Mathew Trueman, by the time you read this, its writer will not be among the living. I will take measures that even you shall not be troubled after my death with any inquiry concerning me. The waters shall be my grave, and may Heaven inspire you with charity towards your daughter as a widow, and her fatherless child, by sending or going promptly to the address hereunto appended.   "FRANCIS RIVERS,

"No. 2, Reed's-court, Blackfriars.

"To Mathew Trueman, Esq.

"Imperial Hotel."

The other letter was to Grace; it was this—

"DEAREST GRACE,—Do not bewail me; fancy that I have but taken a journey for your benefit and that of our child, a journey from which I shall never return; but then, dearest, you will come to me, and we shall never part again. Be of good cheer, Grace. I cannot say more, but I think now that your father may be kind to you.

"Farewell, dear Grace, farewell, but not for ever.   "FRANCIS RIVERS."

Rivers could not trust himself to write more to Grace; he could enlarge upon what he had to say to her father, but to her herself he found the task one of utter impossibility; and with so brief a farewell did he attempt to take leave of her whom he had loved so fondly, and for whom he was about, while on the very threshold of existence, to voluntarily meet the much-dreaded tyrant, death.

CHAPTER XCII.

THE ATTEMPTED SACRIFICE.—THE RESCUE, AND THE STRANGE MEETING.—GRACE'S RESOLUTION.

THE solemn tones of St Paul's cathedral were giving out the hour of ten, when the unhappy Francis Rivers stood upon Blackfriars-bridge. Piles of huge clouds had been for some hours coming up from the south-west, and the temperature was evidently increasing. A cold searching wind swept through the balustrades of the bridge, and thinly clad as was Rivers, he trembled as the blast met his attenuated frame. Deep sobs at one moment would shake his breast, and at another, such a look of calm despair would cross his features, that, could any one have seen him, no doubt could have been entertained concerning the fact that he felt himself trembling on the verge of eternity.

"Oh! Grace—Grace," he reasoned, "have I indeed for the last time looked upon you, and my child too—the dear sacred gift of Heaven, as a blessing to our love? What a hideous fate is mine. Heaven forgive me for the act I am about to commit. It is not for my own sake that I rush from the world, but to secure her whom I love so fondly, and who by my love has been brought to ruin, want, and misery, against more evil. She will be pitied when I am gone. It is not that I cowardly seek to escape the ills that Providence eases to inflict upon me. Oh, no—death is terrible to me, but I die for her. If by living, and enduring still greater suffering, I could aid her, how gladly would I do so."

With such sad and terrible reasoning did poor Rivers keep his mind up to his fatal purpose. The night wore on, but so many persons kept perpetually passing and repassing the bridge, that he began to despair of executing his purpose. About eleven o'clock he left that place, and walked with great speed towards Millbank, where he recollected was a very lonely spot, the river only being separated from the pathway by a low wall, and the passengers few and far between.

As soon as he thought of that place, he resolved that it should be the scene of his self-sacrifice; and having previously posted the two letters so that they would reach their several destinations in the morning early, he told himself there was nothing now to impede his plunging into eternity, and making the frightful effort to save Grace and his child, which seemed to him the only one at all in his power.

Half-an-hour's walking brought him to a very lonely, dismal-looking spot, indeed, not far from Vauxhall-bridge, a spot on which any wild and desperate act might be committed with almost a certainty of secrecy. Rivers leaned over the low wall and saw that the river washed its base. He clasped his hands, and offered up to Heaven a wild but fervent prayer for his wife and child—tears gushed from his eyes, and his deep sobs sounded wofully mournful in the solitude.

Suddenly he was mute, for he heard a footstep near at hand. In the dim light he saw a woman hurrying past.

"That is my last glance at a fellow creature," he said. "Farewell, world, for ever, and for ever—Grace—Grace."

He sprang over the low wall. There was a heavy plash—one bubbling cry, and all was still.

*　　*　　*　　*

When Rivers had left his home, Grace rose and commenced attiring her child in as much warm clothing as she had. As she did so there were tears in her eyes, and occasionally deep sighs came from the very bottom of her heart, while now and then such a heightened colour came across her otherwise pale face, that it was evident some unusual cause of mental excitement had arisen.

Then drawing over her own shoulders a thin, much-worn shawl, which was totally inadequate to protect her against the inclemency of the season, she imprinted a kiss upon the cheek of her infant, and moved towards the door. Her strength and fortitude, however, at that moment appeared completely to forsake her, and staggering to a seat, she burst into tears.

Poor Grace had worked her mind up to a resolution, which to her was a fearful one—a resolution that, rather than see her child want the common necessaries of life, she would humble every proud feeling of her heart, and beg for that bread which there seemed no opportunity of procuring by honest industry.

This was a determination she had shrunk from imparting to Rivers, for well she knew he would object most strenuously to such a course; but she had during the day fully made up her own mind to it; and she thought she might procure some assistance occasionally in such a manner, while he was from home, and free from the heart soreness that would be his, were he to be conscious of the fact.

"Time was," she murmured, when in some degree she had succeeded in calming her feelings—"time was, when my voice was the theme of praise. Alas! I have had no heart to sing for a long, long weary time; but in the days of my own ease and prosperity, I have willingly given to suffering humanity the pittance which now I myself stand so much in need of. Yes, I will beg for Rivers and my child. Farewell, pride—a long farewell."

Pressing the unconscious infant to her bosom, she left the house; but still she could not bring herself to make her first appeal anywhere near her wretched abode. At some distant suburb of the town she thought she could appeal for charity with a lesser pang than that which would afflict her if she had the fear before her eyes that she might be known.

It was strange, but at the very time that Rivers was waiting on Blackfriars Bridge for an opportunity to plunge into the cold deep water beneath, Grace passed him on the other side of the road-way, and each not for a moment suspecting the other's presence, never glanced round sufficiently to know who was passing and who was not.

How far she wandered, poor Grace scarcely knew, for, in addition to not being well acquainted with the suburbs of London, she soon became bitterly cold, and half blinded by a dashing shower of sleet that came down from the accumulating clouds with fearful and terrific violence.

All her exertions were concentrated in protecting her child from the fury of the elements, and she murmured to herself—

"On such a night as this was it that my father spurned me from his door because I loved him whose hands were without a stain, and who had given me a heart that should have been prized Alas—alas! father—father, surely you knew not what you did."

The sleet soon gave way to the increasing coldness of the air, and snow began to fall unmingled with rain, though yet it soon lost its form when once in the damp streets; but after a time the keen wind brought a freezing blast that began fast to harden the mud, and that which was before a mass of sloppy mud now became thicker and heavier; the snow did not melt so quickly, and as that which had fallen became not so readily convertible into moisture, it froze, and the earth soon became a mass of encrustation and snow.

As the wind whistled through the streets it carried the falling flakes in eddying whirls along the deserted streets. The face of the town became quickly changed, as if by an enchanter's wand, the dark mass of mud that might be said to form the road became in a short time of a pure and virgin white, without addition of a single ornament or break.

The lamps shone dimly and sickly; they seemed but to mock the wretched creature who trod the street through dire necessity on such a night a this with its tiny flame, and brightness, and mimic warmth. The small, starlike light that was thrown from these conveniences was dull, and confined to a few, very feet beyond its own post— indeed, the reflection of the post on the earth was often the extent of its power, and the crown above it seldom came in relief, except by an accident, as the attendant now and then committed destruction among them.

Cheerless, melancholy, and very cold was the night; the searching wind struck a death-like chill to the heart; the soft but lightening mass of snow beneath the tread of the foot, with its crump-like sensation, would call the mind from the contemplation of one suffering to that of another. Such a night is seldom met with in this country; but when it is, it is sorely felt by the wretched, the poor, and the homeless.

This storm was the more terrible to poor Grace Rivers, from its awful ikeness to the one during the raging of which she had been thrust from her father's home upon the discovery of her marriage with him whose only fault was a dificiency in worldly wealth.

"Surely—surely," she sobbed, "some other terrible crisis in my fate is at hand; and yet what have I now to fear? Can I sink lower than I have? Can there be a degree of destitution beyond absolute want? Oh, no. But for the pangs that rend my heart for those I love, I could lay me down to die, and smile at the impotency of fate in visiting me with greater hardships or terrors than those I have already gone through. Hush, darling, hush! God of Heaven! are you, my dearest one, to perish this night from cold and hunger in a Christian land, where a Heaven of love and mercy is worshipped?"

Benumbed and shivering, Grace scarcely knew which way she went; moreover, the child began in wailing accents to cry for food. Despair came over the mother's heart, and for some minutes she thought what happiness it would be to lie down and die. This feeling was but of short duration. Had she been completely alone, it might have maintained its place; but her feelings as a mother roused her to exertion, and pausing before the first house she came to, from the windows of which there beamed a light, she commenced in a plaintive voice singing the melancholy ditty which fell so sadly and mournfully upon the ears of Mrs. Woodfall.

> "The bleak wind is blowing,
>   And cold is the air,
> Oh, pity—pray pity
>   The children of care.
> The snow it is falling
>   Upon my babe's breast,
> And hunger is breaking
>   Its slumber and rest.
>
> "We are homeless and houseless,
>   A mother and child—
> A long night is coming,
>   The tempest is wild;
> My little one's moaning
>   Is breaking my heart;
> Oh, pity its hunger,
>   And we will depart.
>
> "We are cold, we are weary;
>   My babe's sweet blue eyes
> Are now dimmed with tears,
>   You may hear its low cries;—

> Its soft little hands
>   Are cold as a stone;
> We shall die—we shall die,
>   All friendless and lone."

How painfully these words struck upon the ears of Grace's old nurse, for it was opposite to her abode that fortune had brought her, we already know, and what generous impulses they awakened in the breast of Harry Woodfall have been recorded.

Scarcely, however, had the last words come from Grace's lips, when a rude hand was laid upon her shoulder, and Mark Hilliard, whose voice she knew in a moment, exclaimed—

"Grace Rivers—ha! ha! ha! I have found you at last, have I, and in such a plight as this."

A scream burst from Grace, and she tried to fly from the spot.

"Hold!" cried Hilliard; "my revenge is not yet complete. You will seek to escape me now in vain."

Grace, in trying to rid herself from his rude touch, fell among the drifting snow, but rising again in a moment, she fancied she still held her child, but in the despair and terror of the moment she only pressed to her breast the shawl which she had wrapped round it, and, with frantic screams, she fled wildly along the roadway, not knowing whither she went.

CHAPTER XCIII.

THE BOAT.—THE MELANCHOLY STRANGER.—THE RESCUE.—THE RECOGNITION.

SOME few moments before the unhappy Rivers cast himself over the low wall at Millbank into the river, a boat, in which were two persons, came slowly against the tide through Vauxhallbridge. One of the persons was rowing, and the other sat in the stern of the wherry in so sad and dejected an attitude that it was easy to perceive some fearful horror was upon his soul.

The waterman, from time to time, said something to endeavour to get his fare into conversation, for he was wonderfully curious to know what deep calamity produced such an afflicting state of mind in the man who had hired him. Moreover, he had his suspicions

that some suddden attempt at suicide might be made, so he rowed gently, and kept his eye upon the groaning man, who sat huddled up in the boat as if he were going to execution.

"A rough night, sir," remarked the waterman; but no answer was returned, save a slight movement to indicate that he was heard.

The boat proceeded onwards for some distance, and then the waterman suddenly pulled up, saying—

"Hilloa!—what's that ?"

"What—what ?" cried the man he was conveying. "Not yet—not yet ; do not let them take me yet."

"I don't know what you mean, sir ; but hang me if there wasn't a splash just now as like some one falling or jumping into the river as possible.— There—there's a cry."

"Horror—horror !" said the other ; "and yet how much happier than I !"

The waterman strained his eyes in the direction of the sound, and then, suddenly, he plied his oars with tremendous speed and force.

"Here he comes," he shouted. "Lend a hand—confound you, lend a hand."

Drifting down rapidly with the current was a human body, and the waterman, shipping his oars in an instant, leaned over the side of his boat, and, at a great risk of upsetting it, seized Francis Rivers by one arm.

"Help me. D—n it, man, are you mad ?" he cried. "Lend a hand."

Mechanically the other leaned over and assisted the waterman, who, then, by one powerful effort, dragged the insensible form into the boat.

"He is happier than I—he is happier than I," was all that the melancholy man in the boat said, as he gazed upon the pale features. Then, with a sudden cry of recollection, he added—

"I have seen that face before. Yes, I am sure I have seen that face before."

"Have you?" replied the waterman, as, with a vigour that sent the wherry spinning through the water, he plied his oars towards the nearest stairs; "have you?"

"Yes. Once I made a call to see one who I dread even to name, at a merchant's counting-house in Thames Street."

"The devil!"

"A very devil. His name—but no matter. This young man was a clerk in the same office, and his name is Rivers. I cannot be mistaken, for, somehow or other, his countenance made a deep impression upon me."

The keel of the boat grated against the step of a landing-place; and the waterman, crying out to some men who were there to see to his boat, lifted Rivers in his arms, and rushed up the stone steps with him as if he had been a child. Excitement, and a humane wish to save a life, aiding a naturally powerful frame, enabled him to accomplish the feat; nor did he pause until he reached a public-house, into which he rushed with his insensible burden.

The prompt attendance of a medical man, and unremitting care on the parts of the people of the house, were, in the course of half an hour, crowned with success, and Rivers opened his eyes, groaning sadly.

"He will do now," remarked the medical man; "he has had a very narrow escape. Another five minutes of immersion in the river would have rendered all exertions useless and utterly in vain."

"God of Heaven! where am I?" said Rivers. "Oh, Grace—Grace?"

"You are safe, and will soon be well," replied the medical man. "What is your name?—where do you reside?"

"Heaven help me," exclaimed Rivers, wringing his hands. "I have failed in the only attempt to succour my wife and child, which, I think, would have been successful. Heaven help me and them.'

"Ah!" remarked the surgeon, "I suspected as much—a suicide."

"Yes, a suicide," said Rivers. "Blame me not. You must pass through what I have passed through ere you can pretend to judge of my acts. Let me leave here now; I am poor—utterly destitute. Let me leave at once, for I have not wherewith to reward any one in the slightest degree. You see before you a wretch against whose defenceless breast evil fortune has expended her sharpest arrows. So tortured am I mentally by the sufferings of those near and dear to me, that I am poor even in thanks."

"If you leave here in that kind of humour," said the humane waterman, "my name ain't Bill Whackles. Come —come, don't be down-hearted. Is your name Rivers?"

Rivers started as he cried—

"And do you know me?"

"No, but there was a miserable-looking chap that had hired me to give him a cast from Deptford to Westminster, who knew your name. Where he has gone now I don't know; but as for your leaving here while I can stand the racket of your stay for a few days—I won't hear of it."

Rivers made an effort to rise, but he found his strength utterly prostrated, and he sunk back on the bed again with a deep sigh.

* * * *

Midnight had passed, when, staggering from exhaustion, and looking as pale as a marble statue, Grace Rivers arrived at the door of her poor home. Her feeble knock far admission was answered by the woman of the house, who was then both shocked and alarmed to see Grace, after exclaiming, "Francis—Francis! My child—our child! Lost—lost!" faint on the threshold.

With difficulty she was carried in, and placed upon a humble couch; but it was many, many hours before consciousness returned to her, during which time the people knew not what to do, or how to account for the inexplicable absence of Rivers, for whose return they waited, of course, in vain, as the next morning must come before any intelligence could be obtained of his fate.

But when that terrible morning did dawn, what increased terror it brought with it—what awful horror was the consequence! Grace was just sufficiently recovered to read the note of Rivers. With rapture she had recognised the handwriting; and, imagining that the epistle, of course, contained some rational reason for his absence from home, she eagerly devoured its contents; but what language can describe the terrible shriek which burst from her lips when she became aware of what a sad leave-taking of her and the world that epistle really was.

It was a mercy, indeed, that again she lapsed into insensibility. Those about her thought she was dead, so utterly ineffectual were all means that could be adopted for her restoration. But, if their terror and affliction was great at Grace's condition, surprise overcame all other feelings, when, about half-past nine o'clock, a carriage drove up to the top of the court, and an aged man, getting out of it with difficulty, tottered towards the house in which she was lying. In nearly inarticulate accents he asked—

" Is—is—Mrs. Rivers here?"

The reply was, of course, in the affirmative; and, when some demur was made about admitting him to the chamber where she lay, he said, in such sorrow-stricken accents as made all tremble who heard him—

" I am her father—her most unworthy father. I am a man of sorrow and of crime. Do not—oh! do not deny me now access to my dear child, whom I have, with an awful pride and resentment, left so long to want and misery."

Silently they made way for him, and he kissed the pale cheeks of his once darling Grace, while tears rolled down his cheeks, and he groaned aloud, in the bitterness of his despair.

" Grace—Grace!" he cried; " my Grace—oh! once again look up to say you forgive you old, wretched father before he dies. Grace, Grace, my beautiful Grace, will you pray for me to the Heaven I have offended—my injured—beautiful child?"

She was deaf to the wild appeal, and Mathew Trueman, for it was indeed he, leaned his head upon his hands, and wept like a child. There was a solemn and holy stillness in that chamber of affliction. None spoke to Mathew Trueman after his declaration of who he was, for there was something terrible in his grief as he sat there weeping for his beautiful child, after accusing himself, as he had done, of causing her so much misery.

The nearest medical man was sent for at his request, and some remedies which he applied restored Grace to consciousness, when the first face her eyes rested upon was that of her wretched father; but, oh! how altered was he since last she had seen him. Had not his features been indelibly fixed upon her memory, she would never have recognised in the bent form, whitened locks, and furrowed face of the sorrow-stricken man, who was weeping by her side, the once hearty and opulent merchant, who was her father.

When she did recognise him, it was with a cry of surprise that she pronounced the one word—

" Father!"

" Grace—Grace," said Mathew Trueman, while the tears flowed down his furrowed cheeks; " can you forgive me?"

She raised herself on her humble couch, and flung herself into his arms.

We will leave the reader to imagine the interview that succeeded; to picture the tears of the heart-stricken and repentant Mathew Trueman, who, with trembling hands, produced the letter that Rivers had written to him—an awful confirmation of Grace's worst fears—and what could equal her despair to feel assured that she had in such a manner lost him who had been her young heart's first, only love! Oh, how she longed to die! She called upon him frantically by name; she shrieked, too, for her child; and such a scene of horror as ensued the people of the house declared, poor as they were, they would not witness again for a thousand pounds.

Twelve o'clock arrived, and Grace Rivers was lying in a kind of stupor, while old Mathew Trueman sat still weeping bitterly by her side, when the woman of the house hastily entered the room with a morning paper in her hands.

" He is saved—he is saved!" she cried.

" Who—who?" exclaimed Trueman, springing to his feet. " Speak, woman, speak—who mean you?"

" Mr. Rivers! Look here; here's a whole *pentograph* in the *Morning 'Tiser* about him.

Mathew Trueman snatched the newspaper from the woman's hands, and in a loud, unnatural voice, read the following paragraph—

"ATTEMPTED SUICIDE.—Last evening a respectably-attired man was rescued from the Thames in a state of total insensibility. The usual means were adopted for the restoration of suspended animation, and, we are happy to say, with success. The immersion was at first thought to be accidental; but there is too much reason to fear that the pressure of extreme poverty had induced the commission of the act. The unhappy man was recognised as a Mr. Rivers, once a clerk in a respectable firm in Thames-street."

"He lives—he lives!" cried Grace. "Father—father—Heaven is merciful, and he lives!"

The gush of tears that came to her relief were those of joy, and old Trueman, whose mind appeared to have undergone a great change, rose from his seat, saying—

"Compose yourself, my Grace; I will soon return to you. Your dear child, you may depend, is in safety, if not in comfort. I have now a sacred duty to perform, and perhaps little time to do it in."

Without waiting for a reply he hurried from the house, and directed that he should be driven at once to his solicitor's, where, within one hour, he executed a will, bequeathing all he possessed to his daughter. After this, he was unceasing in his exertions to find out Rivers, and by good luck, he at length hit upon the public-house where he was lying, for the police had taken him into custody, and would not let him leave, except upon the order of a magistrate. When he entered the room, so remarkable a change had taken place in his appearance, that Rivers looked at him for several minutes without knowing him; indeed, it was not until Trueman said, in broken accents—"Mr. Rivers, do you not know me?" that his voice came to the recollection of the young man, and he exclaimed—

"Mr. Trueman! can I believe my eyes? Have you come, sir, to trample over the wreck you have made?"

"No, Mr. Rivers, I have not. My day of triumph is past; I am no longer the proud, vain man I was. Can you forgive the past, and look upon me now as what I ought to have been long ago—an affectionate father to my only child—my much-injured and beautiful Grace?"

"Can I believe my ears? Do I dream?"

"No, Rivers, you do not dream.—I have seen Grace. From this moment your misfortunes are at an end, and I shall be able to lay my head in peace in the grave, if you will forget the past."

"Freely, freely, Mr. Trueman," said Rivers; "Heaven forbid that I should be the obstacle to your peace of mind."

For the first time in his life Rivers shook hands with Mathew Trueman, the rich merchant, and the latter himself went to the magistrate, before whom Rivers was to have been taken for the misdameanor of attempting his own destruction; and upon promising to take charge of him, procured his release. He then drove back to the public-house, where Rivers had been so humanely attended to, and desiring him to remain until he fetched Grace, the old man was about again to enter his carriage, when an elderly woman stepped up to him with a child in her arms.

It was Mrs. Woodfall, with the infant that poor Grace in her despair had left among the snow. She had seen the paragraph in the morning papers, answering Rivers, and had been wandering in search of him for some hours. Her surprise at seeing Mathew Trueman was intense, and she exclaimed—

"Mr. Trueman, Mr. Trueman, tell me, is your errand here one of mercy and humanity, or of vindictiveness? Behold your daughter's child, and may the God of Heaven soften your heart."

Mathew Trueman actually staggered, as these words were addressed to him. Without attempting a reply, he took the child from Mrs. Woodfall's arms, and giving it one kiss, he hurried with it into the house, and stopped not till he had placed it in its father's arms. Mrs. Woodfall followed him, but he was gone again before she could hear from the delighted Rivers what a change had taken place in the feelings of the old merchant.

"I have but two wishes now unfulfilled," said Rivers. "One is to see Grace smile again as she was wont to smile in happier days, and the other is to take Tom Hackey by the hand."

"I know of no means of finding him," said Mrs. Woodfall.

"Nor I, except by an inquiry at Covent-Garden Theatre, where I hope he is still employed."

"I will go at once and make the inquiry," said Mrs. Woodfall. "Do you wait with patience, Mr. Rivers, and this will be the happiest day we have all known for years."

The interview between Grace and her father, when he went to her with the information that he had not only found Rivers, but that her child had fallen into the hands of one who would behave to it with the greatest kindness, was joyful in the extreme. A new existence seemed to have opened upon poor Grace, and as she accompanied her father in his carriage to the public-house where Rivers was so anxiously expecting her, she several times asked herself if all was not a dream, from which she would again awaken, to find poverty and destitution around her.

What pen, then, shall describe the blissful meeting that took place when she arrived, and once more looked in life upon Rivers, who for such hours of mortal agony she had mourned as dead. It was a relief to the gushing feelings of them all when the door of the room opened, and Mrs. Woodfall, accompanied by Tom Hackey, who she had luckily found attending a rehearsal, entered.

Tom Hackey's first act was to throw his hat out at the window, and then he gave three cheers, after which, turning to Trueman, he cried—

"Mathew, Mathew, I forgive you—only, you know, you very nearly made this affair a tragedy in five acts, you sinner."

* * * *

The reader has probably, ere this, surmised who the melancholy man in the cloak was, who came so providentially to the rescue of Rivers. It was no other than the wretched Wilson, who had escaped a watery grave by being picked up by a barge, since which time he had worked under a feigned name, as a day labourer, about Greenwich and Deptford; but remorse for his participation in Mr. Noble's murder

made him sick and weary of life. He never knew a moment's peace, and his errand to London, on the occasion when he was partially instrumental in saving Rivers, was to give himself up to the police, and make a full confession of the particulars of the murder.

While Rivers and his wife were weeping and smiling at their change of fortune, poor Wilson was making his statement, which, of course, awfully implicated Hilliard, for whom so active a search was immediately made, that, as he had no suspicions of danger, he was in custody before twelve o'clock.

Maddened, then, to desperation at finding Wilson alive, and his accuser, he would have murdered him in the police-office, could he have got at him. He sent immediately for Girkins, who refused to have anything to do with him, and then Hilliard himself made a statement of the base conspiracy which had been entered into for the ruin of Rivers.

"You will not help yourself," said the magistrate, "by this, but still the matter shall be seen into. You are committed for trial."

These facts came to the ears of Rivers and his wife the same day, and Mathew Trueman from them found fresh food for regret at his unjust treatment of Rivers. He made the whole party, including Mrs. Woodfall and Tom Hackey, come with him to the hotel where he had been staying. But before retiring for the night, he informed Rivers of the will he had made, and talked long and affectionately with Grace. Even after he had bidden her good night, he returned, and left a tear and a kiss upon her brow.

In the morning he was found a corpse.

* * * *

Our tale is over. Rivers and his beautiful Grace settled down into the quiet calm of domestic enjoyment, blessing their happy home by five more little ones, with all of whom Tom Hackey was a most decided favourite. We need not say that his fortunes, as well as those of Mrs. Woodfall, were well looked after by Rivers.

Wilson was admitted king's evidence against Hilliard, on the trial of the latter, and within five weeks the ruffian expiated his offences on a scaffold. Wilson then disappeared, no one knew where—he was never again heard of.

His villany was of such a dark nature that he had not the hardihood to show his face again where he was better known than respected; and perhaps such a course was the wisest, since on the great American Continent, he would have the opportunity of starting life afresh, and if his resolution remained firm, he would soon be enabled to lead a life of silent repentance, and comparative cheerfulness. America refuses shelter to none, be their crimes ever so black; for when once landed on her shores the criminal of the old country has an equal chance of making honourable progress with the honest labourer, for merit, after arrival, is the only criterion of a subject's worth in the gigantic republic. It is to be hoped that he made all the atonement in his power for his past vices, and became a worthy citizen.

Girkins was indicted for conspiracy, and he in turn implicated his friend in Barnard's-inn. They were both sentenced to two years' imprisonment.

As for Lord Hawksworth, he turned a bankrupt, availing himself of some horse-dealing transactions, to make himself out a trader; and such a disgraceful exposure as ensued during his examination, never had been surpassed in a court of law.

THE END.